# Eboracvm: Carved in Stone

Graham Clews

Stairwell Books //

Published by Stairwell Books
9 Carleton St
Greenwich
CT 06830 USA

161 Lowther Street
York, YO31 7LZ

www.stairwellbooks.co.uk
@stairwellbooks

Eboracvm: Carved in Stone © 2022 Graham Clews and Stairwell Books

All rights reserved. No part of this publication may be reproduced, stored in or introduced into a retrieval system, or transmitted, in any form, or by any means (electronic, mechanical, photocopying, recording, e-book or otherwise) without the prior written permission of the author.

The moral rights of the author have been asserted.

This is a work of fiction. Names, characters, businesses, places, events, locales, and incidents are either the products of the author's imagination or used in a fictitious manner. Any resemblance to actual persons, living or dead, or actual events is purely coincidental.

ISBN: 978-1-913432-13-3

Layout design: Alan Gillott
Cover art: Chris Collingwood

With thanks to John Wallace (English John), Dr. Alan Watt, and Donna Burgeson, who have been so kind as to help in the proof reading of the various books in the three volume Eboracum series. And also, thanks to the many others who have read the stories, and offered their encouragement . . .

Also by Graham Clews

*Eboracvm Trilogy*

*Eboiracvm, The Village*
*Eboracvm, The Fortress*

*Jessica Jones and The Gates of Penseron*
*Politically Detained*
*A Slightly Tainted Hero*

Non Fiction

*The Sound of Silence*

# Foreword

When historical novels are set against a factual background, it is inevitable that the reader will encounter a number of unfamiliar names for both places and people. The Eboracum trilogy is no exception, and at first these names may be hard to pick up on and follow. In the interest of historical accuracy they must be used, however, so the reader is asked to tought it out. The "double-barrelled" names – those of three syllables of more – are those of real people taken from the pages of history, so we are stuck with them. To help, the names of the real characters mentioned in the story are listed below, along with a brief description of what they were.

Also, over the three books in the trilogy, the fictional character have also grown in number. These characters, for the most part, have been given names of one or two syllables which strive to hold true to Celtic or Roman origins. Nonetheless, in order to assist in 'getting them sorted out', a brief summary of the roles they played in the previous two novels is also given below. Perhaps it will help keep track of them.

As to unusual terms and historical place names, the first time they are used in the book they are italicized; definitions and applicable modern names can be found in Appendix II and III respectively.

# HISTORICAL CHARACTERS

**Cartimandua:** "Catey" was the ruler of the tribe known as the Brigantes, and a "client queen" of Rome. She was a 'close' friend of Gaius Sabinius Trebonius in the first two books of the trilogy.

**Galgar:** Latin name, Galgacus. The Caledoni chieftain or king who led the great army that was defeated at Mons Graupius (see *Eboracum, The Fortress*) in A.D. 83 or 84.

**Marcus Ulpius Nerva Traianus (Trajan):** Roman emperor from A.D. 98-117. See write-up under Appendix II.

**Quintus Petilius Cerialis:** Governor of Britannia from A.D. 71-74.

**Gnaeus Julius Agricola:** Governor of Brittania from A.D. 77 – 83/84. Responsible for the defeat of Galgacus (Galgar) in what is now Northern Scotland.

**Titus Flavius Vespasian(us):** Roman emperor from A.D. 69-79.

**Venutius:** first husband of Cartimandua, and likely a Brigantian king in his own right.

# PRINCIPAL FICTIONAL CHARACTERS WHO APPEAR IN THE TRILOGY:

**Cethen Lamh-fada:** The minor Brigante chieftain whose village was appropriated by Rome for the building of the fortress known as Eboracum, in AD 71. His wife Elena and their three children were taken by the Romans during the invasion of the North by Quintus Cerialis.

**Gaius Sabinius Trebonius:** The Roman engineer and eventual senator responsible for the exile of Cethen and his family, and subsequent legate of the Ninth Hispana legion and governor of Britannia.

**Elena:** Wife of Cethen, who was taken along with her children by Gaius Sabinius Trebonius in *Eboracum, The Village*. She first served as Gaius's slave, but eventually married.

**Cian:** Cethen's younger brother, captured by Rome at the Battle of Bran's Beck. He became a Roman auxiliary trooper, first in Germania, then in Britannia.

**Rhun:** Cethen and Elena's oldest son, taken by Rome at the Battle of Stannick. Gaius reluctantly took him under his wing, and he became a Roman auxiliary cavalry officer. He eventually married **Aelia,** Gaius's daughter, in *Eboracum, The Fortress*.

**Coira:** Twin sister of Rhun, who was taken with her mother Elena at the Battle of Bran's Beck.

**Tuis:** Youngest son of Cethen and Elena, who was only five when taken by the Romans. He was adopted by Gaius (a regular Roman phenomenon) in *Eboracum, The Fortress*. His Roman name became Gaius Sabinius Trebonianus, though he maintains the familiar 'Tuis' among friends and kin.

**Marcus Sabinius:** Gaius's son, who was held hostage by the Brigantes for four years when serving as a tribune with the Twentieth Valeria Victrix Legion *(Eboracvm, The Fortress)*.

**Jessa:** A little person in stature, Jessa is the daughter of Marcus Sabinius by the Carveti deceased free woman Fiona, who had the control of Marcus when he was a hostage and slave of the tribes.

**Bryn:** Son of Cethen and Morallta, one of several women who took up with Cethen after his wife was taken by the Romans. He was conceived in *Eboracum, The Village* and played a minor role in *Eboracum, The Fortress*.

**Criff, Borba and Luga:** Three important characters in the first two books, though with minor roles. Like Cethen, Elena and Gaius, they are now much older. Criff is a Brigante bard, the son of the deceased queen Cartimandua. He's a free spirited soul, who crosses between Roman and Brigante lines without rancour or cause. Borba has been with Cethen since the onset of Rome's northern incursion, and in the first two books served as a friend and major ally. Luga, once almost Cian's nemesis, was taken along with Cian by the Ninth Legion at the Battle of Bran's Beck. He became his friend when serving with Rome's army of the Rhine.

**And one final note on names:** To correctly separate two of the fictional characters (Tuis and Gaius), watch for the use of Trebonius/Trebonianus, which is like a surname. The ending *ius/ianus* was used, respectively, by a father and his son. Again, Roman usage and terms . . .

## GENERAL

A final comment: there is a certain amount of profane language in the book. Some people might find it coarse. If such words offend, then the author apologizes; he does not, however, make apology for their use. It is definitely not gratuitous. With a notable exception, the reader will find that such language is employed almost exclusively by the soldiers and warriors in the book, and then merely for emphasis. The author spent sixteen years in the Canadian Armed Forces (Reserve) and, quite bluntly, this is the way soldiers talk. Research shows that two thousand years ago soldiers and warriors cussed with just as much colour. To use their actual words (such as *cunno, futuo, verpa etc.*) would mean nothing, so modern equivalents have been substituted.

*A glossary of definitions and place names can be found in the appendices.*

The forts shown above are the ones mentioned in the book; a score or more other forts lay within the area shown on the map.

# Prologue

## Northern Brigantia, A.D. 89

Cethen Lamh-fada was honing a felling axe when his ears caught the patter of Kelpy's running feet. The door crashed open and his daughter burst into the small lodge, stamping her shoes to rid them of a heavy coat of mud. She looked soaked to the skin as she shook her head, clearing her face of a crisscrossed web of rain-darkened hair. What, he wondered, had the girl done now?

"Da, there's some riders coming." She gestured anxiously over her shoulder toward the head of the valley. "I think they're Romans."

Ficra eased back on her haunches in front of the fire, and stared up at her husband as if gauging his concern. For a moment the only sound in the hut was the sizzle of a rabbit roasting above the embers on a thin, iron spit. When Cethen said nothing she lurched to her feet and with an exaggerated sigh of the hard-done-by, walked to the door and peered into the pouring rain. Cethen sighed in turn and simply shifted in his chair. He had no idea what the Romans were doing here and even if he had, there was little he could do. After a second glance at Ficra, though, he decided that perhaps he should at least get off his rear and look.

Ficra clucked to sooth Kelpy as Cethen stirred himself. He ambled stiffly over to stand in the doorway beside his wife, one hand shielding his eyes. He blinked, vainly trying to glimpse what Kelpy had seen beyond the small cluster of huts, sheds, and pens that was the *kin*'s village. The effort was pointless. Anything farther than spitting distance was like looking into a fog.

Kelpy volunteered the details as the small column of riders plodded along the muddy track that followed the valley floor. Each one sat hunched over the saddle like a half-drowned hound, and the horses hung their heads low against the biting rain. They seemed to be in no hurry and Kelpy again opined that they were Romans.

"No cause to fret, child," Ficra murmured, speaking with false calm. "They've ridden through here before, and done no harm."

Cethen realized he was still holding the axe, and set it down. The last thing a man should be holding when greeting Roman cavalry was something that looked like a weapon – which was ironic, for at one time he would have greeted a Roman in no other way. He shook his head and smiled bitterly. There should be no cause for concern beyond a well-honed and well-earned distrust of all things Roman.

They were probably from the fort at *Epiacum*, Cethen told himself. The buggers posed no threat, not to a man who stayed free of trouble and offered up his tax – something he had done for the past five years, hard though it had been. Nor had they proved to be a threat to the hundreds and hundreds of other tribesmen who eked an existence within a day's walk of their miserable fort. Not as long as each poor, sodding hill farmer turned over an indecent part of what he grew and remained as bovine as the animals he raised . . .

*Hill farmer!* Cethen grunted. Not so long ago, he would have sneered at the word. Yet now, that's what he had become: a dirt-scratching hill farmer, grubbing to raise a family and nothing more. A man that anyone, Roman or otherwise, would not find worth the trouble to even question. But Rome had a long memory, and long memories made a guilty man nervous.

"There's about a dozen of them." Ficra edged back inside the doorway and stood with one arm propped against the crude frame as she turned to face her husband. "You going to stay, or hide?"

Cethen stretched his arms and yawned, exuding a calm he did not feel. "No reason to leave."

Few in the valley or the surrounding hills knew who he was, which was just as well, for there was little trust to be found there. And farther out – well, Borba was the closest, a man as reliable as the sun itself. The twin's farm was a good two days' ride to the east using the Roman roads, and maybe a half-day longer along the back trails through the hills. If ever he needed him. . .

"Da, are you gonna fight them?"

Cethen laughed and glanced fondly down at his son. The boy had wandered from the rear of the hut, with a yapping hound pup in tow. He was a sturdy, chubby lad of six years, with a thick mop of dark hair and even darker eyes that shone eagerly. "No, that wouldn't be fair,

Modan. There aren't enough of them," Cethen said gruffly, and ruffled the lad's hair. "Just do as your mam says."

"And leave the dog alone," Ficra chided as the boy ambled away, dragging the yelping pup by one of its back legs. Her words were blithely ignored.

"They're almost here," Kelpy said, her voice anxious. A moment later she added, "I count fourteen."

"That's good, very good." Cethen praised the girl on her numbers, his voice belying the empty feeling in his belly. It was time to find out just who, exactly, was coming, and what they wanted. "Why don't you and your mam go back inside?"

⸸

The storm had set in soon after Cian and Luga started north from Epiacum following an ancient wagon track strewn with rock and gravel, and packed hard by countless wheels and plodding hooves. The narrow road wound its way beyond the fort, hugging the low banks of a small river that ran high with the spring rains. About seven or eight miles north of the stronghold it bowed slightly to the west, and it was there that Borba had the small column turn.

Cian shifted the reins against the side of the mare's neck and the tired horse plodded obediently onto an even poorer track. Surely, in all of this sopping, windswept waste of hills and valleys, his brother could have found a more forgiving haven? Borba had told him that the dale where Cethen lived wasn't that bad, considering, and that when the sun did find time to shine, which was not often, there were far worse places to live. But even so, it was a long way from the *Abus* . . .

They rode gradually uphill for several more miles along a narrow trail that was nothing but a mire of sloppy mud. At its crest the land fell away, dropping into a narrow, wooded ravine that soon opened into a deep valley. The forest on the steep slopes had been thinned and Cian glimpsed a series of small sheltered meadows, hand-cleared for pasture. The usual valley stream, more like a small brook this high up, emerged from a stand of willows and bubbled toward the centre of the valley floor. Farther down, perhaps half a mile away, stood a cluster of buildings, no more than shadows in the drizzly haze.

"That's it," Borba called out.

Cian acknowledged the words with a casual wave over one rain-soaked shoulder and chuckled in spite of the chill. Cethen would by now have seen their small column. His belly would be spitting bile while his brain dithered over whether he should run or stay put. Though maybe not. It had been six years since Agricola's final battle and the land had been quiet for the most part, especially this far south of where it had happened. There was also a wife now, and at least one youngster. If anything, the poor bugger might have them hide, while pothering his next move – which, in the end, would be to just sit tight and hope for the best. Hoping for the best had always been Cethen's strategy of choice. Or was that a tactic? Cian shook his head. He never could get the two clear in his mind. The chuckle grew louder. If he were to wager coin on it, the odds would find his brother in the doorway of his lodge, carefully watching, and hoping.

Cian halted the mare a good ten yards away from the small round lodge that sat at the centre of a mean cluster of huts. It wasn't near as large as the one Cethen and Elena had called home at Ebor, but for this part of the north it wasn't bad: a stone wall built more than half the height of a man, a conical roof, and no doubt a step-down floor inside to make up the height. Though if there was, it was out of sight, for Cethen blocked the doorway, standing with his arms folded and wearing a dark scowl.

*He doesn't look any older,* Cian thought. That was likely because his brother had gained some of his weight back, which rid him of the drawn, hunted look he'd worn the last time they met when Cethen and his followers had lost their fight with Rome. The familiar long moustaches held more grey, but those lazy, sandy eyelashes hadn't changed at all. They'd always made a person wonder if the man was deep in thought or half asleep.

"What do you want?" Cethen demanded, not giving ground as his eyes squinted upward. He appeared to be alone, for there was no movement inside the lodge.

Cian pushed the hood of his cloak back onto his shoulders and smiled expectantly. Cethen merely stared back. Borba urged his horse forward and was about to speak, but Cian raised a hand, staying him. "I came to see you about your son."

Cethen glanced back over his shoulder and the frown deepened. "Modan? What's he done? The lad's just a child."

"Not that one, oaf, the other. The one you carelessly misplaced at *Graupius*."

"Bryn? He's long dead –" Cethen began then paused, uncertain. He dropped his arms and stepped forward, head cocked to one side and his jaw slack. "Cian?"

"You hid yourself well, big brother." Cian tried to keep his voice casual. "I came across Criff a few months ago, and he said you were still alive. Told me Borba knew where you lived. Then he told me where to find Borba."

"But – Cian . . . and Bryn . . . ?" Cethen fell silent, as if trying to understand. Cautiously, he asked, "What about Bryn?"

Cian turned and waved one of the riders forward: a fair looking youth with a dripping wisp of a beard, and hair that glistened with a hint of copper. "Found the lad in the slave pens after the battle, looking as miserable as you were last time I saw you. Bryn, come meet your da."

"Bryn?" Cethen barely breathed the name.

Cian slid from the saddle, the better to greet his brother, but Cethen's mind was fixed on his son. Close up, Cian saw that the pale blue eyes no longer squinted, they simply stared. He laughed at his brother's stunned expression, feeling inordinately pleased, and slapped him on the shoulder. "The fool boy thinks he wants to come and stay with you for awhile, rather than with his favourite uncle."

"The boy's only got one uncle," Cethen murmured, finally breaking into a broad, sunny smile as tears mixed with the rain trickling down his cheeks.

# Chapter I

## Selgovae Territory, Februarius, A.D. 105

The Roman fort sat downstream alongside a bend in the river. It stood a good mile away, hidden beyond the twisting slope of the valley, and a thick forest of tall pines and bleak shade trees stripped by winter. For Modan, its threat was none of his immediate concern. The stronghold was far beyond both sight and sound of where he stood beside his horse, the animal's soft muzzle covered by his palm. The Roman road that lay before him, unseen beyond the pines and the winter-dead undergrowth, had been cleared of growth close to a hundred paces on either side. Yet the bare expanse would not be sufficient to protect the soldiers who travelled its path, for the forest provided cover in which even a thousand men might hide.

The supply column edged its way down the upper reaches of the valley, the lumbering oxen slowing even further as the road dropped into the silence of the forest. The carters pulled back on the brake handles, the harsh squeal of wood on iron echoing through the trees. Men walking by the yokes pulled back on the leads, holding the huge animals tight against the falling slope. There were pack mules too, Modan had seen them as the column crossed the open moor above the valley, but the wagons clearly held the greater prize. Beside each one marched a squad of infantry, four men to a side, pulling hard on the drag lines; which meant, for the moment, that at least those men were occupied. Satisfied, Modan melted back through the trees.

The squeal of the wooden axles faded as the column slowed, giving way to the soft, rhythmic beat of marching feet. The chatter of a hundred soldiers filtered through the trees, barely heard above the jangle of harness, the creak of leather, and the clop of iron-shod hooves. A couple of troops of cavalry escorted the foot soldiers, Modan had counted about sixty. They rode in front, behind, and in the cleared space on either side of the road, clearly more at ease as they neared the fort. The column's scouts were no longer visible, nor would they be. This close to the fort, only two had been sent ahead. Both lay beside the swollen stream that traced the valley floor, the sound of their death drowned by the rushing waters of the ford.

Modan had kept his men further back in the pines than he would have liked, but they were well hidden. His da had suggested that, telling him that any more than ten men wouldn't keep quiet long enough for a rabbit to cross the road. His da had also given him the unwanted advice that fighting Romans was futile and not worth the bother – which only served to make Modan's blood boil. As had his final snide comment: "Stuff your people's gobs up to keep 'em quiet, or the Romans will know you're there before you do."

The sarcasm had irked, and he'd grumbled as much, but Modan had done as his da said, other than stuffing gobs. And his da's advice was proving sound – which it usually was – and that was also irksome.

A cough sounded as Modan swung onto his horse; Treno telling him it was past the time to move. Which was irritating – he knew it was time; he didn't need Treno telling him! Modan scowled his annoyance but it raised only a lopsided grin in the fellow's bland, tattooed face. Modan grunted, raised his spear, and silently waved it forward.

All along the line, his small army stirred. The cavalry moved first, advancing slowly at a walk. Treno had formed them up in three long, even ranks, each a hundred horse strong. Trailing behind, doing their damnedest not to break a branch or open their gobs, came an equal number of warriors on foot. The widespread ranks were holding even, Modan saw, which was good, very good. In fact, he thought snidely, it was sodding-well amazing!

Daylight showed through the treetops ahead. Knees trembling and lips dry, Modan fought the urge to whip his horse forward. On either side, the eyes of every rider in the first rank were on him – he could feel each one. A branch broke somewhere and he flinched; another sharp crack quickly followed. *Caution the men, but you can't quiet the damned hooves!* Modan cursed and tried to clear his mind of useless hindsight, squinting at the thin screen of trees that remained.

Swallowing hard, he again raised his hand, silently damning any man who failed to keep his place. Most of them couldn't actually see him, of course, anymore than he could see the plodding figures in the Roman column – though he could now glimpse a dim line of shadows beyond the tangled undergrowth. Risking a glance sideways, Modan saw no more than a score of his own people, but they were all there somewhere; he could feel them on every side.

The day was unfolding as it should. Or was it?

Modan had firmly instructed every man that *he* would order the charge when it came, which suddenly struck him as nonsense. That could cost the advantage of surprise! The man who first broke into the open and saw the Romans should order the charge; and that, surely, had happened somewhere along the line by now?

Modan began to fret. At this rate, some of his people would step from the forest before the Romans had even a hint of them being there. What then? Would everyone stand dumbstruck, waiting until their leader arrived to order the charge? That made no sense. The moment a Roman saw them and opened his big, fat gob, the spears and arrows would start flying. That meant any one of his people, once seen, should yell the order to attack if they were to gain the advantage. Modan swore. It was too late to change . . .

The last of the tangled undergrowth fell away, which was a relief for the going had been hard. Nothing remained between him and the Roman column but a few scattered trees. Modan raised his heels and gulped air into his lungs to shout the order, but a terrible scream rang out from off to his right. A moment later another rang out, off to his left. Modan jumped, his head snapping sideways. Riders everywhere were whipping their horses forward, the second rank following hard on their tails.

Damn them! Someone *had* called the charge!

Modan swore and slammed his heels down. The horse, a stolen Roman mare larger than his own herd stud, leapt forward. Modan's eyes flicked wildly back and forth, his senses both numb and alive with a wild excitement. The wind was cool against his face; the saddle sat tight between his knees; the mare's ears flattened above her thick black mane; and the ground rushed by under flying hooves – all of it stark and crisp and clear, yet barely noticed.

He covered half the distance to the column before lifting his shield, and raising his spear in readiness. The Romans were turning, not as one but in a jumble: some were ready, but most fumbled – their plodding column plainly falling apart. The surprise was complete! Only a few were moving to stand firm in front of the wagons: a few riders – no, four, maybe a half dozen – and a wavering gaggle of foot soldiers. Most were running to the far side of the column. Modan's mouth twisted in a grim smile.

Then a single Roman rider – no, several now – galloped back again. More were following while a few more turned away, and some – some were riding straight at him. Modan screamed his courage as his horse closed the distance, his body one with the animal, his mind blind to its headlong speed. Two of the Romans – two dammit!—were headed toward him. Then, to his relief, one broke right, intent on engaging whoever rode there. That would be Treno! He could deal with the threat. The other Roman kept coming, though – nearer, closer, and –

Modan blinked and flinched as something thumped hard on his saddle, low on the left.

The Roman had *thrown* his fool spear, not fought with it. Yet the sod suddenly had another in hand, a small, wicked barb that was more of a dart. The man raced by, clearly intent on the second line, and Modan whirled sideways and thrust. His weapon glanced off the Roman's shield and he was gone.

Modan's horse was closing fast on the wagons, which were relatively undefended. The pack mules had scattered. The Roman infantry appeared to be broken, running like ants to the far side of the road. Yet some were turning despite their panic, and raising their shields. With a taut smile, Modan tried to kick his horse forward; instead, a horrible flash of pain screamed from his leg and he found himself slipping from the saddle. He struggled to tighten his grip, both knees clenching the animal's back for balance; but something was wrong, terribly wrong. His legs pressed inward with no effect and the pain burst in a ball of fire. The spear fell from his grip and he tried grasping the cross horns, yet nothing seemed to be working. He tumbled sideways, spinning helplessly as he toppled from the horse.

A thousand burning needles ripped through Modan's thigh as he rolled across the dirt. The air flew from his lungs as his back thumped up against a large rock. He lay gasping for breath, his eyes wet, his tongue hanging, his world a whirl of black and red light. Then his stomach heaved, spewing its contents over beard, neck, and belly.

For the longest while he lay unable to move, his mind striving to stay with his body as it fought the agony. The hurt would not ease, though neither did it grow; but finally it became bearable. Modan craned his neck sideways and spit the sour bile from his mouth; then, glaring skyward, he screeched a curse at the gods.

"Bastards!"

Gasping with effort, Modan eased himself up on one elbow and peered through eyes blurred by pain. Anything that seemed to be happening, which at first appeared to be very little, was over by the Roman supply column. And he could not see Treno. Where was Treno?

The sod was supposed to be his right-hand man, and he'd buggered off! Granted, the Roman had struck him on the left and Treno, as he was supposed to do, was taking care of the one on his right. But that didn't free the man's reins to go chasing after the faerie. Modan hesitated as yet another thought struck: maybe Treno had got himself killed? He tried to look over his shoulder but the pain screamed once again, and he slumped back against the rock.

The agony came from his left leg!

Realizing that he didn't know the extent of why he was lying there, Modan peered carefully downward, moving as little as possible. He blanched. The foot was skewed slightly sideways which meant the leg might or might not be broken; the wound itself was partway up the thigh – though it was anyone's guess as to what had happened there. Blood soaked through his woolen pants, and there was – Modan closed his eyes to focus against the pain and his stomach heaved again, only there was nothing left to vomit. Panting, he forced himself to look again at the wound. There were no jagged bone ends sticking up through the bloody wool, which was good – a man could lose a leg because of that. But the spear – it must have been that sodding spear – had torn at the flesh as it ripped loose in his fall. He sagged back with a groan.

A moment later it struck him that he could bleed to death – or be slain by any half-crazed Roman that ran his way. Modan again heaved himself up on one elbow, moaning with the effort, and turned his damp eyes on the scattered column.

His people were everywhere. There was little sign of the Romans – live ones, anyway; and there were plenty of uniformed bodies around – which was as it should be. Somebody was rounding up the pack mules. Others were unloading the contents from the wagons – there was no point stealing the big carts, they were too slow – and that was good as long as people's fingers didn't get greedy. But some idiot had set fire to one of the carts, and the smoke might be seen from the fort. The entire attack had been based on surprise and a quick withdrawal, and now some fool had sent a signal . . .

The pain bit deep again, fuelling Modan's anger. He lifted his head and roared "Treno!" at the top of his voice. Then, a moment later, "Treno, where the fuck are you?"

Treno smiled grimly as he saw the Roman cavalryman turn from Modan and ride straight toward him, eyes focused on his new quarry. The man's hand was holding one of those small, deadly javelins they used, all set and ready to throw. Treno raised his own spear as they closed, and made as if to hurl it in his face. The Roman flinched and lifted his shield, but tossed the javelin anyway. Treno's feint was enough to ruin the man's aim, and he easily deflected the barb with his own smaller shield. He quickly brought the point of his spear across, aiming for the throat. The Roman ducked, but the point caught him below the helmet, jamming tight as it sliced through his temple.

Treno tried to hold onto the spear as it whipped sideways – a mistake. The wooden shaft crashed hard across his chest as the Roman's horse flashed by, its rider tumbling from the saddle. The shaft snapped with a sharp crack and the broken wood slapped back across Treno's cheekbone. Dazed, he tossed what remained of the weapon to one side and fumbled for another, but his hand found nothing.

A Roman foot soldier appeared from nowhere, plunging forward with his shield raised and his sword pointed upward. Treno winced, his belly churning ice as he found nothing left with which to fight. He pulled hard on the reins, savagely forcing his horse over to face the man full on. The animal squealed and lurched sideways, its near shoulder falling low as all four hooves dug wildly at the dirt. The beast stumbled and seemed ready to fall, then its chest smashed against the Roman's curved shield. The man tumbled backward and vanished under the flailing hooves. Treno's mount, checked by the collision, found its footing and staggered on, bleeding from a gash in its shoulder.

Other riders flashed by on either side, screeching triumph as they slashed through the muddle of Romans defending the wagons. Close on their heels came the screaming tribesmen who, Treno thanked the gods, gave him time to fumble for his sword. What had happened to that second spear, he had no idea; he was sure it had been there when he started out.

Treno was vaguely aware of a brief clatter of hooves on stone, and realized he'd galloped his horse clear across the road and beyond, where there was nobody left to fight. Which was odd, because hardly a moment ago there seemed to have been hundreds. Treno wheeled his horse and saw why. The Romans had chosen to cling to the useless protection of the wagons, which would do the silly bastards little good. If they stood any chance at all, it was to run for the forest – though they would likely have fared no better. Modan's foot warriors were all over them like bees on a bear, hacking and slashing like madmen.

Modan! Treno groaned. He'd been tasked with protecting Modan's right and he'd made a total bollocks of it. Yet, when he thought more on that, he *had* been there on the man's right and had handled the single Roman who posed a threat. Surely Modan hadn't got himself hurt?

Treno frowned as a distant voice caught his ear. He checked his horse and cocked his head to one side. Someone was calling his name . . .

⸙

Bryn watched silently from a small knoll further up the valley, half-hidden in the cover of a small stand of pine. The brief skirmish had gone well, as he figured it would; but it had not gone so well for Modan himself. Treno was making his way back to help, though, drawn by the angry yelps that could be heard even this far away. It would do. The tattooed Carveti would see his brother safe out of it, long before any Roman troops arrived. Satisfied, Bryn pulled the reins of his horse to one side and gently touched the animal's belly with his heels.

# Chapter II

# Londinium, Februarius, A.D. 105

The *procurator* was a myopic sort of man, both in appearance and in mind. His eyes, when not bulging, were half narrowed as if trying to focus; and his mental wanderings followed far different paths than the man who sat studying the man's proposed budget. Governor Gaius Sabinius Trebonianus was no wonder with a wax tablet, a trait that often found details ranking second to impatience. Yet even he could see that the procurator's proposed taxes were punitive and unwarranted. They were, in fact, nothing more than self-serving sources of extra income, he was certain. *Trajan*'s problems in *Dacia* might well be starting up again, but as yet there had been no demand for increased revenues, only for more troops. So was the procurator set on plumping his own purse by more than the usual bloat, or was he simply trying to make an impression on Rome? Or was it both?

"Cronus, the *legate*'s situation at Eboracum is a house of straw waiting for a spark," Gaius said, his frazzled mind trying to remember what had been said during the last briefing about Brigantia. "Don't you read the dispatches? We're seeing nuisance raids all over the north. Last month the Carvetii attacked a road-building detail in Cumbria. A score of auxiliary troops were lost, and every tribesman south of the *Bodotria* figures Rome is in full retreat. It's madness!" Gaius sighed at the futility of governing these people – *his* people! "The moment we ease back on the sword the dumb bastards think we've gone senile and try to blade our backs."

"Exactly!"

"Huh?"

"That's exactly the reason we should raise their taxes," Cronus said eagerly. "Hit them where it hurts most."

"It hurts a sight more if you bash 'em in the teeth with a solid brass *boss*," Gaius said, wincing at the thought. One of his earliest memories had been a *Batavi* infantryman doing exactly that to his Aunt Nuada. "That lesson is a far more effective reminder to the neighbours when they see the result: a twisted face and no teeth! In the long run it gives them less reason to rebel than plucking the last grain of groats from their granaries."

"You don't store groats in granaries," Cronus said petulantly. "They're husked and broken up –"

"I don't give a sweet Caesar where they stick their groats," the governor cried, his head pounding from the man's incessant quibbling. "The point is, I've been in this province barely three months, and nothing has been done. A greater tax up north might punish, yes, but it will also set their piss to boiling, including anyone *not* thinking about rebelling. I don't want to get them started too, it could –"

"Actually, it's four months," Cronus interrupted. "You arrived toward the end of October, when –"

"I know when I arrived, Cronus, and it feels like four years, not four months. The snow is gone, spring will soon be upon us and so, it seems, will every barbarian north of Eboracum. And I would gently remind you that Eboracum is where I'm supposed to be at the moment, not bogged down in Londinium by tribes of scribes and a parade of pleading parasites, each seeking a self-serving favour from the new governor!"

"Not all are self-serving, Trebo, and the scribes are necessary to –"

"I don't care how necessary the scribes are. I don't want to go north bearing tidings of a new tax. And above all, I don't want to be called Trebo. My father detested the day Cerialis dubbed him with the name, and *I've* hated it ever since."

Gaius Sabinius Trebonianus fell back in his chair in disgust, and glared about the huge room. The *praetorium* was sparsely furnished, probably because it was so large. And though the building was supposed to be *his* residence, the procurator was also housed there, which was proving to be a nuisance. As too, were the hundred or more wax whittlers and stylus stabbers who haunted the place. The building was a warren of humanity that every morning seemed to fill up faster than a forum on Friday. Where, in the name of Minerva, did they all come from? Though most of them did *appear* to be doing something useful.

Gaius belched his irritation. Why had Cronus left his tax as the last item on their agenda? The answer was plain, of course: the man figured there would be less argument at the end of a long, boring session than in the middle of it. He caught the eye of a young slave idling by the doorway and gestured with his hand for a drink; the lad nodded and disappeared.

"If you *must* use a familiar, call me Tuis," Gaius muttered. "I've answered to it most of my life, and my mother still uses it, may the gods grant her favour." It was the name he'd been born with, and one that felt far more comfortable than the adopted name taken at his father's request when he turned sixteen – which was far too many years ago. Though hearing *any* familiarity from Cronus left a sour taste in his mouth.

"I do have the right to levy taxes," Cronus mumbled, his tone prim and defensive.

Tuis saw beads of sweat on the man's pallid brow, and the top of his bald head glistened like Thassian marble. It told him that Cronus was just as upset, which offered some satisfaction. "You make that sound like a threat," he said, forcing his voice to remain calm. Where was the slave with that drink?

"Reminding you of my duties to the emperor does not constitute a threat," Cronus said piously. "I'll make a note of it."

"There you go again: 'I'll make a note of it'!" Tuis imitated the man's snivelling whine and again glanced around the room. The trouble was that both he as governor, and Cronus as procurator, reported directly to the emperor, the two posts together being an infrequent situation due primarily to the large number of troops in the province. The appointments were most often rolled into one and called procurator, which also galled Tuis. His was the senior, in that he also commanded the armies; but Cronus did have the right to levy his miserable, chiselling, sticky-fingered taxes.

When the meeting was over he would have to find out what influence he had as governor in accepting or rejecting the taxes – there must be some sort of veto. In fact, he was quite certain there was, though there would no doubt need to be good reason. The dangerous side of using that blade, though, was getting mired in a turd-tossing contest with the man himself. That would prove not only unproductive; it ignored the basic rule of any cock fight: don't start unless certain of winning.

And where, on the gods' fields of fruitless battles, had that slave gone?

Tuis sighed as the silence dragged, finally breaking it by offering a threat of his own. "I also have duties, Cronus. They include, among

other things, keeping peace and harmony in the province and avoiding insurrection. That means holding all provocation to a minimum unless we actually *want* an insurrection – which at the moment we don't. So, if a tax levy causes one we *don't* want, I'll make one big bitch of a *note* about that, too."

"There's no need to be hostile," Cronus sniffed. "As I said, I have my –"

"Insurrection costs money. A *lot* of money," Tuis said, reasoning that needless expense might cause a denarii-driven desk driver to think twice. But when the same prim, tight-lipped expression reappeared, he again sighed and reluctantly decided to take a half-step backward. "Look, if we can't agree on this, then I'll pass the problem to Trajan. He may agree with you. But it's my guess that he doesn't want to listen to a lot of petty provincial squabbling until he's certain where he stands in Dacia. But if –" he raised one hand as Cronus opened his mouth to protest "—if we implement a tax increase at the end of autumn when the campaigning season is *over*, you'll find that's a much better time."

"So you will do it then?"

"Me? I thought you said it was your task to levy taxes," Tuis said innocently. "My job is to provide you with the soldiers to collect them, should it prove necessary, which no doubt it will." He made a mental note to dictate to his personal scribe that no *actual* promise had been given to implement a single *sestertius* of the man's lousy tax increase – just a suggestion that autumn would be a better time.

As if to signal the end of what had been a thoroughly annoying meeting, the slave finally appeared with a salver containing not only a supply of wine, but a small platter of odds and ends laid out by the kitchen, most of them sweet. That was yet another thing he didn't really need.

"Wine, Cronus?" Tuis asked genially, feeling better for the end of what was a strenuous session. His mind was already turning to Eboracum, where he should really be; if the barbarians were heating their cauldrons then it was his place to be there when they boiled. But arrangements had not yet been made to go, even though the visit was behind schedule.

Cronus's grim face also relaxed, clearly showing his relief that the confrontation was done with – for the time being. Tuis noticed the trace of a smile on the man's face, and it struck him that the procurator had not *actually* agreed to wait for the end of autumn either. Damn him! He bit his lip as the man reached for the wine, wondering whether he should force the matter or not.

Something else had caught Cronus's attention, though, for he dropped his hand and clambered to his feet, muttering excuses. Tuis turned to determine the cause, a move that proved unnecessary. He groaned as Livia's strident voice echoed from a hundred paces behind him.

※

Cronus strolled back to his quarters, the dark mood generated by his meeting with Sabinius slowly lifting. Though he was forced to put up with the new governor, he certainly didn't have to put up with the man's wife! He found a malicious satisfaction in that. She was – what?—the man's third attempt at marital bliss? He wondered what had happened to the other two. If they were anything like this one, the fool probably had them strangled. Cronus chuckled at the notion then shook his head. Impatient as the new governor was, he was a paragon of patience where his wife was concerned.

Cheered that Livia was the governor's woman and his own wife was a comfortable thousand miles away, Cronus turned down the cross hall that led to his apartments. The area was busy even at day's end, though many had already left for their quarters. His slave Erebus, whom he'd named as chief clerk the year before, still sat behind his table on the low *tribunal* off to the right. Which was as it should be, for the man's sense of duty should not permit him to leave until his cohort of clerks had satisfied their obligations.

"I've decided to delay tossing the spears of misfortune for the moment," Cronus murmured as he clambered onto the small tribunal and peered over Erebus's shoulder. The slave was only partly successful in covering the tablet that lay on the desk, and Cronus smiled. The chief clerk had been doodling. "If you can tear yourself away from the task at hand and halt the implementation, your master would be pleased."

"Sir?" Erebus's brow knitted in a frown. "You mean the new tax levy?"

"Your grasp of events never ceases to amaze," Cronus sneered. "The governor doesn't want to set the northern barbarians' piss to boiling – not that it isn't anyway."

"And the ones here in the south?"

"We never did discuss that. I don't think it occurred to him, though I suppose it will have to be the same." Cronus shrugged. "But we'll keep the pot simmering; if the heat is raised slowly, even these people will adjust."

"Er, how slow, sir?" Erebus asked. "The *Felicia* will dock at the beginning of July with your wine shipment, and the olive oil will be here in August. The balance due is payable on arrival."

"That's months away." Cronus blithely dismissed the problem, though his mind and guts were churning.

Most of the goods would be sold through the quartermasters. The army was where the greater gain lay, both in setting the profit margin and juggling quantities. Should it prove to be necessary, an advance from Britannia's treasury to pay for the goods might be arranged. But that would mean fixing records, even if it was only temporary – a small problem, should the goods be delivered soon. But such shipments were consigned to many destinations, and each location had its own budget and its own coin. If one or two commanders were late paying, the funds would have to be covered elsewhere. Maybe he could . . .

No, cutting in one of those leeches would cost far too much!

Cronus absently bit his lower lip as his mood grew thoughtful.

Perhaps the local traders could be pressured for advance payment. But no to that, too! It would only re-open the price – a distinct disadvantage. His mood began slipping. Another tax levy was an easier path that offered more profit; and any cream not skimmed could be held up by a delay in recording its receipt. And if the taxes were received in kind, a further gain could be had when paying for the goods with legion coin. If – no, not if, rather, *when* – certain trade-offs were arranged with the field collectors, a temporary increase in the division could be arranged . . .

Cronus nodded as figures fell neatly into a dozen imaginary holding slots. Any such arrangement was common practice from Judaea to Upper Germania. It was a just portion of the procurator's reward for faithful service to Rome; it also provided compensation for living in the raw wastelands of her empire. Everyone did it . . .

"Just keep the tax order on hand," Cronus muttered, as much to himself as Erebus. "We'll give our friend Sabinius a month or two fighting the barbarian *then* we'll see how he feels about punitive taxes. When is he supposed to leave for Eboracum?"

Erebus chuckled. "About a week and a half ago."

Cronus shook his head and chuckled in turn. "I hope he doesn't get lost trying to find the place."

# Chapter III

## Aricia, Februarius, A.D. 105

"Over there! Take him over there! And hurry!"

Metellus flung the main door open with surprising vigour for a man of his age, and ushered the four men inside. Hovering and bobbing like a bony crane, the slave urged them to the rear of the entrance hall with frantic gestures. Then, changing his mind, he trotted unsteadily ahead, guiding them through the atrium and into the huge *peristyle* that lay at the rear of the sprawling villa. Clucking with concern, he led them along the edge of the colonnaded garden to the family sleeping quarters, where he gestured impatiently to an open doorway.

"Put him on that, over there," the slave cried, gesturing at the enormous bed, the down-filled mattress bare but for a rumpled pile of linen. He turned anxious eyes south, searching a further *heredium* of lush green gardens. A half-dozen other slaves were already running toward him, as surely as if he'd summoned every last one.

"Where is she?" Metellus demanded, glancing back toward the villa. There was no need to mention her name. A chorus of voices replied, but no one seemed to have the answer. Elena, too, had gone riding, but she was nowhere to be found, and that only led to further questions about what had happened.

"Manius, tell Helier to saddle a horse and see if he can find her," Metellus ordered, nodding assurances to himself as his mind started to settle. Then, as one of the slaves sped away, he called, "And find someone to ride into Aricia for the *medicus*. Tell him to hurry, and not come back without him!"

Metellus hurried into the bedroom, where the four men had placed his master face down on the bed. His head was turned to the right, with both arms bent upward on either side as if in surrender. Were it not for a patch of blood a handsbreadth above his ear and the ashen pallor, Gaius Sabinius Trebonius might have been peacefully sleeping. Metellus reached out to touch the wound, which had already swollen to the size of a goose egg. At the last moment he flinched and changed his mind.

"Rollo, we could use a small sack of ice," Metellus called, staring anxiously at the motionless form. The breathing, he saw, was steady.

"Julia, get some clean cloths and water, hot and cold."

"His horse was going to run off, so we stopped it."

Metellus took a deep breath and stood back, for the first time looking directly at the men who had carried his master inside. The four seemed better suited to guarding the door of a dockyard brothel. "Run off?"

The men glanced at each other. As if by tacit consent, one mumbled, "It must've saw something in the ditch, 'cause it reared up and tried to run."

"He come off backward and cracked his head," the largest of the four men growled, glowering at the first as if chiding him for the omission.

"Yeah, that's how he fell."

Metellus frowned. His master was an accomplished rider. Not only that, Gaius had taken the sorrel gelding, an older horse that was so gentle, even he might have considered riding the beast. "And where did this happen?"

"Down the road, maybe a mile," the first man said, gesturing vaguely south toward the estate's huge groves of olive trees.

"And you . . . ?"

"We were coming up the road from Aricia and saw it, so we came and picked 'im up. We brought 'im back to where he lived."

"And you would know that, of course," Metellus said skeptically.

"No, but the horse did."

That, at least, held the ring of truth. But where, amongst the tangled heads of Hydra, was Elena?

"We thought you'd be grateful," the second man added. The others nodded their solemn agreement.

Metellus blinked as his mind digested the story. Better lies, he decided, could be heard at the Ostian slave market. A chill ran down his spine as he realized he'd just dispatched half the slaves who moments ago had come running to help. *So what is one more?* "Ivo, go and find Lepidus." Metellus turned his back on the men and winked at the slave, hoping it would alert the lad to his suspicions. "Tell him what has happened, and say that we must give these men something for their help."

The young slave looked blank for a moment, then nodded his understanding and ran off toward the stables.

"Who's Lepidus?" the big one demanded, suspicious eyes following Ivo through the fluted columns.

"The estate overseer," Metellus replied, then added to the lie, "the man who controls the purse."

"Ah!"

*Oh no, not now,* Metellus groaned silently as he caught sight of Elena entering the villa. She saw him at the same moment and started running.

"Where is he? Is he dead?" she shouted. Without waiting for the answer, she brushed past the old slave and entered the bedroom.

Metellus sighed as he watched Elena bend over his master, one hand reaching to Gaius's forehead as the other fell to his neck, testing the beat of his heart. Her presence was not needed now, not with Lepidus arriving, hopefully backed by a dozen field hands ready to deal with these men and their transparent tale.

"Oh no, no," Elena wailed. She fell forward across Gaius's back, her arms sliding around his shoulders, her body heaving with sobs.

Metellus blinked. Elena? He'd served his mistress for more than three decades, during which time the woman had witnessed battle wounds, bashed heads, death, and destruction enough to last a dozen lifetimes. Was she losing her mind? Elena was the most practical person in the entire household, including Gaius himself; yet there she was, flung across the master's limp body as if hysterical – or . . . as if protecting him. The hairs rose on the back Metellus's neck. With a nervous glance toward the doorway, he stepped backward.

Lepidus burst through first, a cudgel in his upraised hand. Behind him, framed against the bright sun and the garden greenery, were half a dozen field hands, each as handily armed. For the space of a heartbeat, nobody moved; then it seemed as if everyone moved, all at once.

Metellus watched as if no more than a spectator at a Greek drama.

Three of the men backed away, clearly terrified, their arms spread in submission. The larger one drew a long, crude knife from inside his tunic. Lunging sideways, he grabbed for Elena, half an eye on Lepidus and his men.

Elena rolled across the bed, away from the groping arm, but quick as a snake bite, the brute grasped her wrist and hauled her upright. Instead of resisting, Elena tumbled over the mattress, barely clearing Gaius's unconscious body. One shoulder thumped hard against the big man's frame and her free hand flew upward as if clawing for his face. Then her body fell limp.

An odd silence filled the room as everyone tried to grasp what had just happened. By far the most baffled was Elena's assailant. Standing by the bed holding her by the wrist, he let his knife fall as one hand moved uncertainly up to his eye. He flinched as his fingers struck the hilt of another blade. Blood seeped from around it and trickled down his cheek.

Lepidus was the first to move, stepping forward to free Elena's wrist as the huge man staggered sideways, pulling weakly at the knife embedded in his eye. Metellus gaped as the dagger came free and clattered to the floor. Blood gushed obscenely from the socket as the thug's legs buckled, and he tumbled to the floor.

Elena glared contemptuously at the twitching body, then at the dark crimson stain on her tunic. "I'm covered in it," she complained, then gestured toward the corpse twitching its final spasms. "That one bashed Gaius on the head!"

"Are you alright?" Lepidus asked, staring at her blood-drenched clothing.

"Better than he is." Elena nudged the corpse with one foot, then stared at Metellus. "How about you?"

"I-I-I suppose I'm alright," the slave stammered, his head swimming. "What do you mean, bashed him on the head?"

"Just what I said – and he was helped by those gawping apes." Elena waved toward the three men, now down on their knees, then shook her head as she again glared at the body. "This useless turd was the one who hit him with the club."

"Where were you?" Metellus winced as his eyes swept over Elena's clothing, feeling grateful that she'd not been harmed.

"I was off in the bushes."

"What were you doing in the –" Metellus felt his cheeks heat as his mind grasped the obvious.

Elena told him anyway. "I was relieving myself, dammit. Down the road, not far from where it crosses the one coming up from Aricia. The big one came first, dragging a young girl by the hair." She snorted her disgust. "Gaius rode over to intervene, and these three pulled him from the saddle, while this useless lump –" Metellus flinched as Elena kicked at the corpse "—struck him with a club."

"And you . . . ?"

"I was crouched over with my britches – never mind! I saw it all through the bushes. The girl ran off, likely back to Aricia. I thought about mounting up and trying to ride them down, but by the time I was decent, they'd slung Gaius over his horse and were walking this way.

They followed the animal, which of course came home." Elena shrugged as if baffled. "I was astounded when they turned in here, and started banging on the door."

"They said he'd fallen from his horse and banged his head," Metellus explained. "They were looking to find a reward for bringing him back!"

Elena swore her disgust, and turned back to Gaius with a sigh. She leaned over and placed a hand gently on his back, just to the left of his spine. "His heartbeat is steady, which is good. Have you sent for a medicus?"

"Yes, Helier has gone. I'm surprised you didn't see him."

"I was off looking for help myself," Elena muttered, her hand returning once more to Gaius's forehead. "I found Lepidus over by the stables."

*Leaving Ivo running around in panic, trying to find him!* Metellus chuckled wryly to himself, and decided he'd better go and relieve the boy of his misery. Though there was no hurry.

He glanced fondly down at Elena's bent figure and smiled. The woman had more grit than a gravel road. A year or two into her sixties, and she acted as if she had half those years. And to look at her – well, a man might knock ten years off the tally and still believe it; while as for himself, hah! Never mind the aches, the pains, and the tricks of his memory, he was no longer even as tall as he'd once been! Elena always had the better of him there – though of late, he'd seen the gap grow wider. Yet what might he expect? The woman had been a Brigante warrior when his master claimed her as battlefield booty, and in some ways she still was. Metellus's smile broadened as he counted off the years. Thirty-five had passed –

"If I could call you away from the faerie, Metellus," Elena said, her tone indulgent, "we could probably use some food and drink when he comes around."

⁂

Gaius Sabinius Trebonius never came around that day. Elena grew worried to the point of distraction. Everything in her husband's body was working fine. His breathing was shallow but normal; his heartbeat was a slow, steady throb; and his body ejected waste as surely and as regularly as it had ever done. Perhaps more than regularly, Elena mused as the end of that first month drew to a close.

Metellus supervised the daily feeding, which was followed by yet another change of linen. The daily routine began with Gaius carefully propped against a wall of pillows. On a wooden table close by, a thin tube of soft, tightly sewn leather sat filled with a fresh, soupy mash of his favourite foods. The tube was longer than necessary but completely filled, with the first foot and a half soaked in a glistening coat of olive oil. The old slave tilted his master's head and Elena fed the tube gently down his throat, as slickly as a sword swallower's blade. Once in place, Metellus squeezed the thin leather, the excess food at the top forcing the lower contents down into Gaius's belly. Afterward an even thinner, shorter tube was inserted, and a jug of warm, much-watered wine was forced down the same path.

After the feeding Elena found her eyes watering, yet she tried to remain calm. Metellus eased Gaius back down on the bed and a pair of house slaves took over. For the best part of an hour, the two vigorously massaged Gaius's body, a routine they performed twice a day.

When it was done Elena rose to leave, but a hand fell on her shoulder; she silently covered it with her own. There was no need to look up and see who it was.

"He's losing weight, Mam," Coira murmured.

"Ha!" Elena forced a smile. "He was getting flabby anyway."

# Chapter IV

# Carvetii Territory, Februarius, A.D. 105

Cethen Lamh-fada slumped onto the log bench outside the door to his lodge, unwilling to believe his ears – which was idiotic, because he'd known all along about the ill-conceived assault on the Roman supply column. Modan had said he was going to do it; he had lectured the boy long and hard not to do it; and he'd told the boy how badly it would make the Romans' piss boil. Which Modan had now undoubtedly done, for attacking a Roman supply column – especially with any kind of success – was like kicking a bear in the balls. Or more like a herd of bears, if there was such a thing . . .

Still, it hadn't seemed real until it actually happened. Cethen fell back against the wall of the lodge, more drained than angry. Why, oh why, hadn't *some* of his words pierced his son's thick, bone-brained skull?

The fool had his arguments ready, of course, listing a thousand reasons why he was doing the right thing. One contention in particular had stuck in Cethen's mind: Modan's harping on his da's own violent past. Which was more than just laughable; it was mad! His own efforts against the Romans – or deeds, as Criff used to call them – stood far higher in the minds of others than they did in his own. Oh, he had leaned hard against many Roman shields in the old days – often too hard – but there was more to it than that. Somebody else had always been right there, standing behind, pushing him on. And the thought of that, too, was enough to make Cethen laugh: had Modan been alive back then, he would have been one of the pushers!

The boy never could figure out that what a man did had its consequences. Or maybe he did have it figured, Cethen mused, and seen the other side of that blade: the men left to face those consequences were rarely the ones who caused them. Once in a while a person might get away with shoving the Romans gently when they were distracted, but you never pushed hard enough to make their bile bubble – and Modan had done exactly that. And to add to it, the careless fool had gone and got himself hurt. In the leg, yet!

Cethen grunted at the gods' twisted whims. In a lifetime of fighting the sodding Romans, his only real injury had also been to his leg. It still made him limp, but to be honest it wasn't all that bad, not when the odds of all those years were tallied. How serious was Modan's wound? Cethen sighed and squinted up at Treno, a blurred shadow standing sheepishly holding the reins of a horse, his news now delivered. Cethen bit his lip, his belly cold as he asked, "What happened, and how bad?"

"A spear. He took it when we first attacked."

"Weren't you riding with him?"

"Yeah, right alongside, all the way." Treno shrugged, his bruised, tattooed features unreadable. "You know how it is. Things happen fast. And a man's got to look after himself, too. He can't be protecting someone else if he's dead."

Cethen knew how that one stood, for he'd been there often enough. Treno hadn't answered the question, though, and he pushed it. "I asked, how bad?"

"The big bone at the top might be broke in the middle, but it wasn't sticking out the hole. I think it was the way the spear hit him. Or it might have happened when he fell off his horse. I dunno." Another shrug, then silence.

Cethen sighed again and wondered if there was more to it. He didn't like Treno; the youth was bad for Modan. But then Ficra, if she'd still been alive, would have turned the other side of the sword and claimed Modan was just as bad for Treno. The woman might have been a vixen at times, but she'd always been fair. Cethen briefly savoured the years of memory, then forced his mind back to the question. Treno *still* hadn't given an answer. "I said, how –"

"It's turning angry. The bone looks to be in place alright, but I think the wound is like to turn poisonous."

"How are they treating it?"

"They're using poultices, herbs, honey – you know, the usual stuff to bring out the poison." Treno shrugged in a way that said things might go one way or another.

Cethen thought that over for a moment, then eased himself around on the bench and called over one shoulder, "Kelpy!"

A young woman emerged from the lodge, a knife in one hand and the back half of an eel dangling from the other. "Da, I'm in the middle of getting something ready for – oh, it's you." She nodded to Treno, her face expressionless.

"Modan's hurt, Kelpy," Cethen said. "His leg. It got chopped open, and may be broke too. It looks like it's festering."

"The Romans?"

"Uh-huh."

"So the fool went and did it!"

"Did you expect any different?"

"No, I suppose not." Kelpy released her breath in exasperation, cursed silently, then made to go back inside.

Cethen stopped her with another question. "That big fort beyond the *Ituna*." His brow puckered as he tried to retrieve a snippet of gossip from the back of his mind. "Isn't there a woman helping heal the people around there? Trained by the Romans? I heard she might be Roman herself."

"Uh-huh. I was told they built her a small healing lodge in the village outside the walls," Kelpy said. "She's supposed to be good, very good, both with potions and a knife."

"There you go then!" Cethen slapped one hand against his knee and turned back to Treno. "If the boy can't be helped by our own, see if the woman will lend a hand. I've watched how their surgeons work, and they're good."

Cethen's voice faded, his mind drifting to another time, the only time he had seen the Roman surgeons – *medici*, they called them – perform their grizzly work. It was on a soft bed of autumn grass in a lush, open lea somewhere far to the north, in the hills of the Caledonii. The patient had been his first wife, and at first he thought she'd been killed; even when he realized she was only wounded, he still thought it would prove fatal. But this was Elena, and he should have known; the woman was nigh on immortal! Though without the Roman surgeon, Cethen grudgingly admitted, she would surely have died. Even the man's assistant had knife skills that our own people could only wish for!

Cethen's smile was bitter, for the memory cut deep. There had been a brief truce that day; or, truth be known, everyone had simply pretended he wasn't there. His son, Rhun; his daughter, Coira; even Cian had anxiously watched as the Roman surgeon worked to remove the spear rammed through Elena's shoulder. His children and his brother had then forced him to flee, when the Roman commander himself rode up: Gaius Sabinius Trebonius. Cian had actually ordered him carried off and hidden in the trees. "For your own good," the great oaf Luga had told him as he'd pinned him to the ground like a bleating calf until the clearing was once more empty. That was that last time he'd seen either Elena or his children . . .

"I heard the woman wasn't Roman," Kelpy volunteered. "She speaks our tongue as if born to it. I also heard she's a dwarf."

"I don't care what she speaks, as long as she can fix Modan and stop his bitching. I'll ask him what he thinks," Treno said, and grinned. "If the crazy bugger dies, he's going to kill me."

"Yeah, well, idiot that he is, we don't want that," Cethen muttered, not amused by Treno's jesting. "And I mean the bit about *him* dying, not the bit about killing you. Where is he now?"

"They all rode farther north, into the hills. They're about two, three days from here. A Selgovae chieftain called Lagan is building up one of the old hill forts again." Treno's voice grew more enthused. "Modan says the Romans have been sending troops back across the sea, because their empire is crumbling. It seems like every one of their forts has sent men. If we can gather enough warriors now while they're weak, and –"

"*If!* Hah!" Cethen had used that word far too often himself. "*Ifs* are nothing but wishes. Look, do I need to go with you?"

Treno appeared surprised. His eyes ran over Cethen's sparse body, pausing briefly at his belly, which in fairness looked twice its size due to the way he sat hunched over. It was a look that, had Cethen been able to see it more clearly, would have angered him.

"No," Treno said. "There's going to be a lot of hard riding, and a lot of rough country. And the Romans are probably already out looking."

"I can keep up," Cethen muttered, though a long, hard ride, especially for someone who was near blind, would be a challenge. "The trouble with you young warts is that when a man's skin curls up, you think his insides have done the same."

"Sure, sure." Treno grabbed the pommel and swung back into the saddle. "I'll tell you what: if Modan's not healing well, I'll send word, fast."

"You said two or three days. A lot can happen in that time."

"Hey, there's no problem." Treno chuckled in a show of indifference. "It takes the better part of a week to croak from a festering leg."

"Don't worry, Da, it won't happen," Kelpy said, and squeezed Cethen's shoulder; but her face wore her concern, which was just as well left unseen. "This woman – I think she's called Jenna, or Jessa, or something – from what I hear, she's cured a good many –"

"Jessa?" Cethen yelped, and fell silent; then, remembering her earlier words. "You say she's a dwarf?"

"Uh-huh. That's what I heard. Even so, she's able to –"

"Jessa! Well, sod the gods!" A broad smile lit Cethen's face. He leaned back against the wall of the lodge, his mind again flooding with old memories. "The wee lass is back. I wonder if her da is, too."

"Should I care?" Treno asked as he pulled the reins to one side, ready to leave. "I have her name. I know the place. It should be enough."

"No, no, wait." Cethen raised a hand to stay him. "There's one or two other things I should tell you that might be useful in persuading the girl."

※

"Da," Kelpy began later that day, as the two sat together eating the last of the baked eel, "is there going to be as much trouble as they say?"

"Likely more," Cethen replied. "The last time we thought we had them on the run, they chased us all the way to the end of Caledonii territory, where the land falls off into the sea. A battle took place there that was bigger than anything you can imagine. There were thousands of them, and thousands of us." Cethen paused, certain the figures did not do justice. "No, there were tens of thousands; it was thousands that died." He dropped the spine-like bones of the eel back onto the platter, his gaze going distant as his voice fell to a whisper. "And nearly all of them were us."

"You think it will happen again?"

"You mean us, raising a big army?" Cethen thought on that for a moment, then shook his head. "No, not really. Not just the Brigantes, anyway. We don't have the numbers or the will to gather an army that size. And there's too many who still remember. Besides, I don't know of anyone strong enough to lead. *Galgar* was smart in his own way and he could lead, but his head was sometimes numb. Even with all those numbers it was never a fight. And as for Modan and his bunch, it's mainly the young sprouts with hot blood and thick heads who think they know everything." He turned his face toward her and grinned. "You know what I mean, the ones your age."

Kelpy laughed and kicked gently at her da's rear as she rose from the low table and began clearing the meal. Cethen gazed fondly at the blurred shape flitting about the lodge, wishing his eyes could better focus. The girl had been about three or four years old when he and Ficra had found her: a soot-covered bairn wandering the ashes of a burned village, a day's ride south of that final battlefield. It was as if the gods had left her there for them to find as they stumbled home, cloaked in the shame of defeat: a new bairn with which to start life over again. The girl had truly been a gift. His own brood were all gone, lost to the Romans. Kelpy had proved to be the start of his third family. Yet those same gods had not been kind to the lass herself. The girl's own man, a fair lad with not an idle bone in his body, had caught the fever the year their second child was born . . .

Cethen blinked away the blurred memory of the youth's face, for it was painful to think on – as were too many other things. Kelpy had turned to him for help after that, which was all well and good, but one day he wouldn't be there, either . . .

"What are you going to do?" Kelpy asked.

There was bitter irony in her words, Cethen mused, for his wandering mind pondered the same question, only his was about Kelpy herself: what was *she* going to do – when he was no longer there? But that wasn't what the lass was asking, and he forced his thoughts back to the shadowy lodge and the girl's words. "I don't know, Kelpy. I suppose I'll have to do something."

# Chapter V

## Blatobulgium, Februarius, A.D. 105

At first only a single rider appeared in the middle of the trail, his horse turned sideways, blocking the path that led back to the fort. His mount was the usual barbarian hill pony, a stocky beast with a dark brown hide, a black mane and tail, and a cross-pommelled saddle bound to its back. The rider who sat hunched in the saddle was a large and excessively heavy man who seemed to dwarf the poor animal. Two spears were slung casually over one shoulder, and a small round shield dangled low against his hip. Dark tattoos scrolled across his forehead and down his cheeks, disappearing into a glistening black beard streaked with grey. The rider said nothing, staring at them from perhaps a hundred paces away.

Jessa's escort, though only a third of a *troop*, felt no cause to panic. Each man straightened in the saddle and hefted his shield, at the same time easing a spear into his right hand. As they drew close to the barbarian horseman, the Roman she knew simply as Dracus glanced nervously at the tangled wall of undergrowth and the towering, leafless trees that loomed tall on either side. He growled at the others to do nothing foolish.

Licking his lips, Dracus called for a halt when they were less than fifty paces away. "You're in our way," he shouted in Latin, his tone calm – which was just as well, Jessa decided as she urged her pony alongside. There was no point in tossing angry words until they knew what the man wanted. Even so, an uneasy shiver traced her small spine as the dark forest, by its very silence, assumed a menace of its own.

"I need the little one," the barbarian said, using his own tongue.

"What's he saying?" Dracus muttered, and turned to look at the others. "Does anyone understand this shit?"

"The man says he needs the *little* one. Which, I imagine, means me," Jessa said dryly, and called out in the man's own dialect, "Why?"

"There is a man. He is hurt. It's turning to fever."

"You have your own people. I know their skill. A fever is a fever."

"And we know yours," the horseman replied, and shrugged. "Besides, nothing seems to work. Your skill with a knife is what's needed."

"What's the man saying?" Dracus hissed.

"Someone's hurt, and he wants my help," Jessa replied, then called out, "Your name. What's your name?"

"Treno."

"And the man who is hurt?"

"He's that way." The horseman pointed vaguely to the northwest. "A day's ride."

*I ask for a name, and he tells me the way; a simple mind, or simply sly?* Jessa called out again, deliberately defiant, "And if I don't go with you?"

For answer, Treno barked an order. More than a score of riders drifted from the trees on either side and formed up behind the man in a loose sort of order. Dracus stirred and began muttering his own commands, but a further order rang out from the barbarian. A soft humming filled the air above Jessa's head, followed by the hard thud of arrows striking the tree trunks off to her left.

"Come on, let's get out of here. All of you!" Dracus cried and raised his feet, ready to slam them into his horse's gut.

"Nooo! No! I'll go!" Jessa screamed and tried to grab his arm but, small as she was and mounted on her pony, the gesture was futile.

Dracus's heels slammed down and the horse lunged forward. He cast a quick glance at Jessa, saw she was not moving, and instantly hauled savagely back on the reins. The horse squealed and twisted in mid-stride, then bucked sideways across the trail, tossing him heavily to the ground. Free of its burden, the animal trotted on toward the cluster of barbarian horsemen. The others of Dracus's squad milled about the narrow trail in confusion, their eyes darting nervously between the men who blocked their path and the forest on either side.

"Sorry," Jessa murmured, not feeling particularly sorry at all. The man should have listened. She walked her pony forward until it loomed over Dracus, sprawled on the dirt and gasping for breath. "Are you alright?"

"No, I'm fu –" He began, then decided better and broke off. Shifting onto one elbow, he glared at the man Treno and the riders that blocked their path. "I'll live, for a few breaths, anyway. We could have rammed through. Most of us would have made it. But now they're ready, and only the gods know for what."

"There's no point in *anyone* getting killed because of me," Jessa said tartly, and turned her eyes back to the tattooed man and his riders. Without having seemed to move, they had formed two orderly ranks, their spears held ready. The thick undergrowth on either side whispered with the rustle of movement and the impatient murmur of voices. *Some fool trying to keep control over those who were losing it,* Jessa thought, and shook her head, reminding herself that these were her own people. And, as always, they were growing impatient.

"I'd better find out what he wants me to do," she muttered, and urged the pony forward, ignoring Dracus's protests.

Treno was not, as Jessa had first thought, a man who overstuffed his belly. He was a big one, certainly, but what had appeared at a distance to be fat was due to his loose cloak, and the way it draped over a hidden burden slung across the pommel. The grey in his beard was no illusion, though it had come early, for he was fairly young – perhaps even her age which, according to the best reckoning of anyone she knew, was five or six years over twenty. It was an age that was, Jessa reflected, only *relatively* young. There were some days when the joints in a dwarf's bones…

"You're way smaller than I was told," Treno observed from his vantage, towering above her as she reined the small pony in before him. "In fact, I'm surprised how small."

"Many are," Jessa said, irritated at the remark. Deliberately choosing her words, for she rarely swore, she added, "But most are too fucking polite to comment."

For a moment Treno said nothing, but the men on either side sniggered and someone behind burst out laughing. Then he smiled too, an expression that the dark whorls did little to soften, and lowered his head as if in deference. "If I offend, then my apologies."

"How can ignorance give offence?" Jessa snapped, determined not to lose what little edge she might have; the man did say, after all, that she was needed. "You didn't mention who was hurt. Nor did you mention in what manner."

"It's Modan. Modan-mor."

Jessa waited for further explanation, but Treno said nothing and she realized he was expecting her to recognize the name. "And Modan the Mighty's problem?" she asked, deciding that whatever the fellow's claim on greatness, it was of little importance alongside her own predicament and that of the ten Roman auxiliary cavalrymen behind her.

"An open wound above his knee, the bone likely broken."

"Your people can fix that."

"They did, and it's gone to poison. It won't heal."

"Then it will likely have to come off. Your people can do that, too. How did it happen?"

"It seems that the sharp end of a spear somehow got jammed in it."

Jessa winced. "And I suppose it had a Roman trooper on the blunt end."

"Modan didn't skewer himself," Treno said, then added, as if it might make a difference, "He thinks you can fix it."

"My surgery is performed in the small infirmary by the fort. Usually on the local folk who are ailing. That is well known. He can see me there." Jessa knew perfectly well that Modan *the Mighty* would not see her there; whoever the fool was, he wouldn't dare show his face around a Roman fort.

Treno ignored the suggestion. "He asked for you by name."

"He did? What did he call me? The Roman dwarf woman?" she sneered.

"No. He called you Jessa. Daughter of Marcus Sabinius Treber-ar-ius or something."

"He did?" Jessa said, her belly growing cold. Who could possibly remain among the tribes with knowledge of her father's name? "How does he know that?"

"Modan's da told him. Said he knew you."

Which meant the wounded man's father was getting on in years, Jessa thought. There could be few left alive who knew her from those days, not with a son full grown. "So who is this Modan's da?"

"Cethen. Cethen Lamh-fada."

"But . . ." Jessa's mind fogged with a child's memory: a man, one who had seemed old even back then; lazy, long-lashed eyes, drooping moustaches, a fair and kind sort of man, as she recalled. He was tall – they were all tall, of course – and a friend, sort of, to her own da. She was amazed he still lived, and said so.

"Yeah, well, old age is nothing to take joy in," Treno muttered, and glanced anxiously back and forth down the trail.

Jessa saw the uncertainty scribed in the dark shift of his eyes. The man's followers were growing restless, as were those of Dracus, and there was no telling who or what might suddenly appear along the track. "Is he otherwise well?" she ventured, unsure what else to say.

Treno ignored the question. "Are you coming with us, or do we take you?"

Jessa shrugged. "There's no point going anywhere with no medicine or instruments. Without them, I can offer nothing more than sympathy." She nodded in the direction they'd been riding. "What I need is in the village, back there by the fort."

Treno pulled his cloak away from the bundle that lay across the front of his saddle. "Anything you need is right here."

"How did you get that?" Jessa blurted, recognizing the soft leather pack. Yet there was no need to ask, she quickly realized. Her small hospice was in the village itself, not the fort; and those who came to see her there were, after all, this man's people, not her own – no matter how much she might imagine they were.

"So are you coming with us, or –" Treno nodded meaningfully toward Dracus and his men "—do we have to take you?"

"What are you going to do with *them* if I do come?" Jessa waved a hand toward Dracus, now standing in the middle of the trail, leaning on his spear.

"Leave them here."

"In what condition?"

"Alive and well." The dark whorls twisted with Treno's smile and, perhaps because she was growing used to the man's face, it didn't appear nearly as grim. "Perhaps less their weapons. Though for your sake, we'd rather avoid a fight to get them. I don't want to lose anybody, no more than they likely do."

"Then I'll go with you, though they keep their weapons," Jessa said, then grunted her disdain. "I doubt you'd get them without a fight, anyway."

"Er, we will keep the horses, though," Treno added, and shrugged as if apologizing for an inconvenience.

Jessa shook her head. "Those poor lads are going to be in enough trouble as it is, when they go back without me. The horses stay."

"We're not going to pass up ten good Roman horses. I'd have a revolt on my hands if I just rode off and left them."

"Fine then, we fight! And I hope you get killed. In fact, I'll place a curse on you for exactly that, before we even start." Jessa quickly pulled the reins of her pony to one side and kicked at the animal's belly. The small animal started trotting back along the trail.

"Hey! Wait, girl!"

Jessa pulled back on the reins and turned in the saddle, one hand on the pony's rump. "My name is not girl."

"Jessa, then. We'll leave the horses down the road aways. You gotta admit, I can't have those sods," Treno gestured toward Dracus and his men, "tearing back and telling the Romans what just happened. We need a good head start, especially if we gotta drag that toy horse of yours along with us."

Jessa ignored the jibe, satisfied that she'd at least won her point. She couldn't argue with the man's logic. Nor could she resist being smug. "Then why didn't you say so at the start, and save us all a lot of bother?"

※

Modan-mor was a young man, probably in his early twenties. He lay on a blanket, naked from the waist down. His beard was dark and curly and his eyes had the long, lazy lashes of his father, but their black centres were hard, and at the moment glistened with pain. If he could be cured the pain she saw there would disappear, Jessa decided, but the pitiless glare would remain. She'd seen such a hard glint too many times in the eyes of those who followed a cause, men and women alike, and she had no doubt that Modan's cause was ridding the tribes of Rome. The hard stare was now aimed at her, a woman who belonged neither to Rome nor the tribes. Jessa sighed in disgust, feeling no sympathy for a man who held too much hate to think through what he did.

"The leg stays," Modan ordered with no trace of civility.

Jessa nodded and spared him no further glance, choosing instead to turn and take stock of her surroundings. Modan had been placed under a makeshift shelter, set off to the side of a large, natural meadow. Half-hidden by the stark shadows of a thousand budding shade trees, the setting was hauntingly familiar. Jessa sighed as her eyes swept the cool lea: a wide, picturesque glen carved by time, with gentle, wooded slopes that would soon magically billow with lush shades of green. A wide, bubbling stream burbled across the rich valley floor in search of a greater river, while the . . .

While the rest of it was also familiar, far too familiar!

The clearing was crowded with tribesmen, some painted, most of them not. A few wore an assortment of armour, while many were barely clad. Some stood silent, surly with contempt; others simply stared in curiosity. Most did both.

"I said you won't cut the damned thing off!" Modan growled, clearly angry at Jessa's silent indifference.

She turned back to the man, deliberately muttering her impatience. Her eyes dropped to the wounded leg and a huge, festering scab barely a foot below his limp manhood. The gash itself was no longer large. It had been crudely tightened into a black, crusted line and stitched closed. Any broken bone was now well buried underneath. The limb itself looked straight enough, but that was no assurance the bone had been correctly set. The lip of the wound, where it had grown dark and crusted, wept thick, yellow tears. The thigh itself was swollen and hot, and that was Modan's real problem; though the telltale crimson line of death was not yet there. It soon would be. The limb was throbbing fit to burst and certainly not helping the man's temper, which was clearly vile at the best of times.

"I won't cut what off?" Jessa said, her face expressionless as she deliberately turned her gaze to his flaccid organ. Someone laughed, which only served to further Modan's anger.

"The leg, witch. Cut it off, and it's worth your life."

Jessa stepped back, this time loudly snorting her disgust. She crossed her arms and glared. Her heart pounded hard enough to hear, but she was overwhelmed by a flaring anger: a dark, hot rage that flooded body and mind; an anger that, as it had so many times before, swept away both fear and prudence. This ignorant, doltish fool could sodding-well go ahead and do what he liked, she decided, either to himself or to her. It made little difference.

"Then kill me now, and save us both the bother," Jessa heard herself say, her voice a low, shaking snarl. "*I might then find eternal rest. You*, on the other hand, can then rot, fester, and die in demented agony. And I hope it hurts worse than a thousand deaths, you great useless tit. It's too bad I won't be around to see it." She refolded her arms and looked away.

The clearing fell silent as a tomb. Surprisingly, though her anger was fading, Jessa found she truly did not care what the fool did, one way or another. Yet she could feel blood pulsing through her veins like the beat of a pounding drum.

Treno broke the silence, his face anxious. "She can only do her best, Mod."

Modan's jaw clenched tight, and he groaned as yet another wave of pain throbbed through his leg. Jessa could have laughed, had it all not been so tragic. Modan glared at Treno, then at Jessa, and finally around the clearing, where a hundred men stood silently watching. "Just get on with it," he growled.

"And if you lose your leg? Or die?" Jessa persisted, knowing full well she was pushing the man's limits. "Quite bluntly, there's half a chance it *will* have to go. And if the poison can't be stopped, you'll go with it. What happens then, you selfish man? Would you slay me in your folly, so that whatever help I give your people will no longer be there? All because of your ignorant pride?" She paused and took a deep breath, aware that she was backing the man hard against a stone wall. "I knew your da once, you know. He was a good man – a very good man. I don't know how he ever spawned you."

"As I said, just get on with it." The words came through gritted teeth as Modan again winced in pain.

"And . . . ?" Jessa motioned toward Treno. "You tell him."

"Oh for – don't hurt her, dammit," Modan snarled then added in a low growl, "I weren't going to do nothing anyway. I was just making sure."

"Making sure I did my best?" Jessa finished. "Then why not ask me? I'd have told you. I always do my best – particularly when nobody is threatening me." She turned. "Where's my bag?"

The leather pack quickly appeared, and Jessa rummaged inside. "I need clean, boiling water. Two pots of it," she called out, and looked up long enough to see who might offer help. "Treno, have someone start crushing garlic. Here." She handed him a bundle of pale, peeling bulbs. "Skin and clean them first. I don't want a speck of anything left. The mash is needed as a poultice for the dressing."

"Garlic?" Modan mumbled, eyeing the hefty bundle.

"It's to fight infection. And you can swallow some, later. It all helps. And there's also this." She drew a cluster of roots from inside the bag, picked one out, and thrust it toward him. "Chew on that, and swallow the spit you get from it."

"What is it?" Modan demanded.

"Mandrake."

He paled. "That's poison."

"It can be, if you eat the whole sodding plant. Chew it. Swallow some of the pulp, maybe, but not much."

Jessa removed a heavy instrument box and began selecting what was needed for boiling. Every last piece had been cadged from Roman army surgeons, mostly from the hospital at Eboracum when her father had commanded the fortress a decade past. In those days she had been fascinated by the surgeons' work. Yet now, the same work was nothing more than routine; a routine that gave her odd life a small sense of meaning. For when the gods had made her the way she was, there had to be some meaning to it that made sense . . .

She eyed the instruments carefully, picking out what would be needed: scalpels for opening the wound, and most likely for cutting down to the bone; needles for the stitching, as well as thread, which would also need boiling; possibly a bone lever, and a couple of bone forceps too, for something might have been left in there that needed to be moved. Jessa began humming as she laid out the tools: a cautery or two, a couple of long hooks to hold the flesh, and the probes . . .

"Here, drink half of this while I wash my hands," she ordered, once the instruments were in the pot of bubbling water.

Modan peered groggily into the mug. A finger's width of liquid sloshed about the bottom. "What's this?" he demanded, his voice listless.

"Among other good stuff, it's got henbane in it."

Modan squinted blearily at the contents. "Isn't that poison too?"

"Can be," Jessa said as she carefully washed her hands. "But that much won't hurt, it'll just help. Drink it, and if that doesn't do it, I'll give you another." She chuckled and added under her breath, "And maybe a dozen more, if need be."

"Wha-what do you mean by 'doesn't do it'?" Modan asked a few moments later, forcing the question between yawns.

Jessa ignored him. She stepped onto a flat rock that had been placed alongside the makeshift bed, giving her enough height to look down on the injured leg. She studied the wound closely, touched the hot skin, then cut at the stitches. The flesh fell back somewhat as the pressure released, but mostly remained where it was. Modan hardly flinched.

Jessa released her pent up breath, her mind tracing through needed steps: start by opening it all up again, of course, and be prepared to delve down to the bone – which in turn would have to be cleared, cleaned, and set right, if it wasn't already. She hoped it hadn't been set wrong, or if it had, that the knitting of it wasn't too far along; either way, she'd need help to put *that* right again. *If only the ones who first tended the wound were here to talk to; especially if they'd viewed the bone itself!*

Jessa clucked her annoyance as she picked up the scalpel, her eyes still studying the wound. A careful exit to finish, cauterizing and cleaning what hadn't been cleared on the way in: pus, dead flesh, and debris – and there would be lots of pus, she was sure of that, which meant it would likely need a drain afterward. She'd have to boil some sort of tube, only she didn't have one; perhaps one of her metal catheters would do.

With a long, exasperated sigh, Jessa bent over the swollen leg and began to cut.

※

"Where is Cethen living?" Jessa asked as she dried her hands. Everything was in its proper place in the leather pack, and the clearing had once more settled down to whatever passed here for normal. Modan remained asleep, his breathing steady. The curious had all crept back to where they'd been before the first slice of the scalpel, except for a hulking brute with the face of a gorilla who'd fainted when she cut down to the bone. Modan could thank the gods that it had not been snapped, but only mildly fractured.

Treno glanced up, suddenly leery. "Why?"

"I knew the man. I was just inquiring of his health."

"I see." Treno seemed to think that over. "Well, he don't like to make it known where he lives. But as to his health, it's as well as can be expected for an old 'un."

"Which means?"

Treno shrugged. "Other than the usual aches and pains, he's good, I suppose. He limps, but then he always has. His hearing's good too, though he can't see worth a badger's blink."

"Can't see? How bad?"

"Pretty much blind."

"Hmmm." Jessa's tall forehead furrowed as she mulled over how much she should inquire after the man's sight – if at all. What would her own father do in her place? The answer to that, of course, was simple.

"What are his eyes like?"

"As I said, he can't see hardly nothing," Treno replied, then, as if deciding Jessa might need a full description, he frowned and added, "Blue. Kind of a pale blue. But the black in the middle's turned colour."

"Blue," she murmured, smiling as the description brought the distant memory clearer to mind. "The black in the middle. Is it sort of milky?"

"Yeah. Clouded."

"Hmm. I might be able to help. Tell him to come and see me at the fort. Presuming I'll be able to return there," Jessa said, glancing at the sleeping Modan. "Will he keep his promise?"

"Oh yeah, I'm sure of it," Treno said, though his tone didn't sound as firm as his words. "But Cethen can't go to the fort anymore than Modan can."

"Why?"

"Do you know what that man has done, the past thirty, forty years?" Treno's voice held a trace of awe and pride. "He's a legend. The Romans would love to get their hands on him."

"I don't think so," Jessa said, and smiled wryly. "Tell me, what has he been doing the last *ten* years?"

"The last ten?" Treno chuckled. "Just growing older, I guess. And telling his stories. And maybe he gives a bit of advice, here and there."

"Then he can make use of his pardon," Jessa said, "providing he kept it." When she saw Treno's brow lift in query, she explained. "It's a governor's pardon, given nearly ten years ago, all wrapped up in a leather dispatch pouch. I saw it handed to his brother Cian for passing on; and I know it was passed on, because I asked Cian."

"Huh. Cethen never said nothing."

"Find out. But even if I can't help, I'd like to see him. Tell him that Jessa, daughter of Marcus, offers her hospitality. There's much I'd like to talk about."

Treno nodded, his expression one of disbelief, which only increased with her next words.

"And if he's lost his fool pardon, the present governor will no doubt write him a new one."

"Why would he do that?"

Jessa considered her answer. Was it wise to tell the man who, exactly, the present governor was? If she did meet up with Cethen, she could let him know – perhaps. In the meantime, it wouldn't hurt to enhance the old man's reputation; in fact, it would be amusing to do so. "Cethen is well known to the Romans, a man they respect. As you say, a legend. Rome may wish to kill her enemies in battle, but she does respect those who fought well. To them, when you honour a *great* enemy, you also honour the soldiers who fight against him. I have no doubt the governor would grant him a new pardon."

"Cethen?" Treno murmured, sounding doubtful.

"Oh yes," Jessa replied solemnly. "The Romans all know Cethen Lamh-fada."

## Chapter VI

## Aricia, Februarius, A.D. 105

The day was still, neither hot nor cold, and the sun stood four hours from its zenith. Gaius's skull had been shaved clean. Elena, after her initial shock, decided that while her husband's lack of hair made him seem younger, he looked a sight better with it than without. The medicus, a man called Vitus, had insisted that it all come off, just as he'd insisted that the operation itself take place outside in the huge peristyle. Gaius lay prone on a marble table under a tent of bright green cloth imported, at no small expense, from the *Seres*. Vitus claimed that operating in the open helped reduce infection, and the marvelous smooth green cloth, with its fine weave and glossy feel, helped keep the air pure.

Vitus settled himself on a stool at the end of the table and looked down on the back of Gaius's head. One of the assistants quickly wiped the marble-like scalp with a cloth soaked in fresh spring water. The second handed Vitus a scalpel and the surgeon skillfully peeled a sizable patch of skin away from the skull. Then, angling the serrated edge of a crude circular drill slightly to one side, he began sawing into the bone. Metellus soon excused himself, leaving Elena, Coira, and Gaius's son and daughter, Marcus and Aelia, to watch. The instrument took a good quarter-hour to do its work, as the two assistants sweated to keep the skull clear of ground bone and seeping blood. When only a wafer-thin piece of bone remained on one side, Vitus gently raised the disc-like circle of bone as if it were set on a hinge.

The medicus wiped his mouth on the back of his wrist and peered into the dark hole. "Hmm!" he murmured, clearly not happy by what he saw.

Alarmed, Elena peered over his shoulder at the opening, which was twice the size of a *sestertius*. What she saw looked to be a second skin hidden below the bone, a glistening, greyish-white layer barely visible through a slick coating of blood. Vitus gently wiped the area with the tip of his finger, exposing more of the surface. Elena caught her breath, afraid of what the touching might do. "Careful . . ."

Vitus pursed his lips. "No worries. That inside skin is tougher than a rhino's hide. I was merely checking for signs of discolouration. There are none."

"You seemed unhappy with what you found," Aelia observed.

"I am. It looks normal. I was hoping to find bleeding that was pressing the brain down, or maybe a clot – even a splinter of bone. But there's no sign of anything, not even under that second skin you see there."

"So?"

"So I pin back the bone and sew the skin back in place. After that, some rest and –"

"That's it?" Elena snapped.

Marcus placed a hand on her shoulder. "Surely something can be done?" he said.

"Other than making more holes in his head on the off chance I'll find something there, there's nothing. And doing that is not only guesswork, it's hard on his head." Vitus shrugged. "I drilled right on top of where he was hit. Look." He turned the flap of skin so that they could see the scar where the thieves' cudgel had struck. "The most likely place it would have been was where the blow hit the skull."

"But you said –"

"I said his condition was likely caused by accumulated bleeding or a clot. Either could make him black out and not regain consciousness. In other words, I was hoping to find something pressing against his brain." Again Vitus shrugged. "There just isn't any sign of it. If you want to relieve pressure, you've got to have something there to relieve."

"But he's losing ground."

"It must be something deeper inside, that doesn't show. I can't go there, or I'll kill him."

"He might just as well be dead," Coira broke in, and wrapped her arm gently around her mother's shoulders.

Vitus, bloodstained and homely though he was, did his best to offer sympathy, but his words carried all the comfort of a gladiator's apology.

"What do you think?" Coira asked later that afternoon, after Vitus departed.

The household slaves had placed Gaius back in his bedroom, where he lay face down on the bed. Elena simply shook her head, her eyes watering as she stared down at her husband's skull. There was the old, familiar scar from Eboracum that spanned the top of his head, and a second, off to the side, where his helmet had been battered at Bran's Beck. Now, just back from both, would be yet another: a round scar shaped by a heavily-bruised circle of stitches, which for the moment still glistened with a dark ring of congealed blood.

"It's hard to tell which one of those scars will prove to be the greater," Aelia murmured.

Elena continued to stare at the fresh damage to her husband's skull. "I've always said the man had a head made of rock, considering the blows it's taken." She smiled grimly, feeling a tear growing in her eye. "I suppose we've now seen ample proof that it's not."

Aelia shuddered. "It was horrible. And it was all for nothing."

Elena couldn't have agreed more. The ugly, heavily stitched wound seemed far more brutal than the jagged ivory scars received in battle. Yet she remembered a time when the larger scar had made his skull look like a cracked egg.

"Perhaps it's my fault," she said quietly, wondering what part the gods had in all this. "I made light of the old wound when the medicus first got here from Aricia. I told him he'd been struck in the only place that won't do a Roman permanent harm – his skull." She sighed, remembering what had prompted the remark. "Gaius once told me that was the first thing Cartimandua said to him, when he met her. Such words should never be repeated in jest. They serve only to tempt the gods."

"You're getting morbid as well as superstitious," Coira murmured, and pulled at her mother's arm as she made her way to the door. "We should find something to eat – if anyone thinks they can face food."

Coira and Aelia turned to go, and Elena reluctantly moved to join them. All three were nearly through the door and into the garden when a weak, rasping voice caused them to halt.

"D-don't leave," it whispered.

Elena whirled, stunned. Gaius still lay face down, with his head turned away. For a moment she was unsure whether her ears had deceived her, but one of the slaves stood over the bed as if frozen, his mouth open. The words were certainly not his.

"Elena?"

There was no doubt. "Yes."

"Where am I?"

"In your bed."

"Oh." Gaius was silent for a moment as if pondering the words; then, in a croaking whisper, he said, "That's not true."

"What? Being in your bed?" Elena grinned with relief, knowing full well that wasn't what he meant.

"No. The bit about the only place that doesn't do harm to a Roman . . ."

⁂

Gaius's mind was normal, but his body was thin and weak. His first call upon gaining his wits was for water, because his throat was sore and dry. And his second call, while the water was on its way, was to demand, in a croaking voice, what time of day it was. The answer failed to depress him. What did send him into the depths of gloom was Elena naming the day itself, and the slow realization that almost a month had passed since he'd been attacked.

Gaius's hazy, wandering mind eventually decided the blow was without doubt the will of the gods – though which one he'd offended this time, it was hard to know. What had he done wrong? That the blow had fallen square against his head was a sure sign of their meddling. They had played with him in the same manner before, starting that first day at Eboracum; they had done so several times, always choosing his skull. Perhaps Brigantia herself was responsible? Though whichever god did toy with him, surely there was a sign to be found somewhere? What was it?

Maybe the spiteful wretches wanted a greater sacrifice; or perhaps they were simply punishing him, and could not be appeased. Or maybe the gods just didn't give a shit, and were simply amusing themselves. Whatever the reason, Gaius's mood fell sharply over the days of his recovery, and for the first time in his life he began listing the reasons for living. It was a list that grew shorter with each passing day.

In the meantime the dull, throbbing heaviness inside his head seemed to grow; as did the list of transgressions that may have offended the gods. Nobody, oddly enough, had seen fit to inform Gaius that a large, circular wound at the back of his head was slowly healing under the linen bandages that swaddled his skull.

"Where is Marcus?" he demanded. "I haven't seen him."

It was a week after his awakening and the first day of exercise, a mild form of torture inflicted on an aching body by a well-meaning phalanx of slaves. Some fool medicus named Vitus had ordered this excruciating punishment. Gaius sat hunched on the edge of his bed, glum and exhausted after staggering a bare hundred yards around the garden, held upright by a half-dozen torturing hands.

"He was here yesterday," Elena told him, with a quick glance at Aelia and Coira.

"Shit!" Gaius forced himself to concentrate. Had he missed something? It wasn't Marcus who was here yesterday, surely. "What about Tuis?"

"He's in Britannia," Aelia volunteered.

"Oh yes," he muttered, the words mechanical, as if he should know. Maybe it was Marcus yesterday – but no, it wasn't. There was a vague recollection of his other son, Elena's, the one he'd adopted. Yet they were telling him the boy had gone to – to Britannia? Why? "He's, er, doing . . . ?"

"He's the governor there, dear," Elena murmured, her face tight with concern.

"Yes, yes, that's right," Gaius muttered and, to his relief, he realized that was right. Then another name popped into his mind, and it seemed logical to piece the two together, though he couldn't think why. "He's there with Rhun . . ."

"No, Rhun had business in *Ostia*. He's on his way back now that you've . . ." Elena's voice faded as if unsure of what to say.

"Now that you've recovered your senses," Aelia finished for her. "Rhun will likely be here tonight."

Gaius raised a hand to his forehead in confusion. A wave of frustration flooded his mind, and he growled in annoyance. "Where *is* Marcus, then?" he demanded, his voice rising.

"I'll go and find him," Elena said, and quickly turned to the other two, raising her eyebrows in a question.

"He's not here. He went to the city," Aelia whispered.

"*I asked, where – is – Marcus, dammit?*" Gaius shouted, his face crimson.

Metellus stepped from the shadows, a clay beaker in hand. "Perhaps he needs something to calm him down. The poor man looks worn out. He needs rest."

"Then give it to him now," Coira murmured, quickly moving forward as Gaius tried to stumble to his feet. Metellus got there first, only to receive the back of his master's hand as Gaius irritably tried to push him away. The beaker flew across the room, and the old slave tumbled back on his rump.

Gaius staggered angrily to his feet, both his mind and vision a swirling fog. He was dimly aware that his wife was lying to him, as was his daughter, and he wondered what the pair had done with Marcus. Then his old slave attacked him! What was happening? Why were they trying to hurt him? And someone, somewhere, seemed to be crying for help, for he could hear them. For a moment Gaius thought his rescue was imminent. Then several dark shadows appeared from out of the fog, flitting in front of him, dragging at his arms, pulling him down . . .

⁂

"We have to be prepared for the worst," Marcus told them the following day. "Once the mind starts going . . ."

"But he could be fine," Aelia protested. "He was quite alright before becoming violent. It was just the one incident."

Elena sighed and leaned back in her chair. She stared vacantly at the sky as if trying to sweep everything from her mind, which was clearly far too preoccupied – and well it might be. Yet Marcus saw that she was far more agitated than any of them, which for Elena was unusual. If anyone handled trouble without breaking breath or heartbeat, it was Elena. He wondered if something more than Gaius preyed on her mind.

The small family sat at ease in the marble-columned atrium of the Aricia villa, shaded from the afternoon sun by the stone ledge of the west portico. Several small tables dotted the tiled courtyard, each holding food and drink, none of which had been touched. Marcus edged his chair closer to Elena, and asked what troubled her.

"Oh, nothing. Nothing," she replied, adding those two vague words employed by women the empire over: "Not really."

Marcus scratched at his ear to hide a grin, pondering how to find the root of her troubles. He might guess where her mind wandered; it was simply a question of tact in the asking. To do so, however, seemed impossible, and he sighed. "Look, it might not be the time, Elena, but if anything should happen, you will be taken care of . . ."

"Huh?" Elena fell from her reverie and stared at Marcus in surprise.

"What I mean is," Marcus mumbled, suddenly wishing he'd kept his mouth shut, "there is no need to worry."

"Oh, Marcus!" Elena blurted, as if trying not to laugh. She placed a hand on his arm and squeezed. "You took me by surprise. I'm not worried, at least not on that count. I know all about Gaius's will, and I'm grateful. As you know," her face assumed a mischievous grin, "he has been quite generous to both me and his other long-suffering slave, Metellus."

Marcus bowed his head and smiled. "Then . . . ?"

"I was just thinking." Elena's gaze again lost focus as she eased back into the chair. "Pray the gods forbid it, but should something happen to Gaius, I don't think I could ever enter Rome again."

"Oh?" Marcus was surprised. *Is that all?*

"No. Never." Elena's head tilted sideways to face him. "I've always hated the place. Not the city itself." She smiled, as if the vision of it filled her mind. "Rome is alive. All of it is very much alive, from the forum and the Circus to the rotten, choking stink of the river. No, it's not the city, Marcus, it's the people who live there."

Marcus waited. When nothing more seemed forthcoming, he mumbled another, "Oh?"

"Uh-huh. You know, as a slave I could understand. But even after becoming Gaius's wife, I was rudely tolerated at best. And if he wasn't there to blunt the edges, the snide tongues cut worse than a traitor's dagger." Elena smiled, but without humour. "Marcus, there are more two-legged bitches on the *Palatine* than four-legged ones in all of Britannia."

He fumbled for something to say, but the best he could manage was yet another subdued, "Oh?"

"And as for their men," Elena continued, her cheeks flushed in anger, "they think every barbarian female wants nothing more in life than to be plowed by a Roman stud." She paused long enough to shake her head, then laughed bitterly. "Of course, that's not the problem it used to be – even the wrinkled old lechers hardly bother any more."

Marcus blinked, totally lost for words, but Coira certainly was not. She leaned forward in her chair – he hadn't thought she was close enough to hear – and whispered, "That's fine for you to say."

# Chapter VII

## Eboracum, Februarius, A.D. 105

Tuis glanced gloomily upward as yet another bundle of dispatches landed on his desk. The move north to Eboracum had not reduced the flow one jot; if anything, it had increased. With a barely heard mumble of apology Zoticus, his senior clerk, juggled them into three stacks. The first he placed on the right-hand side of the desk, at the outer edge; the second on the left-hand side, also at the outer edge; and the third he pushed to the very middle of the desk. Tuis groaned as his eyes took in all three piles, passing quickly over a good half-dozen already sitting there. They finally came to rest on Zoticus's gnarled hand, which was not yet finished with the small bundle in the middle.

Over the past several months Tuis had learned what that meant. Should a matter be urgent, which eleven times out of ten meant trouble, it ended up near the middle of the desk. And each missive's precise placement – *the things should really be called missiles* – registered the clerk's opinion of its urgency. A dispatch's proximity to the centre, Tuis knew, was a direct ratio of the contents' gravity.

He cursed silently as Zoticus, devoid of expression, slid a single, curled sheet of heavy parchment – there had been only two in the pile – firmly to the centre, and beyond. If anything, it ended up closer to his belly.

"Tell it, and save me the pain of reading," Tuis growled as Zoticus tried to slip quietly back to his own swamp of scrolls.

"It's from up north, sir."

"Which means it's bad."

"Rotten, sir." Zoticus, a *decanus* retired from service with the Ninth legion, tried to appear sympathetic – which, for an ex-soldier nearing fifty, with a broken nose and a face tanned to leather, was impossible.

"How rotten?"

"First off," Zoticus pointed to the message that remained in the centre of the desk, "a mixed force of barbarians wiped out a supply column north of the Ituna. We lost almost a hundred infantry, and nearly half as many cavalry. The wagons were plundered and burned."

Tuis groaned as he absorbed the news, and slumped back in his chair. "What do you mean, first off?"

"It gets worse, sir."

"Worse? How could it get worse? Someone important was killed?"

"It's not that worse, sir. Nobody of importance was killed, just regular troops, all of them auxiliaries." Zoticus shook his head and gloomily added, "Nobody of importance was killed – as yet."

"As yet?" Tuis groaned again and bent forward over the desk, head in hands. "Tell me we don't have anyone of importance up there. Do we? Somebody's son?"

"Daughter, actually. There's a postscript added at the bottom of the second dispatch." The senior clerk pointed to the foot of the parchment where the writing had shrunk to a cramped, multi-line scrawl, much of it angling up the margin as if the writer had been pressed for time and space. "That one's from the fort commander at Blatobulgium. A civilian surgeon was up there helping the locals, and seems to have been abducted from her escort. She was returning from gathering wild medicines and –"

"She?" Tuis demanded, a chill running up his spine. "A female surgeon?"

"Yes, sir. Quite unusual, I know. The commander seems to place great importance on her well-being. Why, I don't know. It's just a –"

"Did he mention her name?"

"Er, I'm not sure, sir."

"Doesn't matter," Tuis groaned, and slumped back in his chair. "Her father is a senator. Marcus Sabinius."

"Oh, fuck – er, damn, sir!" Zoticus finally appeared impressed. "Wasn't he the Ninth's legate, about ten years ago?"

"Uh-huh."

"Isn't – isn't he your brother?"

"Yes, twice over: once by adoption, and the second by marriage. His sister's married to my natural brother. Which also makes the woman who was abducted my niece twice over, I suppose. Her name is Jessa."

Tuis moaned as he conjured an image of the girl: hardly a finger above two *cubits*, but a good-looking lass nonetheless; a small stubborn chin, a determined mouth, and a pair of limpid brown eyes that melted her father's heart one moment, and flashed fire the next. Yet the girl was bright enough, maybe too bright for her own good; and as for the stubbornness, it was monumental. That came not from her father, Marcus, but from his father – the first Gaius Sabinius; a man who had found more trouble in Brigantia than Prometheus ever found with the gods. Was his granddaughter now doing the same?

Tuis's head whirled, his anger focusing on the girl and her headstrong stupidity. Then he thought of Marcus. If he knew her father – and he did know him, and well – the man would go mad!

"What resources do we have up there?" Tuis demanded, orders flowing through his mind like a flood. "We need to mobilize them, immediately. I also need to send a dispatch to Rome, at once. And the legate of the Ninth; I'll need to talk to him, too. Find out what he's got available. We have to find the girl. And there *will* be reprisals."

"The garrison where she was taken is the strongest north of *Luguvalium*, but it's far from being an army. It's where the girl spent her time coddling her barbarians. I believe it's the headquarters of an *equitata*. Germanians, I think. Some of them will be detached to the surrounding outposts, I suppose."

"And the unit itself is no doubt under strength to begin with." Tuis snorted his disgust.

"Aren't they all?" Zoticus murmured. "I would guess the more so now. They were likely providing escort for those supply wagons."

※

"Only the granaries, the residence, and half the headquarters building are complete. The work on the walls is barely begun. And they are the essence of Eboracum's reconstruction, as any fool knows." Marius Appius Tullius, legate of the Ninth Hispana Legion, was indignant. "I need every man I can muster. The quarry at *Calcaria* is in full production. The barges are moving stone every day. The base for the west wall is being excavated as we speak. I need the men! The earth for the berm is being reinforced with –"

"So what will you do if a barbarian army arrives at *your* gates tonight?" Tuis demanded, twitching at the words *any fool knows!* Damned patricians! The pair sat in the huge atrium that lay at the heart of the commander's residence, each nursing a mug of the local beer. The spacious building had been rebuilt with the same Calcarian sandstone that Marius Appius complained he wasn't getting enough of, so his whining had to be an outright lie – or at the very least, an exaggeration.

"Non sequitur," Marius snapped back.

"It does follow, as *any* fool can see! Would you ask your enemy to stop and wait, Marius? Huh? I can see it now: 'Hold on a while, will you? I need to get my walls replaced – in stone, this time, and my men are too busy building at the moment. Come back next year – or preferably, the one after.'"

"But they're not showing up at my gates, are they?" Marius replied, plainly just as annoyed, the more so at the sarcasm, which was as Tuis intended.

"No, they haven't shown up outside *your* gates," he cried. "And for your sake, I hope they don't. Are you telling me that you don't perceive this outrage to be a threat?"

"No, no, I suppose not," Marius grumbled grudgingly. "It's just that the walls have a certain priority."

"Marius, they're not a priority, they're an obsession."

The legate released his breath in exasperation, but Tuis could see the man realized he trod on boggy ground, as he damn well should.

"How many troops do you need?" the legate asked.

"How many do *I* need?" Tuis pretended surprise. "Me? You're the Ninth's legate. How many troops will *you* need?"

"Sir, with respect, as governor, isn't the deployment of troops ultimately *your* decision?"

Tuis, with partial success, curbed his frustration. Marius had been in command of Eboracum almost a year, and had clearly made the fortress's stone reconstruction his focus. Perhaps the man felt it would serve as his monument? Tuis wondered what the fellow would have done with his time if the order to rebuild Eboracum had not been approved! It was hard to imagine him commanding an army in the field! Had the fool been promoted to a post that he found overwhelming? Tuis blinked as another thought crossed his mind, which he quickly rejected: maybe they both had!

The Ninth's legate had made no great show when posted to Hispania ten years ago as a tribune with the Seventh Gemina. Tuis had made enquiries. Yet Rome was not in the habit of sending incompetents to command her frontier legions – though even when she did, the legion's *primus pilus* was an effective counterbalance. To be fair, Marius showed no sign of incompetence. But the man's fixation on rebuilding his fortress in stone *had* been talked about . . .

"Which I'm now trying to do," Tuis said impatiently, and decided that perhaps even a simple question needed clarification. "I'm deploying part of the Ninth to make reprisals, and also to find the missing woman – and to find her alive. I'm asking you how many troops you think you need to do that."

"Why the Ninth? The Twentieth is on the west coast. It's about as close, and it's not trying to rebuild its base. And the Second may be farther south, but it can –"

"Marius," Tuis growled, aware the man might have a point, albeit a very minor one, "this is not a family debate. I'm ordering the Ninth to handle this because I'm here, and this is where the Ninth is. I'm not at *Deva* with the Twentieth, and I'm not at *Isca* with the Second."

"But that isn't a good reason to –"

"By the two jaws of Janus, enough!" Tuis cried in annoyance, even as part of his mind gnawed on compromise. "All I'm asking is what do you need. If you haven't got the men, *maybe* we'll draw others from the Twentieth. Or the Second Augusta. It's not as if I'm trying to raise an invading army." Which might not really be true, he realized as soon as the words were spoken. He shook his head in frustration and muttered, "Not a huge one, anyway."

"Do you have an idea how many troops you want, then?"

Tuis resisted the urge to throttle the man, and instead threw out a figure, the first that came to mind. "It's only a punitive expedition, though it will be in hostile territory. I should imagine four to five thousand troops should do it. Four or five full cohorts drawn from the legions; the rest would be auxiliary cavalry and infantry."

Marius frowned. "I would have thought a thousand or two would have been enough."

"Then why the fuck didn't you say so in the first place?" Tuis shouted.

"I –"

"Fine, fine!" Tuis raised an impatient hand to halt the man's sniveling. "Two cohorts from the Ninth, and at full strength. Your legion's supposed to have ten of the things, isn't it? Free up a couple from somewhere. Plus you'll need a few auxiliary infantry cohorts, and a regiment or two of cavalry. That'll give you more than twenty-five hundred men. There'll likely be other troops you can draw on from the forts up north, and I'll make up the rest from the Twentieth. I don't want to bugger the bull on this."

"*I'll* need another couple of auxiliary cohorts?" Marius seemed to finally realize that *he* was being tasked.

"Sure, if you think it's necessary," Tuis said, blithely ignoring the man's emphasis on the first-person singular. "If you think that won't be enough, let me know. You're certainly going to need the cavalry to –"

"No, what I meant was, I wasn't expecting to lead what amounts to nothing more than a large detachment. The primus pilus can surely handle an expedition that size. Maybe toss in one of the tribunes, gain a bit of experience."

"This isn't just about reprisals, Marius. There's a senator's daughter involved." Tuis raised his voice, wondering how much quibbling his temper – or his heart – could stand. "It requires handling from the top. The primus will go, certainly, but if this turns bad," he glanced upward, silently begging the gods that it would not, "then I want it clearly shown that we've done all we can."

A hint of slyness crossed Marius's face. "So you're going too?"

Tuis knew when he was trapped and answered quickly, as if going north had always been his intention – which, he reluctantly convinced himself, it probably had. "Of course I'm going. That's my niece they've taken."

"Then why don't *you* take the expedition?"

"Because," Tuis growled between clenched teeth, "I've ordered you to do it."

⸸

"The trouble is, the military end of this isn't on the sharpest side of my blade," Tuis conceded that night, as he savoured the warmth of a glowing brazier of coals in the privacy of his own quarters. The weather of late had not been sufficiently cold to fire the *hypocaust*, but it was far too cold to just sit doing nothing and feel comfortable. "I much prefer administration: handling logistics, seeing to appointments, sorting out people's legal differences, that kind of thing. Maybe I should have been a procurator," he added wistfully.

"You did command a legion for three years," Livia murmured without glancing up from her game of knuckle-bone, which she was playing for both sides. "I thought you said that went rather well."

"I had a good primus," Tuis said. "Besides, it was in a much tamer province." He smiled fondly at the memory. "Those were good days . . ."

"Then why did you accept the position?" Livia demanded in that grating tone which inevitably sent Tuis's eyes rolling toward the ceiling.

"I dunno," he growled, and grimaced. "Duty to the empire? Love of the work? Greed and avarice – not necessarily in that order." He shrugged helplessly. "You know the main reason as well as me. I was trapped into it."

"No you weren't," Livia said, reluctantly pushing the bones aside. "You could have said no."

"It would have made Marcus look bad."

"All Marcus did was to refuse the appointment himself, and recommend you. That's the way things are done, Tuis. He was simply doing the family a favour. You didn't have to accept. When all's said and done, it doesn't matter. You're the son of senator, even if it is by adoption." Livia sniffed in a manner that suggested perhaps it did matter. "I don't see how your refusal would have made him look bad."

"Well, I didn't refuse, and now we're here," Tuis grumbled, remembering how flattered he'd been to learn Marcus had even considered putting his name forward. And how do you refuse your own brother? A brother who, when those dispatches he'd just sent to Rome were received, would likely be racing to Britannia, frantic for his daughter's safety. Which raised yet another question: why had the man allowed her to come back here in the first place? The soft sod never could refuse the girl, no matter what it cost him, emotionally or otherwise.

"You could always seek help," Livia said thoughtfully, the harshness of her voice for once muted. "Not for the expedition you're planning with Marius Appius, that's far too late, but perhaps for the balance of your tour of duty."

"From who?" Tuis snorted. "In this world of wolves, a man closes his eyes once to ask for help, and one of them's got his jaws tearing at your neck. Too much is to be gained from treachery. The first sign of weakness, especially from a provincial governor, simply invites it."

"Even from your own brother?"

"Marcus?" Tuis was baffled by the suggestion, but nonetheless paused to consider it. "I suppose my poor brother will soon be flaying a string of horses, in a mad dash for Britannia. Though when he gets here, he's hardly going to be thinking of helping –"

"No," Livia cut in impatiently, "from the brother who did well in the army. The barbarian *praefectus.*"

Tuis quashed his irritation at Livia's choice of words. *Rhun – the barbarian! Yes, a barbarian, just like me.* Yet his mind instantly grasped the possibilities. Rhun would be no less than a gift from the gods, if he could be convinced, and if he was free to travel to Britannia, which he was – and if an appointment could be finagled for him when he got here.

Where could he fit? Would Rhun even accept another posting? Perhaps command of a full *equitatae millaria* might lure him – more than a thousand men! Where was there a unit that size that might be made available? Tuis sucked on his lower lip. What had Zoticus said about the fort at Luguvalium? The place was in the process of being expanded and refurbished; was it finished yet? Surely it was being done to accommodate a milliaria! Who was slated for command?

"I suppose." Tuis deliberately made his voice cautious. The notion held tremendous appeal, but he was reluctant to admit as much to Livia.

As he mulled over the idea, another thought occurred. His mother had asked him to see if his real da's brother was still alive on reaching Eboracum, which he'd done. Surprisingly enough, he was. Cian, his uncle, lived not far downstream from the fortress; and Cian had told him in turn that his da, Cethen Lamh-fada, might also be alive, and living further to the north. Cian said he hadn't seen him for eight or nine years though, when he'd delivered some sort of a pardon, so he might well be dead by now. Tuis had tucked the knowledge in the back of his mind for when – if ever – he had the chance to do something about it. Perhaps now was the time!

He chuckled at the idea. His poor old da would be shocked to see what his son had become. A dim memory flashed through his mind: a tall giant of man with long moustaches and a limp – which was all he could remember. After all, he'd only been, what, five years old when he'd last seen him?

Tuis's mind sifted the possibilities. Even if his da no longer lived, there had been a son. That would make him a half-brother, and any kind of brother was a possible ally in a land as volatile as Vesuvius itself. Bryn – that was the name! Maybe he, too, might prove useful; or, at the very least, offer a friendly ear. Perhaps the time was ripe: he should be seeking out his kin. He'd get Zoticus working on that, though he would keep the knowledge from Livia. She thought little enough about his ancestry as it was, though he supposed she did try . . .

# Chapter VIII

## Selgovae Territory, Martius, A.D. 105

Jessa had no idea where she was, and had lost track of how long it had taken to get there. How many days *had* passed since Treno had blocked her path? It was all so infuriating. She and Dracus had almost been in sight of Blatobulgium's gates when the tattooed creature had taken her. So close! Jessa's anger boiled when thinking on it. She tried to push it from her mind, but it wouldn't leave. It wasn't just her own fate; there had been Treno's treachery with her escort. How had they fared, once they'd trudged back to the fort, empty-handed and covered in shame? And they had to trudge, because Treno, the lying stoat, had kept the horses! She could only imagine the punishment. The post commander would have been livid.

Dracus, who she thought was a *decurio* – at least he was before she'd been taken – would have borne the brunt of it, even though it was not the poor man's fault. The fault was all hers and her troublesome hospice, with its constant need for roots, herbs, wildflowers and even weeds, that could only be found in the forest. When – if – she ever got back, perhaps she could make amends for the poor man.

*If she ever got back!*

The possibility seemed to be fading with each passing day. And the past few had been particularly worrisome, for Modan, Treno, all of them, seemed unconcerned by what she might see as they travelled farther north. That in itself was a sure sign they viewed her presence as permanent. Certainly Modan did, for he had boasted as much, calling her his personal healer. Jessa had been quick to spit her anger, cursing and threatening with Rome's retribution. Yet her rage only added to the fool's amusement. She might well have tossed dust into the wind. How do you warn a man of Rome's wrath when he goes out of his way to incur it? Or how do you threaten *not* to cure a man when he's already healing? One day . . .

Twice on the journey north she had thought that day was at hand. Jessa knew that the hills crawled with Roman cavalry, either seeking revenge for the attack on the supply train, or simply searching for her. Some sort of clash was inevitable but Modan, ape that he was, seemed capable enough when organizing his men. Or perhaps he was merely adept at saving his own worthless hide.

The first time, Treno and his scouts were ranging a mile or two ahead of Modan's slow-moving column, and ran headlong into a strong force of Roman cavalry. Treno, curse him, had simply ordered his men to put their boots to the horses' bellies, and fled along a path different from that travelled by Modan and his people. The Roman cavalry took the bait and followed as if chasing deer. It was costly, certainly; Treno lost four of his people. Yet Modan, who had placed himself in the centre of his own column of riders on a low stretcher tied to a pair of hill ponies, lost none. He took shelter in the forest and remained hidden until it was all over. Jessa saw no trace of those who might have rescued her. She heard only the distant echo of fading hoof beats. The diversion had been so neatly done that she could have wept.

Yet the second encounter proved far worse. It took place in the early morning, soon after they'd broken camp. Treno came thundering down the trail, well ahead of a Roman patrol that numbered no more than a troop. Modan, stupid as he might appear, plainly had his people prepared for such an occurrence. His men melted into the forest on either side of the track, where she was unceremoniously grabbed by an odorous Carveti cavalryman. The man, much to her disgust, placed one hand firmly about her waist and the other over her mouth.

Moments later she watched in horror as more than a hundred riders poured from the trees, falling viciously upon a quarter their number. Neither Modan nor the Romans appeared interested in taking prisoners, though the Roman troopers could offer little resistance. Their single advantage was superior horseflesh. Jessa counted a dozen uniformed bodies on the ground, before the remainder fought their way through . . .

The end of the journey proved to be an old Selgovae hill fort destroyed by Agricola twenty years before, though at first she hardly had the chance to see it. Modan's people plodded in at the end of a long, tiresome day; a day that had been made all the longer by the need to remain hidden. The large, rounded hill, denuded of fortification, was surrounded by farmland; but in the fading light of evening, it appeared as nothing more than a dark mound set against a dying sun.

Modan was expected, for figures appeared from the twilight and led them to an open pasture, bordered on one side by a dark forest of leafless trees. With no apparent orders given, Modan's people began setting up camp: hobbling the horses, digging latrines, kindling fires, and spreading their gear. A dozen or more stood close by in a circle, fumbling with tight bundles of leather, one of which had been unwrapped. It was a Roman tent, doubtless stolen during the raid on the supply train. Jessa smiled grimly as she watched. They had no idea how to pitch the fool thing, and she was damned if she was going to show them.

"One of my men's got a bad boil on his neck." Modan grunted as his men helped him down from the horse-stretcher, and placed him on a grubby ox hide set close by one of the fires. "Get rid of it."

Jessa turned. She'd been standing by the fire wondering where her place was and who would tell her, and she was in no mood to curb her tongue. "Get rid of his neck? Gladly."

"One more like that, and your teeth are grinding my knuckles," Modan said, his voice surprisingly mild.

Soft footsteps crossed the grass behind Jessa. A shadowy figure slipped past and handed Modan a platter of food and a skin of drink. It reminded Jessa of her empty belly, and she looked about, wondering where the food had come from.

Modan noticed, and smirked. "You'll get nothing until it's done, girl."

"Nothing gets done until I get fed," Jessa retorted. "And for what it's worth, I don't care if I eat or not."

"As I said, your teeth –"

"And how would you do that?" Jessa interrupted, deliberately eyeing his injured leg. "You couldn't thump a blind man, let alone a poor sodding dwarf that just saved your miserable life."

Modan's jaw tightened. "Don't lean on my shield, girl. I've just got to call Treno or one of the others, and you'll wish you'd kept your gob shut."

"So, Modan *the Mighty* must send for his men to help beat on a helpless woman," Jessa taunted, the saner part of her mind wondering why she was pushing the man. But there'd been enough times before when, pushed hard enough herself, she just didn't care. Truth be known, there had been too many times . . .

Modan's reaction to the taunt was odd, though. He didn't rant and threaten in turn. Instead he paused and peered at her by the light of the flames as if wondering why she'd said what she had. Had the words fallen on an open sore? She half expected him to say, "I don't need no help to beat on any woman!" Instead, when he did speak, it was to repeat his warning, adding almost half-heartedly, "And it'll be just the start, bitch."

Jessa's mouth tightened. Anger flooded her mind, bringing with it a reckless urge to toss twice the violence back in the man's teeth. With jaw set, she edged forward until her face was so close to his she could feel his breath. "Listen," she hissed, her voice masking the ice that froze her belly, "you can do what you want. I don't give a druid's damn. Beat me, kill me, nothing will change. You'll still be a liar, a coward, and as useless as a toad's tit. And you'll have rid yourself of the only person within miles who can actually help you or your people – which I'm sure will be noticed by others, arsehole."

Jessa defiantly clenched her jaw and quickly stepped back, unsure what Modan would do, and equally unsure of his reach. She knew he was unable to stand or walk, but his long arms could swing a wide arc. For the moment, though, he sat speechless, his mouth gaping. His black eyes had lost focus as his mind clearly tried to figure a response. Then he blinked, and Jessa saw his jaw clench as tight as her own and his chin lift in anger. But before Modan could loose the reins on his rage, a firm, calm voice sounded from behind his makeshift shelter.

"The lass may be small, but her tongue is sharper than my sword."

A twig snapped, followed by the muted pad of feet crossing the damp turf. A stocky man of middle years and average height stepped into the glow of the flames and stood with his arms folded, staring owlishly at them both. He was unarmed, but the two who followed were not: large men with axes dangling from their belts, spears in hand, and shields slung across their shoulders. Both hung back in the shadows, clearly there to guard the newcomer's back.

Modan glared annoyance, but discretion triumphed over anger and he nodded a greeting. "Lagan."

"Modan, good to see you. Heard about the leg. It's healing well?"

"Yeah, it's healing," he muttered, with a grudging glance at Jessa that held no gratitude.

"I hear our small friend is responsible." Lagan bowed his head to Jessa to acknowledge her skill, seemingly oblivious to the tension; then, with the hint of a smile, he said, "You must be hungry." He turned to his two followers. "One of you get the lass something to eat. And she'll be thirsty, too."

*This man must have heard everything,* Jessa mused, and was about to toss a gloating retort in Modan's direction when she caught herself. The words would sound boorish. Instead, she bowed her head in turn as the guard loped off in search of food, and said, "That would be nice. Thank you."

"Er . . ." Lagan looked uneasily about the fire as if searching for something, then beckoned to the guard who remained. "Something to sit on; from one of the wood piles, perhaps."

Jessa resisted the urge to glare scornfully at Modan, whose gorge was surely rising. Lagan, whose obtuseness was clearly pretense, blithely ignored the hostility that was as palpable as the heat from the flames. She could have laughed out loud, only again, with this odd man – who was as much her enemy as Modan – it would be unfitting. Lagan was no more than a Selgovae hill man, she knew that, but his manner seemed to speak of something more. Jessa wondered what, exactly, that was, and where it had been cultivated . . .

"So, what are you, girl? Jessa, is it not? Are you Roman, Brigante, Carveti, or Selgovae? Perhaps we have a claim on you, as much as anyone. They tell me you were born amongst us."

Jessa bridled at the man's choice of words, and was about to snap back that nobody had a claim on her. But she held her tongue as she realized that for this man Lagan, the word "claim" might not be literal. She allowed him the doubt. "Perhaps, as you suggest, there is a claim. I was born in Selgovae territory, though truth be known, I don't know where. My father says it was somewhere southwest of the fort at *Trimontium*."

"Ah, yes, Trimontium." Lagan's tone was reflective. "One of the many forts the Romans have built on our land, all of them without so much as asking."

There was no reply to that, Jessa decided, and it proved unnecessary as the second guard appeared from the gloom carrying two logs, the ends evenly sawn. He set them upright near the fire, and Lagan gestured toward the shorter of the two. Jessa sat down, and Lagan eased himself onto the other.

Modan plainly felt the need to comment on Lagan's musing. "Yeah, the bastards are everywhere," he grumbled. "Like flies on a pile of –"

"And more so, the past week or two," Lagan interrupted. "Which reminds me, where are the rest of your people? I heard that more than five hundred struck the Roman supply column. Yet you come here with less than half that number. Far less."

"Yeah, well, I came mostly with those who had horses," Modan said, and shrugged his indifference over the others. "Most of them on foot went back home. Crops need seeding, and there's the livestock to care for. They'll be there when we need them."

"I trust they will be,' Lagan murmured, and returned his interest to Jessa. "So, tell me about your father. I'm curious. And your mother. I understand she was Carveti. She must have been quite a woman."


Despite Lagan's almost civilized attention, Jessa remained under Modan's charge. Yet perhaps the Selgovae chieftain had spoken to him, for the clod's rancour seemed to abate. She was provided with a small shelter next to his leather tent, which sat pitched under the trees in a state that would have made a primus weep. Her "sack of magic," as Modan called her medical bag, was returned along with a youth of about fourteen called Colm, who Jessa slowly realized had been provided as an assistant. The lad tried his best to be helpful, but he was as thick as *puls*.

More than a week passed, and Modan's camp took on its own routine. Treno disappeared for a while, and she heard that he'd gone south to tell Modan's da how his son fared. From time to time she saw Lagan, and he was always cordial. He would drop by at least once a day to visit Modan, always in the company of others.

There were obviously greater events in the wind than those that affected just the camp and Jessa began to sense that the occupation of the old hill fort was a mere convenience. The feeling came from the comings and goings of strangers, more than anything. Self-important warriors, clearly chieftains in their own right, rode in with their kin in train; but in a day or two they would be gone – only to be replaced by others. It grew common to see men huddled about the camp in their various factions, heartily slapping backs and eagerly clasping wrists. And most surprising of all, Jessa thought cynically, the evenings were turned over to meetings that lasted well into the night, but seldom degenerated into drunkenness.

Yet such activity could not remain unnoticed by the Romans, which surely made the camp vulnerable. Lagan would know that much, Jessa reasoned, for unlike Modan, he was clearly not stupid. She was curious enough to consider asking him what he intended, and would not have been surprised if he told her. Then Treno returned from his visit to Cethen, with a suggestion that caused her to forget completely.

A dozen or more were gathered about Modan's makeshift shelter enjoying the warmth of an evening fire. Jessa was working nearby, and well within hearing. Lagan spoke first, asking Treno how matters stood with Modan's father, and the state of his health.

"He's alive!" Modan answered for him instead, his voice terse. "Still lives in the same place. He'll die there, I imagine."

Jessa knew that Cethen Lamh-fada had been well known to the Selgovae, and Lagan was likely expressing a natural curiosity. Treno saw fit to add his own words to Modan's curt reply. "He's not doing that bad, considering his age. He gets around well, and everything's working except his sight. Even with his bad eyes, though," he waved a hand toward Jessa, who was trying to prevent Colm from scalding himself with a pot of boiling instruments, "there's hope. The dwarf said she might be able to give him some sight back."

"Really?" Lagan was plainly intrigued, and turned to look at her with his brows raised. "How can you restore a man's sight?"

"I can't," Jessa called over one shoulder. She passed a cloth to Colm and faced him toward the pot. "Put this around the hook so it doesn't burn your hand, *then* lift it up off the fire. Once it's firmly on the ground, let it cool for awhile."

"Then why tell someone you can?" Lagan called back.

Jessa watched Colm set the pot of boiling water on the grass then turned to face Modan's shelter. Lagan was there with his usual guards and half a dozen others, none of whom she recognized. "Modan's da still has his sight. It's hidden behind a cloud that sits on the front of his eyes. All I do is push the cloud away. Only the gods can *restore* sight."

"But he could see again . . ."

"Possibly. Never as well as he once did, but if things go well, far better than Treno tells me he can see now."

"How do you push it away?"

Jessa nodded toward the bag. "With the tools of my trade. There are many."

"I've got to see this," Lagan said, and climbed to his feet.

Jessa smiled. She couldn't bring herself to like the man – at least, not for what he was: her enemy – but he did treat her with a respect that she found intriguing. Had this been Modan or even Treno, she would have been ordered over with the bag in tow, which would have led to another bout of verbal brawling. Yet Lagan was coming her way . . .

Jessa delved deep into the bag and retrieved one of several small wooden boxes bound by straps to the stiff leather bottom. In no time at all she had the instruments spread out on a clean cloth, and she was explaining to Lagan the finer points of *couching* a pair of eyes. He seemed keenly interested, his questions sharp and perceptive.

When she was finished he turned to Modan, a broad grin on his face. "So, when are you going to get your da's eyes fixed?"

Modan simply grunted, but Treno took up the cause to the point of picking hard at his patience. "Yeah, Mod, that would be good. Why not lend the dwarf to your da so he can get his eyes fixed?"

The words sounded reasonable enough, but were spoken as if made as a challenge.

Modan took them as such. "Shut your lousy gob, Treno, and tend to your own problems. You've got enough."

"Hey, hey, is this a father's son?" Treno jibed, then softened his tone. "Come on, Mod, maybe your da could see again."

"How bad is he?" Lagan asked, but Modan simply grunted and said nothing, which seemed to annoy the Selgovae.

Treno cut in. "If you stand a step in front of him, you're nothing but a blur. He pretty much has to feel his food, to find out what's on his plate."

Lagan turned to Jessa. "And if you help?"

She spread her arms as far apart as they would go. "Anything can happen, from here, to here." She looked first to her left hand, then to her right, and shrugged. "If it doesn't work at all, then he could go completely blind. But if everything is done clean and correct – and clean is important – the odds are against blindness." She shrugged again as if that was of no concern, and indeed, she felt it was not. "If he can't see anyway, though, what does it matter?"

"And if it works?"

"Then there's the other side of the blade: complete sight could be restored. But –" Jessa paused for emphasis "—but, that is rare. Funny enough, if a person's sight was bad to begin with, the better his chances are of getting good sight after it's done. If it does work at all, though, he should be able to see like this."

Jessa closed her eyes until she was squinting through her eyelashes. Lagan became a blur, certainly, but she could see him looking at her; and she could see Modan scowling over by his shelter; and Treno was right there, too, grinning his fool head off.

"It varies," she said as she opened her eyes and again shrugged her tiny shoulders. "It depends on the person."

"I see," Lagan murmured, and scratched at his chin. Not for the first time, Jessa stared covertly at his face, trying not to be obvious as the man dealt with his thoughts. Lagan was not a handsome man, but his features seemed to fall in the right places: a broad, lined brow; a firm, cleft jaw; long, dark moustaches; and a nose that was perhaps a bit large, and slightly bent in the middle. It was his eyes, though, where she found his character. They were a bottomless greenish grey, set deep and wide, and they were intelligent.

"There, see? It could make him go blind," Modan growled as if that was the end of it.

"Which, from the sound of it, he already is," Lagan growled back. Looking decidedly unhappy, he walked over and stood in front of Modan. "You know, if I still had my da and he was like that, I'd do everything I could to get him to see something again."

"Well, he ain't your da," Modan muttered.

"Oh, fer . . . ! Listen to me, dammit!" Lagan growled, and for the space of a blink his voice grew angry; then he sighed as if exasperated, and crouched down until his eyes were on the same level as Modan's. "I think you're hearing me, son, but you are not listening. Let's try this: I would think that only a self-centred, useless little prick would not help his da to see again. Don't you?"

"I . . ." Modan glanced at Jessa and that vague, blank stare appeared, as if his mind searched for an answer. When it came, it was feeble. "If I let her go traipsing back through the hills, she'll bugger off."

"I doubt it, but we can solve that problem." Lagan turned to Jessa, and she saw his eyes glint with what could only be amusement. "Jessa, if you were taken to treat Modan's da, *would* you promise not to escape?"

Jessa's eyes widened in disbelief. Promise such a thing to Modan, the man who'd broken his own promise? Then she sensed something in Lagan's tone that spoke of there being more to his words. Was it the emphasis with which they were phrased?

"Certainly," she said calmly, following the Selgovae's lead. "I *would* promise to that."

"Swear to it," Modan growled.

Jessa shrugged. "I so swear."

Lagan nodded his satisfaction and, turning his head so that Modan couldn't see, he looked at Jessa and winked.

# Chapter IX

# Rome, Martius, A.D. 105

# I. The Mare Sardoum

Marcus's patience was stretched to near breaking as the small galley finally cleared the northern tip of Corsica. The vessel was barely thirty hours out of Ostia on a favouring wind, but it seemed to crawl past the island as if plowing through a swamp. The captain, a man appropriately named Pelagius, issued orders to reset sail to the west, and in fairness the crew did so with alacrity. Yet Marcus, spurred by a helpless feeling that much more could be done, strode across the deck and stood alongside the man.

"What's your new heading?"

"*Massalia.*"

"Isn't that farther west than *Forum Julii?*"

"Yes, but Massalia is a larger port. It's not much farther, and the road from there is –"

"How much is not much?"

Pelagius paused as if working out the figure, then shrugged.

"About a hundred miles."

"Not by road, it isn't. Head for the port at Forum Julii. There's a fort there. Horses can be had."

"But if the weather holds, we'll be in Massalia by –"

"I don't deal in 'ifs.' We'll land at Forum Julii. How long?"

Pelagius sighed, clearly reluctant to provide an answer. "Could be two days. Three if the weather turns dead against us."

"Tomorrow night." Marcus glanced upward to where the sun had climbed halfway to its zenith; the sky was clear, but for a thin scatter of scudding clouds. "If nothing else, the weather is a good omen."

Marcus turned and stalked over to the stern. He stood with his hands tapping the rail, staring down at the vessel's wake, a lazy trail of white bubbles oozing slowly to the surface with every mile of the ship's passing. The galley felt like an old scow, plodding through the waves as if pushed by a pole; he could have walked faster! Marcus sighed at his impatience. A horse might well travel faster, much faster, but a horse needed rest, as did its rider. A horse didn't plow through the sea on a straight course for every hour of every day, marking off better than a hundred miles, should the wind be favourable. A horse could only . . .

Marcus lifted his eyes to scan the horizon. The faint outline of a small island stood far off to the side, sliding sternward as the vessel heaved over on its new course. Ostia now no longer lay directly behind, nor did Rome, and neither did his father, and Marcus wondered at the perversity of the gods. They waited like hooded snakes until the time was ripe to strike, but why both his father and his daughter at the same time? Was this a final twist of mischief, a perverse taunt, bringing Tuis's message on the very day his father regained his mind? Was it simply good being cancelled by bad, or was it a cruel and unwanted barter: we'll take your daughter, but give you back your father? He shuddered, and forced the notion from his mind.

A gentle breeze blew in across the stern rail as the ship began running with the wind, and Marcus turned his cheek to feel its steady, even coolness. There had been no choice in leaving for Britannia, though he'd pretended that there was. Aelia and Elena had been at his father's bedside, and Rhun had needed no persuasion to come down from the city. Gaius had been sedated for days, relaxed in a world of dreams that the medicus said would give his brain time to heal. And, to everyone's surprise, when the man weaned Gaius off the potions, they appeared to have worked; though he was at first confused when told of Jessa's disappearance.

"We don't know what's really happening," Elena explained. "She got into a bit of trouble in the north, somewhere beyond Luguvalium. I can't remember the name of the place."

"So what are you doing about it, Marcus?" Gaius demanded, turning in his bed to look at his son.

The aim of his father's question was quite clear. There was nothing Marcus could do, not here in Rome, and he was frantic to do something. There was but one choice, and that was to rush off to Britannia, even if only to find his daughter's body. As the thought once again flashed through his mind, Marcus closed his eyes, tapped on wood with crossed fingers, and offered a quick plea for the gods' forbearance. He had to go to Britannia, even if every step of the way was filled with the agony of what he would find there! Yet his father . . . there was a duty here, as well. The man was close to dying, or he had been just the day before, and he could be gone tomorrow.

"I'm sure Tuis will have another message already on the way," Marcus said, which was probably true. But if so, it would likely tell him nothing more than he knew. And in one way he hoped such a message, if it did arrive, would tell him nothing; for if there were no bad tidings, then there would still be hope.

His mind drifted back to his own years in the same land as a young tribune serving with the Twentieth. There had been far too many years in Brigantia then. What had it been? Eight? That was more than twice the number it was supposed to be. He would have been the same age as his daughter was today – no, he'd been even younger when it started. Yet it was undoubtedly the same gods who were now playing their games. Would they protect her , as they had once protected him?

"You're brewing nothing but belly gas," Gaius had exclaimed, his voice gruff. "The girl is in trouble; what are you doing, still here? If I was well, I'd ride with you."

Aelia answered with her ever-impeccable logic: "By the time he gets there, Father, the matter will probably be resolved. In the meantime, you are here and –"

"And likely to croak at any moment," Gaius finished for her. "Or I could live for another twenty years. If a soft living Greek like Plato can make eighty, then I'm good for . . ."

Elena smiled as her husband fumbled with the arithmetic. "That means you're good for another thirteen years, dear."

"That's right. So get on a horse and go, Marcus. I'll stay here with my women." Gaius reached out and laid a hand on Elena's, and smiled. "If the Shades do call while you're gone, take solace in knowing that I died happy."

Marcus had protested, of course, but left anyway, which did not sit well with his mind. Aelia and Rhun had both accused him of flaying himself in order to create sufficient misery to salve his conscience . . . which they told him was clear, anyway. But was it clear? Marcus and his father had not often been on the same side of the battlefield. Never mind those early years, when he'd been a willing prey in his mother's web of spite; that had been his own fault. It was the later years that chafed, though his sister had told him often enough that he found fault where none was intended.

Gaius had never fully accepted Jessa, though admittedly he tried – sort of. Nor did he understand his son's devotion to the girl. And while his father fully sympathized with Marcus's scorn for the politics of Rome, he would not accept his son's aversion to the women constantly thrust his way as "a fitting match." And above all, he could not abide his son's lack of interest in "a fitting career." Marcus often wondered just how badly he'd let his father down, for he was sure that he had. How much trouble would it really have taken to oblige him, at least once in a while? And how would it all sit if his father was no longer there when he returned?

⸸

The ship arrived at thel port of Forum Julii early in the morning following Marcus's deadline; the tall arches of the aqueduct a dark smudge on the horizon long before the town itself appeared. The sails were still filled with wind when the captain, eager to be rid of his passenger, had the oars run out close by the harbour entrance.

Marcus was on the road before noon with four horses provided by the fort's praefectus: two for himself and two for the man he'd brought with him, a soldier named Tycho, invalided after losing his sword hand at the wrist. A squad of cavalry rode escort, straining every mile to keep pace. They covered more than forty miles before nightfall, with a single change of horses halfway through the journey.

The frantic ride across the length of Gaul brought the pair to *Gesoriacum* in less than nine days. As dusk settled over the small port, Marcus dragged himself to the docks and demanded transport, even if it was in nothing more than a rowboat. When a simpering deputy harbour master sarcastically offered precisely that, stating it was all that they'd find at that ungodly hour, tempers flared. Tycho restrained Marcus as he tried to climb the counter, grasping for the deputy's throat. The flustered harbour master, roused from his table, was appalled to find himself facing an irate Roman senator – a Sabinius, yet; a man who could likely have purchased his own galley and the harbour with it.

The following evening found the two men in the province of Britannia, and well on the way to Londinium. Four and a half days later, ten *pounds* lighter, and with the haggard look of a half-starved, wind – broke horse, Marcus arrived at the gates of Blatobulgium. His sharp demand to see the praefectus met a skeptical objection – the praefectus was occupied, hosting a dinner in the commander's residence.

Marcus would not be put off, and wasted no words in saying so. With Tycho trailing at his heels, he stormed through the reception hall, knowing all too well the location of the dining room in a fort commander's residence. The hum of table chatter reached his ears long before he gained the entrance, but his mind only focused on the dread of what he would learn on the other side. Bitter memories of his own time with the barbarians, the years spent wandering these same hills, filled his mind as he stalked inside – and stopped dead, stunned by what he saw.

Finally finding his tongue, Marcus cried, "What are you doing here?"

## II. The Palatine, Rome

Rhun and Aelia left for the Sabinius town house on the Palatine the day following Gaius's recovery. Rhun's own message from Tuis awaited him there, written in his brother's own hand, which meant Tuis had wanted its contents to remain private. It offered a long, rambling opinion regarding Marcus's overindulgence of his daughter, and the considerable effort now being spent on finding her – hopefully, alive. The uneven scrawl finished with an invitation to return to Britannia and take command of a full milliaria, stationed close by the fort from which Jessa had been abducted. Tuis's description of the posting made the offer sound like a fig ripe for the picking, which made Rhun wonder: what kind of trouble was his little brother really in?

Luguvalium was not exactly set in the fields of *Elysium*, though more than one soldier had been left there in search of them. Rhun recalled that it lay just north of the Cumbrian hills, and there was a huge estuary close by bearing the same name as the fort's river. From what he remembered of the place, winter's rage often turned the fort into an oasis of icy misery; and the greatest joy in summer was to actually see the sun shine.

Even so, a full milliaria . . .

"If I did accept, I suppose it would offer a chance to see Clitus," Rhun ventured as he brooded his way through the evening meal. His and Aelia's youngest son had recently been posted to Marcus's old legion at Deva, the Twentieth Valeria Victrix.

"Rhun, he's only just gone. I doubt the poor boy will be pleased to see his father show up at the gates. He'll think you haven't let go."

"So you think I shouldn't accept Tuis's offer?"

Aelia shrugged. "You don't have to, you know."

"I realize that, but how can I refuse?"

"Easy. Tell him it's due to old age and ill temper. Or you can blame me. You will be fifty next year. You can't get around like you used to."

Rhun peered across at his wife, and snorted at the idea. "I'm as good as ever."

"That depends at what."

"At anything!" He rolled over on the dining couch and stared moodily at the ceiling. A few moments later he muttered, "Almost anything. And I'm better at some things!"

Aelia chuckled. "Well, you *are* a lot faster at slowing down than you used to be."

"That's not funny," Rhun growled, his mind brooding. "The little wart means well, but I did wonder when he took the posting as governor if he was up to it."

"Tuis? A little wart? A man who's past forty? And, I might add, one who couldn't fit into his old armour when he took command."

"He wasn't that bad. There's not much leeway in those molded breastplates."

"He was far too heavy." Aelia sighed. "So when are you leaving?"

Rhun ignored the question. He wasn't yet ready to answer, and preferred to vacillate. "He doesn't actually say he wants help. All he's doing is offering me a command – which he must have arranged." Rhun sat up and swung his legs over the side of the couch, frowning as his mind calculated the number of days since his brother had sent the letter. "You know, he couldn't possibly have had time to obtain imperial approval. I wonder what he's up to?"

"If I remember correctly, Luguvalium is not far from where Tuis said Jessa was taken. It does make you wonder, doesn't it?" Aelia plucked at her lip and frowned as she mulled her husband's doubts. "If the commander's time is close to being done, I suppose Tuis could make the appointment, and have it approved later." She grinned at another thought. "Or quite possibly, he simply made a deal. A bribe here, another there . . ."

"Provincial politics," Rhun muttered. "They used to grind my mind worse than a full-scale battle."

Aelia laughed out loud. "Don't tell me you find the politics more civilized in Rome!"

Rhun grimaced, his mind drifting back to his final command, which had happened to be in Britannia: praefectus of a mixed cohort in the southwest of the province. The greed and theft of the *comites* had been far more blatant than farther to the north where, paradoxically, it was supposed to be *less* civilized. At least in the hills a thief used a weapon and looked the part; he didn't skulk behind a table, wielding a stylus. In Londinium, the centre of it all, incompetence was defined as *not* making a fortune before your posting was over.

"I know that's part of the reason Marcus hides himself on the estate, instead of living here," Aelia added, as if reading his thoughts.

"And now he's on his way back there, flogging half the empire's post horses to death." Rhun shook his head as if reluctant to accept a bad choice. But was it? In truth, a return to Britannia held appeal. It was the land of his birth; the land in which he'd spent half his life – or so it seemed. And assuming command of a mixed millaria would be a prize, there was no doubt; particularly for a man who spent his time doing not much more than passing it.

Rhun rose from the couch and stared down at his wife as if burdened with the care of the world. "You'll be sharing the commander's residence with me, I imagine."

"Yes, you poor, put-upon creature," Aelia teased, "but not for a while. With father still recovering, there's too much to do looking after the estate. Perhaps late summer. Besides, you travel too fast."

"I could go slower."

Aelia smiled and shook her head. "Let's see how Father's health holds. In the meantime, there's someone else who will rip your tongue out if you don't at least talk with her before you go."

"I had that one figured, too," Rhun groaned.

⸸

Rhun rode out to the Nepos country estate the following morning, arriving a good hour before noon. At that time of day there was no point going to the main house, so he made his way instead to the stables.

He found his sister Coira exercising a leggy chestnut stallion in one of the small paddocks hidden behind the main building. The horse had a brilliant white blaze and matching white stocking on its hind legs. The beast reminded him of an animal ridden by his da years ago, one claimed in battle from Aelia's father, Gaius Sabinius. *Gadearg!* The name popped into his mind and he smiled, remembering his father's pride and frustration with the animal. The horse was a magnificent beast, but it had been gelded.

Coira continued setting the chestnut through its paces, clearly aware that her twin watched from the edge of the paddock. It was typical of her, Rhun knew, and not meant to irritate. If the reason he stood there was important enough, then it was incumbent on him to yell it out. If not, then Coira would finish what *she* was doing, which she finally did a good quarter of an hour later. In the meantime, Rhun spread both elbows on top of the paddock wall, eased his chin down on his knuckles, and settled down to watch.

"Is Rome getting too cluttered for you?" Coira asked as she left the paddock and walked over to greet him. One of the slaves led the proud stallion to the stable, its coat glistening but not lathered.

"Too cluttered, and too *un*civilized," Rhun murmured, smiling at the opening she'd left. "In fact, I'm fed up. I think I'll go back to Britannia. Want to come?"

"Hah!" Coira said, but otherwise barely raised her eyebrows. "For how long?"

Rhun shrugged. "I don't know. Up to you. I'm probably off for three years. Never know, though. This time it's a full milliaria. An equitata, I might add. It's something I never had the chance to command."

"I thought you were through."

"I was through. I'm also bored."

"Yeah, sure. Tuis?"

"Who else? That's why I say three years. That's about what's left of his term, too."

"He in trouble?"

"I dunno." Again Rhun shrugged. "I doubt it – but maybe. He probably feels the water's a bit deep at the moment, and he'd like a fellow fish."

"He's got to learn how to swim."

"Could drown first," Rhun said, and grinned. "So, you want to come?"

Coira shook her head emphatically even as she asked, "When?"

"A couple of weeks."

"Can't. Not with Publius the way he is." Coira stared hard at her brother, her face troubled as she bit down on her lip. "It all seems to be coming at once, doesn't it? Publius's lungs giving out, Gaius in a coma for a month; both men far from well, and now Jessa. Bad things always come in threes."

"Yeah, I know. Aelia's staying too, at least for the while." Rhun grew reflective. From what he'd seen of Coira's husband, a good fifteen years his sister's senior, the man was close to climbing onto his deathbed. And given the bellows-like wheeze of the man's lungs, once he was under the covers Publius Didius Nepos would not be getting out again. He could linger for months, though. "Maybe I should stay here too."

"Do you not want to go?" Coira asked.

"Do you not want to go?"

"Of course I do, and no doubt Mother does as well." Coira snorted derisively. "But you're the only one who doesn't have a spouse standing on the banks of the river Styx."

"No, but I might as well have. Aelia is concerned for her father. If I do go and she follows, it likely won't be until late summer. And if something happens to her father, I doubt she'll come at all this year." Privately, Rhun thought the coming summer might well be the last for either Publius or Gaius, despite the latter's recovery. A journey to Britannia, for his wife, his sister, or his mother, was in the hands of the gods.

"Rhun, I know you better." Coira's voice echoed her exasperation. "Your mind is made up, which is fine. Only you figure you first have to protest that you can't leave at a time like this, and go through the expected histrionics. Finally, after everyone says, *Go, Rhun – neither man is kin to you, and your brother desperately needs you, and you have to consider what you want to do,* you'll reluctantly agree and piss off back home anyway. So be honest; get back to Aricia and start making arrangements."

Rhun blinked, startled by his sister's outburst. Then it dawned on him just how embattled she must be. He knew that her marriage to Publius – a match arranged by Gaius – had been ten miles short of spectacular, even though it had been favourable by Rome's standards. Rhun had figured that Publius Didius was a poor second choice for Coira right from the start, a fault due entirely to her own blindness.

The impediment was his sister's dark opinion of Marcus. Rhun had always found Marcus to be a good match; someone who understood his sister and her roots, for he had lived them. Yet there was something between the two dating back to that first year after Bran's Beck. Rhun had a good idea what it might be, but that was a lifetime ago. In fairness, Marc also seemed oblivious to such a match. Or was he just too proud to be the first to break ground? Or was the fool still flogging himself with his conscience?

Not that it mattered. Following Gaius's wish, and probably finding her choice limited, Coira had taken poor old Publius. The man should have chosen an old mare, but instead opted for an unbroken filly. Their union had produced only one child, Fiona; a girl who proved to be Publius's joy and his bane. Ironically, she was named after the Carveti woman who gave birth to Marcus's daughter; a woman whom Marcus often described, tongue in cheek, as being 'determined'. And now here was a second Fiona, Coira's Fiona. Well, she was Fiona . . .

Rhun shook the thought from his mind. There were two reasons he was here to see his sister, and Coira had only heard one of them. He was still wrestling with the second. "Supposing I do go to Britannia, then what —"

"Suppose? Hah!"

"Fine." Rhun grinned and bowed his head to acknowledge his sister's jibe. "*When* I go to Britannia, what do you think – should I take the torque?"

"You've taken it with you every time you were posted there."

"And every time I was posted there, I've asked you," Rhun replied, for their father had entrusted Venutius's torque to them both.

"Then take it with my blessing, and do with it as you see fit," Coira replied, intoning the words as if they were a ritual. Her expression turned thoughtful. "You know, we could both die before finding something useful to do with the cursed thing."

"I could pass the responsibility on to Clitus," Rhun said. He hadn't thought on it before, but as he spoke the words, he realized that wasn't a good choice.

Coira voiced the reasons. "It wouldn't be the same, Rhun. Clitus is Roman, even though you're his father. He doesn't know the tribes. Besides, it's too tempting. With something of that value, its purpose might become perverted: politically, or through simple greed." Coira shook her head emphatically. "I'd rather see it lost. Nothing against Clitus, but the torque belongs to the people. It's for one of them – us – to decide its fate. The gods, and Venutius, gave it to Da, and he gave it to us."

Rhun nodded his agreement. "I'll take it, then. I just needed you to say so."

Coira grinned. "I don't suppose you'd take Fiona too?"

"Hah!"

# Chapter X

## Northern Brigantia, Martius, A.D. 105

Cethen glanced upward when his daughter called, and held out a hand. She placed a platter in the outstretched fingers and he drew it up to his nose, smiling at the rich aroma. "Lamb, not mutton. What happened, did it die of bloat?"

"I'm not certain," Kelpy teased, smiling back. "By the time we shooed the crows away, there wasn't much left to tell."

"What have you got with it? Smells good." Cethen swept clouded eyes over the platter, seeing only a vague mound.

"Chopped samphire fried in buttered oatmeal patties, and roast parsnips."

"I don't like parsnips."

"Eat them. They're good for you."

"You're just after revenge," Cethen muttered. "When you were a brat, you never liked the things either." He eased himself down at the low table, and grinned. "I might add that you're still a brat."

"Just eat them, Da, and stop wailing," Kelpy chided, placing her own meal on the table before sitting cross-legged on the floor across from Cethen. She passed a jug of ale and slid an empty clay mug after it.

"Ta, love," he murmured, and gingerly ran the tips of his fingers over the hot food to figure out where, exactly, it rested on the plate.

Satisfied, he carefully sliced off a piece of the lamb.

"Was talking to Treno again," Kelpy said, eyeing her father over the top of her own mug. "He came by while you were up-valley getting the milk cow bred."

"What's the bugger want now?" Cethen asked, his mood falling at her mention of the name. Though in fairness, it was hard to tell who was worse: Modan, or Treno. Alone, they were bad enough; together, they were a pair of wolves circling a flock of sheep. The trouble was, Modan was too much like his mam, Morallta; then he caught himself. *Morallta was Bryn's mam; Ficra was Modan's. Aah, poor Ficra.*

Cethen paused, his mind drifting to when his third woman, no Ficra was his fourth, had died of a fever. It was getting harder and harder to think back without getting muddled as to who . . .

"Eat *some* of it, then," Kelpy said, mistaking his hesitation and clearly wanting to get on with her other news. "Treno said the dwarf woman came and tended Modan. The poison seems to have gone, and his leg's healing."

"Did Treno say how well she fares? The one that treated him?"

"He said nothing, other than she'd made him better."

"Which is good, but it's also bad." Cethen picked up one of the parsnips, bit into it, then stared at the blurred outline. "You know, when you roast some taste onto the outside, they're not really that bad. And as to the other with Modan . . ." He sighed and turned his eyes more or less toward his daughter. "It'll save the boy's life, but he'll just go out and get his leg buggered up again – or worse. It might have been better if she'd taken it right off."

Kelpy raised her eyebrows, plainly surprised. "You are getting old, Da. A man who spent his life as you did . . ."

"Aye, but I was never one of the fearless buggers like him. The boy's all balls and no brains." Cethen grimaced at the thought, and at a thousand memories of his own. "Things just sort of happened back then, and a man went along with them. But it's them like Modan – the fire-brained ones – that make it so a man's got to go along with it, no matter what. I never did see it do a spit-glob of good in the long run, and that doesn't mean I'm getting old, it means I'm getting wise." He bit into the parsnip, shifted his rump on the hide-covered floor, and groaned at the ache. "Or, I suppose, both."

"Which brings me to what Treno was saying – the getting old bit," Kelpy said, and smiled. "The dwarf woman, Jessa, says there's a possibility she might be able to do something about the stuff that covers your eyes."

Cethen stopped with the lamb halfway to his mouth as his mind grew reflective. Not over the idea of fixing his eyes, for he doubted anything could be done there. The Roman healers might be good, but not that good. The meat fell back onto his plate. "Jessa," he murmured softly, and smiled. When Kelpy had mentioned that there was a dwarf called Jessa treating the people, it had been hard to credit that it might be the same wee lass he'd once known. But others had heard of her, he'd since found out, and the description fit, so it must be her. Yet it was still a large bite to swallow. "Treno said she was a Roman?"

"He didn't say that." Kelpy shrugged. "But he did say it was like I'd been told: she speaks their tongue and ours as if she was born to them."

"Which she was!" Cethen leaned back against the wall, his face breaking into a broad grin. "It's good that she's back. I should really go see her."

"Treno says he'll try to get her to come and see you, even if you don't take the help she's offering."

"She'd be willing to come here?" Cethen asked, surprisingly pleased with the notion, though a long trek into the hills would be a burden on the girl. How old had she been when he'd last seen her? Four, maybe? It had been the day before the lass escaped Morallta's clutches with her da, an event he'd had no small part in. He smiled and released his breath. Like so many things, it was all so long ago.

"The lass is not necessarily willing, which is what I wanted to talk about. I think Treno, unlike Modan, may have a grain of conscience," Kelpy suggested. "At first she told him you should go to the Roman fort, where she might be better able to help you. But –"

"I can't go visit a Roman fort, Kelpy," Cethen interrupted, shuddering at the suggestion. "They'd nail me to the front gate."

"Treno says you've got some sort of a pass. The dwarf called it a pardon."

"Her name's Jessa, not *the dwarf*," Cethen murmured as his eyes, even though they couldn't see worth a faerie's fart, moved to the corner of the lodge where his cot stood, his possessions tucked untidily underneath. The leather pouch given him by Cian – when had that been, ten years ago?—lay buried somewhere in that mess. His brother had told him it was his way back home to where their village had been, to where the Romans now had their fortress at Eboracum. Only Ficra hadn't wanted to go, and he wasn't sure he did either, so he'd simply buried it amongst other relics of the past. And now she was dead, and he still wasn't sure. "I don't trust anything that's written down by a Roman."

"Well, you won't have to," Kelpy said, plainly annoyed, and Cethen wondered what he'd said to upset her. Her next words told the story. "Treno said that after she fixed the leg, Modan promised to let her go. Now he's on the mend, he wants to keep her. And Treno, believe it or not, is upset, which is the first time I've seen him that way for a decent reason. Though there might be another. The Romans are already out searching for the dwa – the wee woman, and they're making reprisals." Again Kelpy sighed. "Not that there wouldn't be anyway, not after Modan's fool attack on their supply column."

"Idiots!" Cethen muttered, wondering how long it would be before the whole thing started over again. It would never succeed, of course, not unless the tribes could find a leader – a man who thought with his head instead of his balls; a man who could replace old Venutius. *Ah, if only the tribes could have stood better together. If they . . .*

Cethen forced the thought from his mind. "They'll keep searching until they find her, you know. And they won't stop. Her da's important. Marcus once commanded the legion at Eboracum."

"He what?"

"I said Marcus – that's her da – once –"

"I heard you. Then why, in the name of Dagda, is the woman tending tribesmen in the hills?"

It was a question that had run through Cethen's mind over the past week or two, and he paused again to give it thought. When he answered, it was with an insight that would have made Elena proud. "Maybe the lass finds she doesn't fit in anywhere else; not in their world, anyway. Maybe not even in ours."

Kelpy stared at her father, startled, then slowly nodded agreement. Her voice was soft when she replied. "That might even be why Treno's having a rare streak of decency. Maybe he sees a bit of himself there. You'll have to make sure Modan lets her go."

Cethen sighed and peered at the dark shadow that was his daughter. The girl was right, of course. But what did she expect him to do?

"Mam, what's to eat?"

Cethen turned as Kelpy's oldest child, a pugnacious lad who reminded him of Bryn, burst through the door, his sister hard on his heels.

"You were supposed to be here ages ago," Kelpy chided. "It's all gone."

"Aw, Mam."

Their mother relented. "You might find something over there, alongside the fire, if you look carefully. But," she wagged a finger, "there'll be no sweet afterward!"

Cethen smiled and glanced toward his daughter, wishing he could see her clearly. The girl had always given him pride. Yet now she was pushing him to deal with Modan as if the boy was still his responsibility. The hot-brained fool was responsible to no one. Imagine wanting to keep the young lass! Something like that would stab at the Romans' bellies worse than the attack on their supply column, which alone was enough to bring down the wrath of the gods – or the Romans, it didn't matter which – on the tribes. Maybe that was Treno's real reason for appearing soft.

※

Cethen had almost forgotten Kelpy's tale of Treno, and the notion that Jessa might help with his eyesight. Kelpy had not, though, and on a fair afternoon when the weather was good and she least expected it, she spied Treno riding down the valley. The wee lass trailed behind, riding a small hill pony. They had an escort of about a dozen riders, who looked just as menacing as Treno himself. Nonetheless, she assumed that he was there to fulfill a promise to help Cethen – though in fairness, it had not really been a *firm* promise, other than in her own mind.

For once, he seemed almost civil as she welcomed him. He introduced the tiny Roman woman – for "Roman" was the way Kelpy thought of her – who did not seem burdened with joy about being there. The lass warmed some when she saw Cethen though, and they were soon talking over old times that surely the wee lass could hardly have remembered, other than through her father's stories.

When evening fell and his belly was full, Treno rode out again. He'd be keeping an eye on the dwarf, he warned Kelpy – but if he and his men were to make camp, it would be at a less conspicuous place than this. Some hidden spot in the woods beyond the small valley, perhaps . . .

※

On the following day, in the cool stillness of early morning, Jessa looked at Cethen's eyes.

"I don't like this," she murmured, pausing to focus on Cethen's pupils. "It would be far better and far cleaner in my surgery. But I suppose . . ." She lifted both eyelids at the same time and glanced back and forth, carefully comparing the two spots in the centre. Each was nothing more than a drop of milk. "I suppose that sometimes, if the slave can't travel to see Caesar, then Caesar must travel to see the slave."

Cethen pondered the words then muttered, "I'm nobody's slave."

Jessa stood back and grinned. "Of course not, oh mighty barbarian warrior; and I'm no Caesar, either. It's just an expression."

"Yeah, well I don't –"

"*Can* you do anything?" Kelpy interrupted, her face anxious as she placed a hand on her father's shoulder.

Cethen's eyes did look good for the procedure, Jessa decided. She had witnessed Roman surgeons deal with similar problems and indeed, she'd helped perform the same surgery herself. The marbling over the black dots in the centre had hardened, she was sure. That would make treatment easier and, in turn, his chances better. But Jessa stubbornly decided not to offer any answers until receiving one or two of her own. It had been weeks since she'd been taken by Modan, and she was damned if she'd fix this man's eyes while his son kept her as his own personal medicus! "How about *you*? Or your da? Can you do something?"

"What do you mean?" Kelpy said.

"What about you two doing something for me?" Jessa demanded, and glared down at Cethen. "I've spent the past five days being led here, hiding from my own people every mile of the way. I've been living like a stinking boar, unbathed and eating slops, simply because your ingrate son won't let me go. I'm running out of medicines, and there are people back at my hospice who need attention. Do you not command your son?"

"I sent word telling him to let you go," Cethen protested, then shrugged as if helpless. "I ordered him to, for what good that did. And I warned him of what's going to happen if he doesn't. What else can I do?"

"Am I to guess that the answer to that question is: nothing?" Jessa sneered, finding this infuriating man nothing like the tall, lanky, dauntless warrior of her dim memory. Not waiting for an answer, she turned to face the small crowd that had gathered in the clearing outside Cethen's lodge. They were eager to watch the operation, and likely thought she was about to describe it. Well, they were going to be disappointed. Jessa raised her voice to be certain that every last one could hear what she had to say. "And that's exactly what I'm going to do: nothing! Nothing at all! Which means all of you might as well go home."

She glanced carefully over her shoulder at Cethen, who sat behind her on an upturned log. She stood atop a second, larger log that had been placed upright between his knees. The arrangement enabled her to peer down on his face while leaving her hands at eye level, free to operate – if she could ever get the dithering fool to resolve her problem. An appeal to the small crowd could do no harm.

"I can fix this man's eyes," she declared, silently appealing to the gods to prove that true. The odds were hugely in favour of some improvement. "Only his oafish son won't let me go. Had he done so, then this man," she gestured to Cethen, "could at this moment be at my small hospital, with bandages on his eyes, waiting to see something. As perhaps could others. But simply because his worthless, lying, oafish offspring has —"

"I'll get you back to your wee hospital, girl," a voice that sounded almost bored called from off to one side.

Jessa whirled, almost falling off the log. A young woman stood on the path that ran alongside Cethen's lodge, with one elbow leaned lazily against the low thatch roof, and the reins of a magnificent black horse dangling from her hand. Her hair was raven black, her eyes a deep, smoky grey, and as indolent as her stance. Jessa noticed with some annoyance that the woman was appraising her with an air of total indifference.

Cethen had also turned at the sound of the voice, and Jessa was sure she heard him groan before speaking. "Trista. What brings you here?"

"I heard you were going to get your eyes fixed. I want to watch."

"Well, it's nice to see you," Kelpy said quickly, as if trying to ease a hidden tension. "Modan is well?"

"I imagine Modan is well. I haven't seen him since they carted him off with his gammy leg."

"And how are you going to get me back to my *wee hospital?*" Jessa interrupted, not willing to keep the sarcasm from her voice.

"Probably on your *wee* horse," Trista replied, not hiding her own apparent indifference. Pushing herself away from the thatch, she sauntered over to where Cethen sat. The black horse, a tall gelding that was clearly no hill pony, trailed obediently behind. Jessa noted that the small crowd of curious onlookers parted for her like sod cut by a plow. The woman bent and kissed Cethen on the cheek. "Lovely to see you, too, Da."

Jessa blinked. How many brats had the man sired? He must have been in rut until he was fifty! She addressed Cethen, not concealing her doubt. "Your daughter can help get me back?"

"I'm not his daughter," Trista replied, rising to face Jessa. With the help of the log, they stood almost eye to eye. "I'm married to his worthless, lying, oafish son. I think that was what you called him. It's not a bad description, actually."

"And *you* can command him to let me go?"

"Command?" Trista repeated the word wistfully, as if relishing its taste; then she laughed and shook her head. "I might persuade, threaten, cajole, and argue; or I may simply grow sullen, surly, and contentious. That usually gets me what I want. But I never command. Right, Da?"

She turned and flashed Cethen a brilliant smile that held not a trace of warmth.

"Aye, that's the right of it," he murmured.

Jessa decided the woman thought too much of herself. "How does that get him to do as you tell him?" she asked, realizing as she spoke how naive the words sounded. "From what I saw of him, he'd knock you silly with the back of his hand."

"Ah, but then he wouldn't have me, would he?" Trista said, as if disinterested. She was staring down at Jessa's bag, which had fallen partially open. "Above all else, Modan doesn't want that to happen."

"I didn't mean he'd kill you," Jessa said, uncomfortable with the sudden turn of words.

"I didn't either, for if Modan did that, then Bryn would surely stretch his neck from here to the Ituna. No, what my husband is afraid of is that I'll bugger off. And I would, if the sod ever hit me." She snorted at the very notion, but added, "Again!"

"That's enough of that horse shit," Cethen mumbled as his eyes, unseeing as they were, swept the small crowd of spectators, none of whom seemed inclined to leave. "This is neither the time nor the place."

"Who's Bryn?" Jessa was intrigued, for the name was vaguely familiar.

"He's Modan's half-brother," Trista replied, shrugging.

*And Bryn would kill his brother!* Jessa wondered at the words, but not enough to shift from the track she was intent on following. "Why would *you* be willing to see I got back to where I came from?"

"Because," Trista said slowly, as if mocking her reasons, "it will turn Modan's belly sour for a month! That alone is worth the deed." Then she settled one hand on Jessa's shoulder and stared directly into her eyes. For the first time, Jessa saw a hint of warmth there, a look of sincerity that made her heart jump. The woman was either an accomplished liar or, for the briefest of moments, was baring her soul. "But there's another reason. Modan is wrong on this."

Jessa felt her eyes grow unexpectedly moist, a strange and rare event. She slowly nodded her understanding, finding speaking suddenly difficult. There was nothing more to say anyway; there was nothing more she *could* say.

※

Trista watched carefully as the dwarf woman made herself ready. She first cautioned Cethen to be still, then lifted a long, needle-like tool from the cloth-covered tray. It was wide on one end, about the width of a fat stalk of straw, while the other narrowed to a point so sharp it was barely visible. The woman glanced up at Kelpy, who stood behind Cethen with one hand clasped firmly under his chin and the other holding his right eyelid wide open. The left eye, for the moment, was covered with a patch of wool and bandaged. Nodding to reassure Kelpy that everything was just fine, she told Cethen once more to remain as still as stone, then leaned forward over his face. With her left hand resting against his cheek, the right hand firm on his forehead, and the base of her thumb pressing against his nose, she began to probe.

Trista watched in fascination as the needle, guided by a tiny hand as steady as the earth, prodded the eye at an angle where the small circle in the middle began. The tip magically disappeared into the orb's liquid-like surface. There was no gush of blood, as Trista had expected, or of anything else, for that matter. The thread-thin instrument simply joined up with the eye where the blue met the tiny, clouded hole in the centre.

The woman began working the tip gently up and down, as if coaxing a sliver loose from under the skin. Her tongue appeared in the corner of her mouth, her concentration hard and unbroken. After a while she pulled the needle back long enough to make another hole, and the to and fro motion continued. The procedure seemed to drag slowly on, yet it really took no time at all – as Trista suddenly realized when the milky cloud seemed to fill only the bottom part of the tiny circle in the centre of Cethen's eye. She was barely able to breathe as the pale cloud edged its way downward until finally, mysteriously, nothing was left of it at all. In some vague manner it reminded Trista of the magic witnessed years earlier, when one black, terrifying night the moon itself had slowly vanished from the sky. Yet even though the milky centre was gone, hopefully never to reappear, the woman continued to work the needle until finally she nodded her satisfaction.

Trista stepped back and released her breath. Then she saw the woman was not yet done. Jessa turned and picked up another small tool, not unlike the first, except its thin tip had been blunted so it resembled a tiny chisel. It had been resting above a bed of red-hot charcoal coals glowing in the bottom of a small iron pan. She raised the instrument in front of her eyes, nodded at the dull glow that could be seen there, and again bent over Cethen. Very carefully, Jessa touched the end to the points where the needle had penetrated Cethen's eye: three tiny indentations that only she could see. There was a faint, sizzling hiss each time it was done, and then the small woman again nodded her satisfaction. Trista realized it was over. Almost.

"The egg whites; the boiled wool," Jessa commanded.

Trista, who'd been primed for this part, picked up a bowl containing three small balls of wool soaked in raw egg white. The inside of the bowl, like everything else it seemed, had been carefully washed out with boiling water.

"Use the forceps – that two legged thing."

Trista selected the instrument from the tray, mildly irritated at being told, for she had been about to do that anyway. She plucked one of the wool balls from the bowl and offered it to the young woman, who instead nodded for her to place it on top of Cethen's eye.

"You've done well, Cethen, but now keep your eye closed," Jessa murmured, and began working the soggy mass into a smooth poultice that covered the eyelids. Then she carefully daubed away the sticky excess with a cloth that had also been boiled. When it was dry about the edges, she trickled a thin coat of honey on top, and bound everything with a freshly boiled bandage that ran diagonally around Cethen's skull.

Once done, Jessa finally turned to face Trista with a huge smile on her face, and said, "There, that's one. Ready for the second?"

Trista stared at the woman and smiled in turn, realizing that each of them was as relieved as the other. The tension that had hung over the small clearing seemed to vanish like a windblown mist and with it, the complete silence that had followed each move of the needle. Everyone began talking at once, as if a hard fought race was suddenly over, and the result now open to debate. Trista found herself staring down at the bowl and the two remaining balls of sticky wool. She saw, with surprise, that her hand was trembling.

"Just set it down again for a while, maybe where it was," Jessa suggested, her voice now gentle.

"Oh." Trista looked up and found she was staring into a pair of brown, doe-like eyes that were full of concern. Which irked, for she needed no one's solicitude. Then she found it really didn't matter; though reluctant to admit it, there was something about this tiny woman, this dwarf, that, well, that impressed her. And nobody anywhere, with perhaps a single exception, had ever impressed her. She glanced down at the bowl again. "Er, what's the third ball of wool for?" she asked, for the sheer lack of anything else to say.

Jessa grinned. "You're allowed to drop *one*!"

※

A week and a half later, Jessa readied herself to depart for the fort at Blatobulgium. Cethen's eyes had been unbound several days past, and showed no trace of infection. And while his vision had not returned to normal, something it would probably never do, he could see far better than he had in years – a condition that Jessa was sure would still improve. All things considered, she was happy with the manner on which events had turned.

Her days in the small village had passed pleasantly enough, despite her status as Treno's prisoner. The weather had remained fair; the food was familiar – if not as varied as she had grown used to with her "other" people in Rome; and Cethen, surprisingly, had proved a good enough host, though mainly through the auspices of Kelpy. The only real complaint she could bring against the man was his continuing blindness regarding his youngest son, a malady that no simple eye surgery would cure. Not that he seemed to have much sway, she readily admitted; but he could make an effort. Certainly his daughter by marriage had done so.

Her initial dislike of Trista had eroded, sparked by the startling recognition of a possible kindred soul. Jessa had always felt apart from just about everyone she knew, with few exceptions. One, of course, was her own father, whose unfailing devotion was indubitable, and often embarrassing. There had been occasions when he would rush to her defense against any slight, real or imagined. And in doing so, he was never mindful of his own interests – or, sometimes, hers.

And there were others, too, who, for lack of any better phrasing, treated her as a normal human being. Yet those people were nearly all kin. At the top of the list was Elena, her grandfather's wife, followed closely by her children who, when the spear struck home, were all born barbarians – which perhaps explained much. And of course, there was Aelia. But then there was her grandfather . . .

Back in Rome, in the circles where her grandfather travelled, she was an oddity, and not only for her size. There was the silent implication that her *barbarian* side had undoubtedly caused her stature. This was a belief that she knew was shared by Senator Gaius Sabinius Trebonius, though he had never voiced as much. But her grandfather didn't have to; he was a Roman patrician, and that was simply the way he rationalized . . .

Ah, the bitter joys of Rome; she missed them like a sore tooth.

Britannia, Jessa had to admit, *was* her home. She found a certain comfort here, a comfort at least partly achieved by doing something useful. Which now she could perhaps return to doing, she decided as the morning of her departure dawned.

That departure, Jessa knew, might not prove easy, nor was it certain. She would be leaving without Treno's or Modan's knowledge, which was cause for unease. Trista had grown moodier as the days passed, and was now plainly unhappy with her choice. Or was she simply nervous?

The black gelding was already saddled when Kelpy brought the animal to the front of the lodge, as was Jessa's pony. Trista tossed both her pack and Jessa's leather bag behind the cantle. She was still tying them down when Treno appeared, squashing any notion of secrecy.

He rode in with the same band of riders that had escorted Jessa through the hills more than a week before. He'd risked moving his camp closer a few days earlier, and had shown up at Cethen's lodge several times. But to get there so soon, this early in the morning, he must have had someone watching. Jessa took some satisfaction in realizing that Treno, too, was expecting to find a path strewn with stones.

"Ready to return?" he asked pleasantly enough, though his voice was strained.

"What are you doing here?" Trista continued testing the snugness of the fastenings, jerking the pack sharply back and forth behind the saddle.

Treno chose to answer the question with sarcasm. "Hello, Treno. Good morning, Treno. How are you, Treno?"

"Sod off."

Treno eyed the saddled horse and the packs, scratched thoughtfully at his chin, and chose optimism as the best path. "I see you are ready to return. Modan will be pleased to see us all back again."

"To this woman," Trista nodded to Jessa, who stood off to one side holding the reins of her pony, "'ready to return' means she's going back to where she lives."

"She's going back to Modan."

"Only if she wants to, which I doubt; and even she did, only after she's first been returned to where she came from." Trista refused to look at Treno and simply moved to tending to the saddle, which Jessa thought was already quite firmly secured.

"Look, Trista, you know I've got no other choice," he said, lowering his voice as if trying to hide the disagreement from his men. "And you don't either. Stop being stubborn and —"

"Being stubborn," Trista interjected in a firm voice as she swung up onto the saddle, where she finally stared directly into Treno's eyes, "is *not* defined as failing to do what you or Modan want."

"Take her back where she belongs, Treno." Cethen came from the lodge with Kelpy, where they'd been preparing a small bundle for the ride back. He'd been about to hand it to Jessa, but turned when he caught Trista's words. "I'm telling you that. And I'll answer to Modan for you."

"Cethen, you know I can't do that," Treno said, his voice revealing irritation. "And even if I did, he'd tear into your hide as well as mine. I promised him I'd bring her back. He specifically told me –"

"*He* promised *me* I'd be allowed to return home," Jessa said, shouting the words in anger. Her gut had told her from the very beginning that Modan would break his word, and now it was Treno doing it for him. Damn the man. Damn them both.

"And you promised him you wouldn't escape!" Treno shot back, as if it mattered.

"No, I didn't. Lagan phrased it so I wouldn't have to!" she said derisively, knowing full well she was juggling words. "He asked me if I *would* promise not to escape, and I said yes I *would*, and I did exactly that. Do you want it again? Here: I promise that I'll promise not to escape! There! That's all I ever did."

"*What* are you talking about, girl?" Treno said, confusion twisting the whorls on his face.

"Treno, I never did actually promise not to escape," Jessa said. "Not that I suppose it matters, because Modan did make a promise, and broke it. Tell him my word is no worse than his, and I'm gone home to Blatobulgium."

"Today, your home is not some Roman fort; it's farther north in –"

"And I'm telling you this, Treno," Trista said, edging her horse alongside his until their faces were almost touching, "she *is* going back to where she belongs – with me. And if you haven't got the balls to accept that, then scuttle right back and tell your master. And by the time you get to wherever it is he's skulking, she'll be back with her people." She gestured toward Jessa.

"Trista, listen." Treno's voice, Jessa noted with surprise, seemed suddenly to have lost its edge; in fact, it was close to a whine. "You know what he's like. What's the sodding difference? We could use the dwarf. All of us. She's good, real good, at what she does. Modan's not going to let her go."

"Her name is Jessa, arsehole, not 'the dwarf,' and she's not some prize horse for Modan to keep," Trista hissed.

"But she's –"

"But nothing! Modan let her go two weeks ago, when she left his camp to come here. And he *has* let her go, Treno, hasn't he?" Trista stared hard into Treno's eyes as she drew out the last words, and Jessa saw a warning written there. What it was, she had no idea, but Treno saw it too, for he wavered.

"Yeah, I suppose he did. But just to treat his da. And *I've* got to take her back."

"No you don't, not if you've got a spine! And Treno, it's wrong." She sat back in the saddle and stared at him, her chin raised as if in challenge. "And *you*, above all, should know the meaning of wrong. You are not taking her – not while I stand in your way. I have my blade and I have my tongue. I'll use both if need be. And you know which will harm you most in the longer run."

Treno sucked on his lower lip and Jessa, startled, realized he was beaten. Trista's look was alone fit to kill, but there was more to it than that. Her flint-like eyes seemed to be almost mocking the man, cold and hard as she stared him down.

Finally, after what seemed an age, Treno slumped back in the saddle. "Then it's your throat that's laid bare."

꙳

Jessa protested that Trista was placing herself in peril, who brushed the threat aside as nonsense; and oddly enough, the more she insisted, the more Jessa tended to believe her. Certainly Trista seemed to *think* it was true; or, as Jessa had speculated before, she was an accomplished liar.

Trista said nothing about the clash of wills with Treno during the few days it took to reach Blatobulgium. Jessa wondered what axe she held over Treno's head, for surely there was one. He obviously feared Modan and was clearly loath to risk the swine's disfavour, yet the man had bowed – no, he had crumbled – under Trista's wilting glare. Jessa knew she could not approach the reason directly, but she did try drawing the woman out through the back gate. They were riding side by side along a dirt road that was within half a day of their destination. Treno, who had eventually decided his best interest lay in riding with them, had gone ahead; he was impatient and nervous, and constantly calling for them both to keep up – which left an opening for Jessa's curiosity.

"Who *is* Treno, anyway?" she asked, gesturing ahead to where he waited, his horse standing sideways in the middle of the track. "Is he a chieftain of some kind? Modan's right hand? One of his commanders?"

The questions produced the hint of a smile. "All of those, I imagine. Though there is a further hook." Trista half turned to Jessa, clearly amused. "You see no resemblance?"

Jessa stared, uncertain as to her meaning. "To who?"

"To me." The smile turned to a grin that was at least half grimace. "Treno is my brother."

"Ah!" Jessa exclaimed, as if perhaps that explained everything; but as she thought on it, she found it explained nothing. "And . . . ?"

"And nothing, I suppose. Though it was through Treno that Modan met me," Trista murmured, her manner suddenly reflective. And beyond that she would say no more.

# Chapter XI

# Selgovae Territory, Martius, A.D. 105

Bryn rode into Lagan's camp with thirty men behind him, and Trista alongside. The site swarmed not only with Selgovae warriors, but others from the two tribes whose blood had joined to form his own: the Brigantes and the Carvetii. A number of Novantae tribesmen were there from the northwest, and he even saw a few Caledonii, probably down to discover what was happening. Hundreds seemed to be gathered here with only a scattering of women among them. All of which told Bryn that Lagan, rather than forming his army, was here testing the support he might gather from those leading the *tuaths*.

Nonetheless, the old hill fort site was a nest of ants, a tumbling disarray of people, horses, chariots, hill ponies, and baggage. In a small way, Bryn found it reminiscent of Galgar's gathering of the tribes in the years before their thrashing by the Roman general, Agricola. He'd been a child then. His da, who had fought there, would have displayed contempt at the idea of starting it all over again.

The sprawling encampment lay beneath the shadow of the razed fort, which had been covertly reoccupied by the Selgovae. The walls and palisades had not been rebuilt, nor had the huge gates, but new ditches and ramparts were dug below the dome of the hill and they were staked, much like those of a Roman marching camp. A clutter of huts had sprung up behind, and three or four decent lodges stood tall among them.

"I wonder where Modan fits in all this?" Bryn murmured as they rode in through a sea of curious faces.

"He'll be trying to crawl as near to the top as possible," Trista replied, her eyes shifting back and forth; she was plainly ill at ease. Her nose twitched, and she frowned in distaste as her eyes fell on a row of open pits close by the tree line. An enormous heap of rubbish sat alongside. "It stinks worse that a pigsty. There's a small army here, and it's fouling its nest. I'll wager Modan has been helping feed it with his raiding." She glared at a small group of tattooed hill men, who all gaped back, one of them pointing.

"Never seen that before." Bryn grinned. "They're ogling your horse, not you."

"Let 'em dream, they're not going to ride either," Trista muttered, and glanced up to where the fort once stood. "I wonder what's happening?"

"We'll soon find out. I see your husband." Bryn pointed away from the hill, toward a stretch of open ground bordered by the thick forest. The trees were in bud and soon the entire camp would be surrounded by verdant new growth, but it would do little to hide the mess and the stink. Modan had roped off a separate camp by the shelter of the trees, enclosing a long row of tents – Roman tents – and a half dozen horse lines. An ungainly figure hobbled across the grass using a crutch, shouting at several others who followed him like goslings trailing a wounded goose.

Bryn smiled bitterly to himself as the gaggle seemed to shrink under the tirade. He'd always had the measure of his brother. Though large and obnoxious, Bryn had never been afraid of the man. He had readily agreed when Trista asked him to go with her to face her husband, and he well knew the reason. Once more she'd defied Modan, this time with the dwarf girl, a lass he vaguely remembered from his childhood. Trista knew that with him by her side, Modan would hold rein on his temper, though the confrontation would be far from pleasant. And Bryn detested unpleasantness, particularly with family, but this was Trista . . .

"I see he's his usual happy self," she muttered, and offered Bryn an equally bitter smile.

Modan stopped when he saw them and waited, leaning on the crutch, his splinted leg hanging clear of the ground. He glanced coldly at Trista, then stared up at Bryn and nodded. "You here to help, or to offer excuses for my wife?"

"The day your wife needs me to make excuses is the day she loses her tongue," Bryn said mildly, and swung down from his horse.

"Not true." Trista remained in the saddle, staring down at both men. "The day I make *any* excuse is the day I cut out my tongue." She glanced at Modan, her jaw thrust defiantly forward. "I delivered the woman back to her home, *as you promised.*"

Her husband hesitated, his eyes lidded, as if undecided. Then he again nodded, and wagged his injured leg. "That's good. I was through with the wee witch anyway. If I need her again, I know where to find her."

Bryn spoke quickly, uncomfortable with the exchange, though so far it was milder than expected. "So what's happening, Modan? Who's behind this?" He motioned to the teeming camp, then to the clutter of buildings and earthworks on the hill. "Just Lagan, or is there more to it?"

"Lagan and me." Modan shrugged both shoulders as if it was of no importance, which it clearly was. "Lagan is merely rebuilding his home. There's nothing the Romans should worry about. You'll notice he's not doing it in a manner that's offensive. A few drainage ditches here and there on the outside. A place in which to live."

"Lagan!" Bryn remembered the Selgovae chieftain: a glib, persuasive man not long beyond his middle years. Depending on who you talked to, he was a pious savior of the tribes, or a self-serving rabble-rouser. Even so, it didn't make sense. They were less than twenty miles from the nearest Roman outpost – *everything was less than twenty miles from a Roman outpost* – and the man was rebuilding one of the hill forts. There seemed no shortage of help. "He appears to have a few guests."

"He's a good host, very popular." Modan ignored Trista's hoot of laughter, other than to scowl. "He is with the menfolk, anyway. I'd guess he finds women too hard on his head. On anyone's head. You'll notice there's not many of 'em here."

"That's because he's expecting reprisals," Trista said, and finally slid down from her horse. Bryn's people had already dismounted and joined Modan's men, most of them loafing off by the trees. "Surely you don't expect to make a stand here?"

"Maybe," Modan said, though his eyes shifted and Bryn knew he was lying. "Then, you never know. Maybe the Romans think one pissy little raid isn't that important, and will leave us alone. We only –"

Again Trista's hoot of laughter interrupted. Bryn could see she was leaning hard on her husband's patience, and stepped in. "Modan, you *only* killed a hundred or more. Most of them after they were wounded," he said, his voice rising as the grip on his temper slipped. Where was his brother's brain? It was his mother's side, he decided, then just as quickly dismissed that notion as nonsense. Ficra had avoided all conflict as she grew older – it was his own mother, Morallta, who had lusted for it! Bryn shook his head and tried not to figure the ways of the gods.

"So, what's a hundred? They've got thousands more," Modan muttered, and glared at Trista.

"Exactly, you butter-brained idiot," Trista replied, "and they're all going to –"

Bryn again interrupted. "You also plundered the Romans' wagons, burned them to the ground, and killed the oxen. You think they're going to ride in, slap your bum, and say don't do that again?"

Modan's face flushed, showing that he was quickly losing control of his temper. "No, but maybe they'll come looking for us, and find a surprise waiting. Bryn, you're becoming weak and old, like Da."

"Da spit more Romans on his spear than you spit phlegm from your gob. Never forget that, little brother. He just got wiser as he got older." Bryn sighed and decided further argument was futile. It was time to offer Modan a reason for his visit that didn't include looking out for Trista. "The Roman governor is leading an army up from Eboracum. The general who commands there is marching with him. There'll be more than two thousand legion soldiers, and as many again of their auxiliary troops. I figure you can add another thousand to that from the forts around here. Their arses have been kicked, and they'll be looking for blood."

"Shit!" Modan paled, and his lips tightened. "Where are they? How do you know?"

"I told him." Trista stepped forward and tweaked smartly on his beard, her face smug.

"How . . . ?"

"The *'wee witch'* told me. Or at least, I heard it through her."

"Why would she do that? How would she know?"

"She took me inside the Roman fort," Trista said, her voice now dripping smugness. "I was in the commander's lodge. I actually ate there, right in this huge room, with a whole pile of Roman officers."

"The dwarf knows the Roman chief that well?"

"Modan," Trista said patiently, rolling her eyes as if explaining the obvious, "when she rode in through those gates, I thought the Roman chief was going to lift her off her pony and kiss her!"

Bryn smiled as he listened to the two: at Trista because she'd been clearly awed by the experience; at Modan because of his appalling ignorance of the men he'd angered. Only the gods knew what the Romans would do because of the attack on the supply train. If his brother had a seed of sense, he'd be gone when they took their revenge. Yet if he did flee, where did that leave the lesser folk who lived in the hills? Bryn knew that answer all too well, and it was as old as time: burned by the fire that others had lit!

He sighed, deciding that Modan was right on one point: he was beginning to sound like his da. Yet Trista's final comment had struck hard at his mind, and he wondered just who this woman called Jessa was. Could she, in some small manner, be a reason for the alarmingly quick response from the Romans? He'd have to find out more when Trista and her husband finished tossing barbs at each other. In the meantime, Modan appeared to have accepted his loss, for he grimly nodded to his brother and stalked off in search of his men.

⸸

Though she had found the fort exhilarating, Trista grew oddly somber as she recalled the Romans' joy when the tiny woman rode through the gates. It had been startling to realize that enemy soldiers were capable of such emotion: the teasing, the relief, the laughter, the playful banter as they escorted Jessa inside. She was plainly a favourite, and just as plainly, the men were not only pleased to see her, they were downright relieved. As was the fort commander when he took her into his own home and made her doubly welcome. The man had greeted her as if she were a lost spirit returned by the *siths*.

"Kissing Roman boots, were you?" Modan's voice cut into her brief daydream.

Her husband had turned when Bryn rode off, and Trista realized that it was not over. She heaved a sigh and decided on sarcasm. *"Glad to see you, Trista,* he says. *I missed you, my dear,* he adds. *Welcome back."*

"What did you expect, woman? I find a decent meat-stitcher that knows what she's doing, and you return her to our enemies. I could have died but for that woman, and you go and give her away!"

"I know, I know. And I shouldn't. She's the enemy, right?" Trista threw up her hands in disgust. "And she's doing what all enemies do, isn't she? She's helping our people, day and night, trying to cure their sores and sickness, the sly, sneaky bitch! Devious, sodding Romans! Makes you wonder, doesn't it? She's probably a spy."

"I can tell you this," Modan growled back, and his eyes fell to the ground, his mind clearly churning, "the five thousand Romans that Bryn says are coming are sure as death the enemy. We've got some figuring to do."

Trista watched as her husband's face grew thoughtful, and a nagging indifference nipped at the back of her mind. A few years ago, she would have been choked with fire and venom at the notion of a Roman army marching north, ready to do battle. The air would have been alive with rage and retribution, and she'd have been part of it. Now, when she put events in order, it was to see that Modan had been daft enough to kick the Roman bear in the bum and start it roaring. What did the fool expect? It struck Trista, not for the first time, that perhaps other reasons fueled her lack of fire for the Romans. Over the past few years Modan's ardour for "the cause" had turned to obsession, while her passion for causes had slowly waned.

Her mind again turned to Jessa and the life the woman enjoyed at the Roman fort – when she wasn't being abducted by "selfish, oafish" barbarians. Trista smiled at the memory of the woman's words. The small one seemed to have found her own cause inside the walls of her hospice, and was pursuing it alone; that took courage and craw, whatever the reasons buried inside her.

Which made her wonder: was Jessa alone simply because she found it less painful? Finding a man would surely be difficult for the small lass. Was that the reason she'd taken the path she walked? Trista grunted her cynicism at such a need. *Finding* a man had never been difficult for her; losing them was the problem. With the exception of Bryn, they were far too interested in leading you around by the nose once they'd got you into their beds and . . .

Her eyes narrowed as she saw Modan nod to himself, his features firm with decision. He huffed a satisfied grunt through his beard, and without a further word he turned on his good leg and stumped off toward the hill.

"Where are you going?" Trista demanded.

Modan paused, and for a moment she thought he would ignore her.

Then he turned and limped back. "To sort this through," he sneered, his face close enough that she could feel his sour breath on her cheeks. "So just skulk off back to Cethen if you haven't got the grit for this, and keep your gob shut. And I'm warning you," a stubby finger poked her hard on the shoulder, "don't ever use Treno to cross me like that again."

"Cross you? Since when is helping you keep your word crossing you?"

"It was Treno's word, not mine, dammit. Everyone seems to forget that. And you did it in front of the men!" Modan's voice rose to a snarl. "In front of the men! If I'd been there you'd still be wearing the bruises. And the dwarf would still be here!"

"And that's your level, isn't it, Modan – bruising women!" Trista hissed. "Huh! You can't even handle the one you've got. Let me tell you this: try that again and any bruising you do will be the last thi –"

She should have seen it coming, Trista realized, in the quick shift of his eyes to see where Bryn was. In the same moment his free hand arced backward and came forward in a wide, vicious swing. She tried to duck, but not fast enough to avoid the blow. It missed her face, but his knuckles slammed into the side of her head and she tumbled backward onto the grass.

Modan turned and stumped off toward the hill fort.

Trista lay on one elbow, her eyes watering as they followed her husband through a starry haze. He limped across the open meadow, the crutch swinging wide and the injured leg dragging like a broken wing. Cursing his back, she brought one hand up and gingerly touched her ear. It was hot and ringing inside. Rage boiled through her mind and she started to her feet, intent on falling on his back, screaming and clawing. But as she rose slowly to one knee, her head aching, she paused and looked around. Nobody stood gaping or leering, as she knelt there caught up in her self-imposed shame. Hadn't anyone seen the blow? Trista staggered to her feet, unsure. Her anger was fading slowly to disgust, disdain, and determination. The man was a fool, but that didn't mean she was one too.

What, she wondered, was the notion that had suddenly formed in Modan's mind? Something was festering there, for she'd seen it bubble and set. And whatever had suddenly spawned would no doubt affect them all. Perhaps she should find Bryn – not to tell him of the blow, for that would only cause trouble, but maybe to ask him what he thought his half-brother would do next.

# Chapter XII

## Blatobulgium, Aprilius, A.D. 105

Tuis rolled backward on the dining couch, unable to believe his ears. When his eyes confirmed that the voice did, indeed, belong to his brother, he leapt to his feet.

But Marcus barely noticed. His eyes were on Jessa, who stared back with equal surprise from the couch across from Tuis. Marcus's face, which had at first expressed concern, changed slowly to a grim visage of anger. "What are you doing here?"

"Father . . ."

"Marcus!" Tuis cried and rushed over to greet his brother, clasping his wrist with one hand and throwing an arm around his shoulders. "Did you not receive my message?"

"Of course. That's why I'm here." Marcus glared about the small dining hall, clearly caught between relief, bafflement, and anger. Jessa climbed from the couch and approached her father.

"No, that was the first message," Tuis explained. "There was a second."

"No, I . . ." Marcus dropped to his knees and clasped his daughter in a tight embrace, his eyes glistening. "Jess. What madness is this? I heard you'd been taken. I worried – I warned you about this. I told you –"

"Father, I'm fine." She kissed his cheek, then stood back to look at him. "You look as if you've been ridden, not the horses. How did you get here so fast?" She frowned, her mind plainly calculating dates. "The first message couldn't have left here – what, six weeks ago? So, how?"

"I did ride a little on the fast side," Marcus said dryly, then stared accusingly at Tuis. "You said she was being held captive by the Selgovae."

"She was. She rode back in here about ten days ago."

"She what?" Marcus blurted, anxious eyes swinging back to his daughter. "Were you hurt? Did they harm you? How did you get free?"

"I didn't have to get free. They let me go – sort of. They only took me to tend one of their wounded, an oafish slug who decided to keep me on as his personal surgeon. Nobody raised a finger to harm me."

"It does get complicated," Tuis murmured, wondering exactly how he was going to explain his relatives to Marcus. One of his half-brothers had nobbled the man's daughter, while his real father had a small hand in letting her go. And key in helping him, it seemed, had been an attractive woman who proved to be his sister-in-law. A very attractive woman, he recalled, with an appealing, haughty independence in her deep grey eyes that caught a man's . . .

"Try me," Marcus snapped, climbing to his feet.

"The man hurt was the one who led the attack on the supply column," Jessa told him. "He's Tuis's –"

"Attacked the supply column?" Marcus interrupted, turning to Tuis as if only he had the sordid details. "What attack? Is that why there are so many troops here? I see two of the old marching camps are occupied. Are you expecting trouble?"

"As I said, it's a complicated –"

"The attack on the supply column was a couple of months ago," Jessa continued, obviously eager to tell her story. "There's been no more trouble since, but I think that's because the leader was hurt. His name is Modan. He's Tuis's half-brother." She chuckled and waved one hand toward her father. "Just like you are, I guess."

"What?" Marcus raised puzzled eyebrows at Tuis. "He's your da's boy? I thought the lad was called Bryn."

"Yes, well, he had another one later."

"That's right, he did. I'd guess he's a bit younger than me," Jessa interrupted again, much to Tuis's annoyance. "Bryn is out there somewhere, though. Trista says he's quite nice. More like his da. Which reminds me," she snapped her fingers, "I spent a couple of weeks with Tuis's da. I did a couching on his eyes. It turned out really well. He thinks I'm a magician."

"Who's Trista?" Marcus was clearly growing more irritated.

"She's Modan's wife, though I don't know why she stays with the lout. He's nothing but a –" Jessa began.

Tuis decided he'd had enough. The fort commander and his guests were on the dining couches, unattended, not to mention the legate of the Ninth, and nigh on a dozen others. "You must be hungry, Marcus.

Why don't you have something to eat?" he turned toward the low table and stopped, blinking in surprise. The fort commander and his wife, their overweight daughter, Julia, Marius Appius, and the garrison's senior officers all seemed to have lost interest in their food. They lounged silently on the dining couches, staring like a pack of wolves: ears pricked and mouths open. "Er, perhaps we should move to my quarters. I'll have something brought in."

⸸

The reprisals proved ineffective and, in an odd way, distastefully hollow. Tuis had mustered his legions into the field – two cohorts from the Ninth and two from the Twentieth at Deva – and he was not happy; all four were understrength, and he suspected Marius of keeping men back for his sodding stone fortress. He should have insisted on bringing each unit to full strength, rather than just agreeing to take the third cohort and the seventh; he should never have assumed each one would be at full strength! And the Twentieth's legate had played the same game, and both men were going to hear about it. In fact, Marius had already been told in words that were loud and clear, when the Ninth caught up with Tuis at Blatobulgium.

The confrontation had not been an auspicious start to the expedition. With auxiliary attachments and a few more troops from Luguvalium, the strength of the small army was under four thousand when it finally moved north to *Crawdum* in late April. From there, the compact force turned east toward the fort at Trimontium, which had been the site of a major encampment when Agricola gathered his armies to battle Galgar almost twenty-five years before.

The cohort commanders forced the march, the small army tramping through scores of half-hidden glens, each hemmed in by endless slopes of broad, rolling hills. There was hardly a soul to be found. Selgovae tribesmen had long lived here, the green valley floors and the lower slopes providing rich, fertile farmland that teemed with lakes and bubbling streams. But the small farmsteads were now all but deserted. The army trekked onward almost unopposed, burning and plundering all that stood in its path. Tuis, his frustration growing by the mile, reached Trimontium on the eastern side of the hills with little sense of success or direction. He grudgingly housed his army in one of the old marching camps that surrounded the fort, and settled down for two weeks to rest and resupply.

Then, with friendlier Votadini territory to his left, he forced a full day's march south along the road that led to Eboracum in the south, and made camp at *Bremenium*. From there, with growing irritation, he pointed his army west again, this time following a deliberately erratic route back to Blatobulgium. The army marched through similar terrain to that encountered on the march to Trimontium, with no greater success despite an aimless route intended to confuse the enemy. Contact with the tribes was as spotty as before. Worse still, the plunder dribbled away to nothing as every barbarian and his mangiest hound grew aware that a Roman army was on the loose. All that could be done was to pillage and burn and while Tuis knew that did nothing more than grate at the enemy's gut, it at least offered a grain of satisfaction for his frustration.

⸸

"It's like grabbing at quicksilver," Marius complained, groaning as he adjusted his rear to sit easier in the saddle. "You try to grasp it as it rolls across the table, but when you open your hand, there's nothing there."

"We'll have to increase the patrols," Tuis muttered, racking his mind for a strategy that might force the tribes into the open. It was like chasing the faerie: you knew the buggers were there, but they wouldn't show themselves. And the tribesmen might well have *been* the faerie, he decided. Some of their warriors *had* been taken or killed during the two month campaign, but if he was to be honest, they were only the slow, the stupid, and the rabid.

As so often happened with armed reprisal, most of the barbarians who fell into the net were the skivvies and the menials: low-kin field minders caught unaware; drudges cleaning pens or turning dirt; and the poor sods who toiled the farmsteads at the beck and call of anyone with half a *quadron* for an *honour price*. Nonetheless, the centurios gathered them up, culling those that were of no value; all of which would undoubtedly anger the masters they no longer served, but do nothing to keep them from fighting. There would be little profit for the trouble taken. By anyone's standards, the result was a sparsity of spoils and a herd of low-grade, ill-disciplined, ignorant slaves that would hardly bring the cost of getting them to market.

"I increased all patrols the first day the girl was taken." Florian Egnatius, commander of the fort at Blatobulgium, glared his indignation.

"Of course, and you did well," Tuis replied, his tone conciliatory, though he didn't know why. For all the man's supposed efforts back then, the fellow had not had the faintest idea where Jessa was. That meant he didn't have an ear bent toward the locals, as any frontier commander should. Rhun certainly would have. And long before his niece had returned by herself, Rhun would have picked up some intelligence on the lass. Maybe in the same manner that he had planned on trying to find her himself: through his own da. Tuis winced at the thought. Contacting Cethen was another matter he'd left dangling. Even so, there was nothing to be gained in berating Egnatius.

"And soon after you got her back," Tuis continued, which was total rubbish because Jessa had ridden in on her own pony, "one of your patrols found their hill camp. That was a fine piece of work. All I'm saying is, we need much more of that kind of thing."

And that, too, was pure pig swill! Finding a newly abandoned camp was a useless piece of work. Besides, Florian's people should have known what was going on at every last one of the old Selgovae hill forts within a fifty mile radius – you don't just wander out and stumble over one of the things, which he was sure had happened. Finding a hill fort freshly worked but newly abandoned was as useless as arriving late on an empty battlefield. Tuis glanced moodily to his left, where Marius Appius had lapsed into silence, his eyes on the bobbing ranks of Batavi infantry trudging ahead of them. *Oh, well...*

The small army was marching, in column, below the southern slope of yet another tree-covered hill. As the road began to fall away, the top of the gate towers at Blatobulgium appeared, small and hazy with distance. The road had improved somewhat as they neared the fort, and the forest had been cleared well back on either side. The illusion of security, however, simply added to the boredom of the march. Marius, his eyes glazed, was either lost in thought, or in a total trance – either brooding on the futility of the expedition, Tuis decided, or dreaming of his precious stone walls. He didn't begrudge the man his mood, though; it was one that afflicted them all as the final leg of the futile march drew to a close.

Tuis turned in the saddle and glanced over his shoulder at the winding column that followed. Turning forward once more, he shook his head at both the strength and impotence of his small army. Leading the order of march were a half-dozen *squadrons* of *Tungri* cavalry, placed there to protect the head of the column and provide the scouts who ranged ahead through the tangle of fields and forests. The Batavi infantry cohorts were next, followed by three more squadrons of cavalry and the headquarters unit, where Tuis and the other two senior commanders rode. Marching immediately behind were the legion cohorts and an under-strength unit of Germanian infantry gleaned from Luguvalium. The balance of the Tungri cavalry brought up the rear. Strings of pack mules mingled with the marching soldiers; and several hundred captive slaves plodded behind and between the legion cohorts.

The trouble, when it came, was in the vanguard. A large band of barbarian riders flooded onto the road half a mile ahead of the lead cavalry. The auxiliary scouts, complacent at the sight of the fort and eager to reach its comfort, had blithely ridden past the dense forest that hid them. The riders, yelping and screaming, thundered down the road as if intent on striking the head of the column.

The Roman cavalry didn't panic, nor did it rush forward to face the threat. Barking orders that rebounded from the trees, the decurios had their men fall back and form ranks on either side of the road. At the same time the praefectus of the lead Batavi infantry cohort, a Gaul named Ursinus, wheeled his horse, screaming his own orders. The infantry rushed forward and formed ranks four deep, blocking the road and most of the cleared area on either side. The drill was well practiced and neatly done.

The centurios growled orders to ready the first volley of *pili* as Ursinus edged his horse behind the rear rank of his infantry and turned to face the threat. Tuis shaded his eyes and peered toward the head of the column, surprised at how little time had been wasted. The barbarian charge, which appeared suicidal on such a narrow front, was a good two hundred yards from closing – but coming fast. The jangle of equipment and the pounding thump of boots sounded as the second cohort of auxiliary infantry deployed, its commander turning them to face the forest on either side. None of the men, anywhere, were showing signs of panic. Ursinus, his eyes gauging the distance, raised one hand to order the first volley of spears, then promptly eased it down again.

The screeching barbarian cavalry had reined in, the lead horses jerking stiffly to a halt a hundred paces away, just beyond range. For the space of a dozen heartbeats, it was as if both sides were oddly undecided. Each stood facing the other, the air silent except for the soft creak of leather and the dull clatter of shifting weapons. Then the barbarians began to shout and jeer, banging their spears against their small round shields in a steady, thumping rhythm. The loud screeching and the pulsing clash of iron on wood echoed down the road, heightened by the dark forest on either side.

Ursinus, baffled, turned to the nearest centurio, who seemed equally confused. Tuis, further back in the column, frowned. Were they trying to tempt the cavalry forward? If so, the tactic would prove fruitless until the field was more certain. Then, faint above the steady din, a soft rustle of leaves drifted from the forest on either side, followed by the quick patter of running feet. Moments later, a deadly whirring filled the air as stones and arrows spewed from the tangled undergrowth.

⁂

Treno stared hard at the lack of confusion on the road ahead, which was not what Modan had told him to expect. Their cavalry was supposed to be in disarray as it struggled to form up, and their infantry should be milling about in chaos as they tried to organize. It wasn't particularly important that they weren't, granted, because his people were supposed to be nothing but a diversion – but it would have been nice. Modan had told him to hold back and make as much noise as he could, which should have added to the confusion that was certainly not there. He'd also been told to move forward only if the Roman column seemed about to crumble – which it definitely was not.

The soldiers blocking the road had been shaken at first – they must have been – but their ranks had quickly settled, and now looked to be pretty damned steady. To charge now, headlong into a wall of shields . . . well, he might just as well fall on his sword and save himself the ride. At a rough count, a couple hundred of those slim, deadly spears would rain down on the lead horses before they slammed into the front rank – should anyone, man or beast, actually make it that far. Not that it mattered; going further forward had never really been in the plan. Even so . . .

Treno shaded his eyes, the better to see what was happening farther back on the Roman flank, where he could hear movement. That would be the slingers and the archers. Some of the soldiers appeared to have been hit, but they were now dealing with the threat, raising shields as their officers shouted orders. Modan had hoped the cavalry in the centre of the column would move up, joining the riders protecting either side of the forward wall of shields – which, it seemed, needed no protection at all.

Perhaps it was time to move. If he faded into the trees with his men, it might confuse the Romans long enough that he could ride up on their column and attack from the side. It wasn't in the plan, but Modan had said to stay just long enough to make them think that his force was the main attack. If he just sat where he was though, and did nothing, they'd soon sodding well realize he was no more than bait for a trap.

Shouting to the others to follow, Treno turned his horse and galloped into the trees, his eyes half closed against the tangled snarl of spring growth. Moments later, he might have been in another world. The hard going quickly gave way to a forest floor that lay clear and silent under a tall canopy thick with new leaves. He reined his horse to a slow canter, and those behind did the same. The rhythmic thump of hooves echoed off the trees as they pounded over the soft, leaf-mulched earth. The forest itself seemed to tremble, and Treno's chest felt fit to burst.

A slight shift of the reins and the horse turned, now running even with the Roman column. Treno's face broke into a broad smile as the blood throbbed hard through his veins. His feet, hands, legs, arms, every part of him was magically alive, and his mind fought a mad urge to whip his horse to a crazed gallop and shout his joy to the treetops. *And I'll slice the head off the first idiot following me who does!*

Bryn held back in the trees and watched. He wanted no part of it and, because of who and what he was, no one dared voice the opinion that he should. Not even Modan had the will to test him. There was something in Bryn's manner that made a man hold his counsel; a calm, deliberate thoroughness that commanded respect – a respect that was only partly earned, however, for he was also the child of his parents.

The tribes knew that Morallta, his mam, had been Boudicca to the Carvetii; and his da, Cethen Lamh-fada, was a legend himself – a legend that had not suffered with his slaying of Morallta for near killing his first wife. Theirs was a story sung by the bards, and Bryn often figured in the verse.

But there was more to it, and the bards loved the story. Bryn was found on the battlefield following Galgar's great, tragic fight, and had been raised with the Romans. His father's brother had plucked the boy from among the thousands taken or slaughtered that day. It was all the grist of which legends were made. So even Modan, other than voicing his annoyance, said little when Bryn told him he would take no part in a "stupid, witless, pointless, bone-brained scheme" to attack the Romans as they returned to their fort.

"But they've been roaming the hills for a couple of months trying to kill us," Modan had protested.

"Yeah, I know, the battle-crazed bastards. And only because you killed a hundred of 'em and snatched one of their women – whose father happens to be a legate," Bryn told him in an infuriatingly calm voice. "You pig-headed lead-brain," he'd finished, in a deliberately audible murmur.

"He's not a legate," Modan said stubbornly.

"Once a legate, always a legate. And I'll tell you this: you don't know how much power a Roman legate wields, and just how many pates he can piss on," Bryn replied, and tried to salve his conscience by telling himself that he didn't care what Modan was doing. "Not that it matters, but I've seen this all before; and just because I find someone strolling off the top of a cliff, I see no reason to follow."

So Bryn had walked away and abandoned Modan and his ill-conceived scheme, which was to attack the Romans when and where they least expected. But when his brother's plan had been taken up by Lagan and his people, he had come along to witness the attack out of nothing more than perverse curiosity. He supposed that Lagan, unlike his brother, had carefully weighed the odds: a quick victory would bring the tribes flocking to his side, but if the attack failed it could be readily called off, with little loss of face.

"Which side are you cheering for, then?"

Bryn turned and smiled as Trista reined in alongside, her jet-black horse nervously pawing the ground as it sensed the excitement in the air. He was about to offer something profound, such as, "You don't cheer for any side, you mourn for the losers," but the comment struck him as pretentious, even condescending. Besides, this was Trista, the one person he knew who might hold similar views. "Neither. I just don't want to see the silly buggers get killed."

"Modan's people, or the Romans?" Trista asked, and grinned.

"Either or." Bryn laughed bitterly. "Roman reprisals are already past due; this will only add to the tally."

"Well, we'll soon see," Trista murmured, her features suddenly grim.

A man had scrambled back from the edge of the forest, rushing over to where Modan, Lagan, and a dozen others were gathered at the centre of their small army. Some of the Roman cavalry positioned at the centre had moved forward, the runner told them, ordered there, as expected, to help stem the attack on the head of the column. But how many, he did not know.

Bryn cast his eyes over the warriors waiting in the trees before him, and shook his head. But as the small army began to move forward, he had to give his brother credit. He and Lagan might well be employing the same tactic as that used on the supply column, which was not a wise thing to do, but it did appear to be working. Positioned well back in the forest, the bulk of Lagan's army had so far escaped notice as it quietly advanced: the cavalry first, and the great mass of foot warriors trailing close behind.

※

Success repeats itself, Modan decided, his confidence rising as he urged his horse through the trees. Long ranks of cavalry spread away from him on either side, while close behind, urged forward by the kin chieftains, the greater mass of tribesmen kept pace. It was the Roman supply train all over again! The only difference was the great number of warriors and his injured leg. The limb, nearly healed, hung from Modan's saddle as stiffly as the board it was strapped to: a narrow slat of wood that ran from calf to arse, just to be sure the leg didn't get damaged again.

Cursing to boost confidence, Modan broke from the trees, his spear raised, ready to stab or throw; his eyes took in the Roman column at a glance. Some of their cavalry remained, which was not planned, and some had ridden to the head of the column, which was. Their soldiers had already turned and were prepared, though, and that was definitely not planned: four even ranks, two on either side of the column, each facing outward, and every man with a shield raised and a spear ready.

Maybe, Modan thought belatedly, it was a bad idea to have Treno draw attention to the head of the column as a decoy. Maybe he should have consulted with Lagaon on that one. He shook his head; he was thinking too much!

Screaming his rage to the sky, Modan slammed both heels into his horse's gut; and the piercing screech echoed from a hundred others on either side. The animal leapt forward, closing fast on the wall of shields which stood not a hundred paces from the tree line. He'd no sooner gained speed than a hail of spears arced upward like so many arrows, tossed by the first rank of Roman soldiers. He flinched, his groin scrunching, but none struck; his horse faltered, but kept running.

A second volley followed, hissing from the Roman ranks as those who were left were about to close. A single spear thudded into Modan's shield and the long iron head bent almost double as the heavy shaft sagged on its own weight, dragging at his left arm. Cursing again as his rage flared, Modan narrowed his eyes and kicked hard, forcing his horse onto the Roman line. The animal stumbled gamely on and crashed into the wall of shields, just as its legs finally failed the beast.

The first rank of soldiers staggered backward, falling hard against the second – which held steady and pushed on, heaving against those in front to prevent the line failing. A single Roman went down – no, there were several – but those facing the other way turned and added their weight to the wavering ranks.

Modan tumbled sideways, swearing as his horse rolled. He landed flat on his back, winded, amid a whirlwind of iron-shod hooves, kicking fetlocks, and a forest of stocky brown legs thudding about his head like hail. Then others were there, hundreds and hundreds of foot warriors, clashing against the wall of shields, pushing it back – and not caring where or on whom they trod. Modan fought to push himself away from the mad crush, and was surprised to find he was suddenly clear. Unarmed and half stunned, he tried to raise himself on one knee and make sense of what had just happened.

The Romans had broken, surely, for most of them were now a good twenty paces away; yet when his dazed eyes focused, he could see the fighting was still hard. The far side of the roadway was now a confused mass of backs and blades, slashing and hacking at whatever stood in their path. Bodies lay everywhere, some still and some twitching, and most were not wearing uniforms.

Modan realized the Romans hadn't broken at all; they had merely given ground. He staggered up, dragging the splinted leg, and saw that his people faced three or four solid ranks of soldiers. The two on the far side of the road had completely turned, affording twice the strength. Shit! The attack should have been from both sides! Yet the numbers hadn't been there to do that . . .

A spear stuck up from the ground close by, one of their own, the point wedged in the dirt. Modan grabbed the shaft and leaned on it for support. The board that was supposed to protect his leg was proving a nuisance! His eyes swept the ground and found his shield. It lay beside his horse, which was on its belly several steps away. The animal's head was raised, and blood dribbled from its mouth. One of the Roman spears dragged from the beast's chest. Its eyes, a dark, blood-tinted brown, stared accusingly as he limped over and retrieved the shield. He grunted his annoyance at the animal's loss, and again turned to see what was happening.

"Want another one?"

He whirled and found Bryn staring down at him. He held the reins of a second horse. The animal was gashed on one haunch and pawed nervously at the ground, its blood stirred. Bryn informed him, quite unnecessarily, that the beast was a stray, caught as it fled from the field – something he suggested that Modan do, if he had a speck of sense.

"Why would I do that?" Modan growled as he hobbled over to the horse using the spear as a staff. With a good deal of effort and a hand from Bryn, he clambered onto the stray's saddle. Once he was settled, it occurred to him that his wife no longer rode with his brother. "Where's Trista?"

"I convinced her to stay back where she couldn't be seen. You hurt?"

"No, but it's not over yet," Modan snapped, and tightened the reins, trying to steady the horse.

From the height of the animal's back, he saw for the first time the full extent of what was happening. The Romans no longer retreated toward the trees on the far side of the road; they stood fast perhaps thirty, forty paces away. The crash and scream of battle was a steady, deafening roar. Fighting was heavy all along the length of the column, but toward the rear, the Roman infantry was not that hard pressed. It would soon fight its way free and start marching forward to relieve the centre.

The column itself had broken completely in two places, but in each instance it was where the captured Britons had been marching, all roped together. That was hardly a victory, Modan supposed, and probably to be expected, but some advantage could be gained there. If they could free the prisoners, it might be considered some sort of a triumph.

"They're also forming up again at the head of the column," Bryn remarked calmly, his eyes following Modan's as they moved to where the Roman cavalry were regrouping. "I'd say your only option is to face them with a solid, organized front, and overwhelm them. And since you don't have a snail's chance of forming one, you'd best call it off. You've gotta smash a column like this on the first charge, little brother, or you are completely and utterly –"

"I don't need a fucking speech," Modan snarled as his temper flared, fueled not so much by his brother's words as the suspicion that they were true. Their only success, as far as he could see, was that most of the prisoners had been freed – though there was really little glory gained there. Hardly any were real warriors and even if they were, they'd been stupid enough to get caught in the first place. The fools were hardly worth the bother . . .

Modan swept his eyes over the Roman column. The cohort of infantry at the front was hardly threatened anymore, other than by the slingers and the archers on the edge of the forest. Treno, as ordered, had broken off but the fool should have at least stayed there as a threat. Some of the troops were actually advancing on the archers, while – Modan turned to face the rear of the column, drawn by a loud cry of triumph – while the those at the rear were chasing some of Lagan's men back into the trees.

"I'd guess you have them outnumbered about three to two, but it's too little," Bryn said, and reined his horse in the opposite direction from his brother's. "I'd also guess there's as much chance of you calling them off as ordering a fish to fly. Maybe you –"

"Aha!" Modan pointed triumphantly to the other side of the Roman column, where Treno had ridden out of the trees at the head of his riders. Brilliant! "Look there!"

Bryn peered across the Roman line and shook his head. "Modan, Treno's got a couple hundred men at best. And see there – the Romans have the mark of him already. They're falling back from the head of the —"

"Stop your whining," Modan shouted, his eyes only on the rush of riders pouring from the trees on the far side of the Roman column. He lashed his horse forward. "It'll be over before either end of their fool column knows what hit it."

⚔

Bryn watched in disbelief as his brother charged headlong into the fight, his shield held high and the spear poised ready to throw. The Roman wall of shields looked so solid, it was impossible to know where best to strike. Yet the rear ranks were turning to repel the unexpected assault by Treno, which left a part of the line stretched thin. Modan saw the weakness. Screaming for anyone to follow who might hear, he aimed his horse at the Roman line.

Bryn's eyes narrowed and he winced but, amazingly, the line broke before the charging horse. Or did it? More likely, the Romans had opened a gap rather than take the impact against their shields. Modan passed through, lunging forward with his spear rather than throwing it. The point caught one of the Roman soldiers high on the shoulder. The contact jarred Modan, and he jerked back on the reins to check his advance, twisting in the saddle to keep hold of the spear. The point slid free of the Roman's shoulder, and again Modan kicked his horse forward. An officer, the only Roman nearby who sat a horse, took a wild swing with his sword as Modan swept by. Bryn again flinched as the weapon struck hard at the back of his brother's head, but the angle was off, and the flat of the blade struck hard against his skull.

Modan lurched forward and sprawled over the pommel as his horse started to buck. Bryn saw a Roman spear jammed in its neck, flopping wildly as the animal turned. The beast skewed sideways and Modan looked to be sliding, but just then a huge roar erupted from the rear of the Roman column, drawing Bryn's eyes.

Lagan's people were falling back and running. No doubt Lagan was too, for he'd previously told everyone to run should the tide turn. The thunder of hooves, lots of them, sounded somewhere off to his right, and Bryn spun about in alarm. A swarm of Roman cavalry galloped down the length of the column, their weapons growing bloodier with every stride. There was nothing more he could do! Cursing Modan for a fool and Lagan for the idiot who encouraged him, Bryn tugged savagely on the reins.

Trista!

He'd near forgotten. His horse turned on its haunches and there she sat, patiently astride the black gelding, off by the edge of the trees. He wondered how long she would remain before fleeing the field.

※

Modan finally pulled himself clear of the horse. He'd lain helplessly pinned to the ground far too long, lost in a daze of frustration. The animal's neck and the fore part of its chest had trapped him firmly against the dirt, less than halfway between the road and the safety of the forest. At first he'd been stunned, only half conscious, lying still under the dead weight of the horse as he fought to gather his wits. A good deal of hard, steady heaving had followed, his body rocking to and fro as he tried to wriggle from under the stupid beast, which had taken a spear in its windpipe before veering away from the wall of Roman shields.

Gasping for breath, Modan slowly raised his head and gauged the odds of reaching the forest without being seen. He glanced back at the Roman column, perhaps fifty paces distant; there seemed to be nothing but bodies scattered between – most closer to the column itself. He grunted his satisfaction at seeing a good sprinkling of Romans among them, but it was of little comfort. Nearly all of them were still on their feet and they were busy, either shoving their sorry-looking captives together, or . . .

He watched in horror as one of them heaved a groaning tribesman to his feet – Modan recognized Kylta, one of his own people – only to see him sag as one leg gave way. The Roman simply slashed his blade across Kylta's throat, and dropped him. Modan swore as he realized what was happening. *They're taking slaves, but killing off the wounded!*

Growling his anger, Modan leaned up on one elbow, then fell back in disgust. He had no more chance of reaching the forest unseen than a bear fleeing a pig sty. So what would it be: slavery, or death? There was no way he'd take either! Yet when his muddled brain thought it through, if there had to be a choice, for the moment it was slavery. Just so long as . . .

Modan's heart lurched. They were killing off the wounded! *Where did that leave him?* He quickly ran furtive hands down his body, feeling neither pain nor the sticky warmth of blood; then one hand struck the board bound to his leg.

The board! If they see the board . . .

Modan slid the knife from his belt and eased his arm downward, slicing the ties that bound the crude splint. He carefully slid the board aside and again glanced back and forth between the Romans and the forest. No, he had no more chance of gaining the shelter of the trees than a lamb outrunning that same lumbering bear. Perhaps there was another way.

Modan's eyes fell on the dead horse, and the dark trickle of blood oozing from around the spear shaft lodged in its neck. He cupped his hand below the wound until the palm was full then, with a grimace of disgust, he dribbled the sticky fluid over his neck and face. Hoping the gore might pass for a slashed throat, he settled back against the grass, closed both eyelids to slits, and tried to ease his breathing so his chest wouldn't show movement.

An age seemed to pass, his chest still and his mind racing, as he lay motionless on the dirt. The late sun beat down on his forehead and a dark, buzzing swarm of flies fell on the blood congealing on his face and neck. The creeping, prickling host picked like nettles on his skin, and an insane need to claw at his lips and scratch at his neck tortured his mind. And then, just when he thought he could stand it no longer, a slow plodding of hooves drew near and halted just beyond the top of his head. Modan could see nothing and he froze, fighting the urge to turn and look.

"Now take this one," a voice said, speaking in his own tongue. "It lays with its throat cut, its face bashed in, and clearly as dead as a virgin's passion."

"But –"

"I know, I know, don't say it: that's what the fool would have us believe. Now, if he had just stayed still and kept himself buried under the horse he *might* have got away with it. But when a man thrashes around like a lovesick eel and paints his face red like a tart, well, that's no way to hide, is it? You've got to wonder at them sometimes, don't you?"

There was a long silence. Modan continued to hold his breath. Maybe, just maybe, the voice was speaking of someone else. He knew that to be a hopeless fancy, but just maybe . . .

A second voice spoke in a broken accent. "Tell you what, a *denarius* as to who can place a spear closest to his crotch."

"Florian, if he's healthy, you could ruin a perfectly good slave," the first voice said as if chiding, then paused for a moment. "Tell you what, make it ten."

"Done."

Modan lay with a body of stone, his belly and groin churning ice. It had to be him they were talking about, yet what if it wasn't? Then came the familiar thud of a spear striking the dirt somewhere just below his belly, and his entire body twitched in alarm.

"Your turn, Florian."

"No, wait!" Modan screeched and rolled over, looking first downward. The spear, he saw, had landed nowhere near his crotch. Its long shaft rose from the ground beyond his feet. He looked up at whoever had chosen to mock him: two Roman officers sitting their horses, both staring down in amusement.

A pair of foot soldiers ran forward, grabbed him by the shoulders, and hauled him to his feet. "Looks healthy enough, sir," one of them called out.

"Then throw him in with the others," Tuis said, and turned to his companion, this time speaking the language of Rome. "Poor pickings, I suppose, but maybe we'll garner something from this miserable expedition before it's done."

# Chapter XIII

## Blatobulgium, Junius, A.D. 105

Jessa made her way to the parapet with her father the moment she heard that the advance riders had entered the fort. It seemed that everyone with a moment to spare was doing the same thing. The arrival of a dispatch rider was an occasion in the isolated stronghold. An imperial army, newly returned from a two-month campaign, ranked as a major event. She found a place on the walkway above the *Praetorian* gate where they might look down on the column as it marched in, arriving just in time to watch the lead elements of cavalry. Marcus carried a small stool, which he set down alongside one of the garrison's soldiers. Jessa climbed on top so she could see, and all three leaned over the palisade, staring down at the tired troopers.

The soldier, an older decanus, echoed all their thoughts as the column marched under the gate, almost twenty feet below. "None of 'em look over-happy."

"True, though they don't seem that tired," Jessa said. The troopers were waving cheerfully enough to those standing on the walls, and the horses, harnesses jangling, had their heads raised and their ears perked, sensing warm stables and chopped grain.

"This is just the first of them, and they're the ones riding, not walking," the decanus said confidently. "The poor sodding infantry will be dragging their shields and trailing their spears. Look down the road. There's been some fighting. And not long ago, either."

Jessa frowned as she gazed over the bobbing heads of the cavalry to the even ranks of marching soldiers beyond. "How can you tell?"

"Because one of the scouts told me so on my way up here." The man grinned, then pointed to the southeast. "They were ambushed just beyond those hills."

"I'd better go to the hospital, then," Jessa murmured and turned to leave, but her father's words stayed her.

"They took their own medici with them, Jess. Besides, the wounded will be farther back in the column. There's nothing you can do until they're inside."

Which was true, Jessa realized, so she reluctantly pushed back the need to feel busy and remained where she was, her impatience growing as the long column wound its way through the gate. The troops would no doubt form up on the *via principalis* in a totally pointless parade, where they would be subjected to an utterly boring speech before being dismissed. After that, most would march right out again to the temporary camps dug outside the walls, because there was not enough room inside. By then the wounded *might* have been delivered to the hospital where, as far as she was concerned, they should have been taken ahead of anything else.

With these thoughts in mind, Jessa was about to turn and leave anyway when she saw her Uncle Tuis and the headquarters section draw near. He was flanked on one side by the fort's commander, who was beaming as if returning from a triumph, and on the other by the Ninth's legate, who looked as if his belly was brewing vinegar. Jessa said as much.

"I'm certain Marius wanted no part of this," Marcus said. "I don't know if it's because he thinks Tuis is beneath him because of his barbarian background, or he just didn't want to be dragged away from building his precious stone fortress."

"I don't think it's all one or the other," Jessa said, and lifted her hand to wave as Tuis called a greeting before disappearing through the gateway. "I think he just takes advantage, because Uncle Tuis isn't – oh, what's the word?"

"Decisive?"

"Yes, decisive. I also think that's why Tuis sent for Uncle Rhun. He thinks Rhun will . . ." Jessa's voice faded to a whisper as the first section of prisoners appeared, hundreds of them, and an odd sense of sadness swept over her ". . . will be more firm."

"Well, Rhun usually knows what he's doing, and he certainly knows the country and the people here," Marcus said, and smiled wanly as he looked down on the trudging Britons, each man roped to another in a series of long, plodding lines. "You know, rabbit, even after all these years, I can't help looking to see if I recognize anyone."

"That's hardly likely," Jessa said, and punched her father playfully on the shoulder to relieve the somber mood that had fallen on them both. "They've likely all died of old age by now. And even if they haven't, you wouldn't know them if they jumped out and –" She stopped and clutched her father's arm.

"What is it?"

"You might not recognize anyone, but I do."

"You do?"

"That man, the one with blood all over his face." Jessa pointed to a string of prisoners where Modan, slightly favouring his injured leg, trudged at the head of the line. His face, the beard stiff with dried blood, tilted upward as if drawn there by her thoughts. Or was he looking for her? Their eyes met and his dark, bloodied features twisted in contempt, then he spat.

"Who is that?" Marcus exclaimed.

"Modan. Cethen's son."

Marcus at first said nothing, and Jessa thought perhaps he hadn't heard. Then, in a voice that was no more than a whisper, he said, "Then he's Tuis's half-brother."

Jessa nodded, her face grim. "Grandfather always said that our gods in Britannia loved to play games with our family."

"*Our* gods? Not the Roman gods?" Marcus smiled at his daughter's choice of words, then glanced downward as Modan disappeared below his feet. "I'd wager that Tuis doesn't know who he is."

Jessa smiled in turn, quickly picking up on a double meaning. "Do you mean Tuis doesn't know who *he* is, or who Modan is?"

"Either or, I suppose." Marcus laughed, and tousled his daughter's hair. "Though I did mean Tuis doesn't know who Modan is."

"Who was there in the column to tell him? Besides, I doubt if Modan knows about Tuis, either," Jessa replied and, for no reason she could pinpoint, added, "And for the time being, there's no need to tell him."

"Oh?" Marcus stared at his daughter, puzzled.

"I feel I have a claim on Modan for what he tried to do," Jessa said quietly, and her thoughts flitted to Trista and any claim she might have. "Though what it is, I have no idea. I need time to think on it."

⚔

Jessa was not certain exactly where Cethen lived, or how to find him. She knew it was somewhere up in the hills by Epiacum, a small fort south of where Tuis had waged his campaign against the Selgovae. He was her only means of locating Trista, and she wanted the woman to know what had happened to her husband. Any such message sent to Epiacum would be passed on to Cethen, she supposed, which would also relieve her of the responsibility of telling him, too – if indeed one existed. As to Trista, there was Modan's fate to be decided, and she chuckled to herself. Maybe the woman might want a say in what happened to the oaf.

Jessa decided she would talk to her father. A rider might be ordered to Epiacum, and perhaps a native guide found to deliver a message. Surely someone lived close by the fort who knew of Cethen's whereabouts. Not for the first time, Jessa regretted not having discussed a means of contacting either of the two.

The following day, Marcus accompanied his daughter to the pens where the Britons were held pending disposition. The blacksmiths were busy forging leg irons and Modan was already shackled. Jessa had him removed from the pens, and he hobbled over to a nearby bench. Two soldiers were detailed to guard him, one on either side. Marcus watched covertly from the doorway of a nearby stores building, one shoulder pressed against the frame. He was clearly amused by his daughter's staging of what seemed to be an interrogation.

"How's the leg?" Jessa walked quietly up behind Modan and spoke sharply, intending to startle him. When he didn't so much as twitch she hid her disappointment and walked around to face him. He sat silent, staring at the ground, glaring defiance at the dirt. "Your face needs a good wash," she taunted. "You look like you've been savaging raw meat."

Other than a quick glance, as if to confirm who it was, he gave no response. Jessa had chosen the two guards because they spoke Modan's tongue, and she nodded slightly to the larger one. She smiled as he growled his part, exactly as instructed.

"You want me to make him speak? I'd love to. It's easy enough to do." For emphasis, he slapped the knife that hung on his belt.

"Mmm – I don't know." Jessa pretended hesitation. "Perhaps not. When this one does speak he has nothing to say." She replied in the same tongue, shaking her head at Modan as if chiding a child. "See that he's shipped to the arenas with the others. The stubborn fool had his chance, and chose not to take it." She shrugged as if the matter was of no concern, then turned and walked away. She counted off seven steps before Modan could bring himself to speak, his tone nothing more than a sneer.

"What do you mean, shipped to the arenas?"

Jessa turned on her heel and stared. She couldn't resist digging at the man, which was unusual, for it was not her nature. Yet Modan, if given the chance, would still be holding her on a tight, brutal leash were it not for his wife. She placed hands on hips and sneered in turn, "So you do have a tongue?"

Modan scowled and opened his mouth, then seemed to think better of it.

"Well, perhaps not." She again turned to leave. This time it took only three steps.

"Where are they shipping everyone?"

Jessa gave an exaggerated sigh and again turned, assuming a stance that left do doubt Modan was trying her patience. "I would guess it won't be far. Not at first. If there are any slave traders at Luguvalium, they might pick some of you up on the cheap, and ship you from the Ituna dock. If not, perhaps a march south to Londinium. There are better prices to be had there. After that, who knows?" She paused and cupped her chin, pretending to think on the question. "You'll go through the auction block, I imagine. You won't be harmed, as long as you behave. It's all about the money. As far as Rome is concerned, petty vengeance is of no interest. We're different than your people, that way." She tried not to smile at the lie.

When Modan still kept his stony silence, Jessa continued. "As for your final destination," her eyes ran quickly from his head to his feet, then back again, her lips pursed as if she found what she saw distasteful. "I'd guess you're fit for either the fields or the arenas. Who knows? You may get lucky and become a notorious gladiator. The women love them – for as long as they live."

"What did you mean: I had my chance?"

Jessa pretended to ponder that question too, and again shrugged her indifference. "I like your wife – when I'm not feeling sorry for her. And I owe her. I was thinking of asking her if she would want you as a gift, paid for by me. A legal gift. A slave." Jessa took a deep breath and raised her voice in anger as she felt her temper slipping. "After all, she was the one who freed me from your miserable, ignorant, selfish, grasping clutches, you stinking stoat. Though why she would ever take you back, even as a slave, I don't know." She frowned, wondering how Trista really would feel about that, then shook her head, for at the moment the answer was moot. "Who knows? Maybe she doesn't want a slave. Maybe you'll be shipped anyway."

Modan's lip's pursed as if he was thinking through her words, then he slowly nodded to himself. "There's no need to ask her. She'll take me. She'd be a fool not to."

"A fool not to? Ha!" Jessa couldn't hide her astonishment at the man's conceit. "If I was Trista, I'd *steal* money to buy you, just for the pleasure of pushing you off a cliff!"

"That's exactly what I meant," Modan growled scornfully. "If you paid good coin for me, then why wouldn't she take me? If nothing else, she could sell me and get good money from some other Roman. So why not just give me to her anyway, without asking?"

Jessa's jaw clenched as she tried to find fault with Modan's logic, and couldn't. Was the man brighter than he looked, or was it just his natural cunning? She glanced toward her father hiding in the shadows, who was grinning like a slavering hound. The tables had turned in some small manner, and it made her think. She was toying with the man, enjoying a rare, self-serving vengeance. But why? Again, that was not in her nature.

Or was it? She'd never been abducted before, so how did she know? When she'd seen Modan in chains, her first instinct had been to do nothing, let them ship the lout. The man was a lout. But he was also family in a far-reaching way, and that, more than anything, had held her back – or so she'd told herself. He was also the son of a man whom her father respected, a man who had, she'd heard more than once, likely saved her father's life. But Modan was also a man taken in the act of killing Roman soldiers! Jessa sighed. Those same soldiers, in turn, had invaded *his* land, killing *his* people . . .

Why *had* she come down here to talk to him? It was all too complicated for reason. The simplest thing, for the moment, was to leave it all hanging and walk away – and just maybe, at the same time, make Modan's blood run cold for a few days. There was no answer to his question, which was an embarrassment in itself.

Jessa waved one hand as if in dismissal – or disgust – it really didn't matter. "When you put it that way, I suppose I don't know why. I think I'll do Trista a favour, and forget it. Enjoy your journey to Rome."

"Hey. Wait!" Modan called as she strode away.

Jessa kept on walking. Three steps, four . . .

"Don't go, dammit!"

Modan started to rise and the soldiers grasped his shoulders, slamming him back down on the seat; but he would not be deterred. "Whatever you pay, I'll see you get it back," he cried. Then, when that produced no reaction, he called, "Double the money. Triple."

The words were too rich to pass, and Jessa turned angrily. "You promise?"

"I promise. Triple."

"You must think me a fool!" Jessa shouted in disgust. "A promise! From a man who broke his word, after I saved his miserable life. You are pathetic."

She stalked angrily away, ignoring Modan's protest that *'he'd never promised no one nothing'*. Marcus, chin in hand, watched her pass by, plainly confused as to what, if anything, had just happened. Then he shrugged as if shedding his bafflement, and smiled. Jessa hid a smile of her own. It was clear from his expression that whatever it was that his daughter was doing, whatever the problems that plagued her mind, he had full confidence in their resolution.

※

Trista cautiously poked her head inside the door of the small infirmary. Jessa barely gave the girl a glance, her attention fixed on a fat, sweaty leg that leaked pus from an ulcer not far below its owner's knee.

"What are you going to do with that?" Trista muttered, her face showing distaste.

"The usual stuff. Clean up the filth first, then wash it out with water that's been boiled and salted." Jessa proceeded to do exactly that, causing the woman whose leg it was to jump and whimper far louder than was necessary. "Hush, woman. You don't expect to heal without a little hurt, do you?"

"That's it?" Trista asked.

"No!" Jessa said scornfully, and nodded to a clay pot waiting on a nearby table.

Trista leaned over to sniff the contents, then looked up in surprise. "It smells like honey."

"That's because it is honey. There's no magic here. Smear it on with a soft cloth, bind it tight, and let it heal."

"That's no better than what our own people do."

"So who said it was?"

"Yeah, but it doesn't always work."

"It does most of the time. It's the cleaning first that's important. Boiled water – boiled everything. If boiling water will kill us, it will also kill infection." Jessa bent close to peer at the open sore. It was raw and an angry scarlet, but at least it looked clean enough for the honey to work its wonders. The sticky, golden goo did not demand total perfection to perform.

Jessa dribbled the syrup across the livid surface, cloaking the sore in translucent amber. Satisfied with the result, she stepped back and released a deep breath, then looked up at her visitor. Not for the first time, she was startled by the intensity of Trista's deep, iron-grey eyes. "So, I see you got here."

"I suppose it's about Modan?"

"Uh-huh." Jessa pulled a clean cloth from a small, neatly folded pile and dabbed at the honey to make it even. "What do you want to do with him?"

Most of the captives taken by Tuis's army had been shipped, the exception being a batch of the strongest that Marius had grabbed for quarrying stone for his fortress. At the moment, Modan was penned in with them. Jessa was already regretting not seeing the lout shipped with the others. She was certain Trista would be far better off without the man, but if she did want to keep him, the two of them needed to resolve a small problem before she could make her a gift of the man – foolish whim that it was.

Trista looked confused. "I'd heard that everyone taken by the army has been sent off as slaves."

"A few were held back," Jessa murmured, intent on moistening a small square of soft cloth with oil before bandaging it on the glistening ulcer.

"And one of them would be Modan."

"Lucky guess."

"And I suppose you're responsible for that?"

"Another lucky guess," Jessa replied, deftly freeing a ready-cut bandage strip from a tangle of others.

"Am I supposed to thank you?"

Jessa glanced up at her. "Hey, unlike most of Rome's decisions, this one is easily reversed."

"That means you're leaving it up to me, then."

"I gather you'd rather not be faced with having to decide." Jessa grinned as she bandaged the oil-dampened cloth firmly against the leg.

"Why should I have to decide?"

"Because he's yours. I bought him for you. Look on it as a small gift for helping me regain my freedom." And repayment it might well be, Jessa realized, though she hadn't really thought of Modan as such. At the time, she'd thought his purchase impulsive, but perhaps being grateful *was* the reason, even if the gift came wrapped in anger and irony.

"What?" Trista cried.

Jessa could have laughed at the expression on the young woman's face; but there was one more part to the transaction, and it was a difficult one to broach. At first she had been unable to buy Modan, at least not on the premise that he would be given back to his wife. As Tuis had said, "The barbarian was taken killing Romans! He'll just go out and do it again!" So she had felt compelled to tell him that the *barbarian* was actually his brother – or at least, his half-brother.

Once he got over that shock, or at least seemed to accept it, her uncle had reluctantly agreed to the transaction. But he'd set one condition, and it was harsh. Even so, it was a decision that her own father had firmly endorsed with the words, "Look for the sunshine, Jess: at least the 'barbarian' will be alive!"

"Do they know him for who he is?" Trista asked, her voice subdued.

"Yes." Jessa blinked in surprise, wondering how the woman could possibly have found out that Modan was Tuis's brother. She certainly hadn't told anyone. "I had to tell both my father and the governor."

"And they're still willing to let you give Modan – the *barbarian* who was the main cause of all this trouble – to *me*?" Trista said, her tone skeptical.

Jessa grimaced, aware of her error. It appeared that Trista, Cethen, and Modan were all ignorant that the clod was kin to the governor of Britannia. Though how long that would last was anyone's guess. Maybe she *should* have told Tuis that his half-brother was much more than just a low-ranking warrior, which he'd clearly assumed. Jessa dismissed the notion; it was too late, anyway. "Yes, they're willing – on the condition that his sword hand is severed."

Trista's expression turned blank as the words filled her mind, then she rolled her eyes to the ceiling. "Shit!"

"Yeah, I know. It's your decision."

"Shit!"

It was another hour before Jessa found herself free, and able to return to the fort. Trista had helped herself to the contents of a large jug of lightly diluted wine, and sat slumped on a chair close by the entrance to the infirmary. The sun was low on the horizon, silhouetting her spare frame against the open doorway. The wine might have cleared her face of its dark cloak of gloom, but she was still far from happy.

"If you like, I can send him to our estate in Rome. You'll at least know where he is, two hands and all," Jessa offered as she placed the last of her instruments in the familiar leather bag. One of the slaves would carry it back to the fort and see the contents properly cleaned. In the meantime, Trista's mug of wine looked as if it needed company, so she topped one up for herself. "Maybe that would satisfy your conscience."

"It's not that."

"It's the hand, is it? Surely you can see their point?" Jessa tried to explain, not sure how she would have greeted the choice herself. "He'll get used to it."

"That's not the point, either. I've sort of got sick of it all and left him," Trista mumbled slowly, and took another sip from the mug. "Sending him away *would* solve any later problems, I suppose. You know his temper . . ."

"So you don't like my gifts?" Jessa chuckled before tasting the ruby contents of the mug; a bit tart, but not bad. "I understand. How about a horse, then?"

"I already have a horse," Trista replied, and chuckled in turn. "Besides, the ones you ride are way too small."

"Hey, I can find a larger one." Jessa took a long, thirsty pull. "So, then . . ."

"Jessa, he's Bryn's brother. I can't let them sell Bryn's brother into slavery. Not if there's a choice. If Bryn ever found out . . ."

"Then accept him as a gift." Jessa sipped the wine again, and giggled. "He's really not much of a gift anyway. You might gain a slave, but you'd still be short-handed."

Trista was not amused. "By all the gods, Jessa, if I agreed to having his hand cut off . . . if Modan ever found out . . ."

"He doesn't have to know that it was you who decided. Really, if you're after the truth, it was the governor who dictated the terms, not you – or me." Jessa shrugged philosophically. "Modan would get used to it. After all, he'd still be here in Britannia, *and* alive."

Trista appeared to brood on the words for the longest time as the pair helped themselves to more wine. Soon, she began rationalizing the logic in the maiming. Jessa joined in, each woman offering opinions and reasons as they plowed over the same ground. And when Jessa mentioned, for perhaps the tenth time and over the third mug of wine, that it was only the one hand after all, and Modan would eventually get over it, Trista burst out laughing. "If you think he'll get over losing a hand, then slice his balls off too. If he could get over that, then maybe I could live with him."

"I would absolutely not!" Jessa said, her voice pretending shock; but her mind instantly pictured Modan, and she giggled again. "It's the medicus who would do it. Only he can't." Assuming a deep voice, she quoted the law. "Thou shall not remove a slave's testes!"

"I thought you could do anything to a slave."

"To the tribes, maybe, as a form of punishment; but not to a slave. About fifteen years ago, Emperor Domitian decreed we can no longer pluck the plums from a Roman slave." Jessa shook her head, and laughed. "They say that Roman wives have been a lot happier ever since."

※

Trista slept over in the residence and left the next day, with the understanding that she would return in two weeks to collect her "gift." Between them, they had agreed that fourteen days would be sufficient healing time to allow Modan to travel, and his temper to cool to less than boiling.

"He'll gripe that slavery in Rome was the better choice, of course," Trista muttered as one of Jessa's slaves brought the sleek, black horse from the stables. "But that's Modan. He'd gripe about too much froth on a free mug of ale. It's his nature to bitch about anything, once it's done. I'd wager good coin that he'll be squawking about it on his deathbed."

"You don't have to take him, you know."

"Ah, but that's the rub. I do." Trista placed one foot in the slave's cupped hands, and swung easily into the saddle. She peered thoughtfully down at Jessa as she remembered her last meeting with Modan. One hand moved absently to the side of her head, and scratched at her temple. "You know," she began, then hesitated, unsure how her words would be taken. "Do you remember what I said about cutting his balls off?"

"Yesss . . ." Jessa's eyebrows lifted in surprise.

"Can you have the medicus cut just one off? That'll still leave him with the other."

"No. Oh no, Trista, that was the wine talking yesterday." Jessa vigorously shook her head, though she grinned at the same time. "Mind you, that's only half of what I thought you were going to ask."

"It might have been the wine yesterday, Jessa, but today it's not," Trista insisted, shaking her head in turn. She'd spent half the night thinking it through, and convinced herself that the surgery was not vengeance, but assurance. Only she would possess knowledge of it, and with that she could threaten Modan when his temper again ran wild. His humiliation before others would be more than the man could bear. Yet it was a sword that could only cut once, for revealing the truth would render the threat useless. Even so . . .

"A missing hand is there for all to see, Jessa, and Modan will bellyache and bray on it, but only to me. To others, he'll tout it as a brave and bitter trophy: a vicious wound inflicted by equally vicious Romans in a battle almost won. And while he does it, he'll make life miserable for everyone, including me if I'm to be found. But if he's left with a single plum, I'll be the only one that knows, for he'll not flaunt the fact. And that gives me an edge I can use, when needed."

"But . . ."

"Do it. Please," Trista said, each word boosting her conviction. "It won't make any difference to him, really. He'll still function. But just once, I'd like to have *him* by the balls."

"By the ball," Jessa corrected softly. Trista saw that she was at least considering the idea, which made her, for the hundredth time, do the same. "Anyway, we can't. I told you about the law on castrating slaves."

"He's not being castrated; he's only losing one," Trista pointed out, a touch more certain of the right in what she was asking. "Besides, he's not really a slave yet, is he? He's a 'barbarian' prisoner taken in war. If they can *kill* him for that, then it's ridiculous to make a law saying you can't remove one lousy ball."

"I suppose I could point that out to the medicus. Though he'll probably want it in writing," Jessa murmured, but her brow was knit as if she was still thinking it through.

Trista smiled as she saw the small woman nod absently. Modan's being a prisoner was fair comment, and it had struck a mark. She knew how Jessa felt about her husband: he was a bully and a lout, a man who treated his wife like bog wallop, and not one person who knew him, least of all herself, would disagree. Except maybe Treno . . .

"Trista, if he ever finds out –"

"If he ever finds out, he'll kill me," Trista finished and grinned cheerily; she was confident that wouldn't happen. "But who's going to tell him?"

※

Jessa had the sale documents drawn up in readiness for Tuis's approval a day later, with no mention of the partial castration. The scroll transferred title of a slave known as Modan to a freewoman known as Trista, daughter of Necto. Jessa reviewed the agreement that night in the quiet of her quarters, a private room inside the fort commander's residence. The transfer appeared to be in order, as did the report on Modan's condition, written by the fort's medicus, a man called Verus.

Strangely, there was no mention of Modan's hand at all, but it did include the fact that, as instructed, his –

Jessa blinked, read the words again, and gasped. She read them a third time, swore, and climbed to her feet. Barely taking the time to wrap herself in something to make her decent, she stalked from the residence and barged her way into the hospital, where she banged hard on the door of the medicus's quarters. The man's personal slave was clearly surprised to find her there, and equally surprised to find a scroll shoved hard against his belly.

"Where's your master?"

"He's –"

"I'm right here," Verus called, sounding equally startled by Jessa's nocturnal visit, and her obvious annoyance. He nudged his slave aside.

"Is there an emergency?"

"There just may be," Jessa replied, and held the scroll high, jabbing her finger at a single word. "That. Was it full, or partial?"

Verus squinted, reading the word aloud. "Castration?"

"Yes, dammit, castration!"

"Full, of course." He stared oddly at Jessa as if puzzled, then laughed. "Why would anyone do a partial, and leave a man with only one ball?"

# Chapter XIV

## Blatobulgium, Junius, A.D. 105

Why did everyone find it necessary to argue? He was the governor of an entire province, yet every order seemed open to question before the script soaked into the parchment. First it was Marius, sniveling about his precious stone walls: they couldn't be built without him – and specifically not without his miserable, understrength cohorts that were needed further north. A man might have been married to the nagging clod the way he bickered, and Tuis muttered as much as he sorted through the usual pile of parchment littering his desk. In the end, just to be rid of the legate's bleating, he'd sent the man back to Eboracum and his under strength cohorts with him.

That left only the two from the Twentieth, commanded by one of the legion's senior centurios, a man from the ranks. That one, thank the gods, had the sense to keep his grievances to himself, though they were obviously many, for he walked the parade square as if ready to trip over his bottom lip. The cohorts were camped just south of the fort and would remain there until relieved, and he'd take no argument. The man was, after all, only a centurio, regardless of his seniority. The units would not be leaving, not until the tribes settled down in their godless, strife-ridden territories. Though how general that unrest actually was, Tuis was still not certain.

The attack on his column had been a complete surprise, and in the short journey back to the fort his thoughts had brooded over why. They finally settled on his real da, his son Bryn, and the hasty messages he'd finally dispatched from Bremenium, hoping to find both. His timing could not have been worse! Those same messages must have arrived at the very moment the pair was planning to destroy his army. They must be laughing at him!

Yet the irony of catching his da's second son – no, his fourth son, actually – in the middle of the attack was not lost on Tuis. If not for that fool request of Jessa's, he would never have known the truth. And he was still not sure what to do with the useless toad, despite his niece's pretentious notion of giving him back to his wife – minus a hand, and one ball.

Why one ball?

And now there were none! Tuis shook his head in disbelief.

Still, he was unable to steer his mind free of its litany of woes. Cronus was harassing him again with an endless stream of correspondence that found his desk no matter how far north he travelled. Out of view was not out of voice; the man was like a dog on a meatless bone – though procurators never sank their teeth into a *meatless* bone. If he let Cronus have his way, the grain husks would be taxed next. The tribes were bitching enough as it was, anymore would only . . .

Tuis stopped short, his mind shifting. Perhaps acquiescing to the procurator's lust for coin might not be a bad idea. Or better still, a compromise. It would never do to give Cronus what he wanted, of course, but a person could bargain. He recalled one of his father's adages – his Roman father, not the barbarian: a man is forever yours if you give him a taste of what he wants, and let the balance dangle. It wasn't necessary for the man to raise his lousy taxes all over the north, just do it in those places that were a source of trouble, like this one! Maybe the man was right. Strategically, a tax might be used as punishment . . . or was that a tactic?

The thought was still on his mind when he pushed the mounting pile of scrolls aside and left to join Marcus and his daughter for a midday meal. The two were a growing source of irritation, though with this last incident he didn't know whether to laugh or cry. What was the fellow's name again? Modan! His own brother! Well, half-brother, anyway. Not that it mattered, for the man's bloodline had just come to an abrupt halt. For the hundredth time, Tuis shook his head in amazement. How, in the name of every god that had ever played with a man's mind, do you *accidentally* relieve a man of his balls? He muttered aloud at the woman's stupidity, drawing several curious looks as he strode from the headquarters building.

There was one consolation, he supposed: the man still had two hands. Keeping them had been part of the tradeoff he'd proposed to Modan *before* the idiot surgeon pruned his plums. After all, the man was his brother, though the fool didn't know it, so it was only reasonable to give him the choice: slavery or his hand. Forget the idiocy about wifely gifts! Though later on, the poor bastard must have wondered what was happening when they started slicing into his sack! And there was only one man who would get blame for that: the governor of Britannia.

What had the medicus been thinking? Surely a *reasonable* person, on receiving an order that cancelled severing a man's hand, would at least *ask* if castrating the sorry bugger was still on the list? Did everything need his personal attention?

Tuis cursed aloud as he entered the commander's residence. Why did the gods wait until you thought a problem was solved before smearing dung? Modan had been quite amenable to the alternative; in fact, the boy had been visibly relieved. He could see it in the glint in the brute's eyes when given the choice: lose a hand and go home as the slave of your wife – *personally, he'd have chosen death* – or keep the hand and work the quarries at Calcaria. Escape had been plain in those glittering eyes when Modan chose the quarries, which was foolish; the lad didn't realize that he might just as well try fleeing the arenas!

No – he would find the work hard, but he'd be treated well enough as long as he carried his share. Tuis's brow furrowed as another thought crossed his mind: did it make a difference, working the quarries, if a person had his balls or not? Did you lose some of your strength? Tuis shuddered at the thought. Marius might be glad of the extra hand, he supposed, but as for himself, he still felt he'd been told only half the truth of what happened.

*Marius would be glad of the extra hand!* Tuis chuckled as he fell into a chair across the table from Marcus and Jessa. The meal would be as good a time as any to dig for the other half of the truth.

"I really don't see how I can be blamed," he said when Marcus broached the subject before the food was even on the table. "In fact, the man should be grateful. By now he could be halfway to the arenas if I hadn't stepped in." Tuis glanced pointedly at Jessa. "As someone asked me to do."

"Well, he *is* your brother," Marcus countered in defense of his daughter.

"Half-brother," Tuis corrected and promptly wished he'd kept his mouth shut, for the comment wasn't exactly tactful with his adopted brother sitting there. He glanced down at the table, where a bowl of hot puls steamed before him, covered with finely diced dried fruit soaked in a thin, syrupy sauce. It was one of his favourites. He dug in, and finished his point around a mouthful of the gruel-like mixture, "You know, he really might as well be a stranger for all I know of him. I never met the man before – or his mother. I would also remind you that he was caught alongside a dead horse, fully armed, after attacking one of our columns. My column! Marcus, what did you expect me to do? He could have killed me."

"Not cut his balls off, that's for sure," Marcus shot back.

Tuis found that totally unreasonable. "I didn't have anything to do with that part," he insisted, struggling to hold his temper. "And, if a certain someone hadn't asked to have *one* of his apples picked, then nobody would have fucked up and scooped them both!" He quickly held a hand up to Jessa as he saw her face tighten at the language, but what *had* the girl been thinking? "I'm sorry, but I've just spent two months in the field, where no one picks his nose without *effing* at the snot. On top of that, everything else is falling behind, and I'm frustrated. My choice of words may not be the best, but that's the way it is." He frowned, determined to find an answer to the one question that had left him baffled. "Why *did* you want to trim one of his balls?"

"I don't know," Jessa began, but Tuis wasn't done yet.

"And let me tell you this," he pointed a finger, "I was the one who came up with the idea of sending him to Calcaria with *both* hands. I'm sorry if it ruined your gift, but Modan himself took the choice when I offered it. And I did it because he *is* my brother, and sending him off to the arenas or slicing off a hand didn't sit well. I might also add that I wouldn't have *dreamed* of lopping off his balls!"

"That wasn't my idea," Jessa mumbled.

"Then whose was it?"

"His wife's."

Tuis laughed out loud, unable to resist. "Well, I gotta say this. It's the first time I've seen a wife physically do it!"

"The raven-haired lass who brought you back, right?" Marcus asked as if to be certain.

"Uh-huh," Jessa said. "She'll be coming again soon, to get her husband."

Tuis snorted. "I don't know why."

"You know, Jess," Marcus said, shaking his head in reproof, though the corner of his mouth twitched, "I've always found it best not to get involved when a man and wife are having family trouble."

⁂

Trista was appalled by what she saw, even from the distance of the commander's residence. Led from the hospital under guard, his skin was ashen, and his hair had been cut back to less than the width of a thumb, on both his chin and his head. He wore standard issue work dress: a plain, woven shirt, cloth leggings cut at mid-calf, and sandals. It seemed that he'd shed a quarter of his weight in less than a month – though Jessa, her eyes narrowing as she carefully watched Trista, assured her that such was not the case.

"I checked with the medicus," she said quietly, "he's down about fifteen pounds."

"So what does that mean?" Trista asked, her voice hard as she gazed at her husband through the window of Jessa's room.

"It means he's lost the weight of a couple of good, plump roosters." Jessa shrugged as if it was of no consequence.

"Is anything infected? I-I see he's still got his hand," Trista said, and wondered what that meant. She'd never been certain that Modan would consider the loss of one hand a fair price for freedom; and even if he did, his strutting pride would prevent him from admitting as much. Personally, she would take the loss of one hand any day rather than spend the balance of her life as a slave – or an even shorter span in the arena, though the arenas would not have been her fate. Her mind flipped to some of the women her own people had taken from the Dumnonii, and she shuddered. Death was preferable.

"No, no infection," Jessa said, her brow furrowed. "He's actually doing very well, considering."

Trista was quick to note Jessa's lack of detail which, with Modan's hand intact, left only his dangler to answer for. She winced at the thought. It was the wine that had made her ask Jessa to do it, of course, and she'd rationalized as much over the past two weeks as her resolve slipped. Yet Trista also knew she could have changed her mind the next day. She almost had, yet when she thought it through, especially that parting blow from Modan's fist, the more certain she was with her choice. He would eventually get over it – more or less – and there would be no *real* change. When you got right down to it, one was as good as two. And when she did leave him, the knowledge would be a permanent whip with which to check his vile temper.

And that was all it would ever be, Trista reasoned. She would never mock him with the knowledge, or see him ridiculed. Though an old, taunting rhyme came to mind, and it made her smile. How did it finish up? *A Roman has only got one ball, and the governor has no balls at all!*

She had to be certain. "The, er, matter of Modan's riding gear," Trista ventured, since Jessa seemed disinclined to discuss the matter. She squatted on her heels so they could speak face to face. "Did you do that, or did you change your mind?"

"First off, I told you I wouldn't be doing it. Second, it wasn't *my* mind that needed to be changed. The whole thing was your idea."

Trista decided she didn't like the sound of that. It was as if her finger had jabbed an open sore, and she'd been poked back. "So someone did go ahead and do it, then?"

"Yes."

"And what happened. It got infected?"

"No, the operation was actually quite successful."

"So . . . ?"

"So . . . you could say it was twice as successful as anyone expected."

"That's good, then. Very good." Trista smiled, wondering at Jessa's reluctance. Then, as the double meaning of the words sank in, her mouth fell open. "No! Oh, no! Tell me you didn't!"

"I told you, *I* didn't do anything," Jessa cried, clearly exasperated. "It was the medicus who did the operation. I only wish I *had* done it! He'd still have at least half his stupid gonads."

"Shit!" Trista moaned, then repeated the word, then said it again, shaking her head wildly in a vain attempt to clear it. "Modan is going to be pissed!"

"I believe he already is," Jessa murmured.

"No, I mean later – when he snaps out of his misery, and it hits him full on. Right now, I'd warrant he's just numb." Trista remained still for the longest time, staring hard into Jessa's eyes, vaguely hoping she was jesting. Yet she clearly was not. It was too much to absorb, and Trista spoke the only words that came to mind. "Jessa, you – me, we must never tell anyone."

"Believe me," Jessa said with feeling, "I'm not saying a word. Though there is one other thing I didn't mention."

"There's more?" Trista cried, wondering what, by every god that was evil, the woman was going to say next. "Don't tell me they sliced his prodder off, too."

"No, no, it's not that at all!" Jessa was plainly alarmed at the idea. "The governor changed his mind on what to do with Modan. Actually, it was Modan himself who did."

"What does that mean?" Trista nearly shouted as she stood, raising her hands skyward. "What else could have gone wrong? You ripped his tongue out?"

"No, no!" Jessa raised both hands in protest. "It happened before the, uh, surgery. The governor gave Modan a choice. Lose the hand and go home with you, or keep it and work the stone quarries at Calcaria. They're a few miles south of Eboracum."

"And he took the quarries?"

"Yes."

"Why?"

Jessa stared blankly, as if the answer was obvious. "Because he'd rather keep both hands, I suppose. And he probably thinks he'll be able to escape – which he won't."

"No, no." Trista shook her head. "I meant why did the governor change his mind? Roman governors don't give a faerie's fart for people like Modan."

For a moment Jessa said nothing, clearly lost for a reply; then, she answered with a question of her own. Had Trista not been concerned with other matters, such as Modan's loss of his manhood, she might have pressed further. "Maybe he's going soft? I've heard that the legate at Eboracum has been bitching because he can't get men for his quarry. Look on this positively, Trista. Working there will keep him alive and intact." Then, because that wasn't quite true, she sheepishly added, "More or less . . ."

Trista thought on that for a moment, and oddly enough, she felt relief. Not that it cancelled out the castration, but if Modan ended up working the quarries he'd be alive, and her conscience would be free. More than that, through no fault of her own, she'd be done with him. As to losing his balls, that was probably a boon for a man who faced a life cutting stone for the Romans!

That was rationalizing, of course, and Trista's breath left her lungs in a rush of air. If she were to wager coin, her husband was already planning escape – and despite what Jessa said, she wondered on his chances, balls or no balls. The odds were likely next to nothing, as the wee girl said, but Modan wouldn't accept that. Yes, perhaps the pruning was all for the best. But there was one question that still puzzled.

Trista again crouched down on a level with Jessa. "So why am I here, then?"

"I dunno. Maybe I felt you should still come, so I could tell you myself," Jessa said, and shrugged. "Or maybe you wanted to tell him goodbye?"

※

As sure as the sun rose in the eastern sky, the gods made sport of man and woman from sheer perversity. Jessa was certain of it early the next morning, when she again climbed onto the walkway that straddled the main gate of the fort. There had been no goodbyes exchanged between Trista and her husband; Modan never knew that his wife was at the fort. Trista simply could not face him and left it that way. Jessa supposed she couldn't blame her.

Trista's head was bent low as she rode out through the gate, her hands loose on the reins. She stared glumly over the head of the sleek black gelding which, sensing her mood, plodded down the road as if pulling a cart. Jessa watched sadly until the bowed figure disappeared from sight where the road sloped away into the trees. Though she knew that none of it was her fault, Jessa felt as guilty as a whipped hound.

Modan departed for Calcaria soon after, with the contingent of slaves held over for the same quarries. By then, Jessa was walking moodily along the *via praetoria* with her father, and happened to pass by the small column as it headed toward the fort's main gate. Modan stopped in his tracks and glared malevolently at them both, then spat. One of the guards slashed hard at his back with a wooden baton and sent him reeling onward. Modan barely seemed to feel the blow. He simply shook his shoulders and trudged on past and through the gate.

"I'd say you've got an enemy for life, rabbit."

"Who, Da? Modan or Trista?"

Marcus smiled and placed a hand on his daughter's shoulder, both of them watching the tail end of the column as it disappeared onto the road south. "Modan. Personally, I think you did Trista a favour."

"I wonder if she thinks so," Jessa said wistfully. "I should never have agreed to sign off on his stupid testes. And it was stupid – all of it. I found out what happened. The scribe used an *i*, making it plural. Tuis almost flayed my skin off – and the medicus's."

"As he should. Modan is his brother."

"Which is the only reason he's still alive, I suppose. Modan's a bully and a troublemaker, Da. I think he remains a threat to all of us. He could still stir things up, even in the confines of a quarry."

"Oh, I wouldn't think so. Visit a quarry, and you'd see why," Marcus said confidently, and squeezed her shoulder. "Besides, I don't think he's got the balls for it."

"Da!" Jessa cried, and thumped the side of his leg. "Be serious. I think Tuis believes he should have done more for Modan. He also mumbled something about his own da and the other son – what's-his-name. You have to remember, these are Tuis's own people."

"His own people? Tuis is a Roman," Marcus said mildly.

"Yeah, just like me," Jessa murmured, and stared down the now empty road, filled with an odd sense of loss. *We – us – them!* When the dice were finally cast who, really, was she? Neither deer nor hound, that was certain, and it was impossible to be both. Even a deer or a hound could find comfort with its own kind.

"True, rabbit, true, but it's Tuis's Roman background that is guiding his next move."

"Which is?"

"On the one hand, he told me awhile back he might try to contact his da and his other brother," Marcus explained, and stretched both arms with a yawn, as if to snap a mood of lethargy. "He thinks maybe he can sort something out with them, and all three can work on getting the tribes calmed down. His father surely retains some status. And if I remember correctly, Cethen prefers to walk a calmer path. Though that was before this Modan thing and the column."

"Cethen walking a calmer path is only the half of it!" Jessa said, recalling the man's reluctance – or was it inability?—to call even his own son to task. "I wouldn't count on anything there. What was on the other hand?"

Marcus sighed. "He figured his campaign didn't punish the tribes enough. He's going to apply Rome's ultimate punishment."

"Oh no . . ."

"Oh yes! He's invited Cronus up from Londinium. To quote your Uncle Tuis: 'If all else fails, I'll tax the arse off them.'"

⸸

"So what's happening, then?" Bryn called from the cover of the forest.

Trista did not bother to look up, but simply turned her horse toward the shelter of the trees. She glanced sideways to be certain that no one watched, but the fort had long vanished from sight, and not a soul could be seen in either direction.

"So where is he now?" Bryn asked as she listlessly pulled back on the reins.

"They're moving him south to work the quarries." Trista shrugged to show there was little else to say. She was tired, dead tired: the inside sort of tired that drags a person down far worse than any other. Her conscience was the cause, and she knew it. One part of her was already thinking on how it would be, once she was rid of Modan, and she felt absolutely no regret; another part beat at her brain for not being worried sick about what happened to the man. And now, here was Bryn, his brother . . .

"With a hand missing?" he asked, his voice incredulous.

"No, he's still got two." Trista raised one of her own to quiet him. "Look, Bryn, I know it was my decision to trade Modan's hand for his freedom. I thought it wasn't a bad trade, but it seems that I was the only one who did."

"So what changed?" Bryn asked, plainly confused. "If he kept both his hands, he was going to be shipped off to their arenas."

"It seems the Roman governor had a change of mind. They're rebuilding the fortress at Eboracum out of stone, and they need slaves for the quarrying of it. He's being sent there."

"When?"

Trista's laugh was bitter. "If you stay here, you'll likely see him pass by before too long. There was a column getting ready to leave when I rode out."

"How big a column?" Bryn asked, his face instantly thoughtful.

Trista sighed. "You're not . . ."

"How big a column? And how many are guarding it?"

# Chapter XV

## Northern Britannia, Junius, A.D. 105

After another sleepless night spent twisting and turning, Cethen decided he had to do something, though what, he had no idea. His mind would not settle, and the more he tried to make it do so, the more the fool thing wanted to think. It was like trying to stop a rolling fog. Yet unlike a fog, the rocks on the road were easily seen and tallied: Bryn had vanished soon after Modan's bone-brained attack on the Romans, and might even have got himself killed there; as might have Modan, who was clearly either dead or taken; then Trista had been seen with wee Jessa at one of the forts since – and had most likely turned her loyalty.

Why couldn't he have raised normal brats, like everyone else's? Though when he looked back on it, and he grunted in disgust as the thought struck him, the only one he'd actually raised from bairn to big'un was Modan. Cethen grimaced and pushed whatever that might mean from his mind, willing it to stay gone.

His thoughts instead turned fondly to Elena and the first three, and the old, familiar image of their lodge perched high in the pasture above the blue waters of the *Abus*. But even as that appeared, as clear in his mind as it had ever been, the Romans' miserable galley thudded against his dock and shattered the dream. How many years ago had that been? It was decades! The sodding Romans just wouldn't go away. And now a Roman governor, a man who controlled the entire land from one seashore to another, wanted to talk to him. To him: Cethen Lamh-fada!

It was ever the Romans! A curse had been placed on him and his family – or families. Like thieves, they had stolen the first one – his wife, his three children, all irretrievably lost – and it now seemed that one way or another he was losing the second one to them, Bryn; and maybe even the third. Except for Kelpy, of course, who, uncharacteristically, was of no help at all.

"There's nothing you can do, other than go find out what happened," she said practically, her voice impatient as she chopped a pile of leafy vegetables for the evening meal.

Modan, Bryn and Trista had all been much discussed the past few weeks, and Cethen knew that whatever happened next was up to him; but he couldn't stop plowing through it, again and again, hoping something might come of words alone. "I don't think either of the boys are dead," he muttered, as much to himself as his daughter. "Bryn is too careful, and men like Modan are just too – well, they're too brash to get themselves killed."

"Brash is not the word you're looking for," Kelpy said quietly.

"Brash, rash, or just plain unruly. How about plain lucky? The gods protect the likes of Modan," Cethen said, and scratched at his chin. What Kelpy meant, of course, was that Modan was bad, and she was unwilling to say as much; but then, so was he. He glanced up at her face, and saw she was annoyed. His vision might still hold a bit of a blur, but it didn't disguise that look! It was time to change the subject. "What do you think Trista is doing?"

"If Trista has any sense, she'll learn something positive from the dwarf and take advantage of it. She's a bright lass and could do well by the lesson. The dwarf herself is a fine example of how a woman can –"

"Her name's Jessa, dammit, not *the dwarf*," Cethen said irritably, though inwardly he smiled, recalling another time when the tiny girl was no more than a bairn, and her father one of the tribes' slaves. "She could speak both tongues by the time she could walk, you know; though she was slow to walk. Then, a year later, she was starting to write them in the dirt!"

"Then go see her – why not?" Kelpy nodded toward the table. A decrepit leather dispatch case sat on the rough-planked surface. After much prompting, her father had retrieved the relic from an equally decrepit sack, long hidden under his bed. "The dwa – Jessa said it should still be of use."

"I wonder where really Bryn is," Cethen mused, choosing to pretend he didn't hear. "I learned through one of Lagan's people that he was at the fight with Trista, but nobody's seen him since. I wonder if they tried to help Modan."

"Uh-huh, and you've wondered that, I'd say, at least a dozen times."

Kelpy was starting to show her impatience again. Cethen sighed, his eyes turning to the leather case. Maybe he *should* take whatever was inside and use it. He knew it was some sort of a pardon; Cian had told him as much, as had Jessa. Maybe he should even use it to go and see his brother, too. It had been years since they'd last met, and even then, Cian had been the one to ride north to see him. But that was a long time ago, and Eboracum was a long way off, and Cian hadn't bothered coming his way since, either.

Kelpy dropped the knife with a clatter, and turned to face him. "Look, Da, if you need to be told what to do, then I'll tell you: take that leather case and travel up to the fort where the wee lass is living. If there's any word to be had of either Bryn or Modan, you might find it there. And if Trista's there too, you'll have it from her mouth, as well. Who knows, maybe one of the boys *is* hurt and the lass herself is tending to him."

"Which lass?" Cethen asked absently, reluctantly deciding that his daughter was likely correct. He'd have to go, only he supposed it would be better not to go there alone. Who else could he talk into going?

"Da – Trista, Jessa, it doesn't matter," Kelpy cried, picking up the knife. She cut hard into a handful of fat-hen. "Just get your hind end in a saddle, and go!"

⁂

Two days later events beyond Cethen's choosing resolved his dithering, which was not an infrequent occurrence. A single rider appeared, travelling south from the head of the valley. The horse had clearly been ridden far, for it plodded listlessly over the sunbaked dirt track, its head hung low. The rider slouched in the saddle, swaying back and forth to the rhythm of the animal's slow gait. Cethen remained seated on the cushioned chair in front of the small lodge, where he sat idly slicing parsnips for Kelpy. The horse halted of its own accord not two steps away.

"I was worried," he said. "There's been hardly a word."

"No one seems to have been looking for me," Trista said pointedly, then saw the mug of ale that sat close by Cethen's hand and nodded toward it. "I could use some of that. It's been a long ride."

"Kelpy! Could you bring some beer?" Cethen called over his shoulder, then turned his eyes back to Trista. "What about Modan and Bryn? There was a rumour Modan was hurt. Maybe even dead."

Trista slid slowly from the saddle, deciding it was better to get the facts out in the open, at least the tell-able ones. "He's alive, Da, though he almost lost a hand. His right one."

"A hand?" Cethen eased back in the chair. His gaze shifted to his own hand as if he might find an answer there, and the questions followed. "A sword cut? A spear?"

Of course Cethen would assume it was a battle wound. Trista sighed, her body suddenly bone tired, and her mind less than willing to offer a long explanation. She decided, for the moment, that a lie would serve better than the truth. "It was nothing. Just something minor after he charged in on the Romans. It was after losing his first horse. I saw it happen from back in the trees, where I was watching with Bryn. After that, he was taken."

"Taken? Bryn?"

"No, Modan," Trista snapped impatiently, then caught herself; the poor man was just asking after his sons. She slumped down on a wooden bench across from Cethen, and released her breath in a great sigh. Since leaving the Roman fort, she'd been angry with herself for every nasty, nagging thought that crossed her mind. "Modan's been sent off to work in a quarry at Calcaria."

"Calcaria?" Cethen seemed to take no offence at her impatience, and sat puzzling her words as if they'd touched his memory. "I think that's what the Romans named Kemoc's village. There's sandstone there." He shook his head in disbelief. "Modan's working a quarry!"

*Yes, Modan is working a quarry,* Trista thought, reminding herself that it was his own fault he was there, not hers. Maybe the Romans could knock the arrogance out of his thick, brainless skull; and if not, they'd certainly teach him the meaning of humility. Though that was going to happen anyway, simply from losing both his . . .

Trista shuddered. She couldn't free her mind of the thought, or of its image, for that matter. All because of some wine and a whim, her husband had lost not one, but two –

Trista sighed and tried to dismiss the memory, forcing her mind to think of Bryn; not that she found any more comfort there. By all the gods, she hoped he wasn't doing something foolish. He'd been awful tight mouthed when the two of them parted, and she had wondered. The man was brooding over Modan, she was certain, for that was what set him off. Surely, he couldn't possibly do anything about his brother's . . .

"Bryn? Where is he?"

Trista blinked and stared at Cethen, her tired mind picking up on his words as if he'd been reading her mind. "Bryn?"

"Yes, Bryn," Cethen said, his voice sharp. "What happened to Bryn? Where is he? Is he safe?"

"I hope so." Kelpy came from the small lodge carrying two mugs of beer and a platter of leftovers.

"I don't know where he is," Trista said, which was half true. She didn't know *precisely* where Bryn was. She just hoped that whatever he was doing, Modan was no longer a part of it. She suspected that was nothing but foolish optimism. All she knew for certain was where he *would* be: the settlement that had grown out of the ruins of *Stannick*. She was supposed to wait for him there, three days from now; and he was supposed to wait for her, if he showed first. How long that took, he told her, didn't matter – whoever arrived before the other would stay. After that, they were to travel to – what was the name of the place? "He's supposed to be going to a Roman fort called E-bar-something. I can't exactly remember the name. It's farther south."

"Eboracum," Cethen muttered. "Why would he go there?"

"To call on your brother Cian. Bryn wants to find out if he knows why the Roman governor wants to see him. Is he in trouble, or something? Aaah!" Trista turned thankfully as Kelpy handed her one of the brimming mugs. The cool ale tasted like iced nectar.

"The Roman governor wants to see Bryn, too?" Cethen blinked, puzzled. "That means he wants to see both of us."

Trista raised her eyebrows. She'd been surprised the man wanted to see Bryn, but his father too? She'd thought that perhaps Bryn had been seen at the attack, and someone had given his name. Yet she could think of no reason why they might want to see Cethen, too. The only common thread that joined Bryn and his da that might offend the Romans was Modan, and Trista said so.

"That makes sense, I suppose. I figured that was why the Roman was after seeing *me*! And now he wants Bryn, too. Modan's Da and his brother. Shit!" Cethen grunted the words as if it was all starting to make sense. "I don't see how either of us can be held accountable for Modan's doings." Cethen fell silent for a moment, brows drawn down as if something else bothered him. "I wonder if it has anything to do with Jessa. I heard the governor was at the same Roman fort that she is."

"Yes, but he left again sometime after Modan's attack," Trista explained. "His brother Marcus is still there, though. I think he's too worried about his daughter to leave. Jessa says you both knew each other quite well in the old days."

"We spent a lot of time together, though Marcus was an unwilling guest." Cethen smiled, then just as quickly frowned. "You have to wonder at the world. His sister married my oldest son, Rhun."

"He what?" Trista was intrigued. Just how entwined *was* Cethen's family with that of the man he claimed stole his first wife? A woman taken in battle, though, was hardly theft. A prize, perhaps, but not even a bard's fantasy would place her as stolen goods. The Roman who took her certainly seemed to feel she was a prize – he'd married her!

Cethen seemed to think that Trista's question deserved an answer though, for he motioned her closer. Or perhaps he just felt the need to unburden himself. Whatever his reason, he took a long pull on the mug of ale and began to speak. It was almost as if he was talking to himself, his head low and his free hand picking at his food.

At first he didn't talk about Rhun's marriage to the Roman's daughter, other than to confirm that it did, indeed, happen. Instead, he went all the way back to when the Roman first came to his home on the Abus, before the fortress was built. Trista listened quietly as she sipped the ale, her attention rapt; as did Kelpy, though she must have known the story backward: the exile of Cethen's family by "the Roman bastard"; the fight at Bran's Beck where his wife and daughter were taken "by the sod"; and the final battle with Rome at Stannick where his oldest two boys "were stolen." Yet all things considered, Cethen told his story with little trace of self-pity, and often in a manner that was both open and self-deprecating. For that, Trista gained a measure of respect for her father by marriage.

But there was more she wanted to know, so when she pressed him about Bryn, Cethen told her of his life, too: how he and the boy's mother, "the bitch" Morallta – Trista noted that he never once called her his wife or his woman – had met at Venutius's lodge; the flight to Cumbria, where he joined her after the defeat at Stannick; and the long running fight to the ends of Caledonii territory, his fortune tied to the destiny of the Caledoni king, Galgar.

His voice grew low when telling of how Morallta joined Galgar's camp, taking Bryn with her, but it grew bitter when telling the tale of the final battle at Graupius. His anger was not because his people had lost, Trista realized; in fact, the enormous defeat seemed to count little for Cethen. His bitterness was directed at Morallta, who had failed to look after their son, a boy not even twelve years old. For he'd lost more than a battle; he'd lost yet another of his children.

Cethen was brief in telling of the final confrontation with Morallta when he killed the woman, and Trista supposed that was natural; nor did he offer further details of his oldest son's marriage to the Roman's daughter, and she supposed that was just forgetful. Cethen did finish the story, though, by telling how he and what remained of their small, veteran troop of Brigante cavalry had dragged their way back to the hills, beaten and wounded, and settled in this small valley under the very shadow of Rome.

When Cethen finished speaking, it was as if he returned from a dream. He stared down at his mug as if baffled by its emptiness, yet Kelpy had refilled both of them at least once. Trista stretched her arms and glanced skyward, surprised to find how quickly the day was passing. She was tempted to ask if she could stay on, but she wanted to arrive at Stannick well before Bryn. Now that Modan was gone from her life, she was determined to take advantage. A journey to Eboracum was the first venturesome step.

Before Trista left the fort, Jessa had been blunt in suggesting she do exactly that, saying a ride south to visit the Roman fortress was just what was needed. She'd even offered a knowing smirk when told that such a trek might be in the company of Bryn, but Trista had ignored that. Whatever was on her mind was of concern to her only and no one else, and that was the end of it! Yet there was nothing on her mind that was really settled, other than the need to learn more about such a great journey. Eboracum was farther than she had ever travelled before.

"Well, lass, I suppose most of all that was what the bards *don't* sing about when telling the story, but it's the plain truth of it," Cethen mumbled later as he cinched the gelding's saddle, and offered one knee for Trista to mount. "Next time you're here, we'll talk more."

"And you'll not get his gob to shut next time, either." Kelpy smiled and handed up a cloth-wrapped bundle that Trista knew would see her through the next few meals.

She smiled her thanks as she took the gift, pleased that she'd followed the less travelled path that took her through Cethen's farmstead – a visit she had dreaded. Telling him about Modan had been her reason for coming, and she had expected nothing but bitterness and accusation. Yet the time spent had not been unpleasant. Cethen had listened to her news as if it had been expected, and it occurred to Trista that perhaps it was. Just maybe – and the thought startled – just maybe he was relieved that his son had been taken, for that meant he was alive. And as long as a man lived, there was hope. A son who was a slave at Calcaria was probably better than no son at all.

Trista's mood grew reflective as she stared down at the two. Modan's death had likely been the most dreaded thought on Cethen's mind! Once she revealed that he still lived – most of him did, anyway – then he had revealed more of himself than he'd ever done. And that had been good, perhaps for both of them.

"Cethen, you should go down there and see the governor too," Trista suggested as she turned the gelding's head toward the foot of the valley. "When you think on it, he did make some allowance for Modan. He could have had him killed."

"A healthy slave is worth far more than a dead barbarian," Cethen said disdainfully, then snorted his amusement. "Tell that to Jessa, next time you see her. She can pass it on to her da! Marcus knows the value of a slave. He should. He was once mine."

"Which is another story." Trista smiled and kicked the gelding's belly, sending it trotting down the track that led south along the valley floor.

"Hey!" Cethen called out before she'd barely started, snapping his fingers as if suddenly remembering. "You said that Marcus was the governor's brother. He doesn't have a brother."

Trista reined in and turned in the saddle. "Maybe he never bothered to tell you." She frowned, trying to remember the man's name. "Gaius – Gaius Sabinius something or other. That was it."

"No, no, that was his da, not his brother!" Cethen told her. "As I told you, I knew the man, but only briefly. He's the one who stole my . . ." It was painfully clear that he had no wish to venture there again, though his face grew puzzled. "I wonder what the old bugger's doing back here?"

Trista smiled at the use of the words "old bugger"; the man Cethen spoke of was Jessa's grandfather and the two of them would be about the same age. But this Roman governor was not Jessa's grandfather, she knew that; he was her uncle, she was certain. "It can't be the same man. This one's younger, maybe forty or so."

"Are you sure?" Cethen frowned, mystified. "Marcus never mentioned a brother. And as to Gaius Sabinius," he shook his head vigorously, "that's a name I'll remember to my dying day."

Trista shrugged her own bafflement, and this time kicked hard at the black's belly. The horse broke into a canter and she let it hold the pace for a short while, then recalled another name that Jessa had used, one that might help Cethen remember. She again halted the gelding, the animal circling, keen to be off as its blood heated with the brief run. "The wee lass mostly called him by a sort of pet name," she shouted back along the trail. "Tuis, I think it was."

"Huh?" Cethen's head shot up in surprise.

"Tuis!" Trista yelled the name once more and for the last time kicked hard at the gelding's belly. The animal leapt forward, the thump of its hooves echoing for the longest time as it disappeared down the valley.

Kelpy, who stood behind Cethen draining her mug of ale, almost choked as she spluttered the dregs across her father's back. "Shit!"

Cethen slumped back down in the chair, his chest tight and his mind spinning. It couldn't be his son, of course. A Roman governor? That was impossible. Yet the gods . . .

He stared pointedly down at his empty mug. Kelpy sighed and went inside the lodge, leaving him to churn the possibilities. Tuis had been raised by the one called Gaius Sabinius, that Cethen knew. The Roman had stolen his sons along with his wife. His own wife!

Elena . . .

The old, familiar rage rose up, and he shook his head. He'd tried to bury that name for thirty years and more, never with success. Though in all honesty, it hadn't crossed his mind so much, the past few years. Could Elena still be alive?

He turned his thoughts back to Tuis. Was it possible that the child had grown up to become governor of Brigantia? Of course not. How would that have come about? Yet – he grinned at the notion – if Elena had a say, then anything was possible. What was the easiest way to find out? Cian would have the ready answer, but he groaned at the idea. Just the thought of a trek to Eboracum was enough to make a man wince. There might be another way of finding the truth, one far better than riding all the way back to the Abus. Kelpy had suggested he visit Marcus, taking the leather pouch with its pardon inside.

Cethen mulled over the idea as Kelpy returned with yet another ale, and he grunted from habit when he saw it was only half full. Marcus! Gaining any kind of help from the Romans was distasteful. Besides, it was likely unsafe to visit the fort. Or was it? Perhaps with that old pass or pardon or whatever it was, going to the Roman fort was a fair enough risk. After all, the lad – no, by now Marcus would be a full-grown man, and then some – owed him his life. In fact, if it hadn't been for him and the bard Criff, Morallta would have slit the boy's throat, all those many years ago.

Whatever had happened to Criff?

Cethen sighed. There was so much to think on. Again he shook his head. It probably wouldn't hurt to take the fool scroll with him, if he did decide to go. It hardly took any room. But the idea of Gaius Sabinius or whoever he was "granting" free passage through his own land rankled. In the old days, Venutius was the only man who granted passage.

Cethen paused as yet another thought crossed his mind. If Tuis was the governor, that meant he held total control over *all* Britannia – or, if worded another way, Tuis, *his son*, now ruled Brigantia! Could it be that the gods had twisted the legend of the ancient torque so that his own son now fit its promise? The druids said the gold neck ring was more than a thousand years old, and had been wrought by the goddess Brigantia herself. According to legend, when the true ruler of the Brigantes wore the torque, the people would be free – or something like that. Maybe he gave the torque to the wrong son. Or – Cethen blinked, startled at the possibility – maybe Rhun *had* given it to Tuis, and now the gods . . .

He scratched the back of his head and tried to think. How long had it been since Venutius died, and he'd found the torque? Thirty years? No, maybe it was a bit more. But it was maybe another seven or eight years before he passed it on to Rhun and Coira. By then it had become a burden – yet to be honest, the fool thing had always been a burden! And he'd passed it down to the two because he figured his own chance of survival wasn't worth a bowl of burnt barley. The odds were that Rhun still had it. But if he didn't, and he'd given it to Tuis, did it mean the legend's promise had been fulfilled?

Cethen shook his head to clear the tangle. It was all too much to ponder on, and a man could never guess what the gods were going to do anyway. It always turned out bad. They just waited until you thought you had it all figured, then they shat on you.

# Chapter XVI

# Northern Brigantia, Junius, A.D. 105

Modan breathed easy once they had stolen past the fort at Epiacum and resumed the trek north into Lagan's territory. If he continued along the same path, he could damned near ride forever and never come across another Roman fort.

He was painfully aware that his father's lodge was less than half a day's ride away and that Trista might be there, but while the notion of going held appeal, he quickly dismissed it. He didn't dare alter course. Besides, bypassing the lodge didn't distress him; he wasn't ready to face either his da or his wife – not now, maybe not ever. How could he tell either of them what the Romans had done to him? Especially Trista! The contempt, the ridicule, the scorn... how could he face any woman again, never mind his wife. He had cursed the Romans a thousand times in the past weeks, calling the wrath of the gods down on every one that walked this land – his land – and upon their miserable, worthless governor in particular.

And though the more time he had to think, the more his mind plowed every possible furrow. When a person is doing nothing but sitting in a cell or a saddle, the mind can do nothing else. The more Modan dwelt on the outrage that had been inflicted, the less sure he was about whom to blame. Did the dwarf have a part in it, for example, or had it really been just the governor?

The Roman governor! The mere thought of that pompous prick made his gut growl. Modan had thought him to be a fair man – albeit a simpleton – for the fool had seemed to shrink at the idea of his mutilation. Yet losing a hand was not an unreasonable trade for freedom, when weighed on a balance. Not that he would have taken it, of course. He had more pride. For some, though, a hand lost on the block was preferable to two wielding a sword in Rome's arenas or, worse still, serving as a Roman slave.

He'd heard many stories of the arenas; they meant a harsh life, but not always death. And a man was a man, after all, and as long as he breathed, he had hope. That was why even slavery was a viable choice – there was always hope of escape. And escape had happened, and much sooner than expected! No, losing a hand was not a man's choice, and Trista should not have made it for him. Thank the gods the Roman governor had, for whatever reason, given in to his squeamish weakness. Though in the end he hadn't, had he, the cunning, two-faced swine! The Roman governor was the only man who had ever made a complete fool of Modan-mor.

When the snake had spared the hand so readily, he'd wondered why. The thought had crossed his mind that Trista was spreading her legs for him; he could find no other rational reason. But he'd rejected the notion at once. She might have done so to *get* him maimed, but certainly not to keep him from *being* maimed. It was all so confusing, and he needed to know. He had to know! Who was responsible: the dwarf woman or the governor?

There was good reason to believe it *was* the woman. From what the Roman had told him, the witch had been about to *give* him to his wife, less the hand, in return for helping her get back home. The very idea made him seethe: *give him* to his wife! Clearly the governor thought so too, for in less time than it takes to string a bow, he'd offered to send Modan off to cut stone at Calcaria – with both hands. At the time, he'd been certain the man was sincere. So what happened next was like a blade that did not fit the sheath. Modan snarled his contempt.

As he rode on through the night, Modan's mind repeatedly turned to the question of what, exactly, had happened. The facts, he reminded himself; always review the facts. Lagan was forever telling him that.

The Roman governor had met Trista, that was clear, for she was the one who had led the dwarf back to the fort. So later when he made the offer, the governor must have been plowing his wife or he'd gone soft. And Roman governors do not go soft – though at the time, he'd thought this one had. The man had come to the slave pen and offered him a choice – an unbelievable gesture: you never offer your enemy a choice! Not unless it's asking if he wants your blade in his belly or across his throat.

Yet once he'd taken the governor's option, oh, how the man had betrayed him! When Modan had realized that Calcaria was not the farthest corner of the earth, he could not believe the alternative: his life, with a whole body, and in his own land. That he was a slave meant nothing; he'd merely bide his time. If a warrior's heart beat and his body was whole, he would rise above his enemies. So he'd ignored the humiliation and agreed. And the man had betrayed him!

It was, Modan grudgingly conceded, a far crueler form of punishment. But he could not rid his mind of the thought that it might have been the dwarf woman, the healer, who'd had the last say.

That was ripe – the *healer*. The wee bitch had been getting even, as sure as gods made thunder. When he lay flat on the surgeon's table, gagged to halt the screeching and bound to stop the thrashing, he'd heard her name. The Roman who'd hacked his balls off had mentioned it not once, but twice, when bantering with the soldiers called in to hold him down on their lousy table. He'd recognized it in the middle of their foreign babble. Was it because she'd had a hand in what they were doing? Who had ordered it: the dwarf, or the governor? Or both?

The woman certainly nursed the greater reason for vengeance. He should never have let her go! Though he hadn't, had he? Trista had done that. And Treno, the fool, had allowed her to do it. He would be punished . . .

Yet Treno rode through the darkness close behind him, after helping Bryn free him from the Romans – which was the only good thing to happen since the ambush on the supply wagons. By the lips of Lug, small though it was, that had been a great battle – planned by him, carried out by him, and finished by him! Lagan had realized that, and willingly given credit. And that was another thing to wonder on: what had become of Lagan? Maybe he was dead. He hadn't asked, and Bryn had volunteered nothing when he'd set him free.

Bryn . . .

Modan smiled grimly, recalling his brother's confrontation with the Roman column. Bryn had freed him, yet the way it happened was not the way Modan would have done it; his brother's way of doing things displayed a distinct lack of balls. Modan winced at his own words, and forced a kinder image to mind; the one in which his brother had magically appeared from nowhere . . .

The small Roman column had been midway between two of their forts, where the road turned eastward and climbed into the great, barren hills that divided Brigantia in two. Bryn had ridden slowly from a large stand of stunted trees as the column passed by, his face concealed with a layer of soot and his spear peacefully slung. Once in view, he halted his horse and sat calmly in the saddle, waiting.

The result was predictable: Roman officers shouted orders, the column crashed to a halt, and the Roman soldiers quickly closed ranks, facing outward with their shields and weapons at the ready. It was no coincidence, Modan realized, that when the column stopped, Bryn's horse stood opposite the small contingent of slaves wedged in the centre. Several auxiliary cavalrymen quickly galloped out to confront him.

At the time, Modan had no idea who the rider was; he thought it might be one of Lagan's men. Though whoever it might be, he suspected he was the reason for the man's presence. What the stranger said seemed to confirm that notion: "I want to buy one of your slaves."

The resulting gabble was hard to follow, but Roman voices prevailed; they were loud and hard, clearly believing they were in command. Bryn quietly raised one hand, waving it lazily forward. A small army of tribesmen oozed from the forest on either side of the road; many mounted, but most on foot. Unlike other times, however, they simply stood in the shade of the trees, staring silently at the Roman column. The image remained vivid in Modan's mind, and he laughed bitterly at the feeling of triumph he'd felt, despite the vicious loss of his . . .

Modan shook his head and focused again on the memory. The air had been sharp with a fresh, morning crispness. Steam rose from the hides of a hundred horses, each one's muzzle a cloud of mist. More than twice as many warriors stood spaced between, each one menacingly quiet, his weapon just as ready as those of the Romans. The odd silence was pierced only by the impatient snort of the horses, and the soft chatter of voices – most coming from the Roman side. *That would have been the moment to charge down and slaughter the whole lot of them!*

"As I said, I want to buy one of your slaves," Bryn repeated, and this time Modan recognized the voice. "Perhaps you should fetch the officer in charge."

Modan had grinned for the first time in weeks, and nudged his neighbour. "That's my brother."

The senior centurio was not long in coming. Bryn remained unruffled as the man neared, even going so far as to yawn, which Modan found hilarious. His glee must have shown, for his brother caught his eye and glared a warning. It was enough to stay Modan's tongue while the two men spoke.

"As I told your men, I'd like to buy one of your slaves," Bryn replied in answer to the centurio's question. "And as to my friends," he gestured absently behind him, "they're not here to fight." He smiled, his teeth glistening white against his blackened face. "I do, however, see that they clearly outnumber yours – though I'll concede a slight edge in discipline."

"Which means you are at a severe disadvantage," the centurio growled.

"Perhaps, perhaps not. I would point to the archers and the slingers." Bryn nodded to where fifty or more men had slipped quietly onto the road, and now confronted the Roman column at either end. "While your men defend themselves against my friends, they will also need to ward off a few stones and arrows. I would guess this might whittle your edge in discipline. In fact, I'd guess it might be completely lost."

The centurio sucked on his lower lip, saying nothing. Bryn continued. "I really don't want to lose any men getting my slave back, but I will. And you'll lose men in turn. Who knows, maybe all of them and the slaves too, which would leave me still in possession of my coin, and with my slave back. But as I said, all I want to do is purchase him. Here." Bryn tossed a leather purse to the Roman. "There are a hundred *denarii* in there, which is more than sufficient for a poorly trained slave, taken on a battlefield . . ." again the glare toward Modan ". . . who really isn't worth two quadrons."

The centurio opened the purse and peered inside. If Modan knew his brother, there had been at least double that amount there. As if to prove as much, the Roman licked his lips, weighed the purse in his hand, and grinned. "You want another one? I could sell you two."

Bryn chuckled. "Just the one." He pointed, saying loudly, no doubt for his brother's benefit, "I want that ugly, yappy lump that's got balls for its brains."

Modan had flinched at Bryn's choice of words, convinced that every last warrior standing there knew the horrible truth. But Bryn had not mentioned his manhood again in the half-day or so before leaving him to the company of Treno and the others. Nor had Treno breathed a word about his humiliation, which he surely would have if he knew, for the man was fond of ridiculing anyone he deemed lesser than himself. Everyone had treated him as if . . . well, as if everything was normal. Yet he wondered. He would always wonder.

## Chapter XVII

## Eboracum, Junius, A.D. 105

Three men appeared from the damp, swirling mist that clung to the banks of the river Abus chilling the evening air. They came by way of a narrow, well-worn bridle path that traced the river's bank. Their presence was unusual for it was a local track, used mostly by those who lived farther downstream with business up at the Roman fortress. The three trod softly on the hard-packed dirt, yet their manner was not covert, as if trying to avoid notice, but light and casual – an easy, loping stride that was as natural as deer coming to water.

Cian stirred and eased his rear on the wood-slab bench, watching through half-lidded eyes as the silent figures made their way along the edge of the river. The three would pass by a good hundred yards away, where the trail marked the limit of his small farm, and then they would be gone. Eboracum lay a mile upstream, on the far side of a second, smaller river, the *Fosse*. The Roman stronghold was likely their destination. But despite the likelihood, Cian was filled with an odd certainty that it was not.

"They'll be coming here," he murmured, as much to himself as the man who lounged alongside. He watched the three figures drawing near to where a well-worn, graveled lane led from the river landing to the farmhouse.

"Huh?"

"Clean your lugs out. I said they'll be coming in here," Cian growled, louder this time. He glanced sideways in time to see a yawn split Luga's huge face, creating a great, gap-toothed cavern almost lost in his friend's grey tangle of beard.

"Who?"

"Those three, you blind blob." Cian nodded toward the river.

The trio halted at the place where the path met the lane. They all began talking, as if the two men sitting on the bench were not there. Then one pointed toward Cian and Luga, and not long afterward they seemed to reach agreement. They turned as one and walked down the lane, the one who had pointed lagging several steps behind.

Cian shifted slightly on the bench, one hand sliding backward to be sure the felling axe was still where it should be. Luga belched and sat upright, his arms casually crossing an ample belly, his fingers brushing the haft of a large knife that hung from his belt. Life along the Abus was peaceful, certainly, but only a fool took that for granted.

"A pleasant evening," Cian said in a neutral voice as the three men halted a half-dozen steps away, a safe distance that allowed him to remain seated and feel no threat. "It will be cold before the night is over, though."

"It's quiet enough."

Cian nodded his agreement as he studied the speaker: a man in his early twenties, stocky and red-headed and of average height, but plainly sure of himself. Like the others, he was dressed decently enough in finely woven britches, softly tanned boots, and a jerkin of thick leather and good cut that might also serve as light armour. A blade hung from his belt that was neither short enough to be a knife, nor long enough to be a sword.

The man standing to his right was younger, slightly taller, and seemed shy by contrast. The youth was smooth-faced, with a straight nose and lips that were perhaps a touch too much – Cian blinked, but otherwise managed to hide his surprise. The fellow was a woman! And if her hair wasn't cut so short, if her figure wasn't so well hidden under a layer of boiled leather, and if he could just wash his mind of that first male image then, Cian decided, she wasn't a bad looking one, either.

He quickly turned his eyes to the man bringing up the rear, as much to clear his head as anything. Though the fading light masked the fellow's face, he was plainly the oldest of the three by a good ten years. And despite hanging back and letting the others do the talking, he was plainly the leader. He stood tall and loose-limbed, his hair tinted by the crimson of the setting sun. Long, fair lashes shaded his eyes, giving him an almost lazy look. They reminded him of –

*By the red hairs of Dagda!* Cian's heart jumped as the truth struck home. Yet he offered no outward sign of recognition other than a slight intake of breath, and a sharpening of his eyes. How long had it been? Cian recovered his wits, which was no easy thing. He smiled, nodded in the man's direction, and in a voice calm enough that it surprised even him, he said, "So, Bryn, it's been a long while."

"Half a lifetime." Bryn smiled in turn, showing no surprise.

Cian hesitated with his next question, almost afraid to ask. "And your da? How's your da? You're not here to tell me . . . ?"

"That he's dead?" Bryn shook his head, and the smile broadened. "No, though he often says he might as well be. Claims he's been ridden hard and poorly groomed. He doesn't fare badly, considering. Aching bones, pees twice a night, but on the by and by . . ."

"He's not bad for a man of his age," the red-headed youth finished. "My da always said Cethen was a survivor. Just like yourself."

"So did his wife. The first one, that is." Cian laughed and turned his head toward the youth, for it suddenly struck him who the lad's da must surely be.

Luga was ahead of him. "So, Gavor, who *is* your da? Borba or Luath?"

"Either one. Depends who you want to believe." The youth grinned in a manner that Cian found both familiar and oddly sad; then the lad shrugged his resignation and his voice turned sombre. "Though I guess it's just Borba now. Luath passed a few years back. Something went wrong in his chest."

"I see." Cian nodded along with Luga, and both paused long enough to show respect. "And Borba?"

"A gimpy leg and a bad disposition, but otherwise fine."

"Good to hear, good to hear," Cian cried and pushed himself from the bench to offer a belated but proper greeting. Then he hesitated, recalling the trio's exchange at the end of the lane. He gestured toward the river and smiled. "Unsure of your welcome?"

⚜

Bryn strode forward and grasped the wrist of the man who was his uncle. He braced himself, ready to pull the older man to his feet, but Cian sprang from the bench clearly wishing to show he was as agile as ever, which was just as clearly untrue. Cian had certainly kept himself lean and trim, but the wrist in Bryn's grip was thin and, close up, he could see that age had cut deep into the leathered face. Cian's hair, tied back in a tail, was more white than grey. Bryn knew his uncle was five or six years younger than his own da, which meant he was something less than the middle of his sixties. So, all things considered . . .

"We left our horses downriver, hidden in the trees beyond the curve where we used to swim," Bryn explained, giving no more details than needed. "I wasn't sure how things stood here, and wanted to ask."

"So you came to see if I was still alive!" Cian grinned.

"No point calling on a dead man," Bryn shot back, though that was not the reason; he'd already determined that his uncle lived. He'd come to Eboracum because he'd been asked by the Roman governor, and he'd called on Cian mainly to see if he might know why. But that was not the whole reason. No, maybe part of the truth lay with Modan.

The road on which he'd freed his brother was the same road that led to Eboracum. He'd found himself almost halfway along it when he set Modan free to fly north with the rest of them, and it was as if the gods had intended him to continue. Or maybe they'd just made up his mind for him, for he'd been thinking on going anyway. So maybe it was the gods and Trista who set him on the journey, for she'd been prodding him to find out what the governor wanted since he'd told her. The woman no longer seemed wary of anything Roman. In truth, lately the woman seemed wary of very little.

"You left your horses downriver?" Luga rumbled in his deep voice. "You'll be lucky to find horse shit there tomorrow, let alone a horse. It's one thing to tempt, it's another to offer."

"The horses are well guarded," Bryn said, which they were, but Cian was curious enough to ask how well. And Gavor, much to Bryn's amusement, supplied an answer before he could tell the truth.

"The rest of the troop is camped there," Gavor said, pointing vaguely downriver, "which is why we're on foot. We didn't want to alarm you."

"A troop?" Cian almost yelped, glancing involuntarily over one shoulder as if he might see them. "You've got a whole troop of barbarian horse camped a mile from the fortress? Are you mad? What, by the black balls of Belenus, are you planning to do?"

"Keep my back covered," Bryn said, which was true, despite Gavor giving the lie with the numbers. There were only four others downriver, making camp. If Cian were to learn how many travelled with him, the lie might prove amusing. His uncle had taught him well: never reveal your true strength. Though of far more importance: never reveal your weakness. "And easy on who you call a barbarian. I'm told the Romans use the name on their own auxiliaries, whether they're retired like you or not."

"There's barbarians, and there's barbarians," Luga suggested blithely. "Up north, you should know as much."

Bryn flushed with irritation, but held his tongue on the big man's lack of tact.

"Roman bastard, Brigante barbarian, where's the difference?" Cian said, easing the awkwardness. "Protect your back from what, Bryn?"

"Treachery, I suppose."

"Treachery is inflicted by friends, not enemies," Cian said, "and I didn't think you had either, this far south." He chuckled. "Other than me, and I'm kin. Kin can be far worse."

"Treachery is practiced by anyone who seeks advantage," Bryn said, and nodded pointedly in the direction of the fortress.

Cian and Luga glanced at each other as if puzzled. "You have dealings at Eboracum?"

"Aye, the new governor had a message sent," Gavor broke in. "It was put out from one of the forts north of the Ituna. And by mouth, I might add," he glared at Luga, "figuring that *us barbarians* can't read."

"Which at least one of you can, thanks to a very patient pedagogue," Cian remarked dryly. "And for that, you're welcome, Bryn."

"All thanks be to the cavalry," Bryn intoned, and bowed his head toward his uncle. "The *verbal* message was that the Roman governor wants to meet with me and Da."

"So where is your da? Is he coming too?" Cian asked, smiling as if he found the idea amusing. So, apparently, did Luga, for a huge grin split his beard. Cian raised a hand as if to silence him.

"He sends his regrets." Bryn shrugged indifferently as the lie slipped from his lips. It was better than telling Cian that his brother couldn't make up his dithering mind; though on reflection, he was damned sure Cian would understand. "I decided to come here myself, and find out."

Cian looked doubtful. "With a whole troop of riders behind you?"

"Why not?" Bryn said, and because he seemed to be weaving a web of lies anyway, he offered an explanation that might prompt Cian to tell him more. "Da says the governor is not to be trusted. And besides, he doesn't see anything to be gained in meeting the man, under any circumstance."

"The governor is not to be trusted?" His uncle at first showed his surprise then he laughed, which Bryn found annoying. He felt as if he was being mocked.

"Yes, the governor!"

"Do you know who this governor is?"

"Yeah." Bryn gestured upstream toward the unseen fortress. "It's the same bloodsucker that started this, those many years ago." Then, remembering Cethen had told Trista that it couldn't be the same man, but only one going by the same name, he added, "Or some other Roman scum of the same ilk."

"Mmm, no," Cian said as if carefully considering his words. "No, I'm sure you've got that wrong."

"No I haven't." Bryn glowered in response to Cian's simpering smile. "Believe me, lad, you've got it wrong."

"The reason I know I didn't get it wrong," Bryn said through his teeth, "is because the commander at Blatobulgium wrote Trista a pass to stay over at their forts on the way down here, if we wanted to – which we didn't."

"With the name of the governor written on it," Gavor added.

"So you can read too?" Luga exclaimed, raising his eyebrows in surprise.

Gavor's cheeks flushed, and he pointed to Bryn. "He read it."

"I see," Cian said quietly. "And in doing so, Bryn read that the governor's name is Gaius Sabinius Treboni*anus*".

"Which means I'm right!" Bryn blurted, feeling vindicated. Remembering his da's stories of the Roman's malice in his previous years in Brigantia, he asked, "So have you any idea why this man might want to see me? Or Da? Hasn't he or his kin done enough harm?"

Cian seemed close to laughing again as he shook his head. Bryn's anger grew. Had his uncle become completely Roman? It was no surprise, he supposed.

But Cian's next words were insistent. "That is not the same man, Bryn. Honest. The man you're thinking of was here more than a decade past – and I suppose a decade before that, too, and twice before that." Cian chuckled and looked toward Gavor. "The first, when he was only about your age. That man's name was Gaius Sabinius Treboni*us*. Not Treboni*anus*."

"What's the difference? Us or anus?" Bryn muttered, now unsure of himself, though the question was still valid. "And why does he want to lay hands on me? Or Da? I was told that the fort commander who issued the pass didn't know – or at least, the messenger who gave it to us claimed as much. Is this Roman set on some cockle-arsed revenge, now he's in his dotage?"

"I told you, this is not the same man!" Cian laughed out loud, and Bryn fought the urge to thump him; instead his uncle thumped Luga on the shoulder, saying, "This is too ripe. You tell him why the mighty Roman governor wants to see him and Cethen."

Luga was equally amused. "My guess is that *this* governor wants to see you because he's your brother. Your da's son."

Bryn blinked. What was the great, over-fed oaf saying? The words played through his mind, as he stood with his mouth open in stunned disbelief. He was vaguely aware of Gavor cursing under his breath, somewhere off to the side. The lad's mind, like his own, was probably sifting its way through Cethen's children. Bryn had always known his da had fathered others. There was the girl Coira, whom he'd met when he was much younger. He'd been quite taken by her. And yes, there was Rhun. He'd been with the Roman army; the cavalry, in fact! But that still didn't explain how the son of a minor Eburi chieftain, a chieftain who had fought the Romans all his life, could become a Roman governor.

When Bryn finally spoke, it was if he was mouthing the words for his own ears. "So my brother . . ."

"Half-brother, actually."

"So my half-brother is sitting in a fortress, not a mile from here, acting as governor of this entire land that the Romans call Britannia?"

"Well, he's not actually there at the moment," Cian explained. "He's still on his way down from the fort that sent you the message. If you'd taken the commander up on his offer, you'd have probably run into *the governor*. But it seems that he finds himself held up at every outpost he stops at, and there's the best part of dozen between here and where he was."

"Which means, as he would tell you himself, he's been *unavoidably delayed*," Luga added.

"Which is not a surprise," Cian muttered.

Bryn barely heard them, still trying to absorb what it all meant. "My own da's son! The governor!"

"I do believe you now have a grasp on the matter, nephew," Cian said cheerfully, and glanced over his shoulder toward the farmhouse. Deirdre had struck a flame, and a soft orange light glowed through the open doorway. "I think you could use a drink, for there's more to the story."

"More?"

"Yes, more. Do you remember some of your other half kin? Rhun?"

"Yes . . ." Bryn cautiously cocked his head to one side, confused.

"If you want to get reacquainted with him, he's at Eboracum at the moment. He arrived this past few days. You'll be in good company until Tuis gets here. In the meantime –"

"Who the fuck is Tuis?" Bryn cut in, his patience again slipping.

Cian's eyebrows went up. "He's the governor."

"But you just said that Rhun was the governor."

"No, I didn't. Rhun is Tuis's older brother. Luga, you explain. But first," Cian turned to face Trista, who'd hung back, silent, as they spoke, "I want to know who the lass is. The short hair might give her the look of a foot soldier, but you can't hide everything." He openly gazed at her, eyes roaming from face to her chest. "Or," he added, now fixed on her woolen-clad legs, "that wonderful pair of stilts."

Trista stepped into the glow cast from the doorway and offered Cian a silent nod, but she addressed Bryn. "You warned me your uncle was a lecherous old bastard." She appraised Cian from head to toe. "I think you have the right of it – on all three counts."

# Chapter XVIII

## Eboracum, Junius, A.D. 105

Livia had never seen a fortress in such turmoil, and she suspected that her husband was a good part of the cause. Tuis exuded authority when striding through a public building – she'd seen as much at Londinium – and he displayed utter confidence when conducting the civil and legal affairs of Britannia from whatever public forum where he presided. Yet a quagmire of confusion always seemed to follow in his wake. Her husband meant well, and he certainly tried hard, yet something was clearly lacking.

She had known Tuis less than a year before they became married, and had never seen him in charge of anything but a horse or a house slave. He had held important posts before; Livia knew that and had been suitably impressed, but she had never been there when he was actually in charge. Now, in close company with Tuis as he bumbled through his duties as governor, it was bothersome to discover that her husband was, well, to put it bluntly, leaving a bubbling trail of chaos in his wake. This was particularly noticeable when in the cultured presence of the legate Appius, where her husband's provincial birth became more apparent.

Livia had come to know Tuis's mother to some extent. Elena was also barbarian born and bred, but there was little there that might explain his endless dithering. Perhaps it was simply because Tuis was the youngest? Whatever the reason, she couldn't set her finger on the pulse of the problem. Maybe she was too fond of the man, and had simply been blind to his faults; and now, perhaps, she was just blind to their cause.

His brother Rhun's brief presence had so far brought a measure of calm and order, which was proving positive, she supposed. His arrival might, in the end, also have a positive effect on the tension that had grown between her husband and the more erudite Marius Appius. *Now there was a man who maintained a correct, formalized chain of command.* Livia sighed. Perhaps that was her husband's primary lack: a decisive, orderly command of his underlings. Of course, if she was to be honest, Marius himself didn't make matters easy on that account.

Livia had noticed a certain vagueness in the way Tuis issued his orders, and there was a definite want of forcefulness in seeing them carried out. It was as if he wanted everyone to agree with him, and worried if they did not. *Personally, I never give a damn.* Yet he was quick of mind. The manner of his thinking was, for example, far more keen than that of his brother Rhun, but also far too flexible. Tuis's mind constantly juggled half a dozen problems and never dropped a one; but when that same mind did finally set those problems down, it was as if they were left to chart their own course.

Her husband was also drinking more than he should, and this evening, his first full day back at the fortress, was no exception. The meal in the formal dining area of Marius's attractive new residence had barely been eaten and both Tuis and Marius were well into the grapes; the governor of Britannia was growing garrulous, while the Ninth's legate spoke with calm precision. *If that man's blood contains a single drop of barbarian ancestry, then it surely predated Romulus.* Livia turned on one elbow to ease her stomach and yawned – and why not? The meal could hardly be called formal; in fact, it had been tense, utterly provincial, and extremely boring. Even Marius had proven tedious, with his obsessed focus on building his fort. Not for the first time, Livia cursed her judgement in accompanying Tuis to this barbarian outpost that was "the home of his kin."

When Marius paused for breath, Livia quickly shifted the conversation. The rebuilding of the fortress was clearly sensitive, though she doubted she'd find any topic that was not. "So is Marcus staying up there with his daughter?" She didn't care what the answer was, as long as it didn't include stone walls.

"He didn't say." Tuis frowned, either at the interruption or his poor memory; Livia couldn't be sure.

"I'm in need of more people at the quarries," Marius said, clearly determined to press on with his griping. "My men are using up the stone faster than it's being cut. If I could increase the output, we might complete the –"

"If your men are ahead of production, then some of them can be released for the business of soldiering," Tuis broke in, not hiding his satisfaction at the chance to pick. "Those troops from the Twentieth are now going back to Deva, because the legate's bitching about the *Ordivices* making trouble – again. That leaves me grubbing around keeping the northern outposts manned – again! Trajan's been bleeding us bare. Maybe I should send –"

"There's more than enough still left up there," Marius grumbled. "You proved it when we went wandering back and forth through the hills, and found nothing more than a handful of poor-quality slaves."

Livia saw Tuis's nostrils flare. She glanced across the low table at Rhun, who simply shrugged. *And that seems typical!* Rhun was far more composed than his younger brother, and would probably wait until the two came to blows before he interfered – and then, probably only if they tumbled over his side of the table. Livia smiled at the image, then pushed it from her mind. Not only were the two men growing more hostile, they were boring, boring, boring.

Tuis opened his mouth to reply and she spoke quickly, before he could throw *his* barb. "Your wife, Marius; is she not coming out here this season?" Livia forced a smile, and was surprised when the legate's mouth twisted with irritation. *That* question appeared to have struck a badly battered target.

"Our commander's wife prefers the opulent comforts of Rome to the rigours of the barbarian frontier." Tuis smirked, getting his barb in anyway. Marius flinched, and Livia winced.

Then the one called Cian, who was Rhun's kin and had been quiet so far, grinned as if ready to throw oil on the fire. "I can understand that," he said. "The trouble with the frontier is that it's full of barbarians. A person can't eat a decent meal without having them in your face, can they Livia?" His mouth twitched at the corners.

*Uh-oh,* she thought, and glanced quickly about the table. She was furious when Tuis laughed far louder than necessary, and Marius's expression turned as grim as a belly wound. Rhun looked as if he'd developed acute indigestion, and the only other guest at the table, the legion's tribune *laticlavus,* was busy feigning interest in the remnants of the pastries.

For once at a loss for words, Livia yawned loudly in the icy silence and hoped Marius or Tuis would take the hint that this meal was over. If her husband opened his mouth again, she'd stick a wine jug in it; and, as much as she respected Marius, if he started in on his infernal walls, she'd climb the damned things. Tuis opened his mouth to speak and she shuddered at what might come out, but a slave padded over and whispered in his ear.

"Bryn?" Tuis exclaimed. "Here? Now?"

"Tuis, you forget." Cian sat up and swung his legs sideways to straddle the couch. "Yesterrday, when you arrived, you told me to get him over here as soon as you were free. You said the earliest would be tonight."

Livia cringed as she noticed the careless manner in which Cian wore his under-britches beneath his short tunic – then she saw Marius's lip curl in disgust and realized his pose was probably not careless at all. The man sat directly across from Marius! Livia couldn't help smiling.

"Oh, that's right," Tuis mumbled, and glanced around the room as if puzzled. "The man's early. It can't be night yet."

*Equivocating as usual,* Livia thought, then wondered if perhaps her husband was simply laying the blame on Bryn for his own forgetfulness.

Or was her piqued imagination just running off with the demons?

"Actually, it is night." Rhun looked pointedly toward the open courtyard that lay at the centre of the huge residence. Slaves were firing the torches around the huge quadrangle, illuminating the fresh-cut sandstone columns with a soft glow that glittered silver in the flames. His face showing no expression, Rhun added, "Time certainly passes quickly when you're enjoying yourself, doesn't it?"

Marius glared, Cian smiled, and Tuis rose heavily from the couch. "Let's have him in, then." He patted his belly and made little effort to stifle a belch. "There's a thing or two we need to talk over, including the tragedy of what happened to his errant brother."

"I've wanted to see Bryn again – though less troubled times would have been preferable." Rhun smiled tightly.

"Yeah, well, better get it over with, bad news and all," Tuis mumbled, and frowned as if deciding what to do; then he patted his belly again and nodded. "Maybe we should adjourn to my quarters. There's a decent wine or two to be found there. It's far more agreeable for a small get-together." He ambled from the room, leaving the others to decide who was supposed to follow.

Livia glanced at Marius, whose face might have been chiseled from marble. Tuis had left the man dangling as to whether or not he was invited to the "get-together," an omission that was clearly rude. She was about to suggest that the legate follow, when it struck her that the snub was deliberate. Tuis had a lot of faults, certainly, but lack of civility wasn't one of them. In fact, she'd heard him assert more than once that if a man of manners was rude, you could assume it was deliberate. Livia sighed and decided to keep her mouth closed and her mind open. Perhaps that was why Rhun was so taciturn.

Marius remained grim-faced and showed little inclination to follow where he had not been invited. Livia decided it was perhaps best to stay and entertain the two males who remained at the table. The young tribune seemed absorbed in a long, sticky, cream-filled almond twist, so she turned to Marius. For lack of any other topic, she swore silently and said, "I see you've started on the foundation of the west wall . . ."

✣

Bryn had often been inside the fortress as a youngster when everything, including the walls, had been built of wood. Cian had never taken him into the main buildings on the *via principalis*, however, and especially not inside the commander's residence. It hadn't occurred to him until now that his uncle – who had always been an awesome, powerful figure of authority in Bryn's young eyes – had no business entering them. Not unless he'd got himself into trouble, which his da had told him Cian was often apt to do.

Bryn stared about the reception hall as he waited. It was a large room with plastered walls painted with columns that looked almost real, and panels skillfully finished with intricate, straight-lined designs, all in a pleasing array of bright colours. The floor had been paved with neatly fitted squares of smooth stone also of varying colours, though not so bright. Bryn had never seen the like of it, and it intimidated him, though he was determined not show the least sign – either to his companions or the Romans.

Gavor didn't seem to care what the others thought. "I don't like this," he muttered, shifting nervously on his feet.

"Maybe we should leave." Trista's wary eyes turned back to the entrance, but just then the flip-flop of sandals echoed from inside the residence. The slave who had greeted them reappeared and beckoned them to follow.

The governor's quarters lay on the far side of a large courtyard, its centre a disorganized square of damp, freshly seeded loam and stone paving blocks waiting to be set. The slave led them around the shadowy portico, where a score of flickering torches cast light on the new stone walls. They approached a set of open doors and Bryn heard several voices speaking inside, followed by a burst of laughter that died when the slave appeared in the entrance. He ushered them through and retreated once they were all in the room, closing the doors behind him.

Bryn noticed Cian first, who simply nodded a greeting. He stood alongside another man, who quickly stepped forward. This one was tall enough to look him straight in the eye, and had clearly spent time as a soldier: his fair, grey-flecked hair was cropped short, and he had the same lean build as Bryn. The man said nothing, but his face was vaguely familiar . . . *Rhun!* Bryn grasped the proffered wrist firmly in the Roman manner as they each spoke their name – it *was* Rhun. The man seemed shy or reserved; either way, he was as sombre as a *libitinari*.

His eyes turned to the only other person there, a man not much older than himself who had remained on one of the couches, watching carefully with the same expression as Rhun. Bryn began to feel uncomfortable; none of the sombre faces had shown so much as a smile. This last one could only be the governor. His short-cut hair was darker than the others', a deep brown touched with grey at the temples, and his ample girth spoke of too much Roman food, or too little Roman discipline – or both. Yet the man wasn't so much fat as well covered. What, by the beard of Belenus, should he call him? Gaius Sabinius, or Tuis?

"Gavor. This is Gavor." Bryn deferred the choice by pushing the youth forward. "Rhun, I believe you knew Borba, his father. And here," he turned and took Trista's arm, pulling her closer, "is our brother Modan's wife, Trista."

The grim smile that had briefly filled Rhun's face at the mention of Borba faded, and everyone grew suddenly, inexplicably, more solemn – even Cian. Bryn stood perplexed, watching carefully as the three men exchanged glances that might have preceded a death sentence.

Tuis rose to his feet, his features set in those reminiscent of a paid mourner. He walked solemnly over to Trista and, placing both hands on her shoulders, moved his head slowly from side to side as if his last friend had died. "My dear, I apologize. I didn't recognize you. The cropped hair, your clothes, the light . . ." Again the slow, sombre head shake. "I'm afraid I have bad news." His eyes slid sideways to Bryn, his expression unchanged. "And for you too, I'm afraid."

Trista's face went slack with shock. "What's happened? Cethen?"

"Cethen?" Tuis blinked in surprise. "Er, no. It's your husband."

*They know about Modan!* Bryn instinctively glanced toward the door, but had the sense not to move. Yet when he thought on it, it couldn't be that. Tuis – or Gaius – whatever his name was – looked sorry for Trista and Bryn, not pissed over Modan's escape. Had they caught Modan? Had they killed him? None of it made sense.

"Modan?" Trista whispered, and Bryn saw that she was as baffled as him. "What . . . ?"

"Yes, Modan. I'm afraid he's dead."

"Dead?"

"Dead." Tuis solemnly shook his head. "I believe you were aware that he was part of a contingent of slaves sent down to work the quarry here.

The tally shows that he died on the march. Some sort of an infection. Likely from . . . er . . ." He glanced almost guiltily at Rhun, then licked his lips. "It was probably from a wound previously received. Perhaps it opened up again with all the walking. I'm sorry."

The centurio! The crafty sod must have used part of the money to bribe the slave master! Bryn relaxed, but just for a moment. *Trista!* He stared at her face, which at the moment looked dumfounded. So far that was good, but what would the woman say?

Trista didn't disappoint. "Oh no," she cried, one hand going to her lips as if in shock. Bryn sighed with relief, but she continued. "Where is he? What did they do with the body?"

Bryn squirmed, willing her to stop. The Romans had Modan listed as officially dead – which was a good thing. Don't poke at the grave, or they might go looking for it!

Tuis looked decidedly uncomfortable and removed his hands from Trista's shoulders, clearly at a loss for words. "I never asked," he mumbled, then shrugged helplessly. "I mean, officially he was just a slave."

⸸

Later that evening in the comfort of the reception room, Rhun watched in amusement as Tuis and Bryn talked. The pair could have been two Roman politicos, each interested in preferment. Tuis was clearly at ease with this sort of thing, certainly more than when leading Roman troops; yet Bryn was clearly no lamb awed by the wolf. Nor did he seem to find the water overly deep on matters involving the military. But there was something bothering the man, something deeper.

What Tuis wanted of him was, on the surface of it, both easily explained and nigh on impossible: stop your people fighting, and make them pay their taxes. There was nothing better for Rome than peace and quiet and taxes, though Rhun found the "peace and quiet" part amusing. *Whenever the Romans are left in peace, they take advantage of the quiet and fight among themselves.*

As the talk ran on and Tuis laid out the details of what he wanted, Bryn seemed to grow more uncertain, and Rhun thought he knew the reason. Bryn didn't have the influence within the tribes that Tuis imagined he had, and knew he was in no position to promise what was being asked. He might even be wondering why he was here at Eboracum in the first place, though Rhun had garnered the answer for that from Tuis. It was because of their da, Cethen, and his supposed reputation with the tribes, though Cian had bluntly stated that any such influence was greatly overrated. Rhun bit down on his lip, and wondered; the man they should likely be talking to was Modan, and he'd just finished dying.

Yet he could see how Bryn might give an impression of influence in the north, and it wasn't something he did on purpose. His half-brother had a presence about him that made you like him; he was the kind of man you instinctively trusted, and he was bright – there was no doubt he was bright. It was in his eyes, and in the way he measured his words before speaking. Perhaps, especially with Modan now gone, Bryn might be the one who, with proper support and direction, could bring some sort of order to the tribes. Maybe with a little help . . .

Tuis took a stiff pull on his wine glass and stared hard at Bryn, as if fumbling to draw his own conclusions. "Tell me," he said abruptly, "what do *you* want? As far as your standing within the tribes?"

The question clearly caught Bryn by surprise. He glanced quickly at Trista as if expecting to find the answer there, which was interesting, Rhun thought, considering she had just received news of her husband's death. Was there something there? Had something been there before? Both Trista and Gavor had said little while Tuis and Bryn exchanged words, but then, both he and Cian had sat in silence, too. Everyone seemed to be listening.

"I . . ." Bryn began.

Trista interrupted. "Bryn will claim his rights with the Carvetii. He has them, as you know, through his mam. He's prepared to take up the burden, but that's how he views it: a burden." Her eyes shifted between Tuis and Rhun, as if to be sure she had their attention. "I think everyone knows that his mother was a Carveti chieftain in her own right. Had she remained in Cumbria, she would have been *the* chieftain – like Cartimandua was to the Brigantes. Her brother Frevan filled that place instead, even before she died; but he's now ailing, and badly. Bryn, if he cares to," she looked pointedly at him, her stare almost a glare, "could take his place."

"And if he doesn't?" Tuis asked as if Bryn was not there.

"Then he's a fool, and the tribes will be the poorer for the loss," Trista said, and leaned back with her arms folded, staring at Tuis as if that was the end of it.

"And are you a fool, Bryn?" Tuis asked blithely.

"We're all fools," Bryn replied, his mouth curled in amusement. "We're human, and we don't always do what's best for us. For example," he inclined his head toward Tuis and Rhun, "you're both here, when you could be elsewhere enjoying a far better life. But you're both back in Britannia for your own reasons, at least one of which is duty. And I could name another." One more nod of the head, this time toward Cian. "This is the land of your birth. Like Cian, you don't easily wash that from your mind. A person can't help what he feels, and that's a curse. Which leaves me, I suppose," he bowed his head to Trista, "who decided long ago to pick up my mother's shield, but only when my uncle – who's a good man – is ready to let it go. I've just never said as much to anyone, including Trista. Doing so before the time is ripe can prove hard on a man's well-being – such as sleeping safely at night." Bryn stretched his arms, sighing as he finished. Was it a sign he'd had enough, and wanted to leave? The lad must be finding this all hard on the mind. "So there you are. I imagine that makes me a fool, too."

Trista turned her gaze on Bryn and smiled, but said nothing. Tuis, however, smacked a hand on one knee, clearly pleased. "Then the sooner we can agree on a few particulars, the better. It helps immensely to work with people you can trust."

"I certainly agree with that," Bryn said, his face blank.

Rhun caught the dryness in his voice and would have placed odds that Bryn was feeling like a rabbit before a fox. He glanced at Tuis, who seemed eager to continue. Yet there was ample time, surely, to discuss the "few particulars" tomorrow, when they were all the more alert and Tuis hadn't been so deep in the grapes. Rhun was more curious about Bryn himself. He smiled to show his interest. "Do you have a woman? Are you married?"

When Bryn smiled back, it was sardonic. "Came close once. No, I suppose it was twice. The same woman. She didn't wait for me the first time, and died a matter of weeks before the second, when she finally changed her mind."

"I'm sorry," Rhun said, and he was. But the man had a future, and was at least fifteen years late in siring sons.

Bryn shrugged it off. "Such things happen."

"And when you do pick up your uncle's shield? A chieftain wants sons," Rhun persisted, expecting to see at least a quick, covert glance toward Trista.

Bryn's eyes never so much as flickered. "One of these days. Who knows?"

"Then you'd better hurry. Some men your age are bouncing grandbairns on their knees," Tuis said, and laughed loudly. "In the meantime, the important thing is, we should be making arrangements."

"Sir, I agree, whole-heartedly." Bryn quickly climbed to his feet, plainly turning Tuis's words to a means of escape. "But my men will be expecting me. I don't want them stumbling about in the dark, and finding trouble. Perhaps tomorrow would be a good time. If you would excuse us?"

"Uh..."

"That makes sense," Rhun said before Tuis could speak. Bryn clearly needed air, and time to think. He sympathized with the man; his chest was likely as tight as a drawn bow. The lad was probably overwhelmed. Too often in his early years he'd felt the same way, and always in the presence of some overpowering, higher-ranked, officious Roman officer – other than Tuis, of course. Your kin can never awe you; you know them far too well.

They made their way back around the portico, the clatter of their footsteps echoing off the flagstones. The torches had burned low, and the stone blocks of the covered walkway glowed dim in the light of the fading flames. Rhun, as he was wont to do, trailed behind with his brows furrowed in thought. He wished his sister, Coira, was here. Between them they carried a burden, a heavy one, placed on them by their da. For the first time his mind played with the notion that here might be someone to rid them both of the torque.

He almost stumbled over the threshold as a further idea popped into his mind. There remained another side to that blade: his da was still alive, wasn't he? His da was the one who'd left them the responsibility of the neck ring, and the superstition that went with it! At the time, Cethen had figured his odds of survival were about the same as a bull's at *Beltane*. But from what Rhun had been told, his da was very much alive. Perhaps the reasonable thing to do was let his da decide what to do with the gold torque of Brigantia.

Rhun reflected on the idea as they crossed the reception room to the main door of the residence. Perhaps, on second thought, his da could *advise* him what to do with the torque.

⸸

Tuis felt uneasy as he returned to his quarters. Too many frayed ends were left dangling and in sore need of being tied. But at least one matter sat easier on his mind: this half brother did not appear to have been involved in the attack that took place by Blatobulgium. He'd figured as much when Bryn had actually shown up; the man wouldn't have dared to do so had he been involved. Though having now met the man, he felt more comfortable. On reflection, he supposed asking him here had been like a test, though at the time it hadn't been intended as one. Yet now, the same test probably applied to his father. Would Cethen dare come down here to Eboracum? The brief discussion held tonight had left him feeling easier about his da, Tuis supposed, but it would still be better to meet up with him. And as for those frayed, dangling ends, a very minor one might still be taken care of before retiring . . .

He decided to stop by the residence dining room before retiring, on the off chance that Livia remained there; if not, perhaps Marius might be. He felt a trace of guilt for abandoning the man in the interest of talking to his kin, and some sort of apology would do no harm. Not that he felt sorry for Marius, because the man could not conceal his distaste in their own dealings – or with any others that involved his barbarian relatives.

When he looked inside the dining room, however, only the menials were there, clearing up the mess, and Zoticus, who was stuffing his mouth – no doubt with the more expensive leftovers. "Didn't you eat earlier?" Tuis growled.

"Mmmm, yes sir. Thank you, sir," Zoticus mumbled, spraying pastry crumbs as he jumped to his feet. "Evening dispatches came in from the south, and there's one from Londinium I thought you'd like to see." A grin puckered the clerk's scarred face. "I was sort of passing time till you came back."

"Yeah, I see that," Tuis muttered, and sighed. "I suppose it's bad tidings?"

"Not really. Or I don't think so, sir," Zoticus said, and held out a single scroll. "The last part at the bottom."

Tuis clutched a hand to his forehead, feeling a headache coming on. "Never mind. Give it to me in ten words or less."

Zoticus airily waved one hand as if the matter was of little importance. "Procurator Cronus and his gang of thieves confirmed they are arriving in three days."

"C-Cronus? Shit!"

"Weren't you expecting him, sir?" Zoticus looked confused.

"I'd forgotten," Tuis said, his voice barely a whisper. Cronus was the last person he wanted to see – not after what he had in mind with Bryn. Bryn was a man he hoped might help bring order to the north, perhaps broker some sort of agreement among the tribes; an agreement that, for once, might last more than a month. How could he raise taxes at the same time? When Cronus was through twisting his rope, he'd have the barbarians screaming all the way to Graupius.

# Chapter XIX

## Blatobulgium, Junius, A.D. 105

Jessa resumed her work at the small infirmary against her father's wishes, insisting that the small rectangular building remain where it was, in the heart of the nearby village. Marcus, since he couldn't persuade her to cease her "foolishness" and wasn't ready to order her to stop, offered to build a larger structure near the shelter of the fort's walls – specifically, close by the main gate. But with Modan dead, there seemed little point and Jessa was persuasive; or, as Marcus phrased it, the more obstinate and stubborn.

Elva, a pretty, grubby-faced child of around six whose clothes were soiled from playing in the mud, was the first to bring warning. Her mother followed on her heels, a young woman Jessa knew well, barely old enough to have birthed the child. Both mother and daughter talked ten words to a finger, and at first Jessa could not understand. Then she heard the phrase "that surly-looking brute with black lines all over his face," and she knew it had to be Treno.

At first she wasn't alarmed. She'd dealt with Trista's brother before, and could do so again. Though this time she probably wouldn't have to; he was likely sneaking down from the hills to deliver some kind of message. It had been some time since she'd heard from Trista, and Treno was, after all, her kin. Any word of the woman would be welcome. But then Elva's mother shook her head vigorously and cried, "Aye, but the one whose leg you fixed is with him."

"Modan?" Jessa blurted. He was dead! "Are you sure?"

"Aye, I couldn't believe it either." The woman nodded eagerly, as if perversely pleased at bearing bad tidings. "It's 'im. I seen 'im from the top of the hill. They all stopped their 'orses to talk. He's the same one that the Romans led away."

"It can't be," Jessa cried, yet instinctively she knew it was true. Cursing under her breath, she fled toward the door; but the rush of hooves pounded the dirt outside, and she backed away. Why, oh why, had she placed no bar on the fool thing? She glanced wildly about the large room, but saw no escape. There were several window openings, certainly, and the shutters were ajar, but the clatter of horses was everywhere. There was nothing left except the ladder up to the loft at the rear. "Be quiet. Not a word," Jessa whispered and ran to scramble up the ladder.

The infirmary had been built by the fort's soldiers, and it was solid. It was also practical. The sloped roof was weatherproofed with shaped wooden slabs that served as tiles. A hatchway gave access to that roof, large enough to take a man and low enough on the slope to make it easy for him. She pushed the cover upward and away, and clambered through the square opening as the door crashed in below. A loud, angry voice roared through the hospice.

Wondering what, if anything, she had gained, Jessa spread her arms for balance and teetered up onto the roof's ridge. With a strength born of panic, she tore off a length of ridge cap about half her height and, carrying it like a cudgel, stumbled back down the slope. She glanced quickly down at a half-dozen horses milling about below, their riders all staring upward. In the middle of the gawping swirl of upturned faces, she saw Treno's.

Their eyes met and held, and each waited for the other to say something. What struck Jessa was his expression. Treno had not worked himself into a mob-induced fit, as had the others; he was calm, almost detached. He simply sat his horse, staring back at her; then his eyes dropped, as if in shame. Jessa blinked in surprise. Whatever was going on here, she realized, Treno was a reluctant accomplice. Not that the knowledge helped, nor did it seem to stop him.

Heavy feet pounded up the ladder. "What is happening?" Jessa screamed at Treno.

He stared up at her again, as if the answer was obvious. "Modan. He's inside."

"By himself?" Jessa asked, knowing the question was not only inane, but irrelevant.

"He said he didn't want no one else with 'im." Treno shrugged as if helpless.

Jessa screamed again. "Why?"

He ran a finger across his throat.

"Shit!" Jessa cried, almost in tears, for she knew the reason – and none of it had been her fault! It had all been a mistake. She glanced downward as movement caught her eye. A dark head was rising through the hatchway. Jessa hefted the piece of ridge cap and, with all her might, swung it in a wide downward arc, as if it were a barbarian broadsword. The impact jarred her hands as the wood slammed against the side of Modan's skull with a satisfying crunch, somewhere between his ear and his right eye. The dark head slipped back inside with yet another roar. Jessa beat down again and again, until a bloodied hand reached up and wrenched the makeshift weapon from her grasp.

"Treno!" Jessa called in desperation.

"I can't do nothing!"

Jessa edged away from the hatchway and looked downward. Treno sat his horse hardly more than a yard from the building, the top of his head about the same height as the eave. She glanced toward the hatchway. Modan was levering himself through the opening on both arms. Without bothering to look, Jessa whirled and jumped toward Treno. There was a loud *oomph* as her feet found his belly and slid sideways. Treno instinctively grabbed at her waist, and she found herself staring into a pair of startled grey-blue eyes that seemed enormous in the familiar web of whorls.

"This isn't going to help, girl."

"Why is the stupid man doing this?" Jessa cried, knowing the question to be insane. She tried vainly to break free of Treno's grip. "It will be his death warrant. And yours. And thousands and thousands of others."

"He don't care. It's revenge he wants. Though why he's so set on it, I don't know. He's mad, and there's no reasoning with him." Treno struggled to hold his horse steady as Jessa fought to break free. "Be still, woman! And don't blame me. I told him: 'Mod, you escaped the quarries, be glad of it. Killing her for being sent there ain't worth the outcome.'"

"Kill her, Treno. Now!" a loud, frenzied voice shrieked, making every man there pause and look. The screech *was* that of a mad man. Modan stood on the edge of the roof, a long knife in one hand, the forefinger of the other pointed at Treno. "Kill her!"

"Kill me for sending him to the quarries?" Jessa blurted, baffled. Then, as if nudged by a cudgel, her mind strung all the beads together on a single string. This was Modan's lie. The reason he was giving for his revenge! Treno, the others – they didn't know what had really happened at the fort hospital! Modan had figured he could kill her before she could tell. She looked into Treno's face and, in her fright, almost blurted the truth.

"Mod, come on," Treno shouted uncertainly; nonetheless, Jessa saw that a knife had appeared in his free hand as if by magic. "The reprisals will be like nothin' we've seen."

Modan, his face livid, slid down to the edge of the roof and appeared ready to leap after her. Near panic, Jessa yelled the first thing that came to mind. "Nobody knows, Modan. Nobody knows. Before I get killed, though, everyone will! Everyone, dammit, and the first will be those here. Right now!"

Modan hesitated, and Jessa cringed. Crouched on the edge of the roof, he loomed above her as if twice his size. Pushing out her words and not caring that she babbled, Jessa rattled on as fast as she could, one lie following another. "And even if I can't tell it first, it's all there, written in my notes at the fort. Along with instructions to tell your brother, your da, Trista, and everyone else in the north, should anything happen to me. So if you kill me or take me with you, it's out in the open."

Modan rose from his crouch, uncertain, but still teetering on the edge.

"I'll scream it out now! Long before you can jump!"

Treno stared down at Jessa, his face scrunched with confusion. "What are you talking about, girl?"

Jessa ignored him, other than to make use of his words. "You want proof it's a secret?" she shouted. "Then listen to Treno. Does he know? Do any of the others? Do you want them to know?"

"Know what, Mod?" Treno called up, his curiosity plainly piqued. Modan shook his head as if trying to rattle his brain into thinking.

"Nothing. It's nothing."

Treno would not be put off. He glanced down at Jessa and the knife moved up to hover alongside her throat. "Then why should I do as you ask, Mod, and kill her? It sounds like a good story. Maybe I should just tweak her neck a bit, and find out."

Jessa closed her eyes and groaned, not knowing whether to weep, laugh, or scream. If only Trista were there, she might have – Trista! Was that the answer? "Modan!"

Modan simply stared, clearly wrestling with the turn of events. Then, when Jessa again called his name, he grunted. That was something, at least; the fool *might* listen.

"I've got notes on Treno as well, Modan. They'll be read, too, if anything happens to me." Then, on the chance it might add the sound of truth to it, she added, "I have notes on quite a few people."

"You've got nothing," Treno growled, but the knife lifted, the hilt turning in his hand so the blade was upright.

"Trista is a good friend of mine," Jessa hissed between her teeth, low enough that only the two could hear. "Friends tell each other things."

Treno stared down into Jessa's face. She lifted her chin, her brown eyes hardening, her gaze steady as she fumbled to recall Trista's words. There had been vague, wispy notions that flitted through her mind, and now they were slowly settling into place. Trista's words had once stopped Treno; would the hint of them do so a second time? Jessa just wished that she knew what, in the dark halls of Hades, Trista held over her brother's head, though she was beginning to suspect. She sneered, gambling on intuition. "Friends let each other know their pain, Treno. The inside kind of pain that haunts a person's mind."

Treno said nothing, his face stony as he looked first into her eyes, then up at Modan. Now both of them were unsure.

Half sprawled across the pommel of Treno's saddle, Jessa heard hooves pounding from the direction of the fort and her heart leapt; but a single rider galloped his horse through the village and jerked the animal to a halt in front of the small infirmary. "Foot soldiers coming. Riders won't be far behind," he shouted.

Modan cursed and ran for the hatchway in the roof. Treno still seemed uncertain, and Jessa knew there could be only two reasons for his hesitation. She sneered, desperately hiding her fear. "Kill me, or take me with you. Either is your death warrant, Treno. And long before that happens, both you and Modan will be shamed."

"Yeah, yeah," Treno growled and, grasping one of her hands, he pulled Jessa clear of the saddle and lowered her, none too gently, to the ground. Incredibly, as if everything was suddenly normal, he asked, "I don't suppose you've seen her lately? Trista?"

"Huh?" Jessa's legs were ready to collapse, and she could barely stand; yet there sat Treno, casually asking about his sister. The question and its delivery were bizarre, yet she found herself answering the man in the same manner. "No, haven't you?"

"Never mind. Lose yourself before Modan comes charging out of yon magic den," Treno muttered, pulling sideways on the reins and kicking at the horse's belly. Most of the other riders had already started along the lesser path that led to the northeast, the distant thud of hooves fading as she scuttled into the trees.

Treno and Modan had barely disappeared when the pounding gallop of horses again echoed through the trees, this time coming from the direction of the fort. A single rider appeared at the far end of the village, and a dozen more trailed well behind. The fellow whipped his mount toward her, careless of the few villagers who had wandered onto the dirt road now that Modan was gone. He pulled hard on the reins as he drew near and the horse jerked to a halt, almost shaking him loose of the saddle.

Jessa squinted upward, one hand shading her eyes as the animal skittered and circled. The rider was a clean-shaven man, an officer of some kind, who was hardly older than herself. His face was flushed from the all-out gallop, and his eyes peered off into the distance, clearly searching – too late – for her assailants. Jessa didn't recognize the fellow, which was odd, because she knew the face of every soldier and trooper garrisoned within the fort. She was still trembling with fright, though, and when she did finally speak it wasn't with a curbed tongue.

"What took you so fucking long?" she demanded, instantly flinching at the profanity. It seemed as if only a week ago she'd never sworn; now her nerves were such a dry bundle of tinder, it was as if every second word was a curse. Yet it seemed so appropriate . . .

"I was riding into the fort when I heard there was trouble." The rider glanced down at her, a long way down, and grinned. "I came as fast as I *fucking* could." Then his eyes switched back to the trail and he murmured, as if disappointed, "I see the barbarian has fled. Maybe when the others get here . . ."

Jessa couldn't have cared less, as long as the 'barbarian' was gone. "Well I'm glad you got here," she muttered, feeling her breathing ease and her pounding heart slow to a canter. Then, because it seemed the thing to say, she smiled and added, emphasizing the word, "And who the *fuck* are you?"

This time the rider laughed, inclining his head to acknowledge the rejoinder. He was a good-looking youth – no, a young man – with the sharp, casual, confident manner of his class that bordered on condescension. Jessa found it detestable. The fellow obviously held the same primped-up opinion of himself as every other cavalry officer she'd met – Rhun being the exception. The way he gave his name, as if it meant something, seemed to confirm as much.

"Kaeso. Kaeso Valerius Parvus at your service," he said, emphasizing the "Parvus" as he offered a flamboyant salute. "With the Tungri Gallorum, at Luguvalium."

Jessa snorted her annoyance. Parvus – *Little!* That was clearly a dig at her size. She was about to swear again, this time telling him where he could jam the effing spear he held ready in one hand, when she realized he was serious. For a moment she wondered how he'd come by the name, but as her eyes swept over the horse, she realized that the animal was a tall stallion – and Kaeso himself sat not so high in the saddle as she'd first thought.

"Well, Kaeso," she said, "there's little point in chasing *the barbarian*. He's long gone. Besides, there's not enough of you – your men, I mean. So, if you can force yourself, haul me up behind the saddle and take me back to the effing fort."

※

"I do not care," Marcus said, and on this issue, like no other before, he was determined. "I've already talked to the fort commander, and he's shutting the place down. You'll come with me, back to Eboracum."

"You can't, you just can't," Jessa cried, her voice emphatic. "The people rely on me. Not just in the village, either. There are others, from miles around. And it's good for the garrison, too. They look more kindly on the troops inside the fort when they're being helped. It wins them over."

"Yeah, I noticed that, rabbit. You're speaking of the same people who attacked your Uncle Tuis's column, *and* the supply train," Marcus said dryly, "then thundered in like a gang of apes and tried to murder you."

"They're not the same people, Da. Animals such as Modan and Treno are the apes, as you call them, who force the regular folk to do as they say," Jessa protested. "*Those* are the ones who need help."

"Perhaps. But I'm not going to stand by and see my daughter slaughtered just for their sake," Marcus said firmly, though he did retreat slightly on one front. In fact, knowing his daughter, he'd been prepared to. "The commander here does agree that some good is coming from your 'venture.' So, when we go, I'll leave a sum of money. He'll see that the building is moved in by the fort, and staffed by one of the orderlies. He mentioned three days a week."

"Da, please, I can't just –"

"That's it, my best and only offer," Marcus cut in, rising from the table. The meal was finished, and he wasn't going to linger for the sake of arguing with his daughter. He'd done that far too often over the years, as Tuis had pointed out. It was time to stop.

Jessa watched carefully as her father stood up, and bit thoughtfully on her lower lip as if gauging his resolve. Then her shoulders slumped, and she sighed. "How about six days?"

"Four, then. Four at the most."

"Five. Come on, Da, it's to help the people. Five days a week isn't too much for the goodwill it builds. Five?"

"Four!"

"Every second day, then," Jessa pleaded.

"Agreed. Every second day."

Jessa paused, her brow furrowed, then she shook her head in exasperation as she saw him smile. "Da! That's not fair. Make it four days a week, then."

Marcus chuckled and sat down again, deciding he'd won his point. Their leaving the fort did, however, raise the question of what his daughter would do next, and he asked her.

"What are you doing?" Jessa shot back.

"I certainly don't want to winter here, it's too cold." Marcus paused, making up his mind even as he spoke. There was a whim he'd been musing on for awhile, and this was likely the best time. "I may go home, but I've been thinking of visiting *Aquae Sulis*. Either way, I'd go by way of *Glevum*. I'd like to look in on the country to the west of there. Want to come?"

"Glevum?" Jessa looked puzzled. "Why all the way down there?"

"Just a fancy. It's not likely I'll find him, but there's an old bear there I'd like to hunt down."

Jessa smiled. "Urs?"

"Uh-huh. What do you say? We could both spend time at Aquae Sulis, even if I did choose to go home."

"Da, if I go with you, you'll be convincing me next to go back to Rome." Jessa shook her head. "He was your friend. I don't know if I even remember him. I prefer to stay at Eboracum."

"What would you do there, Jessa?" Marcus asked, but he already knew the answer: the same thing she was doing here. Admittedly, there would be a difference in dealing with the hostiles – a big difference. At Eboracum the Britons had grown accustomed to Rome's presence, and were starting to reap the benefit.

Marcus's mind turned to his brief stopover at the huge fortress earlier that summer, on the frantic ride to Blatobulgium in search of his daughter. The stronghold had changed much since his tour of command with the Ninth. An enormous dock had been built just downstream from the bridge, along with a row of smaller ones set on the gentler, side-water flow of the Fosse. On the fortress side of the Abus the usual clutter of warehouses, storage sheds, and shops had continued to grow, as had other, lesser structures that were seedy a month after they were built: alehouses, brothels, and a large, seamy inn catering to those who did not merit accommodation inside the fortress. And directly across the river, clustered along a paved road that rose sharply uphill on its way south, a village had sprung up, almost as fast as a field of mushrooms.

Yes, Eboracum was a far safer place than Blatobulgium, but Marcus still couldn't bring himself to abandon his daughter there. While he knew, as surely as the gods set the stars in the night sky, that Jessa was far from happy in Rome, he suspected she wasn't much happier in the land where she'd been born. She had simply found work there that occupied her mind, leaving no time to think of other things. But what could he do for her? Marcus sighed as he listened with half an ear to Jessa as she told him what she *would* do here. He'd heard it all before, of course, and in the end, as always, they'd reach a compromise.

"So the new hospice will be on the north side of the river, close by Eboracum's main gate. Understood?" Marcus said in a voice that left no room for argument.

"Uh-huh."

"And only for as long as Uncle Tuis is the governor here."

"Uh-huh."

"You promise? And don't *uh-huh* me. You promise."

"I promise," Jessa said, and when she saw her father wrinkle his brow, she added, "I promise I'll return to Rome no later than Tuis does."

# Chapter XX

## Aricia, Julius, A.D. 105

"He's staying there until summer is done," Gaius grumbled, casting the scroll aside without bothering to hide his disgust. It struck the top of the side table and rolled off into the grass. He glanced almost accusingly at Elena. The pair lay propped on a pair of lounging couches, placed comfortably in the shade off to one side of the peristyle. "With his daughter safe and his father ailing, I would have thought he'd be coming home as fast as he could."

Elena didn't know what to say, and tried to offer excuses. "Perhaps there are problems. Tuis did offer Rhun a posting, remember. I'm sure it was because was having trouble, and needed help." She shrugged, because her husband could draw his own conclusions as well as she could. "Marcus may have decided to linger and help too. There could be any number of reasons. Tuis said the tribes were causing trouble, when he wrote. He said that lately there were problems with . . ."

"When isn't there a problem over there?" Gaius snapped.

"Exactly," Elena agreed, nodding for emphasis. It was easier to agree than to spark another argument over "barbarian" politics. "Marcus no doubt feels a duty to be of use. And it is the best time of year to be there. The weather can be quite nice, if it makes up its mind."

"As compared to ours? Hah! That's pure wind!" Gaius snorted derisively. "And there's no shortage of that in Britannia. The wind and rain over there might keep the blood flowing, but it's not a place to linger. No, the boy's just caught up with himself and his own doings, and forgets who his parents are."

*As do you, it seems,* Elena thought and smiled as he lumped her in as Marcus's mother. The boy had never called her mother, nor should he;

his real mother was a woman named Helvia, who still lived somewhere in Rome, having recently outlived her third husband. Of late, Gaius failed to mark the difference between the two, which was yet another sign of his failing. She didn't bother to correct him. "The young ones have to carry their own shields, not ours."

"As a matter of fact, they don't," Gaius said, and laughed softly. "When I left Marcus at Eboracum as legate of the Ninth, I let him have my shield. Not that a legate ever really uses one, but you've got to have one as part of your equipment. You know, poor old Metellus carted the thing over half the empire, in his time."

"Yes, well I imagine –"

"Ouch!" Gaius leaned forward on the lounge and scratched violently at an itch that seemed to tickle at the inside of his left arm, then he fell back against the cushions. "Children," he muttered as he closed his eyes. "You'd think the ingrates could spare a little time. It's not as if we're going to be here forever."

A few moments later, as if he'd been pondering his words, Gaius added, "That's a given."

Elena smiled, and continued sewing the finish on a soft leather purse. The colour was a dark oxblood that would go well with the cream-coloured *stola* she'd recently had made. Though when she would wear either the purse or the stola, she had no idea. Neither of them had been anywhere of late, nor did they particularly want to go; Gaius because he was not yet ready and she because she simply didn't care.

"Having another busy afternoon, are we?"

Aelia's voice broke her concentration, and she looked up. The young woman was walking across the garden with a bundle of papers in her arms. Elena smiled. Long before Gaius had fallen ill, Aelia had become indispensable in running the Sabinius estate, most particularly when her father was posted away from Rome. Since his sickness, however, she had taken over his affairs completely, and without complaint. Yet Gaius still liked to keep one eye over her shoulder, even if it was only to agree with her every decision.

Metellus followed on Aelia's heels, flanked by two young slaves. One carried a chair for Aelia and the second a food platter that clinked, even from a distance.

"It's too nice a day to do anything," Elena complained, glancing at Gaius in concern, for despite his protests he hated what he called "the gory details" of running the estate. His eyes were closed, though; he was clearly off with the faerie.

"That's why I brought the chair," Aelia said, and slumped onto the seat as soon as the slave set it down. She ran her tongue over her lips, eyeing the platter. "It's too hot to work. But Father does like to know what's happening, even if he complains about it in the same breath."

The second youth set the tray down and placed a glass goblet beside each woman, which he promptly filled with cool, thinly watered blackberry juice. Elena looked toward Metellus, who was bent over Gaius, one hand on his shoulder. "Don't wake him yet," Elena said, and lifted the glass to her lips. "He's just gone to sleep. The juice will still be here when he's ready."

Metellus ignored her and jiggled Gaius's shoulder as if trying to rouse him. Annoyed, Elena opened her mouth to tell him to stop, but the old slave looked up at her, his eyes wide with disbelief. Then his features went slack and his eyes welled up. "I think he's dead," he mumbled as tears began rolling down his cheeks.

※

Elena and Coira hung back in the atrium as the last of the mourners trudged past the ornate couch that served as the bier, then quietly slipped out onto the street. Night had already fallen, the shadows made even darker by the close-packed houses of Rome. Slaves had lit torches and were handing them out to the paid mourners who would lead the funeral procession. Aelia, who stood by the open door, turned to assure herself that those inside the building were prepared. She received an encouraging nod from the image bearer. Then Titus, her oldest boy and the only male Sabinius left in Rome to help carry the body, smiled to let his mother know he was ready. The other seven bearers, all close friends of her father, stared somberly back, each offering a brief incline of the head.

Aelia licked her lips, clearly nervous, and looked askance at the libitinari, who had gone out into the street to ensure that the procession was ready. With a grave nod of his head he signalled that indeed it was, and she turned and waved the image bearer forward. The man slid a mask down to cover his face and moved through the door, holding the likeness of Gaius aloft before him.

Elena stared glassily at the painted icon that would lead the procession so that all who saw it would know who had died. Though if they did, it was hardly because of the image, Elena thought numbly as she turned for the hundredth time to look at the bier. The stern-faced man on the painted board looked nothing like her dead husband; nor, for that matter, did the corpse itself.

A loud, mind chilling wail began the moment the paid mourners caught sight of the image bearer, their eerie, high-pitched lament drifting in through the open doorway. Elena shivered.

"Farewell, Gaius Sabinius Trebonius, my father," Aelia intoned.

Elena heard the words as if through a fog, somewhere off to one side. The eight men bent as one and lifted the wooden poles that supported the heavy couch.

"Farewell, Gaius Sabinius Trebonius," Coira echoed from her other side.

Elena repeated the words softly as the bier was raised and she reached out, compulsively, to adjust the fabric that hid Gaius's face: a heavy, richly brocaded cloth of crimson and gold. The bearers, grunting with the effort, heaved the couch to shoulder level and moved forward carrying her husband's body, feet first, from the atrium onto the street. The musicians began to play, the slow, mellow tones of the dirge made deeper by the great size of the funeral instruments. Elena fell in behind the bier between the other two women, hardly aware of the hand that steadied her arm. Coira's, Aelia's, it didn't matter. Someone was there, and for that she was grateful.

The bearers moved into the space left for the bier in front of the door. A moment of uncertainty followed as the libitinari made sure that all were where they should be. Then, with nothing more than a brief nod, he signalled the procession to start. The image bearer, his step broken and slow, set the pace and the column of mourners slowly began moving toward the edge of the city. Behind him, the tempo of the music subtly changed to match his slow progress. The wailing voices softened to a dull, background drone, and the masked women mourners began extolling, in poetry and prose, the virtues of Gaius Sabinius Trebonius.

Heads tilted downward, the bier carriers fell into step. The three women, dressed in dull woolen cloth, their bodies unwashed and their hair uncombed, followed. The few relatives who had been near enough to attend the funeral came next, then a small column of family friends, most of them Gaius's. Metellus came last, trailing behind and leading the slaves who had been granted liberty by Gaius's will.

⸙

Aelia had decided not to seek an oration in the forum, even though Gaius would surely have merited the honour. It had not been her father's way to be ostentatious, and Elena certainly was not. Besides, the rite was hard enough on her stepmother as it was, and what was yet to come would prove harder still. She could see the signs beginning already.

The chosen *ustrina*, located just before the junction of the Appian Way and the Via Latina, was visible long before the procession arrived at its gates. The large ceremonial enclosure blazed with the light from a mass of torches that turned night into day. The column fragmented as it marched into the low-walled compound, the musicians and the paid mourners turning off to one side where they continued to earn their pay. The bearers trudged over to an altar-like funeral pyre of square cut cedar, and carefully set the heavy couch on top. Friends and family shuffled slowly forward, solemn and silent as if reluctant to move. As Aelia had already sensed, most of them all but ignored the grieving widow, now that her Roman husband was gone. They directed their low, sombre whispers to one another, or when the opportunity arose, to herself and her son.

Annoyed, Aelia moved closer to Elena who stood gazing silently at the cloth-covered body. She placed an arm around the older woman's shoulders and squeezed, a gesture that clearly showed where *she* stood regarding her father's wife. Elena reached up and placed a hand on hers, as if offering her own assurance. Aelia smiled and tightened her grip, aware of the tension. It would be senseless to ask Elena if she was alright; the question was much overused at these functions, and it was inane. Elena certainly looked alright, for the woman was too proud to look otherwise; but she and Gaius had been together, through battle and balm, for over thirty-five years. Her mind would be numb, and her insides dead; and, though she may not be doing so now, she would soon be contemplating what waited in the years ahead.

The music abruptly died and the wailing, which had risen as they approached the pyre, faded to silence. Titus stepped forward and gravely offered the oration that honoured his grandfather's life: his family, his honours, and his career as a much-decorated soldier who had served the corners of the empire; a loyal provincial administrator, a governor of Britannia, and an esteemed citizen of Rome. A man who had, Aelia was grateful to hear Titus say, been most fortunate – not only in his children, but in the choice of his wife: a woman of wit and courage; a woman as capable of wielding a sword and riding a horse as any man there, and who had done so more than once. Aelia squeezed Elena's shoulder once more in reassurance, and restrained herself from reaching over to wipe the tears that rolled down her cheeks.

Titus finished the oration and the libitinari moved to his side and handed him the ornate torch that would light the funeral pyre. Elena turned to Aelia, clearly agitated. She raised a clenched fist and said, "The coin. Are we sure of the coin?"

Aelia knew exactly what she meant. "I saw the libitinari place it."

"When?" Elena demanded.

"Well, I suppose it was when they were putting the final touches to his clothing."

"How much did you give him?"

"An *aureus*. I wanted to be sure."

"Then here, please, make sure again." Elena opened her fist, revealing another gold aureus lying in the middle of her palm.

"But . . ."

"Please. I don't want him to leave without the passage. He can't."

Seeing that Elena was near panic, Aelia nodded her assent and took the coin. She started toward Titus, but paused when she managed to catch his eye. He hesitated and edged toward her, the large torch held high as the newly lit flame took hold. When Aelia quickly explained, he took the coin, nodding his understanding. *May the gods bless you,* she thought of her son as he walked to the side of the pyre and raised his hand. The gold aureus between finger and thumb glittered in the torchlight.

"My grandfather was a great man," he began, his voice deep and loud. "He was also a generous man. When Charon meets him on the banks of the Styx, his passage across the rivers of the otherworld is assured. But, being the man he is," Titus paused dramatically and gently pulled back the red brocade, just far enough to reveal Gaius's mouth, "it was his wish, and his wife's wish, that he take with him more coin than is needed, to provide for the poor who follow."

He bent over the corpse, deftly parted the mouth, and placed the coin on the tongue. Promptly replacing the cloth and ensuring the head was turned away from the flame, he applied the torch to the lower beams of the pyre. The wood, treated with a pure, clear oil, quickly caught. Head bowed, Titus stepped away as the flames raced up the cedar beams, crackling and roaring as they quickly engulfed the couch.

Aelia, Elena, Coira, and then Titus moved as close as they dared to the intense heat, and tossed perfume, spices, oil, and Gaius's favourite foods into the flames. Others soon began doing the same, and the family eased back to allow them room.

Aelia turned to Titus, whose face had turned doubly grim. There was no need to ask, but she did. "Was it needed?"

Titus nodded, his anger gaining the better of his language. "Would you believe it? Some thieving bastard stole the first one."

Elena heard and sighed in relief. "Thank the gods. He'd have been at the river with no coin."

As the night wore on and the huge fire fell in on itself, the warmth and the wine seemed to mellow the small crowd. Some people, Coira noticed, finally made an effort to talk to her mother, presumably offering condolences which would doubtless ease their consciences the following day – if they bothered to think of them at all. But as the fire died, she glanced anxiously toward a row of *amphorae* that had been lined up like a rank of pot-bellied soldiers. The mourners had made good use of the tables of food, and of the more expensive wine that had been placed there in tall glass jugs. The large amphorae, however, which were filled with a much cheaper vintage, had been reserved for a far less civilized purpose . . .

Elena grew visibly agitated as the flames died to nothing more than embers, and several of the large clay vessels were moved closer to what remained of the pyre. Coira drew a deep, anxious breath and held on to her mother's arm. The most gruesome part of a Roman funeral was about to come, and she knew Elena all too well: the poor woman would be down on her knees as the barbaric rite played out, but not from any sense of expected duty; she would be there vainly seeking solace in the final ignominy of the foolish rite. As the thought crossed Coira's mind, the musicians again began playing, and the wailing mourners resumed their dirge. *And the Romans call us barbarians!*

The libitinari's slaves hefted the huge wine containers and began pouring the dark ruby liquid into a row of ornate urns. Elena, Aelia, and Coira began the ritual, each taking one of the small vessels and pouring the contents on the dying embers. One by one the other mourners followed, each doing the same. As the ritual continued, the air grew heavy with the sour, pungent stink of scalded wine. The cedar smoke quickly faded, replaced by clouds of hissing steam; which in turn, gradually faded to nothing more than tiny wisps, as the glowing embers became a black, mud-like mash.

When the last of the steam vanished, the libitinari crouched over the pulpy ashes and gently turned them with a brass rake, gingerly testing for burning coals. More wine was called for, some poured here and more sprinkled there, until he finally muttered his satisfaction. Solemnly nodding his head, he rose to his feet and beckoned Aelia forward. She hesitated, looking doubtfully at Elena, then at Coira.

"Mam, do you want to start?" Coira asked, deciding that was the cause of Aelia's uncertainty.

"Of course," Elena said firmly and glanced at Aelia, her face devoid of expression. "That is, if you don't mind." When Aelia nodded, Elena stepped forward into the ashes.

"The urn?" Coira looked about, uncertain of what happened next. She'd been to enough funerals over the years, but until you were actually part of one, she realized, you never quite know what to do, and when to do it.

Someone came forward – the libitinari again – with a low wooden stand that he placed at the very edge of the soggy remains of the pyre. Titus struggled forward and set a large, sculpted marble urn on top, its side inscribed with a dedication to the life of Gaius Sabinius Trebonius. Then, with his mother and Coira alongside, he followed Elena into the ashes. She was already down on her knees, with the chalky remnants of her husband's wet, ash-choked skull in one hand and part of a thigh bone in the other . . .

⸸

Elena stared down at the skull, half expecting to find it cracked across the top where Gaius had taken that first blow at Eboracum, what seemed more than a lifetime ago. Yet the only mark she saw was not really a mark at all but a hole, larger than a sesterius – the hole that had been drilled not long ago by the medicus. For all the good it did, the piece that had filled it seemed to have disappeared . . .

Elena sighed and glanced upward as a shadow fell across her shoulder. It was her daughter. No, it was both daughters, for Aelia stood there too. Numbly, solemnly, she handed them the skull and the bone to be placed in the urn.

# Chapter XXI

# Bravoniacum, Julius, A.D. 105

The journey back from Eboracum had at first been heart-stopping, but once Trista overcame her fear she quickly learned to enjoy the advantage. The time spent earlier with Jessa at the Roman fort had helped considerably, yet it had offered no hint of the power of Bryn's brother's word, scrawled like so many bird tracks on what he had called parchment. The small, rolled-up scroll was a faerie's spell that opened gates like magic, only no one had to chant the words.

The fort at Bravoniacum proved no exception, though by the time they arrived the routine had grown familiar. The guards at the gate took the document and scanned it with little hurry and much indifference. After a short but rude delay, one of them trudged inside the gatehouse carrying the scroll as if it was a bucket of stones. Trista giggled and whispered to Bryn that the man had gone to find someone who could read.

What followed was a repeat of their arrival at the previous two Roman forts. A centurio and a decanus hurried to the gate, both cursing the guards for their incompetence. Bryn, Trista, and the others were quickly brought inside, their horses stabled, and each of them housed in one of the many long wooden buildings that seemed to fill the Roman forts. Bryn and Trista were then taken to the officer's mess and provided with food and drink, courtesy of the fort commander, while Gavor and the other four men ate with the other ranks. It was as impressive as it was unnerving, but what happened at Bravoniacum after the meal was subtly different.

Darkness had fallen when Bryn and Trista left the officers' mess, trailing behind a junior centurio guiding them along a well-packed, torch-lit street. As he walked them past the headquarters building, he casually mentioned their destination. "One of the tribunes is on leave. The camp praefectus says he won't mind the pair of you using his quarters. They're right over there, across from the commander's residence."

The young centurio opened the door of a building that was at least ten rungs up the scaling ladder from a soldier's barrack block. Inside was a warm, comfortable sitting room lit by several hanging oil lamps. A small fire blazed in the stone hearth, holding the night chill at bay. Even though they had just eaten, a platter of food and a modest jug of wine sat on a side table covered by an immaculate white cloth. Someone had clearly been there ahead of them, someone who was anxious to please; though pleasing the governor was more likely a motive than pleasing his guests.

Elsewhere on their journey they had shared accommodation with Gavor and the others in pleasant enough quarters that had been far less private. Now, as she looked around, Trista's mind focused sharply on the centurio's words: *"won't mind the pair of you using his quarters."*

The man bid them a goodnight and departed, leaving Trista and Bryn gazing about in amazement. "I could grow used to this," she murmured, for the moment ignoring all other implications.

"I think you've got to be one of the herd bulls to get treated like this all the time," Bryn replied, casually shedding his cloak on one of several chairs scattered about room. He disappeared into a second room, also warmed by the glow of flickering oil lamps.

"That doesn't go here," Trista grumbled, and picked up the cloak to hang it on a row of pegs near the entrance. She turned to find Bryn leaning against the side of the doorway.

"There's only one bed," he said, his lips curled in a mocking grin. "It seems the Romans don't always have things well planned, do they?"

Trista ignored the implication and removed the cloth covering the food. She wasn't at all hungry, but she chose a large dark olive – a delicacy first offered to her by Jessa – and popped it in her mouth.

"These are good. Try one."

"I can't stand the things," Bryn complained, and tilted his head toward the second room. "It is, however, a very large bed. Our absent tribune doesn't always sleep alone, or he's a big man."

Trista glanced about the sitting room but saw nothing to indicate that anyone but a male lived there. "He must be a big man."

"I'm not a very big man." Bryn grinned and patted his belly. "In fact, I'm fairly thin."

"Then don't have any of this, and you'll probably stay that way." This time Trista decided on a square of crusty bread daubed with a fish paste.

"Fine." Bryn shrugged and again vanished inside the room, calling, "Good night."

Trista stuffed the bread into her mouth, snuffed out the oil lamps, and followed. There was indeed a large bed, its carved wooden frame filling half the room. There was really no alternative, she rationalized. "You can have the side against the wall."

"Not a problem," Bryn murmured, and started to undress.

Which was fair enough, Trista thought, but once his tunic and shirt were removed and he undid the belt that held up his britches, she said, "You're not taking those off, too?"

"I never wear anything when I sleep," Bryn explained.

"Then blow out the lamp."

"That wouldn't work."

"Why not? It certainly works for me."

Bryn glanced at the wall by the foot of the bed, where another row of pegs was set in a small recess. "No. I need to see, so I can put my clothes where they belong."

*That, from a man who can't even hang his cloak up.* "Bryn, I've seen better ploys by a stoat bent on taking a rabbit."

"Whatever." He slid his britches off and began placing his clothes on the pegs.

Trista felt her cheeks flush as she became suddenly, acutely, aware of Bryn's lean, naked body half-lit by the glow of lamplight. Behind him was a bed, clean and wide, in a room that was, for this night at least, theirs only. It was an image that defied reality, although it had many times been the focus of her imagination. Such a vision had frequented her thoughts when Modan was rutting over her body, his mind bent only on unloading his seed – which had never taken long, and had never taken root, either. And the same image had been there earlier, even before Modan, when she was younger and Treno . . .

Trista shook her head, vainly trying to clear her thoughts of them both, but she knew they were always there, forever lingering in the back of her mind – the one of Modan now the stronger for the guilt of having him gelded. Much as she might want to respond to Bryn, the passion, the urges that any other woman might feel, were either not there, or buried so deep they refused to surface. And she would die before being nothing more than a cow to Bryn's bulling!

"I think I *will* take the side by the wall, after all," she muttered and crawled across, still fully clothed. She soon had the blankets pulled up under her chin. Bryn turned to face the bed and her eyes dropped involuntary to his maleness, which was far from flaccid. "And as for that," Trista heard her cold voice say, the words sounding as if spoken by someone else, "if you're going to do anything with it, would you please try to be quiet?"

※

Bryn couldn't sleep. The faint glow of the dying embers seeped in from the far room, but that was not what kept him awake. It was his mind; it wouldn't turn off. The cause was Trista, of course, whose steady breathing from the far side of the bed was a harsh reminder of the fool he'd been. After all these years – years in which he'd forced any thought of the woman from his mind – he'd made a foolish, stupid, idiotic, crude, inept, childish gambit that had left him, literally, with his balls on the block.

He rolled over and watched the slow rise and fall of Trista's slim body on the far side of the bed. His movement caused the frame to creak, and the rope that cradled the bedding shifted. She groaned and rolled slowly over on her back, her chin tilted upward. A few more breaths and the soft rasp of snoring filled the room. Bryn smiled and reached over to pinch her nose. Trista stopped breathing for a moment, then her whole body twitched under the covers and she was wide awake.

"What the . . . ?"

"You were snoring."

"Who cares? I was sleeping," Trista whispered, and yawned.

"I couldn't sleep with the snoring."

"You couldn't sleep long before I started snoring." She yawned again. "And now I suppose I can't, either." A hand reached out and touched his bare chest. "Hah! You still living in hope?"

"I told you, I always sleep this way." Bryn paused for a moment but Trista said no more. "Since you're awake anyway," he ventured, "let's talk."

"It's not going to make a difference."

"It might," Bryn said, mildly irritated at the quick reply. "I want to talk about what Tuis and the others want, not about your virtue. Though in turn, I suppose, that raises the matter of your husband. We haven't spoken of Modan since we left Eboracum. They think he's dead."

"That won't last," Trista muttered, and rolled over on her side to face him. "It won't be long before he does something stupid, and lets them know he's very much alive."

"Fine then, so Modan will be out there somewhere doing whatever Modan does, which is boiling Roman bile. What do you think about Tuis and Rhun's suggestion, of working with the tribes? In a way, such a pact is almost tribal in itself: make an accord with one half of the family, while the other half does its best to pitch it in a cesspit."

"Oh, I don't know. I think it has merit. Modan won't win. Your da always said that fighting the Romans was a losing cause," Trista said. "Of course, what Tuis wants from you depends on the health of Morallta's younger brother. I don't know whether you caught the hint, but I'd guess that Tuis thinks giving Frevan a nudge toward the grave wouldn't hurt."

"Hah, that's the Roman way, not the way of the tribes."

"And hah to you, too, if you really believe *that*," Trista snorted. "Bryn, you shouldn't wait for Frevan to die before committing to what you're going to do. By then it could be too late. Go and see him. Find out how things stand. I think Tuis gave you some wise advice there."

"Tuis? Wise advice?" Bryn exclaimed, and rolled over to stare up at the ceiling. "That's amusing. Tuis reminds me of the man who said, 'Let me give you some advice, son; I'm not using it.'"

Nonetheless, Bryn forced his mind reluctantly to Frevan. Rhun had suggested that there was no point in picking up Frevan's sword without also picking up the one dropped by Venutius: the Carvetii and Brigantes, a tribe together. No one had ever done that before, though they had fought side by side . . .

Lagan surely longed to make that happen too, but he was Selgovae. If the man was to gain anything, it would not last long. No, the Carvetii and the Brigantes would hold sway, as they had in the past. They were already half kin and would live far better under a single thatch than ever Lagan's people could. Was it possible to have both tribes follow the same sword? And with Rome's constant meddling, always trying to divide, was it even worth the effort?

*It could work, at least at the tribal level!* Bryn thought ruefully, as he turned his head to stare at Trista and found nothing but further coolness. "You know, I don't know if I truly do want to. I don't mean take Tuis's advice – I mean pick up Frevan's shield."

"You sound like your da. Cethen could have led all of Brigantia, from the stories they tell, but he didn't have the ambition."

Bryn almost laughed. Cian and he had talked that one over many times, along with Luga, Borba, and a few others, some of them long dead. His father was a good man, Bryn had never doubted that, but had he been with the Romans, he would never have been promoted beyond *optio*. Cethen, like Luga, had always needed someone to follow. The greatest irony of his da's life was that, in killing Morallta, he had lost the one person whose lead had kept him on the path that created legends.

"Da was well liked, but he could never lead the tribes – which isn't a bad thing," Bryn murmured, as much to himself as to Trista. He placed both hands behind his head, which always seemed to help his thinking, and carefully chose his words. They would sound arrogant, he realized, but he believed them to be true. "I think that I can lead. I also believe I can muster the ambition. The question is, do I want to? Do I think it's worth the bother?"

"Well, aren't you the selfish sod?" Trista said, her voice sharp and angry.

Her words puzzled Bryn; that wasn't the reply he'd expected. "Selfish?"

"Yes, selfish." Trista raised herself on one elbow, her expression annoyed. "Bad leaders are far easier to find than good ones. The tribes, the people, they need the best that can be had. It's the only way they'll ever flourish. Yet all you can say is, 'I don't know if I want to do it. It's too much bother.' Aah, what a poor, wee, put-upon little bairn we have here, don't we?" Trista sneered. "I'll say this, Bryn. Cethen might not have been able to lead the tribes, but he'd have been proud to be asked."

Bryn said nothing, just gazed sightlessly upward. He didn't know what to say, and even if he did, he didn't feel like saying it. Trista slumped back down on the bed where, after a while, he thought she'd found sleep again. Then he heard her chuckle, but still she said nothing. Finally, irritated, he rose to the bait. "What?"

"I was just thinking," she said, her voice wistful. "You do, in fact, posses the most important qualification necessary to become the greatest leader the people might ever have."

Bryn again waited, but Trista was not forthcoming. He sighed, not hiding his annoyance. "And what, may I ask, is that?"

"You don't *want* the stupid job," Trista snapped, then rolled over as if trying to find sleep, dragging most of the blanket with her.

Bryn pulled it back, and smiled. He would guess there was some truth in what Trista said – though did the comparison apply to him? He did want to take over from Frevan, yet he didn't. So perhaps she was right; perhaps there was too much of his father in him. After all, his da had appeared to have it all in his hands at one time, and failed to do anything with it. Why would his son do any better?

At least one person had thought he might be able to do better: Rhun! His half-brother's final words before leaving Eboracum played through his mind, perhaps for the hundredth time. Words that had first left him stunned: *"If the right one is found to lead the people, it could very well be done wearing the golden torque of Brigantia!"*

He'd thought the words were meant as a tease and nothing more, but Bryn had pried the rest of it from him: how his own da had found the torque alongside Venutius's broken body the day the old king died. Its possession must have clearly gnawed at his father, for he had parted with it, passing it on to Rhun. *How many others would have used if for their own ends?*

And now it seemed that either Rhun or Coira had it in hand – or they had it hidden somewhere. Where, Rhun wouldn't say. But that didn't matter. His half-brother had the right of its worth: possession of the legendary torque might prove the balance in uniting both tribes.

Bryn blinked at the darkness, still unable to find sleep. He glanced sideways at Trista, and wondered if she was still awake. "You're not too warm with all those clothes on, are you?"

"Sod off."

# Chapter XXII

# Blatobulgium, Julius, A.D. 105

Cethen dithered for more than a week before setting out for Blatobulgium. He was first delayed in finding someone who would ride with him. As he told an exasperated Kelpy, unless you were a Roman horse messenger it was more than a day's journey, and the ground was hard to sleep on, and a man needed company. It was best not to ride the roads alone, especially these days, and the more company a man could find, the safer the journey. In the end it was Kelpy herself who left the children with one of the neighbours and rode with him. She found a young lad named Eb from one of the farmsteads who was also keen to go, for he'd never been farther than the end of the valley.

They arrived at the fort two days later and, much to Kelpy's aggravation, this proved to be two days after Marcus and Jessa had departed for Eboracum. The sharp side of her tongue lost none of its edge telling her da what his dithering had cost them.

The Roman commander, a man called Florian, seemed to find her annoyance amusing. "The Sabinius woman mentioned you might ride in here one day," he informed Cethen, and laughed. "She said it might take a year or two for you to make up your mind."

*Typical bull-necked, short-haired, condescending Roman,* Cethen thought; when dealing with the local "savages," the Romans had the tact of a mud hog. All the same, he found himself making excuses. "Jess might think that, but sometimes it's hard to get away."

"You know, it's funny," Florian continued, frowning as he stared pointedly at Cethen as if suddenly weighing judgement. "When you do finally arrive, it's not that long after a band of barbarian horsemen ride into the village," he waved one hand vaguely toward one of the walls, "and try to murder the poor girl."

"Jessa?" Kelpy exclaimed in surprise.

"Who would want to kill the wee lass?" Cethen muttered and slumped back in his seat, baffled. Nobody could possibly want to kill the girl. Absolutely no one! Yet, impossible as it may be, was he being accused of attempting her murder?

He glanced at the table where the old leather dispatch tube lay open alongside a curled scroll covered with a scattering of curly, squiggly lines. A second scroll, one sent by Tuis to the fort's commander, lay alongside. What did each one say? The scrolls had got them into the fort. They had also brought him to the attention of the commander, for he and Kelpy had been quickly ushered to the man's lodge and fed while awaiting his arrival. The leather pouch had worked wonders so far, certainly, but now this? Cethen felt trapped, but he was stunned by the Roman's next words.

"Your son," Florian supplied, his gaze unwavering.

"My son?" For a moment, Cethen was confused. "What about him?"

"Your son. He tried to murder her."

Cethen had four sons, but there was no need to ask which one.

"Modan?"

"Along with some tattooed creature called Treno; though it was your son who was bent on doing the murder. That's why she's no longer here – Jessa, that is. Senator Sabinius insisted she leave." Florian's expression grew wistful. "Which is a pity, really. She was doing a fair amount of good."

"Modan! I don't believe it." Cethen turned to Kelpy, looking for support, but she simply lowered her eyes. Eb sat staring at the ceiling.

"Of course, I don't think this has any effect on what the present governor asked me to do if you ever did come here," Florian continued, rubbing his hands together as if any lingering doubt had been resolved. "It shouldn't take long to put things together."

"This new governor," Cethen asked warily, for he had to know; he had to be certain, "how is he related to the old governor? The one from ten, maybe fifteen years ago; the man who made that old piece of writing."

"He's the man's son. I understand it was by adoption."

"And they also call him Tuis?"

"Yes." Florian smiled. "The senator and Jessa call him that."

Cethen cursed softly, for the first time truly accepting the possibility as fact. Elena must have agreed to it! And yet nobody, not even his own brother, had bothered to tell him.

"Is there a problem?" Florian asked.

Cethen couldn't bring himself to answer so Kelpy stepped in, placing a gentle hand on his shoulder. "This is the first time Da's really heard of this. Or at least, had it confirmed by someone who truly knows. You see, Tuis is Cethen's natural son by the woman who is the wife of the governor who signed that first parchment, years ago." She gestured at the scroll on the table.

Florian sat blank-faced, mentally sorting through the muddle of words. Then, as he grasped them, he leered knowingly. "I see."

"Not when she was married to the governor," Kelpy said impatiently. "She used to be Cethen's wife long before the Romans took her as a slave, north of Isurium. It was later on that the governor adopted Tuis."

Florian's face again went blank. Then he finally seemed to get it figured out. "I see."

For a while nobody said anything, then Cethen glared suspiciously at the Roman commander, remembering his earlier words. "What do you mean, it shouldn't take long to put things together?"

"Oh, that!" Florian waved a hand as if the matter was of no great importance. "The governor has asked me to provide you with an escort to Eboracum. Depending on how fast you want to travel, it could take three or four days to get there. You'll no doubt want to overnight at the various forts along the way." His eyes swept up and down Cethen's lean frame, pausing at his belly, and again at his grey hair. "Maybe five days."

"I can ride," Cethen said sharply, his doubts starting to fade. Surely he could trust Tuis, his own son, not to set a snare; yet he didn't know the lad anymore, not at all. But Jessa, he could surely trust her; after all, his eyes – she'd helped there, and now he could see better than he'd seen in years. "What if I choose not to go? I only came here to see how things stood, and you've told me."

"Then I suppose you'll just return home again." Florian spread his hands and widened his eyes, as if the choice was obvious.

"He'll go," Kelpy said quietly. "We'll be ready whenever."

# Chapter XXIII

# Selgovae Territory, Julius, A.D. 105

It was the beginning of what would prove to be the end and he, Modan-mor, was part of it – though he was prepared to give Lagan due credit . . . grudgingly. Unlike others who had gone before him, Lagan was not just gathering the tribes, he was organizing them; which, once Modan got it sorted through in his mind, was something he could agree with.

Lagan not only had it all figured, he had it written down, and a lot of it had to do with numbers. Those numbers began with the kin and quickly added up, each one building on top of another: twenty warriors here, another thirty there, which in itself wasn't much. Yet each member of the kin, most of them living apart in hundreds of small farmsteads and dozens of tiny settlements, owed loyalty in turn to their tuath. And each tuath, in turn, was scattered among the many more hundreds of hills and valleys that rolled across the north country from sea to sea. Thanks to a Greek called Horus, Lagan was gaining sway over it all, for he and Horus seemed to know more about the tribes than the tribes knew about themselves.

Modan had little grasp of the details concerning how the two were doing this, nor did he want to know. It was far too involved. Nonetheless, he did respect Lagan's newfound love of writing, for that was the tool with which it was done. Not that Lagan himself could write. Horus was the one who did that, but who was the wiser: the scribe, or the man who ordered his labours?

Horus was a Greek who had tallied goods for one of the Hispania traders. The unlikely alliance had come about following Lagan's abandonment of the hill fort. He had journeyed north to the Bodotria to buy an illicit load of long, thin, iron bars shipped in from Dacia. The metal was cheap, and in a form that could be easily beaten into sword blades. Lagan questioned the source out of nothing more than curiosity, and Horus had been immensely amused when giving the answer. The shipment, along with many others, had been slipped out by Dacian traders even as Trajan invaded their land.

"The emperor wanted to annex Dacia, claiming it was needed to defend Rome's borders." Horus had sniffed at the very idea as he wiped his nose indignantly on his sleeve. "Pig shit! It's all about the mines. The Dacians have got more gold, silver, and iron than the Romans got slaves. Trajan can't wait to get his bloody hands on it – but he won't get this lot."

Horus had gestured toward the bay, where Lagan's people were unloading the iron from the ship into smaller boats. The thin bars were being replaced with a full hold of wool bales, and a modest, iron-strapped box heavy with silver. The pair then got to talking, Horus's eyes more than once shifting to the stout box of silver now under the firm control of the trader. The Greek's thoughts were scribed on his face: where there was one box of silver, there would be others.

When the trader departed on an ebb tide, Horus remained. He handed Lagan one of two sheets of parchment, each scrawled with writing containing the terms of his staying. The word "silver" figured five times, though Lagan couldn't tell it apart from any other on the page unless Horus showed him. He supposed the paper might be worth something to Horus, but he knew what he'd agreed to and that was good enough.

When Modan first caught up with Lagan, he was unable to see Horus's worth. The man was Greek and seemed no different from a Roman, other than being willing to sell them iron. Then Modan saw that the man could scribe words on everything from wooden boards to parchment, and days later read exactly what they said – which left no space for argument.

At first that meant nothing, but Horus was fond of saying "If it's written, then it doesn't lie." Modan had sneered at the notion, but grudgingly grew to realize that the flimsy sheets of writing could serve a purpose. When someone like Crom the Surly, whose lodge was at Beaver's Brook, denied that he'd promised to muster twenty foot warriors and ten riders, Horus could find the paper and show him when and where that promise had been given.

This proved of exteme importance to Lagan, particularly when dealing with his own people and their temperament. The word of a Selgovae chief was good, certainly. Each and every tribesman prided himself on that word; but it was often only as good as his memory, or his mood. But if it was written down in Roman scrawl, and another swore to it, then a man was either bound or a proven liar.

In the few months since Bryn had freed him, Modan had learned much from Lagan. A part of the learning was that when all the tuaths were tallied, the sum came to so many thousands of warriors and riders that it was hard for his mind to imagine. In fact, he couldn't. But when Lagan explained that the sum was more than three full Roman legions put together, it was a number that Modan could grasp. It was a figure to make a person think, especially when everyone, from one side of the land to the other, knew the Romans themselves didn't have a full legion anywhere.

"They're sending some of their legion soldiers north to back up their auxiliary troops," Lagan would announce to the tuaths as he and Modan made their way among the tribes, gathering support and obtaining promises, "and it's not just because they're short of soldiers up here."

Then Lagan would pause and say nothing more, sipping on a beer or finding something to keep his fingers busy. He had a habit of wanting people to pry the information from him, and soon someone would ask why and in a loud hard voice he would tell them. It struck Modan that doing it that way made Lagan look as if he was always giving answers; it also made it sound as if he had all of those answers.

"It's because the Romans need the legion soldiers to help collect their lousy new taxes," Lagan would roar, then stand back, listening to the bitching and the clamour. He seemed to enjoy it, sucking it up like fresh air as he kept them going. "It's because they know there's going to be trouble getting those taxes. But –!" He'd scream the word and pause again. "But they're not going to have trouble *getting* them, are they?"

Modan loved that one, because some in the crowd would always shout their agreement. Others, though, the ones who were really listening, would hesitate in confusion. Then Lagan would shout back at them, "No, because long before that, they're going to have trouble getting home with their heads on their shoulders!"

Wherever they went the word had spread, and Lagan found the outpouring of support far greater than expected. In normal times, the chieftains were as hostile as stags guarding their does when it came to following another man's lead. Modan certainly felt that way himself, and yet he was willing enough to cede to Lagan on most points. How had the man been able to get so much agreement, where others had not? Modan asked him one night, and Lagan roared with laughter.

"It's their herds and their gold they love most," he explained, glancing over one shoulder as if someone might be listening. It was late, and they sat by the dying embers of a fire where, earlier that night, a man called Sotal and all his kin had eagerly listened to Lagan's harangue. "Nothing unites our noble tribesmen more than a thief. Sure, they hate the Romans. Sure, they talk of gathering together to rid us of them. But it takes an enemy with a hand in their purses to make them really unite and fight."

"But they . . ." Modan began, unwilling to believe that any tribesman would not fight simply for the sake of ridding his land of invaders.

"No, no, it's true." Lagan shook his head emphatically. "Don't take me wrong, lad. They want to get rid of the Romans as much as you do, but they lack great leaders such as Venutius or Galgar." He shrugged when he said that, which took Modan by surprise; did Lagan not believe himself to be a great leader? "Someone like me needs not only to raise their pride and call out to freedom, he needs to show how badly they're being robbed. Not that they don't already know – they're forever bitching about it. But sometimes they need to be told just how bad it is." Lagan grinned, a lopsided leer that made Modan smile. "I tell you true: when they're being robbed, they'll trust each other just long enough to chase off the thieves. Shit, most of them would even let go of their women before taking a hand off their coin."

Modan nodded his agreement, though not wholeheartedly. Rome's plundering was pressing hard on everyone's shield, certainly; but surely that wasn't the only reason to fight? It was all so confusing. As were Lagan's next words, which at first seemed to come from nowhere.

"Speaking of women, there's another matter you and I need to talk on."

"Women?" Modan frowned, his mood falling, for he had an inkling of what was coming. But he kept his gob shut on the chance that Lagan aimed elsewhere. "What about women? I'm all for 'em, if that's what you're asking."

"I'm for 'em too," Lagan replied with exaggerated patience, shaking his head at Modan as if he were a wayward child, "but I don't go grabbing every half willing skivvy I see, stand 'em up against a tree, and shag 'em like a humpbacked hound!"

"I've never stood anyone against a tree and done that!" Modan protested, because he hadn't. Though if the truth be known, he'd done everything but, always in a dark place far from anywhere, and always at night where nobody could see. It was the only way it now worked for him.

"That's just a saying, lad, an example," Lagan said, rolling his eyes. "The point is, you're humping every one that'll have you – and you're not very particular about who, either." Lagan grimaced as if reminded of someone in particular. "Modan, it's been noticed, and it's not good. It's not good for you, or for me. So watch it! Your pecker's not going to drop off if you don't use it ten times a day!"

Modan bowed his head at the words, and shrugged. He wasn't afraid his pecker was going to drop off; he was afraid it would stop working. The greatest horror of the assault on his groin had been the loss of manhood and all that went with it: women, pride, rutting, and women! He thought he'd lost all of that after the brutal surgery. Then, even before the sack had healed, Modan woke one morning to a full bladder and a pecker as rigid as a pilum. Tentatively, carefully, he'd tried to see if anything else worked, since what was left down there seemed more than willing. He was surprised to find that it did. Hardly any stones flew from the sling, so to speak, but it actually worked. The only question was, for how long?

"Ten times a day!" he heard himself say. "That's ridiculous."

"That's also a saying," Lagan said patiently. "Anyway, stop it, will you? Or at least, don't go sniffing like a bull at the hind end of any cow that's willing to stand. Pick one and stick with her, for the love of Lug. It's not so hard. Most everyone does – most the time, anyway."

But for him, Modan knew, sticking with one woman was impossible – sooner or later she would find out. With different ones, it was easy: a quick bit of passion and some feeling up in a quiet place that was pitch black, then make the lass keep her hands to herself, and go to it. Get it over with. No fondling back and forth, where a woman might find out. No undressing in the light of day, where she could see. Even then, it was bad enough: no, don't do this, and no, don't touch that. That was the worst part, telling them "no" to a whole pile of things. That haunted Modan. That and the overpowering, constant dread: what if one day it *didn't* work?

"Whatever," Modan mumbled.

"That reminds me," Lagan said, sounding almost relieved. "What about your wife?"

And that was another question, one on which Modan also brooded. He had no idea 'what about his wife'; nor, it seemed, did anyone else. She'd last been seen with Bryn, and Bryn had been going to Cumbria to call on his mother's brother, Frevan. He'd heard that from Treno, who'd spoken with one of the men who'd ridden with Bryn to Eboracum. Trista had been with him then, and that had made Modan think long and hard. Such a journey meant the two had been riding together for a long while, which in itself raised further doubt. His half-brother he could trust; it was Trista who bothered him. And worse than that, what if *she* ever found out about his . . . his . . .

"She's fine, but she prefers to stay out of all this," Modan lied.

"Can't blame her, I suppose." Lagan rose, yawned, and turned his back to the fire. He rocked on his heels, soaking up the last of the dying heat before facing the cold inside of the lodge they'd been given for the night. When he spoke, it was as if he was talking to himself. "Well, I suppose we'll have to do something soon. Everything's coming together with the tribes. If we wait too long, we'll start losing them."

Modan took the yawn as a hint and also stood, but his mind was brooding. He and Lagan were not often alone together; tonight had been an exception. The reason was now clear. But Modan had his own questions, and Lagan's words offered the chance to ask them.

When the Selgovae chieftain moved among the tribes, he did not travel with a large following – less than fifty warriors and chiefs, and for a pair of obvious reasons: there was a need to be sheltered and fed; and a small band of armed tribesmen was less conspicuous. Modan knew he was not the most important of those tribesmen, a notion that would never have entered his mind following the successful raid on the supply train. Of late, however, as he listened to Lagan and watched others around the fires, he'd started to wonder just how far down the hill he stood.

"So what's my part in all this, then?" he asked, turning his own back to the fire, both men gazing off into the night.

"Your part?" Lagan glanced sideways as if surprised. "Your part is about to begin, Modan. We're near finished here with my own people. I know where the warriors are, and who I can count on. We need to do more of the same in the north of Brigantia and Cumbria. I don't expect as much support there, not at first. But there are things up here that we can do to get them excited. Deal Rome a great enough blow, and they'll join in."

"And you think I can help do that?" Modan asked. "Get them to join you?"

"Not *you* alone, lad." Lagan chuckled. "But perhaps Modan, *Cethen Lamh-fada's son*, can, with some help from me. And maybe Modan, *brother of Bryn*, son of *Morallta*, can. And, I suppose, Modan the destroyer of Roman supply columns can. You have to get your own word out among the tribes, let them know how great you are." He slapped a hand on Modan's shoulder in a gesture that was friendly enough. "We just won't say what happened the last time you attacked the Romans. Though you did manage to escape, I suppose; we can use that."

"I'm my own man, dammit, without my father and my brother," Modan grated, but he was more troubled by Lagan's reminder of failure. "I can lead men into battle. I can fight."

"Aye, you can do that." Lagan's words were more a sigh than anything else. "No one ever said you don't have the balls, lad. But it's brains that win battles. I want you to start out in Cumbria, with the Carvetii. You need to convince Frevan that when he croaks you're more fit to lead the tribes than your brother."

"But I'm –" Modan caught his tongue before he said that he maybe wasn't.

Lagan murmured something under his breath, and sighed impatiently. "You're Cethen's son, boy. You play on that. And your mam – what was her name?"

"Ficra."

"What was she, Brigante or Carveti?"

Modan smiled. "She was Carveti. Da says she rode with him from the very first day that Morallta joined up with Venutius."

"That was before Stannick," Lagan muttered soberly, as if the name was a curse. Then he shrugged as if that was no longer a concern, and set a hand on Modan's shoulder. "There you go, then, you've got a further claim. It's time to get you started. You'll have Treno with you, I suppose. I'll send some of my own people as well. So sleep on it, lad, and think on anyone else you might take with you." Lagan paused as if considering a further choice, then shook his head and slapped Modan's shoulder as a good night. He turned and made his way to the small lodge, muttering under his breath, "Somebody's gotta be there who can string three words together without starting a fight."

## Chapter XXIV

# Cumbria, Augustius, A.D. 105

In years past, when the sun shone and the air was calm, Cethen believed that the gods had created Cumbria for themselves. A man lucky enough to venture there walked on hallowed ground. Cumbria's countless valleys, each cloaked in the lush green foliage of silent, towering trees, were cavernous temples that humbled a man. Cumbria was truly a land of its own, a land that was almost divine. But to ride through it was as hard on a man and his beast as any place Cethen had ever been.

Every steep forest slope, every rock-strewn, twisting path, and every bogged-in lakeside track jounced an aging back and a butt that was close to being rubbed raw. Yet the rich, rugged countryside, after so many years, was still mostly familiar. And though Borba had found them a guide, Cethen was certain he would have found Frevan's lodge without help.

"So what did you expect to find down there? Barbarians?" Cian snorted.

There were a half-dozen of them camped around a fire, alongside a farmstead that Cethen knew was hardly more than half a day's ride from Frevan's lodge. At one time he'd known the man who lived there. He heard he'd been killed riding north, fleeing the Roman purge. Cethen silently grunted his disgust at the memory. That was more than twenty years ago, and a stranger had since taken it over. What had been the dead man's name? It wouldn't come . . .

"Hey!"

"Huh?" Cethen forced his mind back his brother's blathering.

"The journey down to Eboracum – what did you expect? A band of cutthroats waiting inside every fort?" Cian said impatiently.

"Oh, that," Cethen grunted. "It was no problem." Which was an outright lie! Cethen had found himself in a whirl of confusion when his journey began, as he and Kelpy struggled to keep up with the small cavalry escort provided by Florian. That first night, when he rode through the gates of one of their Roman forts – he couldn't remember the name, they all sounded foreign – he'd been as nervous as a trapped rabbit. The uncertainty had continued all the way to Eboracum and back again.

The men he met along the way were an enemy he'd never known before. Food, lodging, and even drink were willingly provided by each Roman garrison, inside the forts he'd spent a lifetime trying to destroy. The governor's scroll opened gates and larders as if by magic. Kelpy had been equally awed, but was far more willing to talk on it, which she had without end. And both of them – Cethen more reluctantly – conceded that the Roman troops, auxiliaries for the most part, were little different than their own people, once placed around a warm fire with mugs in hand. Amazingly, they had shown as much interest in him as he had in them.

"One fort's the same as another," he continued, pretending indifference, which he supposed was true. Certainly the ones he'd been in seemed to be, and his brother would surely agree. Cian had seen a sight more of them than he had.

"Yeah, just like women," Cian agreed, nodding sagely. "Now, take horses. That's a different thing altogether."

"Cethen was quite good at that," Borba said mildly. "Though if there's a whole herd of the hay burners, don't ask him to count them."

"Good at what?" Cian asked.

Luga laughed, his wit for once ahead of Cian's. "Taking horses. Ask the Roman who built the fort at Eboracum. Cethen took his horse. It was the best animal he ever owned."

"Aye, but the poor sod was cut," Cethen complained, sadly shaking his head at the very idea. "The colts that horse might have thrown! Why the Roman ever had him gelded, I'll never know."

"Because they got a thousand more like him," Borba muttered.

"Aye, that's what Elena said when I first saw the animal," Cethen murmured, and smiled at Borba. It was good to be sitting across a blazing fire from the twin once more, exchanging yarns and lies. They'd done so a thousand times before, always on the run, and wary of any light cast by the flames. Those had been uneasy times, always on the lookout for Romans, and now it felt just as uneasy not to be watching for the buggers.

Cethen had parted company with Kelpy on the way back from Eboracum, soon after leaving the Roman fort at *Lavatris*: she to continue home, and he to find Borba. He'd been pleased that his old friend was willing to travel with him to Cumbria, and had needed little convincing. His sons, or Luath's sons – who knew – were tending the farm; though it seemed that one of the boys, a lad called Gavor, was now travelling with Bryn. Even so, despite Borba's willingness to come, it had been amusing to watch the twin's initial unease riding in the company of two old Roman auxiliaries, Cian and Luga.

It was a strange world that had brought them all together. Cethen had met up with Cian inside the commander's residence at Eboracum, while Luga had preferred to remain on his small farm. Perhaps the man felt uncomfortable inside the fortress, like himself; or maybe he just figured that a lifetime living in them was more than enough. Besides, unlike Cian, the big man didn't have family at Eboracum. Yet when he thought on it, other than his brother Cian, Cethen wondered if he did, either! His mind had become a butter churn, not at all sure where he stood with his first family now that he'd met them again. Did he even know them anymore? Which raised a second question: did he want to know them anymore? It had all been so strange.

The fortress at Eboracum was massive, even more so from the inside! Someone had offered him a glass goblet of red wine almost as soon as he'd been shown into the big building that Tuis named as the residence. They'd set a table beside him bearing a womanish assortment of tiny bits of food, and he sat picking at it while nursing the goblet and staring covertly at his two sons. While his eyes were still slightly fuzzy, he could make out their features well enough – and if his sight was not totally clear, his mind filled in the difference.

The pair might be brothers, but they were as different as chalk and cheese. Rhun, lean and trim, with his hair cropped as short as it had ever been in the army. It was fair and the shortness disguised the grey that had crept in. Tuis's was darker and he had more weight – by far more weight – which showed all the more for Rhun's leanness. He knew there were about ten years between the two – Rhun had to be almost fifty – yet the pair didn't look that far apart in age. Maybe it was the drinking. He noticed that Tuis was prone to empty his measure of wine, while Rhun seemed to nurture it.

The matter of the chestnut had been raised that night, too, Cethen remembered as he turned his eyes back to the glowing warmth of the fire. Cian had been there. His brother had sat beside him when everyone settled down, the pair of them naturally drawn together. It was almost as if the two of them were strangers to the others in the room, even though they were family. Thinking back on it, he must have looked as worried as a whipped hound as what to do next.

"I haven't seen you looking so low since the Roman stole his horse back." Cian had grinned as he straddled a wooden stool alongside Cethen.

"Ahh, old Gadearg." Cethen smiled in turn. "You know, when I found out that Elena was alive, I figured the Roman might trade her back for him."

"I'm sure she'd have been impressed," Cian said, and glanced up as Tuis placed a chair across from them and sat down.

Cethen looked toward Rhun. His son stood speaking to Marcus, who was likely discussing what had happened at Blatobulgium, for Jessa was there talking with her hands as if telling how it had happened. Or she could be describing nothing more than a short walk down to the Abus to catch fish! Cethen shook his mind to clear it, and decided it was all happening too fast, far too fast.

He'd arrived at the fortress with his Roman documents, expecting who knew what, but at the very most, to meet up with his son Tuis. Yet here he was, after half a lifetime, together in one room with two of his children, his brother, and Marcus and the wee lass, Jessa. Perhaps the gods were finally smiling on him. Or maybe they were doing no more than setting him up as a mark for Roman spears – as the sods had always done. Yet there was so much to talk on, to catch up on, and now here was Tuis, the one he knew least of all . . .

"Da," Tuis began, holding up his half empty glass to be filled as a slave edged over with a wine jug, "there's a few things I'd like to talk to you about."

Roman politics! Always his Roman politics! All he wanted to do was talk to the boy about how he'd grown up, did he have family, where were they and – Cethen sighed – and how was his mother? But the lad had gone on about the north, and the tribes, and after a while it just didn't seem important.

And now, Cethen mused as he tilted the mug and drained it, a week or so later, he sat around a fire in the Cumbrian hills, drinking beer with old and trusted friends. Why couldn't it stop there? Instead, the years were galloping back again and it was getting just as troublesome as the old times with Venutius and Galgar and Morallta and the rest of them:

we want you to do this; you must do that; your people are relying on you.

What the boy was really saying was: Da, solve my problems! If the fat was skimmed off the stew, however, Tuis's problems were far more gnarled than any he'd ever faced. And when he numbered them aloud they sounded impossible: help his third son Bryn to gain rule of the tribes; do it at the bidding of his second son, who governed Britannia; and do it while his first son took command of a big fort up by the firth; which stood close to another fort where his fourth son had just been trying to kill the lass who now sat on the far side of the room. A room, he was suddenly appalled to realize, that sat just about on top of his old home, where all he'd ever wanted to do was be left alone to raise his family.

Cethen stared gloomily across the yellow flames at the warm, familiar faces of his brother and his old friends. He lifted the beer mug and drained the dark dregs swirling in the bottom, finishing with a long, comfortable belch. Could he ever trust that other family, he wondered, as much as he did these men with whom he now shared the comfort of a blazing campfire?

† 

Frevan's hill fort was a shadow of itself – the Romans had made certain of that. The huge mound, bereft of defenses, sat in a lushly wooded valley at the southern tip of a long, narrow lake. Frevan's lodge sat on the lower end, where the steep slopes became gentler and wider as they fell away to the south. This was the same lake, Cethen remembered, where the Roman's son Marcus had spent his first winter of captivity. That village, like so many others, was now a circle of ashes overgrown by the forest, a half-day's ride farther north.

Cethen's mood darkened as he recalled the tall wooden palisades that had once crowned the hill, now torn down, along with the gates and about everything else. Even the ditches were mostly filled in, though with the walls gone, that was just as likely a convenience. The once proud hill fort now looked more like a huge pile of cow plop than the home of a Carveti chieftain – or a Carveti king, as Morallta would have insisted.

Frevan's lodge was a new building that sat atop the grass-covered mound like a grave marker, high above the mean scatter of huts, houses, pens, and sheds that crowded the rest of the rounded slope. Cethen told himself the mound was simply the old hill fort without the defenses, but it was hardly recognizable – as Rome had doubtless ordered.

There was something to be gained from the fall of a man's pride, though, and Cethen grudgingly admitted as much as his gaze wandered to the large tracts of farmland cleared between the shoreline and the forest that sheltered the small settlement. The new cultivation had also been pushed south down the valley, and the tawny yellow of ripening crops flanked the wide stream that drained the lake's runoff. And in front of Frevan's hill fort – or village, for Cethen was unsure what to call it anymore – five or six boats bobbed at a gleaming new wooden dock that jutted out into the blue waters of the lake. Where it joined the shore, several women stood gutting fish beneath a whirling cloud of screaming gulls. But most amazing of all, a wide road connected everything like an enormous thread, meandering off in both directions as far as the eye could see – a Roman road, no doubt leading to a string of Roman forts.

If anything was out of place in the rightness of it all, Cethen thought ruefully, it was the clutter on the mound where Frevan's people lived.

"Da!"

The voice rang out long before the horses had plodded up the hill, winding their way through the litter of pens and huts. Bryn stood by the door of Frevan's lodge with Borba's boy, Gavor, waving. It was a modest building compared to the one used by Venutius at Stannick, Cethen thought critically, yet it must have been ten times the size of his own. His son had been grooming a sorrel horse, a tall, well-proportioned animal with a gleaming copper coat and a mane that glistened red in the sun. It had two white fetlocks and a blaze that reminded him, with a pang of sadness, of Gadearg.

"Who'd you steal that from?" Cethen asked as he dismounted and briefly clasped his son. Beside him, Borba did the same with Gavor. Then everyone turned to admire the sorrel.

Bryn grinned. "Didn't have to. It's a gift from one of your other brats."

"Tuis?"

"Uh-huh."

"Hmmph," Cethen muttered as he fondled the animal's mane, the palm of his other hand stroking its soft muzzle. He glanced underneath, and grunted when he saw the animal had not been cut. Ah, if only Gadearg had been intact! "What does he want in return?"

"Not much." Bryn's grin broadened. "Cumbria. Brigantia. Oh yes, he also wants me to stop everyone picking on the poor abused Romans."

"Seems like a fair trade to me," Cian offered from behind Cethen as he dismounted.

"I'd say you got the best of the bargain," Borba suggested, running a hand down the sorrel's front leg and massaging its fetlock. The animal didn't so much as twitch. "If I'd been Tuis, I'd have demanded coin to square the bargain."

Another voice spoke, one that sounded frail and old. "If it was left to me, I'd swap all of Cumbria, bar this lake and its valley, for a mare that matched that stud; and if he wouldn't trade, then I'd give him the place for nothing."

Cethen turned toward a bent figure standing in the doorway of the lodge, leaning unsteadily upon a staff. The man was thin to the point of emaciation and his hair was white, despite a gaunt face that was younger than Cethen's. "Frevan," Cethen murmured in greeting, as did the others behind him, each trying to disguise his dismay. The man was clearly deathly ill.

Frevan nodded his greeting and named most of them; Cethen named Luga and Eb. Then Frevan turned and hobbled back inside, bidding them follow.

"So my nephew contrives to lead the people." Frevan chuckled as he spoke the words. He'd taken them into the main hall of the lodge, where a large hearth blazed despite a day that was anything but cold. Morallta's brother plainly spent a good deal of his time near the fire, for a lounge-like chair sat close by, and a table laden with food scraps, platters, and potions. The air was stale and medicinal, defying the warm, crackling scent of the burning pine.

"Bryn? Contrive?" Trista stepped from the shadows and helped Frevan climb onto the cushioned seat, where he lay back on the pillows with a painful sigh. "You have to want something before you contrive for it."

"A good point, my dear," Frevan conceded. "It's another of Cethen's sons who seems to contrive. What do you think, Cethen; is this son of yours mad, or is it just the other one?"

"I have four sons," Cethen said, looking about for somewhere to sit that offered half the comfort of Frevan's seat. All he could find was a plain wooden bench, and a scattering of low stools. None of them were built so a man might rest his back or an arm – or set a drink. He eased his rear down on the bench and added, "And I only consider one to be mad."

"Ah, Modan," Frevan said knowingly. "I hear he's coming my way, too. After years of neglect, it seems everyone and his favourite hound has concern for the well-being of an ailing Carveti chieftain. A man could believe he was already carrion, the way the crows gather."

Cian laughed. "If you want, you can soon meet Cethen's oldest one. Rhun. He's set to command the Roman fort at Luguvalium. I wouldn't doubt he'd like to speak with you, as well."

"There's a fair-sized town building there," Cethen said, not at all displeased with his son's responsibility. "In the old days, there was a tenth of what can be seen now."

"The gods must be placing wagers on your sons," Frevan said thoughtfully. "Two are on one side vying to lead the Carvetii and Brigantes; and two are on the other, leading the Romans. Bryn and Modan must move fast to catch up."

Cethen was taken aback at the words, and blurted, "The two are doing this together?"

"Hardly!" Trista laughed out loud. "I'd guess that both want the same thing, but each for himself. Bryn, I'm afraid, doesn't care for the task. He feels *obliged*."

"I know Bryn well, and believe that's true." Frevan pursed his lips then smiled, his head moving slowly back and forth. "It's one of the reasons I've agreed to stand behind him."

Cethen stared at the others, who were clearly as surprised as he by the ailing man's declaration. But to what extent had Frevan agreed to help, and what sway did he really hold over his people in making the choice? And there was a further question: Frevan was still alive, but for how long? How do you ask a man when he's going to die?

"Er, how – how are you able to do that, your health the way it is?" Cethen asked cautiously. "I mean, stand behind him . . ."

Cethen felt his cheeks grow warm as the pale eyes turned and stared, glinting with amusement. "I'm dying of something in here," Frevan murmured, smiling bitterly as he placed a hand across his chest, "but I'm not hurrying to get out of Bryn's way, if that's what you mean."

"I didn't –"

"What I'm willing to do, Cethen, is call a gathering and tell the people that I'm favouring Bryn. To be honest, it will be a relief."

"I see." Cethen nodded his understanding, wondering exactly where and when that would be, and how he might ask without giving offence.

Cian had no such scruples. "How soon are you wanting Bryn to give you relief?" he asked cheerfully. Then he looked toward Trista. "It's been a long ride, lass, and all this talk is making my mouth dry."

"Mine too." Luga spoke for the first time, licking his lips.

"Sorry, Cian, I'm a poor host. Would you see to it?" Frevan looked at Trista and pointed her to the far end of the lodge. His hand, Cethen saw, had a distinct tremor. He turned back to Cian. "As to when, that's not important, but it will be well before *Samhain*. What is important, and I've told Bryn this, is that I want to see him here first with a good following, and wearing Brigantia's torque."

Trista, who had started for the kitchen, stopped in her tracks and cursed. Cethen simply bent his head and closed his eyes, wondering how Bryn knew of the torque. It had to be Rhun, of course; that was the only way he'd know. Certainly the others had no knowledge.

Cian, Luga, and Borba stared at each other in bafflement. "The torque?" Cian asked, his voice hesitant, suspicious.

"Aye, the torque," Frevan muttered, and turned to look at Trista. "Don't they know?"

It was Bryn who answered, walking breezily into the lodge. "I think Da was keeping it secret." He clasped Cethen's shoulder, squeezing far harder than necessary. "In fact, he's kept the torque's whereabouts secret for as long as I've been alive. But it can't remain hidden forever."

"Your father's had it all this time?" The angry words burst from Cian. "And you never told me!"

"Shit, Cian, you were the enemy," Borba cried, just as angry. "I was your brother's right hand, and he never told me, either!" The twin turned to face Cethen, poking at his shoulder in annoyance. "Where did you keep it hidden, you selfish sod? We battled all the way up north and back again! You could have told me. If you were killed, it would have been lost. Or worse, someone like Galgar might have had it! You had no right!"

Cethen sighed and lifted his head. "Borba, I don't have it and I didn't have it then. I haven't had it since long before we moved north to fight for Galgar. I gave it to Rhun and Coira for safekeeping, right here in these hills when we met up with that Roman officer. You remember. It was when Cian pretended he broke his leg. You gotta remember that. You were there."

"You gave it to the Romans?" Cian screeched.

"I'm not stupid, Cian," Cethen shouted back. "I slid it over to Rhun; only Rhun, Coira, and I were there at the time. And it looks like I was right in doing it too, you prickly sod. They've kept it quiet ever since. The truth of it is, I'm hearing about it now just like you."

"Bryn already has a following in the hills." Frevan's voice was calm, likely hoping his mood would be catching. "With the Carvetii behind him, I believe the people of Brigantia will follow. After all," his mouth twisted with a sardonic smile, "it was the goddess Brigantia who forged the bauble, for just this moment. Brigante territory is held together by a thread that's grown even thinner since Venutius died; the torque will make that thread stronger. Every bairn old enough to walk has heard of the legend. As I said, it was the goddess Brigantia who –"

"Who wrought the golden torque a thousand years past, melting the blades of a hundred swords prised from the hands of fallen Brigante warriors, and smelting them to gold. Then, twisting the . . ." Luga chanted as if offering up a dirge.

"Then, when Venutius was slain, she retrieved the golden torque with her own hand," Frevan interrupted, his reedy voice loud enough to drown that of Luga, "plucking it from the field of battle where he fell, lest it fall into enemy hands. And Brigantia clutched it to her bosom, where she holds it still in sacred trust for a leader of great courage and pure heart, who will guide the people to –"

"They're saying that?" Cethen exclaimed, incredulous. Frevan's tale sounded as thin as the one forged by the druid Trencoss when the Roman fell in the river Abus; a false vision that had plagued him for years.

"No." Frevan grinned, a genuine smile that lit his wan features. "But before the season turns, I'll warrant they will be!"

"But, to what end? Another bloody go at it?" Cian demanded.

"No, just the opposite." Bryn glanced at Trista as if confirming his words, and Cethen raised an eyebrow; when a man started doing that, a lass has a hold on him. "But when the Romans do confront the tribes across a table, they will not be facing the confusion of many. They will face only one. Imagine it: all the tuaths, from sea to sea, speaking with one voice."

"Isn't that what the Romans want?" Cian asked doubtfully.

"True, that's the way they govern, and are governed in turn; but you can't say it doesn't work," Bryn said. "Just because *they* do it that way is no reason we shouldn't. One good spear striking hard is more powerful than a hundred that fall short of the target. Like Venutius, a single voice that talks for the tribes; only this time, a voice that knows what it is and *isn't* capable of doing."

"One voice is what your brother Tuis wants, so he can control us; he's Roman now, not Brigante." The words came from Borba's son Gavor, who usually sat quiet in front of his elders. "Where's the people's freedom in this?"

"Hey, Rhun hasn't turned Roman, he's taken only the best of it. And Cian certainly hasn't turned though he, too, once wore the uniform." Cethen bent his head to acknowledge his brother, choosing to ignore Gavor's jibe at freedom. "As long as I can remember, Rhun has voiced only one thought: the Romans are here for as long as they want. He's travelled half their empire, and says that's a simple fact; and Cian agrees." He turned to Borba and paused, smiling sadly as he remembered other words spoken by his son. "Rhun says that accepting the truth of that makes his life easier: it forces him to think with his mind, rather than his heart. He claims it's hard on the skull, but easier on the people."

Cian laughed and added his own memory. "And as for the other bit, Gavor, Rhun once said freedom is for kings and chieftains. For the rest of us, it's nothing but the weight on your shoulders of the man above you." He paused, frowning, then shrugged his indifference. "Or something like that."

"But it's still doing what the Romans tell us to do," Gavor grumbled.

"Aye, but if we speak as one people, tens of thousands with a single voice, then that voice will have force," Bryn said. "Granted, how much force remains to be seen, but at least the present governor will listen."

"Tuis would rather travel a road not pocked by stones," Trista added. She had returned from the kitchen and stopped next to Cian, sipping on a mug of ale; when he gave her a questioning look, she chided him, "Patience. Yours is coming."

"You know," Frevan said wistfully, his eyes turning to a half-open door that offered a glimpse of the yellow, sun-touched fields to the south, "oddly enough, I like that road they put in. Before that, there was nothing but a mud track. Now you can travel no matter what the weather, and it leads somewhere. They say you can follow it all the way to far-off seas. They say you can travel for twenty days and never step off it. There are advantages, you know, even if a man has to grow old to find them." Frevan sighed and leaned back on the cushions, his face glum as he shook his head. "Even if the sodding thing passes by a hundred of their lousy forts."

※

They left Frevan's lodge a week later, intending to part company on reaching the Roman road that led north to Luguvalium. From there each would go his own way: Cian and Luga returning to Eboracum; Bryn and Trista and Borba's son lingering on in Cumbria to test the lay of the land; and Cethen, Borba, and young Eb making their way home. Cethen had no idea what he would do once he got there. Nor did Borba. Both men grumbled as much as the small column departed, making its way back along old, familiar trails.

Neither man was happy about the path contemplated by Bryn, because it meant working side by side with the Romans; the very notion stank of defeat. Borba was the more leery of the two, because of his distance from Bryn. The lad was Cethen's son, the twin bluntly observed, which may have obscured his da's thinking; after all, this was the same man who had spent his life fighting the Romans! Cethen in turn pointed out that Tuis was also a son, as was the man about to assume command of Luguvalium, and they were both on the side of Rome, which might actually help clear his thinking. Borba then reminded him of Modan, who was bent on destroying everyone's ambitions but his own – and how was that for muddling a man's mind?

Cian, riding behind with Luga, overheard the exchange, and was about to contribute his two chippets of chat when Bryn, riding in front, raised one hand to call a halt. The rest of them quickly bunched up behind.

Thinking Bryn had overheard and wanting to defend himself, Borba muttered, "Nothing personal, lad. It's just that –"

"No, it's not that," Bryn whispered. "Listen!"

At first they heard nothing in the damp, empty quiet of the forest. The trail, a wide cart track cut through the thick Cumbrian woods, was well used, but the rain-softened ruts showed no sign of recent passage. The broad canopy of leaves that hung above them forming an endless cave only added to the eerie silence. Then, ever so faint, distant cries echoed through the trees: shouting – people in trouble.

Only Bryn and the dozen or so people Frevan had sent with him had arms enough to fight, yet every man carried some sort of weapon. Within moments they all had something in hand, each looking to the other for guidance.

"Into the trees," Cethen suggested, pointing toward the darkness of the forest. "No sense galloping headlong into someone else's fight."

"I'll go scout it out," Cian offered, urging his horse forward.

"No you won't," Bryn said quickly. "I'll go with one of Frevan's men. Wait here."

"I've done this sort of thing more times than you've had your nappies changed," Cian growled, but Cethen took a firm hold on his reins, checking him.

"Into the trees, brother," he muttered. "Let the young'uns have their turn." He cut his horse in front of Cian, forcing them both to move off the trail. Bryn and one of Frevan's men kept on riding, holding their horses to a walk.

Luin was one of Frevan's senior men, an older warrior who deferred to Bryn as they drew near to the harsh, bickering voices. Bryn raised a hand to signal a stop, wondering if he was being tested; Luin seemed to be the far more battle wise of the two. Not much farther down the trail the treetops were sparser, which likely meant a meadow or a marsh. Bryn edged his horse into the silence of the forest, and Luin followed. The pair dismounted and tied the horses to a length of deadfall, then crept forward through the tangled undergrowth.

Beyond a screen of bog-ridden reeds and willows, men on foot and on horseback crowded a small meadow – well over fifty, Bryn estimated, and it took a while for his mind to sort them out.

"Can you name the angry-looking toad on the horse?" Luin whispered.

Bryn shook his head, but it was from despair, not lack of knowledge. "That's my half-brother, Modan."

"And that's Glas, one of Frevan's chiefs that he's arguing with. And – shit, look there! What's going on?"

Bryn asked himself the same question. Five men lay on the ground, barely visible in the tall grass; two were being tended to, three were deathly still. "I don't know," he whispered, "but there's a stink to it all."

"And you say that's your brother?"

"Half-brother," Bryn corrected with a grim smile. "It must be a misunderstanding."

Luin grunted his disbelief.

Glas was beside himself, shouting and gesturing angrily toward the bodies, but Modan had fallen silent, gazing somewhere off into the woods. Bryn recognized Modan's bland, bovine expression: his brother's mind was muddling through its options. *Something had clearly gone wrong*, Bryn realized, *and he's pondering on what might best fix it*. Treno sat a horse directly behind Modan, not moving. Bryn's eyes swept the clearing and he saw that most of the men there rode with his brother. In fact, maybe only a dozen or so were Glas's people.

"It's a mistake, I told you, a mistake," Modan began, quickly raising his voice to a shout.

Bryn groaned and swore softly. His fool brother was working up his own fury, as the implication of what had happened soaked into his thick skull. If he were to guess, Modan had mistakenly attacked the very people he was there to visit. His next words seemed to confirm that.

"My lead riders ran into yours head-on! They thought they were being ambushed. Just look to your own people, dammit! They fought right away, didn't they?"

"That's a pond full of goose shit," Glas cried. "You don't *run* into people if you're skulking in the trees. And your men came charging out of the –"

"That was because you were riding down the track ready to kill – horses running, men shouting. These hills are crawling with thieves, and everyone knows it. Cutthroats, robbers, every slime-coated piece of scum that can find a blade and put an edge on it. For all we knew, you were –"

Glas's voice rose to a screech. "We were trotting our horses. And we were talking, not shouting. You came bursting out of the forest like a . . ."

"Come on," Bryn whispered, his mind turning his brother's words over and marrying them to what Glas was saying. There was no doubt who had attacked who, and the words of the Carveti had a fair ring of truth to them. Modan must have heard Glas and his men coming down the track and, hot-headed and bone-brained that he was, assumed the worst. These hills did, after all, hold their share of cutthroats. Once again, it seemed he would have to pull his brother from the quicksand. He turned to Luin, looking sheepish. "I'd better go and play the peacemaker. My brother's not known for –"

"You're not going out there!" Luin hissed.

Bryn blinked, startled at the hardness in Luin's voice. "Why not?"

"You'll be the death of Glas and his men." Luin glanced through the willows, then tugged at Bryn's tunic, pulling him deeper into the forest. "And likely yourself, too. Right now, they've stopped fighting and they're shouting at each other, and that's good. Your brother made a mistake, and he sees no sense losing any more men for it. As does Glas."

"Look, I'll calm the idiot down anyway and –" Bryn stopped, surprised at Luin's impatient glare. His mind played over the Carveti's words. "What do you mean, I'll be the death of Glas and his men?"

"What did you say your brother's name is?"

"Modan."

"Well, it seems to me that Modan made a mistake, charging out of the trees and fighting Glas."

"Exactly. It was a mistake. And when he realized who it was, he quickly broke off the fight and –" Again Bryn stopped, a cold shiver of suspicion crawling up his spine.

"*Exactly* is dead right," Luin persisted as they reached the horses and freed the reins from the deadfall. "Only the mistake he made was that he thought Glas was someone else."

"You mean me?" Bryn whispered, his mind instantly refusing the thought.

"Maybe and maybe not; but as Glas said, Modan was skulking in the trees. And plainly put, I don't want to get *my* head skulked off; nor do I want to see Glas lose his. So come on, let's leave them to sort it out. We can't do any good here. If there was going to be any more fighting, Modan wouldn't have stopped in the first place, not when he had the advantage. Would he?"

"I suppose not," Bryn muttered, his mind awhirl as he tried to rid it of the sickening idea of treachery. Modan had never borne him any malice. Why would he now? The answer, impossible as it might seem, was suddenly as obvious to him as it had been to Luin: leadership of the tribes. And to further sharpen the point on that arrow, there was now the torque in the offing. Did his brother think he already had it? That could make sense, except how could Modan possibly know? He couldn't, and Bryn muttered as much aloud.

"Bryn, you were here a couple of weeks before your da arrived, and another's passed since. There's been lots of time for word to spread."

"Spread as far as the Selgovae? That's where Modan was going, the last I saw him," Bryn said, his mind flitting back to his brother's flight from the Roman column and the fate awaiting him in the quarries. But that had been more than a couple months past.

"And maybe he went there. But I also heard rumour that Modan was back at the fort the Romans call Blatobulgium."

"The fort?" Bryn frowned. Why would Modan go to a Roman fort? But that wasn't his first question. "Why didn't I hear of that?"

"I dunno." Luin shrugged. "Because that's all it was, I suppose: a rumour? You know what he's doing better than anyone."

"But the fort. Why would he go there?"

Luin supplied the answer. "I heard it was to gain vengeance." He shrugged, as if it baffled him, too. "For what, no one seems to know. There weren't many of them – Modan, the man Treno, maybe a score of others. It was the village they went to, though, not the fort. It's rumoured he was after a dwarf girl that lives there; the one who gives Roman medicine to the people."

"Surely not her. She saved his life."

"Who knows why?" Luin glanced warily toward the clearing, though a good distance now lay between. "Look, what happened here may well be nothing more than a mistake, though I doubt it. Modan, too, has friends among our people, Bryn. He was doubtless coming to visit

Frevan, now that he's dying. There's many who could have given warning of your movements."

"Yeah, but why?"

Luin grasped the cross horns and swung onto his saddle, then stared down at Bryn with an expression that plainly showed what he thought of the question. "Look, Frevan has made it known that you're his choice to succeed. You've accepted that challenge. You have the torque, or you will. Once it circles your throat, it sets your claim above others. But that doesn't mean there are people who won't hunger for it."

"But Modan . . ."

"Welcome to the glories of power, my friend. She's a vicious queen, especially for those who would hold her close. Ask Ilbrec." Luin smiled grimly, but with mention of the name, he grew thoughtful. "If Modan did know you were coming this way, then Ilbrec could just as likely have been the one who told him." For a moment his face was thoughtful, then he shook his head. "Though no, I doubt it it was him. Ilbrec's too ambitious."

Bryn set one foot on a piece of deadfall and heaved himself onto his horse. He felt suddenly tired, though it was his brain that flagged, not his body. Ilbrec. Who was he? The name touched his memory, but the man himself didn't come to mind.

"Frevan's nephew, by another sister," Luin answered when he asked. "The only other kin he has left. Ilbrec keeps to his own lands farther north, but he also has a lodge in the settlement at Luguvalium. Frevan doesn't find him suitable to lead." Luin's smile turned to one of amusement. "He's too much like Modan."

"What's wrong with Modan?" Bryn asked unthinkingly, then immediately regretted the question. He knew full well what was wrong with Modan, he just didn't like anyone else telling him.

"I hope you joke," Luin muttered.

Bryn, with little effort, managed to look sheepish. "Just asking."

✷

"We'll just stay here until they pass," Bryn said when they returned to the others. A host of voices demanded to know what the pair had seen. Bryn brushed them off, insisting that everyone follow him deeper into the forest.

Luin, as if feeling obliged, told them that two bands of warriors, each of different kin, had clashed and were now arguing the toss of the matter. It was best to avoid the whole mess, he said, and leave them to settle it, before moving on. "You know how these feuds play out," he finished.

Trista watched and listened. From the expression on Bryn's face she knew Luin's words were a lie – or, at best, they were a half-truth, and probably less. Bryn looked as if he'd just lost his favourite hound, and for a reason he did not want to share. The man was brooding, and his mood dark. Sometimes she just didn't know what he was thinking, and it was aggravating. If he would just say what was on his mind! Trista sighed at the thought, for Bryn had said exactly the same words the morning after he'd crawled into her bed naked. With a sigh, she kicked her horse's belly, then reined in alongside Bryn, determined to wheedle the cause from him. She had a fair idea where to start.

"So, what's Modan done now?" she asked.

# Chapter XXV

# Luguvalium, Augustus, A.D. 105

Rhun was elated when he set out from Eboracum, travelling first north, then west, to assume command of the fort at Luguvalium. He felt an exuberance he had not felt in years. This regiment would be his final command, he was sure of that, but it was also the largest ever: a thousand men. He found a deep sense of satisfaction in that; a welcome feeling that spoke of once more doing something useful. Adding to the shine on the gold, the posting was in the land of his birth – which was only fitting. And there was a final, trivial satisfaction: Luguvalium was not a command gained through the auspices of his wife's father.

Gaius had always claimed that Rhun's career had progressed on its own merits, but both men knew the truth came short of the telling. Rome demanded that her armies be competent, certainly, but Rome was also a furnace fuelled by patronage and nepotism. Rhun knew that as a barbarian taken in battle, without Gaius he would have progressed no further than Cian – if he'd been lucky. But he felt he'd delivered his worth for Rome's armies and he'd enjoyed doing so. There was a certain amount of guilt in leaving Aelia to the running the family holdings, of course, especially with the tragedy of Gaius's illness. But to be fair, it *was* Aelia's family and she did enjoy her role, just as he had enjoyed his. And if, for the moment, he was a free man with a full command in the land of his birth, he was determined not to feel guilty over the joy of it.

Rhun refused to force the march to Luguvalium, taking advantage of the long string of forts that guarded the way. The column he commanded contained the usual supply wagons and pack mules, escorted by a large contingent of auxiliary troops newly raised in Gaul, mainly from Lower Germania. Mostly recruits and marked as replacements, they were sufficient to fill the ranks of a full cohort. All were assigned to his command for the next several months until they were deemed ready for duty throughout the north. The largely untrained force was not as strong as its numbers, but Rhun was not unduly concerned. The current unrest lay mainly with the Selgovae to the north of Brigantia, and when Rhun passed through the various forts, he confirmed as much.

The column did have some extra "baggage" in its ranks: Jessa and her father. Marcus had been intent on riding south by way of Aquae Sulis, leaving his daughter to set up a new hospice at Eboracum. But the lass had again driven her father to distraction by insisting on accompanying Rhun, assuring him that she was far safer under her uncle's care. Marcus saw the logic of her reasoning: Rhun's personal protection in the large fort at Luguvalium, or the less than watchful eye of Marius Appius, whom Jessa claimed had as much sensitivity as the Roman mob.

Rhun saw that Marcus held strong reservations, but was incapable of exercising them. Unwilling – or unable – to deny the headstrong woman, he'd elected instead to remain with his daughter, for the time being. It wasn't so much that he couldn't wean the child; the child couldn't seem to wean him! Rhun kept a tight rein on his tongue, and in all honesty, he didn't mind her company for he liked her. Jessa was good to talk to, she played a mean game of *Latrunculi*, and she was kin. Her presence would relieve the boring evenings that were part of service on the frontier. Rhun's only aggravation was her small pony: the animal barely managed the day's march that distanced each fort.

His aggravation grew, however, the moment he rode through Luguvalium's gates. The fort commander, a man called Decius Attius, did not expect to be relieved until some vague time in the future, following an even vaguer promise of promotion from Tuis. Furthermore, the fort was garrisoned by a Tungri cavalry regiment and a small detachment of Batavi infantry, which wasn't even within hailing distance of the milliaria that Rhun had been promised. And even if his milliaria had been there, the stronghold was short of space. The fort was in the process of being rebuilt, certainly; but the new building was designed to hold the same cavalry regiment, and perhaps a third of a cohort of infantry – not a full milliaria!

Where was his promised milliaria?

Ironically, even without it, space was still needed to house one! When all put together, the present under-strength garrison and the cohort of raw replacements Rhun had brought with him raised the numbers to slightly more than a thousand. Granted, it was only temporary, and one of the old marching camps could solve the problem. But neither he nor Decius Attius had received instructions concerning where to assign the new body of recruits, once they'd been trained up. Decius, in fact, hadn't even known they were arriving.

This was far worse than typical army, this was typical Tuis; for worst of all was the plight of Decius himself. The poor man had not been officially relieved, which theoretically left him still in command. The man clearly felt as awkward as Rhun did. Thank the gods that the fellow was reasonable . . . once he'd calmed down.

Cursing every word, Rhun angrily composed and dispatched a note to Tuis the morning after his arrival – and only then, because it was too late to send it the same day. Not wasting parchment, and suspecting he knew the answers in advance, he demanded to know:

> I. *What do I do with the Germanian recruits, once basic training is complete?*
> II. *Where is my promised milliaria?*
> III. *When and if I get my milliaria, how do I house it in a fort designed for a cavalry regiment, and a few measly squads of infantry?*
> IV. *What the fuck do I tell Decius Attius?*

*Rhun*

With no regrets over either the content or the language, Rhun watched the dispatch rider leave for Eboracum at a fast gallop that would doubtless slow the moment he vanished over the first hill. The man would have to, of course, or he'd kill his fool horse. Rhun's sole regret as the man sped through the gate was that he had not added the line: *I don't need this posting, nor do I give a shit about keeping it – your loving brother, Rhun!*

He received the reply, succinct and to the point, within five days, for Tuis still lingered at Eboracum, seemingly unable to drag himself away. As Rhun read the response, he didn't know whether to laugh or fume:

*Rhun:*

> *In respective response:*
> I. *Keep them.*
> II. *See item I., you now have it.*
> III. *Expand the one you've got so it fits.*
> IV. *Tell Decius I order him to Eboracum for promotion/reposting.*

*I had thought the above was clearly understood. I trust the Change of Command ceremony runs smoothly. Sorry I can't be there.*

*Carpe diem,*
*Tuis Sabinius Trebonianus,*
*Imperial Governor, Britannia*

It was so typical of the man. No apology, just *I thought the above was clearly understood.* Yet at the end of the confusion it would likely all work, Rhun decided, shaking his head nonetheless. The overt juggling effectively summed up the ox-turd luck that his brother seemed to enjoy. Even Decius would be pleased in the end, probably with an easier posting to the south, but Rhun knew precisely what had happened.

Tuis had balanced matters in his fecund brain until the last possible moment, the primary problem being the offer to Rhun of a prize posting in Britannia that wasn't available. The solution had doubtless nagged at his mind ever since, delayed and delayed again, for two reasons: first, he didn't have a full milliaria to give; second, he couldn't decide what to do with Decius. It was no wonder his brother drank! Reinforcements had then arrived from Germania, a single cohort that must have left Tuis inspired. Only he'd put off telling anybody what he planned on doing with it, because its arrival solved only his first problem – Rhun. The one with Decius still remained, but Tuis had now gained a week in which to solve that one too.

Rhun's elation had faded as he waited on Tuis's response, but he found a surprising ally in Marcus. Aelia's brother had once been posted to the old fort at Luguvalium; it was where he'd been taken hostage by Rhun's da, and the woman Morallta. While Rhun grew more impatient, Marcus seemed to find a renewed interest in the stronghold and the growing native settlement that lay not far from its gates.

Cerealis had built the fort between two small rivers that joined up with the much larger Ituna, several hundred paces to the north. Marcus claimed that Luguvalium had been the most remote outpost in Britannia at the time he was there, as desolate as a shipwreck on an enemy shore. But not long after, Agricola had pushed even farther north, and a string of forts now lay beyond. In many ways, the garrison and the land that surrounded it belied Marcus's tales of desolation when posted there as a young tribune.

Rhun said as much in the commander's dining room, a sanctuary that he felt was finally his own after Decius departed for Eboracum.

"Oh, I don't know, in some ways it's still the same," Jessa said cheerfully, and gestured vaguely to the north. "Father says the hills were an ant's nest of *barbarian* warriors then, only you couldn't see the ants. Nothing changes."

"I can't say he's wrong now," Rhun said.

Jessa nodded. "Kaeso says hardly anyone fit to be a warrior can be found on the farms and villages where they should be, yet none of them can be found where you figure they might be."

"Who's Kaeso?" Marcus asked sharply, his interest clearly aroused, but Rhun broke in, absorbed by Jessa's quandry.

"The tax levies have given them new cause, but it's got to be more than that," he suggested. He'd tried to change Tuis's mind, but his brother had simply shrugged and said it was out of his hands: *'The procurator – carrion-feeding vulture that he is – got his approval for his lousy taxes.'* Though from whom, Rhun noted, Tuis failed to say.

"Uncle Tuis said they were needed," Jessa said, and casually added, "I heard him. He said it would *teach the bastards a lesson*."

Rhun's brows rose. "He did?"

"Yes, he said that to Cronus when he was at Eboracum. I don't like the man." Jessa shivered before finishing her wine and placed the empty goblet on the table. "It was after the two finished arguing about the commission on the olive oil."

A silence fell over the table, broken when Rhun, against his better judgement, asked, "The olive oil?"

Marcus frowned at his daughter as if uncomfortable, but she blithely continued. "Yes, the olive oil. Cronus has a shipload coming in, but it won't arrive until after the one with the cargo of wine. I think that's the way it was."

Rhun stared at his niece, wondering if she was being obtuse – which was unlike her – or if she was simply letting him and Marcus know that Tuis was somehow engaged in the import of olive oil and wine. Surely Jessa knew how her words sounded, all in the same breath: a head-to-head with Cronus, additional taxes, then wine shipments and olive oil . . .

There was nothing wrong with the governor or the procurator engaging in trade, Rhun supposed, but that depended on what was happening to the goods. His question sounded harsher than intended. "Come on, Jess. We don't need a game of guess the battle. What's Tuis up to?"

"Up to?" Jessa's eyes opened wide. "What do you mean?"

"Oh, I imagine –" Marcus began, but Rhun interrupted.

"Tell us the whole story," he growled, allowing his impatience to show. "Were you actually with Tuis when he was discussing this with Cronus?"

"No." Jessa looked back and forth between the two, and shrugged. "I was sitting close by where they were walking, and they stopped to talk. I guess they didn't know I was there."

Rhun glanced at Marcus, who looked thoughtful. He finally spoke, as if the matter was of little concern. "Interesting, my dear. Could you hand me one of those berry pastries."

Jessa seemed grateful for the change in tone, which lacked the asperity of her uncle Rhun; but she wasn't finished. "I'll say it was interesting. Especially when he finally gave in on the taxes."

"Gave in on the taxes?" Rhun blurted. That wasn't what he'd been told!

"Tuis really didn't want to put the taxes into place anymore, not now that he's talking to his da and his brother, er . . ."

"Bryn," Rhun muttered, rolling his eyes.

"That's right. Tuis said it was going to mess up his plans for calming everyone down, and if necessary he'd write Trajan to stop it. Then Cronus said he'd change the deal on the wine and olives, if Tuis didn't argue about the taxes," Jessa grinned impishly, "though he didn't use the word argue."

"Change the deal on the wine and olives?" Rhun cried, his mind sliding to a grubby image of Tuis and a vulture-like procurator, heads huddled, haggling over profits that might cause grief for thousands. And there were those damned taxes too.

"Jessa, you said, 'if Tuis didn't argue about the taxes'?"

"Cronus added another five percent for Tuis on what he called the 'net' on the shipments; though at first he offered only three." Jessa frowned as though puzzled, but there was an amused twinkle in her eye as she continued. "How on earth a net figures in with wine and olives, I have no idea. I thought they were used to catch fish."

Marcus chuckled at her play on words, then he leaned forward, clearly wanting to add to the conversation; at the same time, he seemed oddly reluctant to speak. "I see . . . And, uh, that made what, in total? The percentage?"

"Thirteen."

"The sly snot!" Marcus blurted.

Rhun listened to the exchange, lost for words. His mind tried to absorb what Jessa was telling him, but there was something missing – as if something had been left unspoken. Marcus was not finished, though.

"So that's how much Tuis is getting on the wine and olives," he said caustically. "How much is he getting off the new taxes?"

"Ten percent."

"Ten percent!" Rhun and Marcus both exclaimed, and looked at each other as if stunned.

"Not on the whole lot," Jessa quickly explained. "Only on what Cronus said he could bubble off the top of the pot. Tuis agreed, as long as he got to see the records."

"Well, I suppose there's nothing wrong with selling wine and olives," Marcus muttered, and leaned back in his chair as if considering all that he'd just heard; he seemed willing to give Tuis benefit of the doubt on at least part of his dealings. "A procurator can be a trader too, though it's not without risk. But the taxes, and especially now . . ."

Rhun shook his head. "I don't agree. It depends on where the wine and olives are being sold."

"To the army," Jessa volunteered, for the first time showing a hint of disapproval.

"Tuis must have found out Cronus was going to do it anyway, and demanded his cut off the carcass," Rhun muttered, though that didn't excuse his brother.

"No, that wasn't it," Jessa said. "Cronus couldn't raise all the money to pay for the first shipment. That was the cargo of wine. And he was maybe going to be short on the second one, depending how long the army took to pay for the first. The traders want hard coin when they turn their cargo over to Cronus, and that's the problem. It's first got to be transported to the different units for receipt, and Cronus wasn't sure he could falsify the books long enough to –"

"Yes, yes," Rhun interrupted, "but what's that got to do with Tuis?"

Jessa readily supplied the answer. "He advanced the money."

"Tuis?" Rhun burst out, unable to contain his surprise. "In what bottomless bog did my brother find the funds to finance two shiploads of wine and olive oil? That's a small fortune."

"Er, it wasn't in a bottomless bog." Marcus sighed, clearly reluctant to explain. He turned to Rhun as if surprised at the fuss. "I suppose I arranged for the funds. I have connections in Londinium."

"You did?" Rhun cried incredulously.

"It seemed like a good investment," Marcus said, and shrugged. "Come on, Rhun, such things are expected. You can't go home from the provinces with *any* kind of coin on what the empire pays."

"But he could have raised his shield and blocked the taxes," Rhun insisted. "The last thing we need up here in the north is more oil poured on the flames."

"Yes, that one does bother me," Marcus murmured thoughtfully, then sounded amused when he added, "I wonder if he's going to tell me about the extra five percent he got on the wine and oil."

*A pox on the five percent*, Rhun thought. His own wife's brother had financed a grasping procurator to cheat the army! Yet he really hadn't, had he? It was *his* brother, Tuis, who had borrowed the finances to do it! That was worse! Yet it was really the two of them, along with the stoat Cronus, who had levered the profits against the increase in taxes . . .

Rhun turned on Marcus, trying hard to control the anger in his voice. "You knew about the trade-off on the tax levy?"

"There seemed to be no choice." Marcus shrugged, and at least found the grace to appear sheepish. "Tuis came to me for advice – and the loan. I told him I didn't like the taxes, but Cronus did point out that it was a far more effective punishment on the hostiles than that inflicted by Tuis and his army. Besides, Tuis had agreed to the levy a month or more before matters changed and he met up with Bryn and his da." He shrugged, as if it really didn't matter. "I was helping him out."

The meal continued in silence – it was about over anyway – but it was a silence that stretched on, until it seemed incumbent on someone, anyone, to break it. Marcus spoke, for it appeared that something was bothering him after all. He turned to Jessa and asked, "Who's this Kaeso?"

"I don't believe it!" Rhun, too, finally found his tongue as the implications sank in, and he didn't like a single one of them. "You've got to admit, Marcus, this will make life far more difficult."

"That's true." Jessa was quick to agree. "Far more difficult."

# Chapter XXVI

# Near Epiacum, Augustus, A.D. 105

Bryn rode the hills with a score of his people, moving from farm to farm and village to village, slowly making his way from Cumbria to Brigantia. At each halt the welcome was genuine. Bryn was known to most of those he met, and was now known to be Frevan's chosen. Yet while he was received warmly enough, something was missing, and he and Trista knew most of what it was: Bryn, like Frevan, was known as a good man and a friend; but to angry people his message held little appeal.

Since Morallta's time, Frevan had led the Carvetii along a carefully trodden path – but what he achieved had come with its own cost, for the path taken was low on pride and devoid of glory. Frevan's way did not reflect the nature of the tribes, and many were now more than willing to blame him for that. The Romans had set their wooden forts across the tribe's territory as easily as if they were building cowsheds. More than a dozen now existed, and all were well sited. Roman soldiers patrolled every road walked by the Carvetii. More than twenty years had passed since Galgar's great disaster to the north and, as Frevan had said himself, a rat-nosed Roman now stood watching every time you took a piss.

The younger Carvetii, the ones who had never bled or seen men people in agony, were restless. As they always would be, Frevan told Bryn, until they had felt the torture of a festering belly wound, or limped home with half an arm. And even then, should they live, most would rightly bitch about the wrong of it all, and years later send the next crop of young ones off to gain revenge. Now Modan and Lagan's people also roamed the hills bearing that message, one that those same youngsters were keen to hear.

Bryn found himself fighting both sides of his own mind. When he finally left Cumbria for Brigantia, it was with a plow hitched to his heart. He felt in sore need of advice and rather than travelling east, he turned north to Epiacum. He found his da in no better state than himself, for Cethen still brooded over Modan's encounter with Frevan's man Glas. Both Bryn and his da were reluctant to accept Luin's opinion, but neither had seen each other since to talk it through.

⁂

"I'll be glad to give you advice," Cethen growled when Bryn and Trista arrived at his door, quick to give the reason for their visit. "And you're welcome to take it. It's never done me a single groat of good."

Yet as he listened to his son's indecision, told across a table laden with Kelpy's cooking, Cethen realized that advice of any kind was useless. It was one thing when a son asked his da what might lure a perch on a cloudy day; it was another when he asked how to gain a kingdom, and hold it. For when the fog cleared, the problem was Bryn's to resolve. It was the damnedest dilemma he'd ever heard; and of all people, he was the worst one to ask! Besides, having spent the best part of a lifetime listening to others, including chieftains and kings, he was convinced that any advice other than your own stank like a pig anyway.

Galgar had once made a comment, on the same night the Caledoni chieftain called a counsel before the failed assault on the Ninth legion – which, Cethen remembered with a grim smile, was right on the tail of the horny runt's successful assault on Morallta! What had he said? *"The best advice you ever get is your own."* Cethen shook his head and chuckled, for the words were a circle. Galgar *had* taken his own advice and the gutsy little fox was long dead; while he, Cethen Lamh-fada, seemed to listen to everyone else's advice and still walked on the green side of the weeds – for whatever that was worth.

But he was the boy's da, and he had to say something. His mind churned through the possibilities, only to realize that there was really no one else Bryn might ask for help. Not any of their own people, anyway. Borba was about the only one left of the old wolves, and he'd gone home. Besides, you don't ask a wolf about anything except his next kill. And Cian was no different, only like as not, he'd take half as long to give the same useless answer. The one who could best offer practical advice was probably Elena, but that was out of the question. That left his other son, which made Cethen shake his head and laugh.

"What's so funny?" Bryn demanded, as if offended.

"He does that once in a while," Kelpy teased as she cleared the table; she, too, shook her head. "Something starts tossing about in his mind, but he keeps his gob shut. It makes me want to choke him, because then I have to ask why." She ruffled Cethen's hair as she passed by, and he absently slapped at her hand. "So what's so funny?"

"I was thinking that maybe we should ask my other son what he thought."

"Rhun? What's so funny about that?" Bryn asked.

Trista laughed. "You just gave the answer."

"Exactly. I've got three more sons, but you only mentioned Rhun!" Cethen chuckled ruefully. "You can hardly ask the other two, can you? Modan is part of the problem. We may as well ask a bear where to set a beehive. And as to the honourable governor, a person may as well ask commitment from a sylph. Don't get me wrong, I think Tuis would give sincere, honest advice, I really do; but it would only be good until someone else catches his ear."

"So what's different about Rhun?" Bryn asked. "He's with the Romans, too."

"Aah, but he's as much one of us as he is one of them," Cethen said. "He sees both sides, just like you, only he's more – well, I suppose he's more firm in his seeing. Not only that, he's got the torque. Or I'm assuming he's got it."

Trista blinked as if disturbed. "You think maybe he doesn't?"

"No, no, not the way you mean." If there was one thing of which Cethen was certain, it was that his twins, between them, had kept the trust. "He'll have it. I meant whether he has it here or in Rome."

"Wherever it is, will he hold Bryn to ransom for it?" Trista asked.

"Never, but he will hold Bryn responsible for it. He'll not part with the torque until he's certain that responsibility will be fulfilled. But I think . . ."

Cethen paused, gathering his thoughts. What *would* Rhun demand for the torque before he parted with the bauble? Certainly not coin. Did he still think the same way he had when following the blue and red ribbons into Cumbria with Cian and Coira, all those years ago? His true feeling had shown in the telling of his travels across half the Roman Empire: *"Father, let me say this. As long as they want to, the Romans are here to stay!"* His son had then told why he was willing to serve Rome. If he wore the uniform, the lad said, at least *his* men would be making certain that as few of the tribe got hurt as possible.

Cethen smiled at the recollection as he finished his answer, "In a way, I think he sees things as they were when Cartimandua was queen: the tribes make an accommodation with Rome, but someone strong should sit in her place. If the Brigantes could come to an agreement with the Carvetii – the two tribes are almost kin, anyway – Rhun figures we'd have both a voice and a choice in what happens. There's only one who can do that, Bryn – someone like you."

"King Bryn! It has a sound to it," Trista said, and giggled.

Bryn glared at Trista as if irked by her fribbling. "So how does he figure that's going to happen? I haven't got that figured myself. That's why I'm here."

"There's only one way, isn't there?" Cethen decided it didn't take much figuring. He had four boys and most of them – three to be precise – should be able to find a way of living with the Romans. He winked as he pushed his empty mug toward Kelpy. "Tell him where we're going, lass."

Kelpy shrugged. "I suppose you'll be getting after seeing your oldest."

"Wisdom comes with age," Cethen said piously.

"So you figure I should be asking Rhun how to best go about it?" Bryn looked far from happy.

"Well, you can't ask Modan, can you?"

"There's one other who might also help," Trista suggested. "Her brain's set as firmly in her skull as any of them, and she knows our people."

"Aah, wee Jess." Cethen nodded his agreement. "A good thought."

"You mean the dwarf?" Bryn said.

"Her name's Jessa," Cethen muttered.

"Yes, dammit, not *the dwarf*," Trista added, just as irritated.

⸙

"So what are you going to do?" Trista yawned as she eased herself down onto Bryn's saddle, which sat beside the cloak-covered spruce boughs that formed his bed.

It was late and there was no moon, but a thousand stars dotted the sky. Bryn and his people had taken refuge farther up the valley from his da's lodge, in one of a score of small pastures claimed from the forest. The campfire had died to a glowing pile of embers and the valley lay cloaked in a dark silence, broken only by the soft rustle of the horses as they pulled at the grass. Bryn's men lay sprawled like a circle of dead around the hot ashes, forming a ring of long black shadows that might have been grave mounds. Bryn had placed himself off to the side, close by the trees.

"About what?"

He glanced up as if surprised, which he shouldn't have been, because he'd seen her walking over from where she'd made her own bed. He also knew full well *about what*! But Trista was tired – the inside sort of tired – and felt the need to talk, so she ignored his feigned ignorance. "About going to see Rhun."

Bryn pummelled the bag of clothes that served as a pillow before lying back on his cloak and covering himself with a blanket that he pulled over his shoulder. Then, with infuriating slowness, he finally rolled onto his back, looked upward, and answered her question. "I don't know."

Trista could have booted him in the ribs, but resisted the urge. She'd wandered over just to talk to the man, and here he was, as icy as a mountain stream and as indifferent as a pregnant sow. She took a deep breath, then let it go; but her frustration remained. Yes, she wanted to know what he planned on doing. And yes, she likely knew the answer: he had decided on going to his half-brother Rhun, which only made sense. If you start making alliances, start with who you know. Only Bryn hadn't said so.

Yet she'd come over for another reason than just to talk, and it wasn't because she couldn't find sleep. She felt a need to be there with him, to say something – anything – rather than climb under her own cold blanket and stare at the stars.

The meal with Cethen had gone well earlier, as had the talk afterward, softened by a few mugs of warm mead that Kelpy had brewed from last year's jealously hoarded honey crop. Trista was feeling a glow of well-being as she and Bryn had walked the short distance back to where the others had made camp, her cheeks flushed with the warmth of an evening well spent. They had said little as they came into the clearing, where everyone but the two guards had already fallen asleep. She had been careful not to wake the others when she had wandered over to sit beside him.

She was, Trista realized – perhaps – maybe – willing to go further than just talk, should he show the least inclination. In fact, *be honest*, tonight she did want more. A warm glow of longing had flooded her mind, with an intensity that was far more than just the effects of the mead. It was Bryn she wanted, his warmth and his closeness, and her pride could go rot! Tonight, she felt an overwhelming fondness for the man that, damn him, was not being returned in the slightest.

And damn Modan!

And damn Treno, too!

Bryn might be the only one who might ever make her forget that dark pair of lads; and here they were, everyone asleep, and the guards off in the distance where the clearing opened on the trail . . .

"I guess I don't either," Trista heard herself say as she found herself climbing to her feet. She glanced coldly down at Bryn, who stared back, his features unreadable in the shadows. She shrugged and said good night, then walked quickly back across the pasture.

⁂

Bryn lay watching as Trista crossed the short distance to her bed, then he rolled onto his side and gazed blankly at the dark wall of trees. His jaw clenched suddenly, and his eyes squeezed shut. One hand formed a fist that slammed down on the ground beside his bed.

"Dammit!" he groaned in a voice that was barely audible, and again he rolled onto his back. He gazed up at the stars, his face contorted with frustration. Why, oh why, could she never speak what was on her mind? He certainly wasn't going to; it had been humiliating enough the last time. Yet . . . and yet, he'd known full well what Trista was thinking on, and he'd kept his gob shut! Bryn cursed and snarled his frustration to the darkness, as his chest tightened and both fists thumped hard on the grass beside him.

⁂

Modan passed through Cethen's small village two days after Bryn departed. He rode in from the north, intent on giving the fort at Epiacum its distance. Cethen figured his son had at least a hundred men with him, though that was a wild guess; tallying any kind of number was low on his list of skills. More than half the men were Selgovae, and the rest were a pish-podge from the other tribes, mainly Carvetii. It was clear that his son was angry, even as he dismounted in front of the small lodge.

"I heard Bryn and my wife were here. Are they still?" Modan demanded as he slid from the saddle. Treno was right there behind him, as were two or three others; the rest of them hung back by the stream, watering their horses and for the most part behaving.

"They left a couple of days ago," Cethen replied, and gestured toward the small lodge. "Something to drink? Eat, maybe?" He cast a meaningful glance toward the stream. "I can't do much for the rest. We're mostly living on what's left of last year's crops."

"Where did they go?" Modan's second question was as blunt as his first.

"Back to Cumbria," Cethen said truthfully. There was no point mentioning that the pair had gone back to find Frevan's man Luin, before taking him up to the fort at Luguvalium. Nor was there anything gained by telling Modan that at dawn the next day he and a few of his own people were setting off in the same direction, hoping to meet there with Rhun.

Modan seemed to have no interest in food or drink, however, or anything congenial. His next question was again blunt and to the point.

"Is the prick humping her?"

Cethen was about to deny it, but Kelpy stepped forward to answer and her anger was clear. "No he isn't, though I wouldn't blame him. They stay apart, bedding with their own band of followers, and there's the end of it!"

"Did he tell you he's not, or was it her?" Modan demanded, and he glared at Kelpy as if she was lying. "And why would she bring it up, if there's nothing –"

"There was no need to bring anything up. A woman knows. In fact," Kelpy's voice turned to a sneer, "I don't think she likes any part of that side of life. What happened, did you ruin it for her?"

Modan's lip curled back and Cethen thought he was about to strike her. He moved forward to place himself between the two, but Treno clearly didn't like the direction of the talk either. He grabbed Modan's arm, holding him back.

"Come on Mod, let's go," he muttered, "there's nothing more to be had here. We've a way to travel."

Modan grumbled and reluctantly heaved himself back onto his horse, his mood as black as a bog. He stared down at his da, as if unsure what to say. Then, as if looking for something, his eyes wandered slowly about the tiny village.

Cethen simply stared at the ground. Part of him was fighting his own rising anger, while another part felt as if his belly was torn out, and his heart with it. There were questions he needed to ask – yet if he was honest with himself, he knew the answers. It was important, though, that one be confirmed: what had happened in the forest the day they were leaving Cumbria? He started to ask, but Modan had other things on his mind.

"I thought Gavor was with you."

"Huh?" Cethen was surprised by the question and glanced about the small cluster of huts, but didn't see the youth. Borba's boy, oddly enough, had wanted to remain here in the valley and then catch up with Bryn, and Cethen had agreed; the lad was certainly worth the feeding of one more mouth. He was about to tell Modan where to find him, when Kelpy answered for him.

"He's gone too," she said, gesturing vaguely toward the west.

"Oh." Modan looked uncertain for a moment, then asked, "When did you say Bryn left?"

"A couple of days ago," Cethen replied and then, simply because he was curious, asked, "Where are you away to now?"

"Yeah, I'll be sure to tell that," Modan muttered and with no word beyond a grunt, turned his horse toward the stream. Treno was already ahead of him, shouting the order to ride.

"You could tell us a place, and we wouldn't know if it was a tale or the truth anyway," Kelpy scornfully called to his back.

Cethen watched silently as the horses cantered off down the valley floor, Modan taking the lead. Kelpy moved to stand close by her da as the pounding of hooves died on the chill morning air. A dozen or so villagers soon emerged from the rude buildings, and several more came back from the nearby forest where they'd fled when the small army of riders had first appeared.

"Modan?" one asked.

Cethen simply nodded, and the man spat. He didn't ask the reason for the boy being there, for there was no need. Those who had taken to their homes had plainly heard; those who hadn't would soon be told. Cethen had a question, though, and he asked it of Kelpy. "Why did you tell him Gavor had gone with Bryn? The lad said he was off to the beaver pond on the other side of Cogan's crag. That's less than half a morning's walk."

"I didn't say where he went, I just said he was gone. If Modan thinks he went with Bryn, then too bad." Kelpy shrugged her indifference, but she did look thoughtful. "Besides, I didn't like the way he asked."

# Chapter XXVII

## Eboracum, Augustus, A.D. 105

Tuis flinched as Zoticus entered his quarters carrying a single scroll. It wasn't so much the message itself as the manner in which it was carried. The veteran's features were again scribed with the self satisfied smirk of a man bearing bad tidings.

Zoticus drew himself up in front of the desk and, without bothering with the usual sly sliding, set the offending message square in the centre. "A dispatch arrived late last night, sir."

Tuis groaned. "Give me the sordid details," he mumbled, forehead in hand.

"It's sealed, sir."

"Then give me the rumours that came with it."

"It's from the commander at Bremenium."

"And . . . ?" Tuis asked peevishly.

"It appears that he's in possession of new intelligence from the Votadini. The barbarian Lagan – the one that attacked your army of reprisal, sir, along with your, er . . ." Zoticus coughed as if suddenly unwilling to finish.

Tuis cursed under his breath. Was the man throwing salt on open sores, or had he let his gob get ahead of his gorm? *Along with your brother, whom you caught and let go* – that was what the fool clearly had on the point of his tongue.

The clerk quickly retraced his steps. "It would appear that the barbarians have convinced themselves the attack on your army contained an element of success. In fact, they seem to think they didn't do too badly, all things considered. And –"

"How's that?" Tuis exclaimed. "They lost over a half-dozen men for every one of ours, including that brother of mine whom you not so delicately avoid mentioning."

"Well, that was only temporary, sir, wasn't it? He . . . er, he did appear to have escaped and rejoined his fellow barbarians after we thought he was dead. I believe the family held a sort of wake, did they not?"

"Careful where you shake the salt, soldier," Tuis growled.

"Er, yes sir. Though perhaps I should mention that if we are to believe the commander at Bremenium, your brother's reputation was somewhat enhanced by the experience. The escape bit, I mean, not the attack."

"Did we ever find the man who 'lost' him?" Tuis asked irritably, uncomfortable with the truth of what his clerk said.

"The praefectus who investigated determined that his fetters were poorly secured. He got loose during one of the rest halts, then appears to have hidden himself in the bushes and –"

"That stinks like a pile of pig shit."

"—and the column marched on. He wasn't missed until the count that night. Two of the guards were flogged."

"And I'll wager it wasn't too heavily, either," Tuis muttered, then laughed softly to himself. "Oh well, at least we *hung* on to part of him – if you'll pardon the pun."

"Hung on?"

"Yeah, *hung* on." Tuis chuckled and, since it seemed such a good story, told Zoticus how Modan lost his testes, and his wife's role in their removal. When he was done he frowned, pondering the paths that some people pursue in order to gain revenge.

"This man Lagan, sir," Zoticus said after a polite laugh. "The commander says he's been moving among the tribes, garnering support. The man claims to have more than fifteen thousand ready to answer the call. Oh, and he's got your, er, brother doing the same thing among the Carvetii, and those Brigantes living toward the northeast. Another commander at *Vindolanda* forwarded *that* particular intelligence, because," Zoticus coughed discreetly, took a deep breath, and again looked to the ceiling, "your brother was recruiting in his area. Lagan's people are helping him deliver the message. Several tuaths are ready to follow him, especially," Zoticus's eyes briefly closed as he rocked on his heels, "after imposition of the latest tax."

Tuis grunted at the mention of the tax and chose to belittle Zoticus's figures. "Yes, well, fifteen thousand, eh? Sounds a bit exaggerated."

"Perhaps. That's only supposed to be Lagan's people, however, and a few others who arrived from farther north. The Votadini believe he'll muster at least another five thousand, if not more, from the Carvetii and northern Brigantia."

"Can't you bring any *glad* tidings?" Tuis muttered petulantly. "I wonder where he got those figures from?"

"Since you mention glad tidings, sir," Zoticus tapped the scroll, "there are some in there. Your other brother. The one who was down here . . ."

"Rhun?"

"No, it began with a 'B.' Brom, or something."

"Oh, that's Bryn. When I talked to him, he sounded willing to make compromises."

"He is – or at least, he was. That was the glad tidings, though the man's fighting a battle in a bog when it comes to rallying support. There seems to be some help, though. The same report from Vindolanda mentions rumours that an old torque of some kind has surfaced. The barbarians hold it to be some sort of good luck charm."

"The torque of Brigantia!" Tuis pretended an interest, but he already knew as much from Rhun; there was no sense telling everyone where it had come from, though. "If the rumours I heard are true, it's worth a lot of coin." Which was a hard fact, and he had to give his brother the credit for holding onto the bauble. If it had been up to him, well, there were far better uses.

"However!" Zoticus's tone turned heavy, and Tuis pushed all thought of the gold torque aside as the man *finally* came to the main thrust of the message. He sighed as it was delivered. "The Votadini figure less than two months."

"Two months to what?" he demanded mechanically, though just as quickly he knew the answer. Zoticus provided it anyway.

"Less than two months, and Lagan's going to start his campaign. The roads, the small outposts, supply columns, the usual thing. If he's like the others, he'll try drawing us into the open to force the issue, in the hope they'll win." Zoticus clucked disparagingly. "They'll never learn."

"Trouble is, the sods always spill a river of blood before we set them back in their place," Tuis grumbled, his mind running over the options. He'd have to start moving troops north, of course, which was going to send Marius into another tantrum. The other two legions could supply a good deal of the manpower if needed, though ever since the snows melted the Ordivices had been at it again! The lunatics were off on another rampage, dragging their ovine neighbours with them. That meant both the Twentieth and the Second would be tied up to some extent in the west, but maybe two half-legions for a short campaign . . .

Tuis sighed and slumped in his chair, vainly trying to make the latest problem mesh with the long list of others that plagued his mind – including that of Cronus and his taxes, which was quickly rising close to the top of the scroll. He shouldn't have given in to the man. Sometimes, money just wasn't worth the bother.

※

Tuis refused to be cowed by Marius's autocratic affectations; nor would he be distracted by the man's endless whining over manpower and his infernal walls. It was increasingly clear that Marius was determined to complete the stone fortress before his posting ended, and if it could be done in half the time, so much the better. But the legate had other duties, not the least of which was commanding an army. The Ninth was responsible for the northern tribes, not building stone monuments dedicated to the immortal memory of Roman aristocrats.

Tuis had recently discovered a marble slab that Marius had shipped in from Rome: a huge rectangle of the finest Carrara marble, curved on one end and carved with an elaborately sculpted border. Only the dedication remained, and Marius Appius Tullius was doubtless holding back on its final testimony in hope of a battle honour – which could only happen if he got his stone stacking legion out in the field!

Marius was not to be found when he searched for the man later that day. The orderly room informed him that the legate had gone to Calcaria, presumably inspecting the quarry. Tuis had noticed that the neat, square stacks of stone barged in from downriver had been growing low, a condition he attributed to far too many troops using the blocks to build the walls. Marius, as certain as death, would have seen it as nothing more than a supply shortage. Fuming, Tuis stalked down to the south entrance of the fortress, as much to allow his blood to cool as anything else. It was there, atop the walkway that straddled the twin gate towers, that Livia found him, an hour later.

"It does look sort of lovely, doesn't it?" She set her hands alongside her husband's, atop the stone battlement overlooking the river.

Tuis raised his eyebrows in surprise. The Abus stood a little over a hundred paces away. A good length of sturdy dock was built into the riverbank – and he grunted annoyance as it struck him that it, too, was being readied for stone reconstruction. Several ships were moored alongside, and a clutter of cargo littered the shore. Just upstream the bridge, a plain wooden trestle set on stone piers, ended in a road that sloped steeply upward. The buildings on the far side of the river were plentiful enough, considering the short life of the fortress, but they were unattractive timber structures clinging to a narrow stretch of flat land that bordered the river. The trees that lined the road farther up the hill were quite lush and pastoral, Tuis conceded, as were those farther along the riverbanks; but all in all, the scene could hardly be described as lovely, and he said so.

"I don't mean that," Livia said impatiently, and waved a hand along the wall on which they stood. "I mean the new entrance, and Marius's walls. They're coming along quite nicely."

Suddenly his wife's voice was grating again. *Marius's walls!* Tuis sighed and looked out over the battlements, then from side to side, his eyes reluctantly assessing the pristine lines of the new fortifications. Off to his right, perhaps two hundred paces upriver, soldiers were finishing the stone tower that marked the southwest corner of the fortress. The wall that angled northward from there had been started, though most of that side – other than the open space where they were rebuilding the earth ramparts – remained defended by the old wooden palisades.

Tuis reluctantly admitted to himself that the neatness of it did, in fact, look quite "lovely": the long, straight precision of the fresh-cut sandstone walkway; the solid strength of the three interval towers; the perfect rank of crisp, crenellated battlements; and cloaking it all, a sense of indestructible permanence. He sighed, seeing where a man might find himself taken up by such a project – but not if he was commanding an army and an enemy was making ready to batter down the gates. Or at the very least, pound on the gates of your farthest outposts.

"Yeah, I suppose," Tuis said grudgingly. "But there's ample time to build Eboracum into what it should be. In the meantime, there are –"

"In the meantime, there are things that need doing," Livia cut in and laid one hand on his arm, gesturing across the river with the other. A group of riders had crested the hill, tiny with distance and half hidden by the trees that sheltered the road. The tired horses, with warm stables and fresh fodder within easy reach, pricked up their ears with impatience. The riders eased off on the reins and the animals broke into a slow canter for the final stretch home.

"About time," Tuis grumbled, recognizing Marius in the lead. "I wish I could piss off for a day in the country whenever I feel like it."

※

Marius groaned as his horse clattered across the thick wooden timbers of the bridge, and he caught sight of the governor standing atop one of his gleaming stone gate towers. The glow of pride that had filled his chest on viewing the trenchant lines of his fortress escaped him in a single breath, replaced by a brain-dragging gloom that seeped down to his belly. It was ever the way of the gods when a man was blessed with a joyous and glorious day! They shat on you!

What new and imagined problem was Sabinius about to drop on his shoulders?

"There is no way I'm going to the man's quarters," he muttered to his personal slave as the soft scrunch of hooves on gravel replaced the hard echo of the wooden planks.

The slave nodded his understanding. "Your horse, sir?"

"I'll keep him with me. I might be in need of a fast retreat," Marius replied.

He called a greeting as they neared the gate, and pulled his horse to one side so those who followed could pass. The animal chewed at the bit and pawed the ground, clearly annoyed at being held back. Marius tossed the reins to one of the guards and hurried up the steps before Tuis could start back to the residence.

"Ah, good to see you," he lied cheerfully on reaching the walkway. The governor had abandoned the crosswalk above the entrance, and had climbed down as far as the wall. Behind him trailed Livia and he repeated the lie, at the same time wondering, once again, why a woman with such pleasant features and appealing form should be cursed with such a voice and mind. In any case she, unlike her husband, brought a modicum of pleasure to the eye.

"And you, too." Livia, at least, sounded sincere. She placed a hand on his arm. "I trust your day went well."

"Actually, it did." Marius decided that he, too, could be sincere.

"Good, good." She smiled and squeezed his arm before letting go. "Now that you're here, I'll leave you men to discuss your military things. I'm sure I'm needed elsewhere."

*So it's to be military matters, is it?* Marius thought as he stepped to one side. *What godless disaster has happened now?* He caught the faint scent of roses as Livia edged by and wondered, also not for the first time, exactly where the woman stood with her arm-squeezing familiarity. The trouble with the overtly friendly ones was that you never knew: was that precisely what they were, just friendly? Or were they bored, and looking to break the tedium? He shook his head, his nose twitching from the woman's perfume. *The longer a man is away from home, the more his mind –*

"How are things down at the quarry?" Tuis asked, and chuckled at the idiom, often employed by the plebs when feeling abused.

Marius simply smiled, determined not to allow irritation to overcome poise. "Excellent, in fact," he replied. "Several production bogs cleared, a change or two to the duty roster, and I do believe we'll now be doing better than before."

That was not the thing to say, Marius realized as soon as the words had passed his lips. Tuis beamed and drew in his breath. His face – it was florid, which meant he'd been into the grapes – was set in that firm no-nonsense expression the man used when certain of purpose, but weak of resolve. Marius managed to keep the annoyance from his face as he waited.

"That's good, then," Tuis said firmly. "That means you'll have less trouble freeing up the troops you're going to need."

Marius curbed his tongue, deciding for the moment to assume the role of appeaser – not an easy choice. But first there were questions the governor expected of him, picky ones, and he wouldn't disappoint.

"What's happening, then?" he asked, though he knew full well. There had been more than one dispatch to arrive from Bremenium late last night, and he'd read his before leaving for Calcaria.

"Well, we knew it was coming sometime," Tuis intoned gloomily. "Now we have an idea when. It could be just over a month, according to the commander at Bremenium. That's sooner than expected. But I suppose it does fit with what else we've been hearing."

"Well, he should know," Marius conceded, noting that the timing had been cut by almost half. "You'll be drawing troops from the south?"

"As many as I can. I'm preparing dispatches to both legions tonight, but I think I'll leave on a visit myself in the next day or two – follow up on them." Tuis tilted his head and looked pointedly at Marius. "You know how these legates like to hang onto their troops! I won't tolerate it this time, not from any of them. Matters are serious. This is larger than we figured."

"I'll give what I can . . ." Marius started, the words coming out by habit; again he knew it was not the thing to say.

He stiffened angrily as Tuis almost shouted, "None of this *'give what I can'* shit." Marius flinched, glancing about to see who was within hearing; then, thank the gods, the man lowered his voice. "Marius, this could be another Punic war we've got going. I want all work stopped on the fortress until it's over. Every available man will take to the field."

That was far more drastic than Marius had expected and he was about to say so, then stopped. There were other ways. "I'll need to keep two cohorts back," he said.

"You've got how many of them left? Eight?" Tuis asked.

"Correct," Marius said, grimacing in disgust. "There are the two in Dacia with Trajan. Almost a thousand men! Some spit-pickling commander is unquestionably keeping them for his own use. I wrote –"

"Now why would a commander keep men back for his own use?" Tuis drawled, clearly unable to resist picking. "I know you'll give all you can spare. Let's see, if I leave you with two cohorts, we'd only be marching with six. One is enough to defend this place. You've got several cavalry troops attached, and there are four or five other forts within a good day's ride. You'll just have to –"

"To defend this place I need at least two cohorts, including the First," Marius cried, his voice a deliberate whine that sounded, even to his own ears, like the grating tone of the man's wife.

"The first cohort? Marius, that where our service support is – a double cohort. You're a daft-man," Tuis cried, the epithet slipping out in his native tongue. "Two regular cohorts can remain; that's the most to be spared. And they will be the two with the least men on strength."

*Well, that went not too badly,* Marius decided. With those on sick call, that would still provide men enough to keep some sort of activity going. As to the two "under-strength" cohorts, that could be worked around. A few more on the sick list when the Ninth marched, perhaps . . .

Marius was certain that the current threat was vastly exaggerated. The governor would find himself leading nothing more than another barren march through the northern hills, chasing the barbarian faerie. The man's lack of experience was feeding his panic. Such reaction was typical of a man with a barbarian background: bang the shield, wave the sword, and shout the alarm. He'd be off consulting a druid, next! If there truly was such a great build-up of barbarian strength, there would be far more sign of it. The entire exercise was a waste; and the greatest waste of all was that he, Marius Appius, would once more have to tear his men away from the fortress and lead them through the wilds of barbaria in a . . .

". . . heard from Cronus when his shipments are coming in?"

Marius returned his attention to the governor in time to catch the gist of the question. He fought back the urge to shake his head. One moment it was a tale of panic, the next it was fretting over lost *lucrum*. Admittedly, they both had a share in the procurator's rash investment, but as far as he was concerned, his was protected: payment would only be made to the ships' masters on delivery. And as to the rightness of it, the fool Cronus had shorted himself on the coin; it didn't make sense not to throw him a line if there was a profit to be made. Even so, there was a time and a place to talk about such matters.

"My clerk tells me the first vessel is due any day." Marius drew himself up, speaking as if such mundane matters were beneath him. Then, for extra measure, he tossed out another lie just to taunt the man. "I did hear a rumour that there was a bad storm in the *Mare Cantabricum.*"

He narrowed his eyes in amusement, expecting to see anguish on Sabinius's face, but the man surprised him. He simply shrugged and said, "I suppose if the scow sinks, it's one less thing to worry about."

# Chapter XXXIII

## Aballava, Augustus, A.D. 105

They met in a large warehouse built to unload supplies for Aballava and the two small outposts that lay farther along the shore to the west. The fort had been built by Agricola on the south bank of the estuary, a mile and half down from the mouth of the Ituna. The land in between was low and almost level with the shoreline. It was in part fertile, in other parts marsh, and when a cold wind blew in from the sea it was as bleak as a gutted graveyard. Even so, much of the land around the fort was put to crop, more so toward the east where the estuary narrowed and the warehouse had been built. There the trees began to root, growing thicker and taller as the river wandered the half-dozen miles upstream to Luguvalium.

The Ituna's enormous estuary was calm and deceptive, concealing strong, contrary currents that forced incoming vessels to navigate a tide that rose to flood in a third of the time taken to ebb. A wooden dock had been built in front of the warehouse, which was free of water for much of the tidal cycle, and as evening fell it stood oddly isolated: a tall shadow on stark, stilt-like pylons, high above a huge expanse of sandy, mud-slicked flats. A flock of sandpipers foraged close by the hull of a lone cargo ship that lay tilted to one side, hung up on its mooring ropes as it awaited the next full tide.

Inside the warehouse the stale, nose-twitching dust of sacked grain hung heavy in the air, and the sour reek of wine rose from the damp floorboards where hundreds of amphorae stood in fat orange ranks by the duty office. Jessa noted an accumulation of cracked containers, and cynically wondered how many had been fractures of convenience. She smiled and nodded her thanks to Rhun as he held open the door of the office.

The official in charge of the warehouse, likely a centurio, did not lack for creature comforts: a plump sleeping couch lay off to one side, and a long shelf sat crowded with small wine jugs, each probably filled from the "spoilage" outside the door. Numerous clay jars lined a second shelf, no doubt more spoils garnered from cargoes shipped in from the far reaches of the empire. A single table, surrounded by a dozen comfortable chairs and a single tall stool, had been placed in the centre of the room; and though it was not quite dark, a lantern sat in its centre, already lit. A mouth-watering platter of food sat beside it, along with two bulbous jugs of wine, and a dozen goblets made of red-tinted glass. *Where did a centurio acquire a dozen glass goblets?*

"Ah, the fruits of command!" Rhun chuckled as his eyes fell on the food and the wine. Marcus readily agreed. They had entered the duty room through a doorway that opened into the warehouse from landward side, but a second entrance opened directly outside onto a long wooden walkway that led down to the dock.

"For you, or the man in charge of this place?" Jessa quipped.

"Both," Rhun said as he popped an olive into his mouth.

A brazier sat cold in one corner of the room, but whoever had placed it there had also left a neat pile of charcoal ready to be fired, and a fresh taper for the lighting. The evening air held no chill, however, and Jessa shook her head when Rhun picked up the taper and looked askance. "I'm warm enough, but we should set the lantern outside. They may be early."

"I suppose, though it's barely dark yet." Rhun picked up the flickering lamp and set it outside the door, as they'd agreed with Trista.

"Sir, is everything as it should be?"

Rhun turned to the slight cavalryman who stood in the entrance to the warehouse. "Ah, Kaeso. Yes, it seems to be. What about you?"

"All secure. If you'd care to inspect."

"Er . . ."

"I'll take a walk around and see, if you like," Jessa offered quickly, her eyes meeting Kaeso's for a moment. Her cheeks felt suddenly warm.

"No, that's fine, my dear; I'll go." Marcus frowned down his nose at his daughter, then shrugged and wandered back through the warehouse with the small-framed cavalry officer. Jessa smiled, deciding her father was growing wiser as he aged. As, it seemed, had Trista, for she was growing more cautious – though not for herself, but for Bryn.

The young woman had arrived at Luguvalium's gates with what at first seemed bizarre terms for Bryn's meeting with Rhun. Jessa had commented on Trista's new-found vigilance, and had her ears burned for the smirk that went with it. Trista then told her of Modan's mad attack in the Cumbrian hills, and Jessa said nothing. It seemed that they all now shared a common enemy.

Trista at first said Bryn had chosen the warehouse because he refused to meet inside the fort, which was ridiculous, and Jessa had said so. Behind Luguvalium's walls, he was as far from Modan's clutches as he would ever be. But Trista denied that, telling her that Bryn felt the stronghold was intimidating, a place where he would feel trapped. Yet the Roman warehouse was hardly less confining. The dock and the buildings *were* well out in the open, granted, and Jessa supposed there was safety to be found in that. Then it struck her that it wasn't Modan that concerned Bryn, but more likely Rhun. Was the man now looking to his back for imagined knives? Or – and she smiled at the notion, for it was so typical of her people – did Bryn simply want to push a point, and choose his own location to meet? That way, he would appear to be in charge, and forcing the issue.

The chance to find why was not long coming. Marcus returned and the three of them had barely begun sampling the platter of food when footsteps echoed off the wooden walkway outside. There seemed to be more than a few, and Jessa felt a twinge of alarm. Then the outside door opened, and Cethen stood framed in the entrance.

⸸

Rhun contained his surprise and beckoned his da inside. Cethen entered slowly, first glancing around the room, then inclining his head to acknowledge the three of them. Only then did Bryn, Trista, and three others enter, Trista carrying the lantern, which she set back on the table. Rhun recognized Gavor, Borba's boy, but the other two were strangers.

"Er, this is . . ." Cethen began, gesturing absently behind him.

"I know Gavor," Rhun said. "And this is Jessa and her da, Marcus. Bryn, you may remember them from when they were, well, with our da –"

"Of course. Though I haven't seen either since the lass was a bairn." Bryn smiled and bobbed his head toward them both, then turned to the last two, putting an end to his da's fumbling. "This is Luin, one of Frevan's people, and this here is Arlen. Borba figured he should meet up with you. He's of the Votadini."

"Oh?" Rhun's tone made it a question.

"It seems that many of his people are also becoming concerned about the Selgovae."

"Especially if they prove successful," Rhun said bluntly. The Votadini, like the Parisii farther south, were a tribe whose land bordered the east coast. Neither were violently opposed to Rome. The empire was probably a lesser threat than that posed by their more powerful neighbours, be they Selgovae or, ironically, the Brigantes.

Bryn chose to ignore the challenge in the comment, and turned to face Jessa. "And how is the young lady? Last time I saw you, you were . . ." He hesitated as if unsure what to say and both Rhun and Marcus smiled; Bryn's next words would normally have been "you were just a little girl." Instead he finished with, "You were quite young; what, three or four?"

"Four, I believe," Jessa supplied, chuckling at Bryn's discomfort, "and the young lady is doing fine. She's also pleased to see everyone here."

"As we all are." Marcus gestured toward the food on the table. "Why don't we get seated, and enjoy what our ill-used stores keeper has provided."

The talk was at first general, but there was little to catch up on and it quickly moved toward the reason for the meeting. Rhun saw at once that Bryn was less than clear as to his plans for the future. Or was he just being careful? The path he travelled in succeeding Frevan seemed poorly mapped, though he did appear to have given it a good deal of thought. In fact, it seemed as if the man had given it nothing but thought, to the point of miring his mind!

Someone like Modan, or even his brother Tuis, would have simply plunged forward, ignoring the spears and arrows that inevitably followed. Should either succeed in anything, it would be through sheer will, good luck and desperation; yet if they failed, it would not be through lack of trying. Not that their way was any better, but at least there would have been action, and Rhun found the difference disturbing. Bryn's lack of any such action was unfitting, and he struggled to curb his impatience as the talk circled aimlessly around the table. When the words finally halted due to lack of substance there was a long, awkward silence, and Rhun could stand it no more.

"Do you want this, or don't you?" he demanded.

"Yes," Bryn said quickly, and glanced at Trista. Rhun caught Marcus's eye and saw that he had also seen the look pass between the two. Bryn spoke again, this time emphasizing his reply. "*Yes*, of course I want it. There are aspects I don't like, I'll admit. But in the end, I think what I want is best for the people."

*Think?* Rhun pressed, "So what *do* you want, then?"

"Pride. Dignity. Respect."

"You only get that with solid decisions, a firm grip on your sword, and stomping any man who stands in your way," Rhun snapped back, wondering if his half-brother did have the balls to run the tribes – or did that glance toward Trista mean that she had the grip on them? Was this the same man he'd met at Eboracum?

Bryn's next comment surprised him, though. "I don't mean for me! I want those things for the tribes. Rhun, between Brigantia and Cumbria, our people number in the hundreds of thousands. If you add the Votadini," he acknowledged Arlen with a nod, "there are tens of thousands more. None of us intend to stop fighting the Romans just so they can rule us like slaves. When I lead, we either fight, or we have a say in how *we* run our lives. And that will be the least of it."

"So why are you so indecisive?" Marcus blurted, clearly baffled.

Rhun saw both Arlen and Luin nod their agreement. No one, it seemed, was able to understand Bryn's dithering – with the possible exception of his own da. *Maybe,* Rhun thought, and cringed, *Bryn came by it naturally.* Could it possibly be in the blood?

Cethen opened his mouth as if to answer for Bryn, as did Trista, but Jessa cut them both off with a question of her own. "You two," she said bluntly, her eyes shifting between Bryn and Trista, "are you now humping each other?"

"What?" Trista's outburst dispelled any idea that they were.

Even Marcus seemed surprised at his daughter's bluntness, but Rhun carefully watched Bryn as he, in turn, growled his disbelief . . . or was he simply snorting his disappointment?

"It's just the opposite," Bryn protested, and Rhun *did* note a twinge of regret as he added, "believe me. Why would you even ask?"

"You do travel together," Jessa said. She waved a hand toward Trista. "And Bryn, you seem to think she has a say in what you're doing. Is she advising you, or holding you back?"

Bryn laughed. "Again, just the opposite. If anything, Trista is far too hasty. This all takes time."

"Time? Hah! The trouble is, the man thinks too much," Trista said, and turned impatiently to Jessa. "Bryn's going to lead the tribes. He knows he is; I know he is; but he first wants to chart his course all the way to its finish. Nothing can be left to chance."

"Life's a chance," Luin murmured, "and every day that passes lowers a man's odds."

Cethen vigorously nodded agreement. "Then one morning you wake up and find your keel's stuck fast in the mud, and it's too late to move."

Rhun smiled at his da's words. *When does a man start talking old?* More than once, he'd caught himself doing the same. He leaned forward, his eyes boring into Bryn's. "Listen. You can chart strategy all you want. In fact, it's necessary that you do. But any plan of battle is only good until the first toss of a spear. You have to be prepared to –"

"Strategy?" Arlen interrupted, clearly puzzled. "What's that?"

Rhun sighed and leaned back in the chair, recalling younger days when his da was caught up in Venutius's strategy of hope: gather an army larger than your enemy's, and hope for the best. He glanced at Marcus to see if he had anything to say, but all he found was a knowing grin. It was no wonder that the Votadini didn't know the meaning of the word. Would it do any good to explain?

Rhun sighed and said patiently, "Look, say I've got an enemy who has no place to go, but I can't get at him." Lifting a small apple tart from the tray of food, he placed it on the table. "My best strategy probably is to starve him out. That gives me an overall long-range plan, which is what strategy is. So then I figure out my tactics, which is how I'm going to carry out that plan. For example, one tactic is to cut off his supply of apple tarts." He popped the pastry into his mouth and began chewing, his words muffled and spraying crumbs when he continued. "Another tactic would be to eat them all in front of him like this, and make his piss boil. Then my enemy might come out and fight to get them back, because his people see him as starving them to death while we eat."

"Of course, your enemy will do things you don't expect," Jessa said, and lunged across the table to slide the tray of food over in front of her. Grinning from ear to ear, she stuffed one of the tarts in her mouth. "Like breaking the siege, or grabbing further supplies."

"So you adjust. You always adjust." Rhun shrugged and slapped a hand hard on the table. Jessa jumped and almost fell off her stool, and his other hand darted across the table and retrieved the tray. "So you might change tactics by making a sneak counterattack, and steal back his food."

"Of course, you've always got to watch your rear and the neighbours." Cethen pulled the platter over to his side of the table where, much to everyone's amusement, he began picking through what remained.

When the laughter died, Bryn's face turned serious and Rhun decided it was time to push, and push hard. Surely, to be where he was, the man's mind must have more depth than it currently displayed. "Have you given thought to it, Bryn? Some sort of strategy, I mean."

"Of course." Bryn had been nursing half a glass of the wine; now he downed the contents and leaned across the table, his elbows splayed. "The main problem, at the moment, is my own half-brother, Modan."

"That's only the half of it," Luin interrupted, grunting the words. "The sly stoat tried to kill Bryn."

"We don't know that," Bryn retorted, and explained what had happened with Modan on the return from Cumbria.

Rhun listened carefully, though Jessa had already told him what had taken place, after her meeting with Trista. Yet it never hurts to hear one person's story and see how it meshed with another's, and this time it did. Only unlike Trista, Bryn was foolishy unconvinced that his brother was after ending his life!

Bryn did, however, offer a plausible reason for the odd place of the meeting. "A man doesn't want to be seen as being too friendly with the Romans. Especially," his eyes were fixed on Rhun's, "when his half-brother marches an army from one side of Selgovae territory to the other, and follows up by raising everyone's taxes. The first part, the army, was only to be expected; the second wasn't, and that levy has been extended all over the north. Even to the tribes not involved. That was stupid."

The words poured angrily from Bryn's mouth, and there was little Rhun could say; but his mind winged its way back to Luin's story of treachery. He'd not been surprised about Modan. He'd seen more than one brotherly blade buried in a back, and it was nearly always for gain, seldom for hate. When the motive was hate, a blade came from the front where a man could see. If he felt any surprise at all, it was in Bryn's reluctance to believe Modan might want rid of him, now that Frevan was dying.

Yet could Bryn be correct? Perhaps Modan thought his brother had the torque with him, and was merely after taking it? Rhun knew from the rumours circling Luguvalium that the object's whereabouts was common talk, and that was another question he wanted to ask Bryn. Why had he told Frevan? Yet no sooner had the thought occurred than it was addressed.

"As to my strategy, as you call it," Bryn continued when nobody else seemed ready to talk, "I suppose there is one, and it centres upon the torque. I discussed it with Frevan, and he agrees: the torque is the key, if I can get it. He's already spawned a legend that the goddess Brigantia plucked it from Venutius's 'dying hands' and is holding it for the one who will truly lead the people – which, he says, happens to be me."

*So something is being done, which is good,* Rhun thought, but there had to be more. "What else?"

"Can you do anything about the levy?"

"Huh?"

"The levy. The tax increase, Rhun!" Bryn held both hands out, as if to show his sincerity. "Modan is already down here trying to gain support. One of the main bitches he's hearing is a harsh, unfair tax on the people here. Admittedly, they're his people; and his followers may have been the ones who struck the supply column; but he was just showing Lagan what he could do. Those who attacked Tuis's army were mainly Selgovae."

"So, your point?" Rhun asked, and just as quickly could have cut his tongue. The point was obvious, but Bryn told it anyway.

"The Carvetii and the Brigantes feel the tax is punishment for that, when they hardly had anything to do with it."

"Hardly?" Marcus said derisively. "It seems to me there were enough of them there."

"And I had to deal with more of them later," Jessa said grimly.

"Fine, fine, but they were still mostly Lagan's people," Bryn conceded, "and there were those from other tribes, too. The Noventae, for example. Some were even Caledonii!"

"Look," Cethen interrupted, his voice patient and his eyes on Rhun, "it doesn't really matter who else was there. The fact is this: the main bitch out there is the tax. And for the few that it isn't, Modan and Lagan will make sure it is. So can you get Tuis to change his mind?"

"Or better still," Bryn said, "reduce the taxes to lower than they were before."

Both Rhun and Marcus laughed at the naivety of that suggestion. Jessa agreed with a vigorous nod. "Look, Tuis shouldn't have done it; or at least, he shouldn't have let that stoat Cronus do it," she said, "but even if he did eliminate the extra levy, how's that going to change things?"

Trista moved to answer, but Rhun was pleased to see Bryn lift a hand to stop her.

"I think we've got it worked out," Bryn said, "but first we need to agree on one thing. Lagan is trying to build an army, right?"

"We need to agree on that?" Rhun snorted. "It's obvious. Intelligence tells us that he has ten to fifteen thousand committed, and some renegade Greek is doing the tally."

"I'm not finished yet," Bryn said, ignoring the dismissive tone. "Lagan is also getting support from the tribes farther north, and he's sending Modan down to gather more people from the Carvetii and from your own people – the Brigantes. Correct?"

"So that's two things we agree on, not one."

"Yeah, well let's try for three, then," Bryn said, showing his irritation. "My real question is: does everyone agree that Rome is not going to avoid a fight with Lagan and his tribal army?"

"And that, finally, is your point I suppose?" Marcus replied, though it was not clear to Rhun whether he was chiding Bryn or encouraging him.

"So who is going to win that fight?" Bryn asked, looking at everyone in turn, his eyes coming to rest on Arlen.

"Can I ask how many men Rome has in Britain?" Arlen asked Rhun.

"Oh, I don't know," Rhun extemporized, deciding the authorized strength of Rome's three Britannic legions, plus auxiliary attachments, would serve better than the actual count. "Thirty-five thousand? Most of them are in the south, and a lot of them are at the moment building roads." Which he supposed was true, though it was by no means most of them.

"Really?" Arlen asked, plainly astonished.

"Really," Marcus said, and for extra measure, added, "and throughout the empire, she has about thirty legions in total. Two hundred and fifty thousand trained soldiers, who can move anywhere they are told. Does that also answer Bryn's question?"

"How do they manage to pay them?" Arlen blurted, his eyes wide.

"With the fucking taxes that Bryn's trying to get lowered," Gavor said, speaking for the first time.

Other than to chuckle, Rhun ignored the thrust and returned to Bryn's rhetorical question. "Rome will win, if she so chooses."

"Exactly!" Bryn slapped a hand on the table. "And even if the Carvetii and the Brigante did combine with Lagan, Rome will still win. We've all been there before, first with Venutius, then with Galgar, and before that the tribes further south."

"But not all Galgar's people were defeated. Many just walked from –" Luin began, for Agricola's almost casual advance north was a tender spot with everyone, including the Carvetii.

"There are no buts," Bryn interrupted sharply. "Even in the unlikely event the first battle is lost, Rome will come again and win. The reason is simple: Rome cannot afford to lose. And when she does win, what do we have? Maiming, death, and half the population sold as slaves. I want to keep as many of our people out of it as I can – while Modan is trying to get as many of our people *into* it as he can."

Rhun raised his eyebrows as he saw where, perhaps, Bryn was heading. The answer to the next question would be telling. "So I'm to understand that if Tuis reverses the levy, then you . . ."

"We divide them! If I can gain credit for doing that, along with possessing the torque, it will appeal to everyone except the hot heads living near where our lands border that of the Selgovaes. I want to keep as many of our people out of this as possible. And after that . . ." Bryn shrugged as if the answer was obvious.

"After that, when Rome fights Lagan and beats him," Marcus murmured, finishing for him, "*you* will be in a position to prevail."

"There may be no glory in it, at least the way glory is measured by others," Bryn muttered, his features sardonic, "but I will be leading a people who remain strong and unbeaten. Given time, they will understand."

Rhun leaned back in his seat feeling vaguely uncomfortable. Bryn's words had surprised him, not only for their candour, but for their pragmatism. But he also realized why he felt ill at ease: Bryn's words, even though they made sense, sounded weak. Yet they were little different from his own reasoning when first posted back to Brigantia, wearing a Roman uniform. *You do what you can; and the best way is not always the warrior's way.* On the tip of that spear sat the opinion he'd once offered up to his father about freedom.

As if reading his mind, Cethen paraphrased the words. "Glory, Bryn, belongs to kings and chieftains. But the poor bugger working the fields is the one who pays its price." He snorted derisively, as if recalling an old memory. "In the end, we're all dead, so who's the more glorious then?"

"That's shit," Gavor cried. "My da fought Rome for years, and had the honour and glory of it. He still does. And so do you."

"I was with your da every step of the way, lad." Cethen's features showed his impatience. "If you want the truth, most of the time we both thought it was all nothing but a cartload of shit. You get that way, watching men die, while your balls freeze and your belly's empty." He shook his head angrily as if reliving the times. "So pay no heed to old men's stories. They're only told to impress the young'uns. Borba had far more of it than he ever wanted, and I did too. You'd best have a good talk with your da next time you see him."

"So that's your plan, Bryn?" Rhun murmured, glancing at Gavor, who'd clamped his mouth shut and sat simmering his anger. How deep was the boy's rage?

"I suppose." Bryn smiled at Rhun. "Is that a plan, or is it strategy? I don't think that it's tactics."

Rhun didn't answer, instead rising to his feet. He wasn't quite satisfied, but he could understand Bryn's conundrum: something more was needed to combat Modan's growing appeal. And perhaps Bryn needed a sniff of hope as well. He reached around his back with both hands and fumbled under the hem of his tunic, tugging at a string tie. When the ends pulled loose he grabbed a small, heavy package before it could fall, and set it on the table. A hush fell as all eyes turned to a round doeskin bundle, not a great deal larger than a circle made by the tips of a man's fingers and thumbs when placed together.

"Is that . . . ?" Marcus fell silent. Rhun hadn't told him what he carried with him.

Or Jessa. "I don't believe it," she whispered.

"Bryn, it's fitting that you should unwrap it," Rhun said.

Bryn shook his head and turned to his father. "Da?"

Cethen nodded and reverently lifted the package to unwrap the soft leather. A moment later it was there in his hands glittering its glory: a thick rope of twisted gold, bent almost to a circle, with a snarling dragon's head peering from either end, each one's eyes a pair of blood-red rubies flashing anger at the lantern's flame.

No one spoke. Rhun studied each of them in turn, particularly their eyes. Bryn simply stared, his features thoughtful, as were those of his da. Oddly enough, it was Gavor who caught his notice; the lad licked his lips and clenched his fists, clearly coveting the torque.

Rhun broke the silence before his intentions were misunderstood. "Bryn, for the moment you can touch it, hold it, feel it, but the torque is not yet yours. When you show me that you are able to gather five thousand fighting men to your side, then it will be. Brigantia's legacy will appear in whatever manner needed to fulfill Frevan's prophecy. But for now, it's too early – and too dangerous."

Bryn nodded his agreement, and Rhun saw that Trista did as well, though neither made to touch the torque. The two were clearly as one on the matter, which prompted another thought. Rhun voiced it, but kept a wary eye on his father. "Bryn, you've got to accept that Modan, at best, is no longer your ally; and at worst, he's a deadly enemy. And Trista," he raised his eyebrows in question, "is it done between Modan and you?"

Trista bit her lip, then simply nodded. Cethen sighed.

"Then let me say this. Even if there is *nothing going on there*, I suggest that you both act as if there is." Rhun raised a hand as he saw each one prepare to protest. "Look, if everyone believes you're together on *this*." He grinned and pointed to the torque. "Then no one will believe you're not together on *that*. So reap the advantage of it."

"Advantage?" Trista queried, her voice uncertain.

"Yes, the advantage. Look how it appears: Modan's woman has left him, and is offering Bryn her support. That's good. It raises his standing with the tribe. It's good for a leader to have a woman beside him," Rhun inclined his head toward Trista and smiled, "especially one who is fearless. The chieftains think more of a man for that, and so do their women."

"Or the women consider it a challenge," Trista muttered.

"Whatever." Rhun chuckled. "It doesn't matter, as long as you have their attention."

"Is that it, then?" Bryn glanced around the table as if asking not only Rhun, but the others as well. "Because we need to agree on a few other matters."

"Yes, there is one other thing," Marcus said. "Does anyone know if Criff is still alive?"

Luin volunteered the answer. "He came and saw Frevan this spring, when he heard he was ailing."

"Where does he live? Still at *Camulodunum*?"

"I think so, but you know what bards are like. He could be anywhere, especially now it's summer. Why?"

"I can answer that." Rhun grinned as the reason for Marcus's question took root. "If Bryn can enlist Criff's help, it's worth a small army. Bards are like kings: they create legends. I've no doubt he could create some fine ones for Bryn." He poked his father playfully on the arm. "Look at the legends he created for you and your troublesome Roman. I wouldn't be surprised if he hasn't got one or two going for Marcus, too."

⁂

When they finally rose to leave, everyone's eyes turned to the torque as if moths lured to a flame. The warm glow of the yellow metal stood in stark contrast with the glitter of the four ruby eyes; they might have been alive. Trista's hand edged across the table until her fingers rested on the gold surface. It felt surprisingly cold. She lifted her eyes and found herself staring into Rhun's: a blank, expressionless grey that startled her. She realized he was waiting, like a cat, to see what she would do – to see what any of them would do. She shuddered, aware that the man sat there almost alone, or was he? There was Jessa, of course – who was awfully small; and Marcus – who was just as old as Rhun. While on the other side of the table sat Bryn, and Cethen, and three others, besides herself. Acting together they could . . .

"May I?" she asked.

Rhun nodded. She lifted the torque, which was surprisingly heavy, and held it before her with both hands as she stared down at the dragons' heads. No one spoke a word, all chasing their thoughts in silence. Then someone coughed – Trista thought it was Bryn – and she had to shake her head to clear it, as if ridding her mind of a spell. She half turned and reluctantly offered the torque for him to hold, but he raised his palm in refusal.

"No, wrap it again. When the time is ripe . . ."

Trista nodded and set the torque on the square of soft leather, gently folding the corners until it was once more hidden from sight. She lifted it from the table as if it was suddenly fragile and handed it back to Rhun. She hesitated, for in some odd manner he seemed to be looking right through her, his face expressionless. Then she realized that his eyes lacked focus; they weren't looking directly at her, they were taking in all the others around the table.

Rhun took the leather bundle without looking at it, and Trista turned to see what he could see. Cethen, Bryn, Luin, Arlen, each had their eyes fixed on the bundle, as if a ritual had just been completed; Gavor, though, was staring at the four, his gaze shifting back and forth as if agitated. His mouth opened as if to say something, then it closed again without a word. He was plainly unhappy, and Trista knew why. As did Rhun, for when she looked at him, his eyes were again alive and a faint curl of amusement tipped the corners of his mouth.

Later, when they were making their way back to their horses under a cloudless sky lit by a three-quarter moon, Gavor could no longer contain himself. "We could have taken it, there and then," he burst out, "we had the numbers."

"And then what?" Bryn muttered, and Trista could tell he was angry with Gavor.

"It doesn't matter. We still could have had it. There's what – thirty, thirty-five of us?" Gavor gestured ahead to where a line of trees loomed heavy in the darkness, a small forest that followed the river upstream. "We could have grabbed it and walked out of there. We'd have been in the hills long before dawn. Dammit, we could still do it."

"That's my half-brother," Bryn snapped.

"And it's my son," Cethen echoed, and his tone carried a threat. "We don't betray anyone, unless first betrayed."

"Besides," Luin said, "Rhun doesn't strike me as a fool. I'd guess we're not the only ones with people hidden and waiting."

Trista smiled and nodded back toward the warehouse, a dark looming shadow above the stick-like shape of the dock. "We're in no hurry," she suggested.

They waited, hidden in the trees, as the moon moved barely a hand's breadth across the sky. A second lantern soon appeared, swinging high under the roof at the rear of the warehouse. It had to be a second lantern, for the room facing the river remained bathed in light. Its appearance was soon followed by the steady thud of hooves, pounding across the damp river flats.

The eerie shadows of a fair-sized force of Roman cavalry descended on the warehouse, riding in from the direction of the Aballava fort. At the same time soldiers began trickling noisily from inside the dark building, forming up in ranks on the wooden walkway. Several riderless horses were led alongside the loading bay by the newly arrived cavalrymen. Trista watched, amused, as Rhun, Marcus, Jessa – it had to be them – and then a fourth man all swung into the saddles. She saw, even at this distance, that the fourth figure was short in stature, and her amusement turned to a broad smile. Trista knew about that one, too.

"He didn't trust us," Gavor muttered, and Trista laughed at the hypocrisy.

"Sure he did." Bryn gestured over one shoulder toward his own riders: a dark mass of shadows that sat ghostlike in the shelter of the trees. "He trusted us just as much as we trusted him."

# Chapter XXIX

## Stannick, Northern Brigantia, Augustus A.D. 105

The old fortress at Stannick was a ruin. The tall stone walls of the two north compounds had been razed, and the long defensive wall to the south had been torn down. Venutius's old lodge, along with every other building in the fortress, had been sacked and burned to the ground. Cerealis had destroyed the huge stronghold following the ageing king's defeat, and his clear intent was that it never be used again to rally the tribes.

But even Rome's memory can dim, and to many who had once lived there, Stannick was still home. The years had seen them return to the ruined fortress with the quiet tenacity of a creeping vine. They clustered on the rolling slope of the north compound where long rows of rubble had offered material with which to rebuild, while providing a vague illusion of defense. Stubby stone-walled homes, wattle huts, small shops, and a maze of sheds and animal pens had risen amid the debris.

To the south the largest compound, once a cluttered ocean of hovels and pens quickly raised to house the old king's growing army, had been returned to the land. And whereas the older part of the fortress had gradually taken on the appearance of a town, ripening crops now filled the southern enclosure, alongside grazing cows and sheep. The long piles of shattered stone might remain for years, for rebuilding the defenses was forbidden; but much of it was already gone, eagerly snatched from ruin and put to use. Stannick remained the largest tribal centre in the north, and many of those who lived there remembered its glory.

Modan saw as much when he rode in, and soon found his welcome to be a sword honed on both sides of the blade. Some, mostly the young and those yet to see battle, burned with hate and hungered for nothing less than revenge. Others, for the most part those who had lived through the slaughter, harboured their hatred, but the lust for revenge had cooled. For them, anything less than a victory guaranteed by the gods fell on deaf ears; and the only hint that the gods might be listening was the rumour of a torque.

It was at Stannick that Modan, as never before, felt the need to gain possession of Brigantia's golden neck ring. The legendary talisman might not vouchsafe a victory, but it was a damned good start. He began by spreading Frevan's prophesy, remaining vague as to the actual wording. In some manner, when it was needed, he would have the torque; and as sure as death, it would be in a manner that fit with what the gods had foretold. He felt sure Frevan had made up the whole thing anyway, and he was equally sure that Bryn had the neck ring hidden somewhere.

Lagan reasoned that it was best that Modan be first to show himself at Stannick, and he did so with close on two hundred cavalry. Lagan rode in the following day with over twice as many. Between them, they numbered more than half the people who lived there; but the message they carried was also for those who lived beyond the limits of the battered fortress.

Like all the northern tribes, the Brigantes did not confine themselves within villages and towns. The people scratched a livelihood from the farmsteads and the sea, living in thousands of lodges, huts, and hovels scattered across endless hills and dales, forests, mountains, and shores. Lagan and Modan needed the ears of these people more than any, and those who lived within a day or two's journey soon began to gather.

※

"So what makes you think you can drive out the Romans, when nobody else can?"

The words were more a snarl than a question, and came from the fat one called Dag. As far as Modan could tell, he was one of the three or four who seemed to hold authority at Stannick, which was not at all what it must have been like in the old days, when Venutius alone ruled here. It was an annoying shift of power, for the more the men who shared authority, the weaker the people. Modan held his temper, for the question was often asked, and in the same tone. Yet it always picked at his craw, for the question was craven – it stank of rolling over and baring your throat. He glanced at Lagan to see if he should answer, and the older man nodded.

"Because we have the numbers, and we don't intend to fight a pitched battle, like Galgar did," Modan replied gruffly, which was shit; in the end, that was the only way to beat the Romans. But for the moment, because there was no choice, he was willing to follow Lagan's lead. "You saw how they chased us through the hills earlier this year, and what happened? They got nothing. We –"

"They took slaves, destroyed crops, and burned everything that didn't move," Dag called out, his voice a sneer.

Modan assessed the speaker with narrowed eyes. He was just another one of the faint-hearted, an older blob of a man, and as ugly as a neck sore. Both his head and his face were covered in a shaggy black tangle that revealed only a set of broken teeth that glistened with spittle, and a bulging nose that drooped fangs of hair the shape of boar's tusks. If the man's sword arm had wielded anything but a ham bone over the past year, it didn't show.

"I didn't say they never took nothing," Modan growled. "But you never get what you want without sacrifice."

"Like when you attacked the Roman army, just before it got back to the fort at Blatobulgium?"

"Exactly!" Modan said, pleased that the man's words at last seemed positive. "We took casualties, yes, but so did they."

"Yeah, as you said, exactly!" Dag sneered. "I heard you lost ten for every one of theirs. How do you win battles that way?"

"That's a filthy lie," Modan exploded. "We lost one for every one of theirs, and I don't care who says otherwise. I'll smash the bastard who says different."

"Yeah? I heard they took you prisoner, too. Only your brother set you free."

"Whoa. Stop this. Please." Lagan stood up, his arms raised as if offering a druid's blessing. "Rome is the enemy, not us."

"Your brother set you free," Dag persisted, "and now you're pissing on his name, and trying to push him aside. It seems to me –"

"Shut your lousy gob, you spineless prick, or I'll put your –"

"*I said stop!*" Lagan roared, glaring at Modan more than anyone else.

Modan glared back, tempted to tell Lagan to shut his gob, too. Only with a deal of effort did he curb his tongue, his eyes angrily sweeping the small, barn-like structure that these people used as a meeting hall. Like everything else in this now defenceless fortress, it held the stink of defeat. The meeting room, a rectangular stone building topped with a reed thatch, had been raised from the ruins where Venutius's old lodge had once stood proudly in the north compound. The old king would have turned purple.

Modan guessed the place might squeeze in as many as a hundred people, though each side wall had a large entrance that would allow others outside to listen. Only about half that number had come to this first meeting, though. A third of them were his and Lagan's people; the rest were leaders of the kins that chose to live in the old fortress. Lagan had wanted to speak to them first, to gain a sense of the people's temper as they drifted in from the hills. Only three or four were doing the talking, though, and most of it was being done by the fat oaf called Dag.

That kind of talk was bound to happen, Modan reasoned, when you stopped fighting and lived in a pile of rubble at the whim of the Romans. He couldn't help feeling that Stannick, even though now occupied, had truly been abandoned. The place reminded him of nothing less than an empty granary where the rats had moved in, happy to find a stale pile of barley to keep them going.

"Look, we know that all of you here are not with us, and we don't expect you to be," Lagan said, his voice reasonable. "What we need to know is how many *are*. And we need to know now, because," he paused, and when he continued his voice was low, as if his words were not to be repeated, "the call is going out to the tribes in the next few days. In fact," he raised a cautionary hand, as if giving fair warning, "any warrior who wishes can come with us now, for the time is near. Very near."

The muttering that followed could be taken either way, Modan decided. From the looks on their faces, he figured the room was divided. Maybe a small push was needed. Ignoring Lagan's warning glare, he said, "We did well against their army last time. They were within sight of their fort, and we took them by surprise. It was close. We near had 'em."

"I heard your da say that once!"

The voice came from off to Modan's right, and he whirled in annoyance. A heavyset man had slipped quietly into the room; he looked sixty, maybe more. Age padded his belly and his hair, once red, was a thin, sandy thatch. The fellow edged across the back of the room to where a plank bench ran along the wall. He moved stiffly, tiredly, perhaps fatigued from hard riding, and he rubbed his clasped hands together to rid them of the chill. Modan thought he looked familiar, and then it struck him who it was: Gavor's father, Borba! He cursed under his breath.

"Modan's da was there too then, was he? When Modan near had 'em?" the man next to Dag asked.

The newcomer simply laughed as he slumped onto the bench, and sighed in relief. "No, his da wasn't there."

"Hey, Borba," Dag called out, "have a good ride in?"

"Good as can be expected."

The first man was persistent. "Then how did his da know the Romans were near beat, then? Did Modan tell him?"

Borba shook his head. "I was talking of a long time ago, when we were in the hills with Galgar. It was right after Galgar *near had* an entire Roman army, then got his bum booted instead. It was on the far side of the big firth where the Selgovae lands end." He nodded to acknowledge Lagan, then his eyes drifted off to the thatch ceiling. "Yeah, it was his da's woman that got him going on it, that time."

Borba lapsed into silence as if living the time over again in his mind, and Modan hoped he'd stay that way, with his gob shut. Then Lagan opened his mouth to speak, but Dag cut in, plainly filled with curiosity. Modan cursed as he realized Borba was playing them all, as easy as pulling a hare in on the end of a snare. "So what did his da say, then?"

"Oh, that?" Borba glanced that way as if surprised, then shrugged, pretending a reluctance to finish the story. Modan could have choked him. "Well, let's see. We were all sat around a fire as I remember, bitching on going home. We'd just attacked the Ninth Legion in their camp, and got stomped. We'd all had more than enough by that time. Then Morallta comes up out of nowhere, and tells us that Galgar's starting it up again. He wanted Cethen and his people to stay. She said he was going to raise fifty thousand warriors, and push the Romans back into the sea." He chuckled, shaking his head. "She pointed out that we'd almost had the Ninth that time. And we near did have 'em, too."

"And . . . ?"

"Well, Modan's da agreed with her: he said, 'Yeah, we *almost* had 'em!' Then he pointed out that we almost had 'em at Eboracum, and at Bran's Beck, and at *Galava*, and a dozen other places in between. Cethen said he'd lost count of the number of times we'd *almost* had 'em. I just wish that my old friend – and yes, me too – could have *had 'em* at least once before we died. Not that it's going to happen now, though." Borba sighed, then looked directly at Modan and offered a lopsided grin that, oddly enough, reminded him of his da. "I'll give you the credit of it, though, lad. You did have 'em once." He paused long enough to belch before finishing, his words barely audible. "A scratchy arsed ambush on a lousy supply train that was delivering rations."

Modan surged to his feet, his belly churning with rage. "You're a sorry arsed example to follow. No wonder you never won a fight! You shame your own sons! At least Gavor's got the belly to stand up and fight with us. He's at least with —"

Lagan grabbed Modan by the back of his tunic and jerked him violently down onto his seat with a thud that threatened to crack the wood. "Shut your great gormless gob, you stupid git," he hissed; for a moment it looked as if he was going to clout Modan around the head. Then, visibly fighting his anger, Lagan turned to face his small audience, his face crimson as he struggled to regain his composure. When he resumed talking, his voice was surprisingly controlled.

Modan hardly noticed. Immune to Lagan's rancour, he glared at Borba in sullen hate. When the older man rose and made to leave, shortly after Lagan began speaking, Modan's eye caught those of two of his own people standing by the open door. With a bare shift of his head, Modan bade them follow. The pair nodded and casually stepped into the evening darkness.

Several hours later, Modan found them both lying alongside a horse pen less than a hundred paces from the meeting hall. Each had been brutally beaten.

※

Lagan and Modan spent four more days at Stannick, which were two more than the Selgovae chieftain wanted, for time was growing short. Spreading the message among the sprawling ruins had been a calculated gamble, yet not in so far as dicing with the Romans. Lagan had felt safe enough on that score. Not only were the hills in a state of turmoil, four days were insufficient for Rome to gather a force large enough to defeat the number of riders the two men had brought with them. And even if such a force had already been in the field, which he knew to be untrue, there would have been ample warning.

Nonetheless, it had been a gamble to ride into the ruins of Stannick in an effort to recruit. The greatest fear was in losing face before a large gathering of Brigante tribesmen, but Lagan needed to know their temper. More than a thousand souls lived within Stannick's ruins, and those who drifted in from the surrounding lands more than doubled the number. Most were young men, trickling into the settlement over the four days that Lagan had lingered. The odds of recruiting a fair number had at first appeared good. Yet, when he and Modan returned north, only sixty new riders rode with them, and less than a hundred foot warriors were pledged to follow.

That, in itself, was enough to anger Lagan, but other matters pulled hard on his mind. The first was Modan, with his temper and his mindless gob. The fool was proving more an unwitting enemy than a chosen ally. Yet he wanted – no, he needed – those Brigante warriors, but at what cost? If only the man had more of his father in him. If nothing else, *he* had known how to hold his tongue; and the man must have done something right, for they still told the stories.

Lagan swore aloud as he recalled the meeting. It was obvious why Gavor's da had rushed from the hall: Modan, once again, had opened his gob when he shouldn't, and this time it betrayed Borba's son. Which was another thing! Was Gavor failing him, too? There had been fresh talk around Stannick in the last four days that Modan's brother had a way of easing the heavy Roman taxes. Only the sly fox was set on getting them cut only for the Carvetii and the Brigantes! The man was plainly set on building a wall between the Selgovae and his own people, and what better way to do it?

Why hadn't Gavor told him?

The notion rubbed at Lagan's mind, and when he pushed aside the idea that maybe the lad was failing him, the reason became obvious. Such a strategy was probably over the lad's head, for it was too subtle; Gavor wouldn't realize the importance of it. Modan's brother would, however. Bryn was the one spreading tales of less taxes in order to garner support, and others like him such as his own da. Lagan couldn't help chuckling at the irony of that. But if that kind of story could be told, then so could another – one upon which Gavor had definitely not failed him. It was time someone asked why, by the red beard of Dagda, a tax grabbing Roman had possession of a goddess's gift to the Brigantes. On the sharp end of that arrow, Lagan was pleased that at least he knew where the neck ring was – though what good that did him, other than spreading rumours, he had no idea.

As far as he was concerned, Brigantia's supposed torque was the kind of thing that kept a man in power when the land was peaceful, and he needed to keep his back covered. When the land was as at war, then winning fights and killing Romans was what gave a man the clout he needed . . .

# Chapter XXX

## Northern Brigantia, Augustus, A.D. 105

Borba bypassed the fort at Epiacum by riding well to the south, following trails that were familiar only to deer, rabbits, and the few still left who'd ridden with Morallta. The hills had grown more dangerous than ever of late, and it didn't matter a dog's whisker which side you were on. He'd been nervous setting out with only Dag, for there was safety in numbers. Yet even when you had those numbers, he recalled bitterly, they were useless unless they were a bucketful more than the other man's.

Borba cursed loudly, finding it all too familiar. More than once he'd reflected on how lucky he'd been to survive the old days; yet now, here he was at an age when he should have been dead, doing it all over again. And this time it was worse than ever. Never before had he ridden the hills with a heart of lead, and a mind that wouldn't sleep.

Gavor!

He could believe it, of course. Betrayal was the stuff of which the bards made legends – as did the gods, in all their madness. Could it be that the pair of them, he and Cethen, were being punished? Cethen had his Modan, a lad with balls for brains and the instincts of a wasp: roar in, sting, and damn the consequence! He'd been sorry for his old friend, for the youth kept his da's mind mired in gloom. And now he had his Gavor. He didn't mind if the boy chose to fight the Romans – he'd done it himself; more the credit to him, though useless the choice would prove. No, it was the manner of his doing it that dragged at Borba's mind: skulking in the camp of friends and selling them – no, *betraying* them – to those who did no more than disagree. The madness threw kin against kin and no good, no good at all, could come of it.

Borba rode up the valley from the south with Dag, arriving at Cethen's door as the sun was rising. Kelpy was up and about feeding the two children, and told him her da was off with Bryn. That could be anywhere, she said, so he might first try the fort at Luguvalium, for Cethen's son Rhun likely had been the last to see him.

"Go to the Roman fort!" Borba muttered, hardly believing his ears.

"Yes, I know. But you know Rhun better than I, Borba. He's neither dragon nor demon. He commands the fort there, so there'll be no harm."

"Commands the fort?" Dag shifted uncomfortably in his saddle, and massaged his rear. He far preferred a chariot, but there was no using them nowadays. They were far too conspicuous, and besides, the sodding Romans didn't want them being used. "Stuff that, then. Last time I saw the lad, he was just a trooper and *that* was enough to give my belly wind!"

"Then they must have heard the rumble way down at the Firth." Kelpy glanced slyly at Dag's ample girth then, with hand on hip, she assumed a worldly air. "Personally, I quite like the forts. The servants are so polite, and the food and wine are excellent. At least it is at the commander's residence. Though the officers can be a bit –"

"I don't believe it," Dag muttered. "You've been inside one of their forts?"

"Uh-huh. Da too."

"Eating at their chief's lodge?"

"Not just one. We've been in every fort from here to Eboracum," she said. "Or just about every one. A person can get quite used to it."

"Hah, Cethen's been visiting them for years. He was in the one at Isurium half a lifetime ago, when it was only half built. Old Venutius was thinking on taking it for himself," Borba boasted, even as his mind pondered the worth of going to Luguvalium.

Kelpy seemed to pick up on his reluctance. "I can go with you, if you're afraid of the idea," she mocked.

Borba snorted his disgust. If he did go to any Roman fort, it wouldn't be hiding behind one of Cethen's daughters!

꙳

All three knew Borba, yet Marcus perhaps knew him better than any. To Jessa, the old warrior had been an enormously tall, vaguely remembered, red-haired barbarian, last seen when she was only four years old. Rhun had known Borba briefly as one of his da's friends during the year before the fall of Stannick, when he was only fourteen. Marcus, though, had spent more than four long years held hostage – dragged over hill and glen, and through river and stream. Borba had often crossed Marcus's path, and though far from a friend, he'd been one of the better ones. *Yet old memories,* Marcus mused, *like wine, fare better with the passing of time.*

It was his idea to entertain Borba and Dag in the privacy of his own dining room, where both men might feel less constrained. The quality of the meal would not be spared, of course, and neither would the drink. Jessa opined that it might be difficult to awe the men with food, considering the size of their bellies, but they could serve familiar fare, lots of it, with just a taste of something different; as for the drinks, as long as they were wet and potent, she assured Rhun they would not be wasted. And they would eat at a regular four-legged table, not on the couches where likely all of them, including Jessa, would be ill at ease.

Marcus heard it all and readily agreed, amused at the manner in which his daughter took charge. However, he knew that the remaining guest would do far more than any meal to assure Borba and Dag that they weren't floundering in deep waters.

Seven seats were placed about the table, but only six sat down. And though the meal was held inside a Roman fort, with a Roman commander presiding, the language was that of Brigantia. Still, Borba and Dag were clearly uncomfortable as they eased into their chairs for the meal, and the talk was at first stilted. Only Kelpy seemed at ease. Borba carefully sipped on his mug of ale, while Dag drained his in half a dozen gulps and was plainly surprised to find it promptly refilled. An awkward silence followed, somewhat smoothed by a bard who sat by the fire.

The man's head was bent low over his harp, his features hidden under a loose mop of greying hair. He hummed a soft, lilting melody rather than singing, the notes deep and mellow as they blended with the music plucked from the strings. The melody was smooth and relaxing and seemed to calm Dag as he sipped at his ale, and Borba leaned against the back of his chair, his mug resting atop his ample belly.

Then Rhun, cued by an almost imperceptible nod from Marcus, seemed to decide the tune was too dreary and showed his irritation. He turned and roared at the bard, "Hey you, find something lively to strum! This isn't a fucking funeral!"

Rhun's tone and language jarred his guests, as intended, and Dag jumped, the ale slopping down his beard. It left everyone twice as ill at ease, but the bard didn't seem concerned. He simply paused, nodded, and strummed the harp, sharp and loud, three times. Then his voice rose in a loud, raucous song that flooded the room:

> *A tribune one day went a-swimming,*
> *Wearing his armour and sword.*
> *He dove headlong into the Abus,*
> *Rather than using the ford.*
>
> *Now, nearby stood Cethen Lamh-fada,*
> *On the dock where the tribune fell in.*
> *All he could see were the bubbles,*
> *Where the Roman had* taken a –

"*Shiiiit!*" Borba's voice roared across the room as he clambered to his feet, his chair falling backward onto the floor.

Dag was not far behind, an enormous grin on his battered face as he turned to face the bard. "Criff, you sly sod!"

"Quiet, will you? There are at least six more verses," the bard complained as he rose from the hearth, his face dark with feigned annoyance. "It's always the same. You sing from the heart when people are drinking, and all they do is open their gobs and – *oomph!*"

First Borba, then Dag, clutched Criff in a gleeful bear hug, lifting him off his feet and pounding the poor man's back until he threatened to turn blue. Kelpy watched in bafflement as the two finally set him down, and all three began talking at once. Marcus, whose own bear-hugging, back-pounding dance had taken place two days before when Criff had ridden into the fort, sat back and watched, feeling inordinately pleased.

The bard had been quick to respond to his message, and in some small way Marcus had been surprised. Yet he realized he shouldn't have been. Criff was the man who, along with Cethen Lamh-fada, had first saved him from Morallta at Luguvalium; and the words he uttered then were exactly the same words with which he greeted Marcus inside the same fort: *"This has the grist of a fine story!"*

Marcus glanced at Rhun and Jessa, and smiled. "I think the talk will now flow a wee bit easier."

It had been a good evening, Rhun reflected when he finally went to bed, long after the last of the food had been consumed. Whether it would prove fruitful remained to be seen. One issue had been satisfied, however; a matter that had bothered him since the meeting with Bryn, and for that he credited Borba. It had to do with his son Gavor. The man must have fought more than one dragon in his dreams before speaking out, for to admit that a son has his feet in two camps was hard. Not that Rhun was deluded. Borba had not come to Luguvalium to warn a Roman commander about the threat posed by his son; he'd come to warn Cethen. The issue was clearly a point of honour: the twin could not live with the notion that Gavor was betraying every word his old friend uttered.

Yet hard as Gavor's duplicity must have been for Borba, Cethen had a double tragedy: not only was the twin's son betraying him and Bryn, there was the matter of Modan. If his da's two youngest sons continued on the path they'd chosen, they would find themselves on opposite sides of a battlefield. *Yet I did as much with my own da!* On balance, perhaps Borba was the luckier of the two. His burden would be the lighter, once it was shifted onto Cethen's shoulders. And the twin at least had the satisfaction of knowing that his son was holding true to his beliefs!

Kelpy left the table early, seemingly uncomfortable at the turn the conversation had taken with Borba. But once Gavor's stealth was out in the open the talk seemed to flow smoother, perhaps because it had satisfied Rhun's doubts and no longer nagged at Borba's mind. The old warrior had made his admission not long after the meal ended, and following a good deal of drink and no little prodding. Even so, a painful silence followed the declaration, but only Borba's companions seemed surprised. Criff broke the silence with the sort of backhanded, slash of the blade comment with which he'd always brought light to a dark corner: "Well at least he's busy; how are the other kids?"

Rhun had quickly changed the direction of the talk, for there was little more to be said – though how Bryn and his da would deal with the deceit was another matter. The problem had needed to be exposed, but once done it was like a corpse: everyone knows it's there, stink and all, but unless you're going to bury it yourself, it's best ignored.

"Cethen is with Bryn, and while we're not exactly sure where, we know the path he's taking," Marcus explained when Borba asked the reason for the bard being there; the twin seemed glad to talk of something else. "Criff's on his way to join them."

"We think he is. He hasn't really said so," Jessa added. "All he said is, it will make a fine story."

"That's Criff's way of saying yes." Marcus laughed and turned to face the bard. "Am I also right, Criff, in saying you'd as soon chase a fine story as eat?"

"Hardly," Criff said, and chuckled. "Though I'd sooner chase one than work."

"Or would you rather spy?" Borba asked, laughing with everyone else at Criff's reply, but it was as if water had been poured on a fire. Rhun fumbled for something to say as the table fell silent, wondering where – and why – Borba was pointing his arrow.

Criff seemed to know, though, and did not seem offended. "Ah, you remember!" Criff leaned back in his chair, his eyes glinting amusement as they swept the table. "You know, it's odd, isn't it? The warrior who lives by his sword is admired for his bravery. Everyone loves him. But a spy?" He shook his head as if saddened by the notion. "A bard never sings of spies, though they face far greater danger than a warrior. No spy is a hero when folk want a song; no woman fell in love with a spy for the glory of his deeds. And when you think on the word itself," Criff spoke slowly to emphasize his meaning, "a spy is often *dis-spies-ed*, even by his own. Yet he might have saved a thousand lives! Tragic, really."

"So you *were* spying back then?" Borba blurted, making it clearer as to where his arrow had been pointed. Rhun wondered to what extent Gavor's duplicity was pushing his father's words. "I always did wonder!"

The tension seemed to ease, and Rhun relaxed. Criff had travelled often among both the Romans and his own tribesmen, sometimes riding with him and Cian. The bard had been indifferent whether it was in war or peace, or on which side of the path he travelled. It was likely still that way. Both his da and the Roman Gaius Sabinius had spoken of it, each one convinced that the bard was spying for the enemy. The truth was that if you asked Criff a question, he simply answered it the best way he could.

As far as Rhun was concerned, the man had never harmed a soul – just the opposite, in fact. Marcus readily acknowledged that Criff had at one time almost certainly saved his life; and he'd preserved Cethen's hide at least twice, for Rhun had heard the stories. He smiled as the bard confirmed his opinion. Yet deep inside, like everyone else, he still wondered, even as Criff replied.

"What? Me, Borba? A spy?" The bard grinned and shrugged, one hand running through his long grey hair, which he'd tied back in a tail when he sat down to eat. "I've never spied for anyone in my life!"

"But you once told us –"

"Whoa, stop there," Criff cried. "I know where your mind wanders. You're talking about that time at Eboracum, when the Romans first built their fort, right?"

"Yeah, and you told us all about –"

"That's not quite the way it was, Borba. All that happened is you asked questions and I answered." Criff nodded toward the fireplace, where his harp leaned against the hearth. "It's no different than when I amuse people. If asked, I always tell what's true – only when I'm tale-telling, maybe a pinch of salt is added for the flavour." His lean, bearded face split in a grin as his eyes turned to Rhun. "Such as *The Legate That Died in His Sleep.*"

"Ah, Catus," Rhun murmured softly, and smiled.

"If that's what you told Borba, what did you tell the Romans, then?" Dag asked, his voice querulous.

"The same thing." Criff laughed. "When they wanted to know what I'd heard, I told them. Same way I told Dermat – just repeating what I hear. Telling the truth makes life so much simpler."

"But you didn't tell the truth. The Romans moved before you said they would."

"No, that's not the way it was. I told the truth. I always told the truth about what I *heard*, which was what everyone wanted to know." Criff shrugged helplessly, as if it was all none of his concern. "Whether or not what I heard was the truth was never *my* problem; it was everyone else's – yours, for instance. In fact," he frowned, "I think I once said to Rhun's da that sometimes I wondered if I was being fed lies, just so they could be passed on – or maybe it was Marcus's da I said that to. Who knows?"

Rhun rolled his eyes and decided it was time to dampen Dag's fervour before it flamed, but Borba was ahead of him. "It was Cethen you said it to. In that hut across the river from Eboracum, just before you told him his wife was alive, and living with the Roman." The twin chuckled as if seeing it all in his mind. "You sure as shit told the truth that time."

"See? If asked, I tell. It's the best way, considering what I do." The bard stared owlishly back at Borba and his eyes narrowed as if he was puzzled. "But what about you, Borba? Your eyes gaze inward. What else is it that you think you should tell, but hold in your head instead?"

Borba remained quiet but Dag, his eyes red and rheumy above the great mass of beard and nose hair, had been guzzling ale almost as fast as it was poured. He slapped the twin heartily on the back, stifled a belch, and said, "Borba's memory is long and it leaves him muddled. *His* da fought against the Selgovae, not with them."

"That was before the Romans," Borba muttered and glared at Dag.

Dag hiccupped, and shrugged. "Hey, they probably know anyway."

Jessa immediately caught that. "Know what?"

"There, the lady asked a question." Dag beamed blearily and gestured toward the bard. "Now if that were Criff, he'd smile and give the answer."

Rhun took a chance on Dag's inference, for intelligence on Selgovae movements had recently been forwarded from Eboracum. "Don't worry about it, Borba. We heard over a week ago that they'd be ready in less than two months."

"Yeah, well . . ." Dag muttered.

Borba cut him short with, "It'll be about a month from now, if not before." Then, as if feeling the need of an explanation, he added, "There was a meeting, a big meeting, at Stannick. Modan was there, along with Lagan, and both brought a herd of cavalry to impress everyone."

Rhun hid his surprise and instead made a seasoned guess. "We heard there were upward of a thousand."

Borba blinked his surprise. "Yeah, maybe. Lagan said it was soon, but I got the timing of it from the two lumps that followed me out of the meeting after I tugged on Modan's beard a couple times." The twin shifted in his seat, plainly angered by the memory. "Modan sent both the useless tits to rough me up, maybe even kill me. Who knows? I just saw him give 'em the nod. They didn't know I had a couple lads from the farm waiting with the horses."

"Did they tell you what else they were going to do?" Marcus asked.

"They didn't know." Borba smiled grimly. "And I'm damned sure that if they did, the sorry swine would have told me."

A lull fell over the room after that, for it was getting late. Borba was clearly growing less at ease, probably because of all he'd said; and Dag was swimming in a sea of ale. The twin's words had been worth hearing, though; and Lagan being ready in less than a month, not two, was new intelligence. He'd need to send dispatches to Eboracum and Deva . . .

Rhun showed Dag and Borba to their quarters, a decent-sized room at the rear of the residence shared with Criff. What with Marcus and Jessa being also resident, the building was getting full. He lingered for a moment at the door, and suggested that they all continue on and tell Cethen and Bryn what Gavor was doing in person. "Though you might want to warn the boy first, Borba, so he might safely move on. It could save everyone a lot of embarrassment," Rhun advised, then offered a ready reason for his son's actions. "The young lad's only doing what he thinks best for what he believes in. Who's to lay blame?"

Borba nodded agreement, clearly pleased at Rhun's turn of words. Dag staggered past and tumbled backward onto one of the beds, and in no time at all he was snoring. As the others grinned, Criff walked over to a side table draped with a head-mounted wolf pelt, which he lifted and spread over Dag's ample belly, leaving the animal's head just below his chin, jaw to jaw.

"That'll make him wonder when he wakes," Rhun muttered as Criff stood back and admired his handiwork.

"He's woken up with far worse on top," Borba quipped, and all three laughed.

The moment seemed ideal to mention one other matter, and Rhun carefully chose his words as he suggested that Borba and Dag follow Criff and remain with Cethen for awhile. "Maybe a few old veterans – the three of you, and maybe Cian and Luga, though I haven't spoken to them yet – will add reason to Bryn's stance."

"What makes you think we agree with Bryn?" Borba asked.

Rhun blinked his surprise. "Because you're here, I suppose. And you and Da go back a long way. All of you do. I thought the way you..."

Borba waved a hand to silence him. "I can't speak for the others, but I'm confused. It just don't feel right, talking this kind of talk with a Roman." He shrugged, showing his unease. "I guess I do agree with Cethen on where it will end, though. I suppose that means that in some ways I also agree with Bryn."

Borba said he'd think on it and talk the idea over with Dag the next day, when the man's head stopped hurting. Rhun took that as a definite-probable, and wandered back to his own quarters musing over the events of the evening.

It was strange, the way the gods made a man's fate turn on an axle. Before the Romans uprooted everyone, both he and his da were of the tuath led by Dag's father. What had been the man's name? Maeldav! He'd lived at *Isurium*, upstream from Eboracum. And now here was Maeldav's son, under his roof, sprawled on a bed, as dead to the world as a drunken decanus.

Rhun smiled as another image appeared in his mind: he and his da and Dag sitting on a cloak stripped from a Roman corpse at Bran's Beck, each taking time to eat during a lull in the fighting. Dag had complained about a crowd of "hill-climbers" hacking the heads off the Romans they'd killed, and how it did nothing but draw flies. His da had been in a teasing mood and...

"Rhun!"

He glanced up from his daydreaming and saw Marcus standing outside his door holding a small lantern. A dispatch rider stood beside him and a scroll dangled from Marcus's free hand, which hung limp by his side. His face had the look of a man in a daze. Alarmed, Rhun rushed to him, wondering who or what –

"It's Father," Marcus said, his voice edged with disbelief. "He's dead."

⁘

Marcus and Jessa left for Eboracum the following morning, intent on meeting up with Tuis. What they would do after that, neither had any idea. Gaius's funeral was long over, of course, which was the way of the world; nothing could be done about that. On the positive end, Elena would not be alone, for Aelia had certainly been by her side. Coira was also there to offer comfort, though when he thought on it, Marcus realized the three women would be left alone in Rome. Aelia was certainly competent enough to deal with the estate, but with no male of importance to clear the rocks and rubble cast her way by the legal lepers, even his sister might founder. Her son Titus would be of help, of course, but he was young and as yet had little influence.

Criff volunteered to ride with them as far as it took to meet up with Cethen and Bryn, and at the last moment, Borba and Dag decided to take the same path. Rhun had told them that the last he'd heard, Bryn and his da had crossed the northern hills of Brigantia with only a few hundred followers, making their way toward Isurium. From there, they planned on returning full circle to Cumbria, where Bryn would issue a call for the five thousand warriors demanded for the golden torque. And therein, Marcus mused as he mounted up and prepared to leave Luguvalium, was the supreme irony. Rome was actually encouraging the formation of a barbarian army – so she could be left alone to fight yet another such army. It was far from the first time such a strategy had been employed, but it was a sword honed sharp on either edge.

# Chapter XXXI

## The Palatine, Augustus, A.D. 105

Elena knew Gaius's will provided for her, and that the document had been openly witnessed and publicly announced. And even if it had not, all her children were well looked after, the one directly and the other two indirectly, and each would have given her a fitting place to pass her final years. *Which are far from being over!*

The Sabinius estate was large and for the most part divided between Marcus and Tuis, with a handsome portion to Aelia. The will had been scribed and witnessed in Rome, and Rome was where Elena had to be, with Aelia, to have its provisions executed. Elena was grateful Gaius had treated Tuis as his own child, but that was the Roman way. Caesar himself had been adopted. Gaius had treated Aelia with near the same consideration, which meant that in the long term Rhun was also well accommodated. All in all, a mother could not have been happier with a husband's fairness. But two gut-wrenching obstacles had arisen, one of them born of pure malevolence.

The first was an inconvenience, though one of no small matter. Gaius had shrewdly placed his will in the hands of both Marcus and Aelia for its execution, knowing full-well Tuis's tendency to dance around details. He'd also appointed Marcus as Elena's *tutor*. She had known of the clause, and hadn't been at all concerned. While such a step was not required by law, Elena knew that it had been done as much to protect her from the vultures as to ensure that she did nothing rash with her inheritance. Marcus, however, was off in Britannia with Tuis and Rhun, and unable to carry out his part in the will's execution.

Aelia found herself forced to do battle with Rome's legal leeches, and for the first time in her life Elena felt an overwhelming sense of helplessness. A jungle of lawyers and scribes blocked her every turn, each eager to point out that Elena's *male* tutor, Marcus, was absent. Aelia was at first baffled, for her brother's absence should have been of little importance in executing the will's basic terms. Then further documents were delivered to Elena at the estate, and both women were stunned to discover the real cause of the delay.

   Helvia, Gaius's first wife, had challenged the will, claiming that Elena was no more than her husband's concubine. Though Helvia was her natural mother, Aelia was furious. Helvia and Gaius had been divorced for more than thirty years, an event that took place when Gaius was blessed with a son seven months after the pair reunited at Lindum. Helvia's dowry had been repaid, Elena knew, and a goodly sum besides. The woman was the same age as Elena – *"and showing it far more,"* Metellus had confided to her – and had launched a petition for relief. The brazen claim was made even though *"the bitch had exhausted two husbands to the point of death, as well as their estates"* as Tuis once commented, with far less confidentiality.

↟

Lepidus flung both doors open the moment the slave Chilo beat on the wooden frame with his cudgel. It took but a moment to absorb what was happening then he yelled, "Hurry, hurry, come on in."

   Chilo stood to one side and the litter bearers rushed past, each panting under the load. The five slaves provided as escort trailed behind, backing in through the doorway as they hurled insults at the disorderly riffraff gathered in the street. A dozen or so hooligans hurled them right back, along with a handful of stones. They had arrived at the Sabinius town residence well prepared, for the paved street was constantly swept clean, with not a rock or a pebble in sight.

   One glanced off the side of Chilo's head, and it proved to be too much. Enraged, the slave ran forward swinging the cudgel and, more by chance than a warrior's skill, the tip caught the ringleader squarely on the side of his skull. The man dropped like a stone and with howls of glee the five slaves tumbled back onto the street, each eager to do battle. Lepidus, with a sigh of resignation, grabbed the nearest weapon handy – a slim nude statuette made of bronze – and ran to help. With the leader gone the rabble soon fled, loudly pursued by the hoots and jeers of the slaves. Lepidus hefted the nude, shook his head, and beckoned to Chilo.

   "Get them back inside and look after your mistress," he muttered, then he grinned at the sight of Chilo's face. "And you'd better watch who sees you fight. They'll be selling you off to the arenas."

Elena stood waiting in the doorway. The street teemed with human traffic, as did every other in the city. It was remarkable, she mused as her heartbeat settled to a slow gallop, that the violence had not interrupted its flow. In her more *barbarian* country, such an incident would have created a major stir. Oh, several of Rome's fine citizens had stopped to gape, certainly, but once the brawl was over they had simply moved on. Elena glanced at the still form sprawled in the street. That was the one who had spat on her, pulling the curtains aside before Chilo could stop him, and calling her a barbarian whore!

"Is he dead?" she asked Lepidus as he returned to the doorway.

"I dunno." Lepidus shrugged his indifference. "Don't think so."

Elena glanced doubtfully at the still form. "Are you sure?"

"Want me to go and find out?"

Elena shook her head. "It won't make a difference to his condition, I suppose. You might check in an hour or two. If he's still there, I suppose we'll have to get rid of him."

Lepidus nodded. The former slave had chosen to move into the Sabinius home, following his grant of freedom on Gaius's death. Like so many of his kind, he'd moved into the city by choice, preferring the crowds and the excitement and seemingly endless entertainments of its feast days and the games. But to live in Rome was to live in a jackal-like job jungle, and a man needed coin. Lepidus had been grateful to find employment with the family of his former master.

"Are you alright?"

Elena turned to face Aelia. "It's that two legged –" she began, then realized her words might upset the lass; after all, the woman *was* Aelia's mother. "I'm fine, dear; just a bit of trouble in the street."

"Don't worry." Aelia smiled. "I know she's my mother, but when she acts like this, feel free to call her what you want."

"Aye, the bitch must have paid a dozen or more to hound us through the streets," Lepidus growled. "Chilo clubbed one of them. Maybe killed him. But there'll be another to replace him, wait and see."

Chilo shrugged modestly, and suggested that the man was likely already back on his feet. Aelia nodded her understanding, then glared at Lepidus, though her eyes belied her annoyance. "And you, don't you dare refer to my mother as a bitch!"

"Yes, watch your language," Elena echoed. "I'm the only one permitted to do that. Now go and hunt down some drinks. We'll be in the atrium."

Coira rode up from Aricia two days later, disturbed by Helvia's endless harassment and the overt hostility. She arrived late on a hot, stifling afternoon and joined the two women in the gardens at the rear of the house. Elena was looking strained and Coira realized, with a start, that her mother was really showing her age. Her eyes were tired and her features seemed drained of life. Her skin, usually soft and smooth, was lined and dry; and she sat slumped in her chair as if exhausted, something she never did. She had also paid little attention to her hair. Its natural honey colour, of which Gaius had been so fond, had long since been well salted with grey. It was not like her mother to allow the subtle dye that hid it to fade.

"So did Lepidus kill the man?" Coira settled into one of the lawn chairs, deciding it was best to step clear of her mother's appearance. Besides, she was curious about the outcome of the brawl. There was little chance of repercussion from the man who had been clubbed, but would the incident sit on Helvia's mind as some deluded need for revenge?

"Lepidus said he was gone not long after," Aelia replied, "though whether it was on his own two feet, we'll have to wait and see."

"Chilo says the others are still there when he's out doing errands, but they don't bother him," Elena added. "It seems that I'm the only target."

"If Marcus or Tuis were here, they'd know who to get to 'fix' things," Aelia said as she signalled to a young slave to bring refreshments. "I've complained to the magistrates, and even to Gaius's friends. They claim they'll do something, though what I'm not sure. They give excuses even as they agree: *'it's all so difficult, what with the rabble we see on the streets nowadays; and who knows who's doing what; but we'll try, we'll try.'* Which is pure rubbish!" She glanced helplessly at Elena. "They all know of Helvia's claim against Gaius's 'barbarian wife.' They won't admit it, but they just want to stay clear of anything that means taking sides, until they know the outcome."

"Can't you talk to her? Stop her?" Coira asked, though from what she knew of Helvia, she realized that question was absurd.

"I might as well try reasoning with a scorched cat," Aelia said. "One of Gaius's friends did suggest that the only way to stop it is to fight back in the same manner."

"It might be worth a try," Coira murmured thoughtfully. The challenge held appeal, and the conflict would be for a worthy cause.

She looked at her mother. "How do you feel about that?"

Elena offered a wan smile, and shook her head. "It's not going to gain anything."

Coira nodded, deciding that while her mother was likely correct, harassing Helvia in the same manner would offer *some* satisfaction. And something had to be done! She turned to Aelia. "Have you written to Marcus about this?"

"Not about this – not yet, although I have started a letter," Aelia replied. "I did let everyone know about Gaius's death, of course. I used the military dispatch to Marcus and Tuis, and wrote Rhun a letter a few days later."

"Hmmm," Coira said, her mind whirling over the possibilities. "Mam, how much more do you have to do to finish things here?"

"I don't know." Elena turned to Aelia for the answer.

"I think we're advancing backward," she replied, smiling bitterly. "To be candid, I'm thinking of getting other advice. There's a new guild of legal advisors that are supposed to be versed in these matters; though from what I've seen, a donkey might make better progress. However," Aelia took a deep breath, as if reluctant to say what was on her mind, "I'm going to write another letter to Marcus and bluntly tell him to get back home, and to do so urgently."

"Why don't you take it to him, Mam?" Coira suggested. The words came out without thinking, and just as quickly she realized the notion was absurd. The woman was sixty-four! Yet only of late had she begun to think of her mother as aging, the more so today. "Though maybe that's not such a good idea . . ."

"I couldn't ride that far anymore, and it would take a hundred years in a rumbling carriage." Elena shook her head, laughing quietly at the suggestion.

"And it would shake your bones apart, long before you got there." Aelia leaned back as a slave arrived and set a tray on the marble table that sat between the women. Without being asked, he poured three goblets of chilled white wine. Aelia tasted hers then raised the glass to the other two in a gesture of togetherness. "Mind you, while it's still summer the best way to travel is by sea."

"Hah! Stick that up Neptune's nose," Elena snorted. "I get seasick the moment I sniff the Ostian docks."

"I'd go myself," Coira said wistfully, but knew that was impossible; her husband was clearly readying his fare for the Styx, "only of course, I can't."

"How long does it take by sea?" Elena asked, and when she saw the other two stare at her over the rims of their wine glasses, she quickly added, "I'm just curious."

"I have no idea," Aelia murmured. "I wonder where Metellus is? He would know." She looked around, spied him dozing in the shade of the cypress trees that sheltered the far side of the garden, and sent the young slave to rouse him.

Metellus yawned as he shuffled over, looking as if he was still half asleep. He scratched at his chin as he puzzled the answer. "Well, it's about eight to ten days to *Gades*, I do know that." He paused long enough to yawn again, and frowned as he figured the next leg. "I think it could be another eighteen to twenty to *Rutupiae* or *Dubris*, either one. It doesn't matter which, once you get there. Mind you, that's if the weather is good. And you'd want a fast ship to do that, not a fat old merchant." He chuckled, counting on his fingers. "So what's that in total, then? Not more than thirty days? Less, if the gods are kind."

The three women nodded their understanding. Metellus glanced hungrily at the tray of food, and Elena suggested he help himself. Giving a nod of thanks, he filled one of the small plates and shuffled back to the rear of the garden. Coira, seeing her mother's thoughtful expression, decided to probe her reason for asking. "That's hardly more than the time it takes to travel overland, short of killing horses to announce a military disaster."

"Or to report a triumph." Elena managed a faint smile. "And this is neither."

"So there you go, then," Coira said, knowing what was coming. She could see it in her mother's eyes, and hear it in her voice. What had changed her mind?

Aelia stared at Elena too, and asked, "Is there anything else you need to know?"

"Yes, I suppose. How much ginger, peppermint, and fennel does a person need to fend off *mare morbus* for a month?"

⸸

Their men might all be in Britannia, but the Sabinius name still held influence, even if it didn't extend to proving a will. If you knew a senator or two, and the favour cost them neither coin nor conflict, much could be done – for Aelia, at least. The particular senator she asked already felt a tinge of guilt for not solving the Sabinius family's first problem; and it also helped that Aelia's request was to ship that same problem to Britannia.

A naval galley was leaving Ostia within the week, a smaller, faster vessel carrying items too heavy for the dispatch riders, including chests of coin for the army. With emphasis on her status as mother of

Britannia's governor and the stepmother of a senator, Marcus Sabinius, who also happened to be in Britannia, Elena obtained passage.

Coira accompanied her mother to the docks at Ostia, travelling the sewage-laden current of the River Tiber. Metellus, surprisingly, had asked permission to travel with Elena. The aging slave, now free, had spent much of his life in Britannia serving Gaius, and expressed the wish to return once more before he died. Elena was pleased, though the old man would prove more a companion than a helper. To serve her personal needs Elena chose Shayla, a female slave of middle years who had been assigned to the large villa on the estate.

Elena selected Shayla not merely because she was bright. The woman had been taken from the Carvetii during Agricola's campaign a quarter-century before, when she was still in her teens, and Elena had every intention of setting her free before returning to Rome – if she wanted. But that act of charity was only half the reason for her choice; the rest was curiosity, the desire to see what choices Shayla would make along the way, for in many ways the two were almost kindred. Each woman would be returning to the land of her birth, where they had been taken as slaves. And while one was still a slave and the other her mistress, each was of "barbarian stock" in the eyes of Rome. Now, for the first time, both women would be free and unfettered. What choices, Elena wondered, would be made by either?

# Chapter XXXII

## Brigantia, September, A.D. 105

Marius Appius was unusually indecisive: a lone soldier on a new battlefield, unsure if it was wiser to advance or retreat. The governor's woman was the cause, a haunting vision that pushed his patience, while gripping his groin. He found the woman's grating voice increasingly annoying, yet when she shut her ripe, pouty lips, she could be voluptuously appealing. Even so, on such occasions Livia's choice of bed partner – a lowly bred, self-indulgent barbarian governor – did give him pause. Before slipping your blade into another man's sheath, it was wise to look at its owner: if Tuis Sabinius was the best that Livia could do, then what did that say of him?

It was the money, of course, that made the man appealing, and for that the woman might be forgiven. There was hardly anything else to be said for Sabinius except, perhaps, his name, whatever that was worth nowadays. Not a single drop of patrician blood flowed through the man's veins, however, and it was obvious. And now he, Marius Appius, was dousing his candle in the woman's *cunnie*. The trouble with serving Rome was that her frontiers were so far from the glorious city itself. And the longer a man was away from home, the more he was willing to compromise his standards. The woman was well versed in the art of pleasing a man, though, a talent that was doubtless wasted on her fatuous barbarian consort.

Marius sighed as he returned to his bed, impatiently waiting for Morpheus to seize his wandering mind. How does a man become trapped in such parodies? What gods arrange such impossible links? And yet, he was almost certain that the first episode had been arranged by the woman herself. After all, her husband had barely left the fortress.

And that was another matter: was it truly necessary for the governor to travel south, to assure himself that two legion legates would follow orders? The gesture was an insult to those same commanders! It had been the man's own decision, which meant that the woman had not arranged his absence. So perhaps she *hadn't* taken advantage of it . . . or had she? She would certainly have known of the whereabouts of Marius Appius at the time.

He had spent two days at Calcaria, tallying the output from the quarry. That in itself was cause for amusement: Sabinius seemed to think he was obsessed with building the stone fortress, which was drivel! The tasking was nothing more than a diversion, both from the boredom of Brigantia and from the governor himself. Oh, he found a certain relief in creating the great fortress, yes. The structure might be crude by the standards of Rome, but to the barbarian mind it was a worldly wonder. The huge stone edifice would remain long after they were all dead and gone, proof of the greater civilization.

And that brought to mind another, albeit minor undertaking: a suitable inscription to make it clear that the fortress at Eboracum was built by the legate Marius Appius. After all, the new structure was far more formidable than the feeble walls erected by the first Gaius Sabinius . . .

*Damn the woman!*

Marius again found his mind returning to *the* encounter, now more than a week old. He'd been angry at the time, a state of mind that of late was all too familiar. During Marius's absence to visit the quarry, Sabinius had demanded a state of readiness report directly from the Ninth's primus before leaving for the south, once again making mockery of the chain of command. Such a request should have been made through the legate himself – Marius Appius! The slight, like so many others, had to be deliberate!

Though the evening had by then waned, Marius stormed from the headquarters building prepared to do battle with Sabinius, deaf to the primus's explanation that the governor had departed for Gleva that morning. It was an absence he should have realized the moment he crossed the threshold into the governor's spacious set of rooms at the rear of the commander's residence.

It was late, Marius realized that, but it was, after all, the commander's residence, and it was *he* who commanded here! Light still showed inside the man's quarters, but when he strode inside the rooms seemed quiet; something they never were when Sabinius was present, and there was not a servant to be seen. Marius hesitated only briefly, for his mind was in a rare state of indignation that deserved venting. He pushed on through the reception hall, passed through the shadowy dining area, and entered a room at the rear that glowed with a soft, flickering light – a room which was, he recalled, the governor's private office.

Only it wasn't.

Too late, he remembered that the office lay on the other side of the dining area. This particular room had clearly been taken over by the governor's woman as a dressing room. The sweet scent of unguents and perfume flooded Marius's senses as he entered, and he would have promptly turned back, but his eyes fell fleeting on a pair of side tables laden with hand towels, vials of oil, and flickering oil lamps, then quickly came to rest upon a long, wide couch . . .

Livia lay face down on a soft towel with her shoulders hunched, her legs parted, and her stola riding high about her waist. Her lush, pink, beautifully rounded bottom moved back and forth with a slow, undulating rhythm. He glimpsed the fingers of one plump hand, barely visible, in the damp hollow between her thighs; the other hand clutched the side of the couch, the knuckles white as they pulsed with each heavy moan.

Marius gulped, his mouth instantly dry. The woman was oblivious to anything but her own pleasure. And it was instantly clear that whatever mountain Livia climbed, she was near the very top: her hips moved faster, her body spasmed, her breath came short and hard. Marius was acutely aware of a sudden iron-like hardness in his groin. With no thought of anything but what his eyes could see, he edged quietly forward and placed a hand gently over hers. Livia stiffened for the barest moment, then continued.

Marius rubbed a palm hard against her hot wetness and struggled frantically with the drawstring of his under-britches with his free hand. Swearing silently at the stubborn knot, he jerked at it, which only made it tighter. Cursing again, he tore violently at the fabric itself, and the white linen parted with a loud rip. His throbbing member fell through the jagged rent and he tumbled forward, groaning as he worked his way up the couch in search of relief. Livia obligingly raised herself on both knees, the stola falling over her shoulders. With a rapturous sigh, Marius grasped her waist and wildly thrust his way inside.

Their coupling was exquisitely brief: Livia soon cried out – a loud, moaning wail that sent Marius's passion soaring – and collapsed on the couch in a long, violent shudder, her legs rigid, her thighs hard as iron; Marius lay stiffly between, hands on her shoulders, his body wildly jerking in the final spasms of bliss.

For a long while, neither spoke. Each was completely spent; both were gasping hard for breath. Yet Marius's mind was already pondering what perverse god had created this aberration. Livia's hot, sweaty body was still and sticky beneath him – the body of the very same woman whose presence brought nothing but irritation and disdain. *What do I say to her now?*

Livia solved the problem. With a sigh of contentment, she stretched both arms high above her head and tried to turn. Marius warily eased himself back on his knees, his limp manhood falling free as if mocking him. Livia rolled over on her back with a smile, which quickly disappeared as one hand flew to cover her mouth. Her eyes opened wide in surprise. "Oh, it's you!"

Marius blinked, lost for words as he stared down on the woman. Was this going to be all his fault? Surely she'd known who was behind her!

"I thought Tuis had returned," Livia added, yet she just lay there on the couch and made no move to cover herself. The loose folds of the stola had slipped to one side and a pink, round breast with a nipple dark as honey and tight as a rosebud had fallen free. And her legs, bent at the knees, were placed far from modest. In fact, they were –

Marius cursed under his breath as his groin again stirred. What demon's game was the woman playing?

Livia broke into a broad smile, and for once her voice did not grate; in fact it was low and throaty. "Don't be silly, Marius," she purred. "I'm not *that* stupid."

It was only later, vainly seeking sleep in his own bed, that he realized something was amiss. The woman had admitted that she knew it was not her husband who surreptitiously entered her from behind. But how, in the name of all that was truth, had she known it was him?

Marius sighed, a long, thoughtful sigh that bordered on exasperation. What did it really matter? He remembered one of his grandfather's favourite sayings: small gifts are gratefully received; large ones are grabbed at. And there was lots of Livia to grab.

⁂

The slave roused Marius from his bed shortly after he'd tumbled in. His fogged brain quickly settled on Sabinius as the probable cause, a **non sequitur** drawn by a guilty man still warm from bedding the fellow's wife. Which was an addictive event that seemed to be happening more often than was good, he realized as his feet hit the cold stone floor. He was already three hours short on his usual amount of sleep, and near exhausted. The problem, however, seemed to be nothing more than a disturbance at the south gate. Two riders from the north, it seemed. That was surely something the primus could have handled. Marius mumbled as much to the slave, but the man said it was the primus himself who'd given the order to wake him, for it sounded as if there could be more to it.

Marius cursed and reluctantly fumbled for his britches, then staggered to his feet. The slave helped him strap on an ice cold pair of boots, and hurriedly threw a thick cloak around his shoulders. Someone, somewhere, opened a door, and Marius heard the discord of voices – many voices – sharp and loud in the distance.

"What is going on?" he demanded, his fuddled mind clearing. He strode from the bedroom, breaking into a run as he neared the door that opened onto the principalis.

"I've no idea, sir," the slave called after him, but by then the man was talking to himself.

The street was filling with soldiers, many of them half dressed, but each man with his weapon ready, and all looking uncertain. No orderly call to arms had been sounded, a command that would have sent every section running to its station; nor did anyone appear to know what to do. Marius swore again as he crossed to the via praetoria, ignoring the questions that shadowed his passage. He had no more idea than any of them, his own slave included.

He stopped short at the top of the long street, his mind struggling to absorb what the wavering flames of a score or more torches revealed. It was as if the gates had been breached, for the area behind them was filled with troops, most of them cavalry. But when Marius looked harder, he saw that more riders were coming from the direction of the stables, as if they were preparing to leave.

"Form up in ranks! Form up, I say!" a voice shouted behind him.

Marius whirled and saw that several centurios were taking charge, finally doing the job they were paid for. Their men were falling in, jostling and pushing as they sorted out the ranks. Feeling more confident, Marius strode quickly toward the south gate, aware that he didn't hold so much as a blade to shave with. Orders rang out from behind, though, and the reassuring thump of marching feet followed hard on his heels.

"There are barbarians," a voice called from the confusion ahead; then as recognition came that this was the legate: "The primus is there, sir."

Its owner appeared in the shadow of the barracks blocks, running down the street as if fleeing the chaos around the south gate. Marius recognized the man as the senior centurio of one of the cohorts; he couldn't remember which, but he'd better have answers. What, for example, were barbarians doing inside his fortress? And why had there been no call to arms?

He raised a hand, and behind him the rhythmic thud of booted feet fell silent. "What happened to the primus?" Marius demanded, and glanced nervously toward the gate. Several riders were coming his way. "Is he dead?"

"No, sir, he –"

"Then why are there barbarians inside my gates?"

⸸

Marcus's small column left Luguvalium and caught up with Cethen and Bryn at Isurium. Following that, his intent was to drop in at Eboarucm, then keep going south and catch a boat to Gesoriacum. From there, it would be backtracking the mad journey made to Britannia just months ago, only at a much more sedate pace. As the next few days passed, however, he began to wonder: why the haste? His only blood kin was his sister, who probably knew more about the estate's workings than he did, plus his stepmother. Though it had always been hard to think of Elena as being his mother, step of or otherwise. And it wasn't hard, either, to imagine what she'd say about him returning home, leaving both her natural sons in a pinch!

The fort had ample room to house his men, and by the time Marcus rode through the gate, he was full of indecision. As a compromise, he decided to stay over for a day or two and learn how Bryn fared in gathering the tribes behind him. Borba and Dag, at the last moment, had chosen to ride with them. The twin offered the excuse that it would be good to see Cethen again, though his true reason was probably to warn off Gavor. Dag, on the other hand, had simply wanted to see Isurium once more – the small tribal centre where he'd been born. When Cerealis invaded Brigantia, he and his father had fled the settlement in the naive belief that Venutius would push back the Romans, and they would soon return. Now Dag had finally done so, but not at all to what he expected.

Under the tall shadow of the fort, the settlement had grown beyond belief. More than six hundred of the tribe lived in the small town, which had been partly fortified during Dag's long absence. The talk was that the fort itself would be moved a short way to the west and the tribal settlement strengthened with full ramparts, palisades, and gates. A new site for the fort would relieve the town itself of the human dross drawn there by the garrison's soldiers, but the decision lay with the governor. So far it had not been forthcoming.

Bryn had arrived two days before and his visit was proving only a moderate success – though as the distance from Selgovae territory had widened, the warmer his welcome became. But it ever remained warm, never burning with fire. While the tribes were clearly divided on the invincibility of Roman rule, Bryn told Marcus that most would still rise and fight if the odds of victory seemed good. As for himself, when asked, he said that unless the gods personally assured him the Romans would be beaten, he'd remain committed to the course already chosen.

Jessa had passed through Isurium many times, staying overnight at the fort and hardly ever leaving its gates. Now she was surprised to discover how pleasantly the small town had been sited, spread across a broad stretch of fertile land that sloped gently to the River Ur. The slow-moving waters curved around the northeast side of the settlement as they turned to join the Abus less than a mile downstream. The weather had turned fair, and she found Isurium a place to linger. The next halt was Eboracum, where Bryn would turn west in a great, rambling circle that would end once more at Cumbria. What she and her father would do when that happened, neither had any idea – nor, seemingly, did he.

As evening fell, she found herself down by the river. Bryn had made his camp close to the settlement, by a small dock that had been built of enormous, uncut rocks where the riverbank fell away. Jessa sat on the largest with her bare feet hanging over the edge, while Trista cooled hers in the drifting current. Perhaps fifty paces downstream, one of the villagers had moored a small log raft and was setting a fish net with the dubious help of Criff. Far to the west the sky glowed warm and mellow, casting a hint of crimson on the softly rippling surface of the water. Jessa could have cheerfully laid back and dozed in the final heat of the day, but other matters pressed on her mind, none of which were any of her concern.

"Did you and Bryn resolve your differences?" she asked, her voice low so it wouldn't carry over the water to Criff.

"And you – what about you and your wee friend?" Trista shot back, glancing owlishly sideways, her eyebrow arched. Then she sighed, splashing her feet in the current. For a while she said nothing, lost in thought; then she spoke quietly, as if talking to herself. "Sometimes I could kick him. The man doesn't know which end to nock his arrow. The trouble is, he thinks too much. He sees both sides of everything, while everyone else sees only their own. It could –"

"I don't mean that," Jessa interrupted impatiently. "I'm talking about how things stand between the two of you."

"I can't believe this!" Trista cried, then caught herself and glanced downriver to Criff. He didn't appear to have heard, but she continued in a half whisper. "What else do you do for amusement, Jessa? Hide in the bushes and watch people do it? It's none of your concern."

"I know it's not," Jessa said, at the same time wondering why she was pushing the issue. Was it guilt over the woman's husband? No! Then did she feel sorry for the woman? No! There was a practical reason. "Look, if there is a problem, I can help. You do respect the man, don't you?"

"Respect? What's that got to do with it? Why not ask if I love the dithering sod! That's more the problem."

"Actually, it's not, you know." Jessa knew she was being pedantic, but didn't want to desist. "It's respect that keeps two people walking the same path. Without respect, all those warm, horny feelings will one day die, or at least slack off." For some odd reason she was unwilling to use the word 'love.' "Do you figure that his 'dithering,' as you call it, costs him your respect?"

As she spoke the words, Jessa realized that perhaps that was the reason why her own thoughts on Bryn seemed to bend like a reed. The man's lack of resolution came naturally, for it had ever been the way of his father, Cethen. But Trista's reply caught her by surprise, and made her think on what that might mean.

"I grow impatient with it, yes," Trista murmured, then smiled. "Yet it's a part of what makes him Bryn, isn't it? You know, Modan never could see anything but his own opinion, and I hated that. And as I said before, Bryn sees everyone's, and that includes mine. He respects what people say, and he thinks on it. If that seems like dithering, then I suppose I respect him for that." Trista sighed, as if it was a burden only she must bear. "I just wish the maundering ox was quicker to make up his mind."

"Then there's something else." Jessa smiled in turn, and drew a deep breath. "Maybe you can't get over what happened with your time with Modan, and . . ." She hesitated, unsure how far to go, then decided there was no halfway to the journey she had in mind. "And before that you had to put up with Treno."

Trista's eyes narrowed, and at first she said nothing. Then she shrugged, and her eyes lowered to where her feet cooled in the water. "We were both responsible for what happened to Modan."

"You know what I'm talking about, and it's not Modan's pruning."

Trist was silent as if brooding on the words, then she murmured, "I never said anything about Treno."

"Not directly, you didn't; nor do I have to hear. I know. But I also see the way Bryn looks at you, and you look at him. I see two axe-headed horses travelling side by side, only one seems to think it's a mule." Jessa sighed and laid a hand on Trista's shoulder. "And it ain't Bryn, and I'm not talking about being stubborn!"

When Trista said no more, Jessa turned and opened a leather purse that she'd brought with her to the riverbank. She pulled out a linen bag that was drawn tight at the top with a leather lace. Inside were a half-dozen small cakes, each of which could fit in the palm of her small hand.

All had been carefully baked before she'd left Luguvalium. Only two of the ingredients had been difficult to obtain, and these she'd extorted from Verus after reminding him, not too gently, of his error in removing Modan's plums. Every medicus held a good supply of poppy extract, but Verus was reluctant to admit possessing the dried goat weed. Jessa knew full well that he'd have some, and something was needed to motivate Trista's dormant passion. She'd carefully measured the ingredients, hiding the bitter taste in a mixture of flour, raisins, and almonds, heavily sweetened with honey and *sapa*.

"I'm not hungry," Trista muttered as Jessa showed her one of the small cakes.

"Eat it about an hour before you want to be overwhelmed with uncontrollable passion," Jessa said, smiling; then she told the truth. "You'll find it might help a little."

Trista took the cake and held it briefly to her nose. "Smells good." Then she returned it. "So how long is an hour?"

※

Evening had long fallen when the last of the patrols returned to the fort, the lathered horses galloping through the main gate as if pursued. The fort's senior centurio, a man called Servilius, quickly rode out looking for Marcus. He found the Roman senator down by the river where the barbarians had made camp. There were more than two hundred there, Servilius knew, for they'd reported in at the fort when they'd arrived. Now most of them had gathered to watch the dying flames of a huge bonfire, as if reluctant to turn in. Whatever easy mood filled the camp, his news would quickly dispel.

"A large force of barbarian cavalry, sir." The centurio, face pinched with worry, gestured toward the northwest, where the river became lost in the distant hills. "The decurio says there could be five hundred."

"Five hundred!" Marcus yelped, and turned to Bryn, bewildered. There could only be one explanation. "Modan?"

Bryn, like the others, had been freely sampling the local ale. The idea of so many men descending on Isurium could only have one reason, but Borba provided another. "It's no different than what he was doing at Stannick."

"He sent word that he was coming to Stannick, though." Dag clambered to his to feet and stared into the distance as if he might see Modan there. "You don't just ride in with five hundred at your back without first telling why. Not unless you're after someone." His eyes turned meaningfully on Bryn.

Bryn shook his head. "You do if there's a Roman fort where you're going and an even larger one a few miles downriver. Send notice, and you're setting your own trap."

"How many men do you have?" Marcus demanded of the centurio.

Servilius answered immediately. "Well under two hundred. With just that few, we'd be penned up inside until help arrives, and I'm sure whoever is coming knows it. The locals would be laughing at us, and he'd know that, too."

Marcus nodded, considering the odds if he added his own two troops to those inside the fort, as well as Bryn's people. They were good – good enough for a fight, should one prove necessary. And maybe Borba was right; maybe Modan was doing the same thing as he had done at Stannick.

"I think he's coming here to show his strength, and to find how many he's able to rally," Bryn explained, as if it was only natural. "It's the reason I'm here. He'll make a quick stop and be gone before those at the fortress downriver can react. I'll meet with him, and –"

"You're a fool-minded ox, Bryn," Trista shouted. "Is your mind addled?"

Marcus smiled, for he'd been about to suggest much the same thing. The woman and Jessa had earlier been down at the river, and had returned with a few perch that had been roasted and eaten. Criff was with them, as well as Kaeso – the lad who'd ridden to Jessa's rescue at Blatobulgium. Marcus frowned as his eyes fell on the lad; there wasn't the usual *enormous* difference found in his daughter's height and that of another man. *And the boy seems to have grown quite protective of her.*

"You do that, Bryn, and I'm thinking it will be back to Cumbria for me and my people," Luin muttered. Arlen, beside him, nodded firm agreement.

"Aye, don't forget: Modan's the same back stabbing snot that was after flaying my hide at Stannick. And that's the least of it," Borba muttered, glancing reluctantly at Cethen before dropping his eyes. "He may be your son, old friend, but as Trista says, it's the soft-headed who're blind."

Cethen sighed and shrugged. "I suppose you have the right of it, Borba, but –"

"But nothing," Jessa interrupted. "Should we lock ourselves up inside the fort and send to Eboracum for help, or do we go there now?"

Marcus looked from her to Servilius. "How long before they get here?"

"They weren't moving fast," Servilius said. "Two hours? Three at the most?"

"I'm not locking myself up in a fort with the Roman army," Bryn declared, his voice emphatic. "That would be the end of it, for me and any of us – nothing but shame! A weasel has more honour than to hide in a fox's den."

"There's the practical side to consider here," Marcus said calmly. "Modan, Lagan – it doesn't matter who is there. Either can ride in here and show his strength, but only for a day, and maybe not even that. One rider to Eboracum, and the Ninth will be on the march." *Most of it, anyway*, he thought cynically. *Is Marius doing as he was told?* It was clear, though, why Bryn would not fight alongside a Roman army; nor would it help his cause to be saved by one, not from his own people. That changed everything; but there were ways. "Servilius, are you able to hold them off inside the fort? They'll be on the move again by morning."

"As long as he doesn't convince the people here to join in," the centurio muttered, his eyes straying warily over one shoulder to the sprawl of barbarian buildings.

"And you think they will?" Marcus demanded. Would they all be best served by remaining in the fort? His own people would, that he knew; but there was Bryn, and the others with him . . .

"Not in a day," Servilius said firmly, and his face twisted in a sardonic smile. "From what I hear of your talk, they'll just as likely keep on riding after yon Bryn. Though I'm not going to keep my gates open on the chance they don't."

"Then let's leave," Jessa said firmly. "A small civilian settlement sits by Eboracum. Let it be known at Isurium that Bryn rides there, under the very noses of the Romans, to find who dares follow his cause."

Marcus smiled down at his daughter. If her mother had paired with a man other than himself, Jessa might well have taken the place of Cartimandua! Eboracum it would be. But a final matter needed tending, a problem deferred by the sunshine and Borba's clear reluctance to face it. Marcus moved off to one side and beckoned to the twin, who ambled over, his face twisting with anguish.

Marcus placed an arm on his shoulder and spoke low. "Gavor?"

"Aye, I know. I told him when we got here, and therein lies the problem," Borba muttered, glancing furtively north, his eyes following the riverbank.

"So that's why . . ." Marcus groaned as he divined the twin's meaning. "And now we may not have two or three hours."

⁂

"Look, you've got less than sixty men, and I've got near two hundred!" Bryn roared.

"And *you* look," Marcus shouted back. "They're behind us, they've spent the last few hours trying to catch up, and their horses are tired. We can beat the whole lot of them back to Eboracum with time to spare, but we need to get moving – now!"

The pair sat their horses further along the moonlit road – a road crowded with other men on horseback, some in column wearing the uniform of Rome, but most clad in the cloth tunics of the tribes. All, without exception, were impatient; but none more so than Bryn. He gestured toward Criff, quietly sitting his horse, perhaps the calmest of them all. "I will not have the bards tell that we fled to safety sheltered by Romans. Nor will they say that we sat behind a Roman wall when it was time to defend ourselves. We meet them here, on the road."

"Fighting them here, in the dark and outnumbered, is pointless," Marcus cried.

"Then take your hawks, and flock off. In fact, it's best that you do. There's your daughter to look after," Bryn waved his hand toward a distant cluster of riders, then turned to Luin as if Marcus was no longer there. "Start getting our men in line. We know they're not far behind. We'll block the road and wait. If Modan is bent on fighting, then it's time to grant his wish." Only he wasn't sure that his brother did want to fight. Block his ambition, certainly, but surely not kill him.

"He's got you outnumbered, Bryn. More than two to one," Marcus protested, ignoring the snub.

"And his men will be strung out like a herd of hill goats," Bryn replied, his eyes on Luin as he rode off. "If Modan is leading and he really is looking for a fight, then he'll be starting it with fewer men than we have."

"Then get closer to the fortress, where there's an escape. If there's a fight, you could still call it your own."

Bryn saw Trista riding back again with Jessa close behind, and that further goaded his temper. The two should be a mile or more further on by now, and he turned to berate Marcus; but from the look on the man's face, on this they agreed. Where was Arlen? It wasn't his fight; he could look after the women. "You two are supposed to be halfway to Eboracum," he shouted at the pair. "Go."

"It's my fight too," Trista replied.

"At least let's ride until the first of Modan's bunch does catch up," Marcus persisted without looking at her.

Bryn shook his head. That was just another way of phrasing what had already been said. He knew they could outdistance Modan, Marcus was right on that; but that would be seen as running away, fleeing from his brother; a cowardly choice carried out with the help of the Romans! He would never live down the shame. Besides, Modan's fastest horses would likely catch up to his slowest, unless the slowest were abandoned, something he would not do. And while they still might all get to the fortress ahead of Modan, it would be to what end?

"That could be at Eboracum, and then what?" Bryn retorted, his tone scornful. "Hide behind the walls?"

He turned his horse, anxious to see how Luin fared. The road to Isurium had been cleared well back on either side, and the Romans had even added a low ditch. Bryn guessed that it would take fifty or so cavalry to span the space between the trees, which made for a dangerously thin line. A second rank was forming up behind the first, and Luin had found enough to be telling off a third. At the centre of the front rank, he saw that –

"Shit!" Bryn cursed loudly and ignoring Marcus and the two women, he kicked his horse forward. "Da, Borba, Dag – get your fool arses out of there."

Marcus cursed too and turned to his own men. The two troops of cavalry stood in the middle of the road in column of four, the horses restless. Kaeso sat his mount with the two decurios, all three patiently watching and waiting. Venting a huge sigh, Marcus rode over.

"Kaeso, ride as fast as you can to Eboracum without killing your horse," he ordered. "Take one man with you. There can't be more than eight ten miles left to –"

"Sir!" Kaeso raised himself indignantly in the saddle, glaring. "I respectfully refuse. It doesn't require an officer to deliver a message. I will not leave my men or the two women when –"

"Aw, the gods save me!" Marcus rolled his eyes and turned to the nearest decurio. "Trooper, send two of your men to Eboracum. Let the garrison know we need help. Then get your bones back here, and we'll decide what to do with this lot. And as for you . . ." he turned back to the diminutive officer.

"Sir!" Kaeso stubbornly squared his shoulders, as if expecting the worst.

Marcus simply shook his head. "Take command of the women, if such a thing is possible, and get them to Eboracum." He pointed Kaeso to Jessa and Trista who, for once, seemed uncertain what to do. "Take a couple of troopers with you. Mix up the pace: stiff canter, steady trot, you know the routine; don't exhaust the animals. If you hear even the clang of a sword blade, though, put boots to belly and ride like the wind. Got it?"

Kaeso bit his lip, his sense of duty plainly at odds with itself.

"That's my daughter you have charge of there, soldier," Marcus barked, making the small cavalryman jump. "You foul that up, and it's the last thing you ever do. Got that?"

"Yes, sir!"

⁂

They were pushing the horses far too hard, and Treno knew it; his own was labouring, and had been for a while. He didn't dare look over his shoulder to see how many had fallen behind, which was foolish. *Avoiding the truth doesn't change what is.*

Lagan should have been here. He was the only one with a fair load of sense. His man Gobha was as crazed as Modan, who also should have been here; just like Modan, Ghoba couldn't lead a pig to a pail of peelings. And as for Horus, who was pushing all this, when the stupid Greek wasn't doing his sums, he was as much use as the village idiot. The man couldn't wield a sword and he could barely sit a horse, though he'd had the wisdom to acquire one of the best. That was the only reason the fat lump was able to keep up with them. Though where this was all going to end, Treno had no idea. It was Horus who'd convinced Lagan that Bryn needed killing, which could prove to be the most stupid decision the man had ever made – or the wisest. Treno had no idea which.

Not for the first time, he hoped that Bryn had simply buggered off to Eboracum and was out of reach. Maybe he was already there. Those at Isurium had said that was what he . . .

Treno realized that the riders who galloped ahead of him were slowing down. The squabbling was already in full sway as he reined in, and Gobha's voice was the loudest: "There they are! Come on – let's get 'em before they run."

"Wait, you silly man," Horus bellowed. "The fellow is obviously set on making a stand. Wait until all of our people arrive."

Treno couldn't have agreed more. The pale, pudgy Greek might sit his horse like a sack of grain, but he could think right. It was definitely better to wait, perhaps for both sides: Gobha could plainly use more men, and Bryn might get wise and slink off while he could. Yet Treno knew that wasn't going to happen, nor would Gobha wait for reinforcements – not when he'd just been called an idiot by the damned Greek. The fool was again screeching some sort of order to attack, but it made no difference in the end. A gap had opened in the great mass of riders milling about Gobha, and through it Treno saw that Bryn's people were on the move.

There were far more than expected, he realized, and swore. The road, the ditch, the wide verge the Romans had cleared back to the trees, were full of shadowy figures that, for the moment, slid eerily through the moonlight like an army of spirits. Treno blinked, shaking the spectral image. Those shadows were merely Bryn's warriors, whose shields were made of wood and whose weapons were made of iron – and they were tearing toward him like a pack of wolves. He spun his horse, forcing the animal through the gathering ranks of Lagan's cavalry. The clamour of hard fighting followed him down the road: the squeal of horses; the harsh clash of iron on iron; the shouting and cursing; and the wrenching screams of pain.

Treno had no need to turn to know that matters were not going well. He let the horse have its head as it galloped back along the road, and didn't rein the beast in until a good distance back along the road. When he turned though, it was impossible to know what was happening. Whatever order had existed seemed to be gone, replaced by a dark, distant blob ghostly shapes that plugged both the road and the ditches. There was no sense riding straight back into it, Treno reasoned; he might end up inflicting as much harm on his own people as Bryn's – not to mention himself. He should do something, though.

He was pondering exactly what when the steady drumming of many hooves from behind made him turn, sagging with relief. The way back to Isurium slowly became black with mounted men, their horses loping easily along the road as if ridden for pleasure. Most of the others had arrived, but they'd had the sense not to push the tired horses. He lashed his own animal toward them, glad of an excuse for being found away from the fighting.

"Where've you been? Gobha, Horus – these men need help," he shouted and pulled savagely on the bit as he drew near, wheeling his horse around as the animal jarred to a halt. Treno was appalled to find that many of the distant shadows had broken free of the fight and were heading his way; though if they were attacking or fleeing, he couldn't tell.

"What's away?" someone called out.

Treno had no idea what "was away," and was not going to admit it. The newly arrived cavalry was a restless jumble of tired horses and disgruntled riders, all wanting for guidance. He recognized just three of those riding in front. The nearest was Gavor, who was one of his own men; the other two were Selgovae, both of them minor flames in the light of Lagan's eyes. Which was as well, Treno decided; they just might do what he told them. Feeling foolishly like Modan, whose brain could think of no other command than charge, he pointed with his spear and yelled, "There's the enemy. Take them."

Raising his spear, Treno slammed both heels hard against his horse's belly, but kept a tight rein on the animal; the last thing he wanted was to lead a force of one! He threw a wild glance over his shoulder, and was relieved to see that most of them followed. They were slow about it, though, and he pulled on the bit, his horse snorting and shaking its head. Not far ahead, some of those who had ridden forward were turning back, while others had reined in and stood waiting. Which Treno hoped was a good way to tell who was who.

※

Bryn was fighting for his life, as was everyone around him; though against whom each man fought it was hard to tell. It was nigh impossible to figure who was friend or foe. The question had been easy at first: if they were moving south, kill; if they were heading north, assist. But as the battle bogged down on itself, all sense of direction disappeared. Bryn recognized some he came across, and others he instinctively seemed to know. For the most part, his own people wore plainer, solid-coloured tunics and carried oval shields rather than the smaller round ones favoured by the Selgovae – for the most part. But more than half Modan's men seemed to be Brigante, and not a soul wore a uniform such as those worn by the Romans – which was a shame, because it made things far easier for everyone.

"Bryn!" a voice screamed in his ear, and his father appeared in the corner of his eye; that he remained safe was a relief, because he'd told the stubborn ox to go with the women. But his da was pointing north, probably thinking a breakthrough was imminent – which it just might be, for it looked as if Modan's men were losing ground.

Bryn thrust his spear through the ribs of a man intent on smashing his axe against Arlen's shield. The thrust was easy, but the barbed head wouldn't come free and he let it go. Close in, a sword was better anyway. He slid the weapon free of the pommel horn.

"Stay behind me," he yelled at Cethen, and lunged at the back of a rider carrying a small round shield. The tip of his blade vanished maybe no more than a handsbreadth, but it was enough to make the man's arm drop, and someone else's spear slid over the poor sod's shield and into his neck.

"We gotta get out of here," Cethen yelled. "Look."

"Don't panic, da! I can't look. I'm –" Bryn took a blow on his shield from a man he'd thought was one of his own and struck wildly back; the sword missed and slashed down hard in front of the fellow's saddle. The edge bit deep into the horse's withers and the animal squealed. Dropping its head, the beast spun round in a circle, kicking and bucking and throwing its rider clear. Bryn was appalled to see that the man *was* one of his own, who now stared up at him, winded and clearly confused. The fighting eased for a moment as those nearby grew leery of the wounded horse's flailing hooves.

"I'm not panicking, you daft clod," Cethen yelled and caught his son by the shoulder, jabbing his spear violently toward Isurium. "Look! Over there!"

Bryn's eyes followed the weapon's shaft and he swore. *Just when you have everything your way, the gods . . .*

The road to Isurium was awash with Modan's cavalry.

"Fall back! Fall back!" Bryn yelled and turned his horse, frantic to start his people moving south. Then he remembered the man whose horse he'd butchered. The fellow had staggered to his feet, and stood off to one side in a daze. Bryn held out a hand and pulled him up behind the cantle.

"Yeah," he muttered in reply to the man's thanks, and risked a glance toward the north. This was no longer a fight; his men were in a panicked flight. The odds were overwhelming! Which they would have been anyway, Bryn reluctantly admitted, had Modan's men all arrived at the same time. But should that have happened, he would have at least been organized and might have stood his ground. Now his men were scattered, each trying to break free from what was suddenly a rout; a disordered flight, with every man fighting for himself.

Both Luin and Arlen were tearing around, still hacking with swords, their horses circling as they screamed at their men to turn and run. Bryn saw that Borba had already fallen back, sitting his horse on the road behind him – likely waiting for Cethen – and Dag was there too, unarmed and favouring his sword arm. And his da was still screaming in his ear –"Go, go, go."

It was time. Arlen was now fleeing. More men were breaking away, some with small round shields, curse them, all heading toward Eboracum. Then Luin was suddenly there, pushing his horse against his and yelling over the loud clash of battle, "Get out of here, dolt!" He struck the rump of Bryn's mount with the flat of his sword, and was gone.

Bryn's horse leapt forward as another rider hurtled from the ditch, lunging at his back with a spear. The man behind him screamed and Bryn felt something sharp prick hard against his shoulder. Whatever it was, it the pain quickly eased, and the arms that gripped his waist slid away. Bryn winced at the soft thud of the man's body striking the road, and cursed at the loud thump of pounding hooves. He turned in the saddle and saw the same rider who had thrust the spear. Behind him rode several more.

It was enough. Bryn kicked hard with his heels and let the horse have its head, feeling its strength beneath him as it lunged forward. At the moment, he gave not a damn whether the beast raced all the way down the road to the fortress at Eboracum – a road now teeming with fleeing cavalry, though whose, it was hard to tell. Bryn did note with disgust that Marcus and his two troops of auxiliaries had vanished. He'd thought that maybe the man had ridden farther along the road, and held his men there in the event of a retreat. It might have made a difference. How many troops did a father need to take care of his precious daughter? And Trista too, he grudgingly added.

He supposed he *had* told the man he needed no Roman help . . .

⚔

Marcus sat his horse between those of the two troop decurios, patiently watching from the cover of the forest as the inevitable took its course. The numbers and conditions made matters easy to predict, but you could never tell. Sometimes the gods or, more likely, the spirit of a man's will would make the difference – but he doubted this was one of those times. No, this time it was easy to figure, and his mind numbered the reasons: Bryn and Modan's men were evenly matched in both skill and will; there had been no true element of surprise; Bryn's people were outnumbered by more than two to one; and while the moon was nearing its half, the night remained quite dark, which bred nothing but confusion!

And to further hamper Bryn's odds, the proud fool had lost his greatest asset when telling two troops of disciplined Roman cavalry to slink off and look after the women. Marcus *had* looked after the women, for young Kaeso should by now have his daughter well ahead of the pack. But as for the rest of it, he and his men were not where Bryn figured they were, despite the casual dismissal.

The gesture had rankled at the time, but he sympathized with the man's reasoning. If a barbarian warrior wishes to lead his people, he can't do it hiding behind the shield of Rome. Yet neither should he need to die for lack of Rome's shield, even if it should weaken the man's cause; a dead man no longer has a cause; not this side of the grave, anyway. When it was over, if Bryn figured the price of Rome's interference was too high, at least he would be alive to bitch about it. Or he might be, if he was still breathing . . .

One of the decurios stirred and pointed. "It won't be long, sir."

Marcus nodded agreement. They'd all seen the distant road to Isurium darken with more of Modan's cavalry, though the sound of its coming had been drowned by the clamour of the battle being fought between. Too many moments passed before Bryn's people also saw the cavalry. Some immediately began disengaging – fleeing was the better word – but the two sides remained far too mingled and confused for him to begin his own attack. Marcus shook his head, watched, and waited.

The chaos of men and horses that blocked the road slowly began to unravel as if it was a massive ball of yarn. The lead end was a long black thread of riders that fled south along the road to Eboracum; the ball itself was a massive blot of battle that, rather than vanish, was slowly growing smaller.

"Now, sir?" The decurio's voice was anxious, as if the order might already be too late.

Marcus shook his head, though he understood the man's impatience. He had told the decurio that, should Bryn and his men begin to fail, they would attack. The column would strike Modan's flank from the shelter of the forest – *the element of surprise* – and cover Bryn's retreat. But as he watched Modan's pursuit forming, with Bryn's fresher horses still providing an advantage, a further ploy formed in his mind. It was a choice that would do far more damage to Modan, yet would prove safer for his men.

He smiled as the ball of yarn finally finished unravelling and the last of the ragged blot of newcomers joined its end. "Here's what we'll do," he said.

※

Marcus was painfully aware that he was no longer a young man, and he positioned himself accordingly: well back in the column, with the decurio of the second troop. He waited patiently until the road cleared and the final clutter of riders tore off toward Eboracum at full gallop. Modan's people had little choice but to force their horses, even though a decent animal, in good condition, could maintain such a hard pace for not much more than several miles. After that, the beast would start to labour and fail. And Modan's men would find their animals failing first, for they had travelled most the day.

Marcus signalled the lead decurio. The two troops abandoned the cover of the trees at a trot: a dark column of shadows that flitted over the open ground and onto the road. The orders were brief and clear: keep to the road's surface; hold the gait to no more than a canter; avoid the ditches; and above all, resist temptation. If an enemy flees to the forest, let him go; if he turns to fight, cut him down and keep moving; if he isn't dead, don't stop to kill; and if a trooper falls, he's the responsibility of the second squadron.

They fell on the first of the stragglers within the first half mile. The clash was not a slaughter, nor was it a walk through the forum. It was, however, well executed; a word that Marcus decided was appropriate. A dozen or so of Modan's men had been forced to hold their spent horses to a walk, while the shadows of as many more could be seen farther ahead. The distance made no difference as the column rode on at a steady, solid canter, the rested horses and their armoured riders clattering along the road with the force of a battering ram.

Marcus fought to curb his growing exhilaration, in the same breath thinking it all seemed so unfair. It was like chasing tame rabbits. Never before had he directed a strategy with such success and, dammit, it *was* exhilarating! And he could see that the same mood was shared by his men. Perhaps only two or three tribesmen were killed in that first encounter and a few more were probably wounded – most of them unaware that even a single Roman trooper followed behind. Of those who did hear and turned to look, most fled, taking to the forest rather than fight. There, lost in the darkness of the trees, they likely held back and watched as the column rode on, the oiled armour of the riders glinting in the moonlight.

The sense of awe would have cowed them, Marcus realised: more than fifty troopers in mail and helmets, four ranks wide, all heavily armed and unstoppable. What Modan's people must be thinking was almost laughable: *Where did the bastards come from?*

※

Marius Appius glanced sharply up at the rider, who'd whipped his mount forward and was suddenly very near. Behind him, jouncing along on a hill pony, came a small woman, looking ready to fall off at any moment. It was the dwarf! Another Sabinius! Was her father somewhere behind?

"Sir!" A cavalry officer reined his horse in not two paces away, both animal and rider clearly exhausted. Yet the man's voice was cheerful – or was it simply buoyed by relief? "Are we glad to see you!"

"How . . . ?"

"My father should be here soon." The Sabinius woman edged her horse alongside the trooper and swung one leg over the pommel, clearly looking to him for help in dismounting. Behind her, Marius recognized the barbarian woman who'd visited the fortress – when, a month past? Was the entire family again descending on him? Just when he'd grown used to –

Shit, where was Livia?

# Chapter XXXIII

## Calacum, September, A.D. 105

Frevan was dead. Word of his passing swept through the hills, travelling as if borne on the wind. His body was barely cold when word of his death caught up with Bryn at Calacum, a settlement that lay only a short day's ride from the lake that was home to Frevan's small village. The cluster of buildings lay close by the Roman fort, and had been intended as the final stop in the steady progress that brought Bryn and Trista back to Cumbria to see the ailing chieftain.

The long trek had taken them through the tribal settlements at Camulodunum and *Rigodunum,* and what had seemed to be a hundred lesser villages and farmsteads in between. At each one Bryn had been received well enough, but as ever, the enthusiasm was muted. But the final tragedy was that he'd been desperately hoping to confer with the ailing Frevan, eager to hear his advice. And now that was impossible.

"Rhun is the answer," Jessa said firmly. "Get the torque. Show it for all to see. Without it you have only half a cause."

"With Frevan gone, there'll be no holding Modan back," Trista suggested.

"Not just Modan," Bryn said in a tired voice, his elbows propped on the table, his chin resting on his knuckles. "There's Ilbrec, too – Frevan's nephew. He'll be strutting in Frevan's lodge with any kin that support him nuzzling his behind. Mind you, Modan is the stronger of the two, if for no other reason than he has the backing of Lagan."

"But Lagan's a Selgovae, an unworthy neighbour even for Modan," Marcus murmured as he cupped his chin, his features thoughtful. "You once mentioned that Frevan said he would weave a new legend about how the torque would be found."

"Aye, and he made it as fogbound as a druid's prophecy." Bryn smiled, his eyes half closed as he recited:

> *An eagle is wounded, yet the raven falls,*
> *And the gods look down and weep*
> *As fire burns the land by a brother's hand*
> *While another is lost in sleep.*
>
> *But a father's son will go and come,*
> *And the raven soar once more.*
> *A golden gift will rise in the mist,*
> *Borne by the first of four.*

"Not difficult to figure," Marcus murmured, "though how a person creates a mist, I have no idea."

"Not difficult for *us* to figure, but it would be for others," Jessa said. "Frevan was just being the sly one. If you already have the answer, it's easy to make the question a riddle."

"Which he's done," Marcus said, and turned to Bryn and Trista. "Is everyone leaving here tomorrow?"

Trista glanced instinctively toward the door that closed off Marcus's quarters at the rear of the commander's residence. There was nobody around, of course. Her reaction was no more than natural mistrust, yet she wondered if she could ever feel completely comfortable inside a Roman fort.

She and Bryn had gone to the stronghold soon after twighlight, walking up from the settlement in the dark. It was still best that Bryn not be seen as being close with the Romans; though of late, with Lagan's growing army along their borders, many in the tribes were divided on that. You either lived with the Roman invaders, which offered certain advantages in comfort and safety; or you were fighting them – which, Trista supposed, offered the advantages of a precarious freedom. Yet even if the tribes did beat the Romans, what happens then with the neighbours – the tribes further north, and the Selgovae in particular? They would be left ruling the field with a strong and growing army, something they would never had dared do before the Romans came.

Trista was uncomfortable with the notion, and pushed it aside . . .

"I'm leaving at first light," Bryn replied to Marcus's question. "I need to be at Frevan's funeral if I want to claim what's mine."

"What about Rhun?" Jessa asked. "That's just as important. Maybe more so."

"I agree, but Frevan should be first." Bryn mused. "Yet without Rhun, there is no torque. Dare I arrive at the funeral with nothing but its promise? Ilbrec's already spreading his muck: Bryn's too close to Rome; he's unwilling to fight; he's only a half-bred outsider."

"And Ilbrec's an ill-bred insider," Trista retorted, wondering if Bryn was again bending with the wind.

"Half-bred, ill-bred, or *not bred at all*." He grinned, his gaze seeming to mock her. "What does it matter? The way I see it, there's no choice. I'm off to Frevan's lodge, hopefully in time for the burial. I'd guess Ilbrec's blood won't boil over until after Frevan's poor body's in the ground."

Trista flushed at the words "not bred at all," and looked quickly about the table for signs of amusement. But if anyone had scribed something into them other than herself, it didn't show – except perhaps for Jessa, who did glance up and smile before she spoke.

"Look, why not halve the apple, then both can eat?" she suggested. "Bryn, you go to Frevan's lodge, and make your claim. Promise them the torque."

"How can I promise something I don't have?" he interrupted, clearly annoyed.

"Take Criff with you to smooth the way. Maybe Dag and Borba would also go. They're known and respected," Jessa finished, holding both hands out as if the rest was obvious. "As to the other half of the apple, you have half a dozen others more suited to pry the torque from Rhun's hands, without showing him five thousand followers."

"Starting with my da," Bryn said softly.

"And there's his brother Cian. I'm sure Cethen dragged him and Luga along for that very reason. And don't forget my own da," Jessa paused and stared pointedly at her father, "who can order him to turn it over to Bryn."

Marcus looked trapped, and Trista knew why. He had reluctantly chosen to ride with Bryn following the flight to Eboracum, as if there was a responsibility involved. He could have remained at the fortress, and perhaps continued on to Rome. Trista was surprised that he hadn't, considering the death of his father. She could almost feel sorry for the man. Nearly all his kin was in Britannia, including a daughter who had no wish to leave. Yet there might be a further impulse that drove Marcus to remain, at least for the time being. He'd spent many years in this land, and particularly the northern hills. Maybe he was curious enough to want to see the end of it.

"Ordering Rhun to part with the torque could be helping a future enemy of Rome," Marcus observed dryly, and stared at Bryn without expression.

"Father!"

"No, Jessa, hear this." Marcus said, his eyes still on Bryn. "Tell me that it's not true that if Lagan and Modan utterly defeat Rome you'll toss your lot in with them."

"It's not true," Bryn said blithely.

"Liar."

"Now that is true," he said, and grinned. "Though I doubt they'd have me anymore."

Trista watched the back and forth flow of words, realizing just how much was being thrown into an already bubbling cauldron, including the inference of Bryn's final words – and what they might mean for her.

"Which half of the apple will you take?" Jessa asked Trista, as if trying to move the talk elsewhere.

She had no doubt on that one. "I'll be going with Bryn, of course."

"No you won't," Bryn said emphatically. "You'll be going with Jessa, and my da!"

Trista started to protest, but the look in Bryn's eyes stayed her. It was as hard and firm as she'd ever seen it – which did not speak much on what he thought of his chances.

⸸

"I see you slept under the same roof as Bryn last night," Jessa said.

Trista turned her eyes sharply toward Jessa, who had the audacity to yawn as she asked the question. Was she simply bored? Jessa sat slouched in the saddle, her small body swaying to the steady, rhythmic movement of her horse. Her pony had long been abandoned after the chase to Eboracum, and the larger animal with its broad saddle provided an incongruous perch. Even with the extra strapping and the padding that had been added, the contraption would surely make for hard riding.

"Which is another way of asking if he's plowing me," Trista replied, keeping her voice mild, despite the rude intrusion.

"So, is he?"

"So how about your toy cavalryman? Is he plowing you?" Annoyance made her throw the words back far too quickly. Even though the light was fading, she saw Jessa's cheeks flush. Not that it curbed her irritation. She wasn't the one who'd pulled first on the bowstring.

"Ha! So he's not!" Jessa shot back, and her next words made Trista realize that the word "toy" had rankled far more than intended. "So, what's your problem? Still can't get over Bryn's de-balled brother, or is it the stiff-peckered one you were raised with?"

Trista gritted her teeth and said nothing, fighting the urge to curse and hit back. Jessa had fallen silent in turn, as if realizing that this time it was she who had gone too far. *And she had!* The jangle of harness and the clip-clop of a hundred hooves echoed softly in the silence that hung between them, and the rich, heavy scent of the horses filled Trista's nose as she drew a deep, calming breath. A damp evening chill had settled the air, which was not unpleasant. Even so, she stared stonily at the road ahead. The gate towers of the fort at Luguvalium had appeared in the distance, offering what?

When Trista finally answered she was unsure if she was speaking to Jessa or herself. "Maybe both. Or maybe it's just me."

Jessa turned quickly as if startled by the words, then just as quickly turned away. The small woman appeared nonplussed, and it showed on her face as she fumbled for words. Trista laughed, bitterly, and broke the awkward silence. "You're figuring on telling me it's not my fault, right?"

"I suppose."

"That's tripe! What you really want to do is shake my shoulders and say, 'but you already know it's not your fault, you silly bitch; just face up to whatever it is that's haunting you!'"

Jessa smiled. "Not exactly."

"More tripe!" Trista muttered, and fell silent.

"You do want Bryn, don't you?" Jessa asked a few moments later, her voice soft.

"Sure.' Trista glanced sideways, to be sure Jessa understood. "Really. But something inside stops me. Sometimes it's like maybe I want something from him, but I'm not sure what. It's like being hungry and your mouth drools, but when you go to eat you lose your appetite. I just dunno . . ."

Jessa looked vaguely uncomfortable and Trista wondered if her words straddled a path that they both followed. "You're different from me on this, Jessa, I know; yet in some ways you're no different at all. You like your wee cavalryman but I don't see you doing anything about it, other than talking the poor lad's ears off."

Jessa seemed to bristle at the word "wee" and Trista smiled. She could understand why the lass seemed reluctant to move forward with her Kaeso, for she suspected the woman walked untrodden ground. But there was no need to be so sensitive about the smaller things in life.

Even as that thought crossed her mind, Trista cringed at the use of the word "smaller."

"Look, I'm sorry if the 'toy' word offended. I admit it was unnecessary," she said. "But as to the other, it's the way it is. You are small, Jessa, and Kaeso's a long way from big. What I'm saying is, there's nothing wrong with words like 'wee' and 'small.' People say 'wee bairn' and 'tall warrior' all the time if it fits, and nobody takes offense. Fat is fat, thin is thin, and unless the words are meant to harm, it tells things the way they are. Jess, sometimes you've gotta let things soar over your head!" Trista smiled as, belatedly, she realized what she'd said. "And that's a well used expression, not a dig."

Jessa's jaw firmed and Trista braced herself; then Jessa slowly, perhaps grudgingly, nodded her agreement. Trista smiled. It was at least a truce.

Then Jessa's eyes suddenly twinkled, and she turned to Trista and grinned. *"Or not bred at all?"*

"Stuff your gob." Trista grinned back, remembering Bryn's hidden meaning the night before. At the time the words had cut, but now they seemed amusing.

"Did you not sample the sweets I gave you?" Jessa asked, not bothering to conceal her own amusement.

"Yes," Trista said, and tried to shrug off the question. "They didn't taste bad."

"So what happened?" Jessa asked.

"Nothing."

"Nothing?" Jessa asked, her expression incredulous.

Trista sighed. The small cakes had, in fact, tasted excellent. More than that, they had been wonderfully relaxing, and had stirred a delicious tingling sensation in her skin. They had also eased the usual cramps that struck her belly before the monthly bleeding, and for that she was grateful. But as to any other effect, such as a magical urge to hump Bryn, there'd been nothing. Sheepishly, she added. "I fell asleep."

"You fell asleep?"

"So did Bryn."

"Bryn ate one too?"

"Why not? He saw me and wanted to know what they were. I couldn't actually tell him, so I gave him one and told him it was a sweet."

Jessa glared suspiciously. "How many did you have?"

Trista hung her head, feeling like a scolded puppy. "We ate the whole half-dozen. Half each. As I said, they didn't taste bad."

Jessa muttered and clamped a hand to her forehead. "Why can't people follow instructions?"

"But you said –" Trista began.

Jessa snapped her fingers as if remembering something missed. "Were you at the bitchy time when you took them?"

"You mean when everything cramps up just before . . . ?"

"Yes."

"Yes."

"Hmm, then it's partly my fault." Jessa sighed and lowered her voice, though nobody was within hearing. "Look, I've got some more. I'll give you one. Only one, this time. And it's best to use it, well, maybe if you let things happen about a week before your bleeding stops."

"Ah-hah," Trista drawled, her voice also low. "So you've got some more, you wee witch! Is this your own supply, then? The hidden life of Jessa Sabinius, medicus to the people!"

Jessa seemed to ignore the "wee" word and instead rolled her eyes, her cheeks reddening. "I don't even know what they taste like," she hissed back. Then she relented, shrugging as she grinned once more. "But I'm not going to let them go to waste, am I?"

† 

Rhun had the men he needed, though that was all he had, and it was likely no thanks to Tuis. All around him the hills seemed ready to erupt in warfare, while farther south the Second and Twentieth legions were still piddling around preparing to march. Marius continued to blather about readying the Ninth down at Eboracum; but for more than a week, only rumours had been received as to what was happening on the northeast side of Brigantia. All Rhun knew with certainty was that the forts to the north of him were experiencing a huge increase in tribal movement, as were those immediately to the east. Conditions were less volatile in Cumbria, directly south of Luguvalium where the chieftain Frevan had just died – though anything could happen once the man was under the weeds.

But he did have the men! A full milliaria which, with the replacements that Tuis let him keep, was at full strength. That was cause for celebration on any Roman frontier.

Rhun had halted the work extending the size of the fort. The outer defenses were in place, and would serve: the ramparts were firm and sodded, the palisade complete, and the gates functional. The inside structures could wait. The fort could be defended. In the meantime, some troops would have to double up in the buildings, and the rest could remain under their leather tents. That was nothing new for them, and Rhun had the feeling it would not be for long. Something would erupt soon. In the interim, he intensified troop training and drill. Nearly a thousand troops were stationed at the fort, and Rhun was a firm believer that idle soldiers caused trouble.

As opposed to his father . . .

Cethen arrived unexpectedly, accompanied by what could best be described as hostiles, most of them his own kin. He rode in at the end of a long day on the road leading up from the south, having set out from Eboracum with Bryn's people several weeks earlier. And what his da now demanded, along with every last one of the others who were with him, Rhun found impossible to give.

"Father, you entrusted the torque to me, to do with as I see fit. That should be the end of it," Rhun protested, not bothering to hide his annoyance. "I don't see turning it over to Bryn until he has a following."

"I gave it to Coira too," Cethen said stubbornly.

Rhun glanced impatiently about the great cross hall of the headquarters building, and decided it was no place for such a discussion. All of them – the two women Jessa and Trista; his own father; Cian and his great, hulking shadow Luga; and even his brother by marriage – had all arrived at the building as if dropping by for a family visit. Their horses were likely still outside waiting to be stabled!

"Let's get out of here," he muttered.

The September evening had remained warm, and the large courtyard that sheltered the entrance to the building offered an element of privacy. In fact, with a senator and the fort's commander sitting under its portico there was absolute privacy, for all other ranks inside the fort made sure they stayed clear. He gestured to a table that was flanked by a pair of benches.

"I have no doubt that Coira would feel the same way," Rhun continued, even before the others were seated. He flung one leg over a bench and sat straddling its plank surface. Then someone did dare venture from the headquarters building, and he scowled in the man's direction.

The senior clerk approached anyway. "Beer or wine, sir?"

"Make mine a beer," Cian called out.

"Mine two," Luga echoed, grinning as he raised two fingers.

Everyone else voiced their choice and the man disappeared. Cian chose the silence that followed to voice his opinion. "I know the lass, Rhun, and I'm not so sure. Bryn has a problem, and it's all about the order in which things must happen. Tell me, which arrived first in the sky: the sun or the moon?"

"What, by Tanit's tits, has that got to do with anything?" Rhun demanded, annoyed that his uncle was being obtuse.

"That's just my point. One of them had to be here first, right? But in what order? The gods likely argued at the time, but in the end, what did it matter? They both shine." Cian spoke slowly, as if trying to match his comparison to Bryn's problem with the torque, but Jessa was less patient.

"What Cian means is this: does Bryn gather a huge following first, then get the torque to secure it; or does he first get the torque, which allows him to secure his huge following." She turned and shook her head at Cian. "The moon and the sun! What does it matter which came first? But with Bryn, it certainly does."

"That's what I was getting at," Cian mumbled, then shrugged. "Myself, I'd say it was the sun, because it's the warmth that gives life to –"

"Get to the point!" Trista exclaimed. "Sun, moon – it's obvious that Bryn alone will never gather his large following because of Modan and Lagan. The tribes are *worse* than divided on that. There are those who think the two of them will push back the Romans, so they support them; but there are others who are just plain afraid they can't, and support Bryn."

"So?" Rhun said impatiently, because Bryn had set the problem out just as plainly. "That was his strategy: he'd bide his time, waiting until we quell the latest uprising. It hasn't happened yet, but appears about to. Then he's –"

"That was before Frevan died." Trista's tone was also growing heated. "That changes things. Someone else may well step in and take his place. There are others –"

Rhun raised a hand to stay her as two troopers entered the courtyard from the street. They hesitated on seeing Rhun and the others there, but he beckoned them over. The pair were dispatch riders, road weary and plainly just arrived. They walked over to the wooden bench and stood awkwardly at attention.

"Relax," Rhun growled, almost afraid to ask what they carried. "North, south, or east?"

"From the south, sir," the taller of the two replied. "The farthest one is from Deva."

He made ready to unsling several sealed leather cases that dangled from his shoulder, but Rhun stopped him. Most would be opened the moment the man walked inside the building. If there was anything private or of importance, his chief clerk knew where he was. Often, more than just the dispatches rode with the rider, including oral messages and gossip. "Anything marked for me?"

"Nothing marked private, sir."

"Verbal messages?"

"No, sir." The man grinned. "Not officially. But units of the Second and the Twentieth marched from Deva yesterday morning."

"About time," Rhun muttered under his breath, relieved. "Rumours on its strength?"

"Over ten thousand with the auxiliaries, sir."

*Which likely means eight,* Rhun decided, for rumours of troop numbers were always exaggerated unless it suited the teller. But he was pleased to know that Tuis had finally got them on the move. Nothing had as yet erupted from the tribes, so it was unlikely his brother would be forcing the march north. If he had left yesterday morning, it might take another five days or so; or if they dawdled – Tuis *was* leading them – then it could be six or seven.

"That's good. We'll be pleased to see them here." Rhun dismissed the pair with a wave of the hand. Perhaps, with a proper show of strength, this could all be resolved with as little damage as possible. "You know, a long march through Selgovae territory, and another across where Modan is raising warriors, might just do it. Make a few examples on the way so they won't forget, and we just might get through this year without trouble. Or we might get lucky, and force this Lagan fellow to fight in the open."

"I don't know," Marcus said, offering his opinion for the first time. "You followed Galgar all the way to the very edge of this land before he'd fight."

"What about Bryn?" Trista persisted. "He needs help now. Never mind Modan and Lagan, Frevan's nephew is also circling his back."

"She's right, you know," Marcus said softly.

Cethen echoed the words, his eyes holding those of his son as if for emphasis.

There was a message in his da's words, and Rhun had no need to ask what it was. There was also another to be found in Cian's level gaze. Even Marcus's eyes held the same steady glare. The first of these men might demand he hand the torque back; the second might simply be pissed if he refused; but the third – the third might just order it done! He didn't want to hear from any of them at the moment so he stood up, looking about for his senior clerk. Where were the sodding drinks?

"Look, let's talk about this tomorrow," he muttered, and slumped back down again. "We all need time to think on this."

He was relieved to find agreement. Maybe it was simply because it was late, and everyone was hungry; but it seemed as if they all thought that tomorrow would be a better day.

⸸

Rhun was roused from his sleep an hour after midnight, and handed a dispatch. He read it by the light of a flickering lantern held above his bed by a nervous duty clerk. Then he read it again to be sure, cursed, and dismissed the man. Four hours later the same clerk came to rouse him again, which proved unnecessary. Sleep had been elusive and Rhun lay fully dressed on his bed, hands behind his head, thinking. The clerk handed him yet another dispatch, which sent his thoughts reeling.

He told the clerk to rouse his other guests and bring them to his room, and when the man asked which other guests, he swore impatiently and told him. As the man stepped through the door, Rhun had second thoughts and called him back. He ordered the clerk to have them gather in the dining room, and see they had something to eat – and drink. It was less than an hour from dawn, and they would all feel better to have something else settling on their bellies than what he had to tell them.

Rhun made a point of not entering the dining room until everyone was there, because he still dithered over what he knew he had to do. When he did arrive he set a leather-wrapped package on the table, then stood back to figure how best to tell them what the dispatches had contained. It was difficult, for no commander likes being forced to change his mind.

"First off," Rhun began, even before he sat down, "I think it's time we got this torque to Bryn."

# Chapter XXXIV

## Trimontium, September, A.D. 105

Lagan's patience with Modan, for a long time dangerously thin, was wearing close to nonexistent. The mere sight of the man's bullish figure filled his belly with bile, and the worst part was in knowing that it was his own fault. Joining up with the erratic, headstrong Brigante – clearly a one-sided alliance – had never sat well on his belly. Yet he'd pushed doubts aside for the sake of convenience, which even at the time he'd known was a mistake. When a man's gut growls a warning it should never be ignored. He'd had good reason to do so at the time, but then, there always seemed to be good reason. There was the influence his brother Bryn possessed, whom the fool had since turned into an enemy, and that of his father Cethen, a name legendary even with Lagan's own people. None of it was now worth even a straw shield alongside Modan's blundering.

But now, were fortunes changing?

Lagan refused to consider such hope as he stood alongside Horus and a few others in front of Trimontium's headquarters building. His eyes gazed spellbound at the towering, crackling column of flame. He should have been elated, but instead seemed able to do nothing but stare – and to brood on what must come next.

The fort had fallen easily enough, and it had happened by stealth, not with a senseless, screeching charge that stumbled through a deep ditch, up the sharp slope of a rampart, and over a mountain-like wall defended by a thousand swords, arrows, and spears. That was Modan's way – his only way. Lagan's was to use the advantage of dawn, and the stealth of a silent army marched in by night – an army that lay waiting until the first grey of morning to execute a simple ploy: two men with a cart, bluffing their way up to the fort's stout defenses, and it made not a dab of difference if they got inside or not. Lagan allowed himself a grim smile as he stared at the flames, despite the weight of worry that now sat deep in his belly.

About a dozen men on horses had been sent after the cart drivers, riding in from the south. That was enough to make the guards wary, Lagan figured, but not unduly alarmed. Those men provided enough time and distraction for the two on the cart to kill their oxen, block the gate, and run as if their lives depended on it – which, Lagan mused, they did.

After that, matters had moved swiftly – and far better than Lagan had dared hope. The dozen riders closed in as the few guards on duty tried vainly to close the gate, held open by the weight of two dead oxen and a cart. The first of a hundred or so foot warriors had started forward by then, springing from concealment in the huge clutter of buildings that sat just a few hundred paces from the main gate. To those first ones fell the glory, for the greater part of Lagan's army, more than three thousand, waited farther out, some as much as a mile away. And while it takes time to run the best part of a mile, it takes far longer to rouse a Roman garrison while the cock is still crowing.

Of course, had the plan failed, he would have resorted to Modan's usual method of attack: a crude, head-on charge with hope, guts, and scaling ladders, and the outcome ever in doubt. Should that have proven necessary, his men would in all probability be still outside the walls, throwing themselves against the tall timbers.

"So we cross the Rubicon," Horus commented, breaking the silence. He flinched as the headquarters' roof collapsed with a rending crash, sending a tower of sparks soaring skyward.

"Huh?" Lagan turned and stared blankly at the Greek. "What are you talking about?"

Horus shook his head. "Let's just say there's no going back. Which means that you can't stay still either, can you? You can only keep going."

"We discussed this."

The Greek smirked and waved a hand toward the blazing buildings. "I know, and you said you first wanted to see how complete the success was at Trimontium. You should have asked me how it would be. I would have told you."

"Yeah, well now it's over and we hold the fort, though obviously not for long as it's burning to the ground." Lagan snorted at Horus's boast, his eyes still fixed on the flames. The man seemed to think that battles were planned and won with as precise a tally as figuring his numbers;

those same numbers being at their most precise, he mused, when the man demanded his silver. And that was another thing. Lagan still hadn't figured out where the Greek was hoarding it.

"I know, and you didn't say what's next." Horus shrugged as if indifferent to the answer, but he pushed for it anyway. "Lagan, we gathered thirty-five hundred men here today. More than triple that number are waiting to see what happens, and now they'll know. But if we want to hold them steady to the cause, we need to give them something to do." The Greek grinned slyly. "Something to attack; something to loot."

Lagan hated being pushed, and Horus was pushing. Not only that, he was quoting numbers again, and he was getting tired of the man's numbers. They never ended: you need fifty of this; it costs five hundred of that; you can't twitch a toe until you have four thousand of these! A chieftain had the need of figures, true, but when the time came to fight, you assessed the enemy's strength with your scouts, and when you saw you had the measure of him once over, you trounced him. Though if it's the Romans, you'd best have the measure of him twice over, and surprise doesn't hurt, either, Lagan admitted. And even when you have all that, the most ignorant hill man learned from Galgar and Boudicca that you never face them in open battle!

Lagan supposed that the Greek deserved some sort of a reply, though, and he was about to give it when Modan's loud voice whooped from the direction of the fort's gates. Lagan groaned, wondering what the fool wanted. The man had gone to oversee the sorting of the Roman prisoners; surely he wasn't finished already? Yet he supposed the lad did have hands-on experience at that sort of thing, for he'd been a prisoner himself. Lagan chuckled aloud at his logic, and tore his eyes from the raging flames.

"Got a count yet?" Horus asked as Modan reined in his horse.

Modan slid from his saddle and grabbed the bridle close by the bit, where it could be held firm. The horse was nervous close to the crackling fire, and shy of the heat. He settled the animal, then glanced at the Greek and tossed out, "Two thousand five hundred and ten, not counting the virgins."

"There can't be. It's way more than –" realizing he was being mocked, Horus tried making the best of it "—than they have in the next four forts combined."

"You should have asked me; I'd have told you." Lagan grinned as he tossed the Greek's words back at him. "I could have at least given an accurate count on the virgins."

"Yeah." Modan laughed more than necessary, and seemed bound to state the obvious. "There ain't no more left."

Lagan was also curious on the number of prisoners but knew there had been no time to tally a count – which made him wonder why Modan had returned. "Problem sorting them out?"

"Naw. Gobha said that about one in five is hurt too bad to bother with. I dunno how many'll be left." Modan did look thoughtful, however, as if something else was bothering him.

"So what is the problem?"

"I was thinking," Modan began.

*Oh shit!* Lagan groaned, and forced a smile. "About what?"

"We took all the weapons and armour from the buildings before we burned 'em, right?"

"I'd like to think so," Lagan said patiently.

"Plus we got what we've been stripping off the Romans that we took prisoner."

"Yeah," Lagan agreed, his mind quickly racing ahead to the point where Modan's slowly wandered. "Yeah – that's right."

"So I was thinking. If we . . ."

And thinking was what Modan was actually doing, for once. Lagan conceded the point as he pieced the idea together himself, leaving Modan to mumble through the rest of it unheard. Maybe this morning's lesson in patience had rubbed some rust off the Brigante's brain which, for the moment, appeared to be shining.

⸎

Attacking a small Roman fort further to the south was his idea but Lagan bulled his way in to take charge and, to Modan's annoyance, started picking at the nits. Not that it came as a surprise, because that was the man's way, but it was no less infuriating. Furthermore, the Selgovae chieftain had laid down stipulations. The honour of leading the bogus band of Romans would not be his unless, as he put it to Modan, "You get rid of that rat-infested beard, cut your hair, and start wearing a helmet so you look like a sodding Roman."

The words cut deep, for that was the last thing that Modan wanted to look like. But he did see the logic, and reluctantly rolled over and bared his throat. Along with a score of others, Modan shaved his beard, leaving only a neat, drooping set of moustaches. He also clipped his hair until it hung no lower than the top of his chain mail – which was an uncomfortable piece of armour. The protection was not worth the trouble of plodding around under its surprisingly heavy weight. Not only that, the piece would rust solid in the first rain, and was probably a pain the arse when it came to oiling and keeping clean.

"You will listen to what Horus says?" Lagan asked when they parted ways from the main body of the army, around mid-afternoon.

Modan had grunted his agreement, noting that Lagan's words may have been phrased as a question, but their tone was an order. That rankled because doing what a pale, flabby, Greek number-scratcher told him to do was humiliating, especially in front of the other men. It was bad enough that Horus sat a horse like a tub of butter and knew nothing about how to fight; he looked as much like a Roman cavalryman as a, a – a tub of butter. When Modan protested as much, which hadn't endeared him to the Greek, Lagan had grown angry and, without paring his words, told him the reason: *"Because he's the only one of the lot of you, Modan, who speaks their fucking language!"*

Which Modan grudgingly admitted also made sense, and was the way it had to be. What had already soured him on the Greek long before they started out, though, had been the man's performance in trying to kill Bryn on the road to Isurium. If he'd been there himself, Modan was sure the outcome would have been different. There would have been no threat to Bryn, and he just might have wound up with the torque; but a violent bout of pit-squats had caught up with him just days before. The illness had left him languishing in Lagan's camp for nigh on two weeks, where he would have willing chosen death by fire, given the choice. The healers were of no help. Vile mixtures of charcoal, dandelion root, and fennel seed had been thrown into his growling belly, washed down with buckets of warm, stinking buttermilk and honey. Just the memory turned his stomach.

The squats finally ended, only to leave his bum hole backed up like a beaver dam. In the meantime Horus, Gobha, and Treno had gone off by themselves to see how it stood with the tribes farther south. They'd stumbled across Bryn when riding into Isurium, and that was when Treno realized that Lagan had it in mind to kill Bryn off. Horus had more than once said to Modan that his brother's death would solve a lot of problems, which was obvious. The man had never suggested doing it though . . .

The Greek was lucky they hadn't caught Bryn, and done as he said. He, Modan, would have killed him for doing that. He figured that a man couldn't stand by and see his brother slain, despite the vicious rumours that he'd been trying to do exactly that in Cumbria – which was pig shit. The fool leading Frevan's men had fought back when he'd rode down on them. All he'd ever wanted was to grab the lousy torque, which was only fair. And Bryn was riding two horses on that one, Modan was certain of it. His brother didn't know whether he wanted to wear the neck ring, or not. Taking it would have just helped him make up his mind.

On the sharper edge of that blade, though, if Bryn had got killed, say by an accident, it would have solved more than just the problem of taking over from Frevan.

Modan shook his head free of that notion. Other concerns were also feeding on his bile, one of which had become a matter of pride. He'd thought a lot on it when he'd been laid up for two weeks with a gammy belly. He was growing certain that it was more than just rumour that Bryn was humping Trista. And that, in turn, led to *the* other thing. He was beginning to think that Trista maybe knew exactly what the dwarf had done to him, because it only made sense. Which led to the next step up the ladder: had the two lit that fire together? Just the thought of that happening led to yet another one: did Bryn know what the dwarf had done to him? Were they all laughing at him, even as he suffered on death's door with a rotting belly and a sore arse?

Modan had also brooded long and hard during the weeks that followed Gobha and the Greek's failure at Isurium. The pair had three times as many men as Bryn, yet lost five times more than his brother in chasing him all the way to Eboracum's gates – where they could do fart-all anyway! All because a Roman patrol had ridden out of nowhere, using their spears like they were herding pigs. If only he'd been there it would have been different – the way things had been today.

Trimontium had been a chance to show Lagan that the attack on the supply column had not been idle luck, and the failure to destroy the Roman army at Blatobulgium had been nothing more than bad luck. So why stop there? Just down the road stood another Roman fort that was, granted, smaller than the one Lagan had just destroyed. It was hardly more than an outpost, its purpose to guard a river crossing. It probably had less than two hundred men inside, which was why it was so close to Trimontium. All of which served only to boost Modan's confidence as he charged headlong toward the fort's gates at the head of his small band of spurious Roman cavalry. Trailing behind by a good half-mile and stretched out like a stag hunt, five hundred of Lagan's riders followed, giving Modan good reason to plead for shelter.

⸸

The garrison's soldiers crowded the defenses, peering warily from the gates' crosswalk and the long palisades flanking either side. A low haze of smoke hung over the distant northern skyline, shrouding the slopes of the three great hills that overlooked what remained of the fort at Trimontium. The garrison here was clearly concerned as Modan pulled up sharp in front of the gates. Horus was alongside struggling to master his horse, and soon all of them were there: twenty men in Roman uniforms, each with a tight rein on his mount as the Greek demanded entry.

One soldier on the walls seemed to be in charge and only he spoke, which was the Roman way of it. Modan often wished it was theirs, too: no bickering, no bitching, and what was said was the way it was. The Roman asked the expected question, gesturing anxiously toward the smoke as if for emphasis. "What's happening?"

"They've burned the fort down," Horus shouted, waving a hand in the same direction. His voice held the edge of panic that Lagan had suggested, and Modan figured it wasn't feigned. Yet the Greek was not dense. He'd known enough to take a uniform from one of the Roman officers, even though he wore it like a sack; and the Roman on the gate, in picking him out, seemed to have taken him for what he was supposed to be. Though other than his first question, the Roman said no more.

"There's nothing left. Come on, open up," Horus cried impatiently, and glanced toward Lagan's thundering horde of cavalry, his face as anxious as that of the Roman. "Let us in, or the bastards will be here."

"What's the name of your regiment?"

"Huh?" Horus was at first nonplussed, then he shouted the answer, plainly losing his composure. "The Second *Vocontian*. Now come on, they're almost here. Who do you think you are, *Cerberus*?"

Modan looked anxiously to the north. Lagan's men were getting uncomfortably close. Worse still, unless his eyes deceived him, the Selgovae were holding back, which was not going to deceive those inside the fort. He cursed, wondering what the Greek was on about, and under his breath urged him to hurry. Horus muttered a curse back, but the Roman's answer drowned his voice.

"Cerberus? Naw. I'm the *one*-headed son of a bitch who guards *this* gate." The slow fool seemed unperturbed. "Who's your praefectus?"

A bloodstained figure heaved itself up beside the Roman, supported on either side by one of the garrison's soldiers. It peered down on Horus, and spat. "Never mind the praefectus. Who the fuck are you?"

Modan had lied often enough to know when it was useless. He wheeled his horse, shouting that everyone do the same, and lashed at the animal's rump. The beast leapt forward, racing back toward Lagan's small army. A haphazard shower of spears and arrows rained down from the fort's defenses, but the Romans seemed as ill prepared for the sudden flight as those who fled. When Modan thought it safe enough to look back, he saw that only two had fallen, and a third was hunched over his saddle with an arrow high in his back. Then he saw that one of the fallen was Horus, and Modan groaned. This was going to make Lagan's brain boil.

※

"It just means an extra day or two," Lagan muttered as he stared down from a low hill that overlooked the small outpost from the west. The odds on an easy victory had seemed even enough, and he wondered if Modan was simply cursed. He also wondered if this place was worth the taking. Then he recalled Horus's words: *"Give them something to attack; something to loot. Keep them occupied!"*

Lagan sighed and glanced northward. The sacking and burning of Trimontium was not over; even this far away, the air was heavy with the stink of smoke. The smell of it still clung to the men who had ridden here with him, men who smoldered with resentment for missing the looting of the burning fort. They set up camp in a wide circle, safely beyond range of the smaller fort's archers. The spoils to be had here were not great and neither was the glory, for this stronghold was nowhere near the size of Trimontium. But there were less of them to share what was taken, a fact Lagan quickly pointed out; for as Horus had said, the poor sod, this was no time to rest. A blaze once set to burning needed fuel.

"It was bad luck," Modan complained. "Someone from Trimontium got here first, and warned them. Then the man saw Horus, and didn't know him. There was –"

"I know, I know." Lagan said curtly. What happened had happened, and only the gods knew why. Casualties were to be expected, he supposed, and he was more resigned than pissed. In a way it was probably his fault.

But Horus!

He should have known better than to send the Greek off with Modan on a bone-brained attack, just because he spoke the Roman tongue. The man would be sorely missed, and not just because of his way with numbers! They were useful, certainly, but once they reached a certain level they became something a man could no longer see inside his head. It was the writing Horus did that was important, and the way he could look at it and see who'd said what, and how much, and when. It was useful. As was what Horus knew about how the Romans did things, and his thoughts on what they might do next. The man would be nigh-on impossible to replace.

And what *had* the Greek done with his silver? Lagan supposed he could now search it out without disaffecting the man.

"We took hundreds and hundreds of their soldiers at Trimontium," Modan continued, as if hoping to find glory at the bottom of a bog. "There's gotta be one of 'em that can do what the Greek did. Maybe even more. Find one, and give him a choice."

"A choice?" Lagan asked absently, surprised he hadn't thought of the possibility. One of their centurios might be willing – an older man who valued his remaining life. The Roman auxiliaries were, as Horus had once said, nothing more than trained tribesmen; they just happened to come from across the seas. He'd wager that more than one had been recruited by force. Such a choice might prove even better than Horus; such a man would know the ways of their army. Perhaps Modan really was starting to use his head. *And he's done it twice in one day!* Lagan chuckled to himself. *That's double the number of times the man has used his brain since knowing him.*

"Yeah. Find a Roman who can do what Horus did and give 'im a choice." Modan leered as he explained and ran a finger across his throat. "Maybe I should get back to Trimontium, and start looking for one with brains."

Lagan bit his tongue. Modan seeking someone with brains was like sending a blind man to find a red cow. He sighed and looked away, his attention caught by the thud of hooves. A rider was racing up the rise, coming from Trimontium. As the man drew near, Lagan saw by the neck scarf he wore that it was one of the group of horsemen Horus had assembled to deliver messages. *Something else learned from the Greek.*

The rider was forcing his horse, which likely meant trouble. "Lagan, Lagan," the man called as soon as he was in hearing distance.

Lagan recognized Gavor and he shook his head in distaste, a feeling that he knew was beyond reason. The man had done valuable service, but it had been carried out by betraying his own kind, including his father. It was hard to warm to the youth. And here he was again, bearing news. *It must be trouble,* Lagan decided, scanning the horizon for sign of it. But as Gavor halted alongside, he looked anything but worried – which he should have been, for his horse was lathered and labouring for breath.

"You trying to kill the animal?" Lagan demanded, raising an elbow to shield himself as the horse shook itself, shedding globs of foamy sweat.

"No," Gavor said, confused by the outburst.

"You need a good reason for flaying a horse like that, boy," Lagan growled. "What is it?"

"I got a good reason," the youth confirmed eagerly. "There's been another attack. On the Roman fort at *Lignum*. It was burned to the ground. Everyone inside was slaughtered."

"Then that's a heart bleeding shame," Lagan growled, his gut heaving – not at the Roman loss, but the attack itself. Who had ordered it? Was it some traitorous weasel honing a blade for his back? Likely not, but if you left some of these people alone for only half a day they started thinking – and plotting. Either way, sloping off to attack anyone without orders was the stupid sort of action that scattered the herd. For an army to remain together, it must have only one leader.

Lagan sighed. He couldn't lecture the youth on leadership, it would boggle his brain. "Killing everyone means valuable slaves are lost for no reason, lad; or maybe people we might have used ourselves. There might even have been a ransom in the offing. Now it's gone, just like that!" He snapped his fingers in disdain. "Who started it?"

"That's just it, nobody did," Gavor said eagerly. "A huge band of Caledonii rode down looking to join with us. Even that far north, the word is out that you're going to fight."

"The Caledonii?" Lagan interrupted, for the moment unsure if that was good or bad.

"Yeah. They met up with some of our men who were out foraging, and they told them about the attack on Trimontium. I guess they were close by Lignum, so they got together and figured on showing everybody they could do as good as us." Gavor shook his head as if clucking at the shame of it. "The hill-climbers lost a lot of people doing it."

*And so they deserved,* Lagan thought, but his mind was also figuring on what this news brought to the battlefield. If the Caledonii were sending people south and saw success, would they start coming down in force? If so, that could mean numbers by the thousands, many thousands. And where would that leave him? Suckling on a dry tit until it was over, that's where. And after that, then what? A common enemy was the only reason that both tribes might walk the same path. In the past, the Caledonii had more often than not *been* the enemy.

Modan, fool that he was, was not at all worried. "This is just the start," he gloated, the stalled attack on the small fort seemingly forgotten. "If they join with us, it will be the end of the Romans. Figure it, Lagan: in one day, we've burned two of their lousy strongholds. Two of them – totally destroyed!" He blinked, as if trying to figure the numbers. "Lagan, even if we only did one a week, by Samhain we'd have them pushed all the way back to . . ."

Lagan sighed, his mind blocking out Modan's dreams of glory. He was more concerned with the present. The way he'd had it worked out to beat the Romans – the burnings, the surprise attacks, the decision never to do open battle – could all be changing, just as it was beginning. The Caledonii! Under Galgar, they'd fought the biggest battle that a man might ever hear of, and they'd lost. What did that mean for him, Lagan, who at best had hoped to raise a much smaller army?

". . . not much of a ride, at a good stiff trot. Get there easy, by evening. The sun'll be well above the hills; and those same hills will hide our coming until we're almost there. We try the same thing, only this time, whoomph!" Modan cried, smashing a fist into the palm of his hand. "This time we'll get to them. And if not," he shrugged as if it didn't matter, "we stop them from going any further." He gestured casually toward the besieged fort. "Just like what we're doing now."

"What are you talking about?" Lagan demanded, scowling.

"Think about it, Lagan. That would be three in one day; four, when this one falls!" Modan said gleefully. "The next Roman fort to the south is about ten Roman miles farther on, in the hills. It's not much different than this one. If we –"

"We haven't taken this one yet, you – you . . ." Lagan managed to curb his tongue, and continued on with exaggerated patience. "We need the men here, Modan. When you're on the outside, it takes three, four men for every one of theirs, in order to get inside. We have only –"

"We've got that many," Modan said blithely, and gestured not only to the fort, but to the north where the beginning of a long, wide column of men filled the road, trudging slowly south.

Lagan turned, startled. Hardly a moment ago, there had been nothing there. He briefly wondered who they were, then realized the newcomers could only be his own. They couldn't possibly be the Caledonii, not yet, though that had been his first concern. It would be Treno or Gobha, or more likely both, and each impatient. Treno was supposed to follow as soon as his people could be dragged from the looting; Gobha had been told to do the same. He turned back to Modan who waited eagerly, his mouth half open like a hound primed for the hunt. If the man had a tail, it would have been wagging.

Lagan pursed his lips. Modan had no real plan of attack, other than to repeat today's recent failure. The fort had not been properly scouted, but its size was known. There would be little light left when they arrived, but that could work both ways. And the Roman stronghold, like every other one they'd foolishly built all over the north, was far from full strength. When all was considered, such an assault might have a chance. And even if it didn't, he supposed that Modan's failure just might solve a problem that was of late growing more and more irritating . . .

"I suppose we have," Lagan murmured, not looking at Modan but instead gazing at the slow-moving army trudging toward him. "I'd say about a hundred chasing you hard, only this time not so far behind. Make it look as if you're desperate," he said softly. *Which you well may be!* "And at least five hundred following, strung out along the road. If you do get past the gate you'll need them there fast, to help secure it."

Modan shouted his delight and would have been instantly gone, but Lagan stayed him. "For the love of Lug, wait until the other column gets here to relieve you."

"I'd like to go too." Gavor's features were full of the same puppy-like eagerness. It was as if the lad felt the need to atone for something. Or, Lagan mused, was it just his own irrational bias?

"No way," he snarled. There was no sense getting one of Horus's new messengers killed off; that was dangerous enough employment as it was. He fumbled for an excuse, and his eyes fell on Gavor's panting horse. "Your animal's blown so bad it couldn't fart. Let that be a lesson to you."

※

The fort sat high in the hills on the Roman road leading from Eboracum. Its wooden defenses offered a commanding view of a long, stark valley that fell away to the east – one of two reasons for its being. The fort at Bremenium lay ten miles farther south, which was thirty miles from Trimontium – a distance greater than a normal day's march. The terrain between was hostile, a condition made all the greater by the wild, mountainous terrain. The small fort served to break such a march, while guarding one of the many fords that interrupted the long road north.

Modan lashed his horse to a gallop the moment he caught sight of the fort's gate towers. He was soon a good two lengths ahead of the others, thundering down the road, bent on gaining the gates before they closed. It would all prove useless, should some fool order them shut – but they wore Roman uniforms, rode Roman horses, carried Roman shields, and Roman weapons. Why should they?

Modan glanced behind, satisfied with the distance. Four, maybe five hundred paces split them from the hundred screaming, shouting riders who chased behind, and the five hundred more that trailed those. He turned his eyes back to the fort, relieved to see both gates were still open.

They were well guarded, as expected, and the inside of the fort was already astir. Tiny figures clambered onto the palisades, and more rushed to reinforce the gates.

Modan cursed. The gates were closing! Once again someone had given warning, laying waste their best-laid plans.

But only one gate had been slammed shut. The second remained halfway open, leaving a gap through which they could ride! Modan smiled, and his heart leapt. The fools were leaving just enough room – they'd swallowed the bait! He pulled back on the bit until he was once more part of the pack. As the distance closed, he turned and screamed at any man within hearing, "Remember! Don't ride inside. You'll be killed. Stay by the gates!"

The one gate opened wider to admit them as the distance closed. The thunder of hooves filled Modan's ears, numbing them to anything but his thoughts and doubts. Some of the Romans were outside the gate – not watching him, but rather the great, charging mass of Lagan's warriors that chased behind. Several were waving, hurrying them on. *Eagerly* hurrying them on! Modan's mind turned back to the attack on the Roman supply column. It, too, had seemed all too easy: was a trap waiting? A hundred men could be hiding just within the gates.

Modan swore and kicked at the horse's belly. When it seemed that there was no other choice than to ride through the gate he pulled savagely on the reins. The horse squealed in pain as its head turned to one side and it staggered, its shoulder thumping hard against the gate that had remained closed. The beast faltered, gamely fighting for its footing. A Roman guard, anxiously waving Modan inside, stumbled backward to avoid the flailing hooves. Modan lowered his spear and took him in the belly.

He wheeled the horse on its own length, ready to charge back, but the gateway was already a jumble of screaming men and horses. Despite being told not to, some of his people had ridden inside.

"Kill some horses, quick. Block the gate!" Modan screamed as he slid from the saddle. Grabbing his own mount close by the bit, he pulled the animal toward the gap. The Roman guards were frantically trying to close it, but for the moment they were outnumbered, falling back under the weight of a score of whirling riders – most of them still sitting in their stupid saddles. Not one of the selfish bastards wanted to kill his horse! Modan threw his spear at one of the Romans pulling on the gate and caught him low above the groin. The man screamed and staggered backward, pulling at the bloody shaft.

Modan plucked his sword from the saddle and pushed on, forcing his horse forward until it was alongside the open gate. Then he turned, his grip still tight on bridle, and plunged the blade into the animal's chest just forward of the cinch. The beast squealed and reared but Modan held on, cursing as it tried to break free. A spear, flung from one of the gate towers, grazed his arm before thudding unnoticed into the dirt. The horse finally buckled and tumbled sideways. Screeching in triumph, Modan released the bit and turned, ready to fight.

Two more animals had been slain, one beyond the arc of the gate, its death useless. Two were not enough. Another horse nudged him from behind, almost pushing him off his feet. Modan whirled, his mind raging, and grabbed the reins from its rider's hands. He thrust his sword under the animal's jaw, up into its brain. The beast hardly seemed to feel the blow; it simply collapsed as Modan fought to hold it in place.

Three!

"Block the gate, block the gate," Modan screamed, turning to see who was next.

Another rider slid from the saddle, but he tumbled to the ground, an arrow wedged in his chest. Modan lunged at the horse anyway but his blade bit into its haunch and the animal bolted into the fort, screaming in pain. Modan's eyes followed its path, and he cursed. The inside of the fort teemed with soldiers, seemingly hundreds of them, all running for the gates. Someone else had the sense to drop another animal, though, and now four blocked the narrow opening. But Roman soldiers were filling the gap, hacking, slashing, stabbing, and pulling at the carcasses.

The man beside him took a spear in the throat and a javelin tore at Modan's tunic, grazing the side of his belly. A sword crashed against his shield and he tried to swing back, but he was pushed aside as a fifth animal fell, its hooves twitching madly. And now his own men – damn their cowardice – his own men were running!

Modan glanced over his shoulder and shuddered. The first of Lagan's people were nearly upon them: a hundred or more, galloping full tilt, and close enough to spit. No wonder everyone was running! He paused, unsure where to turn. The Romans who faced him were just as uncertain, no longer concerned by the few left fighting at the gate. Modan wedged the hilt of his sword into the palm of the hand that gripped his shield, and pulled a spear from a twitching corpse. He stumbled to the open gate and stood with his back against the wood planking, vainly trying to make himself as thin as the gate itself.

The first of Lagan's men raced past, smashing through the Romans pulling at the fallen horses, and crashing into the wall of shields forming on the other side. Modan shrank back and watched, fascinated by the carnage, and unable to move. Horses went down, both riders and beasts screaming as others plunged onward to join the milling, pushing, swirling butchery of flailing hooves and waving spears. And – shit! Modan blinked, unable to believe his eyes. Brug, one of his own people, took a spear from one of Lagan's crazed riders, even as the poor bugger urged the man on . . .

*The uniforms!*

Jabbing, thrusting, throwing their spears, the Romans stumbled back under the sheer weight of the onslaught, even as Lagan's horses and riders crashed and fell in front of their line. Someone forced open the second gate and the crush suddenly eased on the outside of the fort as more riders fought their way through. Modan saw it all and cared little as he slumped low against the gate, his shield across his belly, feigning death. The right side of the Roman line thinned as it tried to fill the gap left by the second gate, and for a moment there was a dearth of riders. Then the first of Lagan's larger force arrived, thundering through the gates and scattering the Romans like sheep.

None of Lagan's people heeded Modan as he eased his body slowly along the bottom of the huge gate until he gained the shelter of the fort. It was like finding safe haven in a raging storm. With heart pounding and body trembling, Modan lay on his back, his face split into an enormous grin. For the first time since charging the fort, he breathed easier.

A single street led inward from the gate, and the fighting had moved well back along its length. The Romans were still retreating and Modan realized the battle was as good as over. Above him the walls had been abandoned, the Romans who had manned them fleeing along the walkway, likely in an effort to reinforce those who still fought elsewhere – which was useless. They were outnumbered, and no longer behind their wall of shields. Lagan's men had triumphed and were everywhere.

Modan snapped from his torpor and remembered Brug; here he was, crouched in a Roman fort, wearing chain mail and a Roman helmet. He might as will taunt the gods! At any time another of Lagan's rabid warriors might try to kill him, and he wondered if the others had the sense to realize the concern. Muttering aloud that it wasn't his problem anyway, Modan quickly cast the helmet aside, then loosened the leather ties of the heavy mail tunic and wriggled free. He stared at the carnage that filled the open gate, hoping to catch sight of a rideable horse. There wasn't an animal to be seen that wasn't dead, or too badly hurt to use.

Modan turned, hoping to find a stray horse somewhere along the narrow roadway that followed the inside of the walls. Just moments before, it had been full of fleeing Romans. Now, other than a few bodies, it appeared deserted. Then a quick shadow of movement caught his eye, off to the left where a row of wooden buildings sat in the shadow of the fort's wall. A figure had slipped into one of the doorways, and Modan was near certain it wasn't a soldier. He glanced at the open gates, where a steady flood of cavalry continued to pour through. They could do quite nicely without him.

The door opened on a soldiers' room, for there were eight bunks and it stank of raw leather and oiled metal. He thought perhaps he'd picked the wrong door, for the room appeared empty. Then, below one of the lower bunks, he saw a twitch of movement. Grinning, Modan stepped forward and pulled hard at a wooden kit box, sending it slithering across the floor. A slim ankle appeared and he grabbed at it, dragging its owner, a plump, squirming, dark haired woman, into the middle of the room. Twisting and turning on the hard planking, she screeched her rage as Modan fought to catch hold of her other leg, which kicked and flailed at the air. A foot slammed hard into his belly, a blow barely felt as he finally grabbed the ankle and held on tight. The woman bucked and thumped against the floor as Modan, swearing, struggled to force her legs apart.

It had been a while – a long while, it seemed – and the bitch's furious terror only added to his hunger. First there'd been the fever, then a week of loose bowels and growling belly pains. That had been followed by day after day of Lagan's obsessive planning, all of it needlessly pounded into an aching brain. It seemed like ages since he'd had time to think of his own needs.

The woman's dress – he barely glanced at her hate-twisted face – had risen with her writhing, and become twisted high above her belly. Modan saw she had some sort of garment underneath and he lunged forward, ripping it away with a single swipe of his hand. The one leg, suddenly free, caught him square on the face. He screeched a curse and lashed out with a foot, kicking high on the woman's thigh. He again grabbed the ankle as she screamed in pain then, licking his lips, he stared down at her nakedness, his groin aching.

She screamed and Modan finally looked at her face. She was older, probably some officer's whore, and not that bad to look at, except for the venom in those twisted features. But the hate only added to his purpose. Wedging one of her legs under his arm, he freed the belt that held his britches. The loose woven fabric fell away and Modan lunged forward, only to realize that something was dreadfully wrong. He looked down, stunned. Despite the yearning ache, what remained of his manhood was near flaccid, drooping toward the floor in a withered, listless arc.

Swearing his frustration, Modan flicked the limp member up and down in a vain attempt to bring life to the dead. Nothing happened. He pulled on it, jerking the loose skin back and forth while staring avidly at the woman's groin for inspiration, but the organ remained as dead as a frozen grave. Drool dripping from his open mouth, Modan stared angrily at the woman's sex until his eyes burned; yet while his mind stirred eagerly at the vision, nothing else moved.

He cursed and stared down at the useless glob of dangling flesh. It had been weeks since he'd felt like using the thing for anything but pissing, and more than once he'd been worried; but with everything else happening, he'd shrugged it off. Now, though . . . what was happening? Modan returned his glare to the dark patch between the woman's legs and tried to focus. But the more his spinning brain demanded his stupid prick do something, the more it refused.

The woman had ceased her struggles and fallen still. Modan's eyes moved slowly upward and met hers. She was not staring at him, but at his groin. He watched as the hate slowly dissolved into a twisted smile. Then she was laughing – she was laughing at him!

Modan snarled and lurched forward, flailing and kicking with his booted feet – only his britches had drooped to his ankles, and he fell on top of the woman. Once more she became a snarling vixen, biting at his face and pounding him with her fists.

A knee caught Modan hard in the groin and he yelled in pain; his world turned crimson, and an enormous rage swept through his mind. Raising himself on one hand and screaming in fury, he pummelled the woman's head and shoulders with the other. Then, as if by magic, his groin stirred and the cursed sliver of withered flesh that hung there grew rigid.

If nothing else, Modan's brutal spark of passion kept the woman alive.

# Chapter XXXV

# Eboracum, September, A.D. 105

The galley slid alongside the crowded dock, an event that only yesterday would have attracted attention. Today it barely received a glance. The sleek vessel bumped against the heavy timbers with a soft thud, the captain's voice lost in the shouts of a hundred others that drifted from the riverbank. The area between the Abus and the fortress gates was packed with soldiers, and all that came with them: light horse-driven wagons, mules on tether lines, and the great clutter of gear and supplies necessary to an army on the march. But no oxen – which told Elena that the army intended to move fast, its march forced.

The training field to the east of the stronghold was also packed: rank upon rank formed up by cohort, each one undergoing final field inspection. Farther behind, the open pasture teemed with men and horses: the attached cavalry units, undergoing the same rigorous scrutiny. It was all so familiar, and Elena was alarmed. She had not seen a legion prepare itself on such a scale since the Ninth had marched against Galgar. And judging from what was taking place, not only was the Ninth readying itself to march, it would be doing so the next morning. *What is going on?*

The rumbling shudder of the gangplank drew her from her thoughts. It was time to leave, but to go where? She searched in vain for Tuis amongst a group of officers gathered near the gate, but he wasn't there; she supposed that if he was anywhere, it would be inside the fortress. Rhun would certainly not be here; he was posted farther north. Marcus might still be around with his daughter, but just as likely not. Though there was always Cian. He would be here, for his farm was just downriver. The ship had, in fact, passed it on the way to the fortress, and someone had been up by the house, but it was a woman, not Cian. Tuis hadn't mentioned it in his letters, but there was a possibility that Cian might no longer be alive. Such an omission would not surprise her at all.

The huge gate with its stone towers was the greatest change to the fortress. Elena saw as much as she passed under one of the great arches, which made the surprise on entering the fort that much greater. The long street was still lined with timber buildings, which seemed crude and dated by comparison. The new headquarters building stood at the very end of it, though, the fresh sandstone brickwork gleaming in the sunlight. Elena started toward it, Shayla on one side and Metellus, his breathing heavy, on the other.

"It's pretty raw," Shayla commented, her eyes taking in the planked barracks and the wooden walkways.

"I'm sure they're doing their best." Elena smiled to herself, amused at the Carveti woman's criticism after her years of living in Rome; she wondered if the poor lass found any irony in her words. "Make allowances, Shayla. It is the frontier."

The commander's residence had also been rebuilt in stone, Elena saw as they came to the end of the street. She was grateful for that, for the building would almost certainly be home until she met up with Tuis. And if her youngest son did not happen to be at the fortress, then the legate would doubtless see to her needs in the meantime. He was an Appius, she recalled, an old family name, which could mean either a courteous welcome or contemptuous tolerance. She couldn't remember his *praenomina*. Not that it mattered, Elena mused. If the man proved to be a real bastard, she could be a real bitch.

The courtyard in front of the headquarters building was an anthill. Soldiers stood lined up in front of field tables staffed by dozens of clerks, each solving problems that ranged from kit shortages to last minute wills. Oh yes, it was familiar, so very familiar. But unlike the last time she'd seen this sort of thing, Elena strode confidently through it all and into the building. She had no doubt that the legate would find her presence as welcome as a swarm of wasps at the garrison baths.

"Ma'am, can I help?" A swarthy, one-armed soldier limped over to intercept her before she'd taken two paces into the building. Despite the "ma'am," the man's eyes fell on Metellus as he asked the question, and Elena held her tongue. *Typical army! Speak to the only male, even if the poor old fellow can barely stand!*

"I wish to speak to the legate," she said with assurance, aware that her accent was not truly Roman even after all these years. She wondered if the clerk knew the difference. Apparently he did.

"He's not available," the man replied. "I'll see if I can find one of the centurios."

"Is the legate at his residence?" she asked, and saw the man's eyes slide to the back of the building.

"Er, he's . . ."

"Inform him that the governor's mother has arrived." Elena kept a straight face as she saw the clerk's eyebrows shoot up. He licked his lips, bobbed his head, and promptly turned on his heel. A moment later he vanished into one of the rooms that lined the rear of the building.

She could imagine what was being said inside, though whatever it was did not take long to resolve. An average-looking man in his early thirties appeared in the doorway. He was clad in full uniform: the molded breastplate strapped firmly in place and his purple ribbon of rank tied across the front. He was tired and harried and Elena could have almost felt sorry for him. Any sympathy ceased when he paused as he saw her and muttered a single, four-letter oath under his breath. Elena caught the word, but held her ground as he strode across the room. His face was grim and his hobnailed boots clattered unnecessarily loud on the stone floor. It was going to be contemptuous tolerance, she decided.

"Er, ah . . ." the man began, as if struggling to remember her name. There was no reason for him to know it, Elena told herself, and offered a dazzling smile. "Elena," she said cheerfully, and the legate's name came to her with the sight of his face; it was well enough known in Rome. "And fuck you too, Marius."

Someone sniggered and she saw he was sheepish enough to blush, "I, er . . ."

Elena had learned a long time ago that in any battle, even if only of wills, one must never cede the advantage. "I take it that Tuis isn't here."

"He was at Deva, but they marched north a day or two ago. To –"

"To Luguvalium, no doubt," Elena said brusquely. "I'll accompany you north – I presume you're going north – and then perhaps go on from there. That will gain me two heads with one swing of the blade. My other son is praefectus Luguvalium."

"Yes, I suppose, but we are –"

"I know, I know," she interrupted. "You're marching at dawn. Anyone can see that. My timing is perfect. We'll be up and about in lots of time. I imagine there's space in the residence for tonight."

"Er, Livia is in residence . . ."

The man's cheeks flushed again and Elena briefly wondered what that meant, but she pressed on before he could gain his tongue. "I should think you'll be meeting up with Tuis's force in the near future. At *Coria*, perhaps, or is it at Luguvalium? Both Metellus and I have ridden more than once with an army going to war." She patted the old slave on his shoulder. "We were with Agricola all the way to the Graupius." Elena offered the legate another wide smile, and decided to let the man speak.

But Marius, for the first time, seemed to find interest in her words.

"*You* were there?"

"There?" Elena hid her amusement at the legate's interest. To a soldier, the mention of Graupius was like dangling a worm in front of a perch. "Certainly I was there. I took part in one of the lesser cavalry charges made by the Fourth Gallorum – ended up taking a spear, for my troubles."

"A spear?"

Marius, Elena could see, had doubts on the claim, and she was unable to resist. She casually pulled on the shoulder of her dress, a tightly knit garment of fine wool, and it slid partway down her arm. Below her collarbone and just above the swell of her right breast – which, as far as Elena was concerned, still stood proudly firm – lay a twisted scar: a pale whorl amid a web of stitch marks that stood vivid against her sun-darkened skin. "The Ninth's medicus did good work, considering how bad it was. The tip came out the other side."

"It did?"

*Yes, it did, and it near killed me!* Elena buried the thought, and instead grew dismissive. "It struck nothing vital, or I wouldn't be here." She smiled again, still bent on giving the man no time to speak. "So we'll ride with you until meeting up with my youngest son, and see what he has in mind."

"Look, I –"

"This time, I promise to remain with the headquarters unit." Elena was willing to concede a point or two, even if it did sound condescending. "If we meet the enemy, the cavalry will just have to charge by itself."

"Oh, we will meet the enemy," Marius said firmly, "one way or another."

"At Coria?" Elena was unable to hide her surprise.

"No, not at Coria. Probably at *Habitancum*. Every fort north of there may have been destroyed."

Elena felt Metellus's hand on her arm. "Trimontium, too?" The last time she had passed through the fort it had been a massive camp, so large that two more temporary camps had been dug close by to contain Agricola's huge army.

Marius shook his head, and his face turned grave. "Trimontium has been confirmed as destroyed, along with the settlement surrounding it."

Elena stood stunned, lost for words. She had almost asked Marius if Trimontium was where he planned on meeting up with Tuis, rather than at Coria. Granted, the fort was located farther north, but it would have made sense; as far as she knew, it was by far the larger garrison. And now it didn't exist! Even Galgar, with all the might of his army, had been unable to accomplish as much. What were her two boys doing?

※

Marius was nervous. To date, his military career had spanned four years. Three of those had been serving as the Seventh Gemina's *senatorial* tribune in Hispania, where the only violence inflicted had been on wolves, deer, and errant soldiers. Marius's tour with the Ninth in Britannia, which he knew could be fraught with danger, had been no different until Sabinius had arrived. And even then, other than the wild attack on the governor's army as it neared Blatobulgium, that campaign had been little more than a hunt through the hills of barbaria. But this, this would be different. Marius could feel it with every step he took; it was in the air, as thick as a winter's fog.

As the Ninth pushed quickly northward, the advice of his uncle came to mind, a man who'd served a term as legate in Judaea two decades past. Delivered the day Marius departed, he'd barely heard the advice. But now, as his horse kept pace with the marching column, the words were vivid in his mind: *Rome placed you in command, Marius, but your primus pilus is the one who rules; compared to him, you know nothing. Listen to the arsehole.*

Julius Fermus was squat, bull-necked, and swarthy. His porcine features harboured not the slightest hint of intelligence, nor did they inspire confidence. The sole glimmer of assurance lay in the man's eyes, which were admittedly quick and sharp; but they peered from a fleshy, battered face that might have belonged to a field hand. Julius Fermus would inspire confidence in an arena, perhaps, but as a legion primus the man was a pleb.

The men took his orders well enough, though, and so far Marius had found him reasonably competent, but his true value remained to be seen. The attack on the column as it neared Blatobulgium, admittedly, had given Fermus little chance to show talent, although he supposed the man must have done what was needed. Marius couldn't actually recall seeing him during the brief battle; he'd been too busy trying to remain alive.

The march north to Coria was almost ninety miles, and the primus wanted it done in three days. The first leg, ending at a small outpost twelve miles south of *Cataractonium*, was the shortest and the primus claimed the distance would give the men a chance to *"shake the lead from their tired, miserable arses."* The second and third, each approximately thirty miles, would then *"clear out the shit, and get most of them there on time, ready to fight."* Marius had agreed, flinching at the man's words. It wasn't so much that he was above that sort of language; it was the lack of respect shown in its use. Nonetheless, Fermus did as he said he would and most of the tired column marched in to Coria as darkness fell on the third day.

Marius decided to pay his respects to the fort's commander while the Ninth moved into the marching camp, a set of embankments thrown up by Agricola's army more than two decades before. The grass-covered ramparts had been dug across from the fort on the southeast side of the road, close by a barbarian settlement. The sun hung low over the hills in a dying crimson smear as the centurios had their men stake the palisade and clear the long berms of the thistle and shrub that had grown up over the years.

Marius chose to stretch his legs and walk over to the fort rather than ride. The inside was packed with troops and he wondered how many belonged to the garrison, and how many had fled south from Trimontium. Wherever they came from, the place was terribly crowded, and there was little organization. Tents had been pitched between the barracks and along the *intervallum*. Cooking fires burned everywhere, as if placed at random. Marius wondered if anything had been done about setting up proper procedures for a call to arms. He supposed it had, but it would need checking.

The Sabinius woman appeared from nowhere, falling in alongside as he made his way into the headquarters building. He found himself inordinately annoyed, and was tempted to tell her that what happened inside the building was none of her concern. Yet a sense of unease made him hesitate. The woman was likely older than his own mother when she had died. And though she was clearly a barbarian, there was much of his mother to be found there: a forbidding, commanding presence that would tolerate no nonsense. It was foolish, but it made him wary.

The woman remained silent as he strode into the cross hall. The cavernous room was filled with people, all flitting about in the eerie glow of a hundred oil lamps. The fort commander stood at the base of the *tribunal*, deep in discussion with his senior officers. Marius was irritated to find Julius Fermus had in some manner contrived to arrive ahead of him, his squat bulk leaning over a table as he studied a map. A tall man with olive skin and dark hair, perhaps five years older than Marius, turned from the table as he drew near.

"Linus Tadius." The man thrust out his hand, a grim smile on his face. "The man who commands this oasis of chaos."

"Legate Appius," Marius replied, unimpressed by the man's greeting. "What is the latest –"

"And this must be your wife," Linus added, teasing Elena with a wink before nodding a greeting. "I won't ask if you had a decent journey. That would be trite. Is there anything you need?"

"Somewhere soft to sit on, perhaps." Elena smiled, then told the praefectus who she was, and why she was there. Marius silently cursed, as the man's next words proved equally annoying.

"You're the Brigante woman, the governor's mother! I'll warrant you know this country better than any of us." Linus's face lit up, and he suddenly snapped his fingers. "Hey, one of my men was in your son's troop, under Agricola." He raised his voice. "Edred! Come over here."

A grizzled, grey-haired trooper turned from the table and ambled over, his bowed legs stiff, as if walking was a chore. He greeted Elena warmly and began telling her how he and Rhun had found themselves alone after Galgar's people struck the Ninth's camp up by the *Tava*.

Marius fumed in disbelief at the man's casual waste of time; as the senior officer present, he decided enough was enough. "They tell me there's a war going on," he growled. "Are we here to do something about that? Maybe win it, for example."

Both men stepped stiffly back, and Linus drew himself erect. "Of course, sir. That's exactly what we were doing." He motioned to the table, over which heads had been lowered in heated discussion – only the talking had now stopped, and Julius was peering at Marius as if in rebuke. Was the primus being insolent?

"Perhaps we'd best get back to it," Linus continued. Then, surely just to annoy, he turned to Elena and said, "You might care to contribute. You did spend a good deal of time in this country."

Marius held his tongue and followed the pair to the table. He was utterly dismayed to find confirmation that not only Trimontium had been destroyed, but also two lesser forts just to the south of it, and another further north. The next in line, Bremenium, was under siege by a massive army that Linus's scouts reported to be growing even as they stood there. That left the commander at Habitancum, which lay between Bremenium and Coria, nervously awaiting direction. The man had neither the troops to relieve the siege at Bremenium, nor cover an orderly retreat by its garrison.

"It would seem we have two choices," Julius rumbled. "We wait here until the major part of the army arrives from Deva, or we advance on Habitancum, dig in, and see if it's feasible to do more. We need to determine if Bremenium is able to hold out, or whether we must try and relieve them. I'd guess it would be at least a week before we're reinforced."

"The fort has the supplies it needs, but not the men." Linus sounded uncertain. "Of course, some of those fleeing the destruction will have sheltered there, but at most there are probably six, seven hundred inside. They can hold out for awhile, I'm sure, but it depends how many casualties the barbarians are willing to take trying to breach the walls."

"It's a matter of attrition, then," Julius muttered, surprising Marius with the use of the word; then he winced as the primus continued. "The men can hold the pricks off, but if the crazed bastards keep at it, they're fucked."

"It would appear that the ten to fifteen thousand they claimed having was far from an idle boast," Edred explained. "The hill-climbers from the north have started drifting down, drawn by the smell of blood. It could well turn into a flood."

"And it gets worse." Linus stared balefully at Marius, again snapping those annoying fingers. "Earlier today we received dispatches from Luguvalium. One of the forts northwest of there has been razed. The Luguvalium commander has ordered the lesser ones abandoned, and the garrisons withdrawn to Blatobulgium."

"He's ordered *what*? He has no authority –" Marius cried, then swore softly as the woman interrupted.

"Luguvalium?" Elena asked, one hand moving to her throat.

"You know someone there?" The primus's voice was sympathetic.

"One of my sons is the commander," Elena replied, then shook her head and waved for the man to continue. "Sorry; go ahead."

"Abandoning the forts further north may be the only choice we have as well, after we get to Habitancum," Julius said, turning his bullish body from the table to face Marius. "Cover a retreat from Bremenium, and consolidate back here until the governor arrives. Then go after them."

"A retreat?" Marius exclaimed, then bit his tongue. What was the man talking about?

"A withdrawal, then," Julius growled, shrugging his broad shoulders. "Same fucking difference."

"You're assuming we advance to Habitancum." Marius vaguely wondered if the man's reply was insubordinate. He pretended to study the map, which seemed to blur as he stared. There sat Coria, and fifteen miles north, Habitancum; maybe another nine miles, Bremenium. Marius grew aware that a silence had fallen around the table. He looked up and found Julius staring at him, his face impassive.

"Yes, I am assuming we will advance – sir!"

※

The column departed early the next morning under a grey sky, after forming up in the fading darkness. The order of march was dominated by the six legion cohorts Marius had committed to Tuis, including the first cohort. Their ranks were bolstered by more than fifteen hundred auxiliary troops garnered from forts closer to Eboracum, and a hefty contingent drawn from the garrison at Coria. The small army totalled almost five thousand men: trained, disciplined troops that flowed onto the road at a slow jog, a pace that would continue for the first mile. Marius intended to cover the entire fifteen miles before midday – which he insisted was important. When the final orders had been scribed, he had solemnly stated that surprise offered the greatest advantage. Julius had simply growled and offered the opinion that any surprise was impossible – in words that made the legate wince.

※

"I'd say at least four hours," the Roman called Bellus suggested, as the last of the soldiers moved out of the camp at a slow, loping run. "In six at most, they'll be settling in at Habitancum."

"They won't last long doing that pace," Modan observed.

"They'll go a mile like that, then walk another two, rest, and pick up the pace again. Maybe next they'll move at a quick marching step," Bellus told him without bothering to turn his head. The Roman had also told Modan that he was a decurio, spoke three languages, came from somewhere called Upper Germania, and was totally indifferent to the rule of Rome – particularly if he had to die to keep it intact.

"How do you figure that out?" Modan growled, and appeared not to hear Lagan's loud sigh.

"It's what they do when forcing a march," Bellus said patiently. "They trot for so long and –"

"No, fool, I mean how do you figure out four hours?" Modan cut in.

"Ah!" Bellus stared at Modan as if assessing a hound's chances of being trained; he seemed to decide it was possible and pointed skyward, his hand moving from east to west. "At this time of year, it takes about sixteen hours for the sun to travel from one edge of the earth to the other. So," he faced south and pointed directly upward, "when it's halfway across, the sun's travelled about eight hours, right?"

"There is no sun today," Modan muttered.

Bellus ignored him. His arm moved east, and stopped when it bisected the arc. "So after four hours, it'll be about there. See?"

Modan sat gazing blankly at the clouds, and again pointed out that there was no sun. Lagan sighed again, and couldn't keep his gob shut. "Modan, look there where the clouds are lighter, close by the horizon. See? That's where the sun is."

"I know that." Modan grinned. "I was just pissing with the man. But what *do* you do when there's big black clouds up there, and you can't see any light through 'em?"

"Then you guess," Lagan grunted, annoyed, though he had no idea either. "But in the meantime, we wait."

Whatever four hours really was, it never came. Lagan figured about half that time had passed when a small Roman cavalry patrol, probably out overnight, came racing in from the east, hotly pursued by Lagan's riders. He swore bitterly, for it meant things were not going as planned – and Horus's brief legacy had left him unusually unsettled when events did not go as planned.

Modan, however, had no such qualms. He watched as the Roman patrol gained the safety of the gates, and clambered to his feet. There no longer seemed need to lurk behind shrubs and underbrush. He stood in the open, staring across the flat stretch of land that separated them from the fort. A huge grin split his face. "It's time to burn another one."

Lagan nodded agreement, and hid his irritation at Modan's crude bluster. More battles had been lost from overconfidence than lack of courage, and the fool should know better. And with this one, it would be no different. He had the advantage in both numbers and surprise and still he wasn't sure – nor would he be, until it was over and done. And the more so now that a good part of the surprise had suddenly vanished. Though if he hurried things along . . .

The men Lagan had brought with him, a large force of cavalry split from the growing army that besieged Bremenium, were the best he had; and he had split them once again as they rode west in a wide arc that brought them to the hills beyond Coria. There, half a day's ride from the fort, they had once more joined forces – and waited.

Lagan had watched as the Roman relief column marched in from Eboracum, and that night he moved his small army down from the higher country. Under cover of darkness, he quietly settled his people in the shelter of a broad, forested ridge that overlooked the fort a good mile to the northwest.

Lagan watched again the next morning, his face unreadable as the Romans marched out to relieve the beleaguered troops at Bremenium. That was expected. Bellus had said they would march, and Lagan had gambled. Bellus had also told him the Romans would take part of the garrison with them, leaving it weaker, so Lagan had again gambled, and he waited. The odds, he figured, were good; in fact, they were excellent. At worst, he had nothing but cavalry and could flee if the army turned back; at best . . . well, he now had fours hours at least – and with luck he had all day.

\*

Elena was in the commander's residence when the attack began, picking at a bowl of puls dotted with raisins and freshly cubed apple. Eating had suddenly become a chore for the air was heavy and tense; and, as ever when an army was away on the march, it would remain so until its safe return. Linus seemed equally ill at ease, talking nothing but trivia: the state of grain supplies, the temper of the garrison troops, and the status of the current crops. Then he paused, cocked his head to one side, stood and nodded his excuses, then hurried from the room. Elena cupped her ear and heard it too: shouting; the drumming of many feet running in the streets; the distant, muffled roar of many voices. Alarmed, she rose and followed.

Men crowded the streets, some fully armoured, others wearing nothing but tunics and britches; each soldier carried a weapon, and most carried more than one. Nearly all were running toward the west wall and Elena moved quickly that way, hugging the buildings to avoid delaying others. The walkway behind the wooden parapet was crowded. As she drew close, she heard the dull, throbbing roar that drifted from the other side. She'd heard that sound many times before, and more than once she'd stood in the ranks of her own people, adding to it. Now, however . . .

The soldiers on the walkways, by contrast, were surprisingly quiet. No one seemed to be fighting yet, though a squad of archers who were shooting their arrows stopped when a decanus yelled at them – probably for the waste of it. Elena saw Linus's tall figure climbing one of the gate towers two steps at a time, and decided that was the place to be. Nobody seemed interested in stopping her. The dull roar turned deafening as she clambered up from the walkway and peered cautiously over the parapet.

The force that had chosen to attack the fort was not as massive, nor as dangerous in appearance, as Elena had feared. Compared to Galgar's army of thirty thousand, it seemed puny. She edged over to where Linus stood and said as much. He turned sharply and cursed, then caught himself and said, "*What* are you doing here?"

"I came to see if you needed any advice," Elena offered dryly.

"I'm not taking any from someone who thinks these barbarians look puny," Linus said easily enough, though his voice sounded concerned. "I have enough to worry about. Please leave."

"I see they're a mixture," Elena observed, ignoring the order as she stared down at the screaming ranks of tribesmen. Not many were mounted, but farther out, the old marching camp was full of horses – hundreds of them, maybe thousands. "And they're all cavalry, too. I haven't seen that many horses since Graupius. They're not much use here, though."

"Aye, but they'll find them handy if the Ninth's legate gets his arse back here," Linus growled. "Which is good, for then they'll all bugger off. Look, I'd feel a lot –"

"Did you send a –"

"We've tried."

"Some of my people are out there, too: Brigantes and Carvetii," Elena said, turning again to the roaring horde, noting the familiar dress and the distinctively shaped shields. Her people did stand out from some of the others, and she smiled as she realized why. "They're the ones wearing the most clothing. The greatest part are Selgovae, but I see we've got Caledonii too. See the small round shields? And look at the paint. How many would you say there are?"

"Upward of three thousand, and that means seven or eight times our numbers. My men tell me a Selgovae called Lagan is likely the leader, though whether he is or not, who knows?"

The tribesmen were still forming, well beyond the range of any arrows. The braver were darting forward, taunting with their spears and slings, and had likely been the ones drawing fire from the archers. Moblike as Lagan's army appeared, it seemed well prepared, for an enormous number of crude scaling ladders had been carried forward. There were crudely built sleds too, stacked with wood, though not harnessed to horses. Firewood. Men would doubtless serve better to place them at the gates than horses, considering the spears and arrows.

The various tribes seemed to have grouped together, making a colourful patchwork of the milling ranks. One group in particular caught Elena's eye, off by itself on the river side of Lagan's army. They were all nearly naked except for loincloths; a few wore cloaks. Most of them were painted from head to toe in a dark, blackish-blue woad. "Those will be Marius's main problem," she said, nodding toward them.

"They look more wild than dangerous," Linus said. "There are hardly more than a couple hundred."

"I don't mean these here, I mean the others who will follow if these successfully taste blood," Elena replied. "Galgar led thousands and thousands of them. Only the gods know how many warriors the tribes can field. The hills are full of – shit!"

A band of slingers, more than a hundred, ran forward with their weapons held taut. A single voice rang out and they halted as one, the long leather thongs already twirling in overhand circles. A blurred, gnat-like cloud of small black spots appeared, growing oddly large as they filled the air. Elena was vaguely aware that the slingers were reloading, and some had released a second missile even as the air around her whirred to the sound of the first.

A dull, wet splat sounded close by, as if someone had thrown a blob of mud against a wall. Linus, who had been listening with his head half turned, crumpled to his knees, and tumbled sideways. A huge roar echoed from beyond the walls but Elena ignored it, staring down in shock at a jagged dent the size of a small apple in the side of Linus's skull. Blood oozed between the shards of splintered bone and ran down past his ear and over his eyes, which were still open as if they could see. Elena had seen twitching limbs enough times to know the blow was fatal. A lousy missile, from a miserable sling! Not the death of a soldier who, if he must be killed, should die by the sword.

"Here, ma'am." A burly centurio had her by the elbow, leading her toward the steps as the roar outside the walls grew louder. "You'd best leave, they'll be charging the walls. Take shelter in the commander's residence. You'll be safe there."

*Safe,* Elena thought as she allowed herself to be led away, her mind numb with guilt. She could give a pinch of pig shit for her safety! What did it matter? For her mind was consumed by what might have happened if she hadn't insisted on talking to the poor man.

※

"Bellus is clever," Modan said, cheerfully willing to cede the compliment to a man who seemed about to succeed, particularly if the success bolstered his own fortunes.

Treno glanced sideways, his expression sardonic. "Lagan is by far the cleverest. He listened to the man."

The two sat their horses off to the east side of the fort, where the attack was concentrated. Bellus's words played again through Modan's mind as he watched the assault play itself out at one end of the wall. He couldn't remember all of it, but several phrases had taken root: "Concentrate on a single point, and confuse them with a half-dozen others; take your casualties, standing on them if need be; don't worry about wasting your missiles, just keep their heads down; don't hit the middle of the wall, take them close to the corner – where they can only shoot at you from one side; and save your best for last!"

Modan hadn't been sure what Bellus had meant by "best for last": save your best men till the last, or the quickly foraged stacks of firewood for burning through the main gate? It had to be the wood, for Lagan had sent his best warriors in where the attack was supposed to succeed. The others, the lesser skilled warriors – including the Caledonii, Modan was smugly pleased to see – had been sent against the other three walls, distracting the Romans from the all-important northeast corner. As to the wood, he watched as the last of it was stacked against the wooden gate, and set fire. A small army of slingers and a few Caledonii archers provided cover – the painted pricks were good for something – launching a steady hail of stones and arrows at the Romans who stood on the wall; Romans who shot back at the men skidding the sleds, with deadly effect.

"We should have set fire to all four gates," Modan observed, biting on his lower lip. "That would have distracted them four times as bad."

"Then we'd need to have gathered four times the wood," Treno murmured, "and there'd be that much more smoke to be seen. Personally, I don't think it's worth the distraction. We took a lot of casualties to get that much wood placed at one gate."

"Four would be better," Modan said stubbornly.

"No it wouldn't. We need to get inside, not stand outside and wait for a bunch of flaming bonfires to burn down."

Modan fell quiet, figuring it wasn't worth the argument. A loud roar filled the air, a great, joyous kind of roar that meant something was going right. The noise came from the south wall, where the attack was supposed to be nothing but a distraction. The two men urged their horses in that direction so they could see what was happening.

Toward the centre of the wall, men were climbing the scaling ladders as fast they could set a foot on them; and just as fast, they were disappearing over the top. Lagan and Bellus were riding their horses back and forth behind the press, frantically pointing and shouting and urging every man they could see to concentrate on the one point. Others came running, some with more ladders, slamming them against the wall and climbing upward before they'd even come to rest. The air itself seemed to crackle and Modan stirred, growing impatient.

Someone was on a horse, off to his left, waving at him. Beside him, Treno swore.

"What is it?" Modan asked.

"Come on," Treno growled, turning his horse. "I think they've got the other gate open."

Modan rode into the fort, sword swinging, and screaming to any who would follow. The streets were already crowded with Lagan's warriors, and almost empty of Romans. The clash and clamour of fighting echoed from farther inside the fort and he turned his horse toward the noise, forcing the animal through the crush. Lagan's warriors had their blood up, but many were intent on the buildings, plunging inside in search of plunder. Modan swore as his horse skittered and pushed a painted Caledoni to one side, sending him reeling. The man turned angrily, swinging an axe. Modan caught the blow on his blade and lunged forward. The point took the man in the throat, but no one seemed concerned.

He whipped his horse onward until it reached the end of the street, where it crossed another that led to the side gates. There he and Treno paused, both staring in dismay. What remained of the Roman garrison had fallen back and formed a strong defensive front at the western end of the cross street. They stood firm and defiant with their backs to the barred gate, in command of both the street and the wall above them. There had to be a couple of hundred of them, which meant their casualties had not been great – they had simply been overwhelmed, and forced back. Now they just stood there behind their thick, miserable shields, which Lagan's men were beating on and getting nowhere.

"Hold off, hold off."

Modan turned and saw that Lagan had arrived with Bellus riding behind, dogging his heels like a favourite hound. Lagan was plainly annoyed. Modan vaguely wondered why, and offered to help. "I can form them up. One good charge will send the sods scattering."

"We need all the men we can hang onto," Lagan shouted, and ordered Gobha and a few others to halt the fighting. The men trying to force the Roman line were a mob, battering against the Roman shields as if trying to shatter a stone wall. More than a few were bleeding and dying, and as Gobha moved among them screeching Lagan's order, most were willing enough to stop.

"I'm not trading half a dozen for one, just to slaughter this lot in one mad charge," Lagan continued and turned to Treno, barking orders. "Send slingers and archers up on the roofs over there – and anyone who can hurl a decent spear. Look to the other side of that gate, too. We can set this one on fire just as easy."

"Tell any of them that if they want to join us, then now's the time," Bellus suggested.

"You do it," Lagan ordered and reined his horse to one side, shaking his head in disgust as he sat hunched in the saddle, watching.

Bellus nudged his mount forward and began shouting in a dialect that none of them understood. The answer was clear, or perhaps someone recognized him, for angry shouts filled the air and several spears flew from the Roman ranks. But Bellus had measured the distance and turned back, leaving them to fall short.

"Let's hit them, and hit them hard," Modan grumbled, impatience gnawing at his gut.

Lagan ignored him and instead glanced up at the buildings. Modan followed his eyes. Men were climbing onto the roofs and spreading out, but a rustle of movement from the Roman lines made him turn back again. Their officers were barking orders, and the Romans seemed to be backing up and crowding together. The rear ranks raised their shields to cover those in the front rank, who eased back and knelt down with their shields upright. Modan cursed. They were forming their own roofed fortress.

"Let's just set the place on fire," he muttered reluctantly. "We can stay long enough to see a good burn started."

"Let go, you stupid man!"

All four men turned at the sound of the voice. A number of Modan's own people stood in the middle of the street, with a pitiful collection of prisoners huddled between them. Modan counted about twenty soldiers who seemed healthy enough; these would be the ones who valued their lives more than their loyalty, he supposed. There were three others, though: a tired old man with darkish skin and white hair, a woman still young enough to be worth something, and an older one who might once have been something to look at, maybe thirty years ago. The bitch seemed certainly well enough preserved, though, especially her tongue.

"Why," Lagan asked patiently, "are you bringing me those?"

One of the men stepped forward and gestured to the older woman. "She's Brigante, and speaks the south dialect like she was born to it. I thought you might be interested."

"Oh?" Lagan raised his eyebrow as if mildly curious. "Brigante? Did she plead for her life?"

"That would be the day I cut my tongue out," the woman sneered, her arms folded and her chin high in contempt.

"We can do that for you too, if you want," Lagan growled.

"Kill the useless bitch, Lagan, and the old man too," Modan snarled, then turned his eyes on the younger woman. Not a bad prize, though the woman had a good ten years on him, maybe more. "The other one," he shrugged indifference as he looked at her, "she's probably good for something."

The woman made to reply but the older one spoke first, her voice full of contempt. "That *old man*," she pointed to Metellus, "has been a Roman slave for fifty years. And here we are, the moment he gets a chance to be free, you want to kill him! It's no wonder they call you a bunch of savages."

Modan growled, but Lagan seemed to take no offence. He seemed rather surprised. "That true? You've been a Roman slave for that long?"

The old man stared and said nothing, but the younger woman spoke up, her voice stilted, as if she hadn't spoken the Carvetii dialect for years. "It is true. The same as myself."

"You've not been a slave that . . ." Modan began, then realized she didn't mean the number of years, and prudently closed his mouth.

A clatter of hooves echoed between the buildings and Modan turned to look. A rider lashed his horse down the street at full gallop, reining in only when forced to by the crush of Lagan's people. He trotted the lathered animal carelessly through the crowd, and stopped alongside Lagan.

"I hope you got a good reason, Gavor," he muttered, eyeing the lather.

"Aye, I do. The legion has turned about. It's coming back."

"Oh, fer . . ." Modan decided he'd had enough dithering. "Fire the buildings, and kill the old bitch. We'd best be out of here."

One of his men moved forward and the woman crouched low, snarling. The younger one stepped in front of her, and screamed, "Stop, you fools! Stop. Do you realize who she is?"

Modan didn't care if the old woman was the goddess Brigantia and started to say so, but Lagan raised a hand and shouted him down. "Shut your stupid gob, Modan," he snarled, and stared down at the two women. "So who is she, lass?"

"No, no," the older one cried and struggled forward, but a dozen hands reached out and stopped her.

"She's one of your own," the younger one wailed. "She's Cethen Lamh-fada's wife!"

⁂

Elena slumped in relief. Shayla, may she be well blessed and amply rewarded, had the sense not to tell the rest of it. For one horrible moment, Elena had thought the woman was going to scream to the world that she was the Roman governor's mother. Only the gods knew what this mob would do if they knew; or worse still, what her sons would do, or cede, if they had to deal with it. At least her words seemed to give the man called Lagan pause, for he looked at her with renewed interest.

"That true, woman?" he asked.

"I was once his wife, before the Romans took me. Venutius was still alive then."

"Shit!"

The outburst came from the large, hairy one with stubble on his face and blood covering his tunic; the same ape who moments before had wanted nothing more than to kill her and run. She turned to look at him, and was surprised to see him staring at her with his mouth hanging open.

"Does your vocabulary extend to anything other than 'shit' and 'kill the bitch'?" she asked disdainfully, then blinked. The anger had left the fool's face, and he was clearly perplexed. She wondered what was going through the brute's mind. "A badger bite your tongue?"

The brute's response left her completely stunned. "Elena?"

# Chapter XXXVI

# Cumbria, September, A.D. 105

Bryn arrived at Frevan's lodge only to find his body gone. Racked by a hacking cough and with lungs spewing muck, Frevan had died in the sunlit lodge nestled at the end of his distant lake, in the midst of Cumbria's green hills. And while his dearest wish was to have been buried there, high in those same lush hills where his spirit might wander the valleys and dally by the blue waters of the lake, it was not to be. Even in death, Frevan's leadership had proved a burden. Above all he wanted succession to pass without conflict, and his tenuous peace to continue.

The Carvetii settlement at Luguvalium had grown rapidly with the building of the fort, and many considered it to be the seat of whatever power remained with the tribe. The final irony of Frevan's life was in choosing to be buried there, where such hopes were best ensured by the presence of Rome.

Bryn caught up with the body's slow progress as the mourners descended from the hills south of Luguvalium. Nothing had been lost in the delay it seemed, other than a day's peace of mind and a small stride on Ilbrec. His cousin had carried out Frevan's wishes with undue haste, doubtless because he saw the chance to profit from his standing at Luguvalium. Bryn, already nervous, decided there little choice but to make the best of what was. In the presence of his father and, more important, the several hundred warriors whom he'd brought with him, he thanked Ilbrec for bringing Frevan this far. The man was surly and plainly displeased. Yet despite the man's anger, Bryn bade him join the slow progress as *he* took the body along its final path to Luguvalium. With eyes filled with venom, Ilbrec accepted.

Frevan's funeral proved to be a barren performance, and little else. The man left no wife or children to grieve his passing; nor had the gods blessed his rule with glory, as the people well knew. Frevan's leadership had been born in violence, an unwanted legacy bequeathed by Morallta who had chosen to fight the Romans rather than compromise. The cost had been the tribe's defeat and his sister's life a final mockery, for her dying had not been at the hands of those she fought.

Frevan, though a seasoned warrior, appeared tired and feeble in contrast. There could be no other way. The Carvetii were a defeated tribe, a people whose land had been ravaged and their warriors weeded by Rome. Unable to fight, forced to accept terms, Frevan had no choice but compromise from the day he picked Morallta's sword from the dirt. He kept the peace and his people lost the glory. Frevan had been a man respected for fairness and wisdom, certainly; but he was a man maligned for his refusal to fight. That he had once, in the distant past, faced Romans with sword in hand and shield raised high was hardly even a memory, all but buried with his bones.

The morning of the funeral feast was Bryn's fourth visit to Frevan since his corpse had been laid out on the funeral bier the same number of days before. The man's pale, emaciated body was even more wasted than it had been in life, which seemed impossible. When Bryn had last seen Frevan alive, he had already the appearance of death.

The visits had been to keep company with the dead chief: to share with Frevan a drink, and to share with him the tales of the past. On the first day Bryn had straddled one of the chairs set by the corpse for those who would linger, his arms folded over the backrest and a mug of ale in hand. His eyes at first avoided the body, eerily lit by the flames of a dozen lamps arranged about the pine platform. There seemed little to speak of, for Bryn had spent half his life with the Romans, a time when Frevan had been in his prime. So, for lack of anything else to say, he began talking of the earlier years with Cethen and his mother, Morallta. He grew more comfortable in the dead man's presence as he rambled on, from time to time sipping on the large mug of thick brown ale. When he left it was with a dry throat, a thick tongue, and a bloated bladder, but his mind was comfortably at ease and his burdens lighter.

The second visit had been with hope of gaining advice and inspiration. Of course, as he sat beside Frevan's wasted body, Bryn knew that no advice was forthcoming. Inspiration, however, might be hoped for; and as the hours passed, he felt sure he'd received it. As Bryn mumbled through Frevan's years as leader of his people, he realized the man did not deserve praise so much for what he had done, as for what he'd tried to do and could not. There was no doubt in Bryn's mind, as he glanced sideways at Frevan's pale, wasted remains, that if there had been a decent chance of overpowering the Romans he would have called on all the tribes and led them to victory. And as always, that made Bryn think.

*If there had been a decent chance!*

Frevan had recognized what was impossible. He had swallowed his pride, and taken advantage of what *was* possible. The man had the courage to do that, and the sense to spurn the failings of seeking glory simply for its own sake. For that, he deserved respect. The path taken was selfless, and once Frevan had taken it, it was the people who had gained, right down to the lowest skivvy. Yet many did not realize that, Bryn mused, and therein lay the hub and the rub of the troubles he now faced!

As Bryn sat silent in the shadows of the empty room, the dead man's wan features reflecting the flames of a crackling fire, he recalled Cian musing over the same quandary. His uncle had once served Rome across the seas, and spoke of a huge river near the fortress he'd been sent to protect. To the south of that river, the soil was fertile and ripe with fruit and crops. The Romans built roads, and there were villages and towns, and people lived in relative peace – though Cian had grinned at that, and stressed the word "relative." To the north of the river the land was equally fertile, but remained less tilled, more wooded, and the people savage. Yet they fought like animals to remain that way. Why?

Cian claimed that it was not just their chiefs who fought with such fury, either; it was also the lowest of the kin, who had nothing to gain and their lives to lose. It was a puzzling question, and Bryn supposed there were many answers. Now it was his turn to provide them – perhaps.

✝

Bryn took the place of honour at the funeral feast, for it was his by Frevan's choice and no one, not even Ilbrec, had challenged his right – as yet. He sat with his father at his right hand, and in a gesture of goodwill, Ilbrec at his left. It was a chore to keep the man talking, for he was sullen and clearly remained unsatisfied. Nine others filled the table, Carveti chieftains known to Bryn, some well, others only by name; none could be called an enemy, yet he could not name one as a trusted friend. The hall itself was crammed with mourners, as was the cluttered compound outside, for many had come to pay their respects if for no other reason than to be seen. All of them, in turn or together, had shared their memories with Frevan over the past days, and they were now there to share a final meal.

Bryn knew that was the way of it and watched as the rite played out: the steaming left foreleg of the largest bullock was carved off, and placed beside Frevan to cool as the night wore on. The joint would be buried with him the next day, and serve him well on his journey, as would a host of other grave goods, some already piled at the foot of the bier.

The feasting was at first sombre, as those who felt the need told tales of Frevan's past. His early years fighting the Romans were not forgotten, and his later years were selectively remembered. But more than Frevan's passing hung in the air. Word had spread through the settlement of a massive uprising to the north, and talk at the tables quietly turned to stories of Roman forts destroyed, and soldiers retreating south. Bryn said little beyond speaking of Frevan, though he probably knew the truth more than anyone there concerning the havoc wrought by Modan and Lagan, and their unbroken trail of success.

Oddly enough, he found his belly stirring with a vague longing: this time would they, could they, succeed? And even if they did not, would it have been for the lack of more warriors? The Carvetii and the full might of the Brigante, for example? And, most important, would *he* in his reluctance have made the difference?

Bryn grew anxious as the drink flowed and the huge room became rowdy. Before long, the drunken bickering would begin and some fool would doubtless start a brawl. He glanced toward bier. The dead chieftain, with his silent presence, would help keep the waters smooth; or at worst, help keep a degree of calm. But by this time tomorrow, his corpse would be deep in the side of his grand-da's burial mound, rotting away as Frevan began his final journey. By then Bryn's own journey would have started, on a path that remained to be seen. His eyes wandered to the side of the lodge where a fire blazed in a huge open hearth. He saw Borba walk casually in front of it on his way to the door, tossing what appeared to be a small log on the flames. Bryn wet his lips. His own private ritual had just begun.

Thick smoke billowed from the hearth and spread through the lodge. Those closest cursed and several rose to their feet, coughing and edging away. Bryn rose too, and yelled for order. The smoke did not last long, thinning as it spiralled upward into the huge oak rafters, where it swirled high above the hall. The main door, which had been quietly closed as Borba passed by, swung open with a resounding crash. A tall figure stood in the entrance, a Roman officer clad in parade uniform, flanked on either side by two more. Formed up behind in two ranks stood a full squad of infantry: eight men, each bearing a painted shield and wearing a sheathed sword.

The hall quickly filled with loud, guttural growls as men everywhere climbed to their feet, some in anger, others in confusion. Bryn bellowed for silence and stood with both arms raised, waiting. More from bafflement than reason, a grudging silence fell as the nervous shouts and grumbling faded.

In a strong voice Bryn demanded, "Who is it that dares come here?"

Rhun replied in the same tribal tongue, his voice ringing through the hall. "I, Rhun, son of Cethen Lamh-fada, would bid farewell to a fallen warrior."

"And I, Cian, brother of Cethen Lamh-fada, would do the same."

"As would I, Marcus Sabinius, once a slave of Frevan's people," Marcus finished in the same firm tone and tongue.

The murmur rose once more to a low, steady babble, but now the talk held more bafflement than bile, and Bryn felt his chest sag with relief. "Then step forward and bid Frevan farewell, if your father finds no fault in the doing."

Cethen rose unsteadily to his feet, for his leg had cramped. He placed a hand on Bryn's shoulder to hold himself firm, a gesture that was seen as assurance for his son. "I find no fault. Let us do so together."

Rhun whispered the order to move and they marched forward, in step, passing through the hall to the bier in front of Bryn's table. Each of the three men took one of the seats placed near the head of the body, left there for those who might still wish to speak with Frevan. The squad broke off in file and faced inward, one man standing at each corner of the bier, the remaining four in line at its foot. The four at the corners drew their swords and held them in salute, the glittering blades pointed upward. Bryn, as he made his way down to the bier, decided that the whole thing was very impressive. And it was even more so when Criff, who had taken a place by the fire, added the dulcet tones of his harp to the strained silence.

They had all agreed that what was said to Frevan would not take long. The number of words spoken would be determined by others in the hall, and when the hushed murmur of voices began to rise, the three men rose to their feet and gazed down on Frevan. The rush of voices again fell silent.

"Frevan, may your journey be brief and free of trouble," Rhun intoned. "To defend you on your way, I offer a sword."

Rhun nodded to the first of the men standing at the foot of the bier. The soldier removed a weapon from behind his shield, a long, gleaming Carveti sword, its hilt inlaid with silver. The man briefly raised the weapon high so that all might see, then stepped crisply forward and placed it with the other grave goods arrayed below the bier. He paused as if paying his respects, then straightened, slapped his free arm across his chest in a final salute, and stepped back.

Cian continued. "A cloak to keep you warm."

Marcus said, "Drink to slake your thirst."

And all three finished with, "And food to fill your belly."

As each offering was called a soldier stepped toward the bier and added to an already substantial pile of gifts. Once it was done, each man drew his sword and, like the four at the corner of the bier, held it upright before his chest in salute.

Bryn then stepped forward, amused by what must come next, for he was the host, and a host had certain duties. He stared sombrely at the three men as he extended the lodge's hospitality. "Will you stay and eat and drink with us?"

The silence grew deeper than a grave, and the hall became so still that Bryn could hear Ilbrec breathing behind him. The last thing his people wanted was a bunch of sodding Romans cluttering up Frevan's wake. The corner of Rhun's mouth twitched as he spoke, a slight tic that only Bryn could see. "I would be honoured, Bryn," he called out so that all could hear, and lowered his head as if in gratitude; then he raised it again, and sighed his regret. "Alas, we have other commitments. There is news of trouble to the north that requires attention."

The relief at Rhun's regret was palpable, but his words raised the level of chatter and some began to shout. Turning to face the packed hall, Rhun raised both hands, calling for quiet. The rumble of voices slowly faded, everyone curious and waiting. "I'm truly sorry. We mean no disrespect to Frevan by taking our leave, but I am needed. We are all needed," he said, then cocked his head to one side, as if seeing their interest for the first time. "There is no need for concern."

Rhun paused, his lips unconsciously moving as he silently counted to five. Bryn resisted the urge to look at Borba, who stood by the door. The twin would be doing the same count. If he reached five without disruption, then Borba would call the question. But as expected, someone else called it and the question was quickly taken up and shouted about the hall: "What's happening in the north?"

Again Rhun raised his hands for silence, and when it came, he told them the truth. "The army of the Selgovae chieftain, Lagan Trenlaimh, along with some of my own people," as if to be sure everyone knew exactly who that meant, Rhun specified, "a smaller army of Brigantes and Carvetii led by my brother Modan, have burned four Roman forts that border the land of the Votadinii." He paused before giving the last of what was a terrible admission; however, if the tribes did not know it today, they would certainly know it on the morrow. "A further outpost has been destroyed to the west of here, across the Ituna at *Charia*."

The rumbling began again, much louder this time, and Rhun made to move, as if that was all – but it wasn't supposed to be. Bryn tensed, waiting, then another voice rang out from the rear of the hall, loud and clear. Dag!

"So what are you doing about it?"

Bryn smiled his relief and Rhun turned back, his voice crisp and confident with the answer. "We'll stop it, of course. The Ninth Hispana legion already has the uprising in hand. The legion has relieved the garrisons at Coria and Habitancum, and there has been fighting south of Bremenium, where Lagan still has the fort under siege. Casualties on the Roman side have been light."

Bryn blinked in surprise. That last item was new to him, and he'd talked with Rhun and Marcus only this morning. He waited, now as curious as anyone else in the hall. Rhun must have sensed his surprise, for he shrugged helplessly as if to show there had been no choice. Then he continued, topping one disaster with another. "The Ninth itself will relieve Bremenium, then torch the fort to deny it to the Selgovae. For the time being, the garrison there will fall back on Habitancum with the Ninth. The legions do have a firm grip on the situation."

Bryn looked to the back of the room as everyone sat speechless, clearly stunned by the candidness of Rhun's words. And perhaps Dag was stunned as well! The fool seemed to have forgotten his part in this, which was to be the crux of the ploy. Finally the man appeared to remember, and his gravelly voice barked from the rear of the hall, "So what else is happening?"

Rhun pursed his lips in understanding and rubbed his chin, pausing as if deciding if the question should be answered. Then, as if making up his mind, he nodded and finally spoke. "Further reinforcements are being sent from the south. Order has to be imposed." His voice was curt. "The Second and Twentieth legions will arrive here tomorrow, more than ten thousand strong."

Which Bryn knew to be true, though he also knew the number might be a small lie; but who was going to know the difference when eight or nine thousand troops marched through Luguvalium rather than ten?

And as to the timing, Tuis may have been on the road for near a week – but if he arrived tomorrow as Rhun promised, it would seem as if the two legions had wings.

The surprise was total, for the hall again erupted with voices. Now was the time to move quickly and fulfill Frevan's prophecy, before the questions grew hard and the talk hostile. Bryn glanced anxiously at Rhun, who again had his hands raised in a call for silence.

"Before Frevan crossed over, he made known a prophecy," Rhun began, his voice almost a shout. "A foretelling of his people's destiny, and that of Bryn. As I leave, as we leave, we clasp our brother to our hearts, and wish him its fulfillment. Come," he turned to Bryn, his hand extended, "step closer, so we might part as kin."

Bryn moved forward, cynical at Rhun's use of the word "brother." It was meant for the crowd, of course; but only one man there was his brother: Rhun himself, and that was only half true. Cian was kin, he supposed, but the Roman Marcus didn't fit either description. Nonetheless, he edged closer to the bier. As he did, he slipped a hard cake-like disc into one of the lamps, so that its side nestled against the flame. The decanus caught the movement in the corner of his eye, and barked an order. The eight infantrymen snapped to attention and again formed two ranks. Each man slapped his sword against his shield once before sliding the weapon back into its scabbard. The crash of arms echoed through the building, and the chatter died as everyone in the hall looked their way.

Bryn, Marcus, Rhun, and Cian turned to face each other, standing so close that each man's shoulders touched those of the men beside him. White smoke slowly rose around them, swirling upward from the lamp as if it were steam wafting from a cauldron. An arm reached upward from between the four, the forearm bare, and the hand formed a fist. It stayed but a moment then dropped from sight, only to reappear, slowly rising upward with the glittering gold torque of Brigantia clasped firm in its grip. All about the hall men climbed excitedly to their feet, shouting and pointing.

The hand and its precious burden sank once more, this time to vanish completely. The hall grew quiet, a silence broken only by the crackle of the fire. The torque's appearance had been so brief, it might never have happened; and if it had, it might have been held there by a bodiless limb.

Each of the four men solemnly placed his arms on the shoulders of the men on either side. For a moment they stood silent, huddled together as if the four were suddenly one. The white smoke turned slowly grey, spiralling upward to join the wisps from the fire that still drifted through the rafters.

"I gotta piss," Bryn whispered, trying hard not to cough as the smoke teased at his nose.

"Arsehole," Cian murmured, and sniggered.

"Shut up, you fools," Marcus hissed, and pulled away.

Each man took a step backward. Rhun, Cian, and Marcus turned on their heels to face the hall. Each slammed one foot hard against the floor, then began marching from the room. Behind them, the decanus snarled an order. The squad of soldiers slammed to attention and followed in step, the rhythmic beat of hobnailed boots almost lost in the din that suddenly filled the hall. For Bryn remained standing alone beside Frevan's bier, his arms folded, and the gleaming torque firmly circling his neck.

## Chapter XXXVII

## Bremenium, September, A.D. 105

Lagan might have felt vindicated, but self-righteousness came with a price. A thousand men had died just days ago – *there had to be at least that many, if not more* – and twice the number bore wounds that needed more than a stitch and a clean bandage. Of those, more than a few good men would gasp their last breath in agony, and all because he'd eased his grip on the monster that was his army. Mob was more the better word, he reflected, and an unruly one, now that the Caledoni hill-climber called Uepo had put his head together with Modan's bone-brained skull. He should never have given in to the two following the success at Coria, and tried to do what he knew was impossible. What he should have done, months ago, was kill the fool Modan when his brother freed him from the Romans.

Lagan lifted the mug of ale and drained its contents, his mind on the day of Modan's escape, which seemed years ago. The man had limped back to his camp with Treno, and Lagan figured something bad, really bad, had happened, for Modan's usual spite had turned to venom. It took more than a beating to hate like that, and Lagan figured it had to do with the man's wife. If that was so, it explained the one change in the man that might yet prove useful. Of late, Modan was easing up on his principles concerning killing his brother, and the reason was not hard to figure.

While everyone was out fighting Romans, brother Bryn was in Cumbria taking advantage of Frevan's death – and Modan's wife. For the while, Modan's simmering rage put them both on the same side of the battlefield; but Eupo had since come along and caught the fool's ear, and now the clod wanted to return to Cumbria and claim what he figured was his, the torque, the leadership, and maybe even his wife. Lagan shook his head in despair. The stoat didn't deserve even a sniff of his imagined claims; and even if he did succeed, it would only bring further disadvantage. Any kind of success would just make it harder to deal with the headstrong fool.

"I've often wondered why men want to lead other men," Elena said, watching carefully as Lagan frowned and upended the dregs of his mug on the ground. They sat beside a fire in front of the lodge taken over by the Selgovae chieftain, in the small civilian settlement outside Bremenium. For the moment the fort was under siege. "I don't believe I've ever seen a single one the happier for it, not when the sun finally sets. Neither of my husbands were, anyway; though Cethen always had such things thrust on him. He never sought the responsibility."

"It's far better to lead than to follow," Lagan muttered, though the words rang false in his ears; at the moment, they were actually a blatant lie! *Though there were the other times* when . . . "If you're in charge, you do what you want, not what some other idiot is telling you."

"Some *other* idiot?" Elena chuckled.

Lagan smiled at her across the dying flames. He liked talking to the woman. The way he figured it, she was about the right age to be his mother, even though she didn't look it, and her mind was as sharp as a honed sword. *Shit, it's probably sharper than any other in my entire army!* He sighed as she reached out and refilled his mug, motioning her to stop when it was only half full. "You may have a point."

"I wonder why the gods make it that way. You know: some men want to lead, while others are content to follow. The numbers don't add. Only one man can lead an army."

"Ah, but most are content to lead just a few within that army. Though there's always a Modan, for example, the son your first husband sired, who fits somewhere between." Lagan closed his eyes for a moment, deciding it was best to say no more; the woman was clever enough to form her own opinion. "But I will say this. When a man does have charge of so many, it's a heady brew." He shrugged, grinning. "Besides, if no one is leading, then nothing gets done."

"Mmm . . ." Elena looked thoughtful as she pondered Lagan's answer. "No battles would be won without a leader, that's certain; but then, none would be lost either, for there would be no leader to start one. Each man would have to settle his difference with the next on their own terms. And they likely wouldn't kill each other doing it. Their wives wouldn't let them."

"Ah, so you're saying it should be the women who lead?" Lagan laughed, his mood growing lighter.

"Never," Elena said, her eyes twinkling. "Not from the front, anyway."

"Aye, you've the right of that one," Lagan acknowledged, an image of his own wife coming to mind. She was gone five years now from birthing, but he still missed the woman, for all her brooding moods. "They're not slow in letting you know what *not* to do. *And* they don't seem to need words to say it."

"So what are *you* not going to do?"

Lagan smiled to himself. For the first time in a long time, he didn't know one way or another. Certainly in the near future, assaulting the walls of Bremenium was what he was *not* going to do, though he had yet to tell anyone. Without the element of surprise, to do so would be too great an obstacle with too high a cost. Yet beyond that? Lagan found himself telling the woman the truth. "That's a good question. Everyone wants to know what I *am* going to do, and I've got no idea."

"I don't think it matters." Elena's eyes grew suddenly distant, as if her mind was far away. "The Romans will win anyway. I've seen it before, not only here, but across the sea. It's inevitable. Even if you gain a mile's march on them," she gestured vaguely northward, where the ashes of at least four Roman strongholds lay hidden in the distant darkness, "they'll only return and push you back another ten. They can't afford otherwise, or they lose everything."

"You say that as if with regret," Lagan murmured, and yawned. He was tired, but unwilling to leave the warmth of the fire and Elena's company. Over the past several days, he'd learned much from the woman – about the Romans, and his own people, and about the woman herself.

"Not really. There's good to be found on both sides, along with the bad. It all balances, and makes no difference in the end."

"You're drifting toward the morbid – or the maudlin," Lagan replied, and turned his arrows on another target. Yesterday he'd talked to Modan about his father, intrigued by the fact that he'd once been married to this woman who was . . . Who was what? The most knowledgeable of her sex he'd ever known? The most world-wise? Or just the most interesting? "Your Roman husband died, but there's another waiting in the hills. Are you going to seek him out?"

Elena snorted. "I can hardly do that, being held here."

Lagan chuckled. While the words were true, they were also an invitation to tell what he had planned for her. And that was something he couldn't do, for he had no idea about that, either. "I doubt you'll be with us for long. You're Roman now, and likely of some value."

"So was my stepson, a Roman lad called Marcus. He was with the army. He spent more than four years in captivity."

Lagan ignored the comparison. "We can always sell you to your first husband."

"Cethen?" Elena laughed. "You're assuming he'd want me back."

"Ah-hah! That begs another question. Do you want him? He's out there somewhere, but . . ."

Lagan stopped as several shadows loomed on the far side of the fire, quickly followed by a rustle of movement from behind, over by the door of the lodge. He didn't need to turn and look; those behind were his people, who stood there ready. But those shadows . . .

Modan and Treno sauntered into the firelight with Eupo stepping purposely between the pair, which told Lagan who was feeding whatever flame they carried. Two others trailed behind, Gobha and a Caledoni whose name Lagan couldn't remember: a small, wiry creature, whose eyes glinted in the firelight as they shifted from side to side. He was Eupo's fetcher and bum-nuzzler.

Without asking leave, all five crouched down on the far side of the fire and for what seemed the longest while, nobody spoke. Lagan was at first angry, then found himself fighting to keep from snorting his derision. The three had obviously come to challenge him, yet the half-baked bread-heads had arrived with an arrow nocked but no agreement on who was supposed to shoot it. He eyed them all carefully. Modan would eventually do the talking, he was almost certain. But he was just as certain who'd goaded him, and it was typical Caledoni: place the arrow on the string, and shame someone else into pulling the bow.

Eupo did speak first, however, glancing disdainfully toward Elena. "This is none of the woman's concern."

"Oh, I dunno." Lagan scratched his chin, deliberately drawing out his reply. "You're here for a reason. I'd guess that part of it concerns *the woman*."

"It don't matter, there's no need –"

"Modan, what do you think?" Lagan raised his brow and nodded toward Elena, who seemed to have decided to remain silent. "This is your da's wife. Or she was. I think she's a good deal wiser than any of us. Maybe she can offer us all counsel. What do you say?"

"I . . . she . . ."

Modan swung confused eyes toward Eupo, confirming Lagan's opinion as to which hound led the pack. It was time to stop trifling with the man, before the rest got itchy and scratched. "Never mind, Modan. Give it to me. Why are you here?"

Again silence, then Treno opened his mouth to say something, but Elena spoke first, her voice full of disdain. "They're here for one of two reasons, Lagan: they want to challenge your decisions as leader, or charge off in all directions and slay the giants by themselves."

Lagan was quite sure Elena was wrong on the one count; they weren't there to challenge his leadership. If that was true, it would have been done behind his back, not to his face. "It's Frevan's funeral that's got them all twitchy," he said, and motioned to Modan, speaking as if the man wasn't sitting across from him. "He figures to go back and gather the tribes to his call, now there's a row of burned Roman forts for which he can claim the glory. I'd guess he'll start by attacking Luguvalium to get Brigantia's torque for himself, before it can get to Bryn. It seems your oldest son has it there. What do you think?"

Elena covered her surprise at Lagan's knowledge of a torque, for it was something she hadn't known. But she replied quickly enough, her answer short and simple. "He won't take Luguvalium."

"There you go, then." Lagan turned to Modan and shrugged. The expression he found there clearly showed that he'd guessed right. "You have it, and ahead of time. You want to charge off on your own and try doing the same in the west as we both did here, only this time you won't succeed. You no longer have the advantage of surprise, or the skill. The woman's saved you a lot of trouble, hasn't she?"

Modan ignored the question and asked his own, one that had been obviously discussed. "So what are you going to do? Continue running?"

Lagan cursed softly to himself. There it was again! There was no use in saying that he was not, in any manner, running. So far, with his guidance, they had achieved unmatched success, right through until they'd left the fort at Coria burning and half its garrison dead. Then, with blood hot and their bellies boiling, everyone figured they could go off and conquer the whole rotten Roman world, and attack a fucking legion! Lagan shook his head as he pushed back his anger and sighed. Because he'd been unable to do anything else, he'd given in. Why, oh why, had he done that? Maybe it was easier to die true to your beliefs than to cede to the weakness of others.

But he hadn't. Against his better judgement, he'd given in to the fools. He's reluctantly pulled most of his damned army off the siege at Bremenium to attack the Ninth legion as it *again* marched north following his own successful raid on Coria. Had it only been Modan goading him, he could have dealt with it and said no. But the man was backed up by a snivelling, scornful Caledoni chieftain called Eupo, who had arrived at the head of an even larger force than the one that had burned the fort at Lignum. The man had sneered, boasting he had brought with him only warriors who fought bravely, not crows that pecked at eggs, fed on carrion, and cawed at the first sniff of a wolf. And Lagan's own people had been quickly caught up in the man's stupid, yapping chorus.

There seemed to be no choice, which had been galling. He'd given in, striking the Roman army halfway between the two Roman forts: a large disciplined body of soldiers, who were expecting an onslaught every step of the way. It hadn't taken the gods to foretell the result. Lagan's own army, admittedly not a small one, had effectively challenged a Roman legion to do battle in the field. That was something he had sworn never to do; it was something that time and again, he'd told his people he *would* never do!

Eupo! He, more than anyone, should have known better. He was a Caledoni, one of Galgar's tribe! Stupid, hill-climbing, bone-brained savages . . .

Lagan sighed anew, his anger now nothing more than frustration. "No, I'm not going to stop running, Modan. I'll keep running, and I'll keep winning every little stinking battle that *I* choose to fight like a sneaky, cowardly wolf: one bleeding bite at a time, and from behind if I have the chance."

"We made the Romans go back," Modan argued. "They're still hiding in their hole at Habitancum."

"And look at the cost of it. The ground was littered with our people, and hardly any of theirs," Lagan growled, though there was some spark of merit in what Modan said. The Romans had clearly won the field, but they'd turned about and gone back to the nearest fort. The only reason he could figure was that they were unsure what lay ahead. Even so, why the commander had turned, he didn't know.

Eupo rose silently from his crouch, not bothering to hide his disgust; the others quickly followed. Lagan heard the soft tread behind him as his own people moved quietly forward, crowding in to protect him. He smiled, for he trusted those who guarded his back. Nonetheless he stifled a shiver, on the chance that this just might be the one time he shouldn't . . .

"We'll take my da's wife with us," Modan growled, though he kept his eyes fixed on the ground as if afraid to meet Lagan's.

"You will not," Lagan stated, climbing to his feet. "She will not be going anywhere."

"Under what conditions?" Elena interrupted, leaning forward on the bench with her hands folded primly in her lap.

"There won't be no conditions," Modan muttered.

"Then I'll not go," Elena said, almost in regret.

"What do you mean, ma'am?" Treno spoke for the first time, his politeness belying the ugly tattoos that scarred his face.

"What do *you* mean, young man? The statement that I will not go, or my question about conditions?" Elena's words were as precise as her questions.

Lagan had been about to reaffirm that the woman was not going anywhere, but he waited, intrigued, and broke into a grin at Elena's response. As did Treno, the dark tattoos twisting as he answered, "I meant your conditions."

"I'll want a good horse, some light armour, a weapon, and the right to ride unfettered," Elena said, and turned to Lagan. "Could I entrust Metellus and Shayla to your care, until I send word for them?"

"Of course." Lagan's grin broadened, and he sat down again. The woman must have passed sixty, yet she stood her ground like a she-bear. "And I'll gladly provide the first three conditions, along with my sincere advice that you would be best off remaining here. However, I'm unable to offer the fourth."

"And she ain't going to get it, neither," Modan growled, cautioning Eupo to remain quiet with a wave of his hand as the Caledoni opened his mouth. "She'll run at the first chance."

"I will not, and you have my word." Elena sniffed her disdain. "There will be no need to run. To the contrary. Before your fool errand is over, you will be looking for me to beg the Romans to have mercy on you."

*And that's the truth,* Lagan thought as his mind continued to churn over what he was going to do. Elena herself was one of the issues. Should he – could he – consider keeping her, both as a bargaining token and for her own good? Yet why should he, other than for his own fancy? Several critical problems seemed to be solving themselves here without moving his rear from the log it sat on. Modan was the prime one, and he would be well rid of the man. And the violent argument brewing over *not* asssaulting Bremenium seemed to be resolving itself at the same time.

His greatest concern would be what path he should follow if the major part of his army disappeared on a fool's journey. What choices remained? Carry on sniping at the Romans from the hills in the hope that one day they'd give up and go away? The woman was right on that! The Romans would only go when they wanted to. Lagan sighed. Some days, a man just wanted to get up and go home. The notion made him smile, and he saw that she did too. Perhaps he should make matters easier for everyone, including himself.

He nodded at Elena. "If she wants to go, I'll not stop her. In fact, I'll do better than that," Lagan said, and turned to Gobha, addressing only him. "So nobody can say I was the cause of your failure, take any of the Selgovae who want to go with you. You can go ask them."

Gobha's face split into a huge grin. "Really?"

"Yeah, really," Lagan said, ignoring a vague feeling of uneasiness that could only be his conscience.

※

Marius hadn't kept count, but he was willing to wager good coin that a week had passed since he'd had any sleep. He lay on his bed, staring at the ceiling, which he couldn't see anyway because it was dark inside the room. Even carnal visions of Livia couldn't gain him rest. The subtle sounds and smells of a waking fort filtered into the room, as if the walls did not exist. The noise and stink of overcrowded troops were all out there: the waft of human sewage, the stale odour of boiling barley, the shouts of any man who held a shred of command, and the snivelling of those who did not. And all of it, for at least a good half-hour, had been overlaid by the steady tramp of boots, the nicker of horses, the thud of galloping hooves, and the sporadic crack of thunder.

A flash of lightning reflected through the open doorway. A figure hovered outside in the hallway, half hidden by the glow of a lamp. It was likely bringing food for his belly, and he wasn't hungry – or thirsty. What he wanted most was a piss. Groaning, he pushed the blankets aside and swung his feet onto the floor, shivering as the soles touched the cold wood.

Another bitch of a day, and more bitching meetings!

Fermus, the bull-necked, bull-brained primus, figured there was a fair number more than the expected ten or so thousand barbarians at Bremenium, and fresh blood was arriving every day. The man was a squawking parrot: every morning, the same message. The pilus still brooded over the decision to turn back to Habitancum, insisting they had the enemy on the run – which was rot. How do you march forward with maybe fifteen thousand screeching barbarians ahead of you, thousands behind that have just sacked your fort, and thousands more that you've just fought off? You don't! Not when two legions are only days away and marching hard to join you.

Granted, the attack on the column as it moved to relieve the Bremenium garrison had whittled the barbarians' numbers, as Fermus said. But by how many? His own forces had also suffered. With what he'd brought with him of the Ninth, plus what they had picked up on the way north, he'd marched out with around five thousand. There hadn't been that many killed, but there were the wounded and sick – almost one man in ten was unfit to some degree. Fermus and his centurios had fought a fair enough battle, Marius supposed, but that only left him with –

An orderly ducked inside. "The primus asked me to give his respects, and could you come outside? There's something he says you need to hear."

Marius swore under his breath. Was the man still pressing to march off and do battle before the governor arrived with his legions? Once Sabinius got here, the outcome of any fight would never be in doubt. But Julius Fermus, and clearly most of his centurios, wanted to march their small army into the open and form ranks before Bremenium, inviting the barbarians to do battle. The man was confident of victory, and claimed it was best to stop them now, before more of them arrived. And that might make sense, Marius supposed, if two more legions were not raising dust to get here. The trouble was, Fermus was still pissed because he'd been overruled.

"Tell him I'll be there shortly," Marius muttered, his mood as cold as his feet, "but help me get dressed first." He stood with his arms upraised, allowing the man to slip his under-tunic over his head. It occurred to Marius that he should ask why the primus felt the need to see him, so he might be prepared.

The slave shrugged. "A dispatch rider has ridden in from Bremenium, sir. The barbarians appear to have vanished."

# Chapter XXXVIII

# Luguvalium, September, A.D. 105

The arrival of two Roman legions reduced the Carvetii to sullen silence. Agricola himself had not fielded as many troops here before uniting with the Ninth and marching north to Graupius. The army arrived exactly when Rhun had said it would, for he'd known it had camped the previous night at *Brocavum*. Nothing short of disaster would have prevented its arrival on time, and at the moment disasters were occurring on the east side of Britannia, not the west.

Rhun remained worried over the outposts further north of Luguvalium, doubts that were reinforced when riders clattered in from *Nithius*, having driven their horses hard for nigh on forty miles. The garrison had pulled back to Blatobulgium after fending off heavy attacks by local tribesmen that left part of the fort destroyed. The centurio in command set fire to what remained and withdrew under cover of night, and was awaiting further orders. The fellow recommended that his small force remain at Blatobulgium until it was known just how far the reed was bending, and Rhun was grateful for his opinion. That fort, like every other in this whole sorry province, had been understrength, thanks mainly to Trajan and his endless Dacian war. The extra troops would help.

"How serious is it?" Jessa asked.

"I dunno. All I know is something's happening, but I wouldn't worry," Cian said confidently, though he licked his lips and stared nervously toward the sprawling tribal settlement that lay close to the fort.

"What do you think, Criff?" Jessa smiled at the expression on his face. The bard looked as if his belly churned with too much beer.

"I don't think, I just sing and tell stories," Criff said soberly, which told her his mind was troubled too. The bard was never serious unless singing of lost love and tribal tragedy.

Cethen, riding on her other side, said nothing, but he was plainly doing his best to appear unconcerned – and just as clearly, he wasn't. She followed Cian's eyes as if she might find something there. The settlement looked peaceful enough. The hall where Frevan had lain stood tall over the sprawl of lesser buildings, many of them little more than huts. Most were spaced to accommodate the clutter of pens and sheds that housed the livestock which made the growing town appear much larger than it was. More than the usual number of people filled the dirt streets, which was to be expected, Jessa reasoned. Frevan had been buried only two days, and many mourners still lingered. How many, Jessa had no idea, but it was a good number and she could understand why they were there. The very air had grown heavy with reckoning.

As they made their way toward the hall, Jessa turned her eyes to yet another sprawl, this one on the far side of the small river that flanked the west side of the fort. A larger, makeshift camp had grown there the past week, thrown together by Frevan's mourners on the pastureland that served as the tribe's common. The camp should have all but disappeared by now, but it was still there, as if everyone waited for something, though unsure of what. Those who were left were certainly no longer in mourning. They were more like crows, gathering to peck at the carrion. But that wasn't fair, Jessa supposed. They were, after all, Frevan's people. Most were doing no more than linger to see what path their lives would take.

Trista greeted them from the lodge door and told them not to dismount, but to wait. She disappeared inside, and soon after rode around from the rear of the building on the black gelding. The horse was unsaddled and unbridled, but for a rope halter. Motioning them all to follow, she kneed the animal to a canter, heading directly toward the river.

The water was low and easily crossed. On the other side, instead of riding toward the makeshift camp as Jessa expected, Trista turned her horse south, where farmsteads and open pasture dotted the countryside.

"W-what're you doing, girl?" Jessa demanded, clinging grimly to the pommel crosses as her horse trotted to keep up.

Trista laughed and eased her own horse back to a walk. "I need to get away from the foul smell of it all."

Cian fell in alongside. "Put that many in one room and what else are you going to get?" He chuckled and nudged Trista's shoulder. "Especially if they're Carvetii."

"I don't mean the foul-smelling stink, I mean the foul-smelling talk," she grumbled.

"I suppose every chief with a loud voice and a hot temper is still arguing?" Jessa said, though she was surprised. Tuis had remained only one night and a half day at Luguvalium with the combined army, and the display of force had been intimidating, even for her. The sight had certainly daunted the people at Luguvalium: thousands on thousands of armoured troops, all marching in ranks, with their supply wagons, mules and long, jingling columns of cavalry. So why the change of heart? The combined armies had marched east just yesterday morning, which meant it should be nearing Coria by nightfall today. Just because it was no longer in sight, surely it had not been forgotten? "That's idiocy."

"I can sympathize, but I agree," Cian said. "But don't worry. They'll talk it out and when they run out of spit and bile, it'll all die."

"I dunno. Ilbrec is doing a lot of shouting, and people are listening." Jessa murmured.

"Where's Bryn on this?" Cethen finally spoke, pulling on Trista's arm and everyone reined to a halt. The horses dropped their heads and began tugging at the grass.

"He's shouting back when there's no other choice." Trista rolled her eyes, but her mind was clearly elsewhere. "The soft voice of reason is drowned out if he doesn't."

"So what's happened to change it all?" Jessa asked, then stared hard at Trista's twisted features; it was as if the woman felt tormented. "Are you battling a brain-crossed conscience?"

"What's a conscience?" Cian leered, then his voice softened. "What's happening, lass?"

Trista didn't answer. Instead she nodded for Cethen to follow, and urged her horse farther down the cow track leaving Jessa and the other two behind. The pair stopped once they were out of hearing and began talking. Trista gestured with both hands as she spoke, as if haranguing Cethen. Jessa had to smile, for he sat in the saddle as if helpless, shaking his head, his shoulders slumped. Trista threw her hands in the air, glanced briefly at Jessa, then pulled the reins over until her horse faced south. She thumped her heels hard into the animal's belly and it leapt forward, following another path that shadowed the riverbank.

Cethen turned his horse and let the animal walk back, his features drawn in misery. He glanced moodily at his brother and muttered, "Let's go back."

"What's the matter?" Cian and Jessa asked together.

As they started back, Cethen just shook his head. "The gods should have given me nothing but girls."

Jessa turned to Criff and asked the same question, but the bard just shrugged. "As I once said, I repeat only what I hear. I've heard nothing."

"Bryn's got problems?" Cian asked, turning his horse to ride alongside his brother, who seemed set on going back across the river.

"I gotta think things over," Cethen muttered.

Jessa, with a good deal of kicking and rein-pulling, guided her own mount to his other side. She studied Cethen's face. The man's eyes were tired; in fact, his whole face looked tired and beaten. "No, it's not Bryn. It's Modan, isn't it?"

Cethen said nothing, which made Jessa certain that it was. Her heart thumped an extra beat.

But it was Cian who asked the question: "He's not dead, is he?"

"Naw, it's something else. I gotta think."

"Then what's happening with the man?" Cian demanded in frustration.

Cethen also raised his voice. "I said I gotta think!"

Jessa was surprised at the outburst, though she knew that Cethen's skin was thin when it came to Modan. For all she cared, the gods could wring the man's neck. But Modan was not dead, for Cethen seemed to know that, which meant he had other news of him – probably something that Modan was doing that his da didn't want him to do. What could distress his father so badly? Whatever it was, it had to affect Bryn, because Trista was also upset, and she'd unloaded a wagonload of rocks on Cethen. The two must go together, Jessa mused: Bryn and Modan. What could Modan do to piss on Bryn, when the fool was already riding tall in the saddle on the glory of burning Roman forts?

Which he'd been a fool to do, what with one Roman army advancing from Eboracum, and two more on their way from the south . . .

Jessa's eyes opened wide and she swore under her breath. Modan probably had no idea that not one, but three legions were converging on him! He would expect retaliation, yes, but after Tuis's lame march through the hills over the summer, he probably believed that only the Ninth legion would be delivering it.

Or did he?

Rome often tended to underestimate the tribes. Was she doing the same? There was the man Lagan to deal with, and having met him, she knew he was no fool. The man was too bright to fight even one legion in the open, never mind three! Yet knowing Modan, Lagan was surely being prodded hard do to exactly that. Tempers would be hot, for even small success would make the fool more unbearable than normal. Combine that with rumours of the arrival of hordes of Caledonii from the north, and what do you have? Modan and Lagan may have –

"Ilbrec's had word that Modan's on his way here, Cian," Jessa said, trying show confidence. "And probably with every warrior from Lagan's mongrel army he could get to come with him."

"To fight Bryn?"

"Probably not; not at first, anyway. But he wants the leadership and the torque, and one way or another he's out to get it." Jessa closed her eyes, trying to imagine what Modan and the men of Lagan's army might do. They'd just burned four forts; their blood was likely running as hot as Vesuvius; and it would be just as ready to erupt. "We know others from the north were flocking like sheep to join him, and they've done nothing but kill Romans and burn forts ever since. By now Modan will believe he's invincible. I'd lay coin that he's already on his way to destroy this one, even if Bryn does cede to him first. In fact," Jessa shook her head in despair, "I'll bet Bryn is wavering again, and that's why Trista was tossing turds at Cethen."

"But he won't even get here. Modan will run head on into Tuis," Cian said, "Surely he doesn't think he's going to beat him?"

The barest grunt came from Cethen. Jessa stared it him. His face remained grim, but he'd heard what they said and Jessa could see that her words had struck a target. The man's mind surely churned above a bile-filled belly, and she knew why.

"You'd be wrong, Cian," Jessa said, her words meant equally for Cethen. "I'd guess Modan doesn't even know about Tuis's army. Though it won't matter, because Tuis marched straight east, taking the road to Vindolanda. From there he'll go on to what's left of Coria, then follow the road north to Habitancum and join up with the Ninth. While Modan . . ."

Cian nodded his understanding. "While Modan will cross the hills in a straight line from Bremenium."

"They'll pass each other going in opposite directions, missing by maybe fifteen or twenty miles," Jessa said. Cethen mumbled something that sounded like *hrumph,* and she reached out to pat his arm. The distance was farther than she judged, and she almost fell.

"I suppose there's some consolation to be found, lass." Cethen's hand shot out just in time, steadying her before she slipped from the saddle. When he had her settled again, Jessa saw he was shaking his head, as if resigned. "It will save having to decide whether or not to tell Rhun."

"You know what he will have to do, don't you?" Jessa said quietly, suddenly feeling deeply sorry for the man.

"Oh, aye," Cethen sighed, his shoulders drooping. "And ten blinks of an eye after you tell him, there'll be riders beating their horses eastward."

⚔

Bryn met up with Trista as she returned to Luguvalium. He told her he'd been looking for her and he'd been worried, and she grunted that she didn't care. Neither, really, did Bryn, for his mind was clearly elsewhere. Not that it mattered. She could take care of herself. Though when she looked closer, she realized he probably just wanted to talk to someone – and she was the only person to whom he could bare his mind. And that meant the man was likely changing it again, a reed blowing in the wind. Yet to be honest, Trista mused as she dropped the reins and slid from the horse, there were times when she didn't know which way to bend, either.

The black gelding dropped its head to the grass as they both, without a word, turned and walked down to the river. They stood on the bank saying nothing, staring at the listless current. Trista perversely decided she wasn't going to break the silence and dropped onto the grass to tear off her boots. Casting them aside, she dangled her feet in the cool water. A few moments later she decided the water was more than cool, it was freezing; but she was determined not to remove her feet until he said something. She plucked a few pebbles from the dirt and tossed one in the river, then sat brooding as her annoyance grew. Bryn remained standing over her, staring at nothing.

Finally, unable to bear the silence, she snapped, "So, what happened?"

Bryn heaved a sigh and sat down cross-legged beside her. His eyes remained fixed on the middle of the river, where a gull perched on a large rock, preening its feathers. Trista thought he was going to remain silent and was about to flay him with her tongue, when he finally spoke. "What you said would happen."

"So Ilbrec has them all boiling for battle! And neither you nor Luin nor any of those who support you have the voice to drown his, torque or no torque." Trista angrily tossed the last pebble at the gull and the bird flew off, squawking in protest. "Modan's on his way here with an army, and all Ilbrec and the other hot heads see are Roman forts burning all the way from Luguvalium to – to . . . ah, shit!" She fell silent, not knowing where the last of the Roman forts could be found, or what its name was.

"You know, the man's a fool."

"Who, Modan or Ilbrec?" Trista demanded.

"They're both fools. They're all fools. We're all fools." Bryn smiled wistfully, his eyes still on the rock. "Yet all of them are willing to fight for what they believe in, the moment they see a chance of cracking a Roman shield. There is –"

"So what are you going to do?" Trista asked sharply, as a sinking feeling chilled her insides.

Bryn continued as if he hadn't heard. "There is honour to be found in that, compared to living like sheep, guarded by wolves. The tribes may be far safer under Roman rule, they may even grow fatter, but at what cost? We're all going to . . ."

"The gods save me from the likes!" Trista muttered.

". . . going to die one day, so what does it matter in the end if it's sooner than later? You know, you've got to give him one thing." Bryn tore his eyes from the slow current swirling around the rock and looked into Trista's eyes. "Modan may not have the brains of a gnat, but he's got the balls of a bull!"

Trista snorted her disgust, and the words were out before she could stop them. "Hah, that's a laugh!"

"Huh?" Bryn stared, baffled. "The last thing you can call Modan is a coward."

"Yeah, well, I suppose . . ." Trista's eyes shifted, and she felt her cheeks flush as she stared down at her feet dangling in the icy water. Certain things didn't need saying to Bryn; yet others she needed to hear. What was happening to the man? He wore more skins than an adder. Was he shedding yet another? Only a week or so past, he had been the old Bryn again; now . . .

Trista let her breath go in a great sigh, her mood falling. When they had journeyed across Brigantia she had watched Bryn carefully as he spoke, and at every halt he seemed to gain more certainty of purpose. More than that, he was stronger, much stronger, and far more sure of himself. His father, his brother, the other men who were a part of his past – even the Roman Marcus – had been there, and she could see they shared her feelings. In many ways, it was a return to the days before this whole thing started, when she had looked to Bryn with eyes that were . . .

Trista smiled: with eyes that were warm.

On that last night, the one before he left to mourn Frevan, Bryn had been given a small lodge in the settlement at Calacum. It was crude and not overly neat, but there were several rope-mattressed cots and they had their own blankets. There had been some drinking at the fort, admittedly, but not much; just enough to fill both with its warmth, which was still there as the guards let them out through the gate of the fort. It was there, as Bryn bid them goodnight, that she'd eaten Jessa's small cake, even though it was days past the best time.

It had grown obvious over the past weeks that if ever there was going to be anything more between them than conversation, it was up to her to get it started. She could understand that. Bryn had suffered one humiliation, and he had gone out of his way to show that he would not be subjected to another. Each night was the same. Sometimes Bryn would disrobe in the shadows, and other times it was by the soft yellow light of an oil lamp, for he still insisted on sleeping with no clothes. She wondered if it truly was his habit, or if he simply felt obliged to maintain the lie because it would feel foolish to deny it. Whatever the reason, on the long trek through Brigantia, Trista had seen enough of Bryn's bare butt to last a lifetime.

She sent him to the stable on the pretext of fetching her saddle bag, and the moment he was gone she shed her clothing. The glow was not near as warm as it had been at the fort, and Jessa's concoction seemed to do nothing but make her feel more tired. It was a delicious sort of tired, though, and Trista felt more like stretching out and languishing on her bed than sleeping. *Perhaps that's all the little cake does?* In the meantime the air was cool despite the embers of an earlier fire, and the skin on her arms grew goosebumps as she busied herself laying out the bedding, making a point of keeping her back to the door.

And she waited. Bryn seemed to take forever and she began to feel foolish, standing in the lamplight with her naked body hanging over the bed, settling the blanket on the freshly stuffed pallet of straw for the tenth time. More than once she told herself to sod it; and more than once she was about to do exactly that. Then Trista heard Bryn open the door – *by the gods, I hope it's Bryn!* – and just as she had planned, she whirled about, pretending surprise.

"I wasn't expecting you so soon." Even to herself the words sounded hollow as she half turned, giving Bryn a glimpse of breast and basket before sliding under the blanket where she huddled and, of all things, began to shiver.

"Sorry, I . . ." Bryn said out of reflex, then his mouth tightened and Trista was sure it was to hide his amusement. *Or was he just plain riled?* Then the callous oaf shrugged and tossed the saddlebag on the foot of the bed. "I thought you wanted this."

"I did," Trista said. "I spilled wine on myself, and needed a change."

"Yeah, I can see that."

With infuriating slowness Bryn turned away and began his nightly ritual: boots and liners first; jerkin over the head, followed by undershirt; britches; then finally the underdrawers. Again the tight buttocks glowed in the lamplight, just a glimpse before he slid under his blanket. Bryn had not, Trista noticed, bothered to snuff the lamp. Then he appeared to notice that it was still lit, and asked, "You going to get the light, or me?"

"You."

"Fine, then."

This time Bryn made no pretence of turning, but rose from his bed with an exaggerated sigh, walked to the lamp, and blew out the flame. His body was a shadow as he made his way back, his skin a faint crimson in the glow from the embers of the fire. Bryn might be showing that he felt bored and put-upon, Trista mused as he lay back on the bed and covered himself with the blanket, but there was enough light to see he was not *totally* bored.

She let the silence drag to see if he would say anything, though she knew he wouldn't. Finally, reluctantly, she muttered, "I'm cold."

"You want another blanket?"

*Callous clod!* Trista muttered the words silently to herself, then, aloud, she cried, "No, arsehole, I need someone to warm me up."

"Then why didn't you say so?" Bryn said and again rose from his bed and padded over to hers, where he stood staring down at her; there was enough light to see his cocky grin of amusement as he asked, "You want me to go find someone?"

Trista briefly wondered what he'd do if she told him to do exactly that, but she bit her tongue – he just might. "No, it's probably too late to find anyone worth the having. You'll have to do."

"I thought you'd never ask."

Trista smiled as she remembered the battle of wills, though it was mainly her own that she battled. Their coupling had not been the wild excitement that some of the women talked about. It had, in fact, been nothing extraordinary at all, only with Bryn her mind never wandered and there had been no sullen revulsion as it was with . . .

Trista shook her head and turned her thoughts to the better part of that night, when she lay soft and warm in Bryn's arms as they drifted into sleep. The closeness of his body, the touch of his skin, had been wonderful. And as for the other, well, she supposed that like most things, it was perhaps a start . . .

Trista's wandering mind returned to the stream and her icy feet. She grew aware of Bryn's long silence, and she glanced upward. He continued to stare, his gaze guarded, as if still pondering her words. "What do you know about Modan that I don't, Trista?"

"Not much." She shrugged, wishing he'd just shut is gob.

"How much is not much?"

"Aaahg!" Trista groaned and looked skyward, as if she might find an answer there. One day he was going to find out anyway, she rationalized. It was probably far better that he heard it from her own mouth.

"I asked how much is not much." Bryn spoke sharply this time, and Trista held up a hand. Then, in a mumble, she told him the most of it.

Bryn paled and continued to stare, but it was as if he looked straight through her. After what seemed like an age, he turned his gaze back to the rock in the middle of the stream. For a long while neither said a word. Then, clearly holding back his anger, Bryn raised his hands helplessly, and blurted in a voice that was almost a shout, "Why would they do that?"

"It was the price of letting him live?" Trista shrugged as she spoke, her voice rising to make her words a question. A question could never be a lie.

But Bryn shook his head. "That doesn't make sense. He was on the way to the Roman quarries. Cutting a man would only weaken him." Again Bryn seemed to lapse into thought, then he turned on Trista as if a keystone had been dropped in its frame. "Tuis, his own brother, must have signed the order. How could he do that to his kin? *Why* would he do that to his kin?"

Trista took a deep breath then let it go. Perhaps, in a way, it might be a relief to tell it all, but she quickly found herself passing the blame. "It was Jessa who signed the order."

"Jessa?" Bryn's voice was full of disbelief. "Why would the dwarf order Modan's balls cut out?" Then he promptly answered his own question, and he seemed to accept the sense of it. "Because he tried to kill her!"

"That was after they were plucked," Trista mumbled and immediately wished she'd kept her gob shut. "Plucking them was why he tried to kill her."

"Then she did it because he took her that time, and wouldn't let her go?" Bryn seemed to be looking for excuses, but his tone plainly showed that Jessa's reprisal far outweighed the offence.

Trista clutched her forehead and shook her head in despair. "No, it was because I asked her to do it."

"You what?" Bryn stared in disbelief. "Your own husband!"

"We'd been drinking," Trista mumbled, which was a half truth; there was no need to mention that the final order had been issued in the cold, sober light of morning. "For the love of Dagda, I only asked her to remove one! And believe me, Modan deserved to lose one of his stinking balls, just to curb his arrogant pride. But . . ." she shook her head again, wishing she could change things that could not be changed, "the medicus's clerk skewered the instructions. The Roman healer snipped them both off by mistake."

"Healer? Ha!" Bryn rose to his feet and glared down at Trista, his face twisted in anger. "You castrated your own husband – my brother – because you decided he was too arrogant!"

"There's more to it than that," Trista cried, her own anger rising as she remembered the bone twisting, the bruising, the pain; the harsh, cutting words and the humiliation; and the mad, brutal rutting – whether she was willing or not. "And I didn't say to have him castrated! Not totally!"

"All this, on the back of everything else!" Bryn said bitterly.

For a moment he just stood there, as if deciding what to do. Then he spat on the ground, turned on one heel, and strode over to his horse. Muttering words that Trista could not hear, he swung into the saddle and wrenched the animal's head sideways to face Luguvalium. Without another word, he lashed the end of the reins down on the animal's rump, and it leapt forward.

Trista climbed to her feet and watched numbly as horse and rider raced off along the riverbank. The inside of her belly felt empty; yet, in some odd manner, her mind felt both sadness and relief. She started toward her horse, tripped, and almost tumbled; she glanced downward, suddenly aware that she wore no boots, and her feet had no feeling. Heaving an enormous sigh of exasperation, Trista sank down on the grass, then fell on her back and lay gazing blankly upward at the scudding clouds. What next?

# Chapter XXXIX

# Luguvalium, September, A.D. 105

Lagan had insisted on one unbreakable rule when leading his tribal army, and he'd worded it plainly enough: he, Lagan, was that army's head, and everybody else was the body and the tail. The canny chieftain had told his people that this was no different than a man himself: the head might listen to what the body tells him, but the head tells the body what to do, and if the result is a wagging tail, then so much the better. Modan had found the comparison simple enough, and the wagging part amusing. Then he and Eupo had abandoned Lagan, taking everyone with them but some of the Selgovae, but a good many of them had come along, too.

Oddly enough, Lagan wasn't that concerned with losing a major part of his army and for that Modan was relieved. Had the Selgovae held his sword firm on that one, then blood would have flowed by the bucket, and only the gods knew whose. Eupo had been prepared to challenge Lagan, though the Caledoni claimed it was not for the leadership, because that would have been far too bloody. It was because of the manner in which Lagan was leading, and Modan agreed. Both of them were no longer willing to simply peck at the Romans and hope they'd bleed to death; not with Frevan now dead and the torque promised to brother Bryn. This was the time for a man strong enough to lead the tribes to seize Brigantia's neck ring, and wear it proudly.

Yet on the march down to Luguvalium, Modan began to suspect that Eupo figured on tying a rope to that neck ring, and holding it like a leash. He was uncomfortably reminded of Lagan likening an army to a man's body, with only one head needed to guide it. The trouble was, this new army seemed to have two heads, and sometimes more like a dozen; and as to the part about controlling the body, sometimes that was like trying to lead a squealing pig.

By force of will, he and Eupo had prodded the ant-like army through the countless hills and glens that lay to the northeast of Luguvalium. The trek had taken nigh on four days, and even at that it had been a hard push. It ended when the colourful procession forded the Ituna a good four hours march upstream of the fort, and edged its way toward the stronghold under the doubtful cover of darkness. Modan and Eupo made camp that night less than four miles away, within sight of the settlement's flickering fires. And it was there, despite a firm belief that the final leg of the march had been secretly carried out in the black of night, that Modan received visitors.

He was surprised – no, stunned – as the three shadowy figures were led into the circle of light cast by the campfire. As always, when words of wisdom failed, Modan lashed out. "Are you here to admit defeat or to join us? Or did they toss you out and you're here begging shelter?"

A hundred or more crowded the small fire and their voices, which moments before had been baying a chorus, fell silent. Modan was grateful, for his voice had been loudest among them, gaining nothing as he argued the following day's assault on the fort. Now the whole lot of them sat staring like a pack of drooling wolves. He blinked, more than ever aware of the likeness. There was a growing division between his own people and those who followed Eupo. It wasn't lost on Modan that the fickle horde of Selgovae chieftains that abandoned Lagan had for the most part fallen in with the Caledoni. It made his gut boil! The bone headed hill-climber was as ignorant as a swamp toad. Lagan would not have put up with him, and for that Modan missed the man. The more so now . . .

He glared at Treno, who sat with his ugly mouth open off to his right, and said, "Well don't gawp, get something where they can set their arses."

Treno rolled a log forward so that Bryn, Cethen, and Criff could sit down, then he quietly disappeared into the darkness. None of the three said a word and the hum of chatter began again, this time more subdued.

Modan spoke, his voice again edged with sarcasm. "So which is it?"

"I came to visit my brother, that's all." Bryn's eyes swept the sea of faces. "Da came to see his son and Criff's here because he's Criff. We hoped to see you with less of an audience."

"Yeah, well, at the moment that doesn't seem possible," Modan growled, though as he followed Bryn's eyes he wished it was.

The likeness to wolves was even more apparent, and if the clods had pointy ears they'd all have been pricked. Modan felt uneasy at the image, for this was his kin and he needed to talk to them. Yet of late a man couldn't even have a decent piss without fifty or more watching him. He could see why Lagan insisted that no more than a favoured few be present at such gatherings; numbers like this were only seen when the Selgovae chieftain was giving orders. Even then, the man had always made a point of visiting each group first, to talk about what was going on. That seemed to satisfy the clods, and it made everyone feel they were special. Maybe he should . . .

"Then I'll make it brief," Bryn said, his voice just as curt. "You will attack Luguvalium tomorrow, but you won't succeed. The stronghold is heavily defended by trained troops. I just wanted you –"

"So what are *you* doing, then? Helping the Romans, or cringing in the hills with the rest of the tribe while you strut about with the torque?"

"Hey," Eupo sneered, calling out from the far side of the fire where he sat with his own people. "You come here under no agreed truce. You're either with us, or you're dead."

"And hey, you! This is my da and my brother!" Modan glared at the man and rose to his feet, his voice just as hard. There was a matter of pride here. If anyone was going to threaten his kin, it would be him. "You raise even a fist and there'll be no battle tomorrow, because there'll be one tonight. And a great big bloody one, starting right now. So either . . ."

A low growl rumbled around the fire and people began climbing to their feet. Cethen reached up and pulled sharply on Modan's belt, forcing him down again. "Son, listen to your brother, for once." He glared at Eupo and spoke louder, sprinkling in words from the Caledonii dialect. "And you! I fought with Galgar, a great Caledoni who could control both his temper and his people. Let us all do the same."

"Hah, listen to that!" an older, grey-haired man sitting beside Eupo said, his voice full of scorn. "You couldn't even control your own wife. Galgar was humping the hide off her, and you killed the poor woman for it."

That was too much for Modan. He lurched forward, restrained only by Cethen's hand on his belt. "That's a snivelling lie, you prick – nosed gobby! My da spared Galgar's life! He had his sword poked up the man's arse, then *made* him take the woman off his hands! It was –"

"Listen to you! Listen!" Bryn was on his feet with his arms outstretched, shouting to be heard; he turned first to Eupo, then to his brother. "Your enemy isn't here! He's over there!" He jabbed a finger across the river, anger making his voice hard. "Keep brawling like this and tomorrow the Romans will bury your dead, without having tossed a spear or drawn a sword."

Bryn paused, waiting, his relief obvious as the shouting slowly faded and a few of the Caledoni sat down. He looked toward Modan, who sat muttering under his breath, his face hot and angry. Bryn shook his head impatiently. "So let's say you do breach the walls tomorrow. What's next? Are you hoping to do it in one day then fly off with the faerie before the Roman governor's army gets back here from Coria? Or do you plan on fighting it, too?"

Modan looked at Eupo and saw the Caledoni was equally surprised. What did Bryn mean: *gets back here?* "It depends on how large his army is," Modan improvised, as he tried to make sense of what he was hearing. That a Roman army would be sent from somewhere had never been in doubt; but he and Eupo figured it had already been sent, and sat at Habitancum, too frightened to move. That fact alone showed who had who by the ears! And if another army was to follow it, by then the whole north would be aflame . . .

"I don't believe they know," Criff murmured, in a tone that suggested an amusing story might be in the making.

"Shit, they don't!" Cethen muttered, loud enough to be heard all around the fire.

"Know what?" Modan blurted, annoyed at the disdain he heard in his da's voice.

Bryn answered. "I guess we thought you were being brilliant, little brother, cutting through the hills and bypassing the governor while the main Roman army marches east to Coria." He laughed at the irony. "I thought you'd deliberately given him the slip after he left here."

Modan curbed his tongue before the words "what main Roman army?" could bumble from his mouth, making them all even bigger fools. Ignoring the rumble of concern building around the flames, he tried to absorb what Bryn had just told him; and when he finally did, he tried to figure what, exactly, had happened. Another army had been here ahead of them! But if the Romans were still marching east, then maybe there was still . . .

"When did they leave?"

"Yesterday, around midday."

"How many?"

"About ten thousand."

"Fuck!" Modan felt a shaft of ice spear his back. He glanced at Eupo, but the man was hotly arguing with those sitting nearby – as, it seemed, was everyone else within hearing. "And you came to tell me this?"

"He's lying," Eupo shouted, a sentiment echoed by a score of others.

"Hey, I've nothing to gain in telling you; and it's easy enough to confirm." Bryn gestured toward the settlement downriver then shrugged, as if to show that none of this was his concern. "You've probably got one –"

Bryn quickly shut his gob and Modan was sure he knew why. "We've probably got one good chance at it, and if that doesn't work, we slope off," he said, finishing Bryn's words as the idea settled on his mind. He locked eyes with Eupo, and he saw that their minds were for once one on this: *The glory to be found, should such a deed succeed!*

Modan's gaze shifted briefly to Criff, then back to his brother. "If we take this place, it will just be the start. And we'll do it right under their Roman noses!"

"Songs of glory will be sung, for certain." Criff grinned as if seeing Modan's vision of triumph. "*If* you take the fort at Luguvalium."

"Not if, when," Modan growled.

Eupo ignored the bard as he sat nodding agreement. He'd clearly had enough of Criff and Modan's kin. "We need to talk, Modan; all of us, and only us. Your brother's given his news."

"That's not really why we came here." Bryn raised a hand to stop further talk. "We figured you already knew about the Roman army wandering the hills." He seemed unable to keep the wonder from his voice, and Modan could have bashed him for his smugness. "I came to tell my brother that I'm no longer part of this. To be honest, I'm tired of the whole mess."

Modan blinked, then stared at Bryn in surprise. What was the fool saying? "How can you say that?" he blurted, even as his mind churned over the advantages. "You owe it to Frevan."

"Frevan would have agreed with what I'm doing," Bryn replied. "He knew what could be done and what couldn't, and he accepted that. Just like me. You're going to lose this tomorrow, Modan, and I know the best thing for our people is to stay out of it. They'll suffer less, and there'll be no reprisals."

"They'll not stay out," Modan growled, for Treno had assured him that some, maybe even most, were already waiting.

"Not all of them," Bryn conceded, and shrugged as if helpless, "and I understand that. There's no honour to be found in not fighting; in fact, many will find only shame if they don't. So I told Ilbrec, Luin, and the others to do what they want. I'll not challenge their right to choose. You might even want to meet with them." Bryn smiled, and added dryly, "To be honest, I wouldn't be surprised if Ilbrec was already on his way here."

"But you're not going to take sides?" Modan muttered, just to be certain, though he wasn't surprised. And his brother was talking about his people being shamed! Bryn's stance did solve the problem of what to do with him, though, especially with Eupo across the fire looking for blood. Allowing his brother to leave here might not pose a problem after all...

"How can I? I've got a brother here," Bryn bowed his head toward Modan, then placed a hand on Cethen's shoulders, "and my da will also be outside the fort's walls. Inside, though, is another brother, along with an uncle who found me after Galgar's defeat, and raised me. If I fight on either side, I'll be fighting kin." Bryn shook his head. "I don't want to do that."

"So what about the great torque?" Modan's eyes narrowed, for its present whereabouts had been yet another surprise. There were getting to be too many surprises, and he wondered what others lay hidden along his path. "They tell me you now have it."

Bryn shook his head. "Not with me, but that's a fair comment. Modan, should you win tomorrow and drive the Romans from our land, then it's yours – but not until then." He grinned wryly. "It's better that way. It gives you something to fight for."

"Da, does he really not have the sodding thing with him?" Modan tried to stand and found he couldn't move. Cethen shook his head, but still held tight to the belt. Modan turned, resisting the urge to thump the man. "Let go, will you?" He forced his way to his feet and stared down at his father, keeping his voice low and the words private. "Where do you stand on this?"

Cethen rose and placed a hand on Modan's shoulder, as if in apology. "I know how Bryn feels on this. I'll likely be with him."

Modan reluctantly nodded his understanding. "And where will that be?"

"It doesn't matter what happens tomorrow, once it's over Bryn will be going back to Frevan's own village – the old hill fort, back in the hills. It seems like a good place to live."

Modan grunted as the image came to mind: a cosseted lodge overlooking a distant lake surrounded by steep hills, and boats tied to a long, narrow dock. He looked disdainfully at his brother. "Bryn, you'll be an old man before you're forty. Are you taking my wife with you?"

"At the moment, we don't appear to be speaking to each other." Bryn smiled, a lopsided smile that made Modan's heart lurch, for it reminded him of kinder, younger days. "We seem to have a disagreement on how the Romans treat their prisoners." He placed a hand on Modan's shoulder, and held it there. "As to the next few days, I wish you the luck of them. Who knows, you may prevail. I know you've truly got the balls for it!"

※

Modan ordered one of his men to lead the three back through the sprawling camp to where their horses had been taken from them. They had hardly started out when Treno loomed out of the darkness. Following him was a Roman woman, who walked between two other men who appeared to be her guard. Her features were dimmed, for she trailed several paces behind the flame of Treno's torch, hidden by the shadows. Cethen was at first unable to see who it was, beyond registering an older woman with finely chiselled features of the sort that held back the years; a woman who moved with an ease that defied even the years she did have.

Bryn stopped and said, "Ma'am."

Criff chuckled and bowed his head. "Elena. This will make my tale a legend."

Behind him, Cethen muttered a single, barely audible expletive.

"I thought you should know who's also in our camp," Treno said. "It might temper matters, should things go wrong for us."

Cethen nodded, barely hearing the words above the thumping of his heart. *What twisted, witless, ill-humoured god had brought Elena here? And what, in the name of the same god, does it mean?* He stood numbly staring at his wife as if lost in a dream. Then he smiled, for it was Elena who broke the long silence and that was the way it had always been; only this time it wasn't because he was being stubborn, but because he had simply been struck dumb.

"You look well, Cethen," she said softly.

*Her voice hasn't changed.* "So do you," he murmured, vaguely aware that Bryn had turned and was staring at him. Cethen shook his head to rid it of dust, and grasped his son's arm. His eyes still locked on Elena's, he said, "Bryn, this is the mother of my first three children."

"Bryn." Elena nodded, then chuckled as she turned and replied to the bard's greeting. "Criff, the last thing I want to be is a legend."

"Aye, but what a . . ."

"Elena?" Bryn's voice sounded as stunned as his own; and his next words came without thinking. "That makes her the mam of the Roman governor."

"And also of the man who's defending Luguvalium," Treno observed, and laughed at the admission. "It took a while, but Modan already knew from Gavor who the governor was, and he figured out the rest. Mod's not the fastest thinker, but he's a vicious one. He has a rare hatred for the governor."

"Which means?" Bryn asked and Cethen, his mind half frozen by the ice that gripped it, realized the question's target.

Elena answered. "Eupo and Modan thought they might ransom me for the fort," she said contemptuously. "An old woman for a thousand men! That's a notion even more absurd than assaulting the place. The trouble is, once you name a ransom you're stuck with its terms."

Bryn smiled bitterly. "And if you're stuck with the terms and the ransom is not honoured, you must kill the hostage. However, if you . . ."

"If you already know that the ransom will not be honoured because it's a bone-brained demand to begin with," Elena glared at Treno, who merely smiled, "you might just as well murder the hostage and save the oratory."

"As the lady explained to Modan in great detail," Treno added, his tattooed face splitting in a hideous grin. "She also explained that killing the mam of a Roman governor would assure the death of every barbarian man, woman, and child between here and – as I recall the words – the arse end of Caledonia." Treno laughed as he finished. "It was decided not to ransom the governor's mam, at least not for the fort. Modan listened to her other suggestion instead."

*Which means he's finally using his brain*, Cethen thought. "And Eupo listened too?"

"Him too. The lady pointed out her value should our fortunes fail, though she phrased the words much riper." Treno grinned.

"Have you seen Rhun, Cethen? Is he well?" Elena asked.

Cethen nodded. "Yeah, he's fine. So was Tuis, but I haven't seen him for weeks and weeks." He tried to make light of the question. "He's got more fat on the bone than's good for him." He looked at Treno. "I don't suppose there's anything we can offer you to let her go with us?"

Treno shook his head, plainly amused. "Not unless it's worth more to me than my life, and I can't think of anything that is." He gestured in the direction Luguvalium. "I suppose you'd best leave, if we're expecting more visitors."

"Yeah, I suppose," Cethen muttered, his tongue seeming to have abandoned him. The last he'd seen of Elena was on yet another battlefield, and he smiled at the memory. She'd called him a daft bugger then, though she hadn't meant it. "It was good to see you before a battle, Elena, rather than after. Be safe."

"And it was good to see you, Cethen. Be safe."

All the way back to the settlement, Cethen's thoughts were of nothing but his former wife. He'd heard from his oldest son about the death of her – her what? Husband? Lover? Owner? Cethen sighed. The Roman was her husband, he had to admit it; though whatever he was, Cethen supposed it no longer mattered. The man had obviously done well for Elena, something that had once rubbed as hard on his mind as a festering saddle sore. The very idea had made him feel helpless, less than a man. Yet now, oddly, he wished her the best of what the Roman had given her. Maybe it was because the the poor bugger had finally died – an event he'd once dearly longed for. And if he was honest, there was a certain satisfaction in learning that he'd outlived the thieving stoat. It might be the only matter on which he'd ever bested the man!

That less than worthy notion had flitted through his mind as he stood alongside Treno, gazing at Elena, and he knew what she would have said if she'd known. His wife was a woman who could trade words with any man she chose, and in years past that had certainly included him! Cethen smiled as he remembered. She'd no doubt done equally well in Rome. That had always been the way of it, ever since they were children. His da had more than once told him to watch out for "the woman," warning, *"Her blade's honed sharper than yours, son."* Cethen smiled at the memory; he'd taken a certain pride in that.

But what now?

Cethen was certain that he and Elena would survive the next day or two, for with a Roman army so near that would be the end of it – unless, of course, Modan backed off, which he was clearly not going to do. Then what? After all these years, what did the gods have in mind? Their hands were clearly deep into this, all the way to their scheming armpits. Surely they hadn't brought the two of them together as a prelude to death? Bards did sing of such things around the campfires . . .

Cethen vigorously shook his head to rid it of the notion. Yet if that wasn't the reason, then what was? Another thought struck ice in his heart. Was it to witness the death of one of their sons, or more than one son?

He shook his head even harder. It had to be something else! Perhaps the gods were just being kind, and had brought them together to rekindle the embers of old fires? Hardly! After all this time, Cethen had been surprised to find no stirring of passion on seeing Elena – something he'd imagined often and fondly over the long years. No, for the first time, Cethen realized that was not to be. If anything, he felt only an odd need to gain her approbation.

# Chapter XL

# Luguvalium, September, A.D. 105

Luguvalium was blessed with water. The Ituna River flowed a few hundred paces to the north of the fort before winding a half-dozen miles to the west, where it emptied into its huge estuary. Two lesser rivers flowed directly from the south to join with the greater river. One ran close by the west side of the stronghold, and the other a short walk to the east. The fort itself sat between them all on a broad rise. The view from any one of the four gate towers could be breathtaking, the more so when an enemy army massed thousands of warriors on the fields below.

The sun was barely a thumb's width clear of the horizon, revealing a day that had dawned with a crisp freshness in the air. First light had seen the broad pastures cloaked in a thick coat of rime from an early frost, which the rising sun had softened to a glistening dew. That, too, would quickly disappear with the soft morning breeze that blew in from the sea. A mere speckle of hazy white clouds dotted the sky, promising fair weather and the blessing of the gods. Though whose gods remained to be seen, Jessa decided as she climbed the last few steps leading up onto the fort's wall.

She rubbed her hands together for the warmth, her breath clouding as she peered over the wooden parapet. Standing on her ever-present stool in order to see, she was struck by the incongruity of it all. As Modan's army assembled on the field, a pish-posh of bright colour and chattering, shouting voices, the atmosphere was almost one of a fair. Like everyone else inside the fort, she wondered just what he and his mongrel force of warriors hoped to gain.

Modan could only figure on a speedy attack, and an even speedier burning. But this was Luguvalium. It was not the poorly manned forts he'd found so far. There were enough of them out there, certainly; only the gods knew how many thousands had gathered. And to nobody's surprise, many of the Carvetii from the settlement were joining in, under the prodding fingers of Ilbrec. Since first light they had been seeping across the small river from their makeshift camp; but as Rhun had said, if they had the faintest hope of success, it lay with a single, overwhelming attack. If that didn't carry the day, then Modan had better flee like the whipped hound that he was, before he found two legions clawing at his back.

The move was so bold that even Rhun was haunted with the notion that he might have missed something. Jessa, however, was sure that Modan was simply puffed up following a string of cheap victories, and now looked for the golden torque through greedy eyes. Yet even so . . .

"Frevan's funeral should have been back in the hills," Trista complained. "All his bleating mourners would still be there, nursing headaches and sour guts."

"This is where he chose to have it, though," Jessa murmured, and glanced over her shoulder. The sun sparkled across the deep blue of the river, and in the distance the north shore of the broad estuary lay cloaked in a hazy blanket of purple and green. "There are far worse places to be buried." Then her eyes fell on the jumble of the civilian settlement, and she sighed. "For the most part, anyway."

"Not at the moment," Trista muttered and shivered, her arms folded as she stared at the crowded fields.

"Where's Bryn on this?" Jessa asked, returning her gaze to where Modan's lines were forming, well beyond the range of missiles.

"Last I saw of him was late last afternoon. He was fit to bend horseshoes on his teeth. He – he was upset."

"Like a raging bear or a frightened rabbit?"

"A raging *she*-bear. It slipped out about Modan's loss."

*How does something like that slip out?* "Didn't you explain?"

"He wasn't listening by then," Trista said, and smiled wanly. "Before that, he was bitching about everyone wanting to fight rather than bide their time; then he said there was honour to be found in that. The fighting, I mean. The man didn't know his own mind from a mule's."

"You sound like Cethen's first wife." Cian's voice startled them, his arrival masked by the clamour both inside and outside the fort.

The walkways along the parapet were crowded with soldiers readying their weapons, or just staring out over the palisades. The fort's *ballistae* had been deployed, spaced along the wall close by the stairways, the weapons loaded and the two-man crews sighting the bolts. Hundreds of soldiers were stationed along the intervallum, for the most part doing little other than looking occupied; they'd be responsible for relieving any part of the wall that became hard-pressed. Toward the centre of the fort horses waited, their saddles loosely cinched, their riders ready to burst through the gates in pursuit of a defeated enemy or, if the gods were unkind, try clearing him from the streets.

"You come to move us off the walls?" Jessa asked. She'd been expecting somebody to do that, but so far nobody had shown up with the rank to dare.

"That depends. Which side do you want to be tossed?" Cian wedged himself between the two women and set his hands on top of the parapet. "There's a lot of them."

"You worried?"

"Naw. There was far more at Graupius, and we didn't have a fort to hide in." Cian gestured vaguely toward the east. "And there was no hope of the cavalry coming to the rescue. In fact, we were the cavalry." He glanced sideways at Trista. "You don't know where Bryn's got himself to, then?"

Trista shook her head.

"Cethen came by late last night," Cian continued, his voice full of regret. "He says Bryn went over to Modan, and he –"

"He went over to Modan!" Jessa shouted, stunned that the man would do such a thing. Not after all that had been done for him! And there was the torque. Had the torque blinded him?

"Have patience, lass, have patience," Cian chided. "He *saw* Modan last night, and told the lad that he'd had enough. He's backed off on telling people what to do and told Ilbrec, Luin, and the others to take their choice. That's why you saw so many creeping over the river this morning. Not that it matters." He snorted as if at the waste of it. "It's like they're all farting in the wind: we might catch the smell, but no one's going to get covered in – well, you know."

"Do you know where he is, Cian?" Trista looked worried.

"Don't worry, girl. Other than giving up on leading people, he's not done anything rash. He'll be going back to Frevan's old hill fort to chew his nails, pick his nose, and dwell on the future of Rome and the tribes. He should have just come and seen me first, I could have told him. I came to terms with it years ago." He grinned and slapped her on the back. "But that's not why I'm here. I wanted to talk to you about what else Cethen told us. Or I should say, the part he decided to tell us."

"Us?" Jessa asked.

"Yeah, Rhun and me. He came here in the middle of the night waving Gaius's old pardon like it was a token for a seat at the games. It seems . . ." Cian paused, as if to give more effect to his words, "that when Marius Appius marched north with the Ninth, he lost Rhun and Tuis's mam on the way. Modan has her."

Jessa and Trista stared at each other in disbelief. Jessa glanced instinctively toward where Modan must be, lost somewhere in the middle of the sea of tribesmen. She grew numbly aware that something was happening out there, for a rumble of noise was building – yet all she could think of was that Modan had the governor's mother! It was so tragic it was almost laughable. Yet at the same time, it might explain the man's boldness.

As if reading her mind, Cian spoke again. "If you think the gods don't have their hand in that one, consider this!" He almost choked as he told the rest of it. "You were right. Modan didn't even know there was a second, larger Roman army on his arse, yet he passed it by as if he'd planned it!"

*And that, more than anything else, explains why the fool is here!* Jessa realized.

"What are you doing, girl?" a voice roared, making them all jump. "The gods are fickle enough. There's no need to pick their noses with a needle!"

Jessa groaned at the sound of the voice, and turned. "We were just getting ready to leave, Father."

"And none too soon," Marcus said as the nearby walkway magically cleared of soldiers, leaving ample room for a senator to peer over the parapet. A loud, steady chanting had started among the ranks of Modan's army, vying with the dull, throbbing beat of weapons hammering on shields. "It won't be long before they'll have themselves worked up enough to try."

The two women made their way down the ladder, and for once Jessa found she was quite willing to obey. Marcus leaned down and whispered as she passed by, "I imagine you're on the way to the hospital?"

"Yes."

"Then you might want to keep an eye out on the street in front of the commander's residence."

"Is that where the cavalry grouped?"

Marcus raised his eyebrows, feigning surprise. "Hmm, I suppose it could be."

Jessa smiled, and continued down the ladder. Her father had seemed obtuse for the longest time, but he finally seemed to be catching on.

Modan's doubts faded as the roar of voices numbed his ears, and the rhythmic thump of pounding weapons flooded his brain. His blood flowed hot and he laughed at Eupo, who sat his horse a hundred paces away. The man's face split into a wide grin and he raised his spear in a wild thrusting motion, then turned his horse toward the walls of the fort. Modan did the same, both men screaming the order to advance, their voices lost in the din. On every side the great mass of warriors surged forward, roaring and screaming as they ran across the open turf. Modan felt the thumping pulse of life fill his veins like never before.

Hardly a man was mounted, for the animals were useless against the walls. But someone had to see what was happening, and Modan pulled back on the reins as his horse found itself swept up in the flow. He saw Treno off to his left struggling to do the same, each of them weaving like a small ship tossed on a boiling sea. A hundred other riders, each one a chieftain leading his kin, rode high above the swollen ranks, most choosing to be swept forward with the tide. There could be no stopping this, Modan decided, as warriors raced by all around him, each one determined to breach the wall.

Modan blinked as a half-dozen small, dark shadows seemed to leap from the ramparts, and a hail of arrows arced upward from beyond the notched openings that topped the wall. A loud thud, followed by a sickening scream, sounded just off to his right, and his horse lurched sideways as if hit. Modan cursed, then saw that two writhing men had been flung against the animal's rump as they tumbled, spitted by the same huge bolt. Modan blanched, realizing the force of the weapon. For the moment the sight unnerved him, for it was different than any other he'd seen; compared to an arrow or a spear, it was oddly unfair. Then his horse carried him past, and he quickly forgot the two dying men.

He squinted ahead, grateful to find that the barrage was not one-sided. A steady stream of tiny black dots flitted upward as the slingers launched their small, deadly missiles. Only they weren't so deadly now, for the slingers were being pushed along with the rest of them, forced to fling the heavy stones on the run. It was impossible to see what effect they had. As he watched more arrows flew from the wall, and some arched back, as a second dark volley of the lethal bolts erupted from the wooden crenellations. The forward ranks were closing, though, running into what would be the most deadly rain of all. Modan watched and waited, tensing as it came.

A ragged volley of spears spewed from the battlements, as each Roman manning the wall stepped forward and launched a *pilum*. The advance faltered for the first time and he saw men drop – or just as bad, struggle to free a bent Roman spear, now wedged in a shoulder or dragging on a useless shield. But the chieftains screamed their anger and the relentless army of thousands would not be denied: the headlong charge gushed on.

A second volley of Roman spears arced out and more men fell away as the advance disappeared into the deep ditch that ringed the fort. Men reappeared, scrambling up the far side of the steep rampart and closing on the wall. This, Modan knew, was where most of the dead would later be found. He held his breath. The wooden barrier was not high. The lowest parts of its notched crest stood hardly taller than a man's chest; the highest, not much above his head. But the earth rampart in front dropped sharply, the steep slope near doubling the height. And when a man did gain the top, the sharp incline left him an arm's length from the wall, and the top well above his head. All advantage lay with the Romans, especially with a shield thrust forward and a sword poking a man's eye.

There were too few scaling ladders, Modan realized. They were needed not only for the wall, but the slope leading up to it so men could gain a firm footing on the dew soaked sides of the ditch. Lagan should have told him that! A warrior was already disadvantaged when he reached the wall: the man on the slope stood head and shoulders below the defending Roman, and didn't need his feet slipping at the same time. Nor did the ones who followed him: each of them pushing the man ahead, and all trying desperately to boost someone, anyone, over the wall.

Modan anxiously bit down on his lip. Maybe there were enough men to offset the lack of ladders, for he was sure the wall could be breached – he had no doubt of it. But how many dead would it cost first, and would the men stand for it?

☩

Rhun had worked long and hard during his younger years to maintain a calm, confident mien in battle, even as his gut churned and his mind threatened panic. There was little to be done about the churning; that happened all by itself. But if a man caught the panic before it seized his mind, then he had it mastered. Rhun's means was threefold: think first, be decisive, and keep the mind occupied. And maybe a fourth factor was in there, too: optimism. There was always a way out of a crisis; sometimes, it just wasn't obvious. Besides, when it came to *appearing* calm, it was far easier if a thousand men were looking at you – even if thousands more were clawing at your walls.

Training had also taught Rhun early that a commander had no business on the walls, despite an inbred instinct to be there. To do so placed him in the same position as the soldier he led: aware only of what was happening within yards of where he stood. One thrust of a spear could leave his command headless. It was a miracle that Alexander lived as long as he did; though history, Rhun knew, was written by the victors and the flatterers, and perhaps he never did fight in the front ranks....

When word of Trimontium reached him, Rhun remembered *Vetera* and the razing of the huge fortress by its own troops thirty five years ago. Tall, shielded platforms had later been raised in the intervallum, close by the main gates. Each provided a clear view along every wall, and most of what lay beyond. Rhun had done the same at Luguvalium. It was from the top of the east platform that he spied the vanguard of Tuis's army, long before Modan or any of his people were aware of it. Rhun simply smiled and ordered everyone to keep their hands down and not point, and their mouths shut. In the meantime, he breathed easier . . .

The tower-like structure was not large. Only a half-dozen officers crowded the deck at any given time. Runners and aides came and went, frantically climbing the ladder-like steps as orders were bellowed down to others on the ground. The attack had not long been underway and Rhun, now far less concerned, saw that the frenzied assault was being pressed hard and making surprising progress.

A thunderous roar erupted from south of the gate. A good part of the wall had been overrun, the gap spreading like fire to a stretch maybe twenty, thirty yards wide. Britons were tumbling over the top, falling every which way as they were pushed upward by those on the other side. A dozen squads of infantry reserves were already closing in, running along the intervallum below. A contingent of archers burst from between the rows of barrack buildings, then a second one, bows strung and arrows nocked. Rhun watched calmly, but with hands tight on the railing, as hours of drill played out . . .

The Britons seemed at first confused but most kept going, stumbling down the short rampart and dropping the last several feet where the earthen bank was shored and cut short. Beyond that, they met slaughter. The infantry was merciless, the front rank grimly stabbing as the rear hurled heavy, iron-tipped spears upward at the Britons still pouring over the wall. Then the archers began firing, a steady volley at a range so short it was deadly. The walkway topping the rampart clogged with bodies, both wounded and dead. Some of the Britons climbing over the top tried to turn back, others pushed from behind, and still more tumbled over the wall and down the rampart.

Despite the slaughter, the spears and the arrows were not enough. The narrow breach slowly widened, as those beyond the wall rushed to reinforce what doubtless appeared from the outside to be a major breach. Rhun turned to order more men up – the centurios on the ground should have been handling that – then he saw they already were. More infantry were streaming up the steps down by the gate, and some had already gained the walkway. Rhun recognized the centurio leading them, a man called Donicus. *Remember that name for later!* The centurio hurried along the walkway, bullying his way behind the men defending the wall, pushing and shoving as he struggled toward the breach. Behind him trotted an endless line of infantry, shields facing the battlements and swords ready.

Donicus reached the first of the tribesmen, a man still struggling to his feet. Rhun winced as the centurio's sword stabbed out as he stepped deftly to one side, roaring at the men who followed, his voice lost in the din. The line of infantry began hacking its way along the walkway, slowly cutting into the stream of Britons clambering over the walls. The archers continued their vollies from between the buildings, and the soldiers defending below on the intervallum were finally holding steady. And more were arriving, as Rhun heard the steady tramp of running feet echo from behind the tower.

His grip eased on the rail and a grim smile crossed his face. Someone had finally organized the soldiers on the other side of the breach, and men were now fighting their way across to Donicus. The gap was closing fast, and the luck of those caught on this side of the walls was fast running out. Some were already trying to give up, mainly those who'd just tumbled madly over the wall into a hail of arrows and discovered what awaited. But it was too soon, there were still too many, and his infantry were still fighting for their lives. When the fury eased and centurios on the ground had the fighting clearly in hand, then some of the poor fools might be lucky . . .

Rhun nodded his satisfaction and turned his attention to the thousands hammering at his walls. Modan's warriors had become an unruly, screaming mob that swept like a bubbling current around three sides of the stronghold. At first glance the attacking horde seemed almost aimless, intent on engulfing the fort rather than fighting to get inside. Yet it was only because none of them, try as they might, had forced another breach. The steep ditch was clogged with men and . . .

Something bounced with crushing force off Rhun's shoulder and he staggered, his arm too numbed to register pain. He glanced downward expecting to find blood, but there was nothing. Then one of his centurios bent down and lifted a rock to his eyes, and he realized he'd been struck by a slinger. A touch higher and off to the right – Rhun smiled and shrugged. The shoulder would hurt like daggers later on. He flexed the arm and hoped the bone wasn't damaged.

"Sir, sir," a new voice called out from behind, cracking with excitement. "The governor is here. Look. Look."

"Put your fucking hand down!" Rhun snapped at whoever it was, for the moment losing his detached calm. Then, quickly regretting the sudden outburst – it was young Kaeso, no doubt sent here for orders – he placed a hand lightly on the lad's shoulder. "He's been there for a while, lad, but there's no sense telling the world that, is there? The longer we keep the enemy occupied, the closer the governor gets before he's noticed. This early, it's probably no more than the legions' cavalry, anyway."

Red-faced, Kaeso nodded. "The praefectus sent me to get an update, sir."

Rhun's eyes returned to the dark smudge that edged across the horizon. So far, there *was* nothing but cavalry to be seen out there. Had Tuis sent them ahead of his army to relieve the fort? Was the infantry marching right behind? It made little difference. Just their presence would cause panic among Modan's people – which would signal the time for the fort's own cavalry to reap the advantage. "Yes, report to your commander, and tell him to assemble all the riders he can muster – half at the south gate, the other half here at the east gate. You, young man, will ride with those at the east gate. There is something I need done."

Kaeso drew himself up to his full height. "What is that, sir?"

"You'll look for my mother." Rhun smiled, amused at the absurdity of the order amid the din of a full-blown battle. "Report back here when all's ready, and I'll tell you how."

"Sir." Kaeso scrambled from the tower so fast that Rhun was afraid he'd tumble.

Moments later another figure appeared, his head rising over the top rung of the ladder. "It's getting thick and heavy, how are we holding out?" Marcus shouted while still three rungs from the top. "I saw there was a breach. Your assessment?" He clambered onto the wooden deck, his breathing heavy, and fixed worried eyes on the horde of screaming tribesmen pounding against the walls.

Rhun face turned grim, deliberately offering a vague answer. "I'd say less than a half-hour, and it'll be all over."

"Huh?" Marcus swung his gaze to Rhun, his expression shocked; then he glanced at the others on the platform, frowning his concern. "We can hold out longer than that!" He lowered his voice to a hiss. "What kind of talk is that?"

"Me? The words 'hold out' are yours, Marcus, not mine." Rhun lightened his tone. "But if you want to talk about just holding out, I suppose we can do that all day, if you want. I'm talking about ending it."

Marcus's expression eased. "So how do you figure on doing that in a half-hour?"

"I sent young Kaeso off to ready the cavalry. I'm sending them out the south gate, as well as this one." Rhun waved a hand airily toward the east gate, where the fighting was the fiercest. "They'll have them on the run all the way –"

"You can't do that." Marcus lowered his voice, glancing warily about the tower. "What are you trying to do, kill the boy?"

"Marcus, I'm not that inept." Rhun grinned, and nodded casually toward the horizon. "I'm not going to order him out there until Tuis's cavalry strikes them from the rear."

"Wha . . . ?" Marcus whirled and his eyes narrowed as they focused on the growing black blot edging over the horizon; then he noticed that everyone else on the platform was staring at him in amusement.

"Arsehole!" he muttered.

※

Though he was in charge of only half of a full-scale battle, Modan felt oddly left out; and it wasn't due to Eupo looking after the other half. Normally Modan would have been in the front ranks, savagely hacking at the Romans. Instead he was caught up in the chaotic, swirling ranks toward the rear, with little to do but urge everyone forward, and watch as they either succeeded or failed. Eupo seemed of the same mind, for he was working his way over to Modan, his face showing that he was far from pleased.

"We should have had the walls by now," he called out, the moment he was within hailing distance.

"We almost had them," Modan cried, trying to maintain his optimism; then he bit his lip as Borba's words from Stannick shot through his mind. He pushed them away, his eyes on the walls. The breach had been closed and the parapet was again lined with Romans, but it wasn't hopeless. The only way to take those walls was to lose men; and there were lots of them to lose; and they were all still fighting. And as long as enough of those men were left standing to take the fort, it would be called a victory...

A fire had started up in front of the east gate, tongues of flame rising above the heads of those crowding forward to feed it. Modan could see bundles of wood moving forward, vanishing into the mob as they neared the blaze. The flames leapt higher and he felt a surge of hope, but then the Romans were throwing water, protected by a screen of those infernal shields. It wasn't just a few cauldrons of water pouring down, either, but a steady, gushing stream. Modan cursed. How did they do that?

"So much for burning our way in," Eupo muttered as he finally pulled alongside. The Caledoni rode with roughly a dozen other men around him, as did Modan, all either kin or favourites. Modan could hardly name any of those with Eupo, but he saw that the wiry little runt who Lagan despised was there.

"They'll start falling back if they don't get inside soon," Modan growled. The ramparts in front of the wall remained crowded, but other than the single breach that had set his heart thumping, both sides were just picking at each other. There was no doubt which one was taking the greater casualties. "There's only so much they'll stand. We've got to do something different."

Modan, for the first time, longed for Lagan; and, though it was impossible, Horus might also have proved valuable...

Bellus would have been better, though, but Lagan wouldn't part with the man; nor did the traitorous stoat want to go, which maybe said something...

They should have just said sod it and taken him, though that would have been a direct challenge to Lagan, and Lagan was well guarded...

Modan sighed, his mind whirling uselessly. Perhaps some sort of tower like one the Greek had once told him about, though that would take time they did not have. Maybe next time, and concentrate on one section of the wall only; and maybe use bundles of wood to help climb those ramparts. In the meantime, if enough bundles were brought up and set in one place...

"They've giving up," Eupo grumbled. "So are the cowards leading them. Look!"

Modan had already seen it. Those on horseback, most of them the chieftains who had been urging their men to battle, were turning. The crowding at the rampart was rapidly thinning, enough that now he could see bodies littering the ground. Everyone, the whole cowardly lot of them, were giving up!

"Come on, let's push them back," Eupo shouted.

Modan didn't move, suddenly baffled. The tribes were more than falling back, he realized, they were running like cattle. This wasn't a retreat, it was a stampede! Men were fleeing everywhere, in a panic that was spreading like fire. He'd never seen the like. Modan glanced at Eupo, who sat back in his saddle looking just as baffled.

"There's a Roman army coming!"

The shout didn't come from those fleeing the field. Modan whirled and saw Treno galloping toward him as if chased by demons. He cursed loudly as the fool pulled hard on the reins, his horse skittering sideways, almost crashing into his own.

"Roman cavalry, Mod! The whole Roman army is on its way," Treno said again, as if nobody had heard him screech the words the first time.

Modan looked over his shoulder, but he and Eupo were on lower ground than those who had been attacking the rampart. He could see nothing but open land, and the small river in the distance with its stand of trees on the other side. His eyes turned back to the fort. The east gate had been forced open, and the firewood pushed aside. Roman cavalry was pouring through.

Even as he cursed, he caught sight of movement among those fleeing to the south. The head of a second column of riders was forcing its way through the cowards fleeing the walls. Modan's temper flared, his blood instantly boiling. "Treno! It's just their local cavalry coming out. That's what we want – get them out in the open!"

"Not there, you blind git," Treno shouted. "Over there!" He pointed wildly toward the east.

Modan again turned in the saddle, still unable to see anything but the smaller river and the trees. "What . . . ?"

"Your brother's here with his lousy army!" Treno yelled, as if in some way that was Modan's fault.

Modan stared back at Treno, his mind going blank. Around them, like a fast-ebbing tide, men were running away, many toward Treno's mysterious, unseen army. The thunder of hooves pulled Modan from his sudden numbness, and he saw that Eupo and his covey of arsenuzzlers were also fleeing. Oddly enough they, too, were headed in the direction of the Roman army . . .

*The woman! The spoils from the burnt Roman forts!*

Cursing, Modan pulled brutally on the reins and kicked hard at his horse's belly, the animal squealing as the bit savaged its jaw. The horse leapt forward and was soon galloping headlong after the Caledoni. As if pulled by a leash, Treno and the others followed, heedless of the many who stood in their way. Modan's mind raced blindly over what was happening, then focused on nothing more than Eupo.

A small camp had been set up in a clearing in the trees, during the dark hours of early morning. He'd left the woman there under guard, along with whatever worthwhile baggage he and Eupo had hauled with them: mainly spoils from the destruction of the Roman forts, neatly divided in two – and all packed, ready for taking! He tried to remember how many of his *own* men were there. He and Eupo had left the clearing on good terms, certainly; but they had been like two sated wolves edging cautiously back from a kill.

Modan forced his horse into the river, the animal near lost in a spray of water as it splashed across. On the far side, two riders stood guard at the small opening that led to the clearing – probably watching for him! Modan swore and lashed the end of the reins hard on his horse's rump. For a moment the two men seemed uncertain, then they turned about and disappeared into the forest. Modan cursed aloud, again kicking at the animal's belly. The terrified horse lunged onto the riverbank and into the darkness of the trees, running hard on their tails.

He caught up with the rear rider as all three thundered into the open. Without stopping to think, Modan rammed his spear into the man's back. The Caledoni screamed and fell from the saddle, and his horse galloped on, crashing into a cluster of others that had been herded to the back of the clearing. The animals squealed and balked, most pulling free of the handlers who controlled them. Several crashed off through the undergrowth, followed by a chorus of ripe curses.

Modan pulled up sharp, his horse squealing as he rived hard on the bit. He glared wildly around the clearing, ready to fight and kill, but it seemed that no one was ready to oblige. Some men ran after the horses as others rushed for weapons. In the middle of it all, standing by the two piles of plunder, Eupo gaped in amazement. The only calm figure in the sunlit meadow seemed to be the woman. She stood between two of his own men, in the middle of the divided plunder, her chin high and her arms folded.

"What are you doing?" Eupo screamed, rushing forward with his spear ready, and clearly prepared to use it.

Modan heard Treno shout his name, urging him to caution. He glanced about the clearing, his eyes blinking as if that might help make sense of what was happening. He saw that both Eupo's men and his own had been strapping the more easily packed spoils onto horses. Now the stupid animals were all over the clearing. Nobody appeared ready to kill anyone else, nor did they seem to be stealing each other's share; not unless his own men had turned on him, and their puzzled faces said that had not happened.

"I thought . . ." Modan began, but Eupo was not having any of it.

"You thought I was here stealing your share and killing your men, you stupid, stinking pig!" Eupo screeched, and pointed his spear toward the fallen Caledoni who writhed on the ground, whimpering in agony. Modan turned to look, just as the fallen man's fellow guard dismounted and quietly put an end to the man's misery. "And now you've killed Ferg, you – you – you sorry arsed prick!"

"But you sent him –"

"I sent the poor bastard to watch out for the Romans, you bone-brained bastard. He was doing his job!" The second guard swung grimly back onto his horse and headed off through the trees to resume his watch. Eupo glanced quickly about the clearing, as if trying to figure who was still there, and what might be done.

The man was wondering whether to make a fight of it, Modan decided, and he, too, looked around the clearing. But he and Eupo had left their plunder to the care of the same number of men, and neither side had the odds – and there was a horde of vengeful Romans hot on their heels anyway. Modan blinked. Even his own men, those not helping Eupo's people round up the horses, were glaring at him. He thrust his jaw forward, unwilling to admit his wrong. "I want the woman. She's kin."

"She's not kin," Eupo growled and glanced toward Elena, though he seemed more interested in the dwindling pile of plunder beside her. "The woman just happened to be your da's first wife a hundred years ago, who couldn't possibly have birthed a witless clod like you."

"That still makes her mine," Modan growled, too impatient to figure through the insult.

"To do what with? Are you so . . ." The steady thud of hooves made Eupo stop and turn.

The man who had gone to stand watch rode into the clearing, holding his horse to a fast canter. He reined in alongside Eupo. "We have to go. Roman cavalry are all over the place, and now foot soldiers are coming out of the fort. They'll be on this side of the river before long." The man added a few more words, gabbling on in a broad northern dialect, and Eupo nodded.

He glanced up at Modan, and said, "Fine, then. We've got what we want. It's not worth the bother of arguing. She's yours." Eupo stared hard into Modan's eyes, then shook his head as if in despair. "But if I was you, I'd leave her right where she is and fly like the faerie. Rome's blood is already boiling, as it is."

"What else did he say?" Modan demanded, ignoring Eupo's suggestion, his eyes fixed on the guard.

Someone brought Eupo a horse and at first he said nothing as he swung up into the saddle. Once there, he looked across at Modan. "He was urging me to take what we can carry, and leave," he replied calmly. "No woman is worth fighting over."

Eupo turned his horse down a trail that led off through the trees, a trail that would place him closer to the oncoming Roman army, no matter where it led. Even so, Modan supposed that a man's chances were better in that direction than in returning through the gap to the river. Stay in the cover of the trees then head south, maybe. The hills there would be safe enough, at least for a while . . .

He watched as the last of the Caledonii disappeared, then moved his horse closer to the plunder and stared down on what remained. Eupo had taken just a part of his, though probably the most valuable. He supposed he would have to do the same. Treno seemed of like mind, for he was ordering everyone to stop what they were doing and mount up. It seemed such a waste. Was there time to hide any of it?

"Agricola spent two years fighting the Caledonii. I often helped the Romans with their questioning."

Modan glanced at the woman, and his lip curled. "Yeah? So you helped him fight your own people!"

Elena ignored the thrust. "What the man told Eupo had nothing to do with fighting over women." She shrugged, raising a hand to cup one ear. "Can you hear that?"

Modan paused and raised his hand, though there was really no need. The pounding of hooves sounded from the direction of the fort, drowning the dull, screaming roar of battle that drifted through the trees. They were close, very close; in fact they were –

Modan glanced frantically about the clearing and saw Treno bolting, lashing his horse down the trail taken by Eupo. He turned angrily to Elena as she again spoke, though he barely heard her words in his panic.

"What he told Eupo was: we've got to leave now! Roman cavalry is heading straight this way."

"Shit!"

Modan spun in the saddle as a dull thunder shook the ground, and the crash of breaking branches echoed from the undergrowth. His fool horse was facing the wrong way! He jerked wildly on the reins, the animal shaking its head against the stabbing pain that once more lanced through its jaw. The stupid beast turned sharply, fighting the bit, and Modan lifted his legs, ready to kick down, hard.

⁂

Kaeso would have been there first, but a half-dozen other riders pushed in front of him, including two of the decurios, and he knew what had likely happened. Rhun, the fort's praefectus, had probably primed them, ordering each to "protect the little fellow." It hadn't helped when his fool horse balked at the river, either. A dozen others galloped past in the short moment it took to force the animal down the bank and up the other side. It was all so damned unfair, because he was the one who had spied the barbarian horsemen doing exactly what the praefectus had told him they would do: put their fool heads together and agree the battle was lost, then slam boots to belly and gather up the woman as they fled.

He'd spotted them almost the moment he led the cavalry through the gate. Hundreds of barbarians on horseback were scattered throughout the milling horde, but only in one area could he see a large group gathered together: more than a score, looking oddly like an island in the sea of fleeing barbarians. About half of them turned almost the moment he saw them, plowing through their own people as if they were no more than vermin. The rest seemed hesitant, but followed moments later. That they were after the woman seemed clear as the first of them rode headlong for a gap in the woods, on the far side of the river.

The decurios had by then deployed several squadrons in line four ranks deep, and began a steady sweep across the field. Kaeso briefly thought of trying to stop them, and charging straight for the woods. But this was their regular drill, and there were screaming barbarians on every side, and the formation was heading in that direction anyway. Stopping to change tactics might not gain the river any the faster. Kaeso slid his horse alongside the senior decurio, a grizzled veteran twice his age, and tried to curb his impatience.

The ranks of cavalry cantered swiftly across the field, each man tossing off his quiver of short, iron-tipped javelins, most them aimed at the backs of fleeing barbarians. Kaeso and the decurio exchanged glances as they closed on the bank of the narrow river.

"There. That's where they are!" Kaeso cried, pointing to the dark pathway into the trees.

The decurios shouted an order, which was promptly picked up and echoed down the line. The great sweep of cavalry, which seemed to stretch forever across the field, crumbled inward. The senior decurio hared off toward the river as, behind him, each trooper broke ranks and urged his horse to a gallop, quickly angling inward until the formation became a broad, thundering column.

Kaeso cursed as he found himself behind the leaders, hemmed in on either side by cavalrymen far larger than him. He lashed gamely at his hammer-headed, water-shy horse when it balked at the edge of the river, nearly throwing him. And he swore at the gods as he lashed it forward, ducking through a thick tangle of low-slung branches on the far bank as the fool animal finally made its way clear of the water and into the trees.

※

Elena grew nervous as she felt the ground tremble. Only the gods knew how many charged down that path, or the slaughtering mood they were in. After all these years, what a tragedy to be killed by a bunch of battle-crazed Romans! She smiled grimly as her eyes slid sideways.

Only a few of Modan's riders remained: those who were ill-prepared, or just plain slow of wit. The clever one, the one with the tattooed face called Treno, had been the first to vanish, galloping off at the first sound of pounding hoofs. Elena had been quick to note that, of them all, his pack bulged largest with plunder. Most of the others had quickly followed and none seemed to care where they went, as long as they could gain the cover of the trees. They scampered off like rabbits fleeing a warren. Soon only a few of the most useless remained, including the one called Modan, who'd dithered far too long.

"They say a barbarian treats his horse and his woman the same way!" Elena shouted over the crash of hooves, as he savaged the animal's mouth. She would never see the man again, yet she felt an inexplicable need to lash out, to show him, just for once, his own ignorance. Not that he would ever see it, not if he lived a hundred years.

But her words, surprisingly, seemed to touch an open sore. Modan had managed to gain a firm grip on the pommel, but he paused and glared at her as he raised his heels to hurry his horse. "Shut your gob, woman, or I'll shut it for you."

"You've not got the time to do that," Elena replied and snorted derisively, unable to resist striking back. Modan seemed to realize he was losing his hostage, knew he'd not got the time to take her with him. Maybe he was heeding Eupo's warning of Rome's anger. Whatever the reason, she could not quell the urge to goad the man before he disappeared. "And you've not got the balls for it, either."

Modan's legs eased back, and he glared. Elena shrank back when she saw that her words had struck far more than an open sore. Modan's face darkened to a mottled purple and he pulled cruelly at the reins, clearly intent on running her down as he fled. But the horse squealed and shied as its ruined mouth fought the bit, shaking its head wildly as it skittered sideways. Caught off guard, and with the reins wrapped around his hand, Modan fought to gain control.

The Roman troopers erupted from the pathway like the wrath of the gods. Elena stumbled backward and fell, as they charged into the clearing as if borne on a flood. The two or three barbarians who remained were brushed aside, spitted like slaughtered sheep.

Someone was pulling at her arm, hauling her to her feet, and in a daze she saw it was Modan. He'd slid down from his horse – or maybe he'd been thrown – and he now held her tight above the elbow. His free hand brandished a long-bladed knife, and for a heart-stopping moment Elena thought he was going to cut her throat. She clawed her hand ready to slash at his eyes, but then saw that Modan wasn't looking at her. He was gaping up at the Roman cavalry that ringed them in, crouching low as he circled with the snorting horses, vainly trying to hide behind her body.

"Don't harm the man," a voice roared out in the Roman tongue. "Don't harm him. Take him if you're able."

Elena heard the words in disbelief. "Don't just sit there, get him off me!" she yelled back in the same language, glaring up at the circling riders.

A horse broke through the ring of riders and the young officer who had spoken slid from the saddle, his sword drawn and his face angry. He was a very *short* young officer, who strode forward until he stood in front of them both, looking incredibly inadequate as he gripped his weapon in both hands. "Tell the man to release you, ma'am, and he'll live," he said, his eyes steady on Modan's face.

"You tell him," Elena snapped. "At the moment, I don't particularly care if he lives or dies!"

"What's he saying?" Modan mumbled, his eyes darting back and forth. "What'd he say?"

"He said drop your weapon, and you'll live," one of the decurios called in a stilted translation.

"You should care whether he lives or dies, ma'am, he's your son's –" the short officer began, but Modan interrupted.

"Fuck off," he said in clear Latin, probably the only words he knew, for then he lapsed into his own language. "I'm taking the woman with me. Give me a start, and I'll let her go as soon as I –"

"You will not, you gormless toad," Elena screeched, then glared at the officer. "Get him off me. I don't care if he does get hurt."

"You don't?" he said, his voice incredulous. "Your sons' brother?"

"Listen," Modan began again, "I want –"

"At the moment, I don't care," Elena cried angrily. "He's after killing me!"

"Tell the Roman to let me ride out, woman," Modan cried, panic cracking his voice. "Now! Or I'll slice you right here." He lifted the long knife high, as if ready to slash it down across Elena's throat.

The officer spun on one heel, his sword arcing upward impossibly fast, turning at the last moment to cut sideways. Blood sprayed from Modan's forearm in a crimson fountain, and he stared down in horror at the stump where, only an instant before, his hand had held the knife. Elena's eyes widened as the small trooper turned again and for a moment she thought his next blow was heading for her. But the blade twisted in his hand and, with a resounding clang, the flat of it crashed down on top of Modan's skull. The man crumpled like an empty sack, and the clearing fell silent.

Elena stared down at the diminutive cavalryman as he knelt and wiped his blade on Modan's tunic. Then, with a shake of his head, he said the oddest thing. "The silly ass lost the damned thing anyway."

## Chapter XLI

## Luguvalium, September, A.D. 105

For the last mile the three had not spoken, for to say anything would have seemed profane; but Bryn broke the silence as they closed on the fort's east gate. He lurched sideways in the saddle and wretched, spewing what was left of yesterday's food onto the road. It was little more than bile for he'd eaten nothing that morning, not with a stomach made of knots and a mind that couldn't be reined in. But he seemed the better for it, Cethen thought, even though he was groaning and cursing, and his face the colour of ash.

"Not sweet to look on, is it?" Borba muttered, his eyes casting about a battlefield that was already baking under an unseasonably brilliant sun. Its warmth was horribly at odds with the carnage it revealed. Bodies were strewn as far as the eye could see, though most lay close against the walls or piled up in the ditch that ran in front of them. Those farther out told the grim, tragic story of panicked flight: men cut down as they ran, some in dense clusters where they had turned to fight, and others scattered at random on the ground far beyond the three rivers.

"They're taking the wounded in this time," Bryn said, grimacing as he spat the foul taste of vomit from his mouth.

"That'll be because of Rhun," Cethen murmured, as he finally raised his eyes from the road ahead to see what was happening. Hundreds of soldiers moved among the dead like an enormous murder of crows, their heads bent and their swords ready. Those who still lived were being raised to their feet, as Bryn said, and taken to an area south of the fort, which already held a thousand or more of the healthy. As for the dead, teams of horses hauled logs to points close by the river where men, some of them Britons, were building bonfires.

"When Modan was taken after attacking Tuis, they killed the wounded," Bryn continued, shaking his head at the memory. "They just slit their throats. Even so, this . . ." He cast a hand at the endless sprawl of bodies that covered the ground as thick as autumn leaves, "It was nothing like this."

"Graupius was worse," Cethen muttered, though truth be known, he'd never seen the end of it. He'd left that battlefield before the peak of the slaughter. But Bryn's mention of Modan set his mind on the reason for going to the fort. Trista had sent word that his son lived, but had been hurt. Was it the sort of wound that would finally do for the fool? Or worse still, was the wound slight, but he'd finally pushed the Romans too far? How many times does a dog get to bite before someone does away with it? "If it was any other in charge but Rhun, they'd have killed him by now."

"You mean Modan?" Borba asked, then blithely added, "I hear they take the important ones back to Rome, and do it in public."

Bryn snorted. "That leaves Modan out, then."

Cethen smiled, his face wan. "The boy's a legend in his own mind, I do admit," he said, and as they neared the gate he fumbled with the old leather tube that carried the wrinkled parchments containing Gaius and Tuis's scrawl. But there seemed to be no guards there when they rode through, or if there were, they were lost in the crowds of soldiers going back and forth and didn't care about three barbarians who acted as if they belonged. Cethen now knew enough about Roman forts to know where he should go, and continued on to the large building at the end of the street where those in charge seemed to spend their time.

"Maybe we should try the one off to the side." Bryn motioned toward the residence, for the headquarters building, both inside and out, swarmed with soldiers.

One of them, a grey-haired cavalryman with a look of authority, paused and beckoned them over. "What do you want, old man?" he asked as Cethen stopped in front of him, the parchment ready in hand.

"I'm looking for my son," he replied, and glanced along the busy street, wondering where to start. Should he tell the man it was Modan, the idiot who'd misjudged all this and got everyone killed? Definitely not!

"Where do you expect to find him, with the living or the dead?" The man's voice was abrupt as he waved a hand toward the walls. "Those taken live are gathered outside the south gate; the dead you'll have to pick through, though you'd better be quick. They'll be burned soon, before the stench sets in." His eyes narrowed. "What are you doing here, anyway?"

Bryn spoke before Cethen could answer, talking in a precise Latin. "As my father said, he's looking for one of his sons, though perhaps two of them are here. One is, we know for certain; he's the praefectus who commands this fort. Another may have ridden in with the Roman cavalry. He's the province's governor."

*And there is a third*, Cethen mused, as he watched the Roman's face. The man plainly thought Bryn was pulling his wick, yet he couldn't be sure. Just then a loud voice called his name, and solved the Roman's dilemma – or perhaps gave him cause for more concern. Cian sauntered out of the residence with Luga on his heels, both of them wearing huge grins.

"Glad to see you on the green side of the weeds," his brother said as he drew near.

"That's what you said at Bran's Beck," Cethen replied as an old memory leapt to mind. He couldn't resist looking at the Roman and adding, "We were both fighting the Romans, then."

"Aye, and with the same result," Luga snorted. "You're here about your lad Modan, I suppose."

The Roman trooper seemed to recognize the name and stared hard at Cethen. "That's the bastard who –"

"Yes, I know, I know," Cethen said patiently, then asked the dreaded question. "Does he still live?"

"Yes, but I don't know why. Last I heard, the medicus had him with a hand missing." The trooper's eyes narrowed. "Is he really your . . .?"

*They took the hand off after all; yet, on the good side of that, maybe it means they're going to let him live.* Cethen sighed, a long sigh that continued as he slid from the saddle and set both feet hard on the ground. He squinted up at the trooper, who stood above him on the walkway of the headquarters building, and answered the unfinished question as best he could. "My sons are a varied lot!"

※

They held Modan in the commander's residence, and it was at Elena's insistence. "If anyone is going to do the ingrate in, it'll be me," she'd told Rhun, and she could see he didn't know whether to believe her or not. "I'll not give the satisfaction to a vile-tempered centurio who can't control his temper."

"And you can control yours?" he'd asked, smiling grimly as they both stared at Modan, who stood beside Kaeso like a great, wounded bear.

Unlike a bear, though, Modan was subdued and clearly in pain as he clutched his forearm to stop the bleeding.

"Of course I can control my temper, I'm a mother," Elena had replied, her face equally grim.

Rhun had Modan taken to the fort hospital. When the stump had been treated he was escorted, none too gently, to the residence, where he was held under guard in the atrium. It was a place where, for the moment, he could be easily watched; and it was there, when the sun was drifting down to the horizon, that Cethen found him. Modan was clearly full of whatever magic the medicus had given him. He lay on a wooden cot staring listlessly at the sky through half-closed eyes, his jaw slack in an ashen face, and the stump of his right hand swathed in bandages.

A small table sat on the other side of the enclosed square, surrounded by chairs. It was out of place in a building that bustled with soldiers. Plates of half-eaten food, clay wine goblets, and a good half dozen open jars of wine littered its top. Criff sat on one side, restringing his harp. Elena and Trista sat on the other with their heads together, each holding a goblet.

Elena looked up as the three men stepped into the atrium with Cian and Luga, their eyes at first on Modan; then, one by one, they turned and saw who else was there. Cethen and Borba simply nodded a greeting; Bryn looked away the moment he saw Trista.

Elena smiled in amusement as their eyes, almost in unison, swung back to Modan: Borba because he was as ill at ease as an old cow in a pen full of bulls; Bryn because he pretended not to care that Trista was here, which clearly showed that he did; and Cethen because – well, just because. Elena saw that he'd managed to find a new jacket and boots, only the gods knew from where, and he was freshly shaved and his moustaches trimmed. He'd even combed his hair, plainly trying to look his best – and she was certain it wasn't just to come and see what was going to happen to Modan.

Elena felt her eyes moisten and she blinked; damned if that was going to happen! "Trista, I think your lad is being stubborn," she said firmly, and climbed to her feet. "Come on, lass, let's get this sorted."

"He's not the only stubborn one," Trista muttered and remained in her seat, glaring as Criff strummed the half-strung harp and crooned something about the bane of willful women.

"Pick your battles, girl," Elena hissed. Grabbing her arm, she pulled Trista to her feet. "You can't win 'em all, so lose the small ones and win the ones that count. It doesn't matter who speaks first, as long as you speak." Then, barely audible, she added, "He's just like his father."

"... in the next few days, and as long as infection don't set in, he'll be fine."

Elena crossed the atrium and stopped alongside Cian in time to hear the last of his opinion. She added her own. "Oh, I don't know. From what Trista tells me, Modan's just been having a bad year, and it isn't over yet." She leaned past Cian and spoke to Bryn. "What do you think, young man?"

"I – er, I think he'll be fine," Bryn murmured, then added, "for the time being."

"What're they going to do with him?" Cethen asked.

Elena smiled, for Cethen's eyes were on Modan's chest, and his head rose and fell almost imperceptibly with his son's breathing. *You could always tell where the man's mind was!* "That is a matter that needs talking on," she said. "You have any suggestions?"

Cethen admitted that he didn't; nor, it seemed, did any of the others. There was no reason not to just tell them all straight out, but Elena couldn't resist stretching the bow string. There was a good chance Modan was listening to every word spoken, even though he looked as if he was off with the faerie. "Rhun's decided that there's no choice but to make an example," she began, her voice neutral but firm. "Modan will be –"

"He's gonna kill his brother, then?" Cethen muttered, looking sharply at Elena. He was more dismayed than angry, and she realized that death was what he'd been expecting. She sighed impatiently and glanced down at Modan. The man hadn't so much as twitched, and she supposed he really might be off with the faerie.

"Can't something else be done with him?" Bryn demanded, and Elena saw that he was also troubled, but hid his anger. As well he might do, she supposed, because the fool had no sense. This was the idiot who'd freed him from the Romans in the first place. She'd learned that much from Lagan, though at the time it meant little. If Bryn was angry with anyone, it should be with himself.

"An example must be made, or the Romans figure they might just as well lay down their swords and leave," Elena said sharply, though there had been many times that she'd wished exactly that. She shook her head at the hypocrisy, and relented. "There are other ways to make an example. Publicly hauled off in chains and sold in Rome as a slave is one of them."

"Which at least means he'll still be alive," Trista pointed out, and Elena saw that the lass couldn't hide the wisp of a smile, for she knew where Modan was going.

Bryn saw it too, and scowled at Trista. "That's nothing to be fu – to be happy about."

Cethen was not happy either and his feelings were clearly scribed on his face; but, as ever, he seemed ready to rationalize. "As the lass says, he'll still be alive."

"Rhun will have the orders scribed, and he's giving first offer of purchase to the Nepos estate," Elena continued, and again threw what appeared to be salt on a wound. "It sits not far from Rome, and is always in need of field hands. The woman who presently finds herself in charge is pitiless."

"The woman?" Cethen cried, and Bryn and Borba echoed his words.

"I think that's only fitting," Trista said, and didn't bother to hide her smile.

"But –"

All three men spoke at once, but Elena's voice was louder. "Yes, a woman! And Trista has the right of it; it is only fitting," she said, as if savouring every word. "This particular woman is the wife of a man called Publius Didius Nepos, who happens to be dying. He may, in fact, already be dead, but the lass herself is more than a match for yon Modan. I'm sure she'll continue the old Roman tradition of starving her slaves, when she's not beating them to death."

"Elena, really . . ."

Elena turned her eyes to Cethen, who stared back looking dumbstruck. The poor man looked so crestfallen that she couldn't play the game any longer. "You, you daft bugger, know her better as Coira, daughter of Cethen Lamh-fada."

# Epilogue

## Eboracum, A.D. 122

It was yet another spring, and Elena supposed that she should be grateful to be alive; though more often than not, especially in the morning, she saw little cause to find joy in such a small mercy. Aching bones, an indifferent palate, and the energy of a tortoise were just a few of the reasons. One of the most painful, though, was that she was the last of them. So many had died: friends, kin, husbands, and old enemies too. It was hard not to think of them, but all too often there seemed little to do but exactly that. Time weighed heavy on her mind, which was ironic, because so little time was left. Yet if she were to place all the reasons in order, perhaps the most painful of all *was* that mind. Her memory and her tongue were sharp, quite sharp, considering her age; yet everyone, most particularly those wearing an army uniform, were determined to treat her as if half that mind had vanished with the faerie.

The pending visit was no exception, and the military had taken it on with all the usual fuss and fanfare. She'd seen battles fought with far less preparation. Though in fairness, not since Claudius, nigh on eighty years ago, had an emperor come to Britannia. Not when he *was* the emperor, anyway. Julius had been the first before he made himself Caesar; she knew that from reading Tacitus's nose-nuzzling scribings. But great as Caesar was supposed to be, he never did make his invasions stick. Then Vespasian had been here, who'd done quite well for himself later in life, but he was a legion commander under Claudius at the time. But Hadrian – well, Hadrian *was* the emperor, and had been these past five years. And from what Elena had heard, he wasn't a bad one either, at least as far as emperors went. The man was supposed to be cultured and well-read, and if his carnal preferences were more in line with what she'd heard about the Greeks, then she supposed that was fine, too. She didn't have to see it, and nor did she have a handsome young son to worry about.

"They want you as the honoured guest at the official welcoming banquet," Shayla had said when breaking the news.

"Here?" For a moment, Elena felt the old panic. When Gaius had reluctantly taken his turn playing host on the social circuit, or when somebody of political importance dropped by the house on the Mons, she had hated it. In fairness, both of them detested the politics and the pretence, but Elena had in particular, for it had always been accompanied by condescension.

And now an emperor was coming!

Her home was, admittedly, the finest in Eboracum outside of the commander's residence at the fortress. *Will he come and visit me here?* The villa was large enough: a modern building constructed of the same stone as the fortress, perched partway up the hill that lay south of the river. A small suite of rooms was heated by a hypocaust, for the winters could be bitter; but in the summer, on a warm sunny day, the wide balcony presented a strikingly beautiful view. The Abus flowed gently at that time of year, meeting the Fosse just to the east of the fortress, before wandering slowly seaward through a lush patchwork of green fields and tall shade trees.

And at the centre of it all stood the fortress: more than a dozen *heredia* enclosed by neat, manicured grass berms and tall stone walls; a huge, pristine structure that glowed in the setting sun and reminded Elena of Rome itself – a city that was more perfect for its absence. Surely the gods had done right by her, for in the end they had left her with the better parts of both worlds. Though sometimes, she thought, the gods sodding-well owed it to her.

"No, not here. It will be at the commander's residence." Shayla smiled when asked. "And by the way, Kaeso rode down last night to help the legate organize Hadrian's journey further north. I imagine he'll drop by later today."

"Did Jessa come with him?" Elena asked hopefully. It had been months since she'd seen her granddaughter, the only close kin she had left in Britannia. Though she supposed Kelpy and Trista were now near the same as kin, but it wasn't the same as her own . . .

"No, she stayed," Shayla said, her tone revealing her own disappointment. "But Kaeso said she sent her regrets, and will be down around Beltane. I don't think either wanted to be tripping over each other, not when he's busy organizing all this. I do think Kaeso would rather fight a full pitched battle than face the emperor."

"Which he's done," Elena mused, as had all of them, with no idea what fighting their battles did to their women – especially the mothers. Yet she understood the way of it. When she had been young herself, she cared little about anyone getting hurt – including herself. All she'd ever worried about was killing Romans, and the safety of her own children.

Yet when the fighting was done, the women were left to mourn. She could thank the gods that she'd been spared that side of the shield, for Shayla had not. The poor lass had moved into the large villa after burying the second of her two husbands, four or five years ago. The north had again flared, and again the Ninth had taken a battering, as had the long line of auxiliary forts that stretched north to Habitancum and beyond. Shayla's husband, a junior centurio called Noster, had lived long enough to be invalided to Eboracum, only to die there of infection. The poor old Ninth . . .

"There's never an end to it, is there?" Elena murmured as Shayla made herself comfortable on one of the leather chairs before picking up the embroidery she'd left there.

"Nor will there be; not until mothers hold the reins."

Elena laughed scornfully, though that conversation was an old one. "Boudicca was a mother, and look how that went!"

Shayla smiled as she threaded her needle on the first attempt. "Aye, but she had cause."

"I suppose, but the time was ripe, you know," Elena murmured, thinking through the numbers. The trouble with getting older was that too often there was nothing to do but think, and sometimes it was on the oddest of matters.

"The time was ripe?" Shayla asked absently, absorbed in laying out the cloth she was working.

Elena decided she needn't reply, and instead pondered the notion that for Boudicca the time had indeed been ripe. As it had been ripe for Agricola and his campaigns – which had been about forty years ago. It seemed as if every time Rome beat the tribes into submission, they remained relatively quiet for somewhere around twenty years. That was about the time it took for another generation to be raised – a generation that grew up with no memory of war, other than the glorious, stirring tales of their elders.

When she thought back far enough, it had all started with the Roman invasion, eighty years ago. She'd been a small child then and remembered nothing of it; nor should she, for that had all been in the south. But she did remember the Iceni woman's uprising that followed, nearly twenty years later; that had been sixty years ago, and also further south. There were few left alive today to claim they remembered that! Elena sighed, and leaned back in her chair. Another twenty years passed, then Agricola and Galgar had fought it out, razing the land as far north as anyone cared to live. She chuckled to herself at the memory, for she had been there with poor Gaius, every step of the way.

There had been Venutius in between, of course, but that had simply been one man, who caused a good deal of unrest that ended in a single, easily won battle – one that she'd been a part of. As such, it didn't count; and besides, it didn't fit in with her figuring. Elena closed her eyes. The greatest tragedy of Venutius was that it had cost Cethen the raising of his two boys – the first two, anyway – along with the rest of his family. Though truth be known, Rome was to blame for it all by coming here to begin with. At the time, she would have cheerfully seen every last one of the invaders dead, including the man who became her husband.

As far as Elena was concerned, what happened next did not need a seer's prophecy. After Agricola, another twenty years passed before the tragedy of Modan. Everything north of Brigantia had been in flames, some of the fires lit by the Roman army as it abandoned its understrength garrisons. The uprising had all been in vain, though. Cethen's bone-headed son and his cohorts had no more chance of defeating Rome than a rabbit did a fox, and neither did the Selgovae Lagan, though the man himself was never defeated. Elena smiled at that, pleased with the notion, for she'd quite liked him.

And as always, when she thought of Lagan, poor Linus came to mind. There was another one she had "quite liked," and she'd barely known him. She would take the memory of his death to her grave.

Elena hastily shook the name away, for it had ever haunted her. And as to Lagan, above all she remembered the man for honouring his word. Both Shayla and Metellus had been returned as promised, left within walking distance of Habitancum. That was when Lagan faded away, after being abandoned by Modan and that Caledoni chieftain – she couldn't remember his name. The Selgovae had continued their raiding, and Lagan had no doubt been involved, but those raids also faded to nothing – until four or five years ago, when it all started up again. By then Lagan was either too old to fight or dead; yet with the gods' blessings he might still be hanging onto life even today. That last one hadn't taken twenty years though, had it? It had only been a dozen or so. That was likely because it hadn't truly been finished with Modan, and the unrest had still festered . . .

Elena sighed, her mind returning to Modan. That had been yet another tragedy for Cethen, for though his boy was a fool, that had been another of his sons lost to Rome.

Poor Cethen!

Elena sighed and shook her head, her mood suddenly wistful, perhaps even sorry – but not for Cethen himself! A woman should never feel sorry about any man she cared for, particularly her husband. It chipped away at his self-respect, and it chipped at the respect his woman held for him. And Cethen, in his own easy way, deserved a good deal of respect!

He was the greatest regret of her life, and her eyes grew soft as an old, vague image crossed her mind of a young, gangly, sandy-haired youth whose moustache might have been spun by a spider. Under the right light, there was a faint reddish tinge to his hair that had always caught her fancy. "You never do get over that first love," Elena whispered softly to herself, causing Shayla to look up from her sewing, and smile. Cethen was the most honest and open man she'd ever known, which had ever been his attraction – all the way back to when they were children. If only . . .

Elena smiled in turn. Those 'ifs' again! *Ifs are only wishes . . .*

⚜

The meal was military, and since the weather was fine, they held the reception in the huge atrium at the centre of the commander's residence. Hadrian had arrived with a large following, though by far the larger part had preceded him: a complete legion. By the emperor's own choice, the *Sixth Legio Victrix* had marched into Eboracum, transferred from *Lower Germania*, where it had been stationed for more than fifty years. Ironically, the legion had originally been posted there from Hispania only one year before the Ninth had been repositioned north to Eboracum. And now it was replacing the poor old Ninth, ostensibly because of the Sixth's exemplary record along the *Rhenus*.

What if it had been the other way round, Elena mused, would it be the Ninth that now proudly marched in with its emperor?

Legend already had it that the gods had found disfavour with the Ninth. Or as Gaius had once phrased it, even the men figured she was a "hard luck" legion. The regiment had received yet another pounding when the northern tribes had last risen, and Elena was ready to believe the superstition. But it was tragic to see the Ninth replaced, and Gaius would have been distressed.

Nonetheless, the last rebellion had been quashed and Rome's greatest cost, as ever, had been the soldiers stationed closest to where it happened. If her figuring was correct, though, the Sixth should find the frontier calm for a further fifteen years. By then another generation of hotheaded tribesmen would have grown to be young men, none having seen a festering belly wound or a bludgeoned skull, and all of them ready to sally forth with a sodding sword.

The Ninth, which was down to nearly half its authorized strength, had been shipped off to Germania to replace the Sixth, though Elena had been told that its ultimate disposition remained to be seen. She supposed that might depend on its record or, if a person was a cynic, on a sudden disastrous need for troops elsewhere. More likely it would depend on whether the legion could rid itself of that vague sense of failure that seemed to have followed it since first moving north to Lindum, when Boudicca went on her rampage. Not all the Ninth had been sent to Germania, though. Transfers to the Sixth had been approved for some of the older men, including a certain senior centurio.

"You're looking well."

The older she got, the more that greeting irritated! It translated as, "Maybe you shouldn't be looking well, because you're so very old!" This time Elena turned and laughed as she recognized the voice, for Trista stood at her elbow and the greeting was deliberate. She offered her thanks, and sighed. If the truth be known, she was getting too picky, especially when her mind was on edge. It was ever her way with formal receptions for she abhorred them, and this one was no exception. She glanced past Trista's shoulder. "I presume your husband's with you?"

"Yes . . ." Trista looked about the crowded atrium, and shrugged. "He's somewhere here. All senior officers are. Attendance was mandatory."

Elena's eyes followed her gaze, but was unable to find Varro anywhere. She was also looking for another man, and wondered if Trista knew he was here, too. She was going to find out anyway, and Elena watched carefully as she spoke. "Bryn was invited down, you know."

Trista smiled, but her cheeks coloured and her jaw tightened just enough to notice. "Yes, Varro told me he was on the guest list. I was quite surprised."

"I believe it was a matter of presenting petitions to the emperor. Bryn wasn't sure how far Hadrian's itinerary extended to the north, and wanted to make sure he received an audience." Elena smiled as she watched Trista's features. "I would guess he was horrified to receive an invitation down here instead."

"Hmm," Trista murmured, as if not particularly interested; which, from the way her eyes had glanced instinctively back to the crowded room, was not quite true. "To present petitions? I would have thought Hadrian's staff would have waited until he got to Cumbria."

Elena laughed. "Bryn likely received his invitation for the same reason that I got mine: influence within the family."

"With the emperor?" Trista sounded incredulous.

"Yes, with Hadrian." Elena assumed the same snobbish tone as the tail-wagging women of the Mons. "It seems that at the last moment the emperor felt the need of a man of experience to accompany him, one well acquainted with Britannia, to oversee the imperial visit." Then she smiled, and continued in her normal voice. "And you won't find a more experienced man than one who was born and bred here."

"Oh, you're talking about Tuis being here."

"Yes, Tuis," Elena smiled and placed a hand gently on Trista's forearm. "By the way, he also mentioned that your first husband still lives, fat and docile, on the Sabinius estate."

"Yeah, well, that happens when your balls . . ." Trista began, then her voice faded as if she thought better. "Tuis, I see he's lost weight."

"Surprising, no?" Elena said, and grinned. "He's actually quite trim. I think it's due to getting married again. I'd guess this one has him well in hand. Either that, or she's wearing him out. He looks really quite fit. On the other hand . . ." Elena smiled mischievously ". . . I'm sure you'll be quite pleased to learn that Bryn has not aged very well over the years, and is the owner of a nice, round belly."

Trista grinned and meowed like a cat. "I'll be the judge of that when I see him."

Elena paused thoughtfully and looked into Trista's eyes, suddenly curious, for she realized that there might, in a way, be some of herself within her. "Any regrets?"

Trista didn't hesitate, she just shrugged and the grin grew lopsided. "No more than anyone for their first love," she said, and cocked her head to one side, amused. "How about you? Any regrets?"

"No more than anyone for their first love," Elena repeated, and was surprised to feel her cheeks grow warm. It was best to talk of other things. "How about Varro. Is he settling in with the Sixth, after his transfer?"

But she saw that Trista no longer listened, and was instead staring past her shoulder. Her face had paled, and her mouth had fallen open.

"And this is my mother, Elena," a deep, familiar voice intruded. Elena turned knowing who to expect, but not what to expect. Either way, she was determined not to show the least hint of being awed by a Roman emperor.

Her first impression was that Tuis stood the taller of the two, which made her maliciously pleased as her son beamed down at her. By his side stood a man of average height, perhaps nearing fifty, with thick, curly hair and a neatly trimmed beard. He was one of the few Romans of any standing who she'd seen wearing a beard. Then her eyes narrowed as she realized that the beard covered what appeared to be a spatter of warts scattered on and below his chin. She saw that Hadrian, in turn, had noticed her rudeness, and his eyes – they were a deep, intelligent grey, which reminded her of Rhun – twinkled at the blunder.

He grinned. "I've heard a good deal about you," he said, and bent his head slightly.

"And I of you," Elena replied, and raised an eyebrow toward her son. Tuis took the hint and introduced Trista, offering the further detail that Hadrian had already met her husband, the man transferred in as the new camp praefectus for the Sixth.

The conversation was at first light. Hadrian was plainly being escorted about the courtyard so that everyone might say a word or two to an emperor, and tell of it time and again in the years to come. But he had questions for her, and they were not frivolous ones that might be meant for the failing mind of an old lady. After asking about the early history of the fortress, they turned to conditions in the north, and he asked Elena what she knew of the tribes that lived there.

The words flowed easily as she found herself almost garrulous, telling Hadrian of the destruction of Stannick, the defeat of Venutius, and the final battle with Galgar. He teased her in turn about her short captivity with the Selgovae, which told her that he'd been well-briefed; and she replied by telling of her treatment by Lagan, and what a fine man he seemed to be. After all, she said deliberately, it was his land that was invaded. The sharp jab caused a smile.

"And will they ever by subdued?" Hadrian asked, when she told what she knew of the most recent uprising, which was actually little more than what she'd heard from the officers at the fortress.

It struck Elena that, in all the unrest that had taken place in the north, this last conflict was the only one in which she had played no part. The insight prompted her to mention her thoughts on the timing of each revolt, and Hadrian seemed intrigued. Strangely encouraged, she explained her reasons and he nodded his understanding, one hand cupping his chin and rubbing thoughtfully at his beard.

"So if you're right, we have another fifteen years before the young ones start it all up again," Hadrian murmured.

Elena suddenly flushed as she realized she'd probably been babbling on, and the emperor was simply catering to an old woman – or worse, amusing himself. She shrugged as if it was of little import. "I suppose we'll have to wait and see."

"I hope we have no other choice." Hadrian grinned. "And if it does happen that way, I'll add your theories to the strategy manuals."

Now he is being condescending, Elena decided, and found herself growing irrationally irritated. Why didn't Tuis get the man moving on to what must be a hundred other obligatory introductions? "I'm sure they'll prove of great value," she said, which sounded pompous when the words were meant to be light, but she felt some sort of reply was necessary.

Hadrian's next question surprised her, however, and she was unsure whether he was serious or simply amusing himself. She decided he was amusing himself. "My commanders tell me that the tribes further north are wild, and beyond reason. Do you agree?"

"Well, I can't disagree."

"So how would you keep them in their place?"

"Me?" Elena shrugged and shot back the first thought that came to mind, and she didn't care how it sounded. "I'd build a fuc – flaming great wall from the Tinea to the Ituna, and have nothing more to do with them!"

# Appendix I

# A Brief Description of the Roman Legions, Early Second Century A.D.

A Roman legion did not march alone. A legion would normally have auxiliary units attached. Such forces were generally raised from the population of a territory other than where the legion was stationed, in order to minimize insurrection. The units were both infantry and cavalry, and might double a legion's strength. To some extent these units were organized on lines similar to the legion itself, especially the infantry, but there were differences. The following briefly details the strength and organization of a legion such as the Ninth Hispana, as well as an auxiliary cavalry *alae* (regiment) and an auxiliary infantry *cohort* (about half a modern battalion). In order to make the story flow, modern equivalents have been used for some of the legions' elements rather than the original lengthy and unfamiliar names (such as *squad* instead of *contubernia(e)*; or a *troop* or *squadron* instead of a *turma(e)*).

## The Legion

Each *legio(n)* was made up of ten *cohort(e)s*, which were officially 480 strong, except for the most senior cohort – the first cohort – which had 800 men. There appears to be some debate about the reason for the extra-large first cohort. Based on modern army needs, the author has adopted the position that those extra numbers likely contained service support or specialist soldiers, much like those found in a modern service battalion. In total, the basic legion strength was just over 5,250 men, though 4,000 seems to have been its normal garrison strength, perhaps dipping as low as 3,000 after hard campaigning.

The legion was commanded by a *legatus legionis* (legate), who was of senatorial rank. He was assisted by officers who were mainly ex-rankers, the most senior being the *primus pilus*. This rank might be compared to a supercharged regimental sergeant major, and in many ways equivalent in power to that of the legate himself. Close behind was the *praefectus castrorum*, another senior ex-ranker who remained in charge of the base when the legion was in the field.

Each cohort (except the senior cohort) consisted of six *centuriae* (companies) of eighty men. It was commanded by a *centurio(n)*, who was assisted by a second-in-command (*optio*), the latter word being a general term. A regular cohort was normally commanded by a senior centurio, and the larger first cohort by the primus pilus himself, though a military tribune might also command.

Each company of eighty men was made up of ten 8-man *contubernia* (squads). The leader, or "squaddie," was called a *decanus*.

The legion strength also included six *tribunes* of varying seniority and career paths, including a young tribune of senatorial rank (*tribune laticlavus*) who was beginning the military portion of his patrician career; four 30-man cavalry *turmae* (troops) used primarily for general duties; the artillery, which was dispersed amongst the cohorts; and a complement of musicians.

## Auxiliary Cavalry

Cavalry cohorts (regiments) were called *alae*, and were normally of two sizes, though each regiment was made up of 30-man *turmae* (troops or squadrons). A 480 man cohort of 16 troops was an *ala quingenaria*, and a 720 man cohort of 24 troops was an *ala milliaria*, though each would have had extra men for administration, etc. These cohorts were commanded by a *praefectus alae*, the position normally being the career peak of an officer of the equestrian order. His second-in-command was called an *optio*. The *turmae* or squadrons were each commanded by a *decurio*, and his second-in-command was also called an *optio*. There were also musicians and other supernumeraries, all of them fighting in the ranks.

## Auxiliary Infantry

The auxiliary infantry units were also grouped in *cohorts*, which like the legions were of two sizes: a *cohors quingenaria* of six companies (*centuriae*), totalling 480 men, and a *cohors milliaria* of ten companies, totalling 800 men. The *cohors quingenaria* was usually commanded by a *praefectus cohortis*. However, if honoured with the designation *civium Romanorum*, which effectively gave the unit the status of a legion, the cohort might be commanded by a *tribunus* or senior tribune. The larger *cohors milliaria* were also, normally, commanded by a *tribunus*.

## Combined Auxiliary Units

The auxiliary cohorts regularly consisted of a combination of both cavalry and infantry units, which might vary in mix, but with the same general grouping of companies (*centuriae*) and squadrons (*turmae*). This was particularly useful and common in the garrisoning of the forts and outposts such as those described in the story. Such units were referred to as cohors equitata.

Imperial Rome kept a standing army of around 250,000 men at the time of the trilogy. It was largely funded by the people she was conquering, plundering, or protecting, the description likely determined by which side you were on. A small and easily understood softcover book, *The Armies and Enemies of Imperial Rome*, by Philip Barker (Wargames Research Group, ISBN 0950029963), provides a very quick and readable reference for not only the Roman forces but, as the title indicates, those of her enemies. A more detailed but still easily readable book is *The Complete Roman Army*, by Adrian Goldsworthy (Thomas & Hudson Ltd., ISBN 0500051240).

# Appendix II

# Glossary

Note: The territories of the various tribes mentioned in the story can be found on the map of Northern England and Southern Scotland at the front of the book.

*amphora(e):*

large urn-shaped wine vessel with two ears (carrying handles). What is particularly unusual about them is that the bottom was pointed, rather than having a flat base. At the time of the story, the vessels had the typical narrow neck of such a container with a narrower rather than a bulbous "belly." Essentially a huge wine jug, the contents were standardized for most shipments at around six gallons, or twenty-four litres.

*Aureus (aurei):*

a gold coin that was worth twenty five denarii. See its place in the monetary system under *quadran*, which was the lowest denomination.

*ballista(e):*

a war engine resembling a huge crossbow that hurled large, dart-like missiles. They were quite accurate, and depending on the size, had a range of over 500 yards. In combat the practical range was likely half this or less, firing comparatively light bolts. Skilled operators could pick off a single target.

*Batavi:*

auxiliary troops, infantry for the most part. See below, *Tungri*.

*beaver:*

it is often thought that the beaver is only native to North America. The beaver became extinct in Britain around the sixteenth century. As a point of interest, during the past decade or two the beaver has been brought back to Britain, and not without controversy. Anyone familiar with the animal's habitat and habits will tell you that the animal can be quite destructive.

*Beltane:*

the celebration of life, fertility, and the spring season (most crops would have already been planted); traditionally thought to be celebrated on the first day of May.

*boss:*

a forged metal piece set in the centre of a Roman infantryman's shield. It was rectangular and averaged about eight by ten inches; there was a raised dome in the middle that acted like a club when thrust violently forward by the holder.

*Cerberus:*

originating in Greek mythology, Cerberus is the three-headed dog that guards the gates of Hades.

*comites:*

at the time of the story the *comites* were subordinate officials in the offices of a Roman magistrate or a provincial governor. In the later empire, this became *comes*, the name given to a high military or civil official.

*couching:*

an operation that shifts impaired lenses. See details under Trivia etc., Appendix IV.

*cubit:*

this measurement varied over time and country – for example, Egypt versus Rome. It was based on the width of a person's palm and at the end of first century Rome, it would have been six palm widths. This equates to 18-20 inches or 45-50 centimetres.

*cunnie:*

a slightly anglicized version of a Latin obscenity referring to a woman's private parts.

*decanus (plural, decani):*

a leader of one of the ten 8-man infantry sections called *contubernia*, or what a modern army might call a squad, or a section (see Appendix I, The Roman Army).

*decurio:*

the leader of one of the sixteen cavalry *turmae* that make up a basic cavalry regiment. In terms of nineteenth century cavalry units, these might be equated to a squadron or a troop (see Appendix I, The Roman Army).

*denarius (plural, denarii):*

a coin that would, in terms of today's value, purchase around US$30 of bread. At the time of the story, it was approximately a day's pay, before deductions, for the common soldier. See *quadran*, below, for its place in the monetary system.

*Elysium (fields of):*

for the Greeks and the Romans, this was the fifth area in the underworld, reserved for the dead who had found the favour of the gods. For the Romans their soldiers were the favoured ones who received this Idyllic afterlife.

*equitata (milliaria):*

a mixed cavalry/infantry auxiliary unit, in total around the strength of a full cohort of 480 men plus administration; the added 'millaria' denotes a double strength cohort of a thousand men with all attachments. See Appendix I, for the basic structure of auxiliary cohorts.

*heredia (singular, heredium):*

a Roman unit of measurement, equivalent to about four acres.

*honour price:*

this is a little difficult to describe in today's terms, but it was an assessment of a man's worth in terms of his dignity (face), or present weight in the community; it was also directly related to his material worth. In this way a prosperous man might ascend considerably in rank, but his honour price fluctuated according to his fortunes. This was particularly important when considering compensation for wrongs committed, and in awarding redress.

*hypocaust:*

translation: "heat from below." The Romans had central heating, though it was expensive and labour-intensive and therefore probably found only in public buildings and the properties of the wealthy. The hypocaust refers to the space under the raised floors or in the hollow of the walls that trapped and vented heat from a furnace fed by manual labour.

*intervallum:*

a clear space around the inside perimeter of the walls of a fort(ress), containing a road that was called a *via sagularis*. It was useful in providing an open area to protect buildings from missiles flying over the walls, and to allow easy movement of troops along the inside of the defenses.

*kin:*

the kin could best be described as a smaller unit of related individuals within the *tuath* (see below). It was a very extended family, and in the instance of the *Eboracvm* books has frequently been applied to the Eburii, led by the minor chieftain Cethen Lamh-fada. It would include anyone who is even loosely related (second and third cousins, adoptees, etc.).

*laticlavus:*

a junior tribune of senatorial status, averaging around twenty years old, who is on his first posting with the legions. This would be a three year posting launching a career that might progress to that of legate and possibly governor (nearly all postings were a stint of around three years; a known exception was Governor Agricola, for six years). The latter two postings would be around the age of thirty and forty respectively. In between and following the post of governor would be progressive administrative and political positions that would depend upon both influence and talent.

*latrunculi:*

a game that in many ways resembled chess, the word meaning "robber-soldiers" or "mercenaries." The most common format was played on a board of 8 x 8 squares, similar to a chessboard, with two players and two kinds of playing pieces, a different colour for each side. While the exact details are unknown, it was a military-type strategy game.

*legate (legatus legionis):*

the commander of a legion, at this time a man of senatorial rank. (See further details in Appendix I, The Roman Army).

*libitinari:*

this was the Roman name for the man who was essentially a funeral director, hired to arrange and direct the process of the formal ceremonies of the funeral.

*lucrum:*

the direct translation of this word would be "gain or profit(s)." It is doubtless the source of the expression: filthy lucre.

*mare morbus:*

seasickness, and while the word *mare* means sea, the word *morbus* has clearly come down to us as the root of the word "morbid."

*medicus (plural medici):*

this was a doctor, also a field surgeon, who was quite highly skilled when compared, for example, to mid-nineteenth century physicians. The legion's medicus would be the senior man in a hospital that was usually a building of four wings enclosing a courtyard. There would likely be a large room at the entrance and, in a full-sized fortress, more than sixty small wards, each accommodating four to eight patients. The entire structure might approach 60,000 square feet, and could technically house almost 10% of the legion. The medicus likely ranked on the same level with a fairly senior centurio (*medicus ordinarius*), and many apparently came from the Greek provinces.

*milliaria:*

a double-sized auxiliary unit that might contain either cavalry or infantry, or both. See Appendix I.

*optio:*

this seems to be a general rank assigned to a second-in-command of most designated appointments. For example, a praefectus commanding a cavalry *alae* (regiment), or the decurio commanding one of the *turmae* (squadrons or troops) that made up that regiment, would each have a second-in-command called an *optio*.

*Ordivices:*

one of four known tribes that inhabited what is now Wales, and likely the one that made the most trouble there for the Romans. They were located in the central mountainous hills, with the closest fortress to them being Viriconium, or present day Wroxeter, which lay on the eastern side of their territory. Just as in the north, numerous smaller forts were scattered throughout the lands they occupied.

*peristyle:*

a rectangular colonnaded structure that in the city or towns was usually the central focus of the house's garden. In the instance of a large rural villa such as the Sabinius estate, it might be extremely large, with the villa forming the fourth side to the three rows of columns, with further gardens lying beyond.

*pilum (plural, pili):*

a type of spear, and one of two main weapon types used by the foot soldier (sword and spear). It was a particularly heavy weapon and unique in its construction. The shaft, as might be expected, was of wood, but shorter than most. This was because the tip, rather than being the normal sharp, pointed head about six to eight inches long on the end of a wooden shaft, was instead a small barb at the tip of a long, thin iron rod that comprised up to a third of the weapon's length. It was used in the legion ranks primarily as a throwing weapon that, if it didn't kill or wound, caught and stuck in the enemy shield, rendering his defense difficult. (Note: *pilus* in Latin means "hair," and is today the medical name of a hairlike appendage found on many bacteria.) There were three other types of spear in general use: the *hasta*, a more traditional spear about six feet long, mostly phased out sometime during the early empire;

the *contus*, a longer standard spear used mainly by the cavalry (really a lance); and the *veluti*, which is the javelin sometimes referred to in the book, a lighter, dart-like spear carried in quivers and meant to be thrown, or perhaps used in close-quarters melees.

*pound (Roman):*

from the Latin, *libra pondo*, or pound weight. The word *libra* is where the abbreviation "lb." originated. In terms of comparison, the Roman pound was about three-quarters the weight of today's imperial pound. A Roman mile was much closer, at 95% of today's mile. It is generally considered to have been 1,000 marching paces (a pace being a full left/right step), or roughly 5,000 feet. Modern miles have been used for the distances in the book.

*praefectus:*

the commander of an auxiliary cohort, whether cavalry or infantry. The name is also applied to certain other command rankings, including the legions, such as *praefectus castrorum*, the rank in command of a fortress when the legion is in the field. See Appendix I.

*praenomina (praenomen):*

this was the "first" or personal name of an individual Roman's three names, and there were few to select from (Julius, Lucius, Gaius, etc.). Then came the *nomen*, which was the family name, usually ending in "ius." The third was the *cognomen*, often chosen based on a physical or personality trait, and used like a nickname.

*praetorian gate (porta praetoria), et al:*

the main gate leading into the fortress. In the instance of Eboracum, it was from the south. Using the same fortress as a bearing, the other gates were: north: *porta pecumana*; east: *porta principalis dextra*; west: *porta principalis sinistra*. The word *principalis* was used because these latter two gates opened onto the main street leading east and west, known as the *via principalis*. *Dextra* and *sinistra* respectively mean right and left, the direction determined when standing with one's back to the headquarters building rather than facing it.

*praetorium:*

originally the name of a commander's tent, or his house in a fortification; by the time of the book it had become the name for the house/palace of the procurator or governor of a Roman province.

*primus pilus:*

translation: "first spear." The senior centurio of the legion, who was usually assigned the first cohort. He had powers (particularly over the discipline, operations, and training of the men) that rivalled those of the legate. The position was filled by a man promoted from the ranks.

*procurator:*

a powerful administrative position in a Roman province held by a man of equestrian rank. He was responsible for the finances, taxation, control of imperial property, and census. He also acted as a "check" to the governor's authority, in that he reported independently to the emperor himself. An example of this was the procurator Julius Classicianus, a man primarily responsible for the recall of Seutonius due to his brutal reprisals following Boudicca's rebellion (an uprising that was largely the result of a former procurator's greed and ruthlessness).

*puls (or pulmentus):*

a cereal gruel or porridge prepared from barley or spelt (wheat) that was roasted, pounded, and cooked with water in a cauldron. (Possible ancestor of the word porridge?) The mix is similar to the modern Italian polenta.

*quadron:*

the lowest denomination of Roman money. In ascending value: 4 quadrons = 1 *as*; 2 as = 1 *dupondius*; 2 dupondii = 1 *sestertius*; 2 sestertii = 1 *quinarius*; 2 quinarii = 1 *denarius*; 12.5 denarii = 1 *quinarius aureus* (gold); 2 quinarii aureii = 1 *aureus*. The word *talent* (from the Greek) was used in dealing with large amounts of money, and 1 talent was equivalent to 6,000 denarii.

*Samhain:*

the Celtic festival that marks the end of the harvest season, which is taken to be the final day of October.

*sapa:*

a sweetener for cooking and drinks that consisted of grape juice, must (squeezed grapes), or wine that had been reduced (boiled) down to about a third of its volume. Besides being used as a liquid, it may also have been crystallized. Due to copper and brass cauldrons reacting with the acid in the fruit, the vessel of choice would have been lead-lined, and it seems that lead acetate enhanced the taste. This was not good and long-term consumption may have caused serious effects, though the sapa was likely consumed in small quantities.

*senatorial (rank):*

this rank essentially described the privileged few who belonged to the senate. The senate itself, and membership therein, changed throughout the Republic and into the times of Imperial Rome, and even a basic overview would require several pages. It might, however, be in some ways likened to a Roman House of Lords, with rankings that could determine whether the individual even had the right to speak.

*Seres:*

the ancient Greek and Roman name for the inhabitants of northwestern China (modern Xinjiang). It meant "of silk," or the people of the land where silk comes from. The country itself was known as Serica. The Chinese word for silk, pronounced "si," is likely the root of the word.

*sestertius (or sesterce, plural sestertii):*

a larger coin than the denarius, made of brass or bronze and of a lesser value (the author has one which appears to have a high lead content). See *quadron* for its place in the monetary system.

*sith(s):*

a bit of a liberty has been taken here. A sith is a demigod in Celtic myth, and takes many forms depending on its prefix. It may vary from a faerie to a dog-like creature the size of a cow, or even a vampire-like being. It is difficult to determine to what extent such myths extended back to the first century.

*Sixth Legio Victrix:*

This legion was formed by Octavian in 41 B.C., and served in several theatres before being brought to Britain in A.D. 122 by Hadrian. It served at Eboracum for 280 years, and was likely withdrawn by Stilicho when he was trying to patch up the Roman Empire in the west, around A.D. 402. Historians seem to agree that Britain's Roman rule ended around A.D. 410.

*squadron:*

this is the term used in the book for one of the smaller units that make up a cavalry regiment (see Appendix I), rather than the cumbersome Latin word *turmae*. It has been used interchangeably with the word "troop." This smaller unit, at full strength, would consist of thirty riders.

*stola:*

much like the men's long toga; a rectangular cloth draped around a woman's body to form a long, flowing garment.

*Trajan:*

the emperor in power at the time of the book. He ruled from A.D. 98-117, and was considered to be one of the "five good emperors" Hadrian was one of the other four, and of particular interest (due to Tuis's fictional adoption) is that he was adopted by the weak emperor Nerva, after successfully serving as a general. In viewing ancient adoption practices compared to today, one has to take into consideration the high death rate at the time, not only of children but of the adults, both in their early and middle years.

*tribunal:*

a permanent platform that often served as a podium, commanding any open room that lay before it. Such a platform was standard in the headquarters building (*principia*) of a fort or fortress, and was placed in one corner of the great cross hall (the first room entered once the walled-in forecourt had been crossed). This hall was used for issuing orders, settling punishment, receiving visitors, and other general HQ duties, including smaller parades. Rooms lined the rear of the hall, the central being a shrine (*aedes*) that held the garrison's standards, a statue of the emperor, and likely several altars. Below it was the unit's treasury, and on either side were administrative offices.

*tuath:*

a word that originally meant "people," but which later acquired a territorial connotation. In population and extent it was fairly small, and normally conformed to an area with natural topographical boundaries. Depending on size, it could have its own aristocratic structure that might even extend to a king, nobles (chieftains), and common freemen.

*Tungri:*
    the Tungri were a tribe that inhabited Lower Germania (Germania Inferior). The *Batavi* were also from the same area, which consisted primarily of modern day Holland and Belgium. This part of the empire was fertile ground for raising auxiliary troops.

*tutor:*
    when making a Roman will it was common to appoint a tutor, which would be very close to what we might today call a guardian, even though the beneficiary might have been of age. This was applied particularly to women and in many cases it was mandated; in the instance of an established wife it would not have been. As mentioned in the book, when dealing with Gaius's choice of Marcus, it might have been as much to protect the beneficiary as it was to ensure that the legacy was not wasted.

*ustrina:*
    a compound outside the city walls that was reserved for the cremation of the dead. Whether the corpse was buried (something that became more traditional during the second century A.D.) or cremated, it was always done outside the limits of a city, town, or fortress, etc.

*via praetoria, via principalis:*
    the main streets inside a fort(ress) that met in a T in front of the headquarters. The *praetoria* led from the main gate to form the leg of the T; the *principalis* was the top of the T and connected the two side gates. The *principalis* was also the site of the commander's residence, which usually sat alongside the legion headquarters. There were other streets, including one that led to the rear gate, the number depending on the size of the fort(ress) and the buildings within it. A full size fortess covered approximately 50 acres (Disneyland was originally 85 acres).

*Vocontian regiment (Vocontii):*
    this regiment was known to have garrisoned Trimontium as its cavalry element, and was recruited in the Orange district of southern France. It

was likely sent there after A.D. 105, but it has been used in the book, as evidence of the actual time the unit spent at Trimontium is unknown.

# Appendix III

# Place Names and Detail

*Aballava:*

a small fort at Burgh-by-Sands, about six miles west of Luguvalium (Carlisle). It sat like an outpost a mile and a half back from where the Ituna River flowed into the Ituna Estuary, and would have had an advanced view of the broad estuary and northern shore that would not have been seen at Luguvalium.

*Abus:*

history appears to have left no Roman name for the river at York, which is now called the Ouse. The river flows down to the North Sea, where it first runs into the River Humber, which then becomes the Humber Estuary. It is known that the Romans called the Humber the *Abus*. Since the river Ouse flows uninterrupted all the way from York, the author found it reasonable to speculate that the Romans may have referred to it as the Abus along the entire distance. Eboracum was within the tidal reach; there is no really dramatic site where the Ouse, the larger river, is tapped into by the River Trent to become the Humber; and, as to derivatives – dare it be pointed out that the – *us* at the end of Abus sounds very much like "Ouse"?

*Aquae Sulis:*

translation: "waters of the goddess Sulis." This is now the town of Bath, which in the first century was already being utilized as a resort due to its thermally heated waters. The Romans eventually built sophisticated baths here.

*Aricia (now Ariccia):*

this ancient town dates to approximately the same time as the founding of Rome and, up until the beginning of the Republic, it rivalled that city. It sits on the Appian Way, sixteen miles south and slightly east of Rome. The Sabinius country estate has been located on higher ground just to the northeast of the ancient town, on the slopes of Mons Albinus (the Alban Hills), close to a dormant volcano that forms the cauldron containing Lake Albano.

*Blatobulgium:*

an Agricolan fort that is located by Birrens, in Dumfries and Galloway (southwest Scotland). It was a large structure and eventually housed a full Germanic mixed milliaria-equitata, which stone inscriptions state was "a thousand strong." The actual time of occupation of this unit is not specifically known, and liberty was taken in assuming that the larger regiment was posted after the uprising in the book.

*Bodotria (estuary):*

the Firth of Forth. This is the estuary of the river Forth, in southeast Scotland. Edinburgh is sited on the firth's southern shore.

*Bravoniacum:*

sited at Kirby Thore, Westmorland/Cumbria, the fort sat close to the western end of the long Roman road that crossed the Pennines, the eastern side beginning at what is now called Scotch Corner. There is evidence that the fort was probably home to a cavalry regiment.

*Bremenium:*

this site is just north of High Rochester, in Northumbria, approximately sixty miles south and slightly east of Edinburgh. It is today in open country, dissected by a narrow, winding road, with two small sets of farm buildings set within the confines of what is left of the old ramparts. A 4.25 acre fort, it was probably home to a mixed cavalry/infantry unit (*equitata*) of *Lingones,* a tribe in central France.

*Brigantia:*

the tribal territory of the Brigantes was extensive, and possibly the largest tribal area in Britain. It covered Yorkshire and part of Northumbria in the east; all of Lancashire, and perhaps as far south as the Mersey in the west. The name did not formally exist as a territory but has been simply applied to the area occupied by this large, loosely knit tribe.

*Brocavum:*

now Brougham, Cumbria. This fort sat on the key intersection of the main Roman road leading north on the west side of Britain, and the east/west road that crossed the Pennines. There is evidence of a Gallic cohort stationed here, but its period of occupation is unknown.

*Calacum:*

now Casterton, Burrow on Lonsdale, at the northern tip of Lancashire. It was a larger, 6.25 acre fort that occupied a prominence overlooking the River Lune. It was capable of housing a full cohort or *equitata*, though excavation indicates that the plateau on which it sits may have been extended to house a *milliaria*, a unit a thousand strong.

*Calcaria:*

now Tadcaster, about nine miles south-southwest of York, on the river Wharfe. It was the source of much of the sandstone used in the building of York, both in Roman times and later. York's medieval walls were built of this stone and still stand; of particular interest is that these walls are, for the most part, built on top of the old Roman ramparts. Tadcaster is also the long-time home of the famous John Smith Brewery. A rule of thumb in England: the farther north, the better the beer.

*Camulodunum:*

now Slack, west Yorkshire, and a Celtic tribal centre at the time of Rome's invasion. Some believe that the site was later the focus of the legendary kingdom of Camelot. It is not to be confused with the settlement of the same name in southern England, now called Colchester. The first two books in the *Eboracvm* series had this as the home of the Brigante Queen Cartimandua.

*Cataractonium:*

now Catterick, it sits about forty miles north of Eboracum. It is home to a military base on the main A1 road north (many of the arterial roads in England follow the old Roman roads). Some like to believe that there has been some form of military establishment continually here from the time of the Romans.

*Charia:*

this is an invented name for the fort at present day Glenlochar, using the last four letters of that town. No Roman name seems to have survived. It was a seven acre site and sat in surprising isolation just north of Dumfries (southwest Scotland), ten miles inland from the north side of the broad Ituna Estuary. A large fort, it was established by Agricola around A.D. 80 (Tacitus mentions this: *The fourth summer was spent in securing the ground hastily traversed . . . was fortified this summer with Roman garrisons and the whole sweep of the country to the south secured*). There is evidence that it was indeed burned, probably around the time of Lagan's uprising. Unlike the other forts destroyed in the book, this one was not rebuilt.

*Coria:*

a strategic fort at what is now Corbridge, it guarded the highest fordable point on the large River Tyne *(Tinea)*, on the main road leading north. It was set 2.5 miles behind where Hadrian's Wall would be built; but in A.D. 105 it sat on the east/west Roman road later known as *Stanegate* ("gate" is old Danish for "street"). Stanegate would have been the route taken by Tuis when marching toward Coria, toward the end of the book. The full Roman name for Coria was *Corstopitum*.

*Crawdum:*

an invented name for the fort at present day Crawford, Scotland, where no Roman name seems to have survived. This is a small fort about which little is known, situated about 60 miles beyond Luguvalium on the Roman road leading north. It likely had a short life that became sporadic after the Antonine Wall was abandoned, later in the second century. The site of the fort provided what seemed to be a feasible point for Tuis to turn and march east across what would have been inhospitable country.

*Dacia (Dacian wars):*

Dacia was an area along Rome's northern frontier as defined by the River Danube. Two Dacian wars were fought by Trajan, the first from A.D. 101-102, and the second from A.D. 105-106, both of them successful. (Domitan also fought two Dacian wars between A.D. 86 and 88; the first resulted in a humiliating disaster and the second in a shameful peace; the moral: get it right the first time).

*Deva:*

the city of Chester, in Cheshire, about 120 miles south of Luguvalium, and about 90 miles southwest of Eboracum. Originally a smaller fort built around A.D. 47/48 by Governor Scapula to subdue and dominate the Welsh tribes, this unusually large (62 acres) fortress was the home of the Twentieth Valeria Legion. After abandoning the fortress at Inchtutil circa A.D. 87 (*Pinnata* in *Eboracvm, the Fortress*), it became the legion's home until around A.D. 383 when it was in turn abandoned, perhaps due to silting of the River Dee. It was reconstructed in stone about five years before Eboracum's stone upgrade.

*Dubris:*

the port of Dover. It was one of two major ports for the sea crossing from Gaul (see *Rutupiae*, below), and was the start of what would later become Watling Street, the highway from Dover to London. Dubris was fortified and garrisoned by the *Classis Britannica* (Fleet of Britain, i.e., the Roman Navy).

*Ebor(acum):*

the Roman name for the city of York. The origin of the name is the subject of much debate. Three theories appear most popular. One is that the name was derived from a man called Eburos who, legend says, fled Troy; though doubtful, it seems even more doubtful that he ever lived around Eboracum. The two others are both alluded to in the book *Eboracvm, the Village*. "Ebor" is apparently similar to, or has connotations with, an old German word for boar, which Roman auxiliary troops drawn from that area would have known. "Ebur" is a cognate found in the old Irish word *ibhar* or *iuhbar*, which means "yew." As such, the Ebor/Ebur meaning could be extended to "place of the boar" or "place of the yews." The suffix *ium* or *(a)cum* was normally attached to the end of a place name when a civilian settlement had been built up or was attached (e.g., Viroconium, now Wroxeter).

*Epiacum:*

located just over ten miles south of Hadrian's Wall (built A.D. 122), the fort is odd in that it was constructed in a "squashed" rectangular, almost diamond-shaped, in order to take advantage of the terrain. Today the site is known as Whitley Castle. The name *Epiacum* could be a contraction of *epi-acumen*, which translates as "surrounding the point."

*Forum Julii:*

a small port (now called Fejus) to the east of Marseilles that Julius Caesar turned into a key city when connecting the Adrian Way as a land route to Spain, around 50 B.C. Marseilles had already set up a colony on the site, but it was Caesar who made it prosperous, hence the name: Marketplace of Julius.

*Fosse:*

the second and much smaller river at York which has seen service similar to a canal over the years. The Roman name does not appear to have survived, so an "e" has been added to its modern name (the River Foss) to conform to the spelling of "The Fosse Way." This was the main road leading north, which at the time of the first *Eboracvm* book terminated on the south bank of the Humber, across from *Petuaria* (Brough). Later on, the Fosse Way was extended to what is known today as Wallsend, the termination of Hadrian's wall in the east.

*Gades:*

the pronunciation is close enough to recognize the modern name of this city: the Spanish port of Cadiz.

*Galava:*

this small wooden fort of less than two acres was situated on the north end of Lake Windermere, and is now the site of the resort town of Ambleside, Cumbria. Built in A.D. 79, it was the fort selected to be built by Marcus and Crispus in *Eboracvm, The Fortress.* Little is known of its garrisons.

*Germania (Upper/Lower, or Superior/Inferior):*

Lower Germania (Inferior) was basically the Low Countries where Holland and Belgium are today, south of the Rhine. It was a fertile recruiting ground for auxiliary troops and this is where the Batavi and Tungri cohorts referred to in all three books of the *Eboracvm* series would have originated. Upper Germania (Superior) refers to territory farther upstream comprising the area of western Switzerland, Jura, and the Alsace regions of France, and southwestern Germany.

*Gesoriacum:*

the French port of Calais; it would have been the end of the land route across Gaul before crossing to Britain.

*Glevum:*

now the city of Gloucester, in Gloucestershire, this was a fort established early in the conquest, which later became a full-sized fortress. In A.D. 97 it became a retirement centre for soldiers, and also a market town. It was strategically situated on the River Severn at the crossing of several major Roman roads. At its height, Glevum may have had a population of 10,000 (by comparison, Rome was supposed to have had more than a million).

*Graupius, Mons:*

the Grampian Mountains, which are southeast of Inverness, below the Moray Firth. It is here that the final battle in *Eboracvm, The Fortress*, took place between Agricola and Galgar *(Galgacus)*. The precise site is the subject of much debate, and does not appear to have been proven.

*Habitancum:*

another Agricolan fort, as were nearly all that were founded north of the line later taken by Hadrian's Wall. The fort is near Risingham, Northumbria, and is today in open farmland, roughly a hundred miles north of Eboracum. Remnants of a small civilian settlement have been discovered close by.

*Isca:*

now the town of Caerleon in southern Wales, it was the original home of the Second Augusta Legion. Its present population is around 7,000, which means things haven't changed much over the past 2,000 years.

*Isurium:*

now the town of Aldborough, about seventeen miles north of Eboracum. It was already a substantial Celtic centre before the Romans invaded Brigantia, and grew to be one of several substantial (in tribal terms) centres under Roman rule. The earthen ramparts of the wider fortifications are still readily visible today.

*Ituna estuary/river:*

the large tidal estuary is today known as the Solway Firth, a broad expanse of water that separates Cumbria, in England, from the county of Dumfries and Galloway in Scotland to the north. The Ituna River is now called the Eden.

*Lavatris:*

now Bowes, County Durham, not far west of Scotch Corner. Nearby at the town of Barnard Castle, the Bowes Museum (which has nothing to do with Rome), is a fine stately home built specifically as a museum of art in the latter half of the 1800s. The entire project was a gift of the Bowes family, and well worth a visit.

*Lignum:*

an invented name, for no Roman name survives; it is the Latin for "wood." It was chosen because this fort is located by Oakwood, in the county of Borders. It was likely founded by Agricola, and sat quite isolated in the hills southwest of Trimontium.

*Londinium:*

as it sounds, this is the present day city of London. Little more needs to be said.

*Luguvalium:*

where the city of Carlisle is now located, just below the Scottish border on the west coast of England. The first fort was built by Cerealis around A.D. 72, and was rebuilt on the same site just before the time of the current book. Less than 20 years later, when Hadrian's Wall was built, the fort was relocated (again built in wood) to the north side of the Ituna River, where it was an integral part of the wall's defenses, and became known as Stannix. Luguvalium is believed to have derived its name from the Celtic god Lugus. (A mild expletive used in the *Eboracvm* books is "For the love of Lug!")

*Mare Cantabricum:*

the Bay of Biscay, off the coast of Spain. This area has always been known for its bad weather, and was later known to mariners as The Sea of Storms.

*Mare Sardoum:*

the greater or the largest part of the Mediterranean was cheekily known by the Romans as *Mare Nostrum*, or "Our Sea." *Mare Sardoum* was that part of the Mediterranean north of Sardinia.

*Massalia:*

the port city of Marseilles, in southern France.

*Nithius:*

this is an invented name, for no Roman name survives for this fort. Now Dalswinton, the made-up name is taken from its site on the River Nith. Agricola founded it on his march north; abandoned soon after, it was rebuilt around A.D. 90 by the governor Lucullus. It was situated nearly forty miles (by road) northwest of Luguvalium and at the time of this book was probably the HQ of the military in an area that much later became southwest Scotland.

*Ostia:*

Rome's major seaport sat fifteen miles downriver from the city. It was the place where Gaius recovered Elena from the Neapolitan slave trader in *Eboracvm, The Village.*

*Palatine:*

the centremost hill of the seven hills of Rome, inhabited since about 1,000 B.C. Myth has it that the cave in which the wolf raised Romulus and Remus was located here. During the Republic it was the home of the wealthy, and in imperial times several emperors built their palaces here. The south side of the hill overlooked the Circus Maximus.

*Rhenus river:*

the river Rhine.

*Rigodunum:*

one of nine *poleis*, or towns, attributed by Ptolemy to the Brigantes. It may have been at Castleshaw, located just north of Manchester. There was a small fort (just over two acres) built here, and a second one that replaced it around the time of this book. Excavations in 1990 indicated a civilian settlement. Castleshaw lies on the Roman road from Eboracum to Deva. Bryn would certainly have visited such Brigante settlements trying to gain support!

*Rutupiae:*

now Richborough, this one-time port now sits two miles from the sea. At the time of the Romans (who built a fort here), it overlooked a sheltered lagoon that was a natural harbour. It was an important port, and there has been speculation that it was the landing site for the Claudian invasion that took Britain for the Romans in A.D. 43.

*Selgovae Territory:*

the Selgovae were the tribe(s) whose territory abutted the north reaches of the Brigantes and the Carvetii. The area was later called The Borders, and the Selgovae occupied it all except for a strip about twenty-five to thirty miles wide, on the east coast. To describe it today: all of the middle of southern Scotland beginning at Edinburgh, and a central chunk of northern England, as far as Hadrian's Wall (which did not exist at the time of the story).

*Stannick:*

a Celtic centre before the Roman invasion, located in Durham, not far from Scotch Corner. It seems to have been fortified, or at least built up and strengthened, by the Brigantes following Claudius's A.D. 43 invasion of Britain. There is conjecture that it was the seat of Venutius, and that at one time Cartimandua may have lived there before the two were divorced. The normal spelling is Stanwick. Finding no Roman name for the stronghold, the "w" was dropped in the story simply because "wick" implies an Anglo-Saxon suffix, rather than Roman or Celt.

*Tava estuary:*

the Firth of Tay, approximately thirty miles north of Edinburgh. Agricola built a line of forts here, and it was in this vicinity that Tacitus placed the Ninth when it was attacked by the tribes in the battle described in *Eboracvm, The Fortress.*

*Tinea river:*

the River Tyne, which would eventually be the eastern limit of Hadrian's Wall.

*Trimontium:*

now Newstead, County Borders, southern Scotland, the site is around fifty miles north of Hadrian's Wall. Agricola built a large fort here around A.D. 80 which was subsequently rebuilt on a smaller scale as the frontier was pulled back. It was originally garrisoned by the Twentieth Legion, though the *Vocontii* regiment (see Appendix II), mentioned later in the book, also garrisoned Trimontium, though the precise dates are unknown. The fort was actually burned down in the uprising described in the book. It is of interest to note that, in its subsequent rebuilding(s), the size and significance of this fort is indicated by a fair-sized military amphitheatre that overlooked the River Tweed.

*Vetera:*

a large, almost double-sized fortress located at what is now Birten, Germany, just across the border from Holland. It was taken over and partly destroyed by the local Batavi auxiliaries when Civilis made an unsuccessful bid to be emperor in A.D. 70. This rebellion was put down by Vespasian, who sent his son-in-law Cerealis to do the job (see prologue to *Eboracvm, The Village*). Rhun was stationed there in *Eboracvm, The Fortress*.

*Vindolanda:*

located near Chesterholm, Northumberland, the fort was built around A.D. 90 as part of the east/west road that became known as Stanegate. Hadrian's Wall was built thirty-two years later, and it is thought that Vindolanda may have become a supply base. Two items are of particular interest today: part of the original structure is being reconstructed on site; and numerous Roman writings have been recovered, preserved on thin slivers of wood used as cheap writing paper. The latter's preservation was due to a unique combination in the soil and water in which they were saturated.

# Appendix IV

# Author's Commentary and Trivia

## The Book's Title

The title of this book, *Eboracvm, Carved in Stone*, came about because history records that the fortress was completely rebuilt in stone in the year A.D. 107. However, the uprising (see below) that spread through the north and provides the background for this book actually took place in A.D. 105. This might appear to be a two-year anomaly that some may consider beyond the licence permitted when writing an historical novel. However, Rome was not built in a day, and neither would Eboracum have been rebuilt in a single year. I have taken the position that if history records the rebuilding of the great fortress as A.D. 107, then that was likely the completion date. It would have likely taken a couple of years to reconstruct a complete fortress with stone barged from quarries seven or eight miles away. As such, I have the construction started in A.D. 104-5, beginning with the headquarters and the commander's residence, with concurrent work being carried out on one of the fortress walls.

## Historical Facts and Trivia

In the first two books of the trilogy, *The Village* had as its background the founding of the fortress at Eboracum by Governor Cerealis, and ends with the defeat of Venutius in the battle at Stannick. In *The Fortress*, Agricola subjugated Brigantia and Cumbria, then built his string of forts northward into Scotland, where he fought the battle that defeated

Galgar (Galgacus). History records no battle of major significance in Britain at the time of *Carved in Stone*. However, in A.D. 105, there was an extensive uprising throughout the north that was quite serious.

Excavation has revealed that the forts named as being taken by Lagan and Modan were indeed burned, as were two more north of where Rhun was stationed at Luguvalium. Historians have speculated that some of this destruction may have been done by the Romans themselves, as they withdrew south in the face of this general revolt. Lack of troops would have been a key reason, for resources were being drained elsewhere (the Dacian Wars, for instance). I have chosen the option that at least some of these strongholds were taken and destroyed by the tribes during the uprising. As to who led that uprising, nobody knows; Lagan and Eupo are fictional characters. And as to Cronus, his taxes, and the corruption, well – has anything changed?

Many significant events took place at Eboracum after A.D. 105. The emperor Severus was there for three years at the beginning of the third century with his two sons, Geta and Caracalla (they might have been named Cain and Abel). He used Eboracum as the base for an extensive campaign that had his army fighting as far north as Agricola (the Moray Firth). Amazingly, he concluded a peace with the Picts that endured for many years. While in the north he ordered a complete rebuilding of Hadrian's Wall, and at Eboracum he extended the latter's stone defenses to south of the river, enclosing the civilian settlement. He fell ill and died at Eboracum in A.D. 211.

Constantine joined his father Constantius (emperor of the west) at Eboracum in A.D 305. They campaigned together in the north in much the same area as Agricola and Severus, but in July of A.D. 306 his father died at Eboracum. Constantine was promptly proclaimed emperor (of the west), for at the time the Roman Empire was still divided. He went on to significantly change the course of history by adopting Christianity as the religion of the empire.

A small but interesting vignette of later history is that a great cathedral was built on the site of the old Roman fortress, with construction beginning around A.D. 1215. This magnificent structure still stands today, and is called York Minster. In the nineteen sixties the great central tower (233 feet tall) was felt to be in danger of cracking. The corner foundations were excavated and reinforced with stainless steel and concrete. When burrowing under the tower to carry out the repair, workers found themselves in the ruins of the old headquarters building. As an historic curiosity, this understructure has been left open to visitors; a small part of the old HQ walls may still be viewed.

## Medical Treatment

Almost any reader of historical fiction has come across a story that includes trepanning. The name is derived from the word *trepan*: "a cylindrical saw," which originally came from the Greek word *trypaein*: "to bore." In the book, this operation has been used on Gaius's skull as a means of exploratory surgery.

The surgery on Cethen's eyes (known as couching and common well into the nineteenth century), was first recorded as being practised by the Egyptians. It was quite risky and often went wrong. However, while the operation is fairly straightforward, a good deal of the risk (especially during the last fifteen hundred years) was probably due to lack of cleanliness, and the fact that the operation might be performed by a local crone or the barber. The Romans and the Greeks had, by the first century, standards of hygiene that were phenomenal when compared, for example, to the mid-nineteenth century, which saw such conflicts as the Crimean and American Civil Wars lose many casualties due to lack of cleanliness.

As to Modan's castration, it was indeed forbidden just as Jessa tells it, which indicates that it had clearly become a social problem of significance in Rome. It is interesting, however, that most people assume the operation will make the subject male (victim?) impotent. While it does in most instances, this is not always true. Erectile ability (unless psychological) is not lost immediately; it fades and disappears. However, in a certain small percentage of males, some sexual function will continue with a very small ejaculate that is produced by the prostate. Hormone treatment and stimulation will also negate, to a degree, the effects of castration

## Explanations That Might be in Order

Throughout the book, Eboracum has been spelled with a "u" before the "m." The name on the cover, however, has used a "v": *Eboracvm*. This has been done simply in the interest of "purism". The Romans avoided the letter "u" in their alphabet, using a "v" instead. This has, one is reluctant to admit, caused a wee bit of confusion.

The use of the Roman numeral VIIII is not an error. Nowadays the number nine is expressed as IX. However, the VIIII usage was common with the Hispana Legio. It has been found stamped on their roofing tiles and chiselled into their monuments and other relics.

The smoke generated when the torque was handed over to Bryn was well within the realms of the technology available to Rome. Today's home-based chemistry set would mix powdered sugar with saltpetre (the latter was regularly used by the ancients for such things as lighting fires), and the mixture simply set in a form that might be lit (a small paper cylinder will do). This effectively turns it into a smoke bomb. In this instance, since sugar was not available in Europe until the Crusades, powdered crystallized sapa would have been used.

## A Final Word on the Ninth Hispana Legion

The Ninth was formed by Pompey in Spain in 65 BC. Caesar took the legion to Gaul in 58 BC, where it was present throughout his entire campaign of the Gallic wars. It was brought back to Spain in 49 BC where it remained faithful to Caesar until the civil war, when its soldiers decided to revolt. Brought back into line through decimation, the legion fought at Dyrrhachium and Pharsalus in 48 BC, and in the African campaign of 46 BC. Following its final victory, the Ninth was disbanded by Caesar and the veterans settled at Piecenum.

Octavian reactivated the legion to defeat Sextus, after which it was sent to Macedonia. The Ninth remained with Octavian against Mark Antony and fought with him at Actium. It was then sent to Hispania in a large campaign directed against the Cantabrians (25-13 BC), which is where it likely picked up the name *Hispana*. After this, the legion likely became part of the imperial army on the Rhine border, campaigning against the Germanic tribes until the disastrous battle of the Teutoburg Forest, after which it was sent to Pannonia.

In 43 AD it participated in the invasion of Britain under the titular command of emperor Claudius (and general Aulus Plautius). Eventually stationed at Lindum (Lincoln), the legion put down the first revolt of Venutius around the mid fifties AD, then suffered a serious defeat under Petilius Cerialis by Boudicca, in 61 AD. The Ninth then moved to Eboracum in 71 AD – but of course, a reader of the Eboracum trilogy would know this.

As to the legion's disappearance, this is uncertain. Its destruction in Scotland is a well known fiction created by Rosemary Sutcliff's novel, *The Eagle of the Ninth;* and while the Ninth certainly did suffer ample troubles in the north, **total** destruction was not one of them. Its fate was settled somewhere in the East, possibly during the Bar Kochba Revolt in Judaea, or the ongoing conflict in Parthia. There is ample evidence of its interim presence along the lower Rhine in the first half of the second century, and historians speculate that its fate may have been decided by a strategic transfer from there.

A clue that the Ninth left Britain in a weakened strength and suffered destruction when transferred to Judaea might be read into the words of the Roman historian Marcus Cornelius Fronto, when consoling emperor Marcus Aurelius: *Indeed, when your grandfather Hadrian held power, what great numbers of soldiers were killed by the Jews, what great numbers by the British.*

## The Chronology of Names for the City of York:

- *Ebor(acum)*, the original name; see its history in Appendix III.
- *Eoforwic* came next (note the "wic" on the end; see comment under *Stannick*, Appendix III). Its name came from the Angles (sometime prior to A.D. 627), and may owe some ancestral origins to the Romans, as it was likely pronounced "Evrauc" or "Everwick."
- *Jorvik* (pronounced "Yorewick") followed, and this name was in use under the Danish occupation (beginning circa A.D. 867). It seems to be a slight shift in pronunciation and spelling from Eoforwic. By the end of "Danelaw," which came with the successful invasion of the Northumbrians in A.D. 954, the name appears to have been abbreviated to York.

Other novels, novellas and short story collections available from Stairwell Books

| | |
|---|---|
| My Sister is a Dog | Ali Sparkes |
| Down to Earth | Andrew Crowther |
| The Iron Brooch | Yvonne Hendrie |
| Pandemonium of Parrots | Dawn Treacher |
| The Electric | Tim Murgatroyd |
| The Pirate Queen | Charlie Hill |
| Djoser and the Gods | Michael J. Lowis |
| The Tally Man | Rita Jerram |
| Needleham | Terry Simpson |
| The Keepers | Pauline Kirk |
| A Business of Ferrets | Alwyn Bathan |
| Shadow Cat Summer | Rebecca Smith |
| Shadows of Fathers | Simon Cullerton |
| Blackbird's Song | Katy Turton |
| Eboracvm the Fortress | Graham Clews |
| The Warder | Susie Williamson |
| The Great Billy Butlin Race | Robin Richards |
| Mistress | Lorraine White |
| Life Lessons by Libby | Libby and Laura Engel-Sahr |
| Waters of Time | Pauline Kirk |
| The Tao of Revolution | Chris Taylor |
| The Water Bailiff's Daughter | Yvonne Hendrie |
| O Man of Clay | Eliza Mood |
| Eboracvm: the Village | Graham Clews |
| Sammy Blue Eyes | Frank Beill |
| Margaret Clitherow | John and Wendy Rayne-Davis |
| Serpent Child | Pat Riley |
| Rocket Boy | John Wheatcroft |
| Virginia | Alan Smith |
| Looking for Githa | Patricia Riley |
| Poetic Justice | P J Quinn |
| Return of the Mantra | Susie Williamson |
| The Go-To Guy | Neal Hardin |
| Abernathy | Claire Patel-Campbell |
| Tyrants Rex | Clint Wastling |
| A Shadow in My Life | Rita Jerram |
| Thinking of You Always | Lewis Hill |
| Here in the Cull Valley | John Wheatcroft |

For further information please contact rose@stairwellbooks.com

www.stairwellbooks.co.uk
@stairwellbooks

Ingram Content Group UK Ltd.
Milton Keynes UK
UKHW011835200423
420514UK00001B/120